By Erica Jong

FRUITS & VEGETABLES
(*poetry, 1971*)

HALF-LIVES
(*poetry, 1973*)

FEAR OF FLYING
(*fiction, 1973*)

LOVEROOT
(*poetry, 1975*)

HOW TO SAVE YOUR OWN LIFE
(*fiction, 1977*)

AT THE EDGE OF THE BODY
(*poetry, 1979*)

FANNY: BEING THE TRUE HISTORY OF THE
ADVENTURES OF FANNY HACKABOUT-JONES
(*fiction, 1980*)

WITCHES
(*non-fiction prose and poetry, 1981*)

ORDINARY MIRACLES
(*poetry, 1983*)

MOLLY'S BOOK OF DIVORCE:
A KID'S BOOK FOR ADULTS
(*1984*)

PARACHUTES & KISSES
(*1984*)

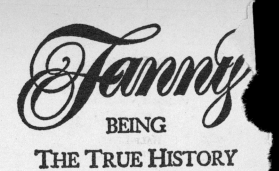

Fanny

BEING
THE TRUE HISTORY
OF THE
ADVENTURES OF
FANNY HACKABOUT-JONES

A Novel by

Erica Jong

A SIGNET BOOK

.NET

...ished by the Penguin Group
...iguin Books USA Inc., 375 Hudson Street,
New York, New York 10014, U.S.A.
Penguin Books Ltd, 27 Wrights Lane,
London W8 5TZ, England
Penguin Books Australia Ltd, Ringwood,
Victoria, Australia
Penguin Books Canada Ltd, 2801 John Street,
Markham, Ontario, Canada L3R 1B4
Penguin Books (N.Z.) Ltd, 182-190 Wairau Road,
Auckland 10, New Zealand

Penguin Books Ltd, Registered Offices:
Harmondsworth, Middlesex, England

Published by Signet, an imprint of New American Library,
a division of Penguin Books USA Inc.

First Signet Printing, December, 1981
16 15 14 13 12 11 10 9 8

Portions of this novel have previously appeared in *Playboy* and *Vogue*.

 REGISTERED TRADEMARK—MARCA REGISTRADA

Printed in the United States of America

PUBLISHER'S NOTE
This is a work of fiction. Names, characters, places, and incidents either are the
product of the author's imagination or are used fictitiously, and any resemblance to
actual persons, living or dead, events, or locales is entirely coincidental.

In which Fanny is introduced . . .

IT IS RAINING at Merriman Park. The green is the green that exists nowhere but in England. Even the tree trunks are green, being kissed with moss. And the steps leading to the little Greek temple are slippery with the same green moss. Across the ha-ha, at the end of the avenue of rain-drenched chestnut trees, cows are grazing, heads down, oblivious of the rain. They are English cows.

A brown and white spaniel with muddy paws bounds into the house, races across the black and white marble floor of the main hall, wholly indifferent to the assemblage of gods and goddesses on the painted ceiling, the scenes from the *Aeneid* on the walls, the reclining marble figures of Poetry, Music, Geography, Astronomy, Geometry, and Sculpture on the pediments above the stately doors. The dog has been eating grass and she stops momentarily to vomit on the parquet floor of the library, then races up the great stairs to her mistress' bedchamber, where she leaps (with muddy paws) upon her silk-dressing-gown-covered knees (marking the rose-pink watered silk with paw prints), vomits some more grass, and in short thoroughly distracts her from what she has been writing. Her mistress puts down her goose quill (now blunt anyway from so much writing) and rises from the walnut writing bureau to chastise the dog, whose name, we now learn, is Chloe.

But who is this lady and what has she been writing? She is too beautiful a lady for us not to inquire. Her hair is the color of autumn. Her eyes are as brown and liquid as her dog's eyes. Her face betrays no years but those required to make a girl into a woman. Perhaps she is thirty, perhaps forty, perhaps thirty-five forever. She is Fanny to her friends, Frances on official documents, and Fannikins to lovers besotted with her charms. There have been plenty of those. She has also been called poetic names like Lindamira, Indamora, Zephalinda, Lesbia, Flavia, Sappho, Candida, by many of her literary lovers (who wrote her into their poems and plays). But no matter. No woman of character ever reaches Fanny's age (whatever it may be) without being ridiculed by some as irrationally as she is praised by others.

So, if she has been called a woman of the town, a tart, a bawd, a wanton, a bawdy-basket, a bird-of-the-game, a bit of stuff, a buttered bun, a cockatrice, a cock-chafer, a cow, a crack, a cunt, a daughter of Eve, a gay-girl, a gobble-prick, a high-flyer, a high-roller, a hussy, a hurry-whore, a jill, a jude, a judy, a jug, laced mutton, lift-skirts, light o' love, merry legs, minx, moll, moonlighter, morsel, mount, mutton-broker, nestcock, night-bird, night-piece, night-walker, nymph of darkness, nymph of the pavement, petticoat, pick-up, piece, pillow-mate, pinch-prick, pole-climber, prancer, quail, quiet mouse, or even Queen—it is not surprising. A woman of lively parts is as likely to be slandered as she is to be praised.

"Chloe—look what you've done to my gown," she says (not really angrily) to the slobbering spaniel; and the two of them leave the vicinity of the writing bureau, the walnut chair (with its ball-claw cabriole legs and its scallop-shell carvings), and proceed to the washstand where the dog will be dried and brushed as lovingly as if it were a child. This enables us to peek at what Fanny has been writing. We do so with only enough guilt to make it more piquant. . . .

The True History
of
the Adventures
of
Fanny Hackabout-Jones

In Three Books

---

*Comprising her Life at Lymeworth,
her Initiation as a Witch, her Travels
with the Merry Men, her Life in the
Brothel, her London High Life, her
Slaving Voyage, her Life as a Female
Pyrate, her eventual Unravelling
of her Destiny, et cetera.*

PRINTED FOR G. FENTON IN THE STRAND

MDCCLI

Dramatis Personae

(in Order of Appearance)

FANNY	*Frances Bellars, also known as Fanny Hackabout-Jones, the Beauteous Heroine of our Tragicomical, Mock-heroical Memoirs*
LORD BELLARS OF LYMEWORTH	*Our Heroine's Step-Father*
LADY BELLARS OF LYMEWORTH	*Our Heroine's Step-Mother*
THE HONOURABLE DANIEL BELLARS	*Our Heroine's Step-Brother*
THE HONOURABLE MARY BELLARS	*Our Heroine's Step-Sister*
ALEXANDER POPE	*The Immortal Poet (but Mortal Man)*
MRS. LOCKE	*The Housekeeper at Lymeworth*
LUSTRE	*Our Heroine's Noble Steed*
LADY MARY	*The Fam'd Rope Dancer, or perhaps her Imitator*
OTHER ACROBATS, CLOWNS, & FREAKS	
DOGGETT	*The Notorious Actor turn'd Fairman*
ISOBEL WHITE	*A Wise Woman of the Woods & Suspected Witch*
JOAN GRIFFITH	*Her Friend*
GRANDMASTER MAIDEN SISTER ALICE SISTER LOUISA ASSORTED WITCHES ASSORTED ROGUES	} *The Coven*

3

of the Bar

n as Horatio, an

llow of Sable

a

Highwayman and

Leader of the

en

LORD RUSSELL

LONGWOOD

LADY HILLGARE

LENGWORTH

THE HONORABLE

LACELLES

The HONOR

ALBERT HENE

Literature Pool

MRS. LACER

Men

A BEGGAR	Carrier of Missives and Messages
THEOPHILUS CIBBER	Infamous Comedian and Son of Colley Cibber
MRS. SKYNNER	Tradeswoman of Dubious Repute who sells "Machines of Safety"
A BAKER	Who assists our Heroine
THE TURNKEY	At Newgate Prison
DEAN SWIFT	The Immortal Author of Gulliver's Travels
HOGARTH	The Immortal Painter
CLELAND	The Infamous Scribbler
HELL-FIRE GUIDE	Who carried our Heroine to the Bowels of the Earth
"MONKS" & "NUNS"	Ye shall learn of 'em soon enough
THE LANDLORD OF THE GEORGE & VULTURE	A Tavern-Keeper
SUSANNAH	Our Heroine's Belovèd Servant
DR. SMELLIE	The Noted Accoucheur
HIS CRONIES	Those who assist and attend him
BELINDA	Our Heroine's Beauteous Daughter
PRUDENCE FERAL	Wet-Nurse, by Profession
MRS. WETTON	A Haughty but Slovenly Cook
THE Cassandra	A Great Merchantman
WATERMAN	Upon the Thames
OLD SEAMAN	At the London Wharves
THE Hopewell	A Brigantine
CAPTAIN WHITEHEAD	A Deist and Sensualist
MR. COCKLYN, THE FIRST MATE	
THE SECOND MATE	The Curious Crew of the Hopewell
LLEWELYN	
BARTHOLOMEW DENNISON, SURGEON	
ASSORTED TARS	
ASSORTED PYRATES, SEA-MEN, SLAVES, & ROGUES	
THE Hazard	A Brig

5

THE *Happy Delivery*
THE *Bijoux*
THE *Willing Mind* } *The Great Pyrate Flotilla*
THE *Speedy Return*
THE *Guarda del Costa*   *A Spanish Treasure Ship*
THE THREE SPOON GALLEY   *Anne Bonny's Noble*
                               Galleass
ANNE BONNY   *The Notorious Female*
                               Pyrate
THE CAPTAIN   *Of the* Cassandra
A PASSENGER   *Upon the* Cassandra
ASSORTED PASSENGERS
    & ROGUES
CHAMBERMAID   *The New Girl at Lymeworth*
LAWYER   *Lord Bellars' Faithful*
                               Retainer

6

Contents

BOOK I

Chapter		Page
I	The Introduction to the Work or Bill of Fare to the Feast.	17
II	A short Description of my Childhood with particular Attention to the Suff'rings of my Step-Mother, Lady Bellars.	20
III	In which I meet my first Great Man, and learn the Truth of that Maxim: " 'Tis easier to be a Great Man in one's Work than in one's Life."	24
IV	Of Gardening, Great Houses, the Curse of Fashion, Paradise Lost, a Family Supper with a Famous Visitor in Attendance, and the Foolish Curiosity of Virgins of Seventeen.	34
V	Of Flip-Flaps, Lollipops, Picklocks, Love-Darts, Pillicocks, and the Immortal Soul, together with some Warnings against Rakes, and some Observations upon the Erotick Proclivities of Poets.	41
VI	Some Reflections upon Harmony, Order, and Reason, together with many surprizing Adventures which follow one upon the other, in rapid Succession.	46
VII	Venus is introduced, with some pretty Writing; and we learn more of the Am'rous Dalliances of Lord Bellars than we, or our Heroine, would wish to know.	52

VIII   Containing the sundry Adventures of our
       Heroine in preparing her Escape, as well as
       many edifying Digressions from Doweries,
       upon Love, upon the Beauties of the English
       Countryside, upon the Wisdom of Horses, upon
       the Necessity for Disguises, and, finally, upon
       the Preferability, at all Times, of being a Man
       rather than a Woman.   57

   IX Containing a most improving Philosophical
       Enquiry into the diff'ring Philosophies of the
       Third Earl of Shaftesbury and Mr. Bernard
       Mandeville, together with an Account of our
       Heroine's sincere Dilemma concerning the Rôle
       of Womankind in the Great World; whereupon
       we follow our Heroine to a Country Fair and
       relate the Misadventures she had there, her
       Début as a Duellist, and, last but not least, her
       most surprizing Rescue by a most surprizing
       Rescuer.   64

    X A Word to the Wise about Gratitude; an
       exciting Chase upon horseback; our Heroine's
       Conversations with two Wise Women of the
       Woods; and a most astonishing Prophecy.   73

   XI Of Prophecies and Herbs; of Witchcraft and
       Magick; of Courage and a red silk Garter.   82

  XII Containing some Essential Information regarding
       the Nature of Esbats, Sabbats, Flying thro' the
       Air upon Broomstaffs, and other Matters with
       which the enlighten'd Young Woman of Parts
       should be acquainted; together with a most
       dreadful Scene upon Stonehenge Down, which
       few Readers should venture upon in an Ev'ning,
       especially when alone.   88

 XIII Containing sev'ral Dialogues concerning Fate,
       Poesy, and the Relations betwixt the Sexes, as
       well as other Intercourse of a more sensual
       Nature (because of which the Modest Reader is
       advis'd to pass o'er this Chapter unread), which
       our Heroine had with Miss Polly Mudge,

Chambermaid, Mr. Ned Tunewell, Poetaster,
and e'en with Herself, at that celebrated
Coaching Inn call'd The Dumb Bell.   103

XIV   In which Lancelot Robinson and his Merry
        Men are introduced and our Heroine meets her
        Fate in all its Nakedness.   118

XV   A short Hint of what we can do in the
        Rabelaisian Style; our Heroine gets her Name;
        Lancelot Robinson begins his astounding
        History.   126

XVI   Lancelot Robinson concludes his astounding
        History, showing that a Man may be wise in all
        Things, both sublunary and divine, yet still be
        a Ninny where Women are concern'd.   136

XVII   An improving philosophical Conversation upon
        the Nature of Orphans, after which the Merry
        Men are introduced, Lancelot discloses his
        future Plans, and Horatio's curious History is
        reveal'd.   142

XVIII   Containing some mischievous and am'rous Play
        in which 'tis presently seen that Lancelot's
        Protestations of sexual Preference are not as
        fixt as he would have had us believe, nor indeed
        are those of our Friend Horatio, whereupon our
        Heroine finds herself in a Predicament which
        Prudes will applaud but the Hot-blooded will
        find (nearly) tragick; after which we ponder a
        prophetick Dream and thereafter begin our
        Voyage to London.   159

Book II

I   In which our Heroine first makes an intimate
        Acquaintance with the Great City of London,
        and what befell her upon her historick Arrival
        there.   173

II   Some Animadversions upon the Author of that
     Notorious Book, *Memoirs of a Woman of
     Pleasure,* or *Fanny Hill,* together with our
     Heroine's True and Compleat Recital of what
     really happen'd during her Initiation into
     Mother Coxtart's Brothel, her first Visit to a
     London Draper's, and a most astonishing
     Message from the Ghost of Robin Hood.   186

III In which our Fanny meets a Frog who thinks
     himself a Prince and loses her Virginity for the
     second Time (which Doubting Thomases may
     profess to be impossible, but Readers wise in the
     Wicked Ways of the World will credit).   198

IV   In which we follow Fanny to Mrs. Skynner's
     Emporium, are initiated into some Mysteries to
     which Wise Women have been privy thro'out
     the Centuries, and subsequently make our
     Descent into London's own Hades, namely,
     Newgate Prison.   206

V   Fanny's Flight thro' London; Dissension in the
     Body Politick, and a most amazing Revolution,
     which Whigs will applaud but Tories may
     grumble of; after which our Heroine learns
     sev'ral important Lessons which we hope will
     help her her whole Life long, but ne'ertheless is
     mov'd to an Act of great Desperation which
     causes her untold Anguish and Agony.   216

VI   Containing a short Sketch of the celebrated
     Dean Swift of Dublin, Author, Misanthrope,
     and Horse-Fancier extraordinaire; together with
     some philosophical and moral Lessons which
     our Heroine drew from her curious Friendship
     with him.   227

VII Of Fanny's Acquaintance with those two
     curious Figures, Mr. William Hogarth and
     Master John Cleland; their opposing Views of
     her Character, their Predilections both in Life
     and Art; together with our Heroine's Motives
     in composing this True and Compleat History
     of her exotick and adventurous Life.   237

VIII   In which we look in upon Mr. Lancelot
       Robinson in Newgate Prison and learn what
       hath transpir'd with him whilst our Fanny was
       very much Otherwise Engaged.   248

  IX   Containing a most edifying Excursion into the
       World of London Clubs, in which our Heroine
       journeys to the Centre of the Earth, meets the
       Devil, and finds him a more familiar Figure
       than she otherwise would have guess'd.   255

   X   Of Love and Lust, Pan and Satan, Longing and
       Loyalty, and other such lofty (or low) Matters;
       together with our Heroine's Adventures at the
       notorious George & Vulture Inn, and how (with
       the Aid of some of the surviving Merry Men)
       she resolv'd the Dilemma of her Destiny.   269

  XI   Containing a most curious Exchange of Letters
       thro' which our Fanny learns more concerning
       the Capriciousness of Destiny than all her
       Adventures have taught her until now; after
       which she is summon'd by her one True Love,
       as the Reader of this most stirring epistolary
       Chapter shall shortly see.   279

 XII   Containing an Incident of a more tragick than
       comedick Kind, the Import of which may not be
       reveal'd for many Years, but which nonetheless
       alters our Heroine's Destiny most profoundly.   289

XIII   Containing a most edifying Comparison betwixt
       Life and a Masquerade, as well as our Heroine's
       Meditations upon Maternity and the curious
       Bargain she struck with the Devil to ensure the
       safe Arrival upon this Earth of her unborn
       Babe.   302

Book III

   I   How our Heroine spent her Confinement; a
       short Description of Her Loyal Servant,

Susannah; some philosophical Meditations upon the Phases of Childbirth, after which your Author enters into the Controversy (which raged thro'out the Age) betwixt Midwives and *Accoucheurs,* and thereafter gratefully ends the Chapter.   311

II   Containing better Reasons than any which have yet appear'd for the happy Delivery of Women by those of their own Sex, together with the Introduction of the newest Character in our Historio-Comical Epick, who, tho' small, proves more Trouble to her Author in her Entrance upon the Scene than any Personage of more prodigious Size.   324

III   In which such surprizing Events occur that we dare not e'en hint of 'em here, lest the Muse of Historio-Comical Epick Writing be very cross with us and flee our House forthwith.   338

IV   We are introduced to Prudence Feral, Wet-Nurse extraordinaire, and your humble Author summarizes the current Controversy concerning Wet-Nursing versus maternal Breast Feeding, to which she appends some Views of her own, drawn from Experience (that greatest of all Teachers).   346

V   Containing the Character of a Cook, some useful Opinions upon the Nature of Infants, our Heroine's Attempts to find a new Wet-Nurse for her Babe, and the compleat Contents of a Mother's Nightmare.   357

VI   In which our Heroine and her loyal Servant, Susannah, begin their Apprenticeship at Sea, and learn that the Sailor's Life is not an easy one, tho' the Ship hath scarce left the Dock.   366

VII   Containing a Storm at Sea, a Scene which should perhaps be skipp'd o'er by those with squeamish Stomachs, and the Entrance into our History of the notorious Captain Whitehead.   377

VIII   In which 'tis prov'd that Sea Captains are as
       lustful as they are reputed to be, that Deists do
       not always make the best Lovers, and that many
       Persons in their Erotick Habits crave that
       Treatment which, in Truth, they deserve, in
       consequence of their Characters.   389

  IX   In which our Heroine learns more than she
       wishes to know about the Nature of Distemper'd
       Lust; debates with the Surgeon (and indeed with
       herself) about the Nature of Evil and whether
       anything we Mortals do can assuage it; and
       loses an old Friend just as she hath made a new.   402

   X   In which our Heroine learns that no Man is
       such a Scoundrel that he doth not wish to be
       an Author, that e'en Slavers account themselves
       patriotick and virtuous, that the Sea is as full of
       Magick and Mystery as the Land, and that Ships
       oft' become Pyrate Prizes as much thro' the
       Connivance of their own Tars as thro' any
       other Means.   414

  XI   Containing a better Explanation for the
       Prevalence of Pyracy than any Authors, ancient
       or modern, have yet advanced; together with
       our Heroine's tragick but true Realization that
       most Revolutionaries are none where Women
       are concern'd, and what ingenious Strategem
       she made Use of to alter this sad State of
       Affairs.   425

 XII   Containing divers Dialogues betwixt Lancelot,
       Horatio, and our Heroine in which the History
       goes backward somewhat and we learn what
       these Gentlemen have been doing whilst the
       Queen of our Narrative was extending her
       Education and Adventures; thereto is added a
       brief History of Buccaneering for the Reader
       who is bent upon the noble Cause of Self-
       Improvement as well as the more pleasant one
       of Entertainment.   440

XIII   In which our Heroine well and truly learns the

Pyrate's Craft, discovers the Joys of Sailing (as
she hath previously known only the Pains),
whereupon our valiant Pyrates meet their Match
upon the Seas, and we disprove that old Maxim,
namely: "Man cannot be rap'd."   454

XIV   Containing Anne Bonny's Legacy to our
      Heroine; better Reasons for Female Pyracy
      than for Male; a very tragical Incident; and the
      Beginning of the Conclusion of our History—
      (but do not fear, we shall not leave our Reader
      without many more Epilogues, Appendices,
      and Farewells).   477

XV   In which we draw nearer and nearer to our
      Conclusion, and certain Omens presage the
      Future of our Heroine, Hero, and their
      Belovèd Babe.   493

XVI   Drawing still nearer to the End.   515

      Epilogue: In which our Author explains the
      curious Chain of Events which led to the
      Writing of this History.   522

BOOK I

Chapter I

The Introduction to the Work or Bill of Fare to the Feast.

I, FANNY HACKABOUT-JONES, having been blest with long Life, which makes e'en the Harshest Events of Youth pale to Insignificance or, i'faith, appear as Comedies, do write this History of my Life and Adventures as a Testament for my only Daughter, Belinda.

I have, in other Documents, left this most Excellent Young Woman my Houses, my Lands, my Jewels, the Care of my Dogs, Horses, and Domestick Animals, and yet I am convinced that the ensuing History shall have more Value to her than all the Riches I have acquir'd in my Life, either by my Pen or by my Person. For tho' 'tis no easy Thing to be born a Man in this Vale of Tears, 'tis more difficult still to be born a Woman. Yet I believe I have prosper'd despite this Capricious Destiny, or e'en because of it, and what better Legacy can I give to my beloved Belinda than a full and true Account of that very Life which hath been so oft' distorted, slander'd, or us'd to inspire scandalous Novels, lascivious Plays, and wanton Odes?

If these Pages oft' tell of Debauchery and Vice, 'tis not in any wise because their Author wishes to condone Wickedness, but rather because Truth, Stark-Naked Truth, demands that she write with all possible Candour, so that the Inheritor of this Testament shall learn how to avoid Wickedness or indeed transform it into Goodness.

All possible Care hath been taken to give no deliberate Offence to Modesty or Chastity; yet the Author avows that Truth is a sterner Goddess than Modesty, and where there hath been made necessary a Choyce betwixt the Former and the Latter, Truth hath, quite rightly, triumph'd.

If some of the Episodes in the ensuing History offend the gentler Sensibilities of an Age less lusty than that which gave me birth, let the Reader put it down to the Excesses of my

17

Epoch, the doubtless impoverish'd Origins of my poor Natural Parents, the Lack of Formal Education occasion'd by my Sex, and the Circumstances of my Life, which caus'd me to make my Living by my Wits, my Pen, and my Beauty.

The World is so taken up of late with Histories and Romances in which Vice fore'er perishes and Virtue triumphs, that the intended Reader may wonder why Vice is not always punish'd and Virtue not always rewarded in these Pages, as in the Histories of Mr. Fielding and Mr. Richardson; to which your Humble Author can only reply that 'tis Truth we serve here, not Morality, and with howe'er much Regret we affirm it, ne'ertheless we must affirm that Truth and Morality do not always, alas, sleep in the same Bed.

'Tis a trite but true Observation that Examples work more forcibly upon the Mind than Precepts; yet whilst the Male Sex hath had no Derth of Examples of Greatness from Jesus of Nazareth to William Shakespeare, the Bard of Stratford, the Members of the Female Sex search in vain for Great Women on whom to model their perilous Destinies.

The Authors of contemporary Novels and Romances do little Service in this regard, for either they prate of Female "Vartue," a Luxury which few Women can afford, and only the dullest and most witless can tolerate, or they condemn Female Vice in such Terms that upon reading these Male Authors, any spirited Young Woman should resolve to slit her own Throat forthwith. Neither Pamela Andrews, with her incessant Scribbling of her "Vartue," nor tiresome Clarissa Harlowe, with her insuff'rable Weeping and Letter-writing, nor yet the gentle Sophia Western of whom Mr. Fielding so prettily writes, nor the wicked Moll Flanders of whom Mr. Defoe so vigorously writes, shines out as an Example upon which a Flesh-and-Blood Female can model her Life. For Life, as the Ancients knew, is neither Tragedy nor Comedy, but an Intermingling of the twain. 'Tis a Feast in which one is serv'd delicate Viands as well as spicy Hashes and Ragoos; rotten Meats as well as exquisite Fruits; exotick Spices and Sauces as well as plain Country Fare. If 'tis thus for Man, imagine how much more so for Woman! Woman who is ev'rywhere in Nature misunderstood and apprehended only as the Embodiment of Virtue or the Embodiment of Vice.

I have endeavor'd in this History to show the Falsity of these Embodiments; for like the aforemention'd Feast of Life, Woman is a Mixture of Sweets and Bitters. I here solemnly

18

protest that not only have I no Intention to asperse or vilify anyone, but that ev'rything herein is copied faithfully from the Great Book of Nature and that I, your Author, am no more than an humble Amanuensis.

Chapter II

A short Description of my Childhood with particular Attention to the Suff'rings of my Step-Mother, Lady Bellars.

I WAS BORN in the Reign of Queen Anne, but the exact Date of my Birth I did not, for many Years, know, owing to the unfortunate Occurrence of my having been abandon'd upon a Doorstep in tend'rest Infancy. Whether my Natural Parents were, as the Saying goes, poor but honest, or whether they were poor and vicious, I could not in Good Conscience say. That they were poor was a fair enough Conjecture, else why would they have left a helpless Babe of their Begetting upon the Doorstep of a Great House in the Neighbourhood?

The Foster-Parents that Fate thus arranged for me were nam'd Bellars: Laurence Bellars and his Lady, Cecilia. Lord Bellars had been born of impoverish'd Noble Ancestry, having had settl'd upon him a Family Seat as heavily mortgaged as our Chestnut Trees were heavy with Chestnuts; but thro' judicious Employment of his Wife's Dowery to finance his Speculations in Stock of the East India Company as well as thro' Holdings in the Bank of England, he had grown extreamly rich, and ev'rything he did, it seem'd, made him richer. So able was he at Speculation, that e'en during the South Sea Bubble, when I was but a Young Girl, he was one of the few that not only prosper'd, but managed to transfer his Earnings into Land before the Bubble burst. I'faith, that Scandal, which was the Ruin of so many, provided our Estate with another two thousand Acres, not to mention paying our Debts and providing us with yet a more handsome Equipage, and still more Footmen in gorgeous Livery.

Lord Bellars chose to live mainly in London, pleading the Excuse of his business Dealings; tho' i'faith, Gaming and Whoring probably occupied many of his Leisure Hours. He left his Wife, Cecilia, to preside o'er the Great House and

Park in Wiltshire and to instruct the Children—Daniel, Mary, and myself—in the Virtues which he had neither Time nor Inclination to impart, either by Precept or by Example.

My Position in the Family was neither that of an Inheritor of the Family Fortune, nor that of a Servant. I was a Found-ling, lov'd for my Quick Wit, my russet Curls, and my play-ful Disposition, yet not granted the Indulgences given to a proper Child, who, for better or worse, is of one's own Blood.

I was e'er a Bookworm, loving to read almost from the Time I was given my first Alphabet. In a Day when Girls were commonly thought to need no Education but the Needle, Dancing, and the French Tongue (with perhaps the Addition of a little Musick upon the Harpsichord or Spinet), I was plund'ring My Lord's Library for Tonson's *Poetical Miscellanies*, new Books by Mr. Pope and Mr. Swift, as well as older ones by Shakespeare, Milton, Boccaccio, Boileau, and Molière. Latin I was left to teach myself; for tho' that Noble Tongue was consider'd the Mark of Erudition in a Man, 'twas deem'd superfluous to Womankind. I'faith, I ne'er could comprehend why Daniel, a rather dull-witted, lazy Boy, but a Year my senior, should be sent to Day School to learn Latin, Greek, Algebra, Geometry, Geography, and the Use of Globes, whilst I, who was so much quicker, was encouraged only in Pastry-making, Needlepoint, and French Dancing, and laugh'd at for being vain of my fine Penmanship. Yet of all the Crafts I learnt in Childhood, Writing is the one that hath stood me in greatest Stead during my whole Life and hath most distinguish'd me from other Women. Beauty, alas, fades; Riches may be lost in one Turn of Fortune's Wheel. A Woman with a fine Dowery can fall into the Hands of a Rogue who will not e'en allow her Pin-Money, and will gamble away her Widow's Jointure and leave her nothing but Play-Debts and hungry Mouths to feed; but a Woman of Learning who can make her Living with her Quill is more se-cure of the Future (tho' all the Coffeehouse Wits may scoff) than any Woman whatsoe'er. For what is Marriage but a Form of indentur'd Service in which the Wife gives up all (her Name, her Fortune, her very Health and physical Con-stitution) to secure the occasional Night-time Visits of a Knave with whom she shares nothing but a Roof and a Nurs-ery full of screaming Babes?

My Step-Mother, Lady Bellars, was one of the most

21

wretchèd Creatures who e'er liv'd, tho' had she been a Man her Fortune and Beauty would have made her happy. Too clever to spend her Life betwixt the Tea-Table and the Card-Table, too sweet of Disposition to nag and scold her Husband for his long Absences, his Whoring and Gaming, and too timid to be a Female Rake in the Fashion of the Day, and use her Married State as a Cloak to cover divers Amours, she languish'd in the Country, devoting herself to her Children far past the Age when they requir'd her Care, and to a Menagerie of Beasts on whom she lavish'd more than natural Maternal Affection.

In addition to three Lapdogs and a Parrot, she kept a Marmoset Monkey, two Paroquets of Guinea, four Cockatoos, three Macaws, a dozen scarlet Nightingales from the West Indies, a half-dozen Canaries (both ash and lemon Colour), two dozen or so white and grey Turtledoves from Barbary, and num'rous Milk-white Peacocks that hopp'd freely around the Park. So devoted was she to her Menagerie that e'en upon the rare Occasions when Lord Bellars sent for her to come to London, she declin'd, pleading the Care of her Animals.

Thus, from my earliest Childhood, I had before me the Example of what a blighted, unloving Marriage could do to a Woman of tender Disposition, and I resolv'd in my Heart ne'er to let become of me what had become of my gentle Step-Mother, who, I sincerely believ'd, was driven half mad by the painful Betrayals practis'd upon her by her Husband.

Where a less tender Soul would have given Tit for Tat and repaid her Husband's Amours with Cuckoldry and Back-Talk, Lady Bellars withdrew into her Menagerie, until at last, when she was a white-hair'd old Woman, she spoke more to her Peacocks and Turtledoves than she did to human Visitors.

. Let that be a Lesson to you, I would silently command my Heart as I listen'd to my Step-Mother speaking to her Menagerie; and tho' I learnt from her the Love of Animals which hath lasted to this Day, I also learnt to be wary of the Male Sex and to view ev'ry handsome Gallant and Man of Pleasure as a likely Robber of my Wits and my Peace of Mind. That Lesson, above all, hath been the Making of whate'er Good Fortune I have enjoy'd upon this Earth.

I'faith, like Belinda in "The Rape of the Lock" (a Poem

22

which I read and read again thro'out my younger Years), my
Guardian Angel taught me one Lesson above all others:

This to disclose is all thy Guardian can.
Beware of all, but most beware of Man!

Chapter III

*In which I meet my first Great Man, and learn the Truth
of that Maxim: " 'Tis easier to be a Great Man in one's
Work than in one's Life."*

THAT LESSON WAS TO BE tested soon enough. Thro'out the
Peace and Plenty of my Country Childhood, I was told I was
growing into a Beauty. I say this out of no Immodesty;
i'faith, I scarce believ'd it myself. Like most Young Girls,
when I lookt at myself in the Glass, I saw nought but my
own grievous Faults; yet was I *call'd* a Beauty so oft' that I
came to understand the World regarded me thus. 'Twas
merely the Condition of my Life that I should set Swains to
sighing and Footmen to fondling my Hand longer than need
be whilst helping me down from Chariots.

Just as my Step-Sister, Mary, was stubby and stout, had a
Face like a Suet Pudding, and Hair of Mouse Colour, I was,
by the perilous Age of Seventeen, straight and tall (*too* tall, I
thought), with flaming Hair (too russet for *my* Taste), the
brownest of Eyes (would that they were *green!*), a Bosom
blue-white as skimm'd Milk (I minded not the Colour but the
Size!), long taper'd Fingers (O my Hands were pretty—I
would grant that!), and slender Legs (but who should see 'em
'neath my Petticoats?) ending in clever Feet that could do
any complicated Dance whatsoe'er (for all the Good 'twould
do me here in the dull Country!). In fact, I was greatly devoted to a Book call'd *The Dancing Master*, which listed no
less than 358 diff'rent Figures and Tunes for Country Dances;
and I knew as well how to twirl, flip and flirt a Fan, how to
behave most fetchingly at Tea-Table, and how to place
Patches to the best advantage upon my oval Cheaks. For all
these Things, I was teaz'd and tormented by Daniel and
silently hated by Mary, whilst my poor distracted Step-
Mother tended to her Animals and seem'd wholly oblivious of
the Fact that her three tender Human Charges were no longer

24

little Babes, but were growing to an Age when all the Envies, Vices, and Temptations of the World might snare 'em.

'Twas about that Season in our Lives when Lord Bellars, who had been chiefly in London o'er the last three Years (with only brief Visits Home), came into the Country for a Stay of sev'ral Months.

When the News reach'd me that he was bringing down from London with him no less a Personage than the Great Poet Mr. Alexander Pope, I could hardly believe my Ears. Mr. Pope—whose "Rape of the Lock" I had got almost by Heart! Mr. Pope, whose Divine Quill had written the Lines:

> Then cease, bright Nymph! to mourn thy ravish'd Hair
> Which adds new Glory to the shining Sphere!
> Not all the Tresses that fair Head can boast
> Shall draw such Envy as the Lock you lost.
> For, after all the Murders of your Eye,
> When, after Millions slain, your Self shall die;
> When those fair Suns shall set, as set they must,
> And all those Tresses shall be laid in Dust;
> *This Lock*, the Muse shall consecrate to Fame,
> And mid'st the Stars inscribe *Belinda's* Name.

Mr. Pope, whose tender Heart had bled for an unknown Lady buried in a foreign Land. . . .

> By foreign Hands thy dying Eyes were clos'd,
> By foreign Hands thy decent Limbs compos'd,
> By foreign Hands thy humble Grave adorn'd,
> By Strangers honour'd, and by Strangers mourn'd!

A Man who could write like that must be the most sensitive Soul that e'er liv'd! He must have Eyes that see ev'rything and a Heart that beats out the Suff'rings of the smallest Creature alive. Here, perchance, was a Man who could understand me, a Man with a great enough Heart, a great enough Mind—not like the foolish Country Boys who gap'd at me in the Village, not like Daniel, who could think of nothing but Excuses for jostling me upon the Stair or thrusting his greasy Hands into my Bosom.

For a Week, the whole Household was engaged in Preparations. Pigeons and Partridges were shot and pluckt. Oysters were brought from Market and boil'd in their own Juices, and extravagant Receipts were taken from Cookery Books. Upon the Day after the Poet's Arrival with Lord Bellars we were to have all the local Gentry in to meet our distinguish'd Visitor and to feast upon Spinach Tarts made with Nutmeg, Cloves, and Lemon Peel, Patty of Calves' Brains with Asparagus, stew'd Oysters, roast Pigeons, roast Partridges, three sorts of Pudding, and a royal Dish called "Fruits with Preserv'd Flow'rs," which took two Days to prepare, being a Concoction of Paste of Almonds, inlaid with red, white, blue, and green Marmalade in the Figures of Flow'rs and Banks, with upright Branches of candied Flow'rs made from glaz'd Cheeryes, Apples, Gooseberries, Currants, and Plums.

But I would hardly be in any Mood to eat.

All Day I linger'd at the Windows of my Bedchamber, dreaming o'er a Book of Mr. Pope's Poetry, fancying myself invited to London to mingle with Wits in a Coffee-House, to stroll thro' Pall Mall or Covent Garden, to go by Wherry to Twickenham with Mr. Pope and be invited to view his fam'd Faery Grotto.

I must have changed my Gown three Times that Day, throwing off Dresses and putting 'em on as if I were a Strolling Actress in a Barn! First, I wore the Dove-grey Saquebackt Silk with the yellow Stomacher and Apron; then I changed into a blue Gown with my prettiest embroider'd Apron and a Tucker of white Lace; but at last, I chose a Cherry-colour'd Damask with no Tucker at all, because I had heard that Ladies in London wore their Bosoms almost bare and I did not wish to be thought a plain Country Wench!

'Twas almost Twilight when the Chariot with six Horses clatter'd into view, greeted by the Barking of all our Dogs. Yet still I linger'd at my Window, dabbing my Bosom out of a Vial of Tuberose Scent, biting my Lips to make 'em redder.

How had I imagin'd Mr. Pope? Can I not have heard till then that he was a Hunchback? Or can it be that Memory deceives me? Ne'ertheless, I fancied him in the Mould of one of the Heroes of a French Romance, perhaps because the Imagination of a Girl of Seventeen is apt to clothe a Poet in Colours of his own Making. His Words were handsome, so should his Figure be! Nothing else was possible. It did not then occur to me that Poets perhaps write in order to create that very Delusion in Wenches of Seventeen and indeed to augment with their Quills the paltry Equipment Nature hath bestow'd upon 'em.

Imagine my Surprize and Discomfiture when I saw the Figure that emerged from the Carriage!

He was not above four and one-half foot tall and his Back hump'd so prodigiously betwixt his Shoulder Blades that his fawn Coat must have been a Taylor's Marvel to accommodate it! He seem'd to be wearing not one but sev'ral Pairs of silk Stockings at once, and yet his Legs were so piteously thin that the Stockings creas'd and hung on 'em as if they were Twigs rather than Flesh. Under his Coat and Waistcoat, he wore a kind of fur Doublet (such as our Ancestors wore), perhaps to bulk out his crooked and wasted Form, or perhaps to guard against the Chills such Flesh must be Heir to. From my Window's Height, I could not see his lower'd Face, but beside Lord Bellars, he lookt like a sort of Question Mark of Humanity standing next to a Poplar Tree. Lord Bellars was tall and straight, with broad Shoulders and manly, muscular Legs. Under his black Beaver cockt Hat, edged with deep gold Lace, he wore a fine Riding Wig, and when he threw his Head back to laugh at some Witticism the Poet had utter'd, I glimps'd a handsome Roman Nose, a clear olive Complexion, glowing with Life and Fire, and Eyes that sparkl'd like Dew Drops upon Rose Petals. His Laugh was as resonant and manly as the Barking of Bull-Dogs. I'faith, the Moment I saw him again, I was prepar'd to forgive, or explain away as vicious Libels, all the scandalous Stories Lady Bellars had told me of him.

O, my Belinda, beware the Lure of a handsome Face, the all too ready Assumption that the lovely Façade must needs have lovely Chambers within; for as 'tis with Great Houses, so, too, with Great Men. They may have grand Porticos and Loggias without, but within may be Madness and Squalor. 'Tis said that by the Cock of the Hat, the Man is known, and Lord Bellars wore his with the Raffishness of a Rogue; yet more gentle Maids of Seventeen have been betray'd by their own trusting Hearts than by the artful Wiles of their Seducers. For, as 'tis usual at that Age to suppose that Nature is ev'rywhere consistent and harmonious, we presume, in our Innocence, that a beauteous Brow contains a beauteous Brain, a handsome Mouth, handsome Words, and a robust manly Form, robust manly Deeds. Alas, my Daughter, 'tis not so.

But I was younger at that Moment than you are now, and I was full of all the Wild Impetuosity of Youth; so I clatter'd at breakneck Speed down the Great Steps and should have run immediately into the Courtyard to greet our Visitors, had not a monstrous Villain upon the second Landing stuck out a Leg to stop me, and sent me toppling headlong down the Stair. Before the World behind my Eyelids went starry as the Night Sky and then black as the Grave, I glimps'd Mary's Face like a boil'd Pudding with a Smile plaster'd upon it, mocking me from the second Landing; and I knew in my Heart, tho' all Proof was lacking, that 'twas she who had tripp'd me. (Ah, Belinda, beware, e'en more than the Wiles of Men, the Envy of Women—for more gentle Maids have been betray'd by envious Sisters than e'en by their own trusting Hearts!)

The Ill-Feeling betwixt Mary and myself had an ancient History. Shortly after she was born—disappointingly enough a Girl-Child—Mary was put out with the Wet-Nurse till she was well-nigh three Years of Age, whilst in the Meantime Daniel was brought to birth and I was found upon the fateful Doorstep.

I'faith, both Daniel and I were suckl'd by Wet-Nurses for a Time after our Births, but wet-nurs'd within the Great House itself (where Lady Bellars could oft' visit us), whilst Mary stay'd away from Home until she could speak. Meanwhile, Lady Bellars, repenting of having lost her Chances at Maternal Affection with her Firstborn, and i'faith feeling cheated by Lord Bellars' Mockery of her Maternal Longings, lavish'd these tender Emotions upon me to such a Degree that Mary envied me extreamly, and doubtless wisht me dead.

To make Matters worse, I was a precocious Child, clever where Mary was dull, able to recite lengthy Passages from *Paradise Lost* and the Sonnets of Mr. Shakespeare, whilst Mary could not e'en remember a simple Country-Ballad; and for this, too, she hated me. I was trotted out in all my babyish Finery to perform before Lord and Lady Bellars' Guests, whilst my poor Step-Sister, whene'er she attempted a Performance, forgot her Lines, lookt Cow-like and dull-witted, causing Lord Bellars to declare:

"La! What a Face! What ails the Child? If I didn't know better, I'd swear the Child was a Changeling and Fannikins my proper Daughter!"

To be sure, none of this was calculated to create Good Will betwixt Mary and myself.

How long I lay unconscious I cannot tell. I dreamt I trav-

28

ell'd to the Moon and back, and that the Face of the Moon was the mocking Face of my Step-Sister, Mary. For a little while, I voyaged to those Spheres describ'd by Mr. Milton and Signor Ariosto, and then I awoke to find the whole Household standing o'er me with great Concern and Solicitude, but especially Lord Bellars and Mr. Pope, whose great, kind Eyes, I now could see, were the all-knowing Eyes of a Poet.

"Come, gentle Nymph," says he to me, extending a Hand which was delicate as a Maid's yet cold and pale as Death itself. I found myself at once repuls'd and attracted by his Delicacy, his Death-like Pallor, his large sensitive Eyes and long quiv'ring Nose, the Physiognomy of Poet within the Carcass of a twisted Dwarf.

"My Dear," says Lord Bellars, aside to Lady Bellars, "you did not tell me our little Foundling was growing into such a Beauty."

"And why should I?" says Lady Bellars; "would you come Home for her when you would not come Home for your own Daughter?"

Lord Bellars made a Motion to indicate that this Remark was beneath Contempt, and, thanking the Poet for his Kindness, he also extended a Hand to me, then swept me at once into his Arms, and in full view of the entire Household, carried me up the Stair to my Bedchamber.

Can you imagine the Fire burning in my Cheaks as this Marvel of Manhood scoops me up into his Arms and carries me thus impetuously off?

"Thou *art* growing into a Beauty," Lord Bellars says, looking down at me from, it seems, a great Height. And then he gallops up the Stair two at a Time, makes haste for my Bedchamber, where he throws me down on the Bed roughly yet playfully, and says, leering like the Devil himself, "I know of but one sure Way to revive a fainting Wench." In a trice, my Petticoats and Shift are thrown o'er my Head, muffling my Protestations of Shock and Alarm, and a strong, warm Hand plays Arpeggios o'er the soft, silky Moss that but a few Years before had begun to spring from the Mount-Pleasant betwixt my youthful Thighs, as velvet Grass springs from a silted River-Bank.

His Fingers play'd and strove to twine in the Tendrils of that womanly Vegetation, but suddenly he begins to insinuate a Finger into the very Quick of my Womanhood, inflaming

29

me beyond the twin Pow'rs of Modesty and Surprize to resist, and causing me to cry out, "O! O! O!" Whereupon he flips the Petticoats back to their Proper Place, surveys my Blushes with Amusement, caresses my Breasts, those great snowy Hillocks tipp'd with rosy Nipples (whose Largeness, i'faith, hath, till this Moment, done nought but embarrass me), laughs, kisses me upon the Lips, and declares, "At least my Beauty is still a Virgin—tho' from the Impatience I feel in her willing Young Blood, she will not be one for long!" Whereupon he makes haste to withdraw, leaving me shockt, speechless, all but mute with Outrage mingl'd with shameful Pleasure. Fire cours'd thro' my Veins, filling me with Longing, Disgust, and Self-loathing.

O, I had heard plenty from the Servants concerning the Evils of giving way to bestial Lust (tho' from the Servants' own Behaviour with each other, one should have thought they were scarce the ones to talk!). Yet I knew that the disorder'd Sensations I now felt presaged my Fall from precious Purity into Ruin and Disgrace, and I wept at my Shame. A Man might vent his Passions unafraid, but a Woman did so at her Peril—particularly before Marriage. E'en my timid Step-Mother had press'd upon all her youthful Charges a Pamphlet entitled *Onania or the heinous Sin of Self-Pollution, and all its frightful Consequences in both Sexes Consider'd*, which told of the Horrors and Distempers which would surely follow soon upon Indulgence in Carnal Pleasure. If Onania might cause Epilepsy, Fevers, Boils, and e'en Death—how much *worse* Horrors the Loss of a Maidenhead might bring! Yet was I verily confus'd o'er all these Matters, for I had heard Lord Bellars' Amours jested of below Stairs as nought but *Bagatelles*, and e'en those of certain married Women of the County more laugh'd o'er than shunn'd. Was Gallantry then a Venial or a Mortal Sin? It depended, i'faith, upon the Committer of the Crime. If he were a Man of Fashion, the Crime was small, but if a Maid of Seventeen, 'twas enormous!

Lord Bellars had not lower'd my Petticoats an Instant too soon, for in a very few Moments, Lady Bellars and Mary arriv'd upon the Scene, and Lord Bellars pretended that nothing untoward had happen'd.

"The Wench is just reviving," says he, with supreme *Ennui*.

"So I see," said Lady Bellars haughtily. And then, under

her Breath, to Lord Bellars, "I wonder why you grace us with your Presence at all, when all you do here is Mischief."

Whereupon Mary peevishly says, defending her Father, as e'er, "I'm sure 'twas Fanny's Fault—the audacious Strumpet!"

"Hush," says Lady Bellars. And then, gently, to me, "Please wear something more modest to Supper, Fannikins. These Poets are a very hot-blooded Lot. 'Twill not do to stir 'em to a Frenzy." And with that she sweeps out, following her Husband. Mary alone remains, sits upon the edge of my Bed, and whispers venomously into my Ear: "You aren't e'en my proper Sister, you saucy Baggage." Whereupon she spits into my Face and turns and runs.

Can you imagine my Feelings as I lay there on the Bed thus humiliated, arous'd, and finally spat upon? Betwixt my Ruminations upon the Consequences of my Lustful Passions, and my Resentment of my Step-Sister Mary, some new Resolution was brewing within my troubl'd Brain.

How should I revenge myself upon Mary for this Humiliation? And how should I resist those Fires of Passion Lord Bellars had, so knowingly, stirr'd? My Step-Father had been Home only a few Minutes and already the entire Household was in a Tumult.

'Twas e'er thus, in the Past, I recall'd. A Semblance of Order and Harmony prevail'd whilst he amus'd himself in London and Lady Bellars, Mary, Daniel, and myself got on tolerably well; but when my Step-Father betook himself to Lymeworth, all the Ruling Passions of his Wards came horribly to the Fore. Daniel, who (tho' ungracefully stout and grievously bespatter'd with Pimples) always essay'd to ape his Father's Manners as a Beau, became frenzied to imitate his Sire's fabl'd Gallantries. Consequently, when Lord Bellars was at Home, Daniel plagued me continuously with his Lustful Attentions. Mary, for her part, became e'en more uncheckt in her Envy of me; and Lady Bellars, who could be tender, e'en witty, when left to her own Pleasures of Animals and Children, responded to her Husband's Presence by becoming once again the prim Puritanical Heiress he had, all lovelessly, wed. Thus 'tis true that tho' People can transcend their Characters in Times of Tranquillity, they can ne'er do so in Times of Tumult. E'en I (I freely confess) became too vain and flirtatious upon Lord Bellars' Arrival, provoking my Step-Sister to a veritable Debauch of Envy.

Poor Mary—whose Passion for Roast Beef and Mutton got

the better of all her Dreams of Slenderness and Grace—had been taking Purges for two Weeks past, in the Hopes of looking beautiful for her Father. But alas, it avail'd nought; for she would purge and purge, and starve and starve, and then, just as she appear'd somewhat more in the Mould of the Belle she ne'er would be, she'd polish off a whole roast Leg o' Mutton, washt down with Claret and the sweetest Port!

As Gluttony was her Ruling Passion, so Riding was mine; Roast Beef could I easily forgo, Horseflesh ne'er. I seldom had cause to fret o'er my Form since exercising my dear Horse, Lustre, kept me as slender as Roast Beef and Yorkshire Pudding kept Mary stout. To be sure, I fretted o'er other Vexations; my uncertain Future, my Lack of Dowery or Prospects, my Dream—dare I confess it?—of going to London to seek my Fortune as a Bard!

For I had conceiv'd the most foolish Passion a Country Lass may entertain: that of going to London as a Lit'ry Wit. O I dreamt of writing Epicks and mingling with the Beau Monde in Town; I dreamt of London Coffee-Houses, Playhouses, Masquerades, and Balls. But chief amongst my Dreams was that of becoming a Famous Scribbler! If 'twas a risible Ambition for a Lad, then how much more ridiculous for a Lass! A Lass in London would be at the Mercy of all Manner of Rogues, Bawds, Sharks, and Sharpers. Lymeworth was Paradise compar'd to London's Hell. In London were gentle Maids corrupted ev'rywhere, and in London (so I'd heard) did all the most voracious Wolves dress as the meekest Sheep.

At least here at Lymeworth I was Home—for all the Vagaries of my Situation. Perhaps Lord Bellars would find a Marriage Portion for me yet; or perhaps, failing that, I might become a Governess in another Country Seat and snag an Heir in Marriage for myself. As some Men of Fashion are said to have a Flair for Heiresses, perhaps I should discover in myself a Flair for Heirs!

So I mus'd for a Time all optimistick, but then Black Melancholy took me once again. Had I been born a Man, I thought, my orphan'd State should not have been so great a Bar to Preferment, but as a Woman, I suffer'd double Disadvantage. Orphan'd, female, and a secret Scribbler—what worse might the Fates bestow? E'en a Hunchback like Mr. Pope had greater Opportunity than a Lass with a straight Back, Quick Wit, but no Dowery! What Choyce had I then but to hold my Revenge 'gainst Mary in check and swallow my o'erweening Pride? Envy was not so unbearable, I suppos'd. Had not Herodotus himself decreed that " 'Tis better to be envied than pitied"? I must learn Stealth and Cunning, Guile and Intrigue—howe'er alien to my Temper these Traits were. Having not one Guinea to my Name, no Experience of the Wide World, and no Skills with which to earn my Bread, I must watch and wait for my Opportunity as a wily General waits for the proper Moment to move his Armies.

And so I wip'd the Spittle from my Cheaks and the Tears from my Eyes, and swore an Oath to God that, above all, I would endure.

Chapter IV

*Of Gardening, Great Houses, the Curse of Fashion,
Paradise Lost, a Family Supper with a Famous Visitor
in Attendance, and the Foolish Curiosity of Virgins of
Seventeen.*

AS HATH BEEN SAID, our weary Travellers were not to be
feasted that first Night, but rather upon the Morrow, when all
our local Gentry would be invited to Dinner to meet our
Great Man, Favourite of both Fortune and the Muses, tho'
not Nature—the Divine Dwarf, Mr. Pope. But upon the
Night of the Poet's Arrival, we were to have a small Family
Supper, after which Mary would divert us with a Concert
upon the Harpsichord (hoping, no doubt, to disguise with the
Beauteousness of Mr. Handel's Musick the Ugliness of her
Form). Whereupon Mr. Pope would discourse to us concern-
ing his fam'd Hobby, namely the Design of Gardens and
Parks according to Nature's own Rule; for Mr. Pope was one
of the most loyal Sons of Flora that e'er liv'd and 'twas his
Delight to help his Friends and Noble Patrons to plan their
Gardens in such a Manner that the Works of Nature and Art
should mutually compleat each other.

Lord Bellars had written Lady Bellars of all this and she
had communicated it to me. Now that he had prosper'd so
greatly and amass'd still another Fortune thro' investing his
Profits from the treacherous South Sea Bubble, Lord Bellars
was eager to pull down the Family's ancestral Mansion, a fine
Gothick Pile, dating from the Time of Elizabeth, standing
upon a Site bestow'd upon one of Lord Bellars' Ancestors by
Gloriana herself, and to replace it with a new House in the
modern Palladian Style. So, too, with the Gardens—those
geometrick Mazes and Hedgerows laid out in the Time of
Charles the Second. They were to be mercilessly uprooted to
make way for a Park in the very latest Fashion, design'd at
great Expence to mimick Nature, with grazing Sheep, little
Temples, diminutive Mosques and Pagodas, a tiny Village,

34

with real Peasants dress'd in rustick Shepherds' Garb, and e'en a Grotto, modell'd after Mr. Pope's at Twickenham. The belovèd Evergreens of my Childhood, (cut to resemble Peacocks with spread Tails, Bears dancing, heraldick Beasts, great Globes, Pyramids, and Cones), were to be consign'd to the Rubbish Heap in the Name of Fashion, and i'faith, Mr. Pope had come for no other Purpose than to help us plan our Garden, such a Devoté was he of the fine Art of making cultivated Parks resemble the very Wilderness from which they had sprung.

Alas, it made me very melancholick indeed—this Deference to the fickle Name of Fashion! Lymeworth (for that was the Bellarses' Country Seat) had been my Home since Childhood, and to say the Truth, the Gothick Style of Building could produce no nobler Edifice. Lord Bellars might call it "a nasty old Gothick Ruin," but to me it had the Smell of History and Grandeur. Elizabeth herself had once been a Guest at Lymeworth and heard Sweet Musick in the Long Gallery under the fram'd Portraits of the earliest Ancestors of Lord Bellars'. 'Twas rumour'd that Shakespeare had been a Visitor, perhaps coming as part of a travelling Troupe of Players. And 'twas further rumour'd that the High Great Chamber (with its Flemish Tapestries depicting the Court of Diana the Huntress, embower'd in a green Wood) was the Room in which he perform'd. But this was the very Room Lord Bellars had grown most to detest as "barbarously old-fashion'd and lacking in Elegance, Proportion, and *Ton*." So 'twas all to be pull'd down, the Bricks and Beams of my Childhood, the long Halls in which I had run and play'd with Daniel and Mary before Age, Envy, and Lust separated us; the vast stone Stair and the carv'd Chimney Pieces, the dancing Stags above the Fire-Place in the Great Hall, that very Fire-Place where we Children us'd to hide from each other (and from our Nurse) in our childish Games, and where once we had e'en burnt a great Full-bottom'd Wig of Lord Bellars' for Sport (and had been severely punish'd for the Prank).

And the Gardens, what Villain could find fault with the Gardens? Lymeworth stood just below the Summit of a pleasing Hillock, shap'd like a plump Thigh, looking down upon a peaceful Valley below, shelter'd from the Wind by a Stand of Ancient Oaks, above a gently rolling Meadow embellish'd with Beeches, Elms, and Chestnut Trees. Besides the evergreen Mazes and topiary Trees of which I have previously spoken, there was a delightful enclos'd Garden, whose Wall was studded with Obelisks at regular Intervals, as well as great carv'd Balls and white heraldick Beasts, all fashion'd of Stone. Within the wall'd Garden was a Bow'r, smelling more sweetly of Flow'rs than anything in Mr. Milton's Paradise. To pull this down was truly like pulling down Eden, and Lord Bellars must needs be our Lucifer, luring us out of this Garden in the Name of Fashion.

"Milord," said the Poet to Lord Bellars, o'er our light country Supper of Broth, Bread, and fresh-churn'd Butter, Pudding with Suet and Raisins, and finally Cheese for Dessert, follow'd by Lisbon Oranges, Muscadine Grapes, Prunes of Tours, and Pears of Rousselet—"Milord, there is nothing more repugnant to the Eye than the Mathematical Exactness and crimping Stiffness of the Gardens of our Ancestors. We must venture, rather, to paint a Landscape out of living Material, as Salvator Rosa, Gaspard Poussin, and Claude Lorrain painted the most romantick Prospects upon willing Canvas."

"Romantick, Sir? Do you use that Term which means 'all that is wild, unrestrain'd, and absurd in Nature'?"

"Nay, Milord," says the Poet, "I mean the Passion for Things of a Natural Kind, where neither Art nor the Caprice of Man hath spoil'd their genuine Order but rather re-form'd 'em closer to the Heart's Desire. I speak of the Beauties of rude Rocks, mossy Caverns, flowing Rivulets, and rolling Waters. . . . I speak of enchanted Bow'rs, silver Streams, opening Avenues, rising Mounts, and glitt'ring Grottoes alive with the Sounds of running Water, like the classical Nymphaeum of Old, the very Haunt of the Muses."

I must confess I was impress'd by this beauteous Flow of Words and in my Mind's Eye began to see an enchanted Garden, despite my previous Reluctance to suffer any Change at Lymeworth.

"Pray, Sir," I askt the Poet (who was sitting on my Right, and had i'faith often allow'd his Eyes to wander downward towards my Bosom, which, notwithstanding the Modesty Piece Lady Bellars had caus'd me to wear, was still quite visible), "describe your Grotto for us, for Lord Bellars hath told us 'tis one of the Wonders of the World, and if I am not mistaken, he means to build one here at Lymeworth, when the new House hath been erected according to the Plans of Mr. Kent and Mr. Campbell."

36

"It gives me great Joy," says the Bard, "to describe my Grotto to a Young Lady of your surpassing Beauty; for Harmony is all in Nature, and what greater Harmony could there be than to describe one beauteous Marvel of Nature for the Ears of another."

I blusht crimson at this gallant Compliment whilst Mary glower'd at me across the Table and Lord Bellars glow'd with Pride (or perhaps 'twas Lust), and Lady Bellars toy'd idly with a Muscadine Grape.

"My Dear," he continu'd, " 'tis the very Maze of Fancy, a subterranean Chamber, craggy and mysterious as if Nature herself had made it, finish'd with Shells interspers'd with Pieces of Looking Glass in angular Forms, and in the Ceiling is a Star of the same Material, from which, when a Lamp of an orbicular Figure of thin Alabaster is hung in the Middle, a thousand pointed Rays glitter, and are reflected o'er the Place. Connected to this Grotto by a narrower Passage are two Porches with Niches and Seats—one facing towards the Thames, made ingeniously of smooth Stones, and the other rough with Shells, Flints, and Iron Ore, like the Cave of the Muses itself. The Bottom is pav'd with simple Pebbles so as not to distract the Eye from the little open Temple it leads to, which is wholly compos'd of Cockle Shells in the rustick Manner, and agrees not ill with the constant dripping Murmur, which lends the whole aquatick Idea to the Place. It wants nothing to compleat it, my dear Fanny, but a Statue of you, in the Garb of a Nymph—or perhaps, if my Eyes do not deceive me about your Natural Beauty, in no Garb at all!"

At this, I blusht still more furiously crimson, and Lord Bellars laugh'd uproariously.

"Sir, you mock me," I protested.

"Marry come up, Fanny, I have ne'er been more serious in my Life."

"But tell me more of the Grotto," I said, wishing desp'rately to move on to less indiscreet Subjects (for little did I suspect in my Innocence that Mr. Pope's Grotto was perhaps a sort of warm Womb to him, who had such Difficulty persuading Ladies to share his lonely Bed).

"There is little more to say," said the Poet. "You must see it with your own Eyes, as Lord Bellars hath done. You will think my Description is poetical, but 'tis nearer the Truth than you would suppose. Moreo'er, I plan to expand the Grotto into no less than five Caverns, each with its own

Beauty lacking in my Person, but certainly the Circumstances of being born an Orphan had given me Knowledge of Sorrow, which perhaps, together with much Practice and the Muses' Blessing, would be enough. I resolv'd to find Mr. Pope privily after Supper and discourse of this with him.

The Ladies (Lady Bellars, Mary, and myself) then withdrew, leaving the Gentlemen to piss and drink, Chamber-Potts and Bottles for the Purposes being produced from the Sideboard. I know 'tis perhaps indelicate to mention this Custom, but as I am writing for my own Belinda, who may be unacquainted with Country Manners at the Time of George and strange." Whereupon she lets out a devilish Cackle, and goads me with: "Come, Fanny, are you such a Coward you will not?" Whereupon she claps her Eye to the Keyhole, and glues it there, whilst I struggle betwixt Curiosity and Disgust.

"Oooh," says she, "what a prodigious Engine he hath, despite his small Stature," and then she falls silent for a Moment, staring thro' the Keyhole with rapt Attention, and then she makes Noises of Mock-Alarm and Surprize, (acting more like a Chambermaid than a Lady—except that a Chambermaid might i'faith have had more Pretensions to the Graces than she).

"Come," she says, "have a Look. You will scarce believe your Eyes."

Reluctantly, foolishly, and with Feelings of Dread and Foreboding, I knelt and clapp'd my Eye to the Hole, thro' which I saw a Sight which scarce was worth the Pain it caus'd me later.

My Step-Father, Lord Bellars, was betting with the Poet about who could most closely hit a Grape thrown into the Pisspott, whilst poor, corpulent Daniel lookt on, with Awe and Admiration for his Father's manly Gifts. As for their Masculine Engines, 'twas hard to tell beneath their long Coats, but Mr. Pope's seem'd a tiny piddling Thing, not deform'd, but Toy-like, whilst Lord Bellars appear'd most mightily well equipp'd. But 'twas the Gaming I wonder'd at, more than the Anatomy. I had little Experience then of confirm'd Gamblers, tho' Today, I know they will lay Wagers upon anything—from twin Raindrops coursing down a Window Pane to fine Arabian Mares. Lord Bellars was surely one of those, and it astounded me that the Great Poet, who just Moments before had discours'd of Nature and Art, should now be taking great Delight in pissing at a Grape in a Chamber-Pott!

"Pray, what are you doing?" came a stern Voice behind me. 'Twas Lady Bellars, suddenly return'd to pry out our Mischief.

I rose and faced her, blushing hotly.

"Fanny forced me to," says Mary, unbidden. "Fanny forced me. I was so frighten'd. I e'en clos'd my Eyes and refus'd to look. I swear it. I swear it upon a Bible."

"Hush," said Lady Bellars. "Fanny, is this true?"

"My Lady," says I, "I cannot plead my own Case. As you saw me with my Eye to the Keyhole, so I was. My Sin was

Curiosity, nothing more. But I swear I did not force Mary's hand."

"Yes, she did! She did!" says Mary.

"Go to your Chambers, both of you," says Lady Bellars. "I will get the Truth of this later."

"My Lady, I am deeply asham'd," I said. "I beg you to accept my Apology."

"Go," says Lady Bellars, "both of you, go."

As we were departing, Mary whisper'd one final Insult in my Ear. "I'll have you banish'd from Lymeworth yet," says she.

"Mary," I said, drawing myself up straight and tall, "you are nothing but a Fool. Having me punish'd will not save you from your own Foolishness. You are a Fool for Life, I fear."

I believe my Dignity alarm'd her more than any Excuses or Insults might have done, for as she blam'd me, she very rightly expected I would blame her, but I had sufficient Understanding of Human Nature e'en then to know 'twould do no Good. Mary had brought her own Punishment upon her Head since, as she had hop'd to win her Father's Favour by serenading him and his Famous Guest upon the Harpsichord, she was now bereft of that Consolation. Had I plotted such a Revenge, I could not have executed it more cunningly than Mary's own Curiosity and Lechery (as well as her Desire to betray me) had done.

If you learn only one Thing, my Belinda, learn that your Enemies will sooner betray themselves than you can help 'em to Betrayal. Accept the Blame for your own Errors and seek to learn from them, but do not try to shift the Blame onto others. 'Twill not only do you no Good (for Blaming can ne'er undo a Wrong), but 'twill cause you to become a Scold and a Coward. When caught in a grievous Error, hold your Tongue and look deep into your Heart. Let Fools scold, and blame; look instead within yourself. A Soul is partly given, partly wrought; remember always that you are the Maker of your own Soul.

Ne'ertheless, perhaps Mary's Rancour was an Instrument of the Fates; for tho' our Concert now was cancell'd, my own Adventures were only just beginning, as you presently shall see.

Chapter V

Of Flip-Flaps, Lollipops, Picklocks, Love-Darts, Pilli-cocks, and the Immortal Soul, together with some Warnings against Rakes, and some Observations upon the Erotick Proclivities of Poets.

BANISH'D TO MY CHAMBER, I ponder'd my Plight. Owing to my Foolish Curiosity, I had lost the Opportunity to discourse with Mr. Pope upon Subjects dearer to my Heart than the Sizes of Masculine Machines. It hath anyway been my Experience, dearest Belinda, that only Fools concern themselves thus with relative Anatomies. 'Tis true there are vast Diff'rences betwixt Men in regard to their am'rous Equipage (which is why Men always wish to be reassur'd to the Contrary), vast Diff'rences betwixt the Pow'rs granted by Venus, and vast Diff'rences betwixt the Native Temperaments granted by their Stars (about all of which I shall have more to say anon), but only Simpletons and Dullards dwell upon these Diff'rences in Size to the Exclusion of other Qualities.

Some Men have stiff staring Truncheons, red-topp'd, rooted into Thickets of Curls which resemble the jungl'd Shores of the Indies; some have pitiful crooked Members, pale and white as unbak'd Bread; some Men have strange brownish Mushrooms upon bent Stalks; and some have tiny pinkish Things, more like budding Roses than Pricks. Also, nothing in this weary World hath as many divers Names as that commonplace Organ; and you will find that the Name by which a Man calls his own hath much to do with how he regards himself.

Doth he call it a Batt'ring-Piece? Well then, he will probably lye with you that way. Doth he call it a Bauble? He is probably vain of his Wigs and Waistcoats as well. Doth he call it a Dirk? He is surely a Scotsman, and gloomy 'neath his drunken Bravado. Doth he call it a Flip-Flap? Well then, be advis'd: you will have to work very hard to make it stand (and once standing, 'twill wish for nothing but to lye down

41

again). Doth he call it a Lance-of-Love? Doubtless, he writes dreadful Verses, too. Nor is a Man's Estimation of his own Privy Member necessarily infallible. The Politician who boasts of his Member-for-Cockshire, the Butcher who praises his Skewer, the Poet who prates of his Picklock, the Actor who loves his Lollipop, the Footman who boasts of his Ramrod, the Parson who praises his Pillicock, the Orator who apotheosizes his Adam's-Arsenal, the Archer who aims his Love-Dart, the Sea Captain who adores his own Rudder—none of these Men, howsoe'er lively their Mental Parts, is to be trusted upon his own Estimation of his Prowess in the Arts (and Wars) of Love!

But, as I was saying, no one but a Blockhead dwells upon Anatomy to the Exclusion of other Qualities. The Soul is far more important than the body in ev'ry respect and e'en a Man of Pleasure (if he is also a Man of Parts) understands this.

Only a Rake cares more for his Privy Member than his Soul, and a Rake, you will find ere long, is the dullest sort of Man. Because he is so devoted to his Masculine Organ, he can think of nothing but finding divers Whores to gratify his Lust for Novelty. He thinks he will find a Woman with a newer, prettier Way of wiggling her Hips, a Whore who knows three score and nine Arabick Love Positions, Tricks with Handkerchiefs, Oils and Salves of the Orient, *Bijoux Indiscrets* (as the French call 'em), or ivory Toys and Gewgaws from China which are carv'd to resemble Elephant Organs or other Absurdities of that sort. Stay away from such Men. There is no Pleasure to be found in their Company, no Wisdom in their Conversation, no Generosity towards their Mistresses, and before long they will surely give you Pox into the Bargain. A dissolute Footman, a Dancing Master with an Excess of Hubris, a Porter with Delusions of Grandeur, makes a better Rake than a Man of Parts and Breeding, because he hath no Education to cause him a Moment's Hesitation in his loathsome, ignoble, and degrading Vices; if you let a Rake into your Bed, you will i'faith often find a Footman in the cast-off Clothes of his Lord.

But to continue with my Tale. I lay abed consid'ring how my Foolish Curiosity (and Mary's Treachery) had undone my rare Opportunity to discourse with a True Poet upon the Habits and Habitations of the Muses, when suddenly the Door sprang open, and who should enter but Mr. Pope himself!

"O Sir," I said, "you were just at this very Moment in my Thoughts."

"And so were you in mine," says the Poet, coming towards me, with a goatish Smile upon his Lips.

"I was just this Moment wond'ring," I said, the Blood flying up into my Face, Neck, and Breasts, "if I might pose you a few Queries concerning the Art of Poesy."

"Pose all you like, my Dear," says he, loping o'er to the Bed, and seating himself upon the edge of it, whence his tiny Legs dangl'd like broken Twigs in the Wind, after a Storm.

"Well, then," said I, so engross'd in my Thoughts of the Muses that I scarce troubl'd to enquire what he was doing in my Chamber, "is it vain for a Woman to wish to be a Poet, or e'en to be the first Female Laureate someday?"

Whereupon he broke into a Gale of unkind Laughter, which made me blush still harder for my presum'd Foolishness.

"Fanny, my Dear, the Answer is implied in the Query itself. Men are Poets; Women are meant to be their Muses upon Earth. You are the Inspiration of the Poems, not the Creator of Poems, and why should you wish it otherwise?"

I confess I was dumbfounded by the Manner in which he pos'd his Query and press'd his Point. I had my own tentative first Verses secreted directly 'neath the Pillow of the Bed, but I was far too abash'd at that Moment to draw 'em out and ask his Opinion. I'faith, with each Word he utter'd, I was coming, increasingly, to disdain those Verses, which only a few Moments before had seem'd touch'd with the Fire of the Muses.

"See these fine twin Globes?" said the Poet, suddenly reaching into my Boddice and disengaging my Breasts. I gasp'd with Shock but dar'd not interrupt the Poet's Flow of beauteous Words:

"See their roseate Nipples, the Colour of Summer Dawn? Why, they are like the twin Planets of an undiscover'd Cosmos," says he, "and these Lips . . ." (he made bold to glue his cold, clammy Lips to one Nipple) "are like unto the Explorer who comes to set his Standard upon their Shores. . . ."

Alarm'd as I was, I could not think of how to interrupt him without insulting an honour'd Guest, and as he suckt upon one Nipple and then the other, firing my Blood and putting all my Thoughts into Disorder, my Resolve grew e'er more befuddl'd. For tho' I found his Person loathsome, his

43

Words were fine and elegant, and despite what he argu'd about the Fair Sex and the Art of Poesy, I was e'er more conquer'd by fine Language than by fine Looks.

"But, Sir," I protested, moving, albeit momentarily, out of his Grasp, "is not Inspiration a Thing which hath no Gender, is neither male nor female, as Angels are neither male nor female?"

"In Theory, that is correct," said the Poet, reaching under my Shift and insinuating a cold, clammy Hand betwixt my dampening Thighs, "but in Practice, Inspiration more frequently visits those of the Male Sex, and for this following Reason, mark you well. As the Muse is female, so the Muse is more likely to receive male Lovers than female ones. Therefore, a Woman Poet is an Absurdity of Nature, a vile, despis'd Creature whose Fate must e'er be Loneliness, Melancholy, Despair, and eventually Self-Slaughter. Howe'er, if she chooses the sensible Path, and devotes her whole Life to serving a Poet of the Masculine Gender, the Gods shall bless her, and all the Universe resound with her Praise. 'Tis all part of Nature's Great Plan. As Angels are above Men and God is above Angels, so Women are below Men and above Children and Dogs; but if Women seek to upset that Great Order by usurping Men in their proper Position of Superiority, both in the Arts and the Sciences, as well as Politicks, Society, and Marriage, they reap nothing but Chaos and Anarchy, and i'faith the whole World tumbles to its Ruin."

So saying, he had managed to wiggle a Finger upward into that tender Virginal Opening which had been unattempted till that very Day (when 'twas visited first by a Finger belonging to Lord Bellars and then one belonging to the Poet himself!), and by wiggling and squirming it and at the same Time intermittently sucking, with renew'd Determination, upon both Nipples, he had made fair Headway against my Maidenhead, whilst speaking of God's Great Plan and the Mighty Laws of Nature.

"But Sir," I said, above the growing Pounding of my Blood in my Ears, like Waves upon the Shore, "cannot this Plan be alter'd? Cannot a Great Female Poet rise up who will give the Lye to these immutable Theories?"

"No," said the Poet, "a thousand Times NO. For whate'er exists in Nature is but an Expression of God's Will, and if He hath placed Women below Men, you can be sure 'tis for a Noble Purpose. In short, whate'er is, IS RIGHT."

Whereupon he loosen'd his Breeches, fumbl'd 'neath his

44

Waistcoat and curious Doublet for his tiny pink Member, threw my Petticoats above my Head, and stood ready to assault my Maidenhead, with the very Weapon made for the Purpose. But my Guardian Angel must have been attending me at that Moment, for just as he drew near my tender Virgin Cunnikin, his own Eagerness brought on the Ultimate Period of his Hot Fit of Lust, of which my firm young Thighs and clean Petticoats receiv'd the egregious Effusion.

"O, Ohhh," he groan'd, part in relief, part in disappointment. And he buried his Head betwixt my Breasts, where his Eyes let fall a few hot Tears of Distress.

"O, my Fanny, you are all the Inspiration I shall e'er wish. Come away with me to Twickenham. You shall be Mistress of my House and my Heart, Queen of the Muses, first amongst Women. I shall dress you in Sattens and gold Lace, cover you with Jewels, adorn you as I adorn my Grotto. . . ."

"O Sir," said I, "I cannot leave the tender Parents who have taken me in and rais'd me to Womanhood. Lady Bellars would be heartbroken. Please, Sir, do not tempt me so." But his Offer put me suddenly in mind of a Plan for leaving Lymeworth and making my Way to London. Consequently, I did not tell the Poet what I thought of his miserable Form and his loathsome Avowals of Passion. I wip'd the sticky Substance from my Thighs with a fine cambrick Handkerchief and begg'd my Admirer to take leave of me so that I might consider his Proposal till the Morrow.

Chapter VI

*Some Reflections upon Harmony, Order, and Reason,
together with many surprising Adventures which follow
one upon the other, in rapid Succession.*

BY THE TIME THE POET took leave of me, 'twas nearing
Eleven o' the Clock; for I could hear the large House Clock,
which we had standing upon the Back-Stairs Head, ring its
eleven Bells shortly after his Departure. Nor did he leave
without putting almost a Handful of Gold into my trembling
Palm and making a thousand Protestations of his Passion for
me.

I must say I found all these Events (together with the
Events preceding them) puzzling in the extream. I could not
make the Poet's Behaviour jibe with his profess'd Philosophies; for, if as he said, Women were below Men yet above
Dogs and Children, why then did he press Guineas into my
Hand and promise me Riches? How is it possible that he
could be at once so lofty and so low—first discoursing upon
his Grotto and the Cave of the Muses, upon Nature and Art,
then pissing into a Pott at a Grape, then finally expiring in a
Hot Fit of Lust into my Petticoats? 'Twas not at all how I
had fancied the Author of those Divine Verses! Where was
Harmony? Where was Order? Where was Reason? All I could
see was Discord, Chance, and Self-Love, in the very Places
where I would have most fervently wisht to see their Op-
posites.

Alas, Belinda, I was Seventeen; and in spite of my
womanly Height and Bearing (and my firm tho' foolish Conviction that Life had no more to teach me than I already
knew), I was but a Child in my Wish for Consistency. I had
yet to learn that the Lives of Great Men are more oft' at
variance with their profess'd Philosophies than consistent with
'em; that their Habits in private mock their Statements in
publick; that their bestial Behaviour in the Boudoir makes a
Mockery of their Angelick Arguments in their Ethick Epis-

46

tles, their Lofty Logick in their Epicks; or their Tragick Pronouncements in their Treatises.

Moreo'er, how can I convey to you my Perplexity about the Spectacle of Masculine Lust I had just witness'd? At Seventeen, I was a Virgin, and my Knowledge of Venus' Hot Fires was slight indeed. O, I had struggl'd with the Demon of Onania (ere I e'en knew the Meaning of the Term), but i'faith before I read Lady Bellars' fateful Pamphlet, I thought myself the first Wench in the whole World's wicked History e'er to give way to such Desires! After reading the Pamphlet, to be sure, I forbade myself that Vice (tho' one of the Housemaids earnestly claim'd it preserv'd Virginity). But I was determin'd to shun all Lustful Practices until Heaven should provide me with a Mate. Thus, I gave myself to Horsemanship instead, exercising Lustre ev'ry Day until I was too weak for Venery.

I'faith, I had witness'd Swiving in my Time—Dogs, Horses, Chickens, Servants, and *Daniel* did it—that I knew. I had come upon him with the Dairymaid in the Dairy (where they were doubtless curdling Cream), but to think so Great a Bard as Mr. Pope should have such low and bestial Proclivities—'twas puzzling, puzzling in the extream.

Thus was I reflecting when once again came a Knock upon the Door of my Bedchamber, and without waiting to be invited, who should appear, but my Step-Brother, Daniel himself, drunk with Port and slobb'ring into his Shirt Front like an elderly Spaniel. (I could not but note with Amusement and Disdain that he had unbutton'd his Waistcoat most rakishly to show the copious Ruffles of his fine Holland linen Shirt, which he presum'd would have a most killing Effect upon the Fair Sex!)

"'Tis a Shame you miss'd the Party, Fannikins, my Lamb," says he, advancing towards the Bed, and looking Goats and Monkies at me. "We scarce miss'd Mary's Concert at all—so merry were we with Drink and Conversation."

"Pray, who bade you enter?" I demanded, leaping up from the Bed, so as to better defend my Person from his intended Assaults.

"Oho," says Daniel drunkenly, picking at his Pustules with one Hand, "do you not wish for my Company?"

"Certainly not," say I. "When I wish for the Company of a drunken Lout, I shall find a prettier one than you at The Bear & Dragon." (The Bear & Dragon, as you may guess, was our local Village Tavern, and a dirtier, more scurvy Hole, fill'd with more drunken country Hobnails, could not be found in all of England.)

"Oho! Do you insult me then?" says Daniel, turning red behind all his Pimples and Pockmarks.

"Call it what you will," I said, haughtily, "so long as you quit this Place at once."

"Oho," says Daniel, "I will not suffer gladly such Insults to my Person and my Parts," and he makes bold to approach me and breathe his pestilential Breath full into my Face (as if 'twould fell me quite—like a Dragon's Breath of Fire!). Whereupon, without further Ceremony or Preamble, he flings his Arms about my Neck, plants his loathsome Kisses upon my Bosom, and attempts to lay me down upon the Bed again and to unlock my Thighs. In a trice, I gather all my Force against his tott'ring Drunkenness, heave myself up with the Puissance which the Goddess of Anger alone makes possible, and kick, with one pointed satten Slipper, straight into his Breech.

"O Jesus, I am kill'd!" he shouts. "Oh, my poor Pillicock, my poor Peewee!" And he reels backwards, holding his Hands to his Breech, and then falls o'er the Washstand, landing in a great Crash and Clatter, with the Wash Pitcher scatter'd in Pieces 'round him.

"Now, then," say I, standing o'er him and pressing my Advantage like Athena the Warrior Goddess herself, "out!"

"O cruel Fanny," slobbers Daniel, "cruel, cruel Fanny. Dost thou not know I love thee?"

"Go make Love to Mrs. Betty the Chambermaid, who is already Great with Child by thee. Or Mrs. Polly the Milkmaid, who soon will be! I have no Use for a brawling drunken Lout who is my own Step-Brother, to boot."

"But not Blood-Brother, Fanny. Come, what's the Harm in it?"

"The Harm is the next Kick I shall give thee, which shall finish thine am'rous Tricks fore'ermore!" said I, savouring my Rage.

"O please," he whimper'd, "please, please," and he commenced to crawl upon his Belly like a Snake towards the Door of my Chamber, whimp'ring and mewling and slobb'ring, until, having reach'd the Doorjamb, he rais'd himself by the brass Door Pull and, with a reproachful, simp'ring backward Glance, let himself out of the Chamber. E'en as he departed, one idle Hand pinch'd a Pustule upon his Cheak.

(If such a Complexion was the Result of Lust, 'twas well indeed I scotch'd it in myself!)

He had scarce been gone ten Minutes when once again the Door open'd, and Lord Bellars enter'd my Virgin Chamber.

My Thoughts were in such a great Turmoil from the divers Events of the Ev'ning, and my Body so weary from my Exertions 'gainst Daniel, that I could do no more than sigh when Lord Bellars came to me, tow'ring o'er my Bed, and looking down at me with those fine sparkling brown Eyes.

"You are so beautiful, my Fanny," he said. "All this Night I have thought of nothing but your Beauty."

"Pray, do not flatter me, Milord. It makes me blush."

And 'twas true, the Blood came as readily to my Face as Moths to a Candle Flame on a hot Summer Night. As their Wings quiver and flutter, so I trembl'd 'neath Lord Bellars' Gaze. My Hands grew cold, my Cheaks hot; the Blood drain'd, it seem'd, from my Feet and Hands, and sped up into my patch'd and painted Visage.

"Nay. Do not forbid me Speech, for if I can possess you only with Words, I *will* speak, despite your Alarms. You are so inimitably fair and lovely. Your Limbs are fine-turn'd and your Eyes run o'er with Liquid Amber. Your Breasts are whiter than Alpine Snow and your Hair flames like a thousand Autumns past, and a thousand Autumns yet to come. You are like a Daughter to me and yet, do I dare dream an Intimacy betwixt us e'en greater than that of Filial Duty and an Orphan's Gratitude?"

He clasp'd me in his strong Arms, and I almost fainted away like one drugg'd.

"O, no, Milord, pray, please refrain. Consider me, I beg you, for I am a Creature who hath no Protection but you, no Defence but your Honour. I conjure you not to make me abhor myself!—not to make me vile in my own Eyes!"

He then fell to his knees at the edge of the Bed and exclaim'd, "I make an Oath at your Feet, to possess you or dye!" Whereupon he removes the tiny pointed satten Slipper from my right Foot and presses his Lips to the Sole of my Foot.

"I beseech you, Milord . . ." I stammer'd. For, had he kiss'd my Breasts directly 'twould have provok'd less Rapture than when he thus abas'd himself to kiss my Foot. How unworthy was that coarse Foot against his fine Lips!

"Please, Milord," I protested.

"My Angel," he sigh'd, now flinging away the other Slipper

and kissing the other Sole. "Please, forgive, if e'er you can, my Coarseness upon that earlier Occasion, for until Supper I did not truly credit what a fine delicate Creature you had become, despite your lusty Beauty. O, for my Presumption, a thousand Pardons! But after hearing you discourse with Mr. Pope upon his Grotto, upon Nature and Art, I knew I had treated you most scurvily. And for that I would sooner drive his Sword . . ." (and here he drew it and it twinkl'd evilly in the dim Candelight) ". . . into my Breast than have you loathe me for a vile Villain, a Common Rake, which surely is your Right, consid'ring what hath transpir'd before Supper."

O what Confusion reign'd in my Breast! First the Poet, then Daniel, then Lord Bellars! Daniel I knew for a Fool and Knave; the Poet seem'd a pitiable Creature, desiring to be above Women because he could ne'er stand equal with Men—but Lord Bellars?—how was I to judge Lord Bellars? Here was a Passion declar'd in Words so tender that one could scarce doubt its Sincerity. (O Lust I knew to be a low Emotion, but Love was all the Poets' highest Good!)

The Sword Tip hung pois'd o'er his manly Bosom. He tore off his Neckcloth, ripp'd open his embroider'd satten Waistcoat, and laid bare his linen Shirt Front, as if to pierce that snowy Field until the red Poppies of his Blood flower'd upon it.

"Well, then, come Death!" he exclaim'd, and with his left Hand tore open the Linen to reveal a fine, reddish Fur, twining here and there into sweet Ringlets, and two boyish Paps of rosy pink 'round which the same reddish Hair did spring.

"Hold!" I cried. "How should I e'er forgive myself if I were to be the Cause of your Death?"

"I would rather dye than dishonour you," he said, "but my Love is such that I must do Violence to one of us—and since I cannot be the Murderer of that fair Maidenhead, which I have rais'd from tend'rest Infancy, I must dye myself. 'Tis a tragick but necessary Choyce! Adieu, sweet Maid! Think of me tenderly, if you think of me at all." And, so saying, he drove the Sword Point into his Chest, whereupon I fell to my Knees on the Floor beseeching him to refrain, to hold, to stop.

He dropp'd the Sword, fell to the Floor, and smother'd me with Kisses. The flowing Blood from his Wound (a surface Wound, I later discover'd) stain'd my Breasts and Gown with its sweet Stickiness. I smell'd the salty Odour of his Blood as he enfolded me, kiss'd me first on the Mouth, then betwixt

50

the Breasts, then betwixt the Legs, where his Tongue thrust upwards into my Virginal Opening, making the Way slick for the stronger Thrusts to follow.

If I bled a little off'ring my Maidenhead, it seem'd as nothing compar'd to the Blood he had sacrificed for me. I'faith, who could tell where his Blood ended and mine began? Enmesh'd, entwin'd in mutual Stickiness and Sweetness, we lay together dying of Love. The Ecstacy was mutual and compleat.

Later, when I was cynical, I would learn to dissect and analyze the Act of Love, to pronounce upon the Techniques of my Lovers, and to judge them in the Lists of Love, because, perhaps, Love itself was lacking. But upon that first Occasion, my Heart no less than my Maidenhead was taken, and I could no more judge than I could resist. If he had askt me to pierce my own Breast, as he had pierced his, I would certainly have obliged him willingly. Afterwards, he fell again to kissing my Feet, this Time in an Attitude of Pray'rfulness.

"I swear my Eternal Love," he said; "I swear by Venus, by Jove, by Jesus Himself that I have ne'er lov'd before as I love now." And I felt for an instant that all the Fulfillment of my girlish Dreams had come true, that I was the Heroine of a French Romance, and that in one Night I had gone from Girlhood to Womanhood, had liv'd a thousand Lives, had felt my Soul incarnate in the Body of Cleopatra, of Desdemona, of Portia, of Eloisa, of Juliet. In me were all the Great Heroines of Romance join'd and combin'd. In me did Juliet mingle with Eloisa, did Portia lend her Strength to the melting Tenderness of Desdemona; in me was there e'en something of mad Ophelia—ready to dye for Love and float away down a mossy Stream 'neath a weeping Willow Tree, whilst drowning Flow'rs dangl'd in my Hair.

Alas! Alas! What Foolish Visions strut thro' the Head of a Maid of Seventeen! Lord Bellars took his Leave and I slept the Sleep of the Innocent, the Sleep of the Lamb who doth not yet know that God hath also created Lions, who doth not further guess that God hath created him King of the Beasts, in that teeming Jungle which we call the World.

Chapter *VII*

Venus is introduced, with some pretty Writing; and we learn more of the Am'rous Dalliances of Lord Bellars than we, or our Heroine, would wish to know.

I AWAKEN'D AT FIVE O' THE CLOCK to the Singing of Birds. My Heart was as light as their Song. I wanted to throw my Cloak about me and run barefoot into the dewy Grass of the Park, skipping along the Velvet Lawns, like a Spaniel Pup, bending down to kiss the Grass, looking up to thank God for the new Day, for my Lover, for my Life.

In short, I was light with Love, skittish and sleepless, full of puppyish Enthusiasm. I dress'd in haste, splasht my Face with the cold Water in the Wash-Bowl, and ran downstairs to greet the Day before the World was up.

The Housekeeper, Mrs. Locke, smil'd at me, yet not without a Query in her Eyes, but I was too taken with my own Am'rousness to answer that intended Query or e'en rightly to apprehend it.

I ran at once to my favourite Spot within the mossy, wall'd Garden. 'Twas a Statue of the Goddess Venus (brought from Italy by Lord Bellars when he was a Young Man making the Grand Tour) and beautiful despite the Fact that she lackt both Head and right Arm. She stood pois'd upon a Scallop Shell surmounting a Pedestal of sculptur'd Waves, and I fancied her freshly born from the Sea.

I fell to my Knees before her and offer'd up a silent Pray'r. I dreamt that she smil'd at me, tho' i'faith, she had no Face. Ruin'd? Was I ruin'd in the World's Eyes? What car'd I for the World's Estimation, when I was now exalted in the Service of Venus? Heroines of Romance were e'er above the World's Laws and if they were made to dye for Love, well then, that only prov'd the Fineness of their Mettle, and the Fineness of their Loves. I, no less than Lord Bellars, could exclaim, "Come Death!"

Ah, Belinda, how eager is Seventeen, so newly hatch'd

from the Void, to quit the World for the Void again! As we grow older, we grow less eager to depart this World. As our Skin grows less firm and the Roses in our Cheaks fade, we cling e'er more tenaciously to Life. But how ready we are to toss it all away whilst those Roses still bloom and the Flesh stands firm as ripe Peaches! It is not a Paradox that the closer we are to the Grave, the more we cling to Life, whilst the closer we are to our Nativities, the more reckless we are with the Gift of Life?

Love, the Poets say, is a Form of Lunacy, a Disorder in the Senses such as one sees amongst the poor mad Wretches at Bedlam; and sure I can attest to the Truth of that.

What happen'd next, it pains me extremely to report, tho' a Quarter of a Century hath pass'd since that Time.

I wander'd, distracted with Love, into the Library, where I meant to seek out a Love Poem by Matt Prior, which, I thought, was a perfect Mirror of my Mind at that Moment. I strove to recollect the Lines. 'Twas something very like,

> O mighty Love! from thy unbounded Pow'r
> How shall the Human Bosom rest secure?

—but no more could I recall. Therefore, I was hast'ning towards My Lord's Library Shelves containing Poetry Miscellanies, to verify my Recollection, when, in all Idleness and Innocence, I pass'd his Escritoire, and spy'd upon it an unfinish'd Letter in his own Hand.

As the Mother Cat cannot neglect her Kittens, but must always be carrying 'em from one shady Spot to another, so the Lover cannot avoid examining anything belonging to her Belovèd—e'en if she will surely come to Grief thereby.

I paus'd, and read the Letter. I remember e'en the Date as if it had been branded on my Brain with a hot Iron. At first Glance, it seem'd intended for me.

Lymeworth
June 21st, 1724

Adorable Creature, thou dearest, best of Women, my Angel, my Queen, my Ruler:

As I am your devoted Slave, and as you have commanded me to report to you all my most trifling Dalliances—as you, I trust, report yours to me—let me tell you what hath transpir'd here this Ev'ning betwixt myself and my enchanting Step-Daughter, Fanny, the Orphan Girl of whom I have spoken, who lives here at Lymeworth thro' the Kindness and Magnanimity of my gen'rous Heart.

I know your Zeal, your ardent Fervour for Conquest, and I fear you will protest that to seduce a Young Girl, who hath seen nothing of the World, who is deliver'd into my Hands as a Lamb to a Lion, and whom a kind and flatt'ring Epithet would not fail to intoxicate, is no Triumph at all, and not e'en worth reporting as a Victory. Madam, you are wrong. This Waif is no Serving Maid, no mean Harlot, but a Devotée of the Muses, well-read in Poetry and Philosophy. Why, e'en as I watch'd thro' the Keyhole of her Closet, she repell'd the Advances of no less a Personage than the Poet, Mr. Alexander Pope (whom I have brought here, as you know, to aid in the Planning of my new Gardens and to lend his valuable Poet's Eye to the Efforts of my Landscape Architects), as well as the Advances of my scurvy Son, Daniel (which, admittedly, is no very Great Thing, because the Lad hath no more Charm than a country Hobnail). But mark you, she is a Worthy Prey, despite her lowly Birth, for by Learning and Application, she hath acquir'd more Graces than my own Children, and tho' naturally hot-blooded, she is also full of Morality (which, as you will remember, is one of the Essential Traits we enumerated when we made up our little Rules for the Sport of amusing each other, each with the other's Dalliances).

I'faith, she possesses all the Requisities: Beauty, Morality, Passion, and she possesses 'em in abundance.

Now, you will wish to know what Strategy I adopted, what Campaign, and what Manoeuvres; in short, by what Means I arriv'd at my Victory, and the total Subjugation of my Prey. I decided upon a Combination of two Strategies: first, the near-Ravishment (which heated her Blood and disorder'd her Senses), then our oft'-discuss'd Strategy of Terror and Astonishment, in which I threaten'd Self-Slaughter and let her be my Sweet Savior, my Minist'ring Angel. It workt better than I might have hop'd! On other Occasions, many Days, e'en Weeks, have been requir'd for Compleat Victory. Here the entire Conquest took only Minutes!

I enter'd her Room, (wearing my Sword!), prais'd her

54

Beauty in Terms borrow'd from the Playhouse, made bold to kiss her Feet (mark you, not her Breasts!), threaten'd to dye for Love unless she save me, actually drew my own Blood, and was rescu'd from the Brink of the Void by the Angel's own Maidenhead. What Capital Sport! Madam, had you yourself been watching thro' a Peep-Hole (as upon that previous Occasion, which I am sure you well remember), you would have commended me most highly. Yes, Friend, she is mine, entirely mine; after Tonight she hath nothing left to grant me.

I am still too full of my Triumph to be able to fairly appreciate it. But I promise you, it shall go down in our little Book of Amours as one of our most enchanting Ev'nings of Sport. Cupid himself prepares a Crown for me!

I hope you are well, Madam, and that your Silence doth not portend a Continuation of that Ague you reported in your last Letter. I'faith . . .

I could read no more. My Eyes brimm'd with salty Tears and my Heart ach'd with Humiliation so great that Death alone could ease it. I ran again into the wall'd Garden, where I wisht to dash my Brains out at the Feet of Venus, and would, no doubt, have done so, had not Cowardice, a base Fear of doing myself bodily Injury, interven'd. The cruellest Phrases from that wicked Letter rang thro' my Brain, like Church Bells resounding in a Belfry.

"Capital Sport"!—I heard Lord Bellars' own mocking Voice say those detested Words. "Subjugation of my Prey"! "A Combination of two Strategies"! "Terms borrow'd from the Playhouse"! Was it not enough that I was ruin'd, that my first, fine Belief in the Pow'r of Love had been betray'd? But must I also be held up to Ridicule in the Eyes of Lord Bellars' London Mistress—no doubt a Woman of Fashion to whom my Ruin was a mere Toy to pass away an Afternoon, or a lewd Playlet, a sort of Afterpiece, to heat the Blood of Jaded Lovers?

O Belinda, ne'er was a Wench so wretchèd as myself! I thought to take my own life ('twas worth nothing to me then) but could not, both for fear of bodily Torment and Torment of my Soul in the World to come! But how should I survive this Humiliation? I could not face Lord Bellars or my Step-Mother again. I could not sit at Table across from the Poet, Lady Bellars, Mary, Daniel, the villainous Lord

Bellars himself, and all our other intended Guests, without showing my Distress. What could I do but flee?

Fortunately, I had the Guineas the Poet had press'd upon me, and I had, besides, some good Clothes and Jewels that might be pawn'd, a silver Snuff-Box, a gold Watch, and sev'ral gold Rings.

I ran back to my Chamber to gather all my Worldly Possessions (including my tentative first Verses) and to plan my Flight from Lymeworth.

I was consid'ring how I might escape to London, without falling Prey to Highwaymen and Robbers, when I recall'd the Custom of certain Famous Actresses in London of dressing up in Men's Clothes to play "Breeches Parts," and I form'd the Idea of stealing Daniel's Riding Clothes and Riding Wig and making my Way to London *en Homme.* Fortunately, I was then, as now, an excellent Horsewoman, but whether I should be able to fetch my own Chestnut Arabian Stallion, Lustre, without incurring Suspicion from the Groom and Stable-Boys, I did not know, and whether I should be able to reach London unharm'd was also doubtful. But what other Choyce did I have? I dried my Tears and set about preparing for my Journey.

Chapter VIII

Containing the sundry Adventures of our Heroine in preparing her Escape, as well as many edifying Digressions upon Doweries, upon Love, upon the Beauties of the English Countryside, upon the Wisdom of Horses, upon the Necessity for Disguises, and, finally, upon the Preferability, at all Times, of being a Man rather than a Woman.

DANIEL SLEPT LIKE A PIG, or still worse, like an old Country Squire, wheezing, sputt'ring, and farting. For all his Pretensions to the Manners of a Man of Pleasure whilst awake, asleep 'twas clear he was more to be pitied than fear'd. From Time to Time, he stirr'd in his Sleep to mutter unintelligible Syllables. 'Twas not much Trouble to take what I wanted without awak'ning him—tho' I did not fail to recall that mere Girls had been hang'd for less than I was stealing now, and that, after my Usage of him Yesterday Ev'ning, Daniel's Revenge might be a terrible one.

The enormous Full-bottom'd Periwigs of my younger Years were just then fading from Fashion (tho', i'faith, some older Folk still wore 'em) and Young Gentlemen of Fashion now wore smaller Wigs, especially for Riding. I snatch'd one of these, a fine black Riding Wig that must have cost a Pocketful of Shillings, and took as well a Pair of Jack-Boots, brown leather Riding Breeches, Stockings, a fine Silver-hilted Sword, a green Redingote, clean Linen, a Cravat, a black Beaver Hat, and a heavy scarlet Cloak against the Rain.

I was too full of Fear about awak'ning Daniel to wonder about the Fit of these Clothes or what sort of Figure I should cut as a Beau. E'en as I left his Chamber, Daniel heav'd and mutter'd, "Fanny, Fannikins, Fan . . ." and for a Moment I fear'd I was lost. But 'twas only a Dream; the scurvy Fellow would pollute me in Sleep e'en as he would awake.

I hasten'd to my Chamber to compose a Farewell Letter to

Lady Bellars and to attire myself properly in these stolen Clothes before setting out.

"My Lady," (I wrote)

The very high Regard I have for your Ladyship, as well as your unfailing Kindness to me upon ev'ry Occasion, compels me to inform you of my impending Flight from Lymeworth. The Cause of that Flight I cannot divulge. Suffice it to say that I have impos'd upon your Good Humour longer than my Unworthiness merits. I should certainly want Feeling were I to fail to confess the Grief which stirs in my Bosom as I bid thee and Lymeworth Farewell. I have known happy Years here, have learnt the gentle Passion of Filial Love, the Gentle Arts of Reading and Writing, the harsher Lessons of History, and the robust Sports of Horsemanship, the Hunt, Angling, and Shooting. I hope with all my Heart you will not deem my Desertion perfidious. Someday, in the Fullness of Time, I shall explain the Causes of my Departure. Until then, farewell Sweet Mother (if I may so call you). I am,

Your most obedient and affectionate
Step-Daughter, till Death,
Fanny.

I seal'd this Letter not without a Tear, knowing as I did the Grief it could not but communicate to Lady Bellars. I wisht I could hide myself in the Skirts of her Gown, as I had when I was small. My Heart o'erflow'd with Melancholick Humours and my Memory brimm'd with the sweetest Recollections. Lady Bellars could have treated me no better had I been born of her own Blood. She had rais'd me as a true Daughter—a Daughter of her Heart, if not of her Womb—and, tho' I had no Dowery and no Hopes of a fine Match, I was in some wise more fortunate than Mary because I was less oppress'd by Familial Duty. Mary should surely be married off to whate'er loathsome Fellow brought Lord Bellars' Dynasty the largest Holdings of Land. And tho' I could not but smile at her Fate, I knew the Injustice of it. E'en she did not deserve such Usage; no Woman did. 'Tis a Paradox that the Lack of a Dowery can be a Boon to some Ladies, for what had attracted Lord Bellars to Lady Bellars but her

Dowery, and should she not have been far happier without him?

Certainly I could carry no Portmanteau upon horseback; thus 'twas essential that I hang all my Belongings about my Person, concealing my Valuables within my Breech, my Coat Pockets, e'en within the Crown of my Hat.

O I cut a fine Figure as a Boy! My long Hair bound up close to my Skull with Ribbands and Pins (so as to remain hidden under my Riding Wig), my Face bare of Paint or Patch, my Breasts hidden 'neath Coat and Cloak, my Hat tilted rakishly forward to shadow my Face, my Jack-Boots and Sword giving me the Assurance of a Beau.

I stood before the Glass and practis'd talking like a Man.

"Stand and deliver," I fancied a Gentleman of the Road demanding.

"Damme if yer not a Rascal and a Knave," I replied in my deepest Voice.

But 'twas no good; I still sounded like a Girl.

"Sir, yer a Rascal and a Knave," I said in a deeper Voice. 'Twas better, if only by an Ounce.

Well then, again.

"Damme if yer not a Son of a Whore!" I said with still greater Assurance and (what I hop'd was) a fine manly Tenor. 'Twas fair enough, tho' not perfect. I should ne'er sing Bass, but perhaps I might pass as a Castrato!

I fasten'd the Letter to my Pillow with a Pin, snatch'd my Poems and secreted them about my Person, bade Farewell to my belovèd Chamber, and crept down to the Stables.

The Clock struck Eight as I let myself quietly down the Back-Stair, and thence thro' a secret Passage which led to the Library. I thankt my Guardian Angel that Mrs. Locke and the other Servants were below in the Kitchen preparing Breakfast, and I took one last Look at the detested Letter as I cross'd the Library to reach the double Doors that open'd upon the Park. I confess I contemplated whether or not to burn it, but decided instead upon Cunning and Stealth for my Revenge upon Lord Bellars; then I made my Escape.

I ran across the Velvet Lawns to the Stables, my small Feet slipping within the large Boots, my Heels sinking into the wet Earth. E'en upon this melancholy Occasion, I could not fail to remark upon the Beauty of the Wiltshire Countryside, the sweet Smell of the Grass in the light Rain.

O Belinda, I have travell'd extensively abroad, have cross'd both North and South Atlantick and the Caribee, but no

Place is as beautiful as this England. Nowhere but here are the Tree Trunks themselves kiss'd with Moss; nowhere but here are the Trees so verdant and heavy of Leaf, the Lawns so green, the Roses so pink, the Hedges so aromatick. Why, e'en the English Cows who graze 'neath the Rain-drench'd Trees are more beauteous than Cows of any other Nationality! Whene're the Mutability of Sublunary Things makes me melancholick, I rest my Mind upon an English Landscape, and once again am peaceful and content. Others may sigh for long Sea-Voyages or the Sublimity of the Alps. O I have been besotted with the Charms of Seas and Sailing Ships in my Time, and I have climb'd many Mountains and admir'd the Clouds from above as well as below; but when all is said and done, an English Landscape is the very Perfection of Nature. 'Tis neither Rude Excrescence nor Gothick Error; 'tis neither too flat nor too high, but a Harmony entire of Serpentine Curves. Whene'er I am the least sadden'd by the Follies of Mankind, I feast upon its wet deep Green, and find myself most blest.

Yet running across the Lawn to the Stables, I experienced a Stab of Indecision. (Pray, why is Home ne'er more beauteous than when we leave it?) On the previous Night, which now seem'd an Eternity away, the Poet had offer'd all— House, Lands, Riches, his undying Devotion. Perhaps I ought then to swallow my Pride, forget my impetuous Decision to flee, and instead go away with him? I doubted not but he would make good his Promises. A Gentleman of his Figure had not perfect Freedom in his Choyce of Ladies, and I suppos'd I might easily manipulate his Good Humour, honey him into parting with his Fortune, and play the splendid Madam to his twisted Goat.

But O my Stomach rose at it! I knew enough now of the gentle Passion of Love to be obliged to reject the loathèd Embraces of a Monster. Lord Bellars had treated me rascally and prov'd to be as arrant a Whoremaster as Lady Bellars had warn'd; still, *I* had felt ardent Affection for *him*—e'en if 'twas only to be dasht to Bits when I learnt of his Perfidy. In short, I had known Love, tho' he had not, and Love, as the Poets say, is like a Flame. Anything which passes thro' it must be changed. 'Tis entirely possible for Love to be true when one Lover feels it and the other doth not. We may know Humiliation and Pain later, but we cannot undo the Love that we felt at first, and sure we cannot undo the Changes wrought in us by the Pow'r of Love. Thus I could

60

not now venture to Twickenham with Mr. Pope. Only a narrow, vulgar Soul could so dissemble. And my Soul, not narrow before, had been further stretch'd by Love.

Belinda, 'tis true that the World is not form'd for the Benefit of Women, and oft' they must sacrifice their nice Principles in order to put Bread into their own Mouths and those of their Children; but I was ne'er so made as to be able to pretend Love of a loathsome Man for Hope of Gain, and it hath been my Experience that I have prosper'd nonetheless.

At Times, I readily confess, I have flasht false Lightning from my Eyes, fetch'd Sighs from my Bosom (which none could have heard unmov'd) altho' I did not wholly mean 'em, and carelessly dropp'd the Handkerchief from my Bosom, in order to win some Point in Discourse, either philosophical or pecuniary. But I swear I have ne'er feign'd Love for one who did not merit it, and I have ne'er us'd the noble Pow'r of Love to obtain rich laced Clothes or Jewels. Had I done so, I might indeed be richer than I am Today. But truly I am rich enough for all my Wants. And what Use is Wealth if the Means of getting it causes us to detest ourselves? Wealth is nothing but the Oil which allows the Wheels of the World to turn.

So I reason'd then and so I reason now; and the Fates surely must have approv'd my Journey, for they arranged it that the Groom and the Stable-Boys were off in the Meadows exercising two prize Arabian Stallions which Lord Bellars wisht to race at Newmarket the following Year, and I was able to saddle my own dear Horse, Lustre, and make my Escape without anyone being the wiser.

How I lov'd that Horse! He was my first, and I shall ne'er forget his rich chestnut Colour, his silken Coat, the Blaze upon his Forehead, and the dear white Stocking upon his left Leg—as if he had stumbl'd into a Bucket of white Paint. He was fleet, too, tho' I should ne'er take him to a Race-Meeting and let all sorts of scurvy Blackguards lay Wagers upon his Flesh. No, to me a Horse was more than an Excuse for Gaming. A Horse was sleek as the Wind, Grace itself; in short, 'twas entirely clear to me why the Ancients had identified Horse with Poesy. Moreo'er, one of the chief Things I had learnt at the Knee of my Step-Mother was the very tender Sensibilities of our four-leggèd Friends. Thus I ne'er fail'd to converse sensibly with Lustre, to inform him of the Purpose of our Journey, and he always serv'd me better for that Reason, because I honour'd him as a Rational Creature.

For mark you, Belinda, Dean Swift (about whose personal Proclivities I shall have more to say later) was entirely right about Horses! Compar'd to their orderly, rational Behaviour, we Humans do, i'faith, appear as Yahoos. Who can be more sympathetick towards the Trials and Tribulations of Love than a loyal Horse (unless it be a loyal Dog)? And who can listen with more Affection to one's Woes than a Member of either of those noble Races of Creatures which we, in our o'erweening Hubris, dare to term subhuman? I avow that *we*, rather, are sub-equine and sub-canine!

What Heavenly Bliss to gallop across the English Meadows upon a June Morning, talking to one's Horse! What a perfect Cure for the Vapours! Ne'er did I mount Lustre without Exhilaration, and ne'er did I gallop upon his Back, the Wind at my Ears, without a Sense of Freedom so compleat it banish'd all Melancholia. Yet suddenly I remember'd this was no ordinary Morning Gallop, but my very last Morning at Home, whereupon the Tears began to flow as if they should ne'er cease!

Adieu! Adieu! Sweet Home of my Youth, and all the Safety I e'er have known! I began then to brood upon the terrible Tales I'd heard told of London. Tales of Highwaymen and Bawds, of Robbers disguis'd as Dealers in Hair or old Clothes, or Procuresses disguis'd as Housekeepers or Decent Matrons. I'faith, I was upon the very Point of turning back when I harshly commanded myself to cease weeping and be brave. Whereupon my old Determination did not fail me (for I had learnt e'en then the curious Knack of commanding myself to appear courageous in the Face of Fear—and lo and behold, the Pretence of Courage almost created it!).

I had travell'd but little about the Countryside in my younger Years, yet I knew that if I could make my Way to the Bath Road, I should be able to follow it easily enough to London. Certainly I fear'd the Highwaymen that infested the Roads to London, and certainly I knew that they grew more num'rous as one approach'd the Metropolis, but I forced myself to feel a certain Safety, dress'd as a Man. Perhaps, as I remarkt to Lustre, 'twas a false Safety. But there is nothing quite so liberating as being free of the Fear of Ravishment—which, unless she dresses as a Man, a Woman can ne'er, not e'en for a Moment, forget. Besides, there is an Exhilaration in leaving off one's Hoops and Petticoats and wearing

Breeches. And there is a Freedom in Disguise that one ne'er knows when one appears as oneself.

"Can you conceive that, Lustre?" I askt my Horse, drying my Tears. "Can you conceive the Freedom of suddenly being disguis'd a Boy?"

He neigh'd in sympathy; sure there was a more than verbal Bond betwixt us. I then tried to find a Metaphor from the Sphere of Horses so that Lustre should entirely understand my Meaning.

"La," says I, " 'tis as if you were to play at being a Brood Mare."

Lustre shook his Head and whinnied; 'twas clear he did not like my Meaning.

"Do you understand now?" said I.

Again he whinnied loudly and shook his Head. I puzzl'd awhile, riding along upon his Back, and suddenly understood his Displeasure. For him to be a Mare was not the same at all—and being a Rational Creature, he very well understood this, (tho' a Man, engaged in the same Dialogue, should not).

To dress as a Boy gave one Privileges no Woman could e'er possess: first, the Privilege of being left in Peace (except by Robbers, who prey'd almost equally upon both Sexes); second, the very substantial Privilege of Dining where'er one wisht without being presum'd a Trollop; third, the Privilege of moving freely thro' the World, without the Restraints of Stays, Petticoats, Hoops, and the like. For I had form'd the Theory that Women should ne'er be entirely free to possess their own Souls until they could ride about the World as unencumber'd as possible. The Hoop Skirt, I reason'd, was an Instrument of Imprisonment. I might shudder with Horror at the Idea of the legendary Amazons cutting off one Breast, but sure I could not but understand their Motives.

"Lustre, I love only you," I said, spurring him on and galloping towards the High Road. "You are my Inspiration, my Lover, my only Friend!"

And the Stallion whinnied his Reply, which I took to be, "Yes! Yes! Yes!"

Chapter IX

Containing a most improving Philosophical Enquiry into the diff'ring Philosophies of the Third Earl of Shaftesbury and Mr. Bernard Mandeville, together with an Account of our Heroine's sincere Dilemma concerning the Rôle of Womankind in the Great World; whereupon we follow our Heroine to a Country Fair and relate the Misadventures she had there; her Début as a Duellist, and, last but not least, her most surprizing Rescue by a most surprizing Rescuer.

I RODE ALL MORNING without Mishap, stopping to water Lustre at Noon (and to buy Bread and Cheese from a Village Market); then I rode again thro' most of the Afternoon.

On the Road, I pass'd many interesting Sights: old Men playing Bowls upon a Village Green; a Stage-Coach rattling along the Highway at great Speed, its Passengers being shaken to Death, most likely, by its rough Ride; Boys angling by a verdant River-Bank; wretchèd-looking Young Girls from a local Workhouse, scrubbing Clothes by the side of the same River.

I remember most vividly the low, rolling Hills and wide Skies, the Villages of warm, golden Stone, the Fields of Corn and winter Barley, the Sheep grazing upon the Downs, and the black and white Cows eating the bountiful moist Grass.

'Twas astounding that the mere Fact of dressing as a Man and having an aristocratick Horse and a fierce-looking Sword (tho' I knew not how to use it), could protect one from most Mischances, and i'faith I was perhaps lull'd into a false Security that first Day, by Reason of my Great Good Fortune in not being stopp'd.

I was able to reflect upon the Beauties of the Countryside and upon my Plight, as well as to consider the Uncertainty of my Future, and to discourse with Lustre upon the opposing Philosophies of the Third Earl of Shaftesbury, who expound-

64

ed the Perfection of the Universe and the Naturalness of Virtue in Man, and of Mr. Bernard Mandeville, who, upon the Contrary, argu'd that Self-Interest was the only Motivation of Mankind. Tho' my Heart inclin'd towards Shaftesbury's Reasoning, my Mind was more apt to favour Mandeville's; ne'ertheless it occur'd to me that neither of these Investigations into the Great Springs of Human Actions seem'd to embrace the Behaviour of Men towards Women, but only the Behaviour of Men towards each other. Was this not odd? Did not Mankind comprise Womankind as well? The Philosophers claim'd 'twas so, and yet e'en the most benevolent amongst 'em, the ones who would most vociferously argue the Universality of Christian Charity and Love, seem'd to disregard the Passions and Interests of one-half the Human Race.

How then could I choose a Philosophy upon which to model my perilous Destiny, when none of the Philosophers had consider'd Woman in their Speculations upon Reason, Nature, and Truth? For, if (as I sincerely believ'd) a Supreme Being of Infinite Wisdom did exist, and if (as I also sincerely believ'd) that Supreme Being had chosen to create, out of all possible Systems, the Best, why, then, must I not devoutly assume that this World in which I found myself was the Best of all Possible Worlds?

And yet, clearly, 'twas not the Best of all Possible Worlds for Women—unless, as Mr. Pope had argu'd, there was a hidden Justice behind this Veil of seeming Injustice. If, i'faith, all Creatures were part of one Great Organism, which, in turn, was part of the Universal Mind, and consequently of God, then our *seeming* Diff'rences were but Harmonies unknown to us. For had not Shaftesbury said that "All Mankind is, as 'twere, one Great Being, divided into sev'ral Parts"? Then Lord Bellars and Mr. Pope and even Lord Bellars' London Mistress must all be Parts of one Great Organism, possessing the Blessings of the Universal Mind. Fie on't! 'Twas not possible that God should approve such goings-on! A Pox on the Third Earl of Shaftesbury and his damnable Optimism!

What did Lustre think? Was he content with his Place in the Great Chain of Being? Did he believe this was the Best of all Possible Worlds? When he turn'd his Noble Head and lookt me Eye to Eye, he seem'd to say that he was happy with his Place so long as I should be his Mistress, but that he should hardly be so happy if a Horse Thief or Robber should take him.

I shudder'd at the very Thought, and threw my Arms about Lustre's Neck. I lov'd that Animal so! What Tenderness we can feel for our mute Animal Brethren! The Thought of losing him (or i'faith of his being harm'd) fill'd me with more Pain than the Thought of my own Death.

Suddenly, as I was musing on these very melancholy Things, my Eyes, those bright Orbs that had so lately been feasting upon the Beauties of the Countryside, began to o'erflow with Tears, which in turn drew a watery transparent Curtain betwixt myself and the World, making the entire Landscape resemble some underwater Faery Grotto. And then, when the Tears began to flow, one Sorrow renew'd another. The Thought of losing Lustre led to the Thought of how I had been betray'd, which in turn led to the Thought of leaving my Step-Mother without so much as a Farewell Kiss. O I was wretchèd indeed! I fell to Weeping aloud, and would perhaps have collaps'd with my Arms about Lustre's Neck, by the mossy Bank of some Stream (into which I might then have thrown myself, Ophelia-like), had not the Fear of being discover'd as a Woman by the Fact of my Weeping, discouraged me. So I put Iron in my Will (if not in my Soul) and dried my Tears. I bit my Lip for Shame at my Melancholy, banish'd all Thoughts of Self-Slaughter, and rode on.

"But of one Thing I *am* sure," I remarkt to Lustre when I had quite o'ercome my Fit of Tears, "whate'er is—most certainly is *not* Right." So much for Mr. Pope. O I was glad to be rid of him and his Hypocrisy. When I became a Great Poet (and I *would* become a Great Poet despite his Snickering about Women Poets) I would not use the Muse to traduce the Truth. For as Horace says, "*Scribendi recte Sapere est & principium & fons*"; or, in plain English, "Of good Writing, the Source and Fount is Wisdom." I devoutly promis'd both myself and Lustre that in all my Future Writings I would ne'er betray that Maxim.

'Twas well past Dinner Time for People of Fashion, and almost Supper Time for the Country Folk—in short, 'twas almost Sundown—when I rode into a bustling country Village, and being persuaded both by the Emptiness of my Stomach and the Weariness of my belovèd Horse, to make a Stop, I began looking about for an Inn.

But a Fair was in Progress in that Town, and the divers Swarms of rowdy, riotous People who fill'd the Streets con-

66

vinced me that perhaps 'twas not the safest Town in which to pass the Night. Nonetheless, I linger'd awhile at the Fair, rejoicing somewhat in my Freedom to take in the Sights of the Great World whilst in a Man's Disguise, but 'twas a sorry Fair and, i'faith, its Wonders made me more melancholick than chearful. There was a constant intolerable Squalling of Penny Trumpets, a Rumbling of Drums, the incessant Shoving and Pushing of the Multitude, and the Air was foul with the Singeing of Pigs, to provide Burnt Crackling upon which the Rabble feasted as if 'twere Manna.

There were, of course, the Rope Dancers, both with and without a Pole, cavorting high above the Heads of the Populace. A droll-looking Italian in fine frill'd Holland Shirt, red Hose, and pink Tights, pranced along the Rope with a red Wheelbarrow before him, and two Children and a Dog in it; as if 'twere not enough, he also balanced a Duck upon his Head. But the Children in the Cart seem'd terrified and clutch'd the little white Dog more in Terror than Merriment, and the Crowd laugh'd raucously and threw Plums and Nuts at the Head of the Rope Dancer to distract him, as if they rather hop'd to see him fall than to perform his Entertainments.

They were soon distracted from his Anticks by a female Rope Dancer call'd Lady Mary (tho' whether she was the famous Lady Mary, or only a crass Country Imitator, I cannot say). In any case, she more distinguish'd herself by her Lack of Petticoats than by her Tricks upon the Rope, for she wore only the scantiest frill'd Pantaloons laced with Gold, and she had dispens'd with Hoop and Petticoats altogether—tho' not with Stays, which she wore without the Addition of Handkerchief, Sleeves, or Tucker, so that her Breasts spill'd o'er the Top of her Stays and flapp'd in the Breeze for all to see.

The Crowd went wild upon her Appearance, the Men remarking lewdly upon her Nudity, and the Women disapproving loudly, calling her Whore and Strumpet, but being unable to unglue their Eyes from her Bosom for all that.

Lady Mary cavorted in the Air above their Heads, seemingly dodging their Insults with her dext'rous Grace, and smiling for all the World as if she saw thro' their false Morality.

There was something in her Spirit I liked, a sort of Mockery of the World's Affectations. Tho' I could no more strip naked and dance upon a Rope than I could take Wing and fly to China, I felt that she mockt her Audience as much as they mockt her, and in this Contest of Wits, she was the Winner. There was Art in her Prancing, after all—tho' perhaps a low sort of Art compared to the Noble Tragedy or the lofty Epick; and there was something in her Visage that seem'd to say we were all Rope Dancers of a sort, prancing a little Time betwixt the Cradle and the Bier, only to fall, at the End, into the Grave.

I turn'd away from this Sight, once again grown melancholick, and led Lustre into the Throng in search of a Pyeman or some other Purveyor of Foodstuffs. The Crowd, howe'er, was pressing towards another Attraction, and Willynilly, my Horse and I were swept along to a Booth which promis'd "a Great Collection of Strange and Wonderful Rarities, all Alive from sev'ral Parts of the World." The Proprietor of the Booth, a certain Mr. Doggett, was a Famous Actor who had abandon'd his Calling in order to grow rich off the Rabble that attended sundry Fairs about the Countryside. He was a strutting Fellow, with an Actor's Hunger for Applause and a Merchant's Hunger for Money, and all the fine Feelings of a hungry Cur scavenging for his Supper.

"Hear ye, Hear ye!" he cried to the Throng, pushing his greasy cockt Hat back on his Head, pulling at the Queue of his Tye-Wig, and screwing up his red Face to intimidate those Members of the Audience he could not tempt with his freakish Wares.

" 'Ere's the Sight of a Lifetime," he declaim'd. "What? Are ye timid? Are ye womanish? Are ye afear'd fer yer Wits?"

The Crowd stood mute and transfixt by his Bullying. I was determin'd to lead Lustre away and escape the Freak Show. But just at the Moment I began to back away, he fixt his terrible Gaze upon me and said, "Won't the Young Gentleman lead the Crowd? Or are ye afear'd, too?"

Thus challenged, I had to make reply, and so, in what I hop'd was my deepest Voice, I said, "Sirrah, my Horse wants Water. I cannot loiter here."

Down comes Doggett from his Pulpit, seizes Lustre by the Halter, praises his Beauty with a covetous Look, and says: "I'll water yer Horse, Boy. Come, see the Show fer not one Farthing." In a trice, he leads Lustre to an Enclosure behind the Pulpit, hands the Halter to his Manservant, and mounts the Booth again before the teeming Crowd.

" 'Ere, Boy," he says to me, "lead the Way, will ye?" I was still too much of a compliant Girl ('neath my Boy's Disguise) to challenge a big, tall Bully when thus commanded,

68

and so I follow'd Mr. Doggett into his great Tent of Freaks and the whole Throng follow'd me. Nay, it engulf'd me in straining forward to see the Freaks.

In the stagnant and fetid Air of the Tent, Doggett display'd his Wonders. He show'd us a Woman having three Breasts, and likewise her little Daughter, also with three Breasts (tho' whether they were of Flesh or Wax, 'twas indeed hard to tell because Doggett ne'er let us get close enough to properly see). He also show'd us a monstrous Child, with a huge Head, who suckt at the Bosom of another Woman, and whose poor Skull seem'd swollen and purple. He then presented a diminutive Black Man, lately brought from the West Indies, whom he call'd "the Wonder of this Age." The little Black Prince was but three feet high, with the Form and Figure of a grown Man, tho' marvellously delicate in all Proportions. There were also two Creatures call'd "Wood Monsters from the East Indies," who lookt rather to me like twin Boys with false Hair glu'd to their Bodies and Harts' Horns affixt to their unfortunate Scalps; and a Marmoset that danced the Cheshire Rounds; and two Dogs, nam'd Swami Bounce and Swami Bark, who wore Turbans and sat upon little Thrones and were said by Doggett to be able to foretell the Future by Barking (howe'er, the Translations thereof could only be constru'd by Doggett!). There were Hungarian Twins, join'd at the Back, who convers'd with each other in High or Low Dutch, Hungarian, French, or English, as the Crowd desir'd. There was also a Hungarian Youth, who had, in the Places where his Thighs or Legs should be, Women's Breasts, upon which he was said to be able to walk (tho' he did no such Thing whilst I watch'd). There was also a Boy who could paint Pictures with his Feet whilst he play'd on a Violin with his Hands, and a Girl born with neither Arms nor Legs, who nonetheless could thread a Needle and sew with her Teeth (the little Black Prince held the Fabrick for her); and finally, there was a Boy cover'd all over his Body with the Bristles of a Boar.

'Twas enough to satisfy my Curiosity for Oddities the Rest of my Life! The pressing Crowd seem'd to me more freakish than the Rarities themselves, for what can prevail upon the Rabble to gape at those less fortunate than themselves, except a gloating Sense of their own Self-Love? What can be the Fascination, the Entertainment, the Surprize in it? Is it merely to bless oneself with one's own Good Fortune in being born with two Arms, two Legs, and the requisite Number of Fingers?

I was musing thus, and trying to make my Way out of the Tent to reclaim Lustre, when a fat, red-faced Village Maid before me, turn'd to me and shouted,

"Swine! Squeeze me Bum, will ye?" And she clouted me with her Basket of Plums, causing quite a Number of 'em to fall upon the Ground.

I was stunn'd. Of course, I had done no such Thing; I had not e'en been aware of her Presence until she clouted me. But her Accusation alerted the rough Country Bumpkin who was her Escort, and he turn'd on me, making the same Accusation.

"Squeeze 'er Bum, will ye? I'll squeeze yer filthy 'Ead till yer filthy Brains fall out!"

What to do? Apologize for a Sin I did not commit, stand and fight o'er a fictitious Wrong—I quickly chose the former Path.

"A thousand Pardons, Madam," said I in what I hop'd was my deepest Voice.

"A thousand Pardons up yer Arse!" her Defender mockt. "All ye fine Gentlemen think ye can grab at any Country Lass an' not be punish'd fer it—well, I'll show ye! A Pox on yer Arrogance! Zounds! I'll 'ave Blood fer yer damn'd Arrogance! Damme if I won't!"

"Sir," says I, "you mistake me. I have nothing but the highest Respect for your Lady's Honour."

'Twas the wrong Tack to take. The Rabble was growing inflam'd with Ale and the Excitement of the Fair, and they wisht for nothing more than a Brawl, no Matter how unjust the Cause. All my Apologies only inflam'd 'em more and made my Adversary more determin'd to fight.

"Draw," he thunder'd. "We'll settle this Lady's Honour 'ere an' now!"

I had Daniel's Sword, but scarce knew how to use it. Would that I had studied Fencing as I had Horsemanship and Dancing! The Crowd was closing in, shouting Encouragement and already laying Wagers for the Fight.

" 'E's a Pansy an' a Fop, I'll warrant," says one Man close to me (speaking, of course, about myself). O I was in a Quandary of Quandaries! Ought I to reveal myself as a Woman and lose my Disguise for the Remainder of my long Journey? Should I fight it out and be flatten'd or possibly e'en run thro' by this Great Oaf?

70

The Many-headed Monster of the Rabble grew larger and larger as the Shouts of the Multitude within the Tent attracted People from other parts of the Fair. The Posture-Masters had stopp'd their Contortions and press'd into the Tent to watch. The Tumblers and Vaulters, Jugglers and Rope Dancers, and e'en the Merry Andrew and his Second, had been drawn into the Tent as well, and now stood at the Sidelines, leering and winking, doing Impersonations of the great fat Country Wench who preen'd and prinkt with Pride that a real Duel was going to be fought o'er her Beauty.

"Damn ye, Sir, fer a Cowardly Pimp," says her Swain. "Give me Satisfaction like a Man of Honour, or I'll cut yer Ears off!"

I thought quickly, my Mind growing clear as Crystal in my Panick. I remember'd that tho' Duelling was i'faith illegal (tho' the Legalities were seldom enforced), there *were* certain Rules which would not be countermanded. A Gentleman was entitl'd to his Second, and to the Presence of his Surgeon; also, he was entitl'd to choose his Spot for the Duel.

"Sir," says I, "I shall meet you in an Hour's Time without the Old Walls of the Town—and I pray you are more a Man of Honour than to take advantage of a Gentleman who hath neither Second nor Surgeon to attend him!"

"Damn yer Second an' yer Surgeon, ye Cowardly Fop!" says my valiant Adversary. "I'll 'ave Satisfaction an' 'ave it 'ere."

Praying to God or the Supreme Being for Aid and Courage, I drew my Silver-hilted Sword, and prepar'd to meet Choirs of Angels and the Almighty Himself forthwith. I blest myself. Ne'er had I more fervently believ'd in the Hereafter.

I stood thus for what seem'd like an Eternity. My Sword pois'd in my Hand, my Adversary glow'ring at me (he was restrain'd for the Moment only by other Members of the Rabble who wisht to clear an Arena so that all might better see the Fight and better lay their Wages), I waited for the End of this Best of all Possible Worlds. Whereupon, just as my fierce Adversary prepar'd to draw, there came a Thund'ring of Hooves in the thick Air of the Tent and a terrifying Neighing and Whinnying—and who should appear but Lustre himself with Doggett's poor would-be Horse Thief of a Servant clinging for Dear Life to his Neck! My belovèd Stallion stampeded into the Center of the Ring, rear'd up, throwing Doggett's Servant clear, whinnied like Pegasus flying across the Skies, dipp'd his Head thrice as if to bid me to mount, slow'd whilst I clamber'd onto his Back, and gallop'd away like the very Wind, with his shockt but grateful Mistress hanging on to his Back.

Within and without the Tent, the Multitude stood and gap'd. Of all the Wonders of Nature they had seen on this remarkable Day, Lustre was surely the most wond'rous.

We clatter'd thro' the Town at breakneck Speed, out thro' the Gates and across the Meadows, where a full Moon was just now rising, and the Road before us lookt like a purple Ribband, shining and beckoning, but leading we knew not where.

Chapter X

A Word to the Wise about Gratitude; an exciting Chase upon horseback; our Heroine's Conversations with two Wise Women of the Woods; and a most astonishing Prophecy.

WE GALLOP'D FOR A TIME whilst I sought to catch my Breath and determine the next Course of Action. I thankt Lustre from the Bottom of my Heart for this amazing Rescue, thankt the Almighty for my Redemption, thankt the Man in the Moon, my Stars, and e'en the Fates themselves for preserving me thus from an untimely Demise. (For I have noticed that altho' Mortals are very prone to beg the Almighty for Aid when they are in some Difficulty, they are equally forgetful of thanking Him when they are deliver'd, and it hath always been my Philosophy, with God as with Man, that an Ounce of Prevention is worth a Pound of Cure.)

Galloping thus, with the Wind at my Back, and my Thoughts all in Disorder about the Events that transpir'd at the Fair, I did not hear, at first, the Noise of Hooves drawing closer, nor did I notice that I was being follow'd.

But presently some strange Sense of Unease made me turn about and lo! I saw behind me, galloping like the very Devil, Doggett himself.

He was swinging a Net as if to catch me, and carrying o'er his Shoulder a Matchlock Musket with a five-foot Barrel, such as an old Country Squire might use to bring down Birds.

I spurr'd on Lustre, who was, anyway, galloping as fast as his weary Legs could carry him, but alas, Doggett kept gaining on us. As he drew closer, he shouted,

"What'll ye have fer that Horse?"

"Nothing," said I, "I'll ne'er part with him!" So that was Doggett's Game—to take Lustre and exhibit him like some Freak in his hideous Display of Grotesques.

"Ne'er!" I swore; and that Resolve giving me the extra

Surge of Pow'r I needed, I jump'd a Fence into a neighbouring Meadow and led Doggett a Merry Chase o'er Stiles and
Streams until we finally reach'd a rapid-rushing River, where
his Horse stumbl'd and falter'd, but Lustre, undaunted,
waded across.

We had lost 'em for the nonce; across the River, I saw
Doggett and his defeated Horse turn back. I devoutly hop'd
we had seen the Last of him. But in losing our Pursuer, we
had also lost the Road. Lustre was tired from the extraordinary Exertions of rescuing me. He requir'd Sleep and Water;
I requir'd Rest. There was no Inn to be found here in the
Wilds, and if we slept in the Open, the dread Doggett might
come to claim us.

I dismounted, kiss'd Lustre upon his blessèd Blaze, ran my
Lips down his gently disht Forehead, and led him to the
Banks of the rapidly rushing River where, by the Light of the
Moon, we both might drink.

I was kneeling thus by the Stream, cupping the cool Water
in my Hands whilst Lustre lapp'd contentedly beside me,
when suddenly I noticed a strange bent Figure in a high-
crown'd Beaver Hat loping along the River-Bank, follow'd
silently by a silky Persian Cat. In one Hand she held an
Elderberry Wand with which, from Time to Time, she struck
the River Water, and she mutter'd curious Syllables I could
scarce, at first, understand.

"Lilith, Ishtar, Ge!" she cried. "Isis hear my Plea! O
boundless bitter Sea! I, thy Priestess, call to Thee!"

The Form and Figure of this Person was so very like Pictures I had seen of Witches that at first I was frighten'd, and
I strove to hide from her. But then suddenly she saw me and
seem'd, i'faith, more affrighted by my Presence than I was by
hers.

" 'Tis not what ye think!" she cried to me. "I'm merely
catching Toads for Soup!"

Toads for Soup? I thought; how very strange indeed. But
as the old Woman came closer, I could see in the Moonlight
that her Face was kind, tho' she smil'd nervously as if to hide
something. She had the ruddy Face of a Countrywoman of
about fifty Years of Age, and 'twas healthy and astonishingly
free of the least Line or Wrinkle. Her Eyes were bright blue
and almost merry; and what was more, the Eyes of her Cat
were the same Jewel-like Colour.

She bow'd ceremoniously, and I could only do the same—

so gentle, almost fragile, was her Manner. 'Twould i'faith have seem'd rude not to bow as she did.

Her Back, it seem'd, had been bent by some childhood Disease, but when she straighten'd up as best she could, her Form was not altogether unpleasing. The Cat leapt up into her Arms and she strok'd it as she spoke to me.

"What brings a Fine Gentleman like you to this part of the Woods?" she askt, her lower Lip trembling slightly despite her confident Manner.

"O Madam," says I, "there was a wicked Man who sought to steal my Horse. He said he wisht to buy him—but buy or steal, 'tis all as bad to me. I'll ne'er part with him, ne'er. He's all I have in the World."

So trustworthy were those blue Eyes that I had blurted all this out in the girlish Voice that Nature herself had given me, whereupon my good Countrywoman lookt me o'er with much Relief and exclaim'd merrily, "A Lass! Of course, you're but a Lass dress'd in your Brother's Clothes!" Then she laugh'd like Wind Chimes jingling on a breezy Day.

"Are you weary? Are you hungry?" she askt, as if she were my own Mother.

I nodded that I was.

Whereupon she put her Arm around my Shoulder, saying, "Don't think you're the first Maid to wear a Gentleman's Garb against the ungentle World. Since Eden fell, there's many have done the same. Come, Child, we'll find Provision for your Horse, and Food and Bed for your poor tired Bones. On the Morrow, 'twill all look brighter."

So saying, she led me thro' the Woods to a small thatch'd Cottage, with trellis'd Roses rambling all about, and Larkspur and Lilies lining the Path to the Front Door.

I was reluctant to leave Lustre, e'en for a Moment, so my Good Woman left him ty'd in the front where I could see him thro' the low Cottage Window, and he soon lower'd his Head and fell to sleeping, e'en before we brought his Oats.

Within the Cottage, all was Simplicity and rustick Warmth. A large open Hearth, with Tea Kettle boiling upon it and also hearty Soup in an open iron Pott. Plain Furniture of Oak and homespun Cloth for Pillows, and a woven Country Rug upon the earthen Floor.

The Good Woman (whose Name, she said, was Isobel White) liv'd with another, a Woman of about the same age call'd Joan Griffith. But whereas Mother White was pink-cheakt and ruddy with Hair of whitish Hue and bright blue

Eyes, Mother Griffith was swarthy as the Night itself, with Eyes like dark Coals. Her Voice was as deep as the other's was high, and she was strong-bon'd and stout as Mother White was small. Her Breasts were large, her Lips large—in short, a Woman of Substance.

But my Eyes were drawn particularly to the Bauble she wore about her thick Neck. 'Twas a little silver Dagger, an exact Replica of the sort that might be worn at the Hip of an Asiatick Prince, and it twinkl'd and glitter'd with each Breath she drew. She, too, greeted me warmly, offer'd to put away my Cloak, Hat, and Riding Wig, e'en help'd me off with my Boots.

As I unpinn'd my long, red Hair, both Women exclaim'd at once of its Beauty. I toss'd my Head, happy to be return'd, for a Time, to my own Identity. But I could not help noticing how intently Mother White studied me, as if she were wond'ring whether we had met before.

O'er a simple Meal of Oxtail Soup, thicken'd with Oat Meal and flavour'd with Thyme and Sage, I told her of my Adventures at the Fair, my wond'rous Rescue by Lustre, and my narrow Escape from the greedy Hands of Mr. Doggett.

"Lucky you are the Rabble did not try you as a Witch," said Mother Griffith in her booming Voice, "for 'tis a Country Belief amongst the Ignorant and Weak of Understanding that any Person of the Female Sex who hath perfect Communion with an Animal must therefore be a Witch and that Animal be her Familiar. Sure, your Stars are most auspicious, for you were spar'd the Ordeal by Water, which I myself have undergone on two Occasions."

She said all this as casually as you please, but I was deeply shockt, for ne'er before had I met a Person tried as a Witch, tho' certainly I had heard tell of such Things. I'faith, I had read horrible Accounts of the Burnings and Hangings of earlier Times and I knew such Things were not yet quite finish'd, tho' the educated Persons of the Modern Age were quite divided upon the Subject of Witchcraft.

Many Persons of Understanding believ'd that tho', in gen'ral, there might be such Things as Witchcraft, Commerce and Intercourse with Evil Spirits, and the like, ne'ertheless they could give no Credit to any particular *Instance* of it. I'faith, whene'er some old Woman had the Reputation of a Witch all o'er the Country, she was found, upon closer Inspection, to be a wretchèd Creature, doting and distemper'd, not so much malevolent as poor and infirm. Certainly, I had heard Tales of some of these old women being hang'd or burnt or committed to Bridewell, upon the Evidence of some Half-Wit Child that he was made to vomit Pins, or the Evidence of some slatternly Dairymaid that the old Woman's Look had curdl'd Milk, or the Evidence of some Town Trollop with Clap that the old Woman's Touch had caus'd her to abort a Babe she doubtless wisht dead in any case—but nothing of the sort had happen'd in our Parish, so I tended to hear such Stories with a Divided Mind. Could such Cruelties really still exist in our Age, which was the Embodiment of Reason and Common Sense? I believ'd, and yet I did not believe. Such horrid Practices and dark Superstitions belong'd, I was sure, to previous Ages.

"Joan," said Mother White to her Companion, "Fanny was disguis'd as a Man, thus the Accusation of Witch did not occur."

"And lucky she was," said Mother Griffith, dishing out more Soup for us all. "The Maid was born under a lucky Star."

"That she was surely," said Mother White, looking at me, as if she wisht to puzzle out a Mystery. For some Reason, her look frighten'd me, so I quickly brought the Conversation 'round to the Fact that I did not know my precise Birthdate, being as I was an Orphan.

"An Orphan?" askt Mother White. "Where then were you rais'd?"

"At Lymeworth, Lord Bellars' Country Seat," said I, all Innocence. But the Looks that the two old Women exchanged upon hearing that News were meaningful indeed.

"Come," said Mother Griffith, as if to distract her Friend from some Troublesome Thought I knew not of, "let me prophesy your Future."

She was, she said, an excellent "Skyrer," or Crystal Gazer, but she had made very few Predictions of late for fear of reviving the Charge of Witchcraft, from which she had so narrowly escap'd.

"Is there such a Thing as Witchcraft?" I askt, sincerely wishing to know.

"Ah, Fanny," said Mother White, " 'tis a Subject so complicated that no two reasonable Persons can speculate upon it and find themselves of one Mind."

"Not true at all," said Mother Griffith, contradicting Mother White like a cantankerous old Husband who doth not agree with his wife's Conversation. "There's but the Explana-

77

tion for Witchcraft and 'tis nothing more than the Enmity and Fear that Men bear for Women!"

" 'Tis not so simple, Joan!" says Mother White, her blue Eyes flashing. " 'Tis a Question of Old Beliefs carried on despite the Preachments of the Church. . . . For doth it not say in *Exodus*, 'Thou shalt not suffer a Witch to live'? And in *Leviticus*, 'Turn not to Mediums or Wizards'?"

" 'Tis not the Point at all, Isobel," says Joan warmly, her Voice becoming fever'd, her Expression serious and intense. "Many innocent Women have been burnt and hang'd thro'out Europe and e'en here in Merry England, because they knew Midwifery or Herbal Cures, or e'en because they were dislik'd and People wisht to steal their Land."

"True enough," says Isobel, "but Fanny wishes to know whether there is such a Thing as Witchcraft or no, and all your Fury doth not enlighten her one Whit!"

'Twas almost droll how they argu'd betwixt themselves. I had not seen the like of it since I had witness'd an Argument betwixt Mrs. Locke the Housekeeper and her Husband Locke the Butler. They had been married upwards of twenty-five Years and were e'er engaged in Domestick Strife, much to the Amusement of the other Servants.

"Fanny, my Dear," says Isobel, "let me tell you my Opinion concerning Witchcraft and then Joan can tell you hers. 'Tis my Belief that in Ancient Times, in the Pagan Albion of Old, Women were not as they are now, subservient to Men in ev'ry Respect. Rather they were Queens and Priestesses, responsible for the Fructification of the Crops, and the Multiplication of the Herds; they were the Leaders of the Holy Rituals—"

"E'en the very word 'Witch,' " Joan interrupted, "derives from our Ancestors' Word 'Wicca,' meaning only 'Wise Woman.' "

Isobel lookt cross. "Are you quite finish'd, Joan?" says she. "Will you hold your Tongue now and let me speak?"

"Yes, yes," Joan mumbl'd, looking not a little vext.

"Well then," says Isobel, "when Christianity came to these Isles, 'twas the Task of the Church to stamp out the Old Religions, but some of the remaining Wise Women would not relinquish their Learning, their Spells, Charms, and Healing Pow'rs, the which they had learnt at their Mothers' Knees—"

" 'Twas all White Magick, too!" interrupted Joan. "Nothing at all for Harm—but the Priests in their Fear told the ignorant Country Folk to fear us—"

78

"Will you hold your Tongue?" says Isobel.

"Very well," says Joan.

"So these Wise Women," continu'd Isobel, "were oft' denounced, tortur'd, or kill'd; but if they were truly wise, they practis'd secretly—"

"As *we* do," said Joan, smiling.

"*Hush!*" said Isobel.

"You—you are Witches?" I gasp'd, suddenly afraid of these two kindly old Ladies.

"Of course we are, Pet," said Joan.

"O dear, O now you've ruin'd it." Isobel sigh'd, burying her Head in her Hands.

"Fanny won't betray us, will you, Dearling?" Joan askt, more with Menace in her dark Eyes than Beseechment. I'faith, I would be afraid to do so, I thought, for fear of Reprisal.

"Upon my Word, I will not," said I. "I swear it by all that's Holy. . . ." I chok'd on that last Word and then was mute.

A sudden Panick seiz'd me. Perhaps they did not believe in God at all, but only in the Devil. Perhaps they were in league with him, us'd his Pow'r to fly thro' the Air upon their Broomstaffs, held Sabbats at which they were defil'd by him and kiss'd his Arse, defil'd the Host, e'en turn'd the Cross upside down! O now I was really terrified! The Devil himself might rise at any Moment, with Horns upon his Head, Fire in his Mouth, a Tail in his Breech, Eyes like Basons, Fangs like a Dog, Claws like a Bear, and Nostrils that breath'd out the Smell of Brimstone.

"Come, Fanny," said Isobel, once again looking up and focussing those bright blue Eyes upon me, "sure you don't believe all that?"

"All what?" I askt, for I had not said a Word.

"All that you are thinking," said Isobel calmly.

"Are you hearing my very Thoughts?" I cried in Terror.

"Dear Fanny," she said, taking my Hand (which had grown quite cold with Fear), " 'tis not as you think. A Wise Woman *can* hear certain Thoughts," she said, "but not because she is wicked, and not because the Devil gives her Pow'r, but because she hath train'd her Mind to it by Extream Concentration, by Meditation in Solitude, and by many other Mental Rigours."

"Then you can perceive what I am thinking?" I askt.

"Not always," said Isobel. "But I can hear *certain*

79

Thoughts as loudly as if they were Words. Thoughts like these are loud indeed. In fact, 'tis always true that Fears are easy to read. Fears are louder than any Thoughts, but e'en so they are the most foolish Thoughts of all."

I star'd at her with Amazement, not knowing whether to credit her as a Genius or to abhor her as a Sorceress.

"Fanny, my Dear, you are too clever a Girl to believe what may have been confess'd under Torture by poor terrified Women examin'd by vicious Inquisitors. The Sisters of Wicca sure ne'er conjur'd the Devil, nor did they use their Broomstaffs except to sweep the Floor! They studied to be wise, to heal the Sick, to preserve their ancient Herbal Receipts, to gain Pow'r o'er their own Minds and Bodies, to bring Babies to Birth, and Crops to Harvest. All the Rest was but the evil Report of evil Men who fear'd the Wisdom of Women, who fear'd Female Knowledge, thus Female Pow'r. . . ."

"Then there ne'er was a Black Mass, nor a Sabbat at which Babies were eaten?" I askt, still shaking.

"Perhaps there was," said Joan, "but those who partook of it were poor deranged Souls, doom'd to imitate the Things of which they stood accus'd by their Inquisitors. They were not the Sisters of Wicca. And, sad to say, they were not Wise Women."

I fell silent now, trying to understand these many Arguments. I was still not sure my Reason was sufficient to grasp 'em all.

Joan clear'd away the Soup-Dishes and Isobel brought out a fine Pudding studded with Currants and Raisins.

"Witchcraft," she said, pointing to the Pudding. This broke the Spell of Silence and we all laugh'd heartily.

For a Time, we amus'd ourselves with humorous Rhodomontade, whereupon at last, when we had quite finish'd the Pudding and once more were merry and gay, Joan went to a large Sea-Trunk lodged under the Bed the two Women shar'd, and from its very Bowels extracted a strange Object. 'Twas the Size and Shape of a Bowling Ball and 'twas nestl'd in a Shroud of black Velvet, inky as the Sky on a moonless Night. Joan carefully unwrapp'd it to reveal a gleaming Crystal Sphere in whose Depths were mysterious Lights, Planets, Stars, whole Worlds.

Isobel rose and blew out all the Candles in the Room but one. Joan sat at the Table, staring into the Heart of the wond'rous Crystal. She grew e'er more pensive and melan-

80

cholick as she did so, rockt back and forth in her Chair, mutter'd to herself, and press'd her Eyes very tightly shut. Then she chanted strange Syllables in a high-pitch'd Voice.

I, too, lookt into the Ball, searching in its mysterious Depths for the Key to my Future. I fancied I saw Seas and Continents swirling within the Ball, but perhaps 'twas just my Imagination deceiving me. I also thought I saw Lord Bellars' handsome Face, then the ugly Face of Doggett, then the Face of a Copper-hair'd little Girl, then the Face of an ugly old Bawd—but all these Visions I discredited as Delusions and Fancies, not true Prophecies.

Finally, Joan began to speak. She spoke in Rhyme and in a Voice not like her own. 'Twas higher and shriller. Her Eyes blaz'd like smould'dring Coals and her whole stout Form sway'd and rockt like a Chandelier in a House that is about to collapse. I listen'd to ev'ry Word as if my Life hung in the Balance. Perhaps it did.

This is what she said:

"Your own Father you do not know.
Your Daughter will fly across the Seas.
Your Purse will prosper, your Heart will grow.
You will have Fame, but not Heart's Ease.

From your Child-Womb will America grow.
By your Child-Eyes, you will be betray'd.
You will turn Blood into driven Snow.
By your own strong Heart will the Devil be stay'd."

Chapter XI

*Of Prophecies and Herbs; of Witchcraft and Magick;
of Courage and a red silk Garter.*

AFTER THE PROPHECY had been utter'd, we three sat in the
dark Chamber by the Light of one flick'ring Candle and
star'd into the Depths of the Crystal Sphere, saying no Word
to each other. A steady Rain began to drum upon the Roof;
a chill Wind flew down the Chimney causing the Fire to
dance madly for a Moment, then leap upward once more;
and Lustre rear'd upon his hind Legs, neigh'd wildly, show'd
his Face at the Window, his Eyes blazing, and then grew suddenly silent again.

"I will lead him to Shelter under the Eaves," Isobel said,
and for a Moment or two, I was left alone with Joan, my
Seeress.

"What doth the Prophecy mean?" I askt.

"It means," she said, her Voice return'd to its normal State,
"whate'er ye take it to mean. You yourself are the Creator of
your Destiny—ne'er forget that."

"But what doth the Prophecy portend?" I insisted. "How
shall I turn Blood to driven Snow? How shall I stay the
Devil?" (I could not but shudder at his very Name.)

Joan lookt at me with all Solemnity and said: "I'faith, Lass,
I do not know. I can only tell ye that when I gaze into the
Ball a Pow'r greater than myself seizes hold of me and what I
say I oft' cannot rightly remember afterwards. My Voice
turns high and shrill as the Wind shrieking, my Throat goes
dry as Kindling, my Eyes burn in my Head like Embers, and
it seems my Brains bubble like boiling Milk. Yet Folks tell
me my Prophecies oft' come true. I can't boast of it myself
because I don't remember 'em."

"But you say they come true?" I askt.

"Other Folks say so," said Joan. "Oft' the Possessor of a
Pow'r is the last Soul upon Earth to credit it. When I come

82

back to my own true Self, as now, I swear I cannot remember the Prophecies at all."

"But I remember 'em," I said. "I shall ne'er forget 'em."

"That's good, Lass," said Joan. "Let 'em seep into your Brain and give ye the Pow'r to seize your Life with Courage. Courage is the only Magick worth having. If I could brew a Potion for kindling Courage in the Heart, I'd be the richest old Lady in all of England. But, alas, each of us must brew it in the Cauldron of her own Heart. There's no other Way. If my Prophecies can do a little to heat the Flames, I'm content."

"This is potent Witchcraft indeed," I said, as the Prophecy silently burnt into my Brain. "Pray tell me, what other Enchantments do you know?"

At that very Moment, Isobel appear'd out of the Rain, where she had tended to Lustre, and hearing the last Query, made quick to answer (as if, i'faith, she had not been out of the Room).

"We know," she said, "Herbs that restore Stolen Goods to their Proper Place and Herbs that reduce Fever and calm the Nerves. . . ."

"We know Herbs to raise Sores on Beggars to promote Sympathy . . . and Herbs to improve the Complexion . . ." Joan added.

"We know Herbs to cause a Death-like Sleep," said Isobel, "and Herbs to cure Warts."

"We know Herbs to treat Flatulence," said Joan, "or cause Abortion . . . or bring Lovers back together . . ."

"We know the Use of Poisons," said Isobel, with a Hint of Mischief in her Voice, "Baneberry, Balsam Apple, Hellebore, Cherry Laurel, Caper Spurge, Christmas Rose, Cuckoo Pint . . ."

"And don't forget Hemlock and Deadly-Nightshade," said Joan.

"And you use all these Herbs just for Good, not Ill?"

"Well, *nearly* always, Dear," said Isobel.

"Yes," said Joan, "*almost* all the Time. But, of course, there *are* difficult Moments in Life that call for strong Measures . . ."

"And then, to be sure," said Isobel, " 'tis good to have some special Wisdom at one's Fingertips . . ."

" 'Tis not pleasant to be ill-prepar'd and totally at the Mercy of the Fates," said Joan.

"Alas," said Isobel, " 'tis a hard enough Thing to be born a

Woman in this Vale of Tears without resorting to some Witchcraft or other to make it bearable. I'm sure Fanny will agree, won't you, Dear?"

"Oh, yes," I said, thoroughly puzzl'd and beginning to grow uneasy again. "Oh, yes, certainly. Indeed."

Isobel lookt at me with her twinkly blue Eyes. "Lustre is well," she said. "He askt after you when I ty'd him under the Eaves. . . . I told him you had been frighten'd, but that you were a stout-hearted Girl and would learn Courage sooner than most. . . . He seem'd content. I promise you, the vile Mr. Doggett cannot follow him here. Come, Fanny, let's prepare a Bed for a sleepy Girl. . . ."

As the two Women took down Quilts and Eider-Downs and laid a Bed for me before the Fire, I thought of all the astonishing Things I had heard that Ev'ning, the strange Prophecy, the Herbal Wisdom of the Witches, Isobel's uncanny Ability to read Thoughts and converse with Animals. . . . What more could these two wond'rous Women do? Could they raise Storms? Could they fly thro' the Air?

"Ah, Fanny Dear," said Isobel, putting a warm Arm around my Shoulder, "you fret too much. 'Tis nothing to worry about. Your Face is the Mirror of your Fears."

"But can you raise Storms and fly thro' the Air?" I askt.

"Perhaps," said Isobel, teazingly, "and perhaps not."

"Only little Storms," said Joan, "no Lightning."

"And short Flights," said Isobel. But 'twas impossible to tell if they were jesting with me or not.

"Here, Fanny," said Isobel, lifting her long Skirt, slipping a red silk Garter down her slender Thigh and giving it to me. " 'Tis all the Magick you'll need Tonight. Wear it and be safe from all Harm."

I lookt closely at the slightly faded red silk Garter with its pink Rosette and silky red Ribbands hanging down; I felt the Silk with my Fingers. Woven into the Band was a Motto almost out of the Cloth with Time: "*My Heart is fixt, I will not range, I like my Choyce too well to change.*"

"Put it on, Dear," said Isobel, "and don't fret."

"Good Night, Lambkin," said Joan, kissing me upon the Forehead.

"Good Night," I said, more puzzl'd than e'er before. But I made sure to slip the Garter on my Thigh as I undress'd for Bed.

Isobel's Persian Cat crept o'er on noiseless Feet and curl'd up in the warm Hollow betwixt my Knees and my Belly. The

Embers glow'd upon the Hearth, and the Cat's Fur seem'd charged with that sort of subtle Fire Sir Thomas Browne had found in Amber and term'd "Electricity." Joan and Isobel sigh'd and roll'd o'er in their Bed. Then one of them—'twas Joan, I guess'd—began to snore mightily. I felt myself secure, protected, as if by two Mothers, and 'twas a pleasant enough Feeling for an Orphan. And so, the ample Arms of Morpheus reach'd out to break my Fall, and I slept; I slept the dreamless Sleep of the Blest.

On the Morrow, I was awaken'd by the Sounds of iron Potts clanging and Buckets of Water being brought from the Well. Joan and Isobel were preparing a fine breakfast of white and wheaten Bread, sugar'd Buns, Lisbon Oranges, and hot Asses' Milk. Save for that humble Beverage, 'twas lavish Fare for two plain Country-women, but I was so accustom'd to Wonders in this House of Wonders that I did not ask where Lisbon Oranges grew in these bosky Woods.

At Table, Joan and Isobel askt me where I was going and what my Hopes were.

"Only the Hope to seek my Fortune in London," I said. Whereupon I recounted the whole sad Story of Lord Bellars' Seduction and Betrayal, Mr. Pope's Hypocrisy, Daniel's scurvy Usage of me, and Mary's Envy.

Joan and Isobel listen'd intently. Isobel's merry blue Eyes flam'd with Anger as I spoke and she seem'd at one Moment (when I mention'd Lord Bellars) to utter a Curse 'neath her Breath. Then she compos'd herself, as if by a Supreme Effort of Will; and when I had finish'd, she said to me: "Oft'times the Strongest and most Beautiful have to bear the heaviest Burdens, because, added to their own Burdens, they bear the Envy of others. But fear not, Fanny, 'twill make you stronger."

"But if you wish to be revenged upon that Whoremaster, Lord Bellars," said Joan, looking like the very Devil, "I can think of a Way. . . ."

Isobel star'd at her, read her Intent in her evil Look, and said, "No. I'll not permit it."

"Permit what?" I askt.

"The Waxen Puppet, the red-hot Pins," said Isobel. " 'Tis Foolishness. Leave him to Heaven. 'Vengeance is Mine, saith the Lord.' Bellars and his London Mistress shall find their Punishments soon enough and at their own Hands."

"Can you truly make a Waxen Puppet?" I askt.

"Joan can," said Isobel.

"Indeed," said Joan, with great Pride, "and an excellent Likeness, too."

"And doth it injure the Person whose Likeness you steal?"

"Some say it doth," said Joan. " 'Tis certain 'twill make *you* feel much better, if not him much worse."

"I won't permit it," said Isobel. " 'Tis uncall'd for here."

"We might put it to the Coven," said Joan, "and call a Vote."

"You belong to a Coven?" I askt.

" 'Tis a fancy Name for a Sewing Circle of old Ladies," said Isobel, looking fiercely at Joan as if to silence her. " 'Twould bore Fanny extreamly."

"On the Contrary, Isobel, my Dear, Fanny will need such Knowledge if she is truly to seek her Fortune in this cruel World."

"I will not risque subjecting an innocent young Girl to the Charge of Witchcraft," Isobel said warmly. She rose from the Table and set her Tankard of Milk loudly upon it to enforce her Displeasure.

"Ask *Fanny* if she wishes to go," said Joan. " 'Tis only right for Fanny to decide."

"Go where? Decide what?" I askt, all in Confusion.

"Are you then agreed?" Joan askt Isobel.

"You play with Fire," Isobel said, sternly. "This Prank could be the Death of Fanny—the Ordeal by Water, e'en Blooding."

"You fret too much," said Joan. "You learnt it at your Mother's Knee."

" 'Tis better than what you learnt at *your* Mother's Knee," said Isobel. "I won't see Fanny harm'd."

"Nor will I," said Joan. "T'faith, I'm fond of the Lass, too. But I say she lacks Experience. What can we give her to take to London but Wisdom of the World?"

"Wisdom, not Witchcraft," said Isobel.

"Oft'times, the two are the same," said Joan. "Come, Fanny, what would you? Join us with the Coven this very Night? Or go straight to London?"

I trembl'd. My Fate was indeed in my Hands. Would I see a Sight few Mortals e'er see and risque the severest Punishment, or would I play the Coward's Part and refuse?

Alas, Belinda, it hath e'er been my Fate, when given the Choyce of Daring or Safety, to choose Daring. "*My Heart is fixt, I will not range,*" may be the Motto on my Garter, but I fear it refers to the Fixity of my Soul in search of Adventure, not the Fixity of my Body in search of Home. Thus I nodded my Head yes to Joan's Query, and I steel'd my Soul to endure whate'er the Fates had in store.

Chapter XII

Containing some Essential Information regarding the Nature of Esbats, Sabbats, Flying thro' the Air upon Broomstaffs, and other Matters with which the enlighten'd young Woman of Parts should be acquainted; together with a most dreadful Scene upon Stonehenge Down, which few Readers should venture upon in an Ev'ning, especially when alone.

THAT AFTERNOON, we prepar'd for the Weekly Meeting of the Coven. 'Twas agreed that after the Meeting, Isobel and Joan should put me on the Road to London (from which I had stray'd in eluding Mr. Doggett) and we three should part—howe'er, not without Isobel's revealing some Mystery which, she declar'd, would both astonish and delight me. Therefore, I was to wear my Travelling Clothes—Daniel's Clothes, to speak truly—and Lustre was to be groom'd and fed and prepar'd for the long Journey. As we made these Preparations, and Joan and Isobel readied divers Ointments and Brews for the Meeting, I was able to ask a few of the myriad Queries that had been seething in my Brain all Day. I wisht to know all about Herbs, all about Divination, and whether 'twas true (as I had heard from my Nurse in Childhood) that a Witch had only to stand o'er her Broomstaff and utter certain Words in order to fly thro' the Air.

Whereupon Joan put a Broomstaff betwixt her Legs and said:

"Horse and Hattock, Horse and go! Horse and Pellatis, ho, ho!" But she mov'd not an Inch off the Ground.

"Then you cannot fly thro' the Air?" I askt.

"See for yourself," said Isobel, laughing.

"But have you not *Flying* Ointments?" I askt.

"Ah, Fanny," said Isobel, "some Ladies in our Coven set great store by an Unguent containing Extract of Monk's-Hood, and Deadly-Nightshade; they say it enables

88

'em to fly; but I say it disorders their Senses and makes 'em *think* they fly. I'd sooner drink good Claret."

"No Subject is more fill'd with Foolishness than Notions of Witchcraft in the common Mind," said Joan, "and, i'faith, many Witches themselves believe that Nonsense. They join the Old Religion, hoping to learn to fly, or set Curses upon their Neighbours, and the Meaning of the True Devotion is lost."

"But do they not worship the Devil?" I askt—for so I had heard.

"One Woman's Devil is another Woman's belovèd Husband," said Isobel, smiling mischievously, "and what the Witch-Hunters call'd the Foul Fiend, the Prince of Darkness, may be just another Name for God."

"Then you believe in Jesus Christ?"

"No," said Joan.

"Well, yes," said Isobel, "but I believe in a greater God, too."

"A Female God," said Joan, "whose Name is too holy to be spoken. She that hath made the World and exists ev'rywhere in ev'ry living Thing. She that is both female and male, with Horns upon her Head, and a Belly that brings forth Young. . . ."

"Hush," said Isobel.

"But this is Heresy," I said.

Isobel lookt at me sternly. "Be not so quick to use that Word," said she, "lest it be us'd against you. The Passion that one Soul hath for God cannot be judged by another."

I held my Tongue. Was it possible that the Great God who made the World was female? Or were these two old Women out of their Wits?

"And what Herb do you use to bring Lovers back together?" I askt, being quick to change the Subject.

"Caraway," Joan said.

"With Lemon Balm," said Isobel.

"But it must be us'd in Conjunction with certain Spells."

"Which Spells?" I askt.

"Fanny, my Dear," Isobel said, "you cannot learn all of Witchcraft in one Afternoon. Come, we must prepare for the Esbat."

"The Esbat," Isobel explain'd, as we two rode on Lustre's Back o'er the rolling Hills, where the Hedges seem'd dark green Velvet to the bright wet Green of the Lawns, where the

Poplar Trees form'd Walls against the Wind, and the stone-roof'd Cottages slumber'd in the Hollows of the Hills, "is the weekly Meeting."

" 'Tis not to be confus'd with the Sabbat," Joan said, riding close beside us upon an Ass call'd Bottom. "Sabbats are held but four Times a Year—Candelmas, Roodmas, Lammas, and All Hallows E'en."

"The most important Times being Roodmas and All Hallows E'en," said Isobel. "And to a Sabbat, many Covens come. The Esbat is only a little Meeting—for weekly Business."

"But where are we going now?" I askt, as we cross'd a grassy Down where a large Flock of Sheep graz'd in the light Rain.

"We are going to a great Stone Circle where we shall meet the Coven," Isobel said. "Hush, now. This is more careless Talk than is wise, here on the open Down."

"But who shall hear us," I askt, "the Sheep?"

"E'en the Sheep have Ears," said Isobel.

The County of Wiltshire was then, as now, Belinda, a vast continu'd Body of chalky Hills whose Tops spread out into fruitful and pleasant Downs and Plains, upon which great Flocks of Sheep were fed. Pleasant Rivers flow'd beautifully into verdant Vales where fruitful Meadows and rich Pastures lin'd the Banks. There were innumerable pleasant Towns, Villages, and Houses in the verdant Vales, but upon the Downs the Country seem'd wild and uninhabited—the proper Resort of Witches, Faeries, and all Manner of Gnomes, Elves, and Hobgoblins.

I had heard, of course, the Country Lore that the "Little People," the green-coated Faeries, and the Witches were wont to meet upon the Barrows and at the Stone Circles; but I had always consider'd 'em mere Country Fictions and Superstitions.

Thro' my prodigious Reading in Lord Bellars' fine Library, I had Knowledge of the Dispute about which England's learnèd Antiquaries had so puzzl'd themselves, concerning the strange upright Stones of great Antiquity upon Stonehenge Down. Some alleged it to be a Pagan or Heathen Temple, some an Altar or Place of Sacrifice, some a Monument for the Dead, and some a Trophy of Victory. Some held it to be Roman, some British, some Saxon, some Danish, some Druid, and some, before 'em all, Phoenician.

But I had ne'er seen this Place of Wonders, and to be sure, I had ne'er seen it just as the setting Sun was sinking below the Horizon, kindling Fire in the Sky. 'Twas a Sight to strike Wonder in the Heart of a shelter'd Maid of Seventeen!

The Stones seem'd at least twice the Height of a tall Man (i'faith, I was surpriz'd that they were not taller) and there were four Rows of 'em, one within the other, some standing singly, some with great Lintels of dress'd Stone, so rude and rugged they seem'd as if the Devil himself had thrust 'em up out of the Bowels of the Earth. As the fiery Sphere of the Sun sank behind 'em, who should come creeping betwixt their shadowy upright Forms, laden with earthen Potts, Horns of Unguent, Baskets of Food and Simples (and trail'd by their Dogs, Cats, Toads, and other domestick Familiars), but true Witches—or so I had come to believe.

They were Women of divers Ages, dress'd in hooded Garments, not unlike those in which Joan and Isobel had attir'd themselves before setting out. Some wore black Mantles, a few wore green, and upon their Heads, they wore Hoods of black Lambskin. They carried tall Staffs, many with Knobs on them, and some had fine Stones set in intricate Brass-Work about the Knobs. Most of the older Witches wore, around their Waists, great fur Pouches, which bulged with mysterious Contents. I fancied Magical Feasts within, or whole Menageries of domestick Familiars, e'en Imps and Devils.

Above the Circle of grey stone Arches, older than Time, of Ancestry unknown, the Sky was bloody with the setting Sun; the billowing Clouds sail'd across it like Pyrate Galleons into a tropical Port, where Witch-Doctors waited to sacrifice the Crew to ravenous local Gods (or so I mus'd at the Time, ne'er having yet seen either a Pyrate, a Galleon, or a tropical Port!).

I trembl'd, as much with Fear as with Cold. The Witches advanced, seating themselves in a small Circle at the Base of the great Altar Stone inside the Circle of Stone Arches. Some were Ancient Crones and some were beauteous and young. There were twelve Women in all, and a variety of Familiars who scurried behind 'em (and curl'd up in the Folds of their Garments when they seated themselves upon the Ground).

But who was this that now appear'd in a dark blue Mantle trimm'd with Fox Fur, with Horns upon his Head, and wearing a terrible Mask of Wrath?

I clutch'd Isobel's Hand.

"Is it the Devil himself?" I askt.

"Shh," said Isobel, " 'tis the Chief, the Grandmaster of our Coven. Sit here and keep still."

The terrible Maskt Man seated himself upon a fallen Stone and a beautiful red-headed Girl came and sat at his right Hand.

" 'Tis the Maiden of the Coven," said Isobel. "She is also the First Deputy of the Goddess."

I'faith, I understood none of this, but I could not draw my Eyes away from the Face of the Maiden. She was a Girl not much older than myself, with Eyes of piercing green, and Skin of a surprizing Fineness and Pallor. She wore a dark green Mantle trimm'd with Lambskin and pointed russet leather Shoes with curious Crosses cut into 'em, and Gloves that appear'd to be made of Cat's Fur. But most astonishing of all was the Ornament she wore about her Neck. 'Twas made of two Tusks of Wild Boar join'd at their curv'd Middles by a Thong of Leather so that, in Shape, it resembl'd two Crescent Moons, dancing Back to Back, or two Scythes, bound into one Weapon.

Upon her Lap, she held a Book into which she wrote at the Bidding of the Grandmaster.

He himself was a terrifying Sight, but whether this was due to the Mask he wore, or to his Person, I cannot say. His Mask was of lacquer'd Wood, japann'd in a purplish Blue, not unlike the Skin of a Plum. From his Skull, two Cows' Horns protruded, as if they would spear the Sky, and cov'ring his Head where Hair would be, was a matted Carpet of Lambswool. Likewise, his Chin, or, to speak truly, the Chin of the Mask, sprouted what seem'd to be a Goat's Beard. His Mouth was terrible, set with black Pebbles for Teeth and parted just slightly to allow his Commands to issue, and his Eyes glow'd red like fiery Jewels. Upon his Feet, he wore pointed Shoes with cleft Toes, and they were of the same russet Leather as the Maid's. They resembl'd Shoes I had seen in old Engravings in Lord Bellars' Library, and the Points were so long 'twas a Miracle he could walk. He carried a forkt Staff which he thump'd upon the Ground to signal that the Meeting would begin.

"Let the weekly Deeds be reported," said the Maiden, speaking for him. Whereupon there ensu'd a Recital from each Member of the Coven of all the Doings of that Week, which the Maiden duly inscrib'd in her Book.

I shall not trouble you, Belinda, with a full Account of all

92

the Conversations which took place at the Esbat. Suffice it to say that as the Witches were telling of their Work in the previous Week and their Work in the Days to come, as they consulted with the Chief and the Maiden about various Herbal Receipts they had tried, new Members they had sought to recruit, and Illnesses which would not yield to the usual Remedies, I took care to hide my Head behind Isobel's Shoulder, praying not to catch the awful Eye of the Grandmaster. Fain would I have got thro' the entire Esbat unrecogniz'd, but that was not fated to be; for presently the Grandmaster turned his terrible Mask towards Isobel and me, pounded the Ground with his Staff, and in a strange, echoing Voice, demanded: "Why is a Man in our midst?" 'Twas the first Time he had spoken out loud.

His Voice sent shivers thro' me. 'Twas neither the booming Voice of Masculinity nor the sweet Voice of Femininity, but a strange Admixture of the twain.

" 'Tis no Man," protested Isobel boldly, "but a Woman dress'd to repel the Wickedness of the World in her Adventures on the Road to London."

"A new Convert?" askt the Maid.

"Yes," said Joan with all Swiftness.

"Well then, proceed," said the Maid, and the Group return'd to their weekly Accounts, leaving me so shaken that my Heart pounded in my Bosom like a defenceless Animal caught in an iron Trap.

When the weekly Business had been compleated and the Maiden had duly inscrib'd in her Book all the new Receipts, the likely new Members who were disillusion'd with Christianity, and new Methods of Divination, the Chief once again thump'd his Staff upon the Ground, and pointed his forkt Stick at me.

"Let the new Member come forward," he thunder'd.

I lookt imploringly at Isobel. By this Time, the bright Moon had risen o'er the black Stones and the Grandmaster's Face glow'd blue and evil in the Moonlight.

"Go," she directed me.

I rais'd myself stiffly from the cold Ground, stepp'd slowly across the Circle, and stood before the Chief.

"Are you born Woman?" he demanded.

"Yes," I replied.

"Will you swear to uphold the Great Goddess, She whose Name is too holy to be spoken, in all Her Works large and small and to do Her Divine Bidding for the Good of all, but

93

most particularly for the oppress'd Members of your own Sex and those less fortunate and more defenceless than yourself?"

"Yes," I said, before I knew quite what Words my Lips had utter'd, whereupon I immediately began to tremble piteously because I fear'd I had forsworn the Saviour and would at once be condemn'd to Hell.

"Hath the Lass a divining Familiar?"

I star'd blankly at the Grandmaster.

"Yes," Joan responded for me, from the back of the Circle.

"Where is thy Familiar?" he askt again of my stupid Gaze.

Joan led Lustre forward into the Centre of the Ring.

"Doth he obey thy Commands?"

"Yes," I said, for so he did.

"Pierce his Flesh then, and thine own."

Joan gave me the small silver Dagger she wore on the Chain 'round her Neck. "You need only draw one Drop of Blood," she directed.

Carefully, as gently as I could, I took the Knife to Lustre's beautiful right Buttock and slit the Skin quickly in the Place where he had most Flesh and would feel it least. Then I drove the Point of the Dagger into my own left Fingertip.

"Press the two Wounds together," said the Grandmaster. Obeying, I held my Finger steady on Lustre's Haunch, whilst the whole Coven chanted:

"By this Beast, I divine,
By this Friend, Her Will is mine."

The Horse stood very still and attentive. It seem'd he had Felt no Pain; my Finger prickl'd, but neither was I in Pain.

"Be seated," commanded the Grandmaster, whereupon Isobel came forward also and both she and Joan escorted Lustre and myself back to the outer Rim of the Circle. We sat down again upon the Ground. Lustre stood above us.

Was there nothing more? No Black Mass, no kissing the Devil's Bum, no wild hoidening thro' the Woods in search of carnal Ecstacy and Transports of the Flesh? I was astonish'd. Had one only to swear Loyalty to the Great Goddess and to one's Horse?

If 'twere Witchcraft, then Witchcraft seem'd not so sinister a Thing. There were many Names for the Supreme Being and just because none I had e'er heard was female did not mean a Female God was impossible. Hath Divinity a Gender? I doubted not but the Grandmaster's Words might accord with some Truth or other, tho' perhaps with one I had not yet encounter'd.

The Grandmaster now conferr'd with the Maid. They whisper'd long and their Whisp'ring was like the Touching of the Leaves of Trees on a Summer Night. Finally, the Maid spoke.

"Hath anyone a Spell in which she requires the Assistance of the whole Coven?" She lookt 'round the Circle at the Witches.

Many of them seem'd about to speak, but thought better of it. Presently, a young Witch with a Heart-shap'd Face, full, plump Breasts, Hair of chestnut brown, and a Belly that was surely Great with Child, made bold to speak.

"I would blind my Master," she said, "for first he ravish'd me, then he cast me out when I was with Child. I would blind his Eyes so that he can ne'er take a Fancy to another Lass and do to her what he hath done to me."

The Grandmaster conferr'd with the Maid, pounded his Staff upon the Ground, then askt of the Girl: "Wouldst thou take the Vengeance of the Goddess into thine own Hands, Sister Alice?" (for that was the Girl's Name).

"The Goddess would approve," said she.

"If the Goddess wishes him blind," said the Grandmaster, "She will blind him."

"But his Pow'r is uncheckt," said Sister Alice. "He can harm other Innocents."

"Are you well?" askt the Grandmaster. "Have you a Place to bear and tend your Child?"

Sister Alice nodded. "Sister Louisa hath taken me as her Serving Maid, and hath provided in her Will for the Child and me."

"And your former Master, how is he?"

"He hath lost his only Son in a foolish Duel, and he is cast down and melancholick."

"The Goddess works in curious Ways," said the Grandmaster. "Her Ways are oft' more subtle than ours, but stronger."

"I have a Request," Joan said, in a trice, speaking loudly from the very back of the Circle where I sat betwixt her and Isobel. "Our new Member requires Proof of the Goddess' Pow'r. She, too, hath been ravish'd and abus'd, but in her case, there is no Redress. She is alone, friendless but for us. I propose we make a Puppet and cast a Spell upon her Deceiver as our first Gift to a new Convert."

"Yes! Yes!" cried the Coven in Unison.

"What Spell dost thou propose?" askt the Grandmaster.

"The Waxen Puppet, the red-hot Pins," said Joan.

"And which Part of him wouldst thou disable?"

Joan thought a Moment and then laugh'd wickedly. "The Part with which he hath disabl'd Fanny!"

The whole Coven now began to giggle and cackle and exchange lewd Remarks.

"Silence!" said the Grandmaster. "And what if another Part of him is harm'd by Mischance, and he cannot walk? Would Justice then be serv'd?"

Joan shrugg'd her Shoulders. "'Tis the Risque we run," she said.

"Let the Coven vote," said the Grandmaster.

The Maid pointed to each Covener in turn and wrote the Answer in her Book.

"Aye," said the first Witch, a wither'd Crone, with a black Eyepatch and Wisps of white Hair peeping out from under her Hood. Her Face was like the Map of the Moon.

"Aye," said the next Witch, who was young and blond and had as her Familiar a furry white Dog with a pink Tongue and black Nose.

"Aye," said the next, who identified herself as Sister Louisa (and was, therefore, I suppos'd, the Benefactress of the young Witch with Child who had spoken before).

"Aye," said the same young Witch, Sister Alice. "Aye, aye. I'm for it."

Around the moonlit Circle they went and ev'ry Witch except Isobel said "Aye."

When Isobel's Turn came, she said: "I cast my Vote with Fanny. Whate'er she wishes, I will second, for 'tis said that the Past cannot be changed, but only the Future."

The Grandmaster then turn'd to me. "What would'st thou, Fanny?"

My Senses were disorder'd and my Heart still pounded in Terror. I knew not what to answer.

"What wouldst thou?" came the echoing Query again from the terrifying Mouth of the Mask.

"Will he be disabl'd fore'er," I askt, "and possibly lame?"

The Witches titter'd. I heard one not far from me say, "The Lass is mad."

Presently the Grandmaster answer'd. "Sister, we cannot predict the Effect of our Spells with utter Certainty. Perhaps

96

he will lose only the Use of his Privy Member, perhaps more. I cannot tell you otherwise."

I ponder'd well. In my disorder'd Mind I consider'd Lord Bellars' Beauty, his fine straight legs, the soft Hair that twin'd on his muscl'd Breast, his manly Charms. He had us'd me rascally, but I still remember'd how I had lov'd him. Was not Love still Love tho' 'twere Love betray'd?

I remember'd back e'en before that tempestuous Scene of Love (and Love betray'd) to the Time in Childhood when Lord Bellars had first taught me to mount a Horse and ride—not side-saddle like a Girl, but with a proper Saddle like a Man. I remember'd how he lov'd the Hunt, how he leapt the highest Hurdles on his own Arabian Stallion, High Flyer, how he had given me Lustre, High Flyer's Foal out of Molly Longlegs, his own prize Brood Mare; how he especially came down to the Country from London to present me with my belovèd Lustre on Christmas Eve of my fourteenth Year. E'en now I could see him leaping o'er Stiles and Hedges, his Cheaks ruddy with the brisk Weather, his Redingote flying behind him, his Boots gleaming in the Sun.

"No," I said. "I would not cast a Spell."

A Gasp of Horror went 'round the Circle of Witches. Some amongst them cackl'd and mockt me for a Fool.

"No," I said warmly. "I would not. I shall not take Vengeance into my own Hands. The Goddess will do what She will."

"So mote it be," said the Grandmaster. "Let the Dance begin."

The Witches rose (some still mocking me) and cast off their furry Hoods, threw down their Magick Staffs and Pouches. Many had Horns of Ointment, Animal Skins fill'd with evil-smelling Unguents with which they rubb'd their Legs, betwixt 'em, under their Arms, upon their Breasts. Sister Alice, the Witch who was Great with Child, offer'd me some of her own Provision, saying, "I pray you don't regret your Soft-heartedness, Fanny."

"What shall I do with this Unguent?"

"Do as I do," she directed me. And she rubb'd ev'rywhere upon the most private Parts of her Body, saying, "'Twill make your Body light for the Dance."

Putting my Cape and Beaver Hat upon the Ground, I took some of the sticky Stuff on my Fingers, reach'd into my

Breech, and mimickt her in rubbing wheresoe'er she did. It prickl'd betwixt my Legs like the Stinging of many little Bees.

Then the Grandmaster march'd into the Middle of our Ring, lifted a rude Pipe to the Lips of his Mask, and began to play the most curious (but withal the sweetest) Tune that had e'er enter'd my Ears. Whereupon the Maiden join'd Hands with us, widening our Ring, and the Dance began.

It began slowly, the Ring first moving in one Direction, then the other, but presently the Dance grew faster and bolder, and i'faith, it seem'd to divert all melancholy Thoughts, to beget wild extravagant Imaginations in the Brain, to raise our Hopes, and to banish our Fears. The Witches pull'd in one Direction and then the other. As they danced, they held fast to one another's Hands. I seem'd to see Forms and Colours in the Air—the brightest Colours my Eyes had e'er beheld and the most jagged Forms. At one Moment our Circle appear'd to be whirling in a dark Funnel, and the Ancient Upright Stones seem'd beneath us as well as above. Then the next Moment, I fancied that the very Stones were alive, swaying against the Sky, that the Sky itself was alive with other Witches riding the dark Clouds. I believ'd I saw Animals dancing at the edges of my Vision, not the Familiars, but legendary Beasts—Unicorns, Griffins, Basilisks. And then, stranger still to tell, I felt I had become united with the Earth, the Stones, the chalky Hills, the grassy Downs; I felt my Heart beat with the Hearts of the Witches, as if we were all one Woman, one Force, one throbbing Heart.

Then a most mysterious Thing came to pass; I felt myself—or truly, that Part of myself which is most myself, my Soul—fly out of my Body and hover o'er the Stone Circle and Barrows, as if I were a Bird, not a Woman. I lookt down upon the dancing Women as if I were a Nightingale or a Dove. I saw their Heads as round Circles of Hair, their Feet as Points of Leather. I seem'd to float, to soar, to dip and dive thro' the Air. The Witches' Dance below grew smaller and smaller as I ascended higher and higher into the Ether, and then, just as I fancied I would ne'er return to Earth, I plummeted in a Blaze of white Light, with the Colours around me those same brilliant Reds, Greens, Blues, or Yellows I had seen before, tho' oddly jagged in Shape, like Strokes of Lightning in a Child's Picture, or squar'd and angular as the Floor of an Italian Marble Hallway, or i'faith, a Board for playing Chess.

Then, in a trice, I was back in the Circle, whirling and

turning, joining the Witches as they made a smaller Circle within the larger Circle, dancing closer and closer to the Grandmaster, who still play'd upon his Wond'rous Pipe.

Now the Maiden took the dark blue Mantle from his Shoulders, and the other Witches remov'd his Undergarments one by one; and thus whilst he play'd, and some Witches whirl'd in place, and others took his Clothes from him, he was reveal'd as—I could scarce believe it—a Woman!

When the Breasts appear'd, the Witches chanted, "She is risen." When the dark triangular Thatch of Hair appear'd, the Witches chanted, "She is born."

Perhaps I have gone mad, I thought. Perhaps my Senses are disorder'd by this Unguent, but despite my Discomposure, and despite the Madness of the Dance, I plainly protest that the Grandmaster was a Woman. Now she twirl'd in place, still wearing the terrible Mask. Witches came forward and anointed her Body with Unguents. She pass'd her Pipe to the Maiden; she receiv'd from that same Deputy her curious Necklace of Boar Tusks, shap'd as a double Crescent. The Maiden chanted: "Behold the Goddess; She is born; She is we; She is One."

The Witches were all in a Frenzy now; but i'faith, my own Wits were so disorder'd that my Judgment was not the best. Ne'ertheless, I recall that Isobel took me aside and whisper'd that now I must mount Lustre and ride far beyond the edge of the Ditch surrounding the Great Upright Stones; for I had not yet been formally baptis'd into the Cult and there was one Part of the Ritual I must not see. But she herself would come to fetch me as soon as this Ceremony was o'er, whereupon a Great Feast should begin which would last until Dawn and the first Crowing of the Cock. Moreo'er, I was not to be cast down, for at the very next Sabbat, I should have my full Initiation, if I wisht it, and then the Sisters of Wicca should have no Secrets from me whatsoe'er.

I put on my Cape and Hat once more, mounted Lustre, and rode in Darkness beyond the outer edge of the Stone Circle. I rode to one of the Barrows beyond that awesome Monument, still looking for all the World like a Boy, despite my Knowledge of the Witches' Female Creed. I shudder'd a little with the Cold and i'faith with Fear of the Dark. Nor had the Stones ceas'd to sway and gyrate 'gainst the Sky, for my Senses were still somewhat inflam'd by the Magical Unguent. 'Twas like a fright'ning Dream from which I could not waken.

I waited thus on horseback, apart from the Mysterious Ceremony, unable to see the Witches e'en as shadowy Forms dancing in the Darkness, and i'faith unseen myself, because of the sloping Bank that surrounds that Mystical Monument, when, in a trice, I heard the Thund'ring of Hoofbeats, and heard Men's Voices shouting to each other, and out of the Moonlight along the Great Avenue, I saw a Parcel of Blackguards gallop straight for the Centre of the Witches' Circle.

What then ensu'd, Belinda, I tremble to recollect, but Truth, my dear Daughter, is a sterner Goddess than either Morality or Innocence, and what I was to learn about Human Nature that Night would have turn'd e'en the Third Earl of Shaftesbury into a gloomier Prophet than the Duc de La Rochefoucauld.

Shots rang out. Bloodcurdling Screams rose to Heaven. There was piteous Wailing and Weeping, and piteous Pleas for Mercy. From where I stood, I could see nothing, but from these Horrid Sounds I deduced that the Witches were being tortur'd or murder'd.

Without thinking of my own Safety, I spurr'd Lustre and gallop'd back towards the Ring, but when we were scarce halfway there, the Horse rear'd up, and would go no closer; i'faith, he froze in his Tracks like a statuary Horse cast of Bronze. Now, howe'er, I had a plainer View of the Battle (due to a Break in the Stone Circle) and fain would I have been blinded upon the Instant than to have seen what my Eyes then beheld.

There were but five Rogues, led by a Boy of Ten, who slobber'd and shook like a Half-Wit, and who continually scream'd, "Vile Witch! She cast a Spell on me!" pointing a crooked Finger at each of my Sister Witches.

In the Centre of the Circle two Men held the beauteous Maiden of the Coven to the cold Ground, whilst the others ravish'd her in turn, with as great Brutality as they could muster; and less, it seem'd, for whate'er Pleasure an unreasoning Beast might find in so forced an Act of Passion than for showing off their Brutality to their Brute Brothers. She was violated perhaps ten, perhaps twelve Times; and whereas at first she whimper'd and fought, after a while she seem'd to lye still, her glaz'd Eyes staring Heavenward, her Mouth mutt'ring, "Gracious Goddess, have Mercy." Whereupon the Brute who then was tormenting her with his swollen red Organ, grew inflam'd by her Piety and, pulling his ugly Truncheon out of her poor abus'd Cunnikin (which now

100

spill'd o'er with dark Blood), he thrust it violently into her Mouth, saying, "This'll teach thee to pray to Devils!" and he ramm'd his Organ so far back in her Throat that she turn'd red and chok'd and seem'd on the very Point of Death. Whereupon he withdrew it, and each of the other Men ravish'd her Mouth in turn, until it bled as horribly as her poor Nether Lips. When I thought I had seen the Worst and could bear to look no more, one of the ugliest of the Lot, a Rogue with a Strawberry Nose and the slitty Eyes of a Pig, extracted his Scimitar from its Scabbard, and, ignoring her most piteous Screams and the Pleadings of the other Members of the Coven, carv'd a Cross into the Flesh of her Forehead, and carv'd it so deep that her whole Face ran red with Blood, and soon she swoon'd in his Arms and expir'd.

"Thus is our Soft-heartedness rewarded!" Sister Alice scream'd, accusing the Grandmaster, who huddl'd in her Nakedness betwixt Alice and Joan. She had done very ill to draw attention to herself with this Scream, for now the same Rogue turn'd his horrid Lust upon her, dragg'd her into the Centre of the Circle, threw her to the Ground, ripp'd her Clothes from her Body, and despite her Screams that she was with Child (which, indeed, could be seen by all), ravish'd her fiercely and hideously; and having done so, offer'd her to the other Men. Three of them refrain'd, owing to her Great Belly, but another hideous Rogue, with a greater Belly than her own, a Beard of flaming red, and Pustules that stood out upon his Cheaks, rose, as 'twere to the Challenge, and ravish'd her both above and below; and not being content with the Conquest of two Orifices, drew her whimp'ring to her Knees, caus'd her to thrust her Bum in the Air and ravish'd that Orifice, too, until it bled copiously and she scream'd for Mercy. Then she was dragg'd to her Feet, pusht down upon the Great Altar Stone, and as the red-bearded Man stopp'd her Screams with his Hand, the Pig-faced Man ravish'd her again, and withdrawing, took his horrible Scimitar and thrust it into her Cunny in place of his Organ, as if i'faith Sword and Organ were but the same horrible Weapon. Alice seem'd to faint with the Agony. The Blood ran down the black Stone and pool'd darkly 'neath the Altar. The Sisters begg'd the Goddess for Mercy, but none was forthcoming, for now the same Rogue rais'd his Scimitar again and stabb'd Sister Alice a dozen Times or more in her Great Belly, surely murd'ring her Child, and leaving her as bloody and limp as a Carcass in a Butcher Shop.

d swift and true,
e Plain, towards
is Back, I pass'd
towards the Up-
Fancy Dress Ball

r'd, thinking me
e's Back and gal-
was to live for,
World.

Chapter XIII

Containing sev'ral Dialogues concerning Fate, Poesy, and the Relations betwixt the Sexes, as well as other Intercourse of a more sensual Nature (because of which the Modest Reader is advis'd to pass o'er this Chapter unread), which our Heroine had with Miss Polly Mudge, Chambermaid, Mr. Ned Tunewell, Poetaster, and e'en with Herself, at that celebrated Coaching Inn call'd The Dumb Bell.

AT LENGTH, I came to an Inn. 'Twas call'd The Dumb Bell, and being numb from my horrid Adventure upon Stonehenge Down, and certain that my Stars held nothing more of Good to tempt me onward upon the Road of Life, I conceiv'd that the Name of the Inn was most fitting for my State of Mind; for truly, at that Moment, I wisht to be deaf, dumb, and blind, and to live out my Days in unthinking Muteness, like a poor dumb Beast at the very Bottom of the Great Chain of Being.

I rode into the Courtyard, enquir'd of the Landlord whether there was room or no, and being told that I might share a Room with another fine Fellow, I accepted in a trice, praying only to fall into Bed in my Breeches and collapse into the Sleep of the Dead. I almost wisht ne'er to awaken.

I ruffl'd Lustre's Mane fondly ere he was led away to the Stable by a Groom. Then, asking that Supper be brought to my Chamber, I trudged up the Stair. The Room was inviting enough, with a Fire already laid in the Grate, and fresh Water in the Wash-Bowl awaiting my dirty Hands. A chearful Tent-Bed cover'd in flower'd Chints stood 'gainst the Wall opposite the Fire-Place.

I had scarce been in the Chamber for two Minutes when a pretty young Serving Maid flounced in holding her Apron and Petticoats above her Ankles flirtatiously, darting Looks at me as if I were the Man I seem'd to be.

"La, Sir! I'll bring your Supper presently," says she. "The

Leg o' Mutton's gone, but what say you to a fine roasted Capon an' a bit o' Barley Soup?"

I said that would be fine, indeed; but before she left, would she enlighten me as to what Manner of Man would be sharing my Bedchamber?

She thought a Moment, flutter'd her pretty dark Lashes, heav'd a Sigh from her ample Bosom, and said:

"O Sir, that would be Mr. Ned Tunewell, Sir; a noted Poet is he, Sir, I mean Mr. Tunewell, Sir. O yes, Sir, last Time he pass'd thro' here on his Way up to London, he composed a Poem for me, Sir, an' a pretty Poem, too, Sir. I'faith, very pretty, I warrant."

"Can you say it for me, Lass?"

"Well, Sir, I'll try, Sir," said she. And drawing herself up to what she deem'd the proper Attitude for receiving the Muse of Poesy, she recited in a sing-song Voice:

" 'Polly, why should we delay'—that's me Name, Sir, Polly is—

"Polly, why should we delay
Pleasures shorter than the Day?
Could we (which we never can)
Stretch our Lives beyond their Span;
Beauty like a Shadow flies,
An' our Youth before us dyes;
Or would Youth an' Beauty stay,
Love hath Wings an' will away. . . ."

Here the Lass falter'd; Inspiration fail'd her, quite as swiftly as Love fled in the Poem.

"I'm sure I don't remember the Rest proper, Sir. . . ."

"Try, then," says I. "Can it be anything like—

"Love hath swifter Wings than Time;
Change in Love to Heaven doth clime"?

"Why, that's it, Sir. How did you know, Sir?" And without waiting for the Answer, she continues in the self-same Sing-Song:

"Gods that never change their State,
Vary oft' their Love an' Hate.
Polly, to this Truth we owe,
All the Love betwixt us two. . . .

104

I'm sorry, Sir, but I fear I cannot say the Rest. . . ."

"What," says I, with Mock-Horror, "a Poet goes to the Trouble to indite Verses for thee and you cannot e'en trouble to remember 'em? What an ungrateful Lass!"

"I'm sure I'm very sorry, Sir," says she, all humbly.

"Can they be anything like this?" And I recited:

> "Let not you and I require
> What hath been our past Desire;
> On what Shepherds you have smil'd,
> Or what Nymphs I have beguil'd.
> Leave it to the Planets too,
> What we shall hereafter do;
> For the Joys we now may prove
> Take Advice of present Love."

"Why, Sir," says she, "that's it, that's it exactly. Why, how did you know?"

"Your Ned Tunewell," says I, "is, in truth, a very noted Poet."

"I *expect* so, Sir," says she huffily, "for so he told me himself, an' I'm sure he's too fine a Gentleman to fib about it."

"Next Time he wants to make love to you," says I, "ask him what he thinks of Edmund Waller, would you do that, Lass?"

"Why, Sir," she said as she blusht hotly. "I'm sure I'm no Trollop, Sir."

"No," says I, "I'm sure you're just a fine healthy Country Lass, but pray do me that one Favour, would you? Ask him what he thinks of Edmund Waller and then ask him if he thinks the Name of Phyllis suits you?"

The Lass was all in a Dither. "An' why should I do that, Sir? What's Mr. Wallow to me or me to Mr. Wallow?"

"Your Mr. Tunewell will know, and I promise you, 'twill be to your Advantage if you use it so. . . ."

"Why, Sir, I'm sure I don't understand you neither."

"You will, Phyllis, you will," said I. "Now, I'll be having my roast Capon, if you please. . . ."

"Certainly, Sir. . . . Right away, Sir, but me name's Polly, Sir." And she flounced out of the Room in Confusion, perhaps e'en thinking that I was a bit mad. She lookt at me queerly before she shut the Door.

Was I indeed mad? I wonder'd myself. How could I be unmarkt by the Horror I had witness'd? The most Melancholick Emotions of Sorrowful Indignation depress'd my Spirits, and 'neath my Jesting with Miss Polly, and Quoting Lines of Verse (which hath e'er been Second Nature to me) there was a Heaviness upon my Heart which would not lift.

What a Swine that Tunewell was! He quotes a Poem by Waller to an ignorant Country Maid and changes the Muse's Name from Phyllis to Polly so she deems it writ for her own pretty Self (and doubtless takes him at once into her Bed). I had been betray'd e'en thus, and 'twas my Duty to help the Lass, but I wonder'd if I could preserve my Mind and Spirit without Bitterness after what I had seen of the Horrors of the World upon Stonehenge Down; and I wonder'd how i'faith I might spare myself from being wholly o'ercome by Melancholick Humours. 'Twas true that Aristotle had said, "*Nullum magnum ingenium sine mixtura dementiae*"; or, in plain English, "No great Wit without Madness intermixt." But was *this* to be the Price of my Education as a Poet, that I should lose my Sanity and rail against the World? I wisht to be Horace, not Juvenal! I wisht to be Portia, not Lady MacBeth! Prince Hal, not Prince Hamlet! Rosalind, not Ophelia! Madness was not to my Taste or Liking. Harmony, Balance, Order—these were the Virtues I admir'd.

O my Mind was grievously confus'd! Were all Men Brutes and Deceivers? Was Goodness nowhere to be found 'neath Sun and Moon and Stars? Were the Witches right in worshipping the Great Goddess rather than Jesus Christ? But, if so, if the Goddess were i'faith so pow'rful, why did She allow Her Chosen Children to perish so horribly? Worse still, I had to reflect upon the Change wrought in my own Nature by wearing a Man's Garb. I had spoken haughtily to Polly the Chambermaid, and watch'd her blush and bow and flutter, as I myself had flutter'd before Lord Bellars once. I had treated her like a poor ignorant Wretch and condescended to her Ignorance of Poetry all because I was wearing Breeches and a Wig, and she was wearing a Petticoat and Apron! What a Diff'rence mere Garments could make! 'Twas true, I had read Edmund Waller and knew that his Poem "To Phyllis" (which that Blackguard Tunewell claim'd for his own) was first publish'd perhaps four score and ten Years ago, but was that a Cause for Haughtiness? I had spent the tender Years of Childhood in a Great House with a fine Library; Polly had not. I had a great Memory for Lines of Verse; Polly had not. But was that Just Cause to scorn her when we were both Sis-

106

ters, equally deceiv'd by the World of Men? Why was it that wearing Breeches and a Wig suddenly conferr'd upon me the Right to order Wenches about in unaccustom'd Fashion?

I askt myself the Question and lo! 'twas as if a blinding Flash of Light flew into my Brain to give me the Answer. 'Twas as if the Goddess Herself had answer'd my Questions to show me a Way out of the dark Tunnel of my Perplexity.

When, in the Development of Human Society (I thought), one Group, Sex, or Class is given Dominion o'er the other, all the Members of that Group become in some Way corrupted by that Unreasoning Pow'r. Most, to be sure, will not rape or murder; only the Brutes will do so. But e'en Good Men will be a little haughty upon Occasion, and e'en fine strong Women a little submissive and foolish in their Flirtations. Thus the Sexes will bear out each other's Myths about each other, and e'en those who wish to escape the Pow'r of these Foolish Conventions will find themselves acting as their Breeches or their Petticoats dictate.

In a Corset, Stomacher, and Panniers, I am wont to flirt outrageously, tossing my Hair this Way and that, showing my Bosom to advantage, laughing secretly at the Way Men stare into the Cleft betwixt my fine white Breasts when they think I do not detect them doing so. But in Breeches, I am haughty and impudent; I walk the World with Authority—almost as if my Jack-Boots made up my Character rather than my Immortal Soul. Thus in a Society in which Women are gen'rally scorn'd, some few Men who love Rapine, Torture, and Murder will feel themselves free to bleed Witches, slaughter 'em in Cold Blood, and e'en slaughter their Babes (I shudder'd to remember this); but the only Cure for this Heinous Excess is greater Justice betwixt Men and Women upon the Hearth and in the Bedchamber; for if Men may rule Women in Daily Life, then 'tis not surprizing in the least that some few Brutes should blood them upon the Down. Neither Sex must have Dominion o'er the other! Instead, they must fit together, like Lock and Key, both indispensable, both precisely made and well-oil'd.

'Twas fit Matter for a Poem, I thought; my first great Philosophical Poem. I should call it *The Lockiad*, and in it I should expose the Folly of the Age, the Folly of Mankind, the Need for Great Change in Human Society, and I should call for Equality betwixt the Sexes. For, if I truly believ'd that Mankind was essentially good (tho' corrupted by Ignorance, Folly, and false Dominion o'er his Sisters), then surely my Affection for the whole Human Race must make me strive to help that Race perfect itself. And what was Poetry but a rhyming Means of leading the Human Race towards Perfection? And what was the Poet but a Human Creature inspir'd to raise his Fellow Creatures closer towards the Divine Spirit?

Hot with the Fire of the Muse, I sat down to write—but alas, I had neither Quill nor Ink!

I ran to the Grate, found, lying 'neath the Flames, a damp little Twig which had flam'd but slightly before going out, and took it as my Writing Instrument. Paper had I none—but the linen Tablecloth would serve.

I sat down at once and began. "The Lockiad," I wrote, scraping the Letters carefully into the Holland Linen. And then, in a tortur'd Hand, stopp'd ev'ry so often by the Coarseness of the Charcoal 'gainst the linen Threads, I wrote the first four stirring Lines:

> What dire Distress from Women's Bondage springs!
> What Miseries arise from Trivial Things!
> I sing—this Verse to Clio, Muse, is due,
> For she hath all Eternity in View.

A Noble Beginning; but then the Twig snapp'd! 'Twas no Matter, for just at that Moment, there came a Knock upon the Door, and, like a Conjurer at a Fair, I flipp'd the Tablecloth o'er to its clean Side, secreted the charcoal Twig in my Boot Top, and call'd:

"Enter!"

'Twas Polly with my roast Capon.

"If you please, Sir," said she.

"Thankee kindly, Polly," said I.

"Thank *you*, Sir," said she, flashing her Eyes at me. Whereupon she tuckt a linen Napkin into my Shirt Front, taking care to expose her fine, plump Bosom, just below my Nose, and I receiv'd a most Pow'rful Odour of Attar of Roses, and honest female Sweat, o'er and above the Odour of roast Capon; so much so that, 'twas fortunate I was not the Man I seem'd to be, for certainly the mingl'd Lusciousness of their entrancing Odours would have caus'd me to ravish Polly forthwith.

Instead, I made ready to ravish the Capon.

"Sit ye down, Lass," said I, "and talk to me whilst I have my Supper."

"Oh, Sir," said Polly, flutt'ring her Lashes. "I'm sure I daren't. The Landlord would surely turn me out o'Doors for such."

Now, our Polly was not one of those Slender Wenches who put one in mind of an Anatomist's Skeleton, and who would probably seem more like Broomstaffs than Women if one embraced 'em in Bed. No. She was, on the Contrary, so juicy and plump that she seem'd bursting thro' her tight Stays, e'en as the Flesh of the delicious roast Capon was bursting thro' its sewn Trussing. For a Moment, I almost fancied I *was* a Man and susceptible to her Charms. 'Twas all I could do to stop myself from thrusting an eager Hand into that luscious Cleavage.

"Are you quite well, Sir?" she askt, bending o'er me with Solicitude (for, perhaps I lookt as queer as I felt). "Shall I cut your Capon for you?"

"Yes, Lass, please do so, for I have had a most wearying Journey and I can scarce find the Strength to do it myself."

She leant o'er me to pierce the juicy Flesh of the Capon; and, unable to contain myself any longer, I clapp'd my Mouth to the tender Valley betwixt the white Mountains of her Breasts and there insinuated my darting Tongue.

"Sir!" she cried with Alarm.

"A thousand Pardons!" I cried, sinking to my Knees, and kissing the Hem of her Garment. "A thousand Pardons. But I have this Day lost my own dear Mother and Grief hath left me distracted."

"Sir," she says, "I'll have you know I'm no Strumpet!" But i'faith, I could feel her softening a little at this Tale of Grief—which was, indeed, not so very far from being true.

I need hardly say, Belinda, that I was astonish'd by my own Behaviour, and yet, somehow I could not desist. Perhaps 'twas Grief that drove me to seduce a Maid when I was a mere Maid myself; perhaps 'twas something stranger still. Perhaps 'twas the wretched Influence of the God of the Witches (whom some call the Devil), or perhaps 'twas some long-lasting Result of the Flying Unguent, or yet perhaps some Madness brought on by the Horrors I had witness'd. Perhaps e'en 'twas my Muse's Way of showing me to feel both Man's and Woman's Passions. Or perhaps 'twas the mischievous Working of that Great Goddess in whom I only half believ'd.

At any Rate, I threw myself at Polly's Feet, and kiss'd her Hem, and then her Ankles, and then, since she made but little

Resistance, her Knees, and then, since she seem'd to sigh and invite it, her Thighs, and then, since she sat down upon a Chair and spread those Thighs (all the while protesting *No! No! No!* in the self-same Tone as *Yes! Yes! Yes!*), the sweet tender Ruby-red Cleft of her Sex itself, which lay expos'd to my View, since the Wench wore nothing at all 'neath her Shift and Petticoats.

Ah, the poor Capon lay deserted and steaming upon the Table (and 'neath that lay hidden my poor, scarce-started Epick), whilst I bent my Lips to Polly's tender Cleft and play'd Arpeggios with my own astonish'd Tongue. 'Twas salt as the Sea and tasted not unlike sweet Baby Oysters pluckt from the Bosom of the Deep.

"O Sir! O! O! O!" cries Polly, as I dart my Tongue in and out, inflam'd by her Words as well as her lovely ruby Slit. But, since by now her Petticoats are o'er my Head, I cannot fondle the twin Hillocks of her Breasts, but instead make free to stroke her milky Thighs, whilst her Petticoats make a sort of Tent in which I hide from all the Horrors of Mankind.

How warm and sweet it is inside a Petticoat! What Refuge from the Terrors of the World! What great Good Fortune to be born a Man and have such Refuge e'er within Grasp, within the warm World of a Woman's Hoop!

The Sound of Boots along the wooden Floor brought me to my Senses once again.

"O!" cries Polly. "Someone comes!"

But before she can jump up from the Chair and before I can rise from my Knees, the Door opens and we are compromis'd!

'Tis Mr. Tunewell himself! A big strapping Fellow with the ruddy Cheaks of a German Peasant and the Manner and Gait of a blond Viking Warrior. Far from being displeas'd, Mr. Tunewell was fairly transported with Amusement and apparently inflam'd by the luscious Scene before his Eyes. Instead of stopping us, he says, "Pray continue," and forthwith, he locks the Door. Whereupon he sits down in a comfortable Chair at Table, impudently plucks a Leg from the abandon'd Capon, puts his Boots upon the Tablecloth, and awaits the Continuation of the Show as if we were but Strolling Players brought for the King's Pleasure!

"Continue, my Dears," says he again, this Time thro' a Mouthful of Capon. "I'll join you presently." And he sits

110

back to enjoy his Supper, whilst we continue at our am'rous Play.

Polly, for her part, seems more inflam'd than abash'd by his Presence; for now she grows more wanton still, and now she makes for my Breech-Buttons as if she would undo them. This I cannot allow! And so I take her Hand away.

"What, bashful?" cries she.

"Alas," say I, more truthfully than she knows. "Alas, my Sweet, I am but half a Man. My Tongue must do what the other ne'er can!"

"Zounds! A Poet, too!" says Mr. Tunewell, laughing heartily. "Well, I'll relieve you, Lad, now that you've begun what you cannot finish!"

Thus we change Places, I at Table with the Capon, Ned Tunewell making ready to plunge betwixt Polly's Legs with his fierce erect Ramrod already almost bursting thro' his Breech-Buttons.

He takes the madden'd red Member in his Hand (which, by the by, is slick with Capon Fat), seems i'faith to admire it, and freshly parting Polly's ruby Nether Lips, he drives it into her pretty Cleft quite up to the Hilt; whereupon Polly gives a deep Sigh, more with Pleasure than Pain, and e'en seems to assist him by pushing forward her Hips.

Now, for my part, I gnaw upon my Capon Leg more with Lust than with Hunger; for short of thrusting my own Hand into my Breech, or revealing myself for a Woman, what Release have I but thro' my eager Mouth!

I watch 'em, chewing lustily, as they thrust and heave, first in a regular Rhythm and then as if the World should end in a Moment and this were their last Chance to couple for all Eternity.

"Oh! I dye!" cries Polly.

"I too, I too," echoes Tunewell, whereupon he gives one final Thrust, which not only causes Polly to deliver a deep Sob of Ecstacy, but topples the Chair in which she reclines; and with that comes a great Crash, as the Lovers fall backward upon the Floor. For a Moment they are shockt and frightened, but then Terror gives way to Merriment and they both laugh heartily. I join their Laughter, and presently I make bold to offer 'em the Remains of the Capon to restore their doubtless exhausted Bodies.

You may wonder, Belinda, why I do not pass o'er all this in the Interest of Modesty; for surely this cannot be fit Matter for Maternal Instruction to a Daughter. On the Contrary,

111

I say that tho' this Matter may be immodest, yet it deals with Truth; and Truth is ne'er unfitting, whether convey'd from Parent to Child or from Child to Parent. For truly, ev'ry Child hath a Right to know her Parents, as a Means of endeavouring to know Human Nature; and Human Nature is curious, inconsistent, full of Vagaries. What better Lesson can a Mother teach her Child than that Human Nature is replete with Complexity and Contradiction? If Modesty stand in the Way of this Instruction, then surely Modesty is no Friend to Truth, and Truth is all we may with Justice seek upon the Road of Life.

Friends we may find, but also lose. Parents (and e'en Children) may perish before we have had full Measure of Sweetness and Instruction from 'em. Riches do not shelter us from Nightmares and Melancholick Humours. Fine Clothes do nothing to prevent the Decay of our Bodies. But Truth is e'er a Comfort to us—e'en if it be Melancholick Truth. I'faith, as it astonish'd me to find myself in am'rous Play so soon after the Heinous Murders of my dearest Friends, so 'twill doubtless astonish you, my dearest Reader and Daughter. But perhaps there shall come a Time in your own Life when you shall do some strange and unaccountable Thing for which you may feel unaccustom'd Self-Contempt and Guilt, and then I pray you will think of your own Poor Mother and recollect that she hath done the same; and perhaps that will be some Solace to you. For this Reason and this alone, do I contravene the Laws of Modesty, because truly 'tis a Comfort to know that a Parent has suffer'd the self-same Torments before and yet surviv'd and triumph'd despite 'em all.

"Come!" says Ned Tunewell. "Let's all three to Bed!"

Whereupon he blows out all the Candles but one (upon the Night-Stand), strips down to his Shirt, takes his Polly with one Hand and the Remains of the Capon with the other, and verily bounces into Bed. I follow, tho' without stripping off my Clothes.

"What? Modest?" cries Tunewell.

"Alas," say I, "I'd rather watch than play."

"What? Impotent?" cries Tunewell.

"Alas, I would 'twere not so," say I, hanging my Head.

"'Tis no great Matter," says Tunewell. "Not a Man born of Woman but he hath suffer'd the self-same Want of Hardness from Time to Time! Pray, assist me, Master Poet, with Mouth and Hand! The Prick grows tired, but the Tongue doth e'er stand!"

112

Polly giggl'd prettily at this Instance of Tunewell's Wit; and Ned Tunewell, for his part, took her Laughter as another Sign to dive, Cock-first, betwixt her Thighs. I watch'd with more Fascination than I would care now to recall (were I not sworn to Truth).

"What? Lazy?" cries Tunewell. "Pray, Sir Poet, let us have some Assistance here! See these ruby Nipples? Pray tweak them with your Tongue! See these Lips like ripe Cherryes? Pray feast upon them!"

And in order to accommodate me, he rears up like a bucking Stallion (whilst holding Polly's Hips with one Hand so that his huge red Master-of-the-Ceremonies doth not lose its Mooring in her pretty Pudendum—and, with the other, pushes my Head down upon her Breasts).

What innumerable Kisses were then given and taken, I cannot say. We three seem'd i'faith to become a great Mythological Beast with twelve Limbs, three Mouths, six Eyes, and three darting Tongues. Whilst Tunewell pump'd away with his Member-for-Cockshire (as the Saying goes), gathering Votes as lustily as he might, I learnt more Uses for my Tongue than a good Cook hath for Soup-Stock. For if Monsieur Rabelais calls the Privy Member the *Dispensateur des Plaisirs* (amongst a hundred other Terms), surely we may, with Safety, say the same of the Tongue. What a Wonder is that malleable Organ! It licks, it tastes, it wets, it smooths, it slicks; it causes Nipples and Pricks to stand at attention, and sucks the Savour out of Capons and Cocks. The Privy Member is a Specialist; but the Tongue, verily, is a Jack-of-all-Trades!

All this occurr'd, Belinda, in a not very sturdy Tent-Bed, with a metal Frame, Chints Curtains, and Finials of Polish'd Brass. As the Curtains had been hastily drawn shut before our am'rous Play within, a Spectator outside the Bed (had there been such, which I hope and pray there was not) would have seen swelling Curtains, odd Limbs darting betwixt parted Chints, and heard, as well, a Host of assorted Love Cries such as "O! I dye!" and "Ah! I can't bear it! I am going!" and finally mere Grunts, Yelps, and Sighs, fitter for Beasts than Rational Beings.

But were we, in those Moments, Rational Beings? I doubt that we were. There exist Recesses in the Souls of Men and Women which Philosophy can neither probe nor explain, nor Religion rationalize, (tho' perhaps it may forgive). For many Years I felt grievous Self-Contempt for what I did in that

113

shaky Tent-Bed with those two amiable Strangers; but now, with the Perspective of Years behind me, I see 'twas doubtless simple Grief that drove me betwixt the luscious Legs of Miss Polly. Grief is both a stern Mistress and a capricious one. I dare say, more Fornication goes on hard on the Train of the Funerary Hearse than upon that of the Marriage Coach. For, whilst Joy uplifts our Hearts, it doth not always stir us to Venery; but Grief, by low'ring our Spirits, causes Humours to rise from the lower Part of the Human Corpus, which must needs be vented somewhere, and the Bed, dear Belinda, oft' proves the most convenient Place.

During that Night, our Polly fled. Perhaps Fear of Reprisal at the Landlord's Hands banish'd her from our Bed, or perhaps 'twas some other Reason unguess'd at then. At any rate, I awoke in the early morning Hours, beside that hairy blond Giant, with the Face of a Viking and a Member to match, and I thankt Heaven that I still wore my Breeches, for certainly, had he known my true Sex, he would have ravish'd me as well.

Ah, the Remorse I knew then was palpable as a Wound! There was I, just above seventeen Years of Age, banish'd from my Home, having recently seen my dear Friends murder'd most cruelly, and now awak'ning in Bed with a Stranger! I wisht for nothing more than to be Home with my dear Foster-Mother, Lady Bellars! But Home, alas, was far away, and lost to me fore'er by my Indiscretion with Lord Bellars. I curst myself heartily for my loose Morals. Had I not been so quick to succumb to Lord Bellars, my Blood should not have been so easily stirr'd by Polly! O sure I was ruin'd now! Ruin'd, defil'd, unfit for anything but Whoredom. What a Debauch of Self-Hatred now ensu'd, hard on the Heels of that other Debauch! To the Tempo of Tunewell's rhythmical Snoring, I curst myself repeatedly, mutt'ring the most loathsome Names to myself under my Breath.

As Luck would have it, my mutt'ring awaken'd Tunewell.

"What's that, me Boy?" says he (in jovial enough Fashion for one so rudely awaken'd from a deep Sleep).

"O, I am wretchèd with Remorse, Mr. Tunewell," say I, "wretchèd, wretchèd indeed with Self-Contempt!"

"How now, Boy?" says he. "What? Regretting a Bit o' Female Sport? I assure you, Friend, our Polly's a free-hearted Girl. No Virgin, she, I'll warrant."

I groan'd with Grief, so deeply had my Meaning been

misunderstood. Nor had I (without revealing my Sex) the Means to remedy the Misunderstanding.

"Women," Tunewell goes on, "are but Children of a larger Growth. They have no Moral Imagination, I assure you. For a Girl like Polly—who will, I've no doubt, spend the Rest of her Days married to some Country Lout—a Night with two fine, educated City Wits such as ourselves, will be Sport to look back upon her whole dreary Life long. Where's the Virtue in Continence, me Boy? We pass this Way but once, to be sure. 'Tis a Gift to know how to be happy. Few Mortals know it, I'll warrant you. The Grave gets us soon enough."

"But," said I recov'ring my Wits, "have we the Right to assert our Dominion oe'r the Fair Sex?"

"Dominion? Why, Lad, they rule *us!* Can we help it if our Blood is stirr'd by the Way they push their Breasts under our very Noses? Ah, my dear Boy, our Polly was sure *asking* to be toy'd with. Have not a second Thought about it." And with that, he rolls o'er and goes back to sleep.

By then the rosy Dawn was creeping up, and quite unable to sleep, I bethought myself to gather up my few Possessions and quit the Inn forthwith. In a trice, I remember'd my Poem, writ last Night upon the Tablecloth, and hastily flipp'd 'neath the Capon before the foul Debauch.

I clamber'd out of Bed to seek for it, walkt gently upon the Floor so as not to wake Tunewell again, flipp'd o'er the Tablecloth—and lo! found that my Words were smudged out of the Linen! Bits of Charcoal clung here and there where my Epick's grand Opening Lines had been! Whether 'twas due to the Suddenness with which I flipp'd it, or to unremember'd Sliding of the Tablecloth during our Great Debauch, I could not say. But O my Heart came near to bursting with Remorse. That must be a Lesson to me, I thought. Venus had driven out Apollo! A suitable Punishment for my Wickedness! Now I would ne'er be a great Epick Poet, but merely a degraded Sensualist, a Female Rake, the very sort of Creature I most abhorr'd in the other Sex. And what of those Juvenile Verses I had carried with me from Lymeworth? They were gone as well! Lost either at the Fair or at the Witches' Meeting, I knew not where. O this boded ill for my Career as Bard!

With a heavy Heart, I descended to the Stables to seek my belovèd Horse. There, a dim-witted Boy of about a dozen Years of Age sat picking his yellow Teeth with a Straw. He drool'd slightly, and his Eyes seem'd to cross as he humm'd the first few Bars of "Roger of Coverley."

"Boy!" I cried. "Pray saddle my Horse!"

"Your Horse?" says he, coming out of his Reverie. "What Horse is that?"

"A Chestnut Stallion, Lustre by Name. And be quick about it, too. I can't tarry here all Day."

The Boy stood up as slowly as a Body e'er did, dusted off his Breeches, squinted up at me with his pink-rimm'd Eyes, and said: "Would that be the Chestnut Stallion with the Blaze upon his Forehead?"

"Indeed, 'twould. And the white Stocking as well."

"Would that be the *rear* left Leg, Sir?"

"Indeed, 'twould, Boy. Come, why are you standing like that, gawking at me?"

"Sir, I fear another Fellow hath fetch'd that Horse durin' the Night."

"What?"

"Yes, Sir. He swore he was sent at your Command to fetch the Horse."

"And you gave it him without asking me?"

"Please Sir, I had the Kitchen Maid rap at the Door of your Chamber, Sir, but there came no Reply. Only terrible Noises within, Sir, shoutin' an' yelpin' an' pantin' like Dogs, Sir."

I pal'd at this Reminder of last Night's Debauch; the Boy continu'd: "Beggin' your Pardon, Sir, but this Fellow seems a Person of Quality, Sir. He gave me a Guinea an' said he was a Famous Player. He said he was in Partnership with you, Sir. Pray tell me, are you a Player, Sir? For what I wish, Sir, is to go up to London an' see one of the great Playhouses. I wish I might be a Player, Sir. 'Tis all I wish for in the World."

"You Fool!" I cried. "You've given my Horse to a Thief!"

The Boy cower'd in Fear.

"Please, Sir, don't tell the Landlord, Sir. He'll sure send me to the Workhouse. I have a poor sick Mother, Sir, an' five Sisters at Home, one with a sickly Babe. I'm only a 'Prentice, Sir, an' my Life is a Misery."

The Poor Wretch pleaded with me, and I was so touch'd by his pathetick Dream of Acting in a Play (when all he had in Life were cross'd Eyes and a drooling Mouth) that I could not find the Strength to blame him. I'faith, I was more disgusted with myself than I was with the Boy.

So Doggett had come for Lustre! How had he follow'd me here? Had he been on my Trail all thro' my Time with the Witches? Had he witness'd the Meeting of the Coven upon Stonehenge Down? Where had he taken Lustre?

"Boy," says I, "wither did the Man ride?"

"Up to London, Sir. I'm certain of it."

"Have you a Horse for hire?"

"No, Sir, for another Gentleman that was with him took the last of our Hire-Horses. But Sir, in less than an Hour the London Stagecoach comes thro' here. You can take the Stage up to London, an' it please you, Sir."

I curst myself for my Folly as I paced the Stables, trying to decide what to do. Without Lustre, I was truly friendless. My Horse was my Partner, my Familiar (unless the Witches were all mad), my Rescuer, e'en my Coach—for who is the Latin Poet that says, "*Comes jucundus in via pro vehiculo est*"? (An agreeable Companion on the Road is as good as a Coach.) And what was Lustre if not an Agreeable Companion? O I was now more wretchèd than e'er!

"Very well, Boy," says I, returning to the Spot where the poor miserable 'Prentice sat, "I'll take the London Stage."

And the Boy lookt up at me, as to say, "Take me, too, Sir, and I'll serve you faithfully fore'er." But alas, 'twas impossible, tho' my soft Heart e'en wisht it for a Moment.

And so 'twas thus that I came to be riding in the London Stage (with a Fine Lady nam'd Mrs. Pothers and Sally, her Maid—both of whom took frequent Draughts from a silver Bottle which the Lady claim'd was only Hungary Water—a puff'd-up Lawyer from Bath nam'd Slocock and his Black Servant from Barbadoes, a jolly Fellow call'd Paul) upon that fateful Day when Lancelot Robinson and his Merry Men made up their Minds to set upon the London Stage and rob us all.

But so illustrious an Encounter, so destin'd to change my whole Philosophy of Life, surely demands a new Chapter.

Chapter XIV

In which Lancelot Robinson and his Merry Men are introduced and our Heroine meets her Fate in all its Nakedness.

WE WERE RIDING ALONG as roughly as you please, the English Drizzle misting the entire Countryside (in spite of what the Ballad Singers may say about fine June Weather), when, in a trice, there comes a Stampede of Hoofbeats beside us, and a Pearl-handl'd Pistol is thrust in at the Window next to my Nose, and Shouts are heard from the Postilion and Coachman (who presently come flying past the Window and roll Head o'er Heels into a Ditch by the side of the Road), whereupon the Coach begins to move at such a Pace that we are all rattl'd like Apples in a rolling Barrel, and Mrs. Pothers screams (and Sally can do nothing but press the Hungary Water to her Lips), and Lawyer Slocock vows Vengeance in Terms no one but another Lawyer can comprehend, and at last the Door flies open and a very pretty red-headed Fellow (with Hair as curly as Lambswool and Eyes as slant and green as a Cat's, and Tartar Cheakbones like the God Pan himself) leaps into the Coach, saying:

"Not one Move or I'll blow yer Brains to the Moon!"

He slams the Door, points the Pistol at each Passenger in turn, reaches into his embroider'd Waistcoat and removes a folded Sack, made of some homespun Stuff, pulls it open, sticks it under our Noses one by one, and demands:

"Jewels an' Valuables first, then Clothes. An' be quick about it!"

"Must we strip?" cries Mrs. Pothers in a Panick.

"Aye," says the green-eyed Highwayman.

" 'Tis a Capital Crime and punishable by Hanging in Chains," says Lawyer Slocock (as ugly and puff'd-up a Fellow as I have e'er clapp'd Eyes upon).

"I'll hang ye from the nearest Oak an' ye don't keep yer

118

Mouth shut," says the Highwayman, relieving Lawyer Slocock of his Pocket Pistol, then stripping him of his Watch, his Rings, his Snuff-Box, his Silver-hilted Sword, his Silver-button'd Coat and Waistcoat, likewise his Periwig and Beaver Hat, and e'en his Linen—all this as quickly as one might pluck ripe Fruit from a Tree. Presently Slocock sat shiv'ring in the very Skin he was born in, crossing his Legs to make quite certain that his poor Peewee (for certainly one could hardly use a grander Term for his Masculine Equipage) was guarded from both Sight and Assault; whereupon the Highwayman stripp'd his Black Servant quite as expeditiously, but that jolly Fellow made no Effort whatsoe'er to hide his glist'ning black Body; on the Contrary, he seem'd to revel in his very Nakedness, holding his big black Master of Ceremonies in his Hand and pointing it at Mrs. Pothers to make her whimper.

"O me! A naked Man! A naked Savage! O me!" she cried, hiding her Head in her Petticoat (whereas her maid Sally could do nothing but stare in amazement at the great strapping Black Man, and not for a Moment did she take her Eyes away from his prodigious Masculine Member).

"You great Oaf!" cries Lawyer Slocock to his Manservant. "Don't just sit there playing with yourself! Kill the Blackguard!"

"Sir," says Paul, " 'tis Common Sense i'faith to know that Nature and Wisdom ne'er disagree, or, as Juvenal says, 'Nunquam aliud Natura, aliud Sapientia dixit.' And truly, Sir, Nature tells me I am naked as the Day I was born, and quite as unarm'd as a babbling Babe. Therefore, 'tis Wisdom to deduce that I had as soon play with myself as attempt to o'erwhelm this Worthy Gentleman of the Road."

"Scoundrel! Blackguard! I'll have you transported back to the wretchèd Jungle where your wretchèd Ancestors spawn'd you!"

Paul smil'd chearfully, saying, "O no, Sir, anything but that! What a terrible Fate!" Whereupon the Bandit clapp'd him upon his stout Back, saying, "What a jolly Fellow an' Latin Scholar to boot! May I make bold to invite ye to join our Merry Band if e'er ye require new Means o' Gainful Employment?"

"I'll think on't," says Paul, smiling like a Lawyer himself.

Now the Highwayman begins to strip Mrs. Pothers, who kicks and screams as if, i'faith, she anticipates she will be ravish'd forthwith. Off comes her Cloak, her Watch, her Rings, her Earrings, her Shoes with their silver Buckles, her Boddice with its gold Lace, her Gold-embroider'd Stomacher and e'en her Side-Hoops (tho' what use the Highwayman might make of 'em I could not fathom).

"Off with it all!" cries the Highwayman, whereupon the poor Lady whimpers, "Spare me! Spare me! I'm Virgin as the Day I was born!" To which her Maid can only snicker, as she, too, strips off her Clothes (without first being askt) and says, "As for me, Sir, I've no Maidenhead at all to get in the Way, so why not have me here in the Coach and leave my poor Lady in Peace."

"Jade! What makes ye think I'd want ye—or yer Mistress either—with or without Maidenhead! Sorry Slut! D'ye think yer poor Cunny is made o' Gold? Can I fence yer Cunny? Can I melt it down an' coin it into Guineas? Keep it an' be damn'd! Give me yer Gold an' Silver!" Whereupon he turns to me, commanding, "Strip!"

O this is a fateful Moment! My Horse gone, my Friends murder'd, and now stripp'd of the one Thing that guards me from the Evils of the World—my Disguise!

'Tis oft' in Moments like these, when, in Peril for our very Lives, we act purely upon what we term in lesser Creatures, lower down the Great Chain of Being, Instinct. In short, Belinda, I stripp'd.

Off came the scarlet Cloak and black Beaver Hat! Off came the excellent Riding Wig purloin'd from my scurvy Step-Brother! Off came the Jack-Boots, the Riding Breeches, the Stockings, the Silver-hilted Sword, the green Redingote, e'en the Neckcloth and Linen!

With each Article of Clothing I remov'd, the Eyes of my fellow Passengers widen'd. "Bless me—'tis a Wench!" Lawyer Slocock said, looking Goats and Monkies at me; "by my Troth, I wish I had a Writ of Entry into that Abode!" And then he laugh'd, being well-pleas'd with his meagre Wit. Paul, the Black Man, smackt his Lips as if preparing to enjoy a great Banquet of Delicacies, whilst his prodigious Masculine Member stood straight up, like unto a Compass pointing True North; Sally, the Lady's Maid, lookt on my Breasts as if she would steal 'em for her own; and Mrs. Pothers sputter'd and mumbl'd, "O! I am mortified! O! That it should come to this! O! O! O!"—to which the Highwayman replied, "Fie on yer damn'd Sputt'rin!"

At last, when I had stripp'd entirely naked but for my Garter and sat demurely (demurely as a naked Body can sit in a

120

Stage-Coach rattling along the Highway at top Speed),
Lancelot lookt straight at me saying, "I might have known
'twas a Lass!" Whereupon, staring at my red Garter, he says
with a Wink, "I shan't be needin' that for *me* Bewitchments!"
To say the Truth, that Remark terrified me more than all my
shiv'ring Nakedness. Did he know it for a Magick Garter,
and me for a Witch, or was that merely a Jest?

"A scarlet Garter and a scarlet Fleece as well," says Paul,
looking straight at my Boskage of Venus (if I may so call it).
"Damme if Jason wouldn't have sail'd for that Fleece as well
as the Golden one! Here, let's have a bit of it. . . ." But before Paul could reach out to stroke my poor naked Belly-
Whiskers, the Highwayman interceded.

"None o' that! D'ye hear? We'll have no Cunny-Catchers
in this Coach! 'Tis Golden Fleece I'm after, not Fleece-
Hunters! Hands off, d'ye hear, or I'll blow yer own Captain
Standish to High Heaven. I'll have no Cunny-haunted, Cunt-
struck Rogues in this Coach be they black or white!"

"Begging your Pardon, Sir," said Paul, quite wither'd from
the Tongue-lashing, "I was merely admiring the young Lady's
Plumage and thinking how rare 'tis, i'faith, that the Tail
Feathers are of the self-same Hue as those on high, for, as
Horace says, '*Mutum est pictura poema*,' or, for those igno-
rant of Latin, 'A Picture is a silent Poem,' and what is this
Lady's precious Cunnicle but a Picture, which e'en if we
ne'er enter it, we can nonetheless enjoy with our Eyes."

"What an Excellent Fellow!" said the Highwayman. "By
Jove, I like yer Wit!"

"His Wit," says Lawyer Slocock, "will be but half as great
when I see his wretchèd Skull split with an Axe!"

"Come now, Mr. Slocock," says Paul. "Pray where will
you get the Axe in your present Condition?"

"Quiet!" shouts the Highwayman, and in a trice he leans
his Head outside the Window of the Coach, shouts something
to his Confederates, and lo! the Coach begins to slow. Whereupon the Highwayman puts a Gun to the Lawyer's Head and
says:

"Out, or be blown straight down to Hell—fer I ne'er met a
Lawyer yet who would go to Heaven!" And then he opens
the Door of the Coach, and as nicely as you please, pushes
Lawyer Slocock out into the Road, after which he puts a
Gun to Paul's Head, saying: "Are ye with me or against me,
Horatio?"

"Sir, in a Word: *with*."

"Very well then," says the Highwayman, "but I'm expectin' no Mutinies nor Insubordination, nor Cunny-catchin' neither."

Then he turns his Pistol on Mrs. Pothers and her Maid, Sally. "Out with the both of ye!"

"O Sir, spare me! I can cook for your Troupe. I can sew. My poor dear Father himself was a Highwayman and transported to the Plantations."

"'Tis a Fetch," says Paul to the Highwayman. "These Wenches are full of Tricks."

"D'ye fancy I don't know me own Business?" says the Highwayman, whereupon he adds, "Sorry me Dear," to Sally, and without further Ado pushes her out the Door. Mrs. Pothers cries after her: "O you ungrateful Wench! Traitor! I'll ne'er take you back!" But presently the Highwayman also throws her out the Door and the two Women are soon embracing each other in a Ditch, made Friends again by their Common Fate.

Now he turns the Pistol on me, saying, "Are ye with me?"

"Sir," I say, "I know nothing of Highway Robbery."

"Nor did I once," says he. "But ye seem a quick Learner to me."

"Sir, I'm a Law-abiding Girl."

"An' what's the Law but a nasty Tangle o' Injustice fer the Poor an' Justice fer the Rich? 'Tis nothin' to abide. 'Tis a Bauble fer the Wealthy, the First-born, the puff'd-up Legal Thief who steals with Writs and Settlements instead o' Pistols. Come, ye don't mean to tell me ye love the Law?"

"I don't know, Sir, but I want to be an Honest Woman."

"An' if ye were an Honest Woman, ye wouldn't be here, dressin' like a Man, wearin' red Garters! Come, Girl, ye have no Choyce in the Matter. Yer comin' with us." And he gave a Signal to his Confederates to hurry the Horses. In a trice we began to roll at top Speed again and the Coach rattl'd along the Highway as if 'twould fly apart at its very Seams, and I silently pray'd for Mercy to the Great Goddess of the Witches, and presently we rode off the Highway into a Thicket where the Coach bump'd to a Stop and Lancelot held the Pistol to my Head, saying:

"Now, I'll not be bubbl'd, bamboozl'd, nor troubl'd by a mere Wench—Beauty tho' she be. So I'm tellin' ye to swear. An' ye don't swear by the Ghost o' Robin Hood, an' I'll blow yer Brains to the Moon—if ye have any. . . ."

"I swear," says I, without my usual Ponderment. Robin Hood, the Great Goddess, Jesus Christ—what's it to me as long as I stay alive?

"Hold! I haven't given ye the Oath yet neither."

And then with all Solemnity, as if he were standing in a Church, he recites:

"I swear by the Ghost o' Robin Hood
That I shall steal—but steal fer Good,
That I his Creed shall e'er uphold:
An' love True Justice more than Gold."

Whereupon he presses the cold Pistol right up against the thin Skin of my Forehead and commands me to repeat the Oath (which I assuredly do), whereupon he also commands the same to Paul, (who doth the same), whilst we both sit shiv'ring in our very Skins.

The Oath once sworn, the Highwayman gives Paul his Clothes again, but curiously, he doth not return mine to me. Only the scarlet Cloak doth he return, tho' under it I am still naked as the Day of my Nativity. Yet soon I am to discover the Method of his Madness, for he leads me out of the Thicket into the Highway again, takes my Cloak away despite my shiv'ring Protestations, directs me to lye in the Ditch by the side of the Road and to wave my Arms in dire Distress, whilst he makes haste to hide in the adjacent Bushes. Then he calls to Paul and his Confederates to join him. Before too long—tho' surely it seems longer to me in my Nakedness—a Coach comes rattling down the Highway, whereupon the Postilion claps his Eyes upon me in my trembling Condition, stops the Coach to offer Kind and Christian Assistance, and is forthwith set upon by the Highwayman and his Merry Band, which now includes Black Paul, or Horatio, as Lancelot calls him. In almost less Time than it takes to recite the Oath of Robin Hood, Lancelot, Horatio, and the Band have reliev'd the weary Travellers, the Coachman, and the Postilion of all that they possess, including the Horses that lately drew the Coach, and they have also rescu'd me, wrapp'd me once more in my scarlet Cloak, and gallop'd off into the Woods with great Dispatch to divide the Booty. Not a Shot hath been fir'd—for Lancelot (as I now learn) takes the greatest Pride in sparing the Lives of his Victims.

" 'Tis true," he says, "that the Punishment fer Theft as well as Murder is Hangin', yet I am a True Christian e'en if the Law is not. The Gentlemen o' the Law are no better than the Gentlemen o' the Road. I'faith, they are worse. Fer we have Honour an' Loyalty an' they have none. They are Whores fer hire to anyone that fees 'em, whereas we are fer hire to no Man, an' whilst we may mimick the Manners o' High Life in our Clothes an' Baubles, yet we are proud to be Low Life in our Morality. Fer what is a Gentleman, after all, but a Thief? A Thief o' Love, a Thief o' his Wife's Inheritance, a Thief o' his Children's Peace, his Servant-Girl's Virtue, his Manservant's Honour an' Manhood? Whilst we, who freely admit that we are Thieves, are truly Filchers o' nothin' but Toys. They steal Love an' Honour an' Life; we steal nought but Baubles. We but retrench the Superfluities o' Mankind."

Whereupon he offers me first Pick of the Booty. 'Twas a vast Array of Snuff-Boxes, Patch-Boxes, Sword-Hilts, gold Watch-Cases, cambrick Handkerchiefs, Earrings, Rings (both Wedding and Mourning), brocaded Boddices, Gold-laced Aprons, Coats with Buttons of Gold, Tye-Periwigs, Full-bottom'd Wigs—all the *Accoutrements* of the World of Fashion that any London Coach might handsomely provide.

I lookt at this glitt'ring Array of Baubles and Gewgaws and said plainly: "No. I'll none of it."

"A Girl after me own Heart," says Lancelot, not without Irony, "but pray, take at least enough to clothe yer poor shiv'rin' Self—fer I hate to see a Naked Woman."

"O Lancelot, Sir," says Paul, "there we must part Company, for I love the Sight better than the Sight of my own Native Island from the Deck of a Sailing Vessel. As Lucretius speaks of those Things touch'd with the Grace of the Muses—'*Musaeo contingere cuncta lepore*'—I perceive that this young Woman's Body is Muse-touch'd also, like unto a Statue of a Goddess in Parian Marble; and I bow down before it, as I would bow down before a Representation of Venus herself."

At this Lancelot scowls. "An' I suppose ye don't find me a pretty enough Fellow to bow down before?"

"But, Sir," says Paul, "you are a Man."

"Precisely, Horatio, precisely," says Lancelot, with a Twinkle in his Eye. "An' yer dear Friends, the Ancient Greeks, were Men, too," says Lancelot, putting an Arm on Paul's stout Shoulder.

"Sir, begging your Pardon, but 'tis the Ancient *Romans* I

124

most admire." And so saying, he disengaged himself from Lancelot's Caress, adding, "*De gustibus non est disputandum,*" which, I trust, requires no Translation for those present?

Chapter XV

*A short Hint of what we can do in the Rabelaisian Style;
our Heroine gets her Name; Lancelot Robinson begins
his astounding History.*

BY NIGHTFALL on that first Day, we had robb'd no less than
three Coaches (not counting the one from which Paul and I
were abducted), and in each Instance, Lancelot's Method was
the same: to wit, I was the Decoy, shiv'ring in my Skin to
kindle the Pity (or the Lust) of the Coachman and Postilion;
but no sooner had that Pity or Lust been kindl'd than
Lancelot, Horatio, and the Merry Band of Twelve fell upon
the Coach with Pistols and Bludgeons, stripping the Travellers stark naked, stealing their Horses, and e'en smashing a
Skull now and again, tho' taking care to murder no one.

By Dusk I was in a sorry State indeed. I'faith, 'twas a
Wonder I did not catch my Death that first Day, for it rain'd
intermittently thro'out our larcenous Adventures. Truly, I
would have suppos'd that such Willingness to risque my very
Health and Limb would have endear'd me to Lancelot's
Heart (or, at the very least, induced him to trust me as a
loyal Confederate), but 'twas not so; for when our Day's
Work was o'er, and 'twas Time for us to retreat to our
Thieves' Hideaway, Lancelot caus'd me to be blind-folded so
that I should not see whither we rode—e'en tho' 'twas Twilight and I knew the Countryside rather ill myself. 'Twas the
final Insult, after all I had borne, and I fear, Belinda, I did
not take it with the Grace befitting a Lady.

"Villain!" I scream'd at Lancelot as he bound my Eyes.

Lancelot laugh'd. "Ne'er trust a Woman, not e'en a dead
one, as me good old Father us'd to say."

"Blackguard!" I shouted again.

"Madam Jade," said he with that mocking Tone I had
grown to hate.

"I'm no Jade, nor Hussy either. I pray you, call me by my
right Name: Mrs. Frances—Fanny, if you must."

"Madam Fanny," says he, obliging me, but with the same ironick Tone. "D'ye know what that means in the Vulgar Tongue?"

"Yes," says I, still in a Huff.

"Well then, what?"

We rode in Silence, for truly I did not know, being Innocent then of all such Knavery.

"Well, Madam Fanny?" says Lancelot.

"I know not," I confess'd.

"It means the Fanny-Fair," says Lancelot, "the Divine Monosyllable, the Precious Pudendum, the Chearful *Cunnus* (in Latin, that is, as our Friend Horatio could tell us), an' in French, *l'Autre Chose*. O 'tis the Aunt, the Arbor, the Attick, the Bath o' Birth, the *Belle Chose*, the Best-Worst Part (accordin' to Dr. Donne), the Bit o' Fish or the Bit o' Mutton (dependin' on whether ye are a Meat-Eater or no), the Bottomless Pit, the Bow'r o' Bliss, the Brown Madam. 'Tis likewise the Earl o' Rochester's Bull's Eye, an' Shakespeare's Circle (the little *o* to his great wooden one). 'Tis Cock-Alley an' also the Confessional; 'tis the Crack, the Cranny, the Cradle, the Cream-Jug, the Cuckoo's Nest, the Cuntkin, an' also Cupid's Alley. 'Tis the Dearest Bodily Part (at least to Mr. Shakespeare o' Stratford); an' some have call'd it Diddly-Pont, Doodle-Case, Dormouse, Duck-Pond, Dumb-Oracle, e'en Dyke! 'Tis the sweet Et Cetera, the E'erlastin' Wound, the Eye that Weeps Most when Best Pleas'd, the Faucet, the Fiddle, the Flapdoodle, the Fly-Trap, the Fortress, the Fountain o' Love, the Funniment, the Furrow, the Gap, an' o' course, the Garden o' Eden. 'Tis a Gravy-Giver, a Gold-Finch's Nest, a Grotto, a Grove o' Eglantine (at least so it seems to Mr. Carew), an' also Safe Harbour an' Happy Huntin' Grounds. 'Tis the House under the Hill an' the Ivory Gate an' e'en Itchin' Jenny! 'Tis the Jacob's Ladder, the Jampott, the Jelly-Bag, an' the Jewel o' Jewels! 'Tis a Kitty an' a Kitchen an' a Kettle. 'Tis a Lather-Maker, a Lamp o' Love, a Little Sister, a Lock o' all Locks, a Lucky-Bag, a Maryjane, a Masterpiece, a Milkpail, a Moneybox, a Mole-Catcher, an' e'en Molly's Hole. 'Tis a Mossy Bank, a Thankless Mouth, a Mustard Pott, a Mutton Roast, a Needle Case, a Nether Eye (to Mr. Geoffrey Chaucer), an' a Nether Lip as well! 'Tis a Nest, a Niche, an Old Hat, an Omnibus, an Oyster, a Palace o' Pleasure, a Peculiar River, an' also a Pen-Wiper (if ye scribble Verses, that is). 'Tis at once a Pleasure-Boat an' a Plum Tree, a *Portal* to the Bower o'

127

Bliss (or so says Mr. Herrick) an' a Pulpit, a Purse, a Pussy-Cat. 'Tis the very Queen o' Holes, the Quim, an' the Queynte. 'Tis also the Ring, the Rose, an' the Rufus. 'Tis a Saddle to ride in, a Seed Plot to hide in, a Scabbard, an' a very Seminary o' Love. 'Tis a Slipper, a Slot, a Slit, a Snatch-Box, an' a Socket. By Jove, 'tis the South Pole, the Sperm-Sucker, the Split Fig, the Spot o' Cupid's Archery, the Sugar-Bason, an' the Temple o' Venus! 'Tis also the Tit-Mouse an' the Tool-Chest an' also the Treasury o' Love. 'Tis the Underworld an' also the Undertaker. 'Tis the Vineyard an' the Vestry. 'Tis the very Water-Gate o' Life, the Wicket, an' also the Workshop. 'Tis the Yoni o' the East Indies an' the Passion Fruit o' the West Indies—but as fer me, I ne'er found a Use fer it, an' I'd sooner have a Boy or a Sheep!"

I stood mute and astounded by his Monologue. What a String of Wond'rous Words. The Poet in me was charm'd e'en whilst the Woman was sore insulted.

"Be that as it may," he continu'd, "but I must call ye somethin' new as well as Madam Fanny, for 'tis me Practice to rename me Pupils in accordance with their Attributes. An' so, Black Paul shall be Horatio, first because he hath prodigious Learnin' in Latin, but second, because I pray he shall play Horatio to me gloomy Prince Hamlet an' tell me Story when I am gone perhaps to Tyburn Tree. I have, as well, nam'd all the Members of me Band, as ye shall shortly see. But yerself, Madam, I christen Fanny Hackabout—because ye have, in truth, been cruelly hackt about by Fate, an' fer yer Surname shall ye be: Jones."

"Why Jones?" say I in Astonishment.

"Because 'tis a plain Name an' 'twill teach ye Modesty."

"And, pray, why should I require Modesty?"

"Because yer too vain of yer Beauty already!" Whereupon he spurs the Steed we share and gallops on thro' the heavily pounding Rain (which I can feel upon my Cheaks, but not, alas, see).

We rode then for many Days, stopping only to water our Horses, perform Nature's Necessities, and eat a bit of Bread, but since I was blindfolded most of the Time, I no more knew our Route than a Blinder'd Horse. Depriv'd of Sleep, Conversation, or any Information about our Destination, I was truly wretchèd. Weary, Rain-pelted, out of Humour at Lancelot's ill-Treatment of me, and seiz'd with Ague Fits, I fear'd I should truly perish due to Lancelot's unkindly Usage

128

of me, and in my Mind, I began to form a Bitter Resentment of him.

O he was a great Witsnapper indeed and a very learnèd Tonguepad, but I fear'd he had spoken the Truth when he said he had no Use at all for Women, and I fear'd he should use me as a Decoy only until my Health gave out and I should expire, and then he should kidnap another Unsuspecting Innocent and do the same to her.

If I have given a very loose and uncorrect Account of the Robberies we accomplish'd when first I met Lancelot Robinson and his Merry Men, 'tis because I was in no Condition to observe very closely, being mostly occupied with my own extream Cold and Discomfort, and concentrating all my Pow'rs merely upon remaining alive. You will wonder, my dear Belinda, why I neither sought to run away nor protested this Ill-Usage more severely, and I will reply that in part 'twas a case of my being helpless, but also that I was as much fascinated by this beauteous red-headed Fellow as I was outraged by him. I seem'd to know him from another Life, as 'twere, or know him as a Brother; and if the Truth be told, I was not a little challenged by his Refusal to fall down before me, raving of my Beauty, as all the other Men I had known were wont to do!

At length our Caravan of Horses and Riders came to a Stop. Lancelot help'd me from the Horse, unbound my Eyes, and what I saw before me in the Darkness seem'd a pleasant half-timber'd thatch'd Cottage in the Tudor Style, with a large Barn attach'd to it. Where we were—whether in Wiltshire, Hampshire, or e'en Dorset—I could not tell. But to say the Truth, I was more occupied with my Ague Fits and Discomfort than with observing the Landscape. I had always been a healthy enough Girl, and in the Manner of the Healthy, had taken Health itself for granted. But now I was, for the first Time, beginning to know that 'twas a precious Gift from the Almighty.

Lancelot carried me into the Cottage, whose Rooms were low-ceiling'd, after the Tudor Style, tho' not without Chear. The Furniture was plain yet serviceable in the rustick Manner; the Floors were broad Oak Boards.

Yet what was most amazing about the Cottage was that it resembl'd a vast Warehouse of Goods; 'twas indeed a kind of Lock or Respository of Stolen Goods, for I presum'd that all these Objects were stolen. Ev'rywhere, on ev'ry Table Top and Bureau Top and Mantelpiece, Objects were pil'd, oft' one atop the other. There were silver and pewter Goblets, gilt Salvers, silver Sugar Bowls and Tea Kettles (with and without Stands). There were silver Tea Caddies and Ewers, Casters, Spoon Trays, Inkstands, and Loving Cups. There were silver Centrepieces and Candlesticks, Tapersticks, and Snuffers. There were silver Cream Jugs and Cake Baskets, engrav'd Beakers, Tankards, Cups, Wall Sconces, Chocolate Potts, Flasks, and a great Variety of Snuff-Boxes. One that caught my Eye bore the Arms and Crest of the Weavers' Company. "Weave Truth with Trust," it said, almost as if in satyrical Commentary upon the Company of Stolen Articles in which it found itself.

Nor were the Stolen Articles confin'd to domestick Plate, for there were also Clocks of ev'ry Description, gold Watch-Cases, Chains, Jewelry of all Sorts, and also an amazing Array of Periwigs, set up on Periwig Blocks, as in a Shop. There were Full-bottom'd Wigs, and Campaign Wigs, Ramillies Wigs, Bob-Wigs, Tye-Wigs, and Bag-Wigs. There was also rich laced Clothing of ev'ry Type: Men's Suits embroider'd with Silver and Gold, Women's Boddices and Aprons, Doublets and Petticoats, Fans and Hats, and Muffs.

Lancelot set me down upon a rustick Bed, cover'd me at once with an Eider-Down Coverlet, whereupon he strode away, mumbling Promises of Tea, which Promises, I was, by that Time, too weaken'd either to applaud or gainsay.

He return'd not long after with a silver Pott upon a filigreed Stand and Chinese Porcelain Tea Dishes—all doubtless stolen. By then I had grown e'en weaker and I could scarce lift my Head to sip the Tea; I had, as well, a raging Fever, Fits of Trembling and Shiv'ring which seem'd to throw Terror into his stony Heart. I'faith, I believe, 'twas my Illness which just began to melt him towards me, for he show'd an Apprehension that I might be carried off by it, and not only did he nurse me with his own Hand, but he sat by my Bedside, speaking to me betwixt Fits of Fever that whole first Night. 'Twas thus that I learnt about Lancelot's Life; for I truly believe that but for my weaken'd Condition, the Hardness of his Heart might have been such that he should not have reveal'd his History to me. And what a History 'twas! E'en thro' my Fever and Trembling, I could come to understand how his Soul had been shap'd and indeed warp'd.

"I was born," he began, "in the third Year o' the Reign o' William an' Mary durin' the hot Month o' August, under the

130

Sign o' Leo—tho' damme if I believe one Whit in that Parcel o' Lies call'd Astrology. Me Mother was a prim Popish Heiress, me Father an agin' Restoration Rake who would ne'er confess that the Age o' the Wits had pass'd, an' who sought to make our decayin' Family Seat in Oxfordshire—a ruin'd Gothick Pile known as Wilderknoll—into a little Replica o' the Court o' Charles II, with ancient decayin' Courtiers scribblin' their execrable Verses an' agin' Belles playin' nauseously at bein' irresistible young Mistresses. I was the youngest Son o' Seven—an' a Rebel from Birth—which me Mother's Strictness only serv'd to inflame. 'Twas clear I should ne'er inherit anythin' but me Father's Affectations—fer me Brothers—damn 'em all—were too disgustin'ly healthy, so I early conceiv'd the Fancy o' runnin' away to Sea, an' at not much above thirteen Years o' Age I ran away with a Strollin' Player I met at a Country Fair, journey'd to London with him, bound meself as a 'Prentice to a Ship's Surgeon an' shipp'd out on a West Indiaman, headed, I thought, fer Jamaica. But, alas, not before it stopp'd upon the West Coast o' Africa to fetch a Cargo o' Black Human Bein's call'd Slaves."

I shut my fev'rish Eyes and let myself drift amidst the Visions Lancelot's History conjur'd. Sick as I was, I seem'd to enter his Fancy as if 'twere my own Dream. No wonder I had felt this Highwayman the Brother of my Heart; why, he was orphan'd, too—in Spirit, if not in Law—and his Adventures had taken him e'en farther from Home than mine!

"Ah, to be apprenticed to a Surgeon on a Slave Ship at Thirteen is to know, ere the Waters o' the Womb are fully dry behind yer Ears, the full Extent o' the Degradation o' the Human Heart!" Lancelot went on. "Like many another Seastruck Lad, bound to a Home he hated, a Father he fretted o'er, a Mother to make him mutter under his Breath, I read Dampier's *New Voyage Round the World* an' dreamt o' driftin' from a Jamaican Plantation to Campeachy, o'er the Isthmus with Buccaneers, back to Virginia, 'round Cape Horn, across the Pacific to the Philippines, an' thence to the East Indies, Land o' incredible Riches, Jewels, an' Spices, an' strange slant-eyed brown-skinn'd Boys in Turbans an' with bare Breasts (for e'en then, at the tender Age o' Thirteen, I had forsworn all Womankind, havin' been cruelly spurn'd by me first True Love in Oxfordshire! An' lucky 'twas, too, fer a Boy bound to Sea fer seven Years!)."

"Then did you love a Woman once?" I askt Lancelot, com-

131

ing back to Life most suddenly (for I reason'd that if he had done so once, he might again).

"I have no Use fer Womankind!" he snapp'd. But the very Swiftness of his Protestation made me doubt his Words, and e'en as he spoke of Slaves and Voyages, I dreamt myself his own True Love drifting on exotick Tropick Seas. Lancelot knew nothing of this; he continu'd with his Tale unaware of the Fancies brewing in my fever'd Brain.

"Imagine then me Astonishment," he said, "when after all me Readin' o' the Marvels o' Sea-Travel in Dampier, I found meself on a Slave Ship—nam'd, with pow'rful Irony, the *Grace o' God*—with a Cargo o' dyin' Africans, manacl'd to each other in the stinkin' Hold, beaten within an Inch o' their Lives by Men not fit to be their Masters (fer they were not e'en Masters o' themselves), forced daily into the Hold to provide Rancid Food an' Fruitless Medicine for Men who needed nought but Air an' Space an' the Sight o' their own Native Lands, who could not speak me Language, nor I theirs, but who, in their mass'd black, naked, shiv'rin', vomitin' Humanity, seem'd far superior to the Englishmen who lorded it o'er 'em. No, Lass, I'll not trouble ye now with Stories o' the Horrors o' the Slave Trade, sick as ye are. 'Tis one o' those Tales, which, tho' we know it to be true—still it strains our very Bein's to believe that Men like ourselves, might to this very Day, practise it."

"Ah, Lancelot, 'tis true, 'tis true," I sigh'd, tho', i'faith, I knew little or nothing of the Slave Trade then.

"Me Surgeon's Crafts were well-nigh useless on a Slave Ship," said he. "I had learnt o' Cuppin' an' Bleedin' an' the Use o' Cordial Powders, Dulcifers o' the Blood an' such. Likewise I knew the Use o' Jesuits' Bark fer Ague an' Fever, Volatile Spirit o' Viper 'gainst all Faintin's, Sweatin's, an' Lowness o' Spirits, Powder o' Burnt Toads 'gainst the Smallpox, as well as Powder o' Goose Dung 'gainst the Yellow Jaundice. Besides, I knew the Use o' Lancet, Forceps, an' Saw as well as—nay better than—any o' yer Black-Velvetsuited, bewigg'd Physicians an' Surgeons with their Coaches an' Four, chargin' Guineas fer their Visits, an' their useless Medicaments."

"Useless?" askt I in a Sweat. "Wherefore useless?" O I took this Word as fearful Portent of my own Fate.

"Aye, useless," said Lancelot. "Fer mark ye well, Madam Fanny, most o' these Remedies are wholly fruitless, whether on a reekin' Slave Ship or no—an' as our Friend Voltaire

132

says, the Physician but amuses the Patient whilst Nature makes him better!"

"Dear Goddess!" I cried.

"Alas," said Lancelot, " 'tis true: most Illnesses get better despite all the Doctors do to kill the Patient, an' others get worse, quite independently of his lethal Remedies—whereupon the Gen'rous Earth hides his Errors at the Last, an' the Survivors pay his Bills or go to Gaol."

These last Words quite penetrated my delirious State, whereupon I sat up suddenly in Bed and star'd at Lancelot with burning Eyes.

"Pray, what of me, Sir Lancelot? Am I to perish, too, and the Earth hide your Errors?"

"Nay, Fanny," said he, with unaccustom'd Gentleness, "I shall use all me Arts to get ye well, I swear it." So saying, he call'd for Horatio to bring more Tea and hot Compresses, and he gave me as well, dried Powder of Rosehips to eat and whole West India Limes. The Limes stung my Tongue sorely, but Lancelot assur'd me that of all the Remedies he had met with on his Travels, none was so sovereign for Chills and Fever as the simple West India Lime. Moreo'er, he swore that tho' Apothecaries, Physicians, and Surgeons might scoff, the Lime would one Day be seen as a Cure-All beyond any on Land or Sea, for entire Crews of Ships had perish'd that might have been sav'd by this simple Fruit and instead they were cupp'd and blooded, purged, and cover'd with Leeches.

I hardly believ'd him then, but thought him merely pacifying me that I might dye in Peace. O I abus'd Lancelot sorely, as a fever'd Child will abuse the most loving of Mothers. Whilst my Fever rose, I ranted, rav'd, and saw Visions of Fantastical Sailing Ships with royal purple Sails and golden Masts. Lancelot, meanwhile, washt my fever'd Body with Lavender Water and ne'er suggested the least Lewdness to me—tho' Black Horatio, I remember, stood by, lusting mightily, yet restrain'd by his new Master from so much as laying a Finger upon me!

"Me Years in the Slave Trade taught me a Reverence fer Black People which hath lasted to this very Day," Lancelot continu'd, as he bath'd me most tenderly, "fer I truly believe that if we, the English Race, were treated as we treat the Negro Race, we would be nought but Animals grovellin' upon the Ground, whereas they still maintain a kind o' High Spirit, a Love o' Laughter an' Life, such as we ourselves would do well to mimick. But more o' that anon. Durin' me Days at

133

Sea 'twas me Fate to fall in Love with a Pretty Fellow nam'd Martin Faulk, a Boy about two Years me senior, an' with a Family as low as mine was high. O I lov'd him as I ne'er lov'd me Brothers! I mimickt his Dress, his Walk, his Speech (so that if I lapse out o' the cultivated Speech o' my Birth an' into the Gutter-Language o' London Street Urchins, 'tis all fer the Love o' him, me first Lover!). He'd been born in Newgate, Martin had, o' a Mother who was a Cut-Purse an' a Father who was Child-Getter to half the Prison and father'd well-nigh most o' the squallin' Brats in that vile Dungeon. His Mother was due to be transported to the Plantations after her Lyin'-in, but by some Strategem escap'd, Martin with her, an' resum'd her Life o' Crime, bringin' the Boy up in the Trade ere his Swaddlin' Clothes were outgrown or his Bum dry. When his Mum was at last apprehended and sadly hang'd (bein' too old now to avail herself o' the Services o' the Newgate Child-Getter), little Martin ran away to Sea, much like meself, an' 'twas our Fate to meet upon that wretchèd Slave Ship an' comfort each other thro' the Horrors o' that first Middle Passage."

My Fever was subsiding now and I was coming back as from a Dream. What had Lancelot said about loving a Woman once? And could he love one again?

"From then on, we were ne'er apart," he said. "Martin taught me all there was to know about Love betwixt Men, a Catalogue o' Lovin' Practices that would inflame yer Ears, e'en if ye weren't fever'd as ye are. But Martin also taught me about London Low Life, the private Language that Thieves have amongst 'emselves—*Dead Swag* fer Booty that can't be fenced, an' *Clink* fer Gaol, an' *Bridle-Cull* fer Highwayman, an' *Buttock an' File* fer the Bloke what robs a Shop, an' *Priggism* fer Thievin', an' *nubb'd* fer hang'd, an' *Mill-Ken* fer House-Breaker, an' *The Cheat* fer the Gallows."

"The Gallows?" I gasp'd.

"Aye, Lass, the Gallows," said he. "Sure enough, when our Time was up at Sea, an' our Articles were at their End, we went into the Priggism Trade in London in a royal Way. We were proud Fellows an' sure we knew too much to be petty Pickpockets, or *Filin' Lays*, as they call 'em—so we form'd a veritable Army o' Boys and took in more Swag in a Week than most o' yer Newgate Prigs do in a whole Lifetime o' Priggism!"

"Bravo, Lancelot!" I cried.

"Not so fast, Fanny," said he. "Fer we were caught, too,

134

turn'd in by one o' our own Fellows fer the Reward—and we were sent to the Gallows and hang'd."

"Hang'd?" I askt. "But how comes it you are here to tell the Tale?"

"Ah, Lass, 'tis the very Nub o' me Story. I'faith, I cheated The Cheat."

Chapter XVI

Lancelot Robinson concludes his astonishing History, showing that a Man may be wise in all Things, both sublunary and divine, yet still be a Ninny where Women are concern'd.

No SOONER HAD HE SAID those Words than my Body was wrackt with a Fit of Coughing so severe that I fear'd my very Soul should grow faint in me and depart my Body forthwith. Yet as I cough'd and sputter'd and shook with Chills, I retain'd a pow'rful Curiosity to know the Outcome of Lancelot's History, so that, like that fam'd Sultan of Old (who would not slay his Wife because she was such an excellent Story-Teller), I kept Body and Soul together in Hopes of hearing the Conclusion of Lancelot's History. If this were part of his Physick, 'twas extraordinary Physick indeed; whereupon when my Fit of Coughing subsided I begg'd to know how he had cheated The Cheat, and, tho' my Eyes water'd, and my Breath wheez'd in my Windpipe like Winter Winds in an ill-clean'd Chimney, I vow'd to stay alive long enough to hear the End of this remarkable Tale. Ah Belinda, I fear that I was more than half in Love with Lancelot and his wond'rous Words; for at that Season in my Life, soft Syllables could woo me more than Sensuality and my Love of Language was deeper than my Love of Men!

"I'faith," Lancelot continu'd, "we languish'd in Newgate fer the better part o' the Year—Martin an' I did—an' I was e'en put to the *Peine Forte et Dure* on account o' me Refusal to plead guilty or no. Fer three Days I was lyin' upon me Back with an iron Plate upon me Chest an' iron Weights placed upon that until me Lungs was fair to burstin' an' Stars twinkl'd before me Eyes an' the Pain gave way to a Numbness so prodigious that I'd have sworn I dy'd an' came back to Life from the Great Beyond. But that was not the case indeed, fer mark ye, Fanny, I was to learn o' the Great Beyond soon enough—an' 'twas nothin' like that."

"Pray what is the *Peine Forte et Dure*?" I askt, puzzl'd in the extream.

" 'Tis a hard Punishment sometimes call'd *Pressin' to Death* which is us'd to make a Prisoner plead guilty or not guilty, an' 'tis barbarick, fer verily 'tis worse than the Rack o' Old. Each Day, they increase the Weight an' each Day they give ye barley Bread alone or Water alone so that indeed ye cannot perish swiftly as ye wish, an' if ye continue in Obstinacy, they leave ye in that Condition till ye slowly an' horribly dye."

"Is that how you dy'd, Lancelot, and return'd from the Dead? Tell me, pray do." I had almost forgotten how ill I was and I wisht to sit up in Bed to better hear the Rest of the History, whereupon Lancelot pusht me back on the Pillows again—but he did so gently enough, to be fair.

"Nay, Lass, 'twas more astoundin' still than that. After the third Day, I gave up me wretchèd Obstinacy an' confess'd, thinkin' that if I was to be hang'd in Chains like a proper Highwayman, I might as well go to me Death in a Blaze o' Glory, an' become a Legend to Posterity."

"A Legend to Posterity?" askt I.

"Aye," said Lancelot gravely. "So we pleaded guilty—Martin an' I did—an' makin' a Lovers' Pact, we vow'd to dye as grandly as two Prigs e'er did and meet once more to love again in the Great Beyond. When the Day o' Hangin' came, we rode in no common Cart with the common Lot o' Rogues, but hir'd a golden Coach an' six white Horses to ride to the Fatal Tree, an' we got ourselves up in gorgeous Gold-laced Clothes—all Snow-white Silk, with gold Embroidery an' white cockt Hats, heavy with golden Lace, an' flutt'rin' Feathers as well. Our Boots were Cream-white Leather, our Breeches milky Satten, an' our Waistcoats Eggshell-colour'd Silk; our Gloves were fine French Kid. We studied rhym'd Speeches to bid Farewell to the World, an' our priggish Friends made certain that all along the Way up Holborn Hill, we should be follow'd by Maids in white, with great silk Scarves a-wavin' an' Baskets o' Flow'rs an' Oranges. Rose Petals strew'd our Way to Tyburn—O 'twas a Grand Spectacle indeed!"

I clos'd my Eyes again and fancied beauteous Lancelot all in white, riding upon Rose Petals in a golden Coach and waving to the Crowd like any King!

"We arriv'd at the Gallows at Twelve," said he, "drank Burnt Brandy very grandly, an' had our Men offer it to the thirsty Throng as well. The Girls threw Oranges at 'em an' scatter'd Rose Petals, an' Martin an' me put up a fine show o' Courage. What animal Faces I saw around us then! Poor Wretches whose only Entertainment was an Execution! The Squallin' Gin-soakt Rabble lusted fer our Blood as if 'twould preserve their own! What makes a Man love Death, Fanny? Is it because he hopes to avert his own by watchin' the Deaths of others? Doth he hope to devour Death by devourin' Executions with his Eyes? I'll ne'er understand it, if I live to be eight hundred Years. The Human Beast is more Beast than Human, 'tis true...."

I only sigh'd in answer.

"By special Permission o' the Hangman," he went on, "(which we paid dear fer, I'll warrant ye), Martin an' I were to dye together in the very same Cart, so after we had said our pretty Speeches, an' been duly blest by the drunken Preacher, we climb'd into the Cart just as jaunty as ye please, kiss'd each other full upon the Lips before the whole Crowd—which, I'll warrant ye, drove 'em wild—(fer ne'er had they seen two lovin' Men, lovin' in Publick before such a Crowd o' scurvy Rogues no less!), an' then the Executioner puts a Noose around each o' our Necks, fastens the other End to that ill-favour'd Beam, an' this done, he gives the Horse a Lash with his Whip, an' away goes the Cart, and lo! we are hoisted up in the Air by our Ears!"

"Dear Lord!" I cried, for as Lancelot spoke, I seem'd to feel the very Rope around my own Neck!

"A piteous Snap o' his Neck told me that Martin had gone to his Reward with Merciful Dispatch—but I dangl'd in grievous Pain, unable to dye, yet unable to live. Some o' our Gang came forward pullin' on me Legs an' poundin' on me Chest to dispatch me, an' still the Pain grew greater, but still I would not dye. The Crowd jeer'd, me Body grew stiff, e'en me Bowels loosen'd an' me Cock stood up, as if I were a Corpse already, but yet I would not dye—an' then, just when I thought I could bear the Pain no longer, the Shouts an' Jeers o' the Crowd were drown'd out by a horrible buzzin' Noise that engulf'd me entire Bein', an' at the same Time I seem'd to be movin' thro' a dark Tunnel, like a Sewer or an underground Cave. . . . Then suddenly, the Pain vanish'd an' I seem'd to be floatin' in a dark Space an' I thought to meself, I am dead, an' yet 'twas not an awful Feelin', 'twas a Comfort to me in truth to be dead; 'twas the strangest Feelin' I've e'er known. I floated o'er the Heads of the Multitude then. I saw the Orange Girls passin' in the Crowd, bein'

138

pinch'd an' grop'd by the Gin-drunk Louts who'd come to watch me dye. I saw the Gin-Sellers with their pockmarkt Faces, their Wigs askew, their greasy Coat Pockets stuff'd with Coppers. I e'en saw the Pickpockets an' Cut-Purses passin' in' the Crowd as I meself had done so many Times, an' I thought to meself how much better a Filin' Lay I'd been in me Time, an' how clumsy these Rogues were, how thick an' fumblin' their Fingers! Almost as if I was a Bird, I saw the Soldiers standin' at attention, their Spears pointin' upward towards Heaven, their three-corner'd Hats near-perfect Triangles from above—but the strangest Thing of all came when I lookt at the Gallows: there hung poor Martin, his Face already black and blue with clotted Blood—and there hung I, surely as dead as he!"

I gasp'd. Lancelot, encouraged e'en more, went on: "How long I floated thus I cannot say. I knew the Body on the Gallows was mine an' yet, I did not properly *care*. 'Twas the strangest Feelin' to see meself hangin' there, lookin' like a proper Corpse, an' know it fer meself yet not feel sad! Lass, i'faith I cannot e'en describe it properly. I was so amaz'd by this State o' Affairs that I resolv'd to try an' inform a Pretty Fellow that was havin' his Pocket pickt o' that Fact. (I knew the Prig that was pickin' it fer a scurvy Blackguard; t'was *he* that first turn'd me in!) But 'twas no Use tryin' to warn the Victim in me present State, fer the Fellow could no more hear me when I whisper'd in his Ear than he could feel me ghostly Hand upon his Shoulder. I'faith, I had no Substance nor Voice at all! So I floated on o'er the Rabble like a Feather, watchin' all the mischievous goin's-on in the Crowd, an' bein' mightily amus'd to be dead—fer mark ye, Fanny, 'twas nothin' like what I expected. 'Twas calm, 'twas painless, 'twas serene!"

"Alas," I sigh'd, "that we should fear Death if Death be so sweet!" And yet I fear'd Death still.

" 'Twas a grey and rainy Day, the Day I dy'd," Lancelot continu'd, "an' I tell ye this because perhaps 'twill help explain the next astoundin' Thing that happen'd. I don't understand it rightly meself, but suddenly, 'twas as if the Sun exploded in me Eyes, an' a great Ball o' Fire, but a *gentle* Ball o' Fire, come to surround me like a glowin' Fog. The Rabble was gone then, an' Martin's Corpse hangin' there, an' mine as well, an' this Light came to surround me, an' 'twas a Godly Light, fer it clearly askt me if I were happy with me Life an' if I was ready to dye. . . ."

139

"Pray, how did it ask you, Lancelot, in Words?"

"Nay, Fanny, it askt clear as ye askt me just now, yet not in proper Words. I'faith, Lass, I can't explain it rightly neither. 'Twas the damn'dest Thing I e'er heard or saw. 'Are ye ready to go with me?' it askt, an' then, as if 'twere the Master o' Ceremonies at a Country Fair, it show'd me whole blasted damnable Life in Review! There was Wilderknoll, an' me accursèd Father! There was me accursèd Brothers an' me accursèd Mother! There was me Cruel Sweetheart, damn her Soul! There was little Pranks I'd play'd as a Child—like stealin' me blasted Father's Snuff-Box an' fillin' it with ground black Peppercorns! An' there were the Rogues I met on the Road up to London, an' the scurvy Captain o' the *Grace o' God*—that wretchèd Slavin' Ship. An' there was Martin himself wavin' an' sayin': ' 'Tis not so bad to be dead, me Lover—we'll be together now fore'er, Lad. . . .' An' there was e'en twelve Black Slaves thrown o'erboard alive fer bein' sick with Pox durin' that blasted Middle Passage. An' I had pleaded with the Captain not to toss 'em to the Sharks, an' he had boxt me Ears, an' now the Blacks was here beside me, thankin' me (tho', i'faith, they could ne'er speak English before). They was thankin' me in a kind o' Silent Language an' tellin' me I was a Good Sort, an' that they had dy'd in Pain but woke to Bliss, an' we would be together now for all Eternity! Lass, 'twas the damndest Thing! Me whole Life, all the Rogues an' Pretty Fellows I had known, was there before me! An' the Ball o' Fire, askin' me whether I was ready to go with Martin, an' me bein' sorely tried, wantin' to go with him, yet wantin' to return to the World o' Men to tell 'em what I knew, to tell 'em that God an' the Angels verily guide our Ways, to tell 'em not to oppress their Fellows an' make 'em Slaves, to show 'em their Cruelty an' Barbarous Treatment o' their Fellows. ' 'Tis yer Mission,' says the Ball o' Fire, 'to spread the Word o' Love an' heal the Sick an' give to the Poor an' be the Heir to Robin Hood's Legacy. . . .' An' I says to him swiftly, 'I accept this Task, I will go back, tho' I have the World an' all its Laws. . . .' An' he bids me then return. Suddenly the Buzzin' starts again, an' I am pull'd, like a silk Scarf thro' a Buttonhole, an' lo! I am back in me own Body, an' in horrible Pain as the Blood returns to its proper Channels, an' with horrible Pain in me Neck as I hang upon the Fatal Tree. An' there hangs Martin dead, swingin' beside me—but I now know 'tis only his Body, not his Soul, an' then, thinkin' me dead, me fellow Thieves lay me in me Coffin, an' I am carried away in the golden Coach with Martin's Corpse, but no sooner do we come down Holborn Hill again than I leap out o' the Coach an' run as fast as me Legs will carry me, whereupon twelve o' me Fellows follow, screamin' o' the Resurrection an' the Messiah, an' I tell 'em to shut their Mouths an' get back in the Coach like nothin' happen'd an' I will send fer 'em by an' by. . . ."

"And did you, Lancelot? Pray, did you?"

"I did, Lass, I did, but not before I had establish'd meself in the Forest an' had me a long Talk with meself about me Death. Fer it changed me Soul, it did, an' made me lose all Fear o' Death. The Curse o' Man is Fear o' Death, Fanny, an' when ye lose it, I warrant ye, there's nothin' ye can't do. Conceive yerself to be God's Tool, nothin' more. He will provide an' protect ye. He keeps ye on Earth to do what He needs ye to do, an' when He lets ye go, 'tis because yer Work is done."

"Lancelot," says I, "did you e'er think that He might be a She?"

Whereupón Lancelot breaks into a Laughter so profound, I think it might cause his Soul to fly out of his Body once again.

Chapter XVII

An improving philosophical Conversation upon the Nature of Orphans, after which the Merry Men are introduced, Lancelot discloses his future Plans, and Horatio's curious History is reveal'd.

HIS MOCKERY MADE ME melancholy once more. For a Time I had thought him the Brother of my Soul, despite his earlier Ill-Usage of me, but now I was pow'rfully disappointed. His Laughter and Mockery reminded me of how far I was from Home, how wretchèd was my Physical State, how truly orphan'd I was by Fate. First Lord Bellars had seem'd to be a God, but then he show'd me his Feet of Clay. Then the Great Poet Mr. Pope had seem'd to possess a more than human Wisdom, whereupon all his lofty Philosophies had turn'd out to be not Nurturance for my Soul, but lowly Snares for my Body! Then the Witches had seem'd to point a Way towards Higher Truth, a Supreme Being of Female Compassion; and yet, despite their devout Prayers to that puissant Goddess, they were cruelly murder'd. At last, Lancelot had seem'd to know about Heaven and Earth, Good and Evil, Life and Death, yet was he not as foolish as the Rest where the Fair Sex was concern'd? O I began to weep, taking such Pity on myself as would make the very Devils in Hell weep piteously themselves.

At once my Tears arrested Lancelot's Laughter.

"Come now, Lass, don't take on so. I meant no Harm."

"No Harm! No Harm!" I said. "You ne'er mean Harm, but you do it!"

Lancelot himself lookt suddenly melancholy.

"How's that, Lass?"

"O I can't make my Meaning clear. I'm so alone!" and I sobb'd and sobb'd until he took me in his Arms and strove to comfort me.

"O Lancelot, I'm an Orphan. No one cares for me. My own Step-Father rap'd me! My own Step-Brother nearly did

142

so, too. I have been betray'd by Men and seen my dearest Friends kill'd and my belovèd Horse stolen! I have no one, no one, no one!"

I sobb'd and shook in his Arms like one possess'd.

"Lass, we're all Orphans, until we come into the Sight o' God an' find our own true Father. Don't ye know that ev'ry Soul on Earth feels itself to be an Orphan? I do—sure as I'm holdin' ye. Me Lover, Martin, did, I'll warrant ye. Those Slaves we toss'd to the Sharks did. . . . E'en the Captain who had 'em toss'd felt so. E'en the *King* feels like an Orphan, I'll warrant ye!"

"Do you truly feel like an Orphan yourself?"

"O' course I do, Lass. Me own Parents are good fer nothin'—hardly Parents to me at all. Me Lover is gone. An' yet I know that he waits somewhere fer me—so, i'faith I'm better off than ye, because I don't believe in the Finality o' Death. . . ."

"And yet you laugh'd at my Female God. You laugh'd when I said the Supreme Being might be a Woman."

"Woman or Man, what's it to me, Lass? 'Twas like a Ball o' Fire, I told ye. It hath no Cock nor Cunny neither any more than that Fire in the Hearth hath one. The Supreme Bein', Lass, is all Heat an' Fire an' Love. That's why when we love one another an' our Bodies heat with Passion, we begin to know the Supreme Bein'. That's why Love is the Path that takes us to Heaven an' not to Hell—as yer Drunken Lout of a Clergyman will say. I'faith, Fanny, I don't care one Fig fer the Sex o' the Supreme Bein'—'twas just Surprize that made me laugh so—I swear it. I may have no Use fer Women in me Bed, but I don't deny they're wily an' shrewd an' oft' have more Brains in 'em than the Gentlemen o' the Species. Yer fine Self, fer example, have the Makin's o' as great a Prig as e'er swung o'er Tyburn. In one Week I could make ye into a Cut-Purse to be the Envy o' ev'ry Female Prig in Newgate—what say ye, Lass?"

"If I live thro' the Night, Lancelot, I'll have no more Thieving and no more Shiv'ring in the Road either."

"An' what o' the Robin Hood Oath?"

"That's your Oath, not mine, Lancelot."

"Ye swore it, Lass."

"Under protest, I swore it, and at Pistol-Point."

"Nonetheless, ye swore. D'ye think ye can shuck yer Destiny? D'ye think the Supreme Bein'—whether male or female, an' beggin' yer Pardon if I offend—put ye in me Path, just fer Foolish Pranks, Rhodomontade, an' such like? No! There's a Greater Plan by which ye fall into me able Hands an' I mold ye an' teach ye me Trade. I'faith, yer a lucky Girl. Not many have the Chance to study Priggism with Lancelot Robinson—an' give their Lives to such a worthy Cause. Now go back to sleep an' get well an' when ye awake all healthy an' sound again, I'll have the Boys in here to parade before ye an' introduce 'emselves. There'll be John Littlehat an' Puck Goodfellow an' Sir Foplin' an' Mr. Twitch an' Beau Monde an' a goodly Parcel o' other Fine Fellows."

"Did you give them all their Names, Lancelot?"

"I did, Lass, includin' meself. An' Horatio o' course, that luscious Black Morsel who, i'faith, wishes I were *ye*. Bless me if he isn't as mad fer ye as I am meself mad fer him! Now you sleep, Lass, whilst I creep into Horatio's Bed—if he'll have me—which is far from likely. Wish me Luck, Lass."

"Good Luck, Lancelot," I said, sinking back on my Pillows, too weak to protest any more that I would not be a Thief and risk The Cheat myself. But in Truth I was growing fonder and fonder of Lancelot (tho' I'd not tell him for all the Tea in China, Limes in the West Indies, or Silver and Gold in this curious Cottage of his).

"Good Night, Lass," he said and crept out the Door.

I awoke the next Morning to see the Sun streaming thro' the mullion'd Windows. My Fever had abated, my Cough was less troublesome to me, and standing before my Bed like a Vision out of some Stage Play were thirteen Highwaymen in all their Finery, standing at attention, with Lancelot saluting me at their Head.

"Mornin' Lass!" said he. O he was all gotten up in his Best as well. They lookt fine enough to be hang'd that Day—all of 'em!

"Here's John Littlehat," said Lancelot, pointing to a short fat Fellow with a black Beard, a scarlet Coat, and yellow Breeches. "I call him that because his Prickle's as small as his Heart is big."

"Old Sot!" says John Littlehat. "Ye lye betwixt yer Teeth." But still he saluted me and wisht me Good Morning.

"An' this here is Puck Goodfellow," he said, pointing to a fearsome, strapping Fellow almost six Foot tall, with a Scar on his Face nearly as long as the Sword he wore at his Waist. "I call him that because he's such a bad Fellow an' his Christian Name rhymes with what he likes to do best."

144

"Blackguard!" says Puck, laughing and saluting me.

"An' this here is Sir Foplin', because he dresses so fine," says Lancelot, introducing a Fellow with a purple Waistcoat embroider'd with yellow Daisies, red Breeches with yellow Stockings, and a Coat of Parrot-green Silk. Sir Fopling wore a purple silk Eyepatch with an embroider'd Eye upon it, a Pyrate's Earring upon his right Ear, and had a Face so pockmarkt it seem'd it might be made of Sponge, not Flesh. He, too, saluted me.

"Mr. Twitch is next," says Lancelot, indicating another Colleague, whose Eyebrows went up and down with each Beat of his Heart. This gave him a constant Expression of Surprize, a kind of Lunatick Glee, such as you might see amongst the Inmates at Bedlam.

"*Enchanté*, Mademoiselle Fanny," says Mr. Twitch, bowing low, as if he were a Courtier in the Time of Charles II.

"An' this is Beau Monde," says Lancelot, pointing to a Fellow with a perfectly curl'd, Full-bottom'd Wig such as Louis XIV himself might have worn. "I call him Beau Monde because he e'er prefers Style to Comfort an' insists upon dressin' as ye see him, e'en on the Road."

Beau Monde bow'd still lower than Mr. Twitch, and with e'en more Grace. He was a Man of medium Stature, much addicted to Snuff, which he kept in a round enamell'd Box, painted with Birds and Bees.

"Next is Grudge because he hath such a sweet Temper, an' Smooth because his Face is so pockt, an' Thunder because he talks so soft, an' Sotwit because he will ne'er take a Dram whether o' Gin or Madeira, an' Sancho because he verily resembles Don Quixote's Squire, an' Sir Francis Bacon because he eats not Meat, an' Caveat because he always bids me beware, beware, an' o' course, Horatio, me darlin' Boy— tho' the Bugger toss'd me out on me Arse last Night merely for failin' to resemble ye! I told him the Colours o' our Hair was the same—but, i'faith, he hardly set much store by that!"

After each of the Merry Men had greeted me in turn, Horatio came forward, saying: "Madam Fanny, I trust you're faring better than you were last Night?"

"Thank you," said I, "that I am."

"Excellent," says Horatio, "for, as Horace says: '*Quaesitam Meritis sume Superbiam*,' or, in our own sweet Mother English, 'Accept the proud Honour won by the Merits'; and

145

indeed what could you merit more than Health? May all the Blessings of the Goddess Hygeiea be upon you!"

"Enough o' yer Latin Palaver," says Lancelot, responding, I fear, to the petty Promptings of the Goddess of Jealousy, if such there be.

"Aye, aye, Sir," says Horatio, mockingly. O what a Lovers' Triangle we'd form'd in so short a Time!

'Twas droll also how Lancelot had nam'd his Disciples. Grudge was kind and had no Grudge anywhere about him. Smooth had a Face more pockmarkt than Sir Fopling's. Thunder's Voice was tiny and squeaky as a Mouse's. Sotwit inveigh'd endlessly against the Evils of Drink, and Sir Francis Bacon was pow'rfully oppos'd to good English Roast Beef. Caveat, for his Part, worried continually about Lancelot's Welfare as if he were Lancelot's own Mother. What a fine Assortment of Fellows! Whate'er their Names had been before they join'd Lancelot's Band, they seem'd so suited to their present Names, that, truly, I could imagine them having no others.

"Very well then," said Lancelot, "let's bring on the Breakfast."

In a trice, Horatio and the Merry Men march'd out of my Chamber and into the adjoining one, busied themselves there for a Time, whereupon they march'd back, carrying a long Trestle Table set with Breakfast for all of us, and serv'd in such resplendent golden Plates and Goblets that I should have thought myself the Queen of England to merit it.

'Twas hearty Country Fare serv'd in Court Utensils, and no sooner had the Table been brought in than two of the Men went out again to fetch Benches. Before long we were all sitting at Table, toasting my new-found Health with Ale.

"Here's to our Fanny," says Lancelot, "the most courageous Wench in all o' England!"

"Hear! Hear!" says Thunder in his tiny Voice.

"And beauteous, too," says Horatio, "for, as Virgil says—"

"Damn Virgil," says Lancelot, "an' be done!"

"Yes, your Highness," says Horatio mockingly.

"Now then, Men," says Lancelot. "On the Morrow, we are goin' to carry all the Swag up to London to deliver it to a Vessel call'd the *Hannibal*, bound fer the Port o' Boston an' the Port o' New York. 'Tis a delicate Operation which calls fer cratin' up the Booty as if 'twere not what 'tis—namely 'Swag.' "

"An' what shall it be, Lancelot?" says Sir Fopling.

146

"That I'll tell ye when the Time comes."

"Pray why do you ship it to the Colonies, Lancelot, instead of selling it back to its proper Owners as most Thieves do?" I askt him.

"Because we get good cold Cash from the Captain an' we ne'er hear o' the Swag again. I'll not be a Blackguard like most o' yer Newgate Prigs an' fence the Swag, then turn in me own Men fer the Reward. I'll not peach on me Fellows—an' if any o' ye e'er peach on me, ye'll regret it in Hell as on Earth. D'ye hear?"

"Aye, Lancelot," said the Men in Unison. "We're true."

"But shan't these Wigs and Clothes be quite out of Fashion when they arrive in the Colonies?"

"Ah, Lass, the damn'd Colonists know nothin' o' Style. Last Year's Fashion Plate dazzles 'em as well as this Year's—nay better. The *Hannibal* sails to Kingston, Charlestown, New York, an' Boston. Horrid Hell-holes all of 'em. 'Tis Wild Land, the New World is, an' full o' Savages!"

"And who is the Captain of the *Hannibal* that he takes such a Risque?"

"Risque! Why he stands to make a great Fortune off this new Shipload. I'faith, Lass, his Eyes light up when he sees me. He's a Fellow I met in me Sailin' Days an' not a bad Sort himself. No Slaver he; he trades in Stolen Swag, not Human Flesh."

"And what do you do with the Money?"

"We distribute it to the poorest Wretches we can find."

"And you keep none?"

"Aye. We keep enough to live. What ye must understand, Fanny, is that most o' yer wealthiest Rogues live by Peachin', not honest Stealin'. They're Thief-Takers, not Thieves. Now, Stealin' is the most honourable Occupation ye can name. Why e'en the Good Lord stole Adam from the Earth an' Eve from his Rib! Jesus stole, ye might say, the Loaves an' the Fishes! But to steal a gold Watch from a puff'd-up Lawyer who has a fine House, a Coach an' Six, an' a Wife who doth nought but visit her Dressmaker, is to do nothin' more than to snap an Apple from a Tree that hath a thousand Apples. 'Twill ne'er be miss'd. 'Twill grow back two fer ev'ry one ye take—an' some poor Wretch (whose Brother that same Lawyer doubtless bled dry) will live instead o' dye!"

"What I love best about Lancelot, i'faith, is how he doth go on about the fine Art o' Priggism," says Caveat. "What a golden Tongue that Boy hath! But, ah, I worry lest the Lad be taken on the Road an' hang'd again despite his fine Philos-ophies."

" 'Tis Drink that's at the Root of the Evils of the Poor," says Sotwit, sadly. "If we could wean 'em off their Mother Gin, in truth, we'd not have to give 'em all our Money."

"*Our* Money? *Our* Money?" says Lancelot. " 'Tis the *Lord's* Money. We but redistribute it! Ne'er forget that, Sot-wit!"

"The Lord's Money, Lancelot?" I askt, all incredulous. I had e'er been told that Money was an Invention of the Devil, not of God.

"Aye, the Lord's Money! 'Tis the Lord's Corn, the Lord's Gin, the Lord's Apples, an' the Lord's Money! We but pluck it from His Tree an' pass it about."

"But is not Money the Root of all Evil, Lancelot?"

"Nay, Fanny, *Mankind* is the Root o' all Evil! Give him Glass Beads to trade with or Barrels o' Herrin', an' I warrant ye, he'll do the same! The loftiest Minds will fall into the Gutter fer the Hope o' Gain. John Locke, fer one, with all his Palaver o' the Natural Happiness o' Mankind an' the Right to the Fruits o' yer own Labor—why, e'en he put Money into the Royal African Company an' profited mightily from the Sale o' Human Flesh! Where was the Social Con-tract fer the Black Man? Where was the Pursuit o' Happiness an' Pleasure fer him? Is the Social Contract only fer the White, the Land-Owner, the Property-Holder? I say: Fie on't! Would ye believe Locke? Well then believe him fer Blacks as well as Whites! Believe him fer the Poor as well as the Rich! Have they not the Right to Life, Health, Liberty, an' Pos-sessions? I hate Philosophers worse than I hate e'en Lawyers an' Priests an' Physicians, because in the Name o' the Mighty Mind, with its Mighty *Tabula Rasa*—or what have ye—they *lye!* Is not ev'ry Man entitl'd to the Inevitable Pursuit o' Hap-piness an' Pleasure? We bring that Pleasure to the Poor as well as the Land-Owner, the Merchant, the damn'd thievin' Lawyer, the damn'd lyin' Priest, not to mention the damn'd Physician who kills ye fer his Fee! Truly, Fanny, we do the Good Lord's Work!"

"Hear! Hear!" squeaked Thunder.

"T'faith," said Mr. Twitch, working his Eyebrows all the while, "Lancelot is a Poet amongst Prigs, is he not? A very Shakespeare of Priggism! I'd go to the Gallows anytime for such fine Speeches!"

"But, Lancelot," say I, "I have read that it is the African

148

Kings *themselves* that sell the Blacks to the English on the Gold Coast, or at the Mouth of the River Calabar or the River Niger."

" 'Tis true, Lass, 'tis true. But I could tell ye Tales about Africa an' the People there. Why Slavery to 'em is not what 'tis in the Wild New World. Such Savagery is quite unknown. Why, an African Slave may be taken in Battle as a Prisoner o' War or bought by Strangers because his Kinfolk are too poor to feed him—yet when he comes to his new Village, he is a Slave, not an *Animal!* An' many, I'll warrant ye, are treated well, adopted into Families, freed after a Time, by workin' off their Bondage with the Sweat o' their Brows—an' some e'en become Tribal Kings! Is this not true, Horatio?"

"In Truth," says he, "I know as little about Africa as you know about Ancient Rome, for I was born in Barbadoes, to a Master who car'd for nothing but the Study of the Classicks, and early he took me from my poor Mama, forbade me to speak ought but Latin, French, or the King's English, kept me in the Great House, and train'd me up to be a Latin Scholar and Tutor to his Children. In truth, I am not sure I'm not a Child of his myself, for my Mother was black as Ebony and my Skin, as you can see, is the Colour of Sweet Chocolate. *'Sic visum Veneri,'* as Horace says, *'cui placet impares Formas atque animos sub juga ahenea Saevo mittere cum joco'*—'Ah the cruel Decree of Venus who takes Delight in yoking together Bodies and Hearts that so ill-mated are'!"

Lancelot frown'd at the Latin, but I was fascinated by Horatio's odd Upbringing. No wonder he was so strange a Combination of Savagery and Civilization! I wisht to hear more of his History.

"But was that not illegal in the New World—teaching Slaves to read and write?" I askt eagerly. "For I have read so."

"My Master was a peculiar Man, Madam Fanny. He believ'd he could create a Little Rome there on the Tropick Plantation. He'd brought marble Sculptures without Heads from his Grand Tour to Italy. Some were Forgeries, I'll warrant, but he lov'd 'em ne'ertheless. He brought Renaissance Coffers of gilded Wood, and gilded Cherubim from Venice, and Paintings of golden-hair'd, blue-eyed Angels from Florence and Siena. When he took it into his Head to rebuild his Villa in the Roman Style, he brought a Family of Italian Painters to his Plantation and there they liv'd painting and drinking and playing their bawdy Games right under his very

149

Nose. I'faith, they could do no wrong—tho' they laugh'd at him behind his Back. What'er I've learnt about drinking and wenching, I learnt from those Tuscan Rogues—and mark you, they knew plenty! But to go on about my Master—why, he e'en built Roman Baths and an Amphitheatre and he e'en wanted his Slaves to play Gladiatorial Games. He was a strange one, my Master was, part Lunatick, in truth."

"Then damn yer Master an' be done!" says Lancelot, perhaps not pleas'd to have another Witsnapper in our midst. But I begg'd to hear Horatio's Tale, for now my Curiosity was e'en more arouz'd.

"How did you leave Barbadoes and come to England?" I askt Horatio.

"I had read Books and Gazettes from Europe and I knew that the Condition of Blacks in the Old World was not what it was in the New. I thought to run away to France, where by dint of my Knowledge of the Classicks and the fine French Tongue I'd learnt at my Master's House (not to mention my Smatt'ring of Italian, pickt up from those roguish Painters), I would be consider'd a Marvel, taken into a Salon as a Pet, and ador'd by Learnèd Ladies for my Colour and my Wit— so I ran away to Sea, but alas, I did not get to France."

"What happen'd, Horatio?" I askt.

"O 'tis a long and breathless Tale, and as Virgil says, '*Ipsi sibi somnia fingnut*,' 'They fashion their own Dreams'—so I, too, fashion'd my own Dreams, made my own Destiny, and all such Poetick Stuff."

"Do tell of it, Horatio," I said.

"But, pray, leave the blasted Latin out," says Lancelot, "fer I love Latin about as much as I love to fuck a Pig's Arse when there's a fine black one in me Bed instead!"

"My Master hath spoken," said Horatio, with all possible Irony, "I must obey."

"Pray tell your Tale!" I begg'd.

"Very well, then. I stow'd away on a French Ship which had call'd at Barbadoes for Careening. 'Twas nam'd the *Esperance* and its Home Port was Dieppe, which I had been told was a fine Modern Town, having been rebuilt after the War of the League of Augsburg. I thought I would sail thither and easily make my Way to Paris, where the French People were said to be very tolerant of Blacks—more tolerant than the blasted English and the cruel, cruel Spanish, by Jove. But alas, my Plans were thwarted, not by Man, but by God, for when I was discover'd (and the Slave-Brand upon

150

my Shoulder seen), the Captain vow'd to return me to my Master on the next Crossing and swore that until then I should be his personal Servant, his *Valet de Chambre*, Man of all Work, and the like. None of this troubl'd me much, howe'er, for I knew that the Winter Months were coming upon us ('twas already September) and that not many Ships made more than one Atlantick Crossing *per Annum*, as we say in Latin—" With this he gave a hasty Look towards Lancelot, who scowl'd now at the slightest Mention of that Tongue, whereupon Horatio smil'd mischievously, then continu'd:

"Verily the Winter Crossings upon the Atlantick are harsh indeed, and only the greediest of Captains—or the most desperate—venture across the Sea in those Months, so I trusted to my own Charm to ingratiate myself with the Captain in the Weeks to come and I doubted not but I should find a Way to escape when we came to the beauteous Shores of France. That was not to be, howe'er, for our Ship was wreckt in a monstrous Hurricano—whilst still in the Waters of the Main, and those of the Crew who were not drown'd were eaten horribly by Sharks, the Waters running red with Blood and the Screams of the Victims echoing in my Ears. . . ."

"Pray, how did you escape?" I askt.

"Again, 'twas my Learning that sav'd me. There was a Sack of Victuals in the Dinghy in which the Captain and I were put o'er the Side—"

"Did he not go down with the Ship, Horatio, as a true Captain ought?" said I.

Horatio laugh'd merrily. "My dearest Girl, he was the first one off the sinking Ship, and in the best Dinghy, too! Do not believe Heroick Tales of Captains going down with their Ships. I've ne'er seen it nor heard of it in all the Time I spent at Sea. . . ."

"Nor I," said Lancelot, agreeing heartily.

"But the Captain," Horatio continu'd, "was swiftly punish'd for his Desertion of his Men—for the greatest Shark I've e'er seen (in Pictures or at Sea) fairly seiz'd him from the Boat and snapp'd him in two! 'Twas verily as if the Devil himself had come in the Guise of a Fish and in an Instant he ate his Hindquarters, then his Torso and his Arms, but left his Head bobbing like an Orange upon the Sea. Then he swam away, contented, for the nonce, this Devil Fish did, whilst I lay at my full Length in the Bottom of the Boat and prepar'd to meet my Maker, for surely the Fish should return

151

to take me as well. But as I lay there in the Dinghy, I chanced to feel in the Darkness a Sack of Oranges left as Food for shipwreckt Seamen, and, remembering Stories I had read of Sharks being deceiv'd by Stillness, the Absence of thrashing Limbs, I resolv'd to remove the Oranges and wriggle myself into the Sack, which, after some Difficulties, I accomplish'd. Whereupon the monstrous Shark return'd in a Feeding Frenzy, butted the Boat with his evil Head, fairly chomp'd into the Wood with his huge Jaws, near destroying the Boat, but at last swimming away, leaving me in my Sack, clinging to a bit of Board (which had once been the Dinghy's Seat), and the Seas all around awash with Oranges, and one ghastly sever'd Head as well—namely the Captain's! How long I waited there (as still-ly as I could, to be sure), I cannot say. The Shark circl'd the Area curiously. I saw his hideous Fin and fear'd for my Life. I pray'd to Jove, to the Supreme Being, to the African Gods of my Ancestors (whose sacred Names I did not e'en know). I pray'd to dye swiftly, if at all, and go to Heaven, there to mingle with Horace and Juvenal, Catullus and Petronius Arbiter—for surely such Great Writers must be in Heaven, must they not?"

"Bah," says Lancelot. "Italian Bastards—all of 'em!"

"So I linger'd in my Sack, keeping still as I might whilst the Shark circl'd closer, toying with the Oranges, but not eatin 'em, coming e'er closer, finally circling me, and then—just as I was prepar'd to dye, and be done—the big Blackguard turns Fin and swims away!

"By Jove, I'll ne'er understand how I came to be sav'd, but surely, 'twas God's Will, and 'twas also His Will that not long after I was pickt up by a Pyrate Ship nam'd the *Good Intent*, flying the red Pyrate Flag (for mark you, 'tis a Lye that Pyrates e'er fly the darksome Skull and Crossbones—they only do so to affright their Prey before Attack), and taken aboard amongst the Buccaneers."

"Bucaneers!" I gasp'd. O few Words struck such Terror in my Heart unless it were the Word "Pyrates" itself!

"Bah!" said Horatio. "I'd sooner see a Pyrate than Politician any Day! Now these were the most Freedom-loving Fellows I e'er met. Black or white, they judged a Man solely by his Learning, his fighting Ability, his Pluck. Many were uneducated Rogues from the Streets of London, Newgate Prison, or runaway Apprentices and Indentur'd Men from the New World. They were amaz'd by my Learning, amus'd by the Stories I could tell at Night to pass away the lonely

Hours at Sea, and not a little impress'd by my physical Strength, which was also great despite the Years I had spent speaking Latin with my strange Master (who, by the by, e'en wore a Toga whilst on his Plantation!).

"We took many Ships in the Time I sail'd with the Pyrates, for as you know, their Slogan is '*No Prey, no Pay*,' and ev'ry Man must do his Share, black or white, literate or illiterate. Had I not had Brawn as well as Brain, they would no doubt have toss'd me o'erboard again. But I did my goodly Share of Work—and into the Bargain told 'em Tales all Night, adapted from the Latin Authors I knew so well—but told in simple English to suit their simple, un-Book-learnt Hearts!"

"Then be brief, fer God's sake," said Lancelot, growing e'er more jealous of Horatio's Skill in Story-telling. But the Faces of the Merry Men clearly pled to hear the Rest. And as for me, I was as fascinated by Pyrates as I was horrified.

"What a Time we had!" Horatio rav'd. "We rais'd Spanish Plate from well-nigh half a dozen sunken Galleons, took Ships with Cargoes as divers as these Merry Men here. We were true 'Sea-Artists'—as the Saying goes. Our Vessel was small—a mere twenty-ton Sloop—but 'twas all the better to come in like the Wind and escape like the Wind after the Capture was made. We fought with Cutlass and Flintlocks. Some Men were equipp'd with Boarding Pikes to cut thro' the Enemy's Rigging (as well as their Nets and Bulwarks), others hurl'd Stinkpotts at the Prey—homemade Crocks of Sulphur with a horrible Smell—or homemade Grenades of Pistol Shot and old Iron. Still others us'd Petereros, firing old Spikes and Nails, Pieces of Glass and Crockery, that could make a Man's Face look like a Swiss Cheese in no Time at all. After the initial Attack, we'd throw the Grapnel Hooks o'er the Side to snare the Prey like a wriggling Fish on an Angler's Line. Then some of the Sea-Artists would drive Wedges betwixt the Enemy's Rudder and Sternpost, jamming it and making Escape impossible. O we were very quick indeed and better drill'd than the King's Armies! Each Man had his Task and each Man did it—and did it swiftly because the first Man on board the Prey got a double Share of the Booty. Once on board, 'twas Hand-to-Hand, Thrust and Cut, firing at close Range, and e'en using the Pistol Butts as Batt'ring Pieces. We were a season'd Crew—Men who had surviv'd Prison, Poverty, many pestilential Voyages—and we were hardy, much hardier than any King's Navy we might meet. 'Twas ne'er a long Contest and when the Prey surrender'd, we swarm'd o'er the Ship looking first for Rum or Wine, then for other Booty, but sometimes the Men got drunk so fast that in their Frenzy they kill'd all the Crew—especially if they were the detested Spaniards—tho' 'twas in fact our Policy to offer 'em to join our Pyrate Company and sign our Pyrate Articles instead of being thrown o'er the Side or strung up from the Yards for Musket Practice! But Men who had drunk too much Rum were ne'er Solomon-like in their Judgement. . . ."

"Amen to that!" cries Sotwit.

"And once or twice the Prey was pistol'd point blank! But many of our Company objected to such wholesale Slaughter, and if a Man was a Surgeon, a Gunner, a Bosun, a Carpenter, or Sail-Maker, his Life was surely spar'd and he was press'd into Service."

"What Booty did you take?" I askt, proud to be using a Pyrate Word.

"O the Booty was divers as the blooming Flow'rs of the Tropicks, beautiful as the Green Isle of Barbadoes! We took Spices, Silks, and Perfumes from the East; Indigo, Cochineal, and Logwood for Dyes; precious Woods, and Sugar; Tobacco, Hides, e'en soft Llama Wool from the Spanish Territories to the South. Sometimes we'd come upon Bales of Damask, Strip'd Silks for the Colonial Ladies, Bolts of sheerest Linen, pieces of cut Velvet; Stands of Arms, Fowling Pieces, Pistols damascen'd with Silver and Gold; or sometimes fine Casks of Wine (which ne'er reach'd Port but in the Pyrates' Bellies!) and sometimes Religious Articles, Statues, Chalices, Missals, and the like.

"We sold the Booty at Auction at Tortuga. The Trollops and the Alehouses took most Men's Shares—and tho' many a Doxy went Home rich to Europe, her Pockets stuff'd with Pyrate Gold, the Pyrates themselves were Spenders, not Hoarders—and few of 'em had anything to show for all their Bravery but Scars and lopp'd-off Limbs!

"But sometimes, we attackt Prey we could do nothing with—a Shipload of fine Arabian Stallions we had no Use nor room for. Some of the Men rode wildly about the Decks for a Time, hollering like Lunaticks, but when one of our Crew was thrown and had his Neck broke, we retreated, leaving the Steeds to their Fate with what remain'd of the enemy Crew."

"O no," I cried, my Eyes filling with Tears at the Plight of these Horses. What if my dearest Lustre should be lost at Sea?

"D'ye weep more fer Horses or fer Men, Fanny?" says Lancelot.

"I weep for both," I said, but in my Heart, I knew that Horses won the Palm.

"Then hear the Rest of my Tale," said Horatio. "For we next met a Shipload of indentur'd English Felons bound for Slavery in Jamaica. Some of 'em begg'd to join us, thinking the Pyrate Life a far better Thing than Slavery in the Plantations, but such Fighting broke out amongst the Lot of 'em concerning who should be taken, who left behind, that we had to leave 'em all, giving 'em Sailing Directions for Montego Bay, where we doubted not but they might escape and hide in the Bush. We had no Love for putting Men in Chains to toil in the Sun, but our Ship was too small to take 'em all, alas.

"But the very sorriest Dilemma came for me when we chanced upon a Slaver fresh from the Middle Passage and the Guinea Coast. She lookt a fine Prize upon the Horizon, but as we drew closer, we saw the Gear all foul aboard her, the Sails backt and gyb'd, and none of 'em trimm'd to the Wind. We boarded her and found a Cargo of Africans that had broken loose from the Holds and slaughter'd all the Crew, but since none of the Slaves was a Sailor they'd floated thus for Days, unable to return to their Homeland, unable to make for Shore.

"O what Turmoil in my Heart when I saw this Shipload of my People and yet could not speak a Word of their African Language, nor communicate my Grief in any Way. All my Latin, my French, my English avail'd me not! And my Skin was almost that of another Race compar'd to their gleaming Ebony, and I knew not whether to love 'em as Brothers or disdain 'em as Savages who knew nothing of Catullus and Virgil! For my Education had verily made me a Freak of Nature—not African, not Roman, nor yet a True-born Englishman; pray then, what was I?"

"A Human Bein'!" cries Lancelot. "A pox on yer Obsession with yer Skin!"

"Ah your Lancelot's a very unfeeling Rogue!" said Horatio to the assembl'd Company. "He knows not what Torture a Black Man feels being e'er a Raven in a Nest of Swans, an Orange in a Basket of Apples. He thinks he loves the Blacks—but how can he love when he doth not understand?

155

Where is Love without Sympathy? Where is Charity without Understanding?"

"Damn ye!" shouts Lancelot. "I'm an Orphan as much as ye, as much as Madam Fanny! She cries always about the Lot of damn'd simperin' Females! Ye cry about yer damn'd Colour—but are we not all the same? Human Souls, orphan'd by our Fates, seekin' Solace, seekin' Friendship, seekin' God?"

"Yea, Lancelot, that we are—but we seek in diff'rent Ways. My Colour will set me apart as long as I shall live and Fanny's Sex shall do the same as long as *she* shall live. . . ."

"But in Heaven yer Soul shall have no Colour an' no Sex neither! Ah, damn ye all with yer Short-sightedness an' yer Whimperin' an' Simperin'! Can ye not see that 'tis all foolish Trifles in the Light o' Eternity?"

"Pray, what did you do with the Slave Ship, Horatio?" I askt politely as I could, hoping to staunch Lancelot's new Tirade; for you have seen that he was a famous Tonguepad himself and 'twas clear he resented Horatio's Skill in Spellbinding the assembl'd Company.

"We boarded her, as I have said, and then, seeing that we could not accommodate the Slaves on our Vessel (and would not auction 'em in Port, Slaving being strictly against our Articles), we tried to teach 'em the Rudiments of Sail-handling, gave 'em Maps of the Guinea Coast, set 'em on course for Africa, and then left 'em to their Fate! What became of 'em, I'll ne'er know. Oft' in my Dreams I see that Ghostly Ship of Africans, sailing fore'er on a Storm-toss'd Sea, unable to make for Home, neither slave nor free, imprison'd by their Fates and by the Roiling Mystery of the Sea! O 'tis a Vision to make a strong Man weep!"

Here e'en Lancelot was silenced by the Ghostly Vision Horatio had conjur'd.

"I sail'd with the Pyrates for more than two Years," Horatio said, "feeling the Pyrate Life well-suited to my Temper and seeing no Need of any other Life. But our Captain, Mr. Thackaberry (also known as 'Calico Thack' because of his Habit of wearing Calico Trowsers), had made too many Enemies in his Days at Sea, had taken too many Prizes, and what was more, had refus'd to pay the expected Share of Booty to the Colonial Governours (calling 'em Cowardly Rogues, who claim'd to hate Pyracy, yet demanded their Share of the Spoils), and so, many a Ship was sent after him in hot Pursuit and a fine Price had been put upon his Head. 'Twas now

156

within the Pow'rs of the Colonies to try Pyrates themselves, without sending 'em back to England—and the Governour of Carolina, whom Captain Thack had especially offended, took it into his Head to have him hunted like a Fox, enlisting another famous Pyrate as the Bloodhound; for he knew that none but a Pyrate could take a Pyrate such as Calico Thack. This Pursuer was a terrible Man, Name of Seabury, with a red Beard to his Waist in which he had plaited colour'd Ribbands, and he was known as a Blackguard who did not e'en keep the Pyrate Code, but play'd into the Plans of the Colonial Governours, e'en turning in his own Men if the Reward were high enough. He was the lowest Sort, lacking the Pyrate's Honour, but he rounded up a Crew of Villains and a light but Sea-worthy Brig call'd the *Devil's Revenge,* and he gave Chase o'er the High Seas till he boarded us and either kill'd or took us Prisoner, to a Man.

"Some he had walk the dreaded Plank, for truly he was the only Barbarian I e'er knew to use that Punishment—contrary to Pyrate Lore. Calico Thack he deliver'd to Charlestown to be hang'd and then left to rot in Chains whilst the Governour chear'd. And my own poor self he sold for a small Fortune to a British Lawyer (who chanced to be in Charlestown then) and who plann'd to use me as a Manservant and also avail himself of my Latin Scholarship to teach his Children. Lawyer Slocock was as surly and stingy as he lookt when you met him on that London Coach! He was the sort of Man who wants one Servant to do the work of ten. I was Tutor, Valet, e'en sometime Cook and Coachman in the Months I spent with him, and I itch'd for my Freedom you may be sure. When I saw your fine fierce Faces, I knew I'd found my Pyrate Band again!

"O what Melancholy I knew when my Belovèd Captain Thack was hang'd! He was the finest Pyrate that ee'r sail'd the Spanish Main! From Barbadoes to Boston Harbour, he was a Legend—and 'twas his Fame that did him in, I fear!"

"Ah, Horatio, thy Tale makes me tremble, too, for Lancelot's Fate," says Caveat, "for that Lad is also too famous for his own Good."

"And haven't I cheated The Cheat once?" cries Lancelot. "Fain would I have the Chance to cheat it again, an' prove meself a walkin' Miracle!"

"The Lad is deluded," Caveat exclaims. "He hath the Notion he is Jesus Christ!"

"Not Jesus," says Lancelot, "but the Ghost o' Robin Hood!

157

I am he that cannot swiftly Dye, an' e'en dyin' I shall live again!"

"If my Belovèd Captain Thack could dye, then so can you!" cries Horatio. "For he also felt himself invulnerable and well-nigh immortal. 'Tis the Common Curse of Highwaymen and Pyrates, that having dar'd so much, they eat Daring as their Daily Bread—and before long someone slips 'em a Poison'd Slice!"

Chapter XVIII

Containing some mischievous and am'rous Play in which 'tis presently seen that Lancelot's Protestations of sexual Preference are not as fixt as he would have had us believe, nor indeed are those of our Friend Horatio, whereupon our Heroine finds herself in a Predicament which Prudes will applaud but the Hotblooded will find (nearly) tragick; after which we ponder a prophetick Dream and thereafter begin our Voyage to London.

YOU MAY WONDER, Belinda, why I grew so fond of Lancelot, Horatio, and the Merry Men in the short Time I spent with 'em, and I will reply that, truly, I did not then understand why, tho' I do now. In the Great Pageant of our Lives, from Time to Time, we chance to meet certain Persons who seem closer to us than our own Kin, and who promise to lead our Souls where they must go. Surely Lancelot and Horatio were such Guides and Teachers to me. Criminal they might be, yet they seem'd to have master'd the World's Vicissitudes, each in his own Way, nor did they seem lacking in Wit and Understanding—tho' these they chose to apply to Lives of Crime. Moreo'er, having lost the Good Witches so recently, and my own adoptive Parents before that, and then e'en my belovèd Horse, 'twas not surprizing that I found in Lancelot and the Merry Men a new Family, to whom I swiftly form'd a most prodigious Attachment. Thus, when Lancelot inform'd us that we were shortly to set out for London with the Swag, my Heart leapt in my Bosom like a spawning Salmon and I fear'd for him as much as for myself.

We were somewhere in the Chiltern Hills of Buckinghamshire ('twas all Lancelot would disclose of the Location of his Hideaway—lest, he said, I e'er be apprehended and put to grievous Torture), and we were to journey by Land to a small Stream call'd the Mill Brook, thence tow the Swag by Barge and Dray Horse to the River Thames, thence remove it to another, greater Barge, and enter London triumphally by River.

We were to be disguis'd as Maltsters and the Swag to be hidden in Barrels 'neath a large Shipment of Malt. Lancelot had a Confederate who was a Maltster at Great Marlowe and would provide us with a spacious Barge to convey us to the Metropolis. 'Twas not an easy Journey, nor lacking in Danger, for the Barges, said Lancelot, had to shoot the Weirs on the River thro' Flash-Locks, and oft' many Barges were lost, their Cargoes capsiz'd and their Sailors wreckt. But 'twas safer than risquing the Turnpikes, where each Gate might conceal a Traitor, ready to turn Lancelot in for the Reward.

All Night the Merry Men were busy crating the Swag, and I was to prepare myself to dress *en Homme* once again for the Journey up to London, which would begin at Daybreak. I was now almost recover'd of my Coughing and felt nearly myself again.

Was I to remain a Member of Lancelot's Band and travel with the Merry Men, robbing Coaches and hazarding my Neck in the Noose? I'd not play Decoy again and shiver naked in the Road for him, but should I travel with the Band as a proper Cut-Purse, or should I make my Escape in London and continue to seek my Fortune?

'Twas a hard Dilemma, for as I have said, I had truly come to know great Fondness for Lancelot, Horatio, and the Merry Men and to feel 'em almost my Brothers. When I had found Friendship again, should I toss it all away so swiftly for nought but drear Loneliness and Solitude? And yet was it not rash indeed to risque Prison or The Cheat all for a bit of Friendship with a motley Assortment of Rogues? I would ponder well all Night and make my Decision come Daybreak, I thought. Morning would be Time enough to make up my Mind.

Just as I was laying out my Costume for the following Morning (for my manly Attire had been restor'd to me by Lancelot, together with the Addition of some still more splendid purloin'd *Accoutrements*), the Door of my Chamber creakt open and Lancelot himself appear'd. He paced the Room with a Degree of Uncertainty, as if not knowing where to alight, or what indeed to say. Then he sat himself down upon the edge of the Bed and began, awkwardly, in Fact—which was scarce his wont:

"T'faith, Lass, I hope ye won't hold me earlier Ill-Usage of ye amiss—fer I confess that tho' at first I thought ye a

160

worthless Baggage, I have come to see the Error o' me Ways an' to know ye fer a fine young Woman, a trustworthy Wench o' great Learnin' an' Sensibility."

He said this with much Abashment—he who ne'er hesitated o'er which Word to choose—and so, inspir'd by this new Humility of his, I clasp'd his Hand warmly, saying,

"And I am fond of you, too, Lancelot. Pray, let us bury the Hatchet and let nought but Good come betwixt us two from this Hour forth."

As soon as I seized his Hand, he drew it quickly away, almost as if 'twere a red-hot Coal, and I was surpriz'd and affrighted by the Rapidity of this Motion, and, to say the Truth, not a little offended.

"Fanny," says he, "forgive me, but the Touch o' Woman's Flesh fills me with Fear. I cannot lye to ye. 'Tis the one Terror neither comin' back from the Dead nor all the Dangers I've endur'd can save me from. I've but to touch a Woman's Skin an' I quake as I ne'er did before the Hangman's Noose."

Now, this strange Tale stirr'd my proud Blood as nothing had since Lord Bellars' false Avowals of Eternal Love, and taking Lancelot's Hand again in mine, I carried it slowly to my Bosom, unpinn'd my Handkerchief, and placed his Hand betwixt the swelling Hillocks of my Breasts.

"There," says I, " 'tis nothing to be afraid of."

Again he drew his Hand away, but methinks he linger'd a Moment first, savouring the Heat betwixt those twin Globes.

Encouraged by this slight Hesitation (which truly, I told myself, I did not fancy so much as feel), I took his Hand again—ah, 'twas not altogether unwilling!—and brought it 'neath my Petticoat and rested it upon my Thigh. There it linger'd for more than a Moment, then drew back, as from a fiery Furnace.

"Lancelot," said I, now much embolden'd by the Pow'r of Injur'd Vanity coupl'd with the mischievous Abandon a Woman feels when she knows she must play the Seducer to an unwilling Swain: "Lancelot, pray help me to undress for Bed."

"Nay, Fanny, 'tis not me Taste nor Style, I swear it. Ladies I revere fer their Wits, their Will, their Cleverness—ye may be sure I give the Sex its Due—but Lust I ne'er felt yet fer one o' the Female Kind. Don't take it to Heart, Lass. If I lov'd Women, I'd take ye to Wife as well as Bed. . . ."

"If you'll be not tempted, what Harm, then, in helping me undress the Way a Brother helps his Sister?"

"Nay, Fanny, I'll be goin' now. . . ."

But I held his Hand, so he could not depart.

"Pray, just this Boddice, help me to unlace it. I have no Chambermaid and I can't sleep like this."

Coming towards him, I bade him unlace my Boddice, the which he did, with extream Caution, as if the Touch of my Skin could Kill. As I felt the Stays loosen, I took his two Hands and brought them to cup my Breasts. Again, he linger'd longer than was needful, almost tempted by the melting Flesh, but then once more, his Fingers flew away like Birds, and I was left alone.

"Fanny, adieu, I go. Good Night. . . ."

Now I fell upon him and press'd my naked Bosom to his Chest. His silver Lace-embroider'd Waistcoat scratch'd my Breasts, but I continu'd and still he did not flee.

"Come, Lancelot," I said (with perhaps more Mischief than Passion), "since nought will come of it, pray, put me in my Bed."

"Nay, Fanny," he protested; but when I led him by the Hand, he follow'd.

I gradually undress'd; my Petticoat, my Shift, the loosen'd Stays—all were thrown upon the Floor. My red Garter I withdrew from my Thigh and placed tenderly 'neath the Pillows. Then I lay at length upon the Bed, and bade Lancelot sit by me and run his Hand along my Body, tracing ev'ry Hillock, ev'ry Plain.

"I cannot, Lass, truly I cannot." Nonetheless, I grabb'd his Hand again and drew it from my Knee upward along my Thigh, ling'ring betwixt my Legs, upward o'er my Belly to my Breasts, where now I tarried, asking that he taste what he had lately touch'd.

"Nay, Fanny," cries Lancelot in a Panick, "that I surely cannot do!"

"What?" says I, challenging those terrified green Eyes, that Mop of curly red Hair the Colour of my own, those Cheakbones like the Great God Pan himself. "What? Not afraid of Death, but afraid of these harmless Breasts? Afraid of this Softness when you are so hard already?"

And 'twas true; his Member-for-Cockshire (as the Saying goes) stood within his Breeches, outlining its own Shape in the silk Brocade. I was almost bold enough to reach within and convert that Merry Fellow to the Love of Females fore'er—when lo! the Door flew open and who should appear but Horatio! Quickly appraising the Situation, he screams,

162

"You bloody Blackguard!" Whereupon he falls upon Lancelot, tearing him from my Body and pulling him down to the Floor with a great Thud.

There now ensu'd such Screaming and Pummelling, so many Blows given and taken, that had anyone been passing by the Neighbourhood, he should certainly have suspected that a Murder was in progress! I wrapp'd my shiv'ring Self in the Eider-Down, and watch'd the Fray as the two Men tore at each other for my Sake, shouting Curses, twisting Arms quite out of their Sockets, beating each other with their Fists. Why the Merry Men were not arous'd I'll ne'er know—unless they had Experience with Lancelot's am'rous Proclivities!

"You rotten Swine!" scream'd Horatio. "You pretend to hate Women so as to creep into their Beds the faster! You and your Robin Hood Honour! You Mountebank! You Charlatan!"

"Ye damn'd Black Prince!" screams Lancelot. "Who says yer Arse is worth so bloody much that ye'll always keep me from it!"

"Yea! And I'll have your Ballocks as Dumplings in my Soup before I eat your thieving Cock!"

With that, Horatio falls upon him again, holding Lancelot immobile on the Floor, pummelling him about the Head and Neck till his Nose runs with ruby Blood and he seems, for a Moment, to be upon the Point of expiring. Then, before I understood just how, the Tide of the Battle turns and Lancelot is atop Horatio, pinning him to the Floor, and the two Men are clinging, for all the World more like Lovers than like Pugilists. Before my very Eyes I see Lancelot grind his Hips against Horatio's Hips, and Horatio at first resist, then succumb, and Lancelot undo his Breeches and stuff his flaming Member betwixt Horatio's Lips, and Horatio at first unwilling, grow more willing, swallowing the redden'd Member as if indeed he quite savour'd it, and then the Thrust and Parry as in a Duel, the Sighs, the Grunts, the Murmurs of "I dye," and Lancelot, like a great Fountain in some engraving of the Gardens of Versailles, shooting a Stream of white Foam high into the Air (his Cock having come unloos'd from Horatio's Lips) and then expiring upon the Floor in Weariness whilst Horatio strok'd his Back more in Love than in Fury.

They lay there for a Time, seeming to have forgotten my very Existence, and presently Lancelot crawl'd along the Floor to press his Lips to Horatio's Breech, and to tease his

Great Black Member into its own Fury of Lust, and to cradle it in his Mouth until it, too, discharged its Fusillade of Foam.

Then the two Men lay in each other's Arms, full of Sweat and the sticky Effusions of Love, whilst I rockt myself to sleep in my lonely Eider-Down, feeling myself to be older and uglier than Medusa herself, and more alone e'en than she.

I fell to sleep and dreamt of Lymeworth. I was walking thro' the Long Gallery, under the fram'd Portraits of Lord Bellars' Ancestors. My Heels echo'd upon the cold stone Floors. I lookt at the Portraits—Portraits of pale Elizabethan Ladies by William Larkin and Nicholas Hilliard, Portraits of Elegant Courtiers by Sir Anthony Van Dyck and Sir Peter Lely, Portraits of Great Ladies and Immortal Wits by Sir Godfrey Kneller—but lo! those familiar painted faces which I had studied and Day-dreamt o'er so oft' in my Youth were suddenly changed! I dreamt I saw Lord Bellars' own Face in one, and the Face of Isobel the Good Witch in another, and Lancelot himself, as if painted by Kneller's deft Brush, in still another—and then (could it be?) my own familiar Face staring down at me from a massive gilded Frame (as if I were—O strange to say!—my own Ancestor).

At once the Portraits seem'd to speak. "Forgive me," said Lord Bellars, "I did not know the Truth about your Birth." "I am with you yet," says Isobel, her blue Eyes flashing. "I love, but fear ye, Lass," says Lancelot. " 'Tis not yer Fault, but mine." And then at last my Portrait spoke, at first so softly that I could not hear the Words; but now I read the moving Lips of my own Image: "I forgive you all," I seem'd to say.

Suddenly I awaken'd, puzzl'd in the extream by the Visions I had seen, and yet with a great Sense of Peacefulness such as Dreams at Times provide when we are sorely troubl'd. I thought and thought, but could not puzzle out the Dream; still I had great Certitude that all would presently be well.

The two Men were gone from my Room; the Sun was rising, an orange Ball of Flame glinting thro' the verdant Branches outside my leaded Window. The Day was fine and sunny. I rose and dress'd almost eagerly and with a Degree of Hope I had not felt in many Days; ne'ertheless, I remember'd to put on my red Garter first, for Luck.

The Journey to London by River was as fright'ning as Lancelot had promis'd. But 'tis a curious Fact that actual Danger is less troublesome to the Mind than the Threat of

Danger, consider'd in Tranquillity, and indeed once we left the Mill Brook and enter'd the River Thames, I was so occupied with the Sights we pass'd (as the Men were occupied with Navigation of the Barge) that I was quite transfixt.

Our Route took many Days and Nights because of the sundry Locks we had to pass. We follow'd the River from Marlowe to Maidenhead to Windsor to Staines, thence to Walton-on-Thames, past Hampton Court, to Twickenham. I had ne'er before seen the fabl'd Hampton Court, nor e'en the mighty and beautiful River Thames, and my Eyes were quite amaz'd and delighted by the Beauty of the Banks, the Glory of innumerable Stately Buildings, Gentlemen's and Noblemen's Houses, sleepy Hamlets, bustling Market Towns and Villages, and withal the Profusion of Boats and Barges that grew more num'rous as we came closer to the great Metropolis.

Hampton Court lyes upon the North Bank of the Thames, close to the Water, yet not so close as to run the Risque of Flood in inclement Weather, and 'tis graced with lovely Gardens extending almost to the Bank of the River. Yet it seems to me that, more e'en than the pleasing Prospect of the Palace, I was taken up with Reveries of the Court of that wicked King Henry VIII, floating up to London in great Pleasure Barges, whilst Minstrels sang and play'd their Lutes, and that I fancied myself a Tudor Lady (with a Ruff about my Neck and a Dress studded with Pearls) chosen to be the King's Mistress and i'faith so well-lov'd by him that he would ne'er behead me as he did those unfortunate others. O I would charm e'en Henry VIII—I who had slept alone whilst two Men clung and kiss'd 'neath my lonely Bed!

We pass'd Twickenham next (and I made a terrible Face towards what I believ'd to be the Villa of Mr. Alexander Pope, Poet and Knave). I could be there as his Mistress at this very Instant, basking in his reflected Glory, enjoying his Faery Grotto! But then I would have to endure his loathsome, Toad-like Embraces into the Bargain! 'Twas better to be here with Lancelot, who was fair to look at, and must, i'faith, love me, tho', alas, he would not touch me!

As we came closer and closer to the Great City of London, my Heart beat faster and faster; and, in truth, 'twas easy enough to tell we were approaching the Metropolis, for the Thames became a Sea of Masts, and the whole Surface of the River was cover'd with Barges, Wherries, Boats of divers Sizes, with grizzly old Tritons rowing, and shouts of "Next

Oars!" and "Skullers!" echoing in our Ears, and such a Volley of Bad Language from the Boatmen that 'twas amazing my Ears did not turn red for Shame owing to the Indignities that enter'd there! Whoe'er would ride in a hir'd Barge had no Choyce but to submit to the Language of the Rogues who rul'd the River, and I o'erheard many Arguments about Rates betwixt the Watermen and their "Bargees"—and not once but sev'ral Times did my Ears hear a Waterman shout, "Ye niggardly Sons of Bitches!" as he attempted to o'erturn his Customers into the Water because they refus'd sufficiently to grease his Palm.

What a Place was this London! The River was apparently the main Thoroughfare of the City and many substantial Citizens sat at their Ease upon Cushions in hir'd Boats whilst their rough and grizzl'd Boatmen row'd 'em skillfully, but grievously assaulted their Ears and Senses by the Curses they exchanged with their Brethren—if not, i'faith, with their Prey. There were also Picknicks and Pleasure Parties upon the River, gorgeous Barges fill'd with Fiddlers, Lutanists and Sweet Singers, Feast Tables and Bow'rs, and Fine Ladies and Gents to partake of all this Delectable Fare. As we pass'd Whitehall, my Eyes spy'd what seem'd a fine Noble Edifice, which lookt to me like a Faery Castle pois'd upon the very Surface of the River.

"Pray, what is that?" I askt Lancelot, who wore his Maltster's Disguise, as he wore everything else—with a Swagger.

" 'Tis the *Folly*, Fanny, me Love. Once, in the Time o' Charles II, t'was the Noble Resort o' Gentry, but now, 'tis a floatin' Bawdy House an' the Lair o' Ladies o' the Town who drink Burnt Brandy (they *say* to defend their Stomachs from the Chill Air upon the Water) an' lye in wait fer such poor Cunny-haunted Fellows as they can infect with the Pox. Fortunately, that ne'er included meself."

"Then how do you know so much of it, Lancelot, my Love?" I askt. O I was beginning to wonder whether the Gentleman did not protest too much—as our own Mr. Shakespeare might say. If he truly detested Women, as he claim'd, why did he bluster of it so continually?

He eyed me coldly. "Because I have been there in the Way o' Business, pickin' their whorin' Pockets!"

I lookt at him steadily—his Hair of Carrot Hue, his merry slanted Eyes of emerald green, his high and laughing Cheaks.

"Lancelot, I do love thee, tho' it be only as a Sister loves a Brother."

166

"An' I love thee, Fanny," says he.

Then in a true Fit of tender Affection, I reach'd to clasp his Hand, whereupon he drew it away with as great Dispatch as e'er. I sigh'd profoundly.

" 'Tis not fer Lack o' Love," says he.

"I know," says I. But did I truly know?

Ah, Belinda, Memory e'er falsifies the Facts, and thus to tell the History of one's Life is e'er a perilous Business. One wishes Fidelity to Truth above all. And yet, knowing the Issue of Events, (of which one could not know the Issue when first they occurr'd), one tends to shape the Story with a Poet's rather than a sober Historian's Eye. But let me give away no more than that. I lov'd Lancelot and he me—and yet we could not touch!

Now we came closer to the throbbing Heart of the Town, and the Traffick upon the River thicken'd. Lancelot began to point out to me the chief Attractions of wond'rous London. O I could not have been more amaz'd if I had lookt on Troy itself or Rome in all its Glory! We pass'd Lambeth House on one side of the River and presently the Parliament Stairs and the Wool Staple upon the other. Proceeding along the Curve of the River, we came at length to the New Exchange, Somerset House, and the Inner Temple. London seem'd a Faery Land to me! The Day was summery and bright; the Sun glinted upon the River, catching, it seem'd, hundreds of tiny Mirrors; and ne'er before had I seen such enormous Structures, such clamorous Crowds of People as fill'd the Boats and Wherries on the River and press'd down the Stairs and Quays lining it!

"O I shall love London!" I cried to Lancelot like one newly fallen in Love. What a splendid City! Why, merely to breathe the Air was to sense an Excitement I had ne'er known in Wiltshire.

"Ah, Lass, wait until ye see the Gin-soakt Rabble, the Beggars, the Sewage in the Streets, an' the muddy Current o' the Fleet Ditch!"

"Pray, what is that?"

" 'Tis the Sewer o' Sewers, London's own River Styx, a fetid, black Stream that rises in Hampstead an' pours its Offal into the Thames at Blackfriars. We'll soon come to it. Pray lookee there, 'tis the Dome o' St. Paul's."

But alas, 'twas not to be my Fate just then to feast my Eyes upon St. Paul's nor to disgust them with the Sight of the Fleet Ditch, for e'en as Lancelot spoke, a Barge came stealthily up beside our own, and suddenly a Parcel of Scurvy Rogues (dress'd as if they were Watermen) boarded us in a trice, screaming for the Blood of Lancelot Robinson!

There were a dozen Rogues in all, grizzl'd Fellows in baggy Bargemen's Trowsers, sweaty Shirts and short-skirted Doublets, with, as well, strip'd Stocking Caps o'er their bald Noodles. Who had sent them? How did they know Lancelot's Disguise? I duckt behind a Barrel of Swag, fearing for my very Life and Limb. O they had come so suddenly that scarce one of us was prepar'd. Yet Horatio was the first to rouse himself to Action. Pyrate that he was, he leapt upon the Foe and wrestl'd one Rogue to the Ground, whereupon he stomp'd him with his Feet. He crackt another's Head with Pistol Butt, and another he engaged in Wrestling, but our belovèd Lancelot was yet in Peril. He was the Prize they sought—he and the Booty. He was the Leg o' Mutton they hunger'd for; the Rest of us were merely Gravy.

Presently the other Merry Men came to their Senses and also began to engage the Rogues in Combat. A Mêlée ensu'd in which poor Sotwit was the first to perish; for he dy'd a watery Death in the Thames after being hit with Musket Fire. And poor Beau Monde was stabb'd, whilst Thunder's Head was dasht against the Barge. My Sweet Lancelot held the Foe valiantly off for a Time; still there came a Moment when he seem'd to weaken (tho' Horatio defended him most fiercely).

"Flee!" he commanded me in the Thick of Battle. "Flee! I'll send for thee!"

"But where shall I flee? Whither shall I go?"

"Jump Ship, Lass," cried Lancelot, "but flee!"

Given this Command, I froze as if my Feet were planted in the Arctick Snows.

"Flee!" he cried again, holding off the Rogues with Good Horatio's Help.

Just then, John Littlehat commandeer'd a nearby Boat, press'd Coins into the Boatman's Hand, said something in his Ear, then took me bodily by my Waist and lifted me across the Water to the hir'd Oars.

"I would not leave thee!" I whimper'd as the Boatman row'd away. "I love thee! O I love thee!" But the Boatman had his Orders and, despite my Pleas and Protestations, he row'd e'er faster. Screams reach'd me from Lancelot's Barge. Now Mr. Twitch was hit and bleeding, then presently he toppl'd backward into the Thames, trailing a Scarf of Blood.

Now Puck and Francis Bacon were thrown o'erboard and made Haste to swim for Shore. As my Boat row'd away, I saw Lancelot and Horatio standing yet upon the Prow of the Barge, defending their Booty, and their Lives—but how long they should hold out, no sane Body could fairly conjecture.

"God's Speed! I love thee!" I shouted to the Figure of Lancelot, which grew e'er smaller as my Boatman row'd swiftly towards the Somerset Stairs (which we had pass'd not long before). I could see two other Barges with fresh Replacements of the Enemy row up alongside Lancelot's Barge and essay to board. My Heart sank in my Bosom like a heavy Stone falling from the Top of a Belfry. O Lancelot was sure to be captur'd now! I hid my Face in my Hands and wept— for e'en if I were to look back, we were i'faith too far away for me to judge the Victor in the Battle that still raged betwixt Lancelot and his Betrayers upon the Watery Highway of the Thames.

BOOK II

Chapter I

In which our Heroine first makes an intimate Acquaintance with the Great City of London, and what befell her upon her historick Arrival there.

PLUNGED THUS WITHOUT WARNING into the very Heart of London, I wander'd lost and lonely past Somerset House, into the Strand, and thence to Covent Garden—tho' I scarce knew their Names then.

The Town assaulted me with its Cries and Smells. The Streets were ill-pav'd and filthy with Offal of ev'ry sort. In the Kennels which ran down the mucky Centres of the Streets, one saw Fish Heads, Orange Rinds, Human Wastes—e'en dead Cats! The Air above was as smoky here as it had been fresh and clear upon the River; and one hardly dar'd look up o'erhead at the Profusion of creaking Sign Boards, hung upon ornamental iron Brackets, which sway'd in the Wind like hang'd Men, and obstructed whate'er Light and Air there might be, especially upon the narrowest Streets. But the Sign Boards were beautiful when one did catch a Glimpse of 'em. The Vintner's was painted with rich purple Grapes; the Peruke Maker's Sign show'd his most elegant Wares all in a Row (as if set out upon Blocks); the Draper's Sign show'd his richest Silks, and the Shops themselves were of such surpassing Splendour that they seem'd more like lofty Palaces than low Places of Commerce. Fine Ladies stepp'd out of Sedan Chairs to be greeted by bowing and cringing Shop Clerks who gave themselves the Airs of Princes. Why e'en the Footmen in London outshone the Country Gentlemen at Home!

Chairs, Horsemen, and Hackney Coaches jostl'd for place in the Streets, and the poor Pedestrian darted where'er he could. "Make way there!" the Chairmen cried, carrying their noble Passengers above the clamouring Throng. "Stand up there, ye blind Dog!" the Fruit Peddlars would scream, as they pusht their heap'd Barrows of Fruit, halo'd with Flies. "Will ye have yer Guts squeez'd out?" others growl'd, pushing their Carts or Barrows with such Roughness that one verily believ'd they had no fonder Wish than to mow one down.

I took the Wall in fear for my very Life, but now and again a Bully came along, brandishing a Silver-hilted Sword, shouting, "Turn out there, you Country Bumpkin!"—and made me yield it. O did I still look so countrified and coarse? I suppos'd I must. I had my Masculine Attire from my earlier Travels, together with some purloin'd Finery given me by Lancelot, but my Hat had fallen in the Thames whilst I escap'd, and my Riding Wig was in so sorry a State that it could hardly be redeem'd by the finest Barber in the Land. My Boots were muddy and scrap'd, my Breeches dirty, my Linen soil'd.

I had some Coins in my Pocket—some of the original Guineas given me by Mr. Pope (and restor'd to me by Lancelot before our Journey)—and likewise a few gold Watches and a jewel'd Snuff-Box from the Store of Stolen Booty. "Take 'em," Lancelot had said. "Who knows but they may come in useful if we are e'er parted on the Way. . . ." What prophetick Words these now seem'd! Was it e'er my Fate to lose my Friends and be left alone? Under what wretchèd Star had I been born only to be orphan'd and orphan'd again?

The Street Cries amaz'd me; I had ne'er heard such a Profusion of Cries. My Ears were assaulted at ev'ry Turning, and 'twas not always easy to make out what they said, for this London Speech was odd indeed and not simple to comprehend like good plain Wiltshire Speech.

"Crab, Crab, any Crab!" shouted a Fishmonger, brandishing his many-leggèd Wares, as if to threaten the Young Maidens with their wriggling Limbs. Wenches fled in Terror at the very Sight. "A brass Pott, or an iron Pott to mend?" croakt a Tinker, pushing his Cart clatt'ring with old Iron Cookery Potts. "Buy my Dish of great Eeles!" sang a robust Country Woman, her Cheaks red with Veins that had once burst from the Cold but remain'd Scarlet as e'er despite the Sweat that stood in Beads upon her Face this Summer's Day. She carried a large flat Basket of wriggling Eeles upon her Head like a Peasant Medusa. "Sixpence a Pound fair Cher-

174

ryes!" cried a pretty buxom Maid, flirting and showing her ruby Fruits to two Swains who, 'twas plain, would rather toy with her than with her luscious Wares. "Old Satten, old Taffety or Velvet!" shouted the poor old Ragman, pushing his Barrow of dirty Muslin and torn Linen, and wearing no less than a half-dozen greasy old Hats upon his bow'd Head. "Fair Lemons and Oranges!" sang an Orange Girl, who kept a Bottle of Gin in her Apron Pocket and drank when she thought no one was watching. "A Merry New Song!" cried the Ballad Peddlar, a Sheaf of Papers in his grubby Hand. "Remember the Poor Prisoners!" came the mournful Cry of a Wretch shaking an earthen Pott full of Pennies. At this Lament, I was reminded of Lancelot's Fate—for surely he was dead or in Gaol by now—and Tears ran down my dirty Cheaks and slid into the Corners of my Mouth.

What a cruel Place this London was! First I saw a poor Chimney Sweep boxt upon the Ears by his Master for nothing more than a Jest; then, I saw a Blind Beggar kickt in the Guts by a Person of Quality who would rather doubt his Affliction than show him the slightest Christian Charity!

"Why, the Rogue sees better than I do!" cried the puff'd-up Punk in silver Lace and red Satten, whereupon he kickt the Beggar with his pointed Shoe, then straightaway disappear'd into a Chocolate House to greet his Cronies.

The huge Stream of Humanity, which flow'd thro' the Streets without ceasing, was predominantly compos'd of the Poor and Wretchèd. For ev'ry Fine Gentlewoman in her Chair and ev'ry Liveried Footmen dress'd like an Oriental Potentate, there were a dozen destitute Wretches guzzling Gin, maim'd Children begging for Pennies, and Ladies of the Town, preening upon Street Corners and showing their blowzy Breasts for all to see. I'faith, I shall ne'er forget the pockmarkt painted Faces that seem'd to mock me as I walkt the ancient long and narrow Road leading to Covent Garden—(where, indeed, my Country Gentleman's Attire seem'd to make me Fair Prey for all the Bawds and Trollops on the Street).

"Will ye have a Bit o' Mutton?" whisper'd one Tart, leering at me with Eyes rolling in a painted Face. Alas, she was more terrible than she was appealing. She had daub'd her Complexion—if such it could be call'd—with white Lead, upon which her Cheaks were painted carmine, her Lips crim-

175

son, and she had sought to cover her Pockmarks with so many Patches of various Shapes and Sizes that she seem'd more like a Plum Pudding than a Woman.

I shrank back in Terror from this Apparition.

"What? Is the Lad afear'd?" she mockt, whereupon she el-bow'd her Sister Strumpet—another ghastly Apparition half-hid in Paint and Patch—and bade *her* essay to tempt me since she herself could not.

"Won't ye have a Nestlecock?" cries the second Tart, "a Climber fer yer Pole, a Pretty Dear, a Naughty Dickey Bird, a Needlewoman fer yer e'er-lovin' Needle?"

I bow'd my Head to the fetid and uneven Cobblestones and walkt away as quickly as my Legs would carry me.

"Afear'd! Afear'd!" they mockt me from behind. "We ought to drag ye Home an' ravish ye!" the first Blowzalinda said. "What Sport that would be!" her sister Blowzabella chim'd, whereupon a Volley of cackling Laughter echo'd thro' the Alley. I did not stop to think at all then, but ran as fast as I could to the next Corner, thinking all the while how mournful if I really *were* a Country Lad and were mockt thus by these Awful Apparitions. I'faith, 'twould turn me off the Love of Ladies fore'ermore.

I ran until I reach'd the Corner of a nearby Street where two pretty Ballad Singers, dress'd like a country Bride and Bridegroom stood, singing their Hearts out. 'Twas such a pretty Air—and one I had ne'er heard before—that I stopp'd to listen, healing my Ears with the Sweet Musick, and think-ing that London was not so bad after all if it could have such Sweet Singers in it, plying their Trade, and such attentive Lis-teners who stood as if transfixt by the Divine Pow'r of Musick.

The Singers were a Boy and a Girl hardly above my own Age. She a tender, flaxen-hair'd Maiden with the bluest, most angelick Eyes, and he swarthy as the Night, but with a healthy olive Complexion and withal a Brow of such Inno-cence as to make Nuns or confirm'd Spinsters throw away their Vows of Chastity and fall hopelessly in Love. They sang of Spring and budding Branches, of Birds, Wildflow'rs, and Young Love; and i'faith, they so resembl'd their Song that it seem'd more than a mere Ballad—but the very History of their Love.

The Crowds jostl'd and press'd against me and the Stream

176

of Humanity ne'er stopp'd flowing at the outer Borders of our Magick Circle; but here within it, the Crowd was still'd and reverent, transform'd and gentl'd by the Song they heard.

How long we may have stood thus I cannot say, but for myself, I would have stood for as long as the two Sweet Singers sang, had not a dark Thunder Cloud cross'd the golden Face of the Sun and a sudden Summer Show'r begun.

The Listeners fled in all Directions as the Heavens open'd up and the Gutter-Spouts began to pour with Rain, sending their Streams not quite clear of the Pavement. Draggl'd Ladies, holding up their Petticoats, ran for Shelter in the nearby Shops. Beaux fretting lest their Wigs be soakt and their Brocades spotted, did likewise. All Gallantry was forgotten in the Rush for Cover, and I e'en saw one Swain filch the oil'd Umbrella of a Sempstress, slapping her Bottom thro' her Petticoats and crying impudently, "Thankee kindly, Ma'am!" as he ran away. For my own poor Self, my dirty Clothes were nearly soakt by the Heaviness of the Show'r, and I duckt into a Baker's Shop for Cover.

What a glorious Shop 'twas! The Cases neatly gilt, the Buns winking their sugar'd Tops at me, the luscious Cakes and Breads making my Mouth water and reminding me how neglected was my poor empty Stomach. 'Twas only when I reach'd into my Pocket for a Guinea (to buy a Bag of sugar'd Buns) that I discover'd it empty! The Guineas were gone and the Watches and the Snuff-Box, too! Had my Pocket been pickt whilst the Singers held me in their Thrall? No doubt, for I was so Innocent then of London Ways that I did not know that Ballad Singers and Cut-Purses were oft' in league with one another.

A Squab-fat Lady of at least fifty, who had also taken Shelter here, saw my Distress, devour'd me with her Eyes, apprais'd my Plight and, handing me a Bun she had bought for herself, said, "Pretty Boy, will you eat my Bun?"

I hesitated, looking the Lady o'er. She wore a garnet velvet Cloak—despite the Warmth of the Weather—and a Commode that surmounted her hennaed Hair, which fell in Curls o'er her furrow'd Forehead. She smil'd seductively, as if to allay my Fears of taking the proffer'd Bun; but two harsh Lines—or, more properly speaking, Furrows—betwixt her Eyebrows gave her a Hawk-eyed Look that put me upon my Guard. Her Eyes were cold; they calculated my Worth and found it wanting.

"Pretty Boy," she said again, "pray, take this as a Christian Gift. It seems some scurvy Rogue hath pickt your Pocket. Pray, eat. 'Twill give me greatest Joy."

My stomach argu'd with my Judgement, and, alas, the Former won.

"Thank you kindly, Ma'am," said I. "But I should like to pay you back when I have recover'd my Fortune."

She laugh'd heartily. "Then pay me back by escorting me to my Home when the Show'r is past. 'Twill pay the Debt most graciously."

The Show'r soon being over, she invited me again, bidding me take her fat Arm; and feeling I could not refuse (for after all, I had eaten her Bun), I did as I was told.

She led me presently to a House in Park Place, St. James', which was so elegant and handsomely furnish'd that I deem'd her a great Lady of Fortune. I remember a wide Staircase (wide enough to accommodate two abreast—a Rarity indeed in Town Houses during the early Part of the Century), beautifully carv'd Wainscotting of Oak, and the newest Wall Paper in the Manner of flower'd Damask.

She told me her Name was Mrs. Coxtart and that she was a widow'd Lady of Means with sev'ral Daughters, and that furthermore she should be pleas'd if I would join them all for Tea, which was the great Diversion of their Day.

I thought nothing amiss here, until I saw the Daughters—or three of 'em at any Rate—for they lookt so unlike each other that 'twas hard to believe they were Sisters.

Druscilla was dark with the whitest of Skin; Evelina seem'd a Creole girl or an Octoroon; and Kate, plain Kate, was as fair and blond as any Swede.

We sat down to Tea, serv'd by a Butler and a Mulatto Maid, and presented in the most gorgeous Chinese Tea Dishes of canary Glaze.

Mrs. Coxtart chatter'd on, speaking of Balls and Assemblies, the fine Equipage she had order'd, the Servants she would soon be adding to her Ménage—as if indeed she were trying to impress me with her Wealth and Station. Did she see me as a potential Suitor for her Daughters? 'Twas most curious to me, for something was a bit amiss about her Chatt'ring. She did not seem like a Lady of Quality with all her boastful Talk, and i'faith her Daughters titter'd behind their Fans in a most disrespectful Fashion, and said nothing

178

but "If you please" and "Thank you," as they pass'd the Dishes of Bohea Tea, the Sugar Bowl, the Cakes, Buns, and Sugar Plums. Moreo'er, I could scarce prevent my Eyes from seeing that all three of 'em lookt Goats and Monkies at me (as did their Mother) and they flirted quite shamelessly, leering o'er their painted Fans (which had shockingly lewd Pictures on 'em), thrusting forward their Bosoms as they pass'd the Cakes, as well as titt'ring, darting meaningful Looks at each other, and, in short, behaving more like Tarts than Ladies.

Druscilla, I recall, devour'd ev'ry last Cake and Sugar Bun, whereupon Evelina, who, all the while, had pouted at her Sister in Annoyance (perhaps she wisht to polish off the Buns herself), now proceeded to eat the remaining Sugar with her Teaspoon—as if in spite. Kate, for her part, dispatch'd the leftover Butter with her Fingers, whilst Mrs. Coxtart stirr'd the Tea Leaves with her Fork, and call'd loudly for more hot Water from the Pantry whilst she blithely spear'd the last remaining Sugar Plum upon the End of her Knife. Could these be Ladies? Their House and Servants seem'd to speak in their Favour, but their Manners (if such they could be call'd) spoke against.

When the Tea was quite finish'd and the Butler was clearing away the Dishes, Mrs. Coxtart privily gave some Sign to her Daughters, whereupon they all rose as one and, with coy Looks, nodded in the Direction of the Stair.

"Will my Fine Gentleman partake of our Afternoon Nap with us?" she askt. Druscilla leer'd peculiarly and Evelina pointed up the Stair with her Fan whilst Kate was lifting her Petticoat far above her Ankles to show a Pair of well-turn'd Legs in red silk Stockings, and at the same Time, she was plainly winking at me.

"Thank you kindly," I said, "but I must be off."

"And where will ye go with yer Money stolen, Lad? Come now. 'Tis best to do as we say."

"No, Ma'am, but thank you kindly," says I.

"Not so fast, Lad," says she, whereupon she grabs me firmly by the right Arm whilst the Butler (who has lately reappear'd) commandeers the Left and I am half dragg'd, half lifted up the Stair, whilst the three Daughters lead the Way gesturing wantonly as e'er before.

I am carried into a great Bedchamber, hung with red Damask, and with a fine Fire roaring in the Hearth, behind an iron Fire-Screen wrought with Bas-Reliefs of naked Nymphs, and a carv'd oak Bedstead no less than seven foot broad and ten foot high, and fairly festoon'd with red Damask, as well as Tassels of Silver and Gold.

I am thrown rudely upon the Bed, my Mouth smother'd with Kisses by the Raven-hair'd Druscilla, who also unlooses her Stays and drops one by one her small uptilted Breasts with their piquant Nipples into my waiting Mouth. Meanwhile, Mrs. Coxtart and the other Daughters are lewdly dancing and disrobing—as if indeed they were Grecian Bacchantes.

Mrs. Coxtart throws off her Boddice, Stays, Petticoat, and e'en Linen to show an awesome Body made of Breasts that reach fair to the Navel, a Belly flaccid as that of an old Spaniel Bitch bred twice yearly, and Legs so cover'd with broken Veins that they might be Barbers' Poles. Kate, with her blond Hair and ivory Skin, resembles a Statue carv'd in palest Marble, whilst Evelina, with her honey'd Skin and ringleted molasses Hair seem'd a Vision from a Book of Imaginary Voyages to Undiscover'd Tropick Isles.

The Butler stood at the Door, as if to guard it, but he had position'd himself to watch the Play as well, and 'twas plain he'd not be cheated of his Afternoon's Amusement.

Now Mrs. Coxtart, Evelina, and Kate leapt upon the Bed and began to pull off my Clothes whilst Druscilla teaz'd my Mouth with her pert Breasts. The Butler's Eyes widen'd and one Hand wander'd deep within his Breech.

Surely I was ruin'd once they discover'd my Disguise! What horrible Things would they do to me when they found out (as they presently must) that I was but a Lass and could not satisfy their sundry Lusts?

Slowly, they remov'd my Boots, strok'd my Legs, e'en suckt my sweaty Toes (which, strangely, sent a potent Fire coursing thro' my Veins). Next, they pull'd off my Breeches but not my Linen yet, and whilst Mrs. Coxtart made fair to straddle my Body with her huge Legs and let her loathsome Self down upon what she hop'd was an upright Cock, Druscilla remov'd the very last Barrier standing betwixt her Dream of my Masculinity and the Truth of my Femininity—namely my Linen—whereupon she gave out a

180

Scream like one who hath fallen amongst Thieves, and cried:
" 'Tis a Wench! By God! 'Tis a Wench!"

At once they all stopp'd their Gyrations, Mrs. Coxtart
fairly dismounted me, and e'en the Butler drew near to see
this prodigious Wonder—a Wench dress'd in her Brother's
Clothes!

"Sly Wench," whispers Mrs. Coxtart, and yet she seems not
put off by the News of my Sex, for she still stands upon her
fat Knees above me on the Bed, fondling her own dark
Nipples with one Hand and laying bare my Breasts with the
other. There are many Oohs and Ahhs of Admiration as the
Ladies (and one Gentleman) expose my entire naked Form,
unbind my Hair, cast away my Clothes, and begin to pay Attention—all five of 'em!—to sundry Parts of my Anatomy.
(By the by, Belinda, you may be wond'ring what became of
the tell-tale Witches' Garter. 'Twas still upon my Leg, but in
their rapacious Lust, my five Seducers paid not one Whit of
Attention to it!)

Mrs. Coxtart usurps from Druscilla the Care of my first
Orifice, stuffing her enormous Dugs into my Mouth and
indeed almost choking me with those pendulous Promontories
of Flesh. At the same Time, the three Graces (for so I had
begun to think of 'em), paid particular Homage to my
Thighs and Belly, and, of course, the chief Attraction which
lay betwixt 'em. Kate fell to her Knees and teaz'd my Cunny
with her Tongue, finding the most Inflaming Spot quite readily. Druscilla strok'd my Thighs, whilst Evelina made fair to
fondle my Breasts, now tweaking my Nipples with her delicate Fingers, now wetting 'em with her warm, slick Tongue.
The Butler, for his part, suckt upon my Toes, as if, indeed
(being just a Servant), he were wary of ascending any
higher!

Ne'er had all my Senses been more inflam'd! These
Nymphs were as skill'd at the Business of spreading Fire as
an invading Army—but could they put it out? My Heart pal-
pitated in my Breast, my Breath came short and in the most
rapid Gasps, and my Thighs strove to close around that Head
whose Tongue provok'd 'em to this Frenzy.

Seeing me so near the critical Ecstacy, Mrs. Coxtart withdrew her Attentions from my Mouth, and extracted from
beneath the Pillows a curious ivory Object shap'd like a Masculine Member (but, i'faith, twelve Inches long and thick as a

clench'd Fist). 'Twas carv'd with strange entwining Figures, diminutive Men and Ladies engaging in the lewdest Practices, and verily its Size fill'd me with both Terror and Lust—for I fear'd 'twas intended for me!

Whilst the Butler and two Graces firmly held apart my Thighs (and whilst Druscilla toy'd with my Breasts), Mrs. Coxtart knelt beside me on her monstrous Knees, parted the ruby Lips of my tender Sex, and fairly thrust the whole carv'd ivory Gewgaw into my Pudendum, burying the devilish Thing quite up to its devilish Hilt! O I cried aloud with both Pain and Pleasure as she did so, and Tears ran out of the Corners of my Eyes. Druscilla lickt 'em with her Tongue (indeed, lickt my Eyelids, Lips, Nipples, e'en my Navel) whilst Mrs. Coxtart, grinning like the very Devil (and smacking her Lips in Lust and Mischief), thrust the ivory Cock again and again into my Cunny, until I was so inflam'd with Pain and Pleasure that I cried out sharply, whilst my Sex contracted like a beating Heart and finally spent its Contractions in an Excess of Pleasure. At last, I dissolv'd into that melting Flow which Nature hath design'd for the Senses' Recov'ry of themselves.

Nor was Mrs. Coxtart content to stop here. Nay, she must now repeat the Endeavour, teazing my most sensitive Spot with her Tongue and taking me again twice more, then thrice, until I was so weak with Pleasure (and my Cunnicle was so sore) that I could do nought but whimper in her Arms at last.

Truly that pleas'd her, for seeing my compleat Submission, she was well-satisfied and now she fell to the Satisfaction of her own Lusts, bidding the Butler to service her huge greasy Nether Orifice whilst her "Daughters" (indeed, I scarce believ'd 'em such any longer) paid particular Attentions to her Dugs, her Nipples, and her bulbous painted Lips.

The Butler had a Batt'ring-Piece—for truly one could call it nought but that—that was not long but extreamly stubby and thick, and indeed Mrs. Coxtart was quite acquainted with it, for she call'd it by a pet Name ("Cockshort" or e'en "Master Shorty") and seem'd oft' to have avail'd herself of it in the Past. She pull'd him down upon her on the Bed, clasping his thin Form to her fat one, manoeuvering his Body this Way and that for her own Pleasure whilst the Bed shook like a Raft upon a Storm-toss'd Sea and the Nymphs left off

182

their Ministrations (indeed Mrs. Coxtart was too lost in her own Ecstacies now to notice 'em) and fell to mimicking her comick Grunts an Gyrations like Merry Andrews at a County Fair! O they were cruel in their Miming! But truly, she was an irresistible Subject for Satyre. Her Eyes bulged as she approach'd her Dye-Away Moment; her Thighs quiver'd; her Mouth slobber'd and she cried out, "O Mother of God!"

When she had had her Satisfaction of the Butler, she bade him roll off her, and she swiftly dispatch'd him to the Scullery again, whilst Druscilla, Kate, and Evelina all moan'd in Misery.

" 'Tis not fair! Not fair! You spent his Seed and left no Drop for us!"

" 'Tis Pity, Girls," says she, sarcastically, "but I'm the Mistress here and have my Rights. Pray, satisfy each other with this Toy!" And straightaway, tossing the great ivory Cock to Druscilla, and gath'ring up her fallen Finery, she waddles out of the Chamber in all her Nakedness and locks the Door behind her. I was so exhausted by then I could scarce move.

"Not fair," grumbles Druscilla, turning the ivory Cock in her Hand. (What a curious Toy it was! The Carvings were so placed as to give Pressure to Critical Spots as well as inflame the Eye, but Druscilla was not enticed by it.) "I like a nice warm Bushwhacker, not a nasty cold one!" she said.

"O do shut up, Dru," says Kate. "Ye know Mother Coxtart will ne'er share her belovèd Shorty. She'd see his Thingum-bob cut off first."

"It looks cut off already!" says Evelina, laughing wickedly. "O Hell, I've got the Cunny-Itch now. Who'll finish me?"

"Not I," says Druscilla.

"Not I," says Kate.

"Do it yerself, ye lazy Thing," says Dru. "Ev'ryone *else* does."

"What about the new Girl?" whispers Kate.

"I wouldn't risque me Neck," Druscilla whispers back. "She seems quite spent. What's more, Mother Coxtart would flog ye for it—at least until she's sold her Maidenhead."

"Maidenhead!" cries Kate. "Why e'en if she had one before, there cant' be much left now. The old Bag is daft. She's so mad to make the new Girls submit that she loses herself a fat Profit into the Bargain."

"She don't care," says Dru, "she can always use the Pigeon Blood and Sponge as she did with you and me. She wants to get their Blood inflam'd is all—to start 'em off."

"Well, she won't be havin' no Trouble with this one," says Evelina. "She's a hot one."

"Redheads always is," says Kate. "Blondes is cool."

"Hah!" says Dru. "That's a Load o' Shit!"

"Come on, Dru, finish me off! I did it fer you last Night," says Evelina.

"An' made me pay a Guinea for it, too, ye Blowzy Tart!"

" 'Tis force o' Habit," says Evelina. "Unless I charge fer it, I don't enjoy it none meself!"

"The Vixen!" says Druscilla. "Always quick with some new Impertinence! Well, I'll not scratch yer Itch again. I've better Uses fer me Fingers. Here—try this instead!"

Tho' I pretended to be asleep during this astonishing Conversation, and had my Eyes shut, I could not resist opening 'em a Crack to see what Druscilla was tossing to Evelina. 'Twas another curious Toy, a series of three ivory Eggs join'd by a red silken Cord.

"Here, stuff this in yer Crack to plug it up!" says Druscilla.

Whereupon Evelina loses no Time, but straightaway lyes down beside me on the Bed, flips up her Petticoat, spreads her Honey-colour'd Thighs, and stuffs the ivory Eggs—one, two, three, into her commodious Cunny. A red silk Cord dangles seductively from her Molasses-colour'd Nether Curls.

"Pray, what now, Dru?" cries Evelina.

"Clasp the silken Cord," says Dru, "and pull it up and down, but pray, take care to keep yer whorin' Thighs together or they'll all come out!"

From where I lay, with Eyes half open, I could see Evelina tugging on the silken Cord and squeezing her Thighs together whilst she moan'd and sigh'd in Ecstacy. Her Mouth was open, her Nipples harden'd until they pointed Heavenward, her Mop of Curls toss'd this Way, now that, as she tugg'd and squeez'd, squeez'd and tugg'd. At last, the Dye-Away Spasm seem'd upon her and, with a piercing Cry, she ceas'd her Motions and lay still.

"Pray, wash it ere ye give it back to me!" Druscilla cried, at which Kate laugh'd merrily whilst Evelina merely groan'd in reply.

Presently I heard the Door to the adjoining Chamber open and Dru and Kate retire therein whilst Evelina and I lay spent with sensual Passion in the huge oak Bed, each pretending to ignore the other, each feigning Sleep, until soon we did not have to feign, for Sleep engulf'd us like an Ocean Wave, and we both sail'd away.

Chapter II

Some Animadversions upon the Author of that Notorious Book, Memoirs of a Woman of Pleasure, *or,* Fanny Hill, *together with our Heroine's True and Compleat Recital of what really happen'd during her Initiation into Mother Coxtart's Brothel, her first Visit to a London Draper's, and a most astonishing Message from the Ghost of Robin Hood.*

THUS DID I PASS my first Day in Mother Coxtart's notorious Brothel. I fear that the World hath altogether a diff'rent Notion of my History from reading Mr. John Cleland's scandalous Book, *Memoirs of a Woman of Pleasure,* for which he stole my History, e'en my Christian Name; but being a Man, and a Man of very Eccentrick Understanding and Questionable Parts at that, he could not but sentimentalize my History, giving me an humble, unlearnt Country Childhood (with Parents conveniently carried off by the Pox) and claiming that I met Mother Coxtart (whom he calls Brown—thus confusing her with another venerable Abbess of the Day) at a Registry Office where I had supposedly gone to seek a Place as a Chambermaid.

The dastardly Mr. Cleland, seeking nothing but to repay his num'rous Debts by writing an Inflaming Book, and understanding almost nothing of the Thoughts and Sensations of the Fair Sex, fashion'd from my Life a nauseously sugar'd Tale (as studded with Inflaming Scenes as a Plum Pudding with brandied Fruits) about a poor Country Girl who comes to the City, quite inadvertently becomes a Whore, but nonetheless is faithful at Heart (if not at some lower Organ) to her belovèd Charles, and becomes an Honest Woman at the Last, concluding her Days in "the Bosom of Virtue" (as Mr. Cleland quaintly styles it).

That the Book was written by a credulous Man, not a

canny Woman, may easily be seen by the excessive Attention Mr. Cleland pays to the Description of the Masculine Organ, for which he hath more Terms than Lancelot Robinson hath Names for the Corresponding female one! Only a Man (and an indiff'rently-endow'd one at that) would dwell so interminably upon the Size and Endurance of sundry Peewees, Pillicocks, and Pricks—for a Woman hath better Things to do with her Reason and her Wit.

Be that as it may, I will soon have Occasion to tell you how I met Mr. Cleland and how the Blackguard came to steal my History. Suffice it for the Present to say that not one Whit of his "Memoirs" is true, save the Christian Name of the Heroine, the bare Fact of her having been driven to a Life of Whoredom for a Time, and certain Features (tho' scarcely all) of the physical Description of his "Fanny."

Her Hair he describes as "glossy Auburn"—which, I suppose, is not too far off the Mark (tho' my Hair was e're more red than brown). But "black Eyes" I ne'er had, nor was my Chin either cleft or pitted as he alleges, nor was I e'er in love with any Person nam'd Charles!

All the most Curious and Compelling Facts of my Life— my Travels with the Merry Men, my Introduction to the Craft of the Witches, my Studious and Learnèd Childhood at Lymeworth, my Love of Latin and English Authors, my Perplexing Meditations on Philosophy—he saw fit to ignore (for a Man can ne'er understand that a Woman may be a sometime Whore and yet love Latin!), and he made me out instead a perfect Ninny.

By Jove! I resent his pallid Portrait by which the World *thinks* it knows me. Innocent of London's Wicked Ways I may indeed have been when first he met me, but surely I was no simp'ring Idiot!

Alas, Belinda, most Men can only see us either as the Embodiment of Virtue or the Embodiment of Vice; either as Bluestockings or unlearnt Painted Whores; either as Trollops or as Spinsters; as Wives or Wantons; as Good Widows or Bad Witches. But try to tell 'em, as I have, that a Woman is made of Sweets and Bitters, that she is both Reason and Rump, both Wit and Wantonness—and you will butt your Head against a stone Wall! They'll have it one Way or the other! Be clever, if you must, and forfeit Reputation for Beauty and Sensuality, as well as all Pleasures of the Flesh. Or have your Pleasures and your Loves—and in their Minds you'll always be a Witless Whore!

(By the by, 'tis not quite so in France, where Women of Beauty and of Brains are not unknown, and oft' the greatest Courtesans have been renown'd for Learning as well as Liquorishness. But here in Merry England, where the Men, I fear, are all a little queer, 'twill never wash!)

But on with my Tale.

I found myself, then, a Prisoner in Mother Coxtart's West End Brothel, a Prisoner of my Poverty, her watchful Eye (and the Eyes of the Girls and the Butler as well). Of Druscilla, Kate, and the beauteous Evelina, you have already had a Taste; there were seven other Girls as well—altho' four of 'em were off in Buckinghamshire at a Private Revel and I was not to make their Acquaintance until later. Three more I met the following Day: Molly, Roxana, and Nell. Molly was very plump and blond, with a turn'd-up Nose and red Cheaks like a Milkmaid. Roxana was pale and dark and seem'd fore'er coughing in her Handkerchief. Nell was scrawny and plain, but as she was reputed to know devilish Tricks in Bed, she was much sought after nonetheless.

The first Morning I awoke in Bed beside Evelina. She was languid and lovely, and with her Honey-colour'd Skin, she put one in mind, as I have said, of Tropick Isles; I made bold to strike up an Acquaintance by enquiring of her Birthplace.

"Martinique, Sweetheart," she replies, rolling o'er sleepily in Bed, "an' I near caught me Death in London many a Time. The Weather here is *fierce*." She shiver'd as if to better make her Point. "What o' yer own pretty Self, Sweetheart?"

"Wiltshire."

"An' where's that?"

" 'Tis a Country to the West of here, methinks, but this being the first Time I am in London, and my Way here having been so curious and indirect, I cannot rightly say. . . ."

"Oh," says Evelina, quite bor'd with my Geography, and plainly not wishing to hear more of my Travels.

"What brings you here across the Seas?" I ask.

"A Man, *bien sûr*," says she. "A wretchèd Englishman that promis'd me a fine Career upon the Stage, a Coach an' Six, an' all me Heart's Desires. He left me quick enough."

"And what of your Career upon the Stage?"

"Poo," says she, "the Managers hire their Mistresses first, an' the Rôles fer Colour'd Wenches is few enough. A Touch o' the Tar Brush makes a Merry Mistress, but a starvin' Player. Most Girls play once or twice, hopin' to snare some

188

Duke fer their Keeper an' leave the Stage. 'Tis no Life fer a Lady."

"And what of this Life?"

"'Tis not so bad once ye learn to outwit the old Bitch. She's a sly one. She'll try to take yer Money fer yer Clothes an' Food before she'll let ye see a Penny. Ye must watch her like a Hawk. She keeps a little Book wherein she *says* she balances yer Keep 'gainst yer Take. Hah! Wait fer her to pay ye and ye'll starve in Hell! The Trick is to get paid *direct*—or have yer Swains put Clothin' on yer Back and Jewels 'round yer Neck. Then ye can fence 'em fer some Cash. Some Girls got Swains who give 'em South Sea Stock, or Bank o' England Notes, or East India Bonds. That's good, but fer me own Part I have a Swain who says he'll set me up. I'll soon be out o' here an' into Keepin', God help me."

I listen'd intently to all this good Advice, wond'ring if Evelina truly had a loyal Swain or if she was merely dreaming.

"An' one more Thing, Sweetheart, be mindful not to get with Child, fer the old Bitch will surely throw ye out an' on the Mercy o' the Parish. She'll no doubt try to sell yer Maidenhead—whether ye have one or not—because, bein' as yer a new Lass, she can claim ye fer a Virgin. She'll give ye Sea Sponge an' Pigeon Blood an' show ye how to stuff it in yer Privy Hole. It makes the Swains think yer a Virgin when ye bleed an' Mother Coxtart gets a double Fee. 'Tis droll. The Men who comes here is a learnèd Lot—Playwrights, Poets, Scribblers o' all Sorts—yet they ne'er suspect Mother Coxtart's false Virgins! She'll have ye play the Virgin half a dozen Times fer half a dozen Swains!

"Mark ye well, keep the Sponge (or buy another at the Apothecary) an' soak it in Vinegar an' put it in yer Privity before ye lay abed with any Man—'twill keep ye out o' the Family Way. By the by, Sweetheart, what's yer Name?"

"Fanny," said I, still marvelling at all she'd related.

"Mark me well, Fanny, Sweetheart, 'twill save yer Life someday."

Just then we hear a Key turn in the Lock, and who should appear but Mother Coxtart, dress'd in her Morning Finery, follow'd by a Chambermaid. The Chambermaid carried a Pitcher of Water and a Wash-Bowl, which she now placed upon the Washstand. Then she knelt at the side of the Bed, extracted the Chamber-Pott, took it to the Window, merrily toss'd its odiferous Contents out into the Street (with a Cry of "Gardy-loo!"), replaced it 'neath the Bed, and

189

presently began to lay a Fire in the Grate. Mother Coxtart also seem'd very hearty and hale after last Night's Debauch. 'Twas nothing short of astonishing how she'd corseted herself to make it appear she had a Shape! The Woman was a Sempstress' Triumph!

"And how be my Beauties?" she askt, coming to the Bedstead and peering down at us with her Hawk Eyes. "Now then, out of Bed with ye, ye lazy Tartlets! There's Breakfast in the Parlour and I'll be wantin' the new Girl—what's yer Name, Lass?"

"Fanny, Ma'am."

"I'll be wantin' Fanny for a visit to the Draper's and the Sempstress. Now, out of Bed with ye!"

Whilst Evelina had her Turn at the Chamber-Pott and the Wash-Bowl, I was made to stand naked as the Day of my Nativity in the Centre of the Bedchamber (shiv'ring, you may be sure) so as to enable Mother Coxtart to examine my Body carefully and to take my Measure with a Tape which she extracted from her Apron. 'Twas so cold in the Chamber (despite the Fire just starting) that my Nipples stood up, and my Skin seem'd as pucker'd and bump'd as a pluckt Chicken's; and indeed, it seem'd that Mother Coxtart was examining me as much for her own lustful Delectation (and for my continu'd Submission) as to truly take my Measure (for could not the Sempstress measure me as well?). She tweakt my Nipples, pok'd a Finger in my Navel, e'en thrust two Fingers into my Privity (she *said* to test my Virginity—but after last Night's Am'rous Play—what Resistance might she hope to find?). I had not disburden'd my Bladder since the previous Night and when she so rudely thrust her Fingers in my Privy Place, I fear'd I might piss upon the Floor, and then my Degradation would be compleat! With much Travail, I held back, biting my lower Lip until it fairly bled.

"I trust the Lass is not with Child," said Mother Coxtart coldly.

"O no," says I, in fear now to be thrown out in the Streets, but her Cold Question set my Mind racing wildly—for 'twas just possible, tho' not likely, that I might have conceiv'd a Child by Lord Bellars. "Goddess preserve me," I whisper'd 'neath my Breath.

"What's that?" says Mother Coxtart.

"I am a Virgin but for thee," I ly'd (with such Readiness, I astonish'd e'en myself).

Mother Coxtart lookt at me quizzically.

190

"I saw no Blood upon the Sheet last Night," says she. "Come now, Fanny, 'twill do no good to lye, for I can find you out quite soon enough."

"Yes, Ma'am," I said, thinking quickly, "but from earliest Youth, I have been a Horsewoman, riding astride like any Man. I'faith, my belovèd Stallion, Lustre, was stolen from me at a Country Inn as I was riding up to London. . . ."

"A likely Story!" Mother Coxtart said, snappishly. "Come, Girls, I'll expect you in the Parlour before long." And she swept out of the Room like the Queen of France, with the Chambermaid following her.

The Chambermaid had gather'd up my fallen Clothes from the Night before, and pil'd 'em upon a Chair. Suddenly missing my lucky red Garter, I search'd for it in the Pile, but 'twas nowhere to be found! Panickt and distraught, I ran to the Bedstead and felt 'neath the Coverlet. My Fingers grop'd for it desperately. Sure enough, 'twas there, at the Foot of the Bed, where I had doubtless kickt it off during the Night that follow'd our Debauch. I breath'd a deep Sigh of Relief as I slipp'd it on my Leg again.

Meanwhile, Evelina had compleated her Toilette, dress'd herself in a Morning Gown of sumptuous yellow Silk, woven to mimick Lace, with pink Ribbands fastening the Boddice. She wore pink Ribbands in her Hair as well, and, i'faith, she lookt so innocent 'twas hard to believe she had partaken of the Transports of the Flesh that I had witness'd here last Night!

"What shall I wear?" I askt Evelina, wrapping my naked, shiv'ring Self in the Coverlet both for Warmth and to hide my red Garter.

"Here ye go, Sweetheart!" cries she, tossing me a Boddice and Petticoat of green Silk. "An' hurry, or the old Bitch will be vext!" Whereupon she, too, departed the Chamber and started down the Stair.

Left alone for the first Time, I ran straight to the Chamber-Pot (where Evelina had already left a steaming Reminder of her Charms) and reliev'd my Bladder of its Load. Then I quickly washt my Face and Hands in the dirty Water in the Wash-Bowl and began to dress myself in the green Silk, (which, you may be sure, was neither the best Fit, nor wholly clean).

As I dress'd, my Mind raced. I tried to recall when I had last been visited by the Monthly Flow'rs, but my Brain was all in Confusion. How long had it been since I left Lyme-

191

worth? The Profusion of Events had been so num'rous and perplexing that 'twas very hard to recall the Dates. How many Days had I been with the Witches? How many Weeks with Lancelot? Had I my Monthly Visitation just a Week before Lord Bellars' return Home, or was it earlier? I seem'd to recall 'twas a Week in advance of his Arrival, for I remember'd my Step-Sister Mary asking me "if the Captain was at Home" and Lady Bellars rebuking her with the Rejoinder that 'twas a scurvy Way to speak of Woman's Domestick Afflictions, and show'd a Want of Breeding. I tried to count the Weeks upon my Fingers, but was defeated by the Fact that I did not know the Date. O I resolv'd to find out forthwith! The Fear of being with Child sent Shivers thro' my Legs as I dress'd. I felt myself weaken, my Brow sweated, my Fingers grew cold as Death (and I near affrighted myself out of my Wits with my icy Digits as I laced my Boddice). I could scarce provide for myself—let alone a Babe!

It cannot be, I said to myself. It cannot be. But e'en as I said these Words, I knew they might be wrong.

Attir'd in the green Silk, with green Shoes (which were indeed too big) and my red Hair flowing down my Back, I ran down the Stair to join Mother Coxtart and the Girls for Breakfast.

Evelina and Druscilla, Kate, Molly, and Nell were there, as was the coughing Roxana—and old Coxtart herself, presiding like a Mother Hen. They were eating Bits of toasted Bread with Cheese, and drinking Chocolate as their Beverage. I wonder'd, as I sat down to Table, whether Coxtart kept Count of each Bit of Bread and Cup of Chocolate and charged it 'gainst one's Earnings at the End of the Month. 'Twas likely, for the sly old Abbess did not seem a charitable Soul. I wonder'd how a Woman became as harden'd as she. Was it the Harshness of her Life, or was it Poverty, Want, Excess of Gin, as well as Lack of Education and Breeding? For in my Heart I still believ'd, e'en after all I had witness'd, that Human Souls were essentially good, but were corrupted by the Evil World.

The Conversation at Breakfast was perfunctory enough. I observ'd how subdu'd the Girls were in Coxtart's Presence—almost as if they fear'd her. They chatter'd readily enough when they were alone, but under her watchful Eye, they were restrain'd, and Roxana and Nell plainly lookt unwell, perhaps consumptive. 'Twas alarming how sick the Wenches all seem'd in the clear Light of Day.

"Now then, Girls," says Mother Coxtart, rubbing her hands together. "I have Assignments fer ye all. . . ." Whereupon she read off a List of Names from a grubby Sheet of Paper, assigning one Swain (or sometimes two) to each Girl. I thought I recogniz'd some of the most distinguish'd lit'ry Names of the Day, but I doubted they would frequent such a Place, so I told myself I must surely be mistaken: these must be their younger Brothers or obscure Cousins.

"And as fer Madam Fanny," she went on, "I shall have an Assignment fer her presently, but first we shall outfit her as befits a Lady of her Beauty. Pray, eat. We must away."

I gulp'd my Chocolate and a Bit of toasted Bread, but i'faith, I was too distress'd to eat heartily. Betwixt my Worries that I might be with Child and my Worries about what had become of Lancelot, not to mention my Worries about what Plans Mother Coxtart had in store for me, I was quite untranquil.

Before long, my new Employer hurried me away from the Table, down to the Streets and into a waiting Chair.

The sly old Fox, being too frugal to call for two Chairs, and telling me I was slender enough to share one with her, bounded into the Chair first, lifted her Panniers and Petticoats to make room, and said, "Here, me Love, there's plenty o' Space."

But 'twas hardly so, and finding no Space to put my Bottom (let alone my Petticoats) I half crouch'd, half stood erect whilst we made our bumpy Journey thro' the teeming Streets of the Town.

We were bound for the Royal Exchange, where, Coxtart promis'd, we should find a dazzling Array of Baubles to outfit me for my new Life. I was content enough just to be let out of the Chair, where I had fear'd I would be squasht, shaken, or smother'd to Death.

The Chairmen discharged us at a wond'rous Arcade of Golden Stone, fill'd with Shops of ev'ry Description. 'Twas a pav'd interior Courtyard, newly built after the Great Fire, and 'twas crowded with Travellers, Idlers, Shoppers, Merchants, Servant-Girls in search of Places, Ruffians looking for Victims to kidnap and carry off to the American Plantations, Spaniards with their Moustaches full of Snuff, Dutchmen in Caps, long-hair'd Jews, Porters, Hawkers, Orange Girls, and Ragmen; there were, as well, talkative Irishmen, taciturn Scotsmen, lazy Apprentices, flirting Sempstresses, insolent

Footmen, Husbands in search of Mistresses, and Wives in search of Lovers.

Little Notes conveying likely Employment were pinn'd to the Columns, where they flutter'd slightly, like dying Moths; these Notices the Crowd consulted indiff'rently if at all. For they had come to talk and tarry, flirt and gossip, not to seek an honest Day's Work!

We hasten'd into a Draper's Shop, where the Profusion of fine Stuffs quite bedazzl'd the Eye. Tho' Lady Bellars' Draper was wont to visit us at Lymeworth with Bolts of Silk, Satten, and fine Muslin, in truth, I had ne'er seen the like of the Selection that a London Shop provided.

The Draper himself, a wretchèdly thin Giant of a Man who seem'd quite compos'd of Angles, greeted us with a prodigious Bow and Cringe, offer'd us Dishes of Tea, and set the Shop Clerks scurrying to take down Rolls of the newest Stuff from the highest Shelves.

"And what shall Madam have Today?" the Draper askt with all possible Deference. If he knew Mother Coxtart's Profession, certainly nothing in his Manner betray'd it.

"I must outfit this fine young Lady—my Niece lately come from the Country—for a Season in Town," says she. Mother Coxtart's Voice became haughty and refin'd when she spoke in publick Places; last Night, in the Bedchamber, and this Morning as well, her Speech had scarce been so elegant.

"Ah, Madam," says the Draper, "allow me to show you our newest Stuffs. We have Pudsway Silks, Mowhairs, Flower'd Damasks, Poplines, Crapes, Plushes, Grazets, Shalloons, and Serges, not to mention the fine new Indian Stuffs—the Sooseyes, Succatums, Taffaties, Seersuckers, Chintses, Morees, and Pelongs."

Then, having first directed a Clerk to bring him some rich, bright Mustard-colour'd Stuff, he spread it before Mother Coxtart, bow'd, and said, "This, Madam, is a diverting Silk. My Stars! What a fine Gown this would make!"

"Not for a red-headed Beauty, I fear," says Coxtart in her elegant Style. "My dearest Niece looks rather ill in Mustard. Better Green or Blue. And Rose, to be sure, sets off her lovely Pallor, whilst a Flower'd Lustring might suit her well, if 'twere pale enough."

"Ah, Madam, I have just the Thing!" says the Draper, and clapping his Hands for another Clerk, he sends him bounding up a Ladder to fetch a Bolt of Silk, bluer than Heaven itself. As soon as the breathless Clerk descends with the heavenly

194

Silk, the Draper gathers it up into a Sleeve and drapes it seductively 'round my Shoulder.

"Behold, Madam! A Vision!"

"'Twill do, 'twill do," Coxtart says without much Enthusiasm. 'Tis plain that she is already preparing to haggle o'er the Price.

This Process continues for at least two Hours as innumerable Rolls of gorgeous Silk are brought down from the Shelves and the tall Draper repeatedly bows, cringes, and grovels before Mother Coxtart. I am us'd chiefly as a Tailor's Dummy, and Stuffs are drap'd upon my Form as if I had neither Will nor Wit of my own. Tired and fretful, I gaze out the Window at the teeming Arcade, where, suddenly, to my considerable Astonishment, I see a tatter'd Beggarman gazing in at me and screwing up his entire Face in a Squint, as if he is trying to determine whether or not he knows me.

He is an old Man, dress'd in piteous Rags, and his Beard is grizzl'd. I turn away, now grown fearful of his Looks, and pay Attention instead to the twinkling Cloth of Silver that is just now being drap'd across my Bosom.

"Ye Gods, Madam," says the Draper, to my "Aunt." "Would I had ten thousand Yards of this! But alas, all that remains you see here, and I doubt that I can get e'en a Yard more. Pray, consider your Niece's splendid Hair against this glitt'ring Silver! She looks a perfect Moonbeam, shining across the Ev'ning Sky!"

"Fifteen Shillings a Yard," says Coxtart coldly. The Draper lookt fair to faint at the very Words.

"Fan me, ye Winds!" cries he. "Why—should I part with it for such a Price, the very Weavers would rise up in Arms against me! Nay, Madam! Four Guineas per Yard is the lowest I can go. And yet, for your Ladyship, because you are a worthy Customer, I shall come down a Shilling or two."

"Two Guineas," Coxtart retorts. "'Tis a Remnant of the Winter Season. Lord knows what next Year's Fashion Plates will show."

"Madam, surely you jest. Cloth of Silver is e'er *à la Mode*."

"Two," says she sternly.

"Three," says he.

"Two and a half," says she.

"Done!" says he. "But you must swear an Oath you'll breathe no Word of this abroad—for just Yesterday my Lady

Farthingswood had it of me for four Guineas! You drive a hard Bargain, Madam."

When the Accounts had been tallied and the Draper and his two Cow'ring Clerks had bow'd, cringed, and clickt their Heels together more Times than I could count, the Trio of 'em escorted us outside the Shop and offer'd to get us a Chair, a Hackney Coach, the very Moon itself if we would but nod our Heads in Assent.

"Nay," says Coxtart, "we'd best walk, for we have spent all our Money here with you!" 'Twas hardly true, in fact, for Coxtart ne'er bought for Cash when she could for Credit; but it had the desir'd Effect upon our Friend the Draper.

"Not a Penny ill-spent," says he, to which Coxtart merely says, "Harrumph," as she leads me away.

Thus went our Visit to the Draper's. Next, we call'd upon a Sempstress, then a Shoemaker, a Toy-Shop (for I must have my painted Fan and Snuff-Box), a Milliner, and finally a Perfumer nam'd Charles Lillie, who sold us Chymical Wash-Balls, Oil of Rhodium and Oil of Roses, a Concoction call'd "*Eau Sans Pareil*," as well as Jessamine and Cordova Waters. Mother Coxtart also insisted that I have a Bavarian Red Liquor to give an added Bloom to my Cheaks, and Rose Lip Salve to stain my Lips. Despite my Protestations, she caus'd me to select an astonishing Array of Patches—some shap'd like Stars, some like Crescents, some like Flow'rs, some e'en like Dogs or Cats.

All the while, as we went from Shop to Shop (sometimes on Foot, sometimes by Chair), I caught Sight of the Beggarman following us and I grew e'er more untranquil. Sometimes we seem'd to lose him; sometimes he lagg'd back behind Corners or behind Peddlars' Carts, but there could be no doubt of it, he was upon our Trail.

At last, laden with Purchases, we prepar'd to find a Chair to take us homeward; whilst Mother Coxtart was engaged in finding a Chairman, the Beggarman made bold to approach me.

"Madam Fanny?" he askt, in a hoarse Whisper.

" 'Tis I," I said, with all unthinking Honesty. Whereupon he thrust a dirty Paper in my Hand and scurried away.

"Damn these impertinent Chairmen," says Coxtart, plainly anger'd by her own Ineptitude at finding a Chair. "We'll be obliged to take a Hackney Coach!" So saying, the sly old Fox walks away and begins to haggle with a nearby Coachman

196

concerning his Fares; thus I am briefly at liberty to read the Paper without being observ'd.

My Love, (it says), I am alive and in Newgate Prison— Come to me presently—Robin Hood.

My Heart heav'd in my Bosom with Passion. Indeed, it seem'd so loud to me that I doubted not but ev'ry Passerby on the Street might hear it. I thrust the Paper in my Boddice to keep it near that passionate pounding Organ.

"Come!" commanded Coxtart, stepping heavily into the Hackney Coach, with the Driver's Assistance.

"I am here," I said, breathing a deep Sigh, but my Mind was in Newgate e'en as I spoke. *He is alive!* I thought; *Goddess be Prais'd!* And I touch'd my own Bosom to feel the comforting Crackle of Paper 'neath the tatter'd green Silk as the Hackney Coach took us back once more to my Place of Captivity.

Chapter III

In which our Fanny meets a Frog who thinks himself a Prince and loses her Virginity for the second Time (which Doubting Thomases may profess to be impossible, but Readers wise in the Wicked Ways of the World will credit).

MOTHER COXTART HAD PLANS for me that very Night—Plans which precluded my going to Lancelot—tho' they certainly did not prevent me from dwelling upon my other principal Worry, namely: was I or was I not with Child?

In that Regard, I must report that, altho' I certainly could not confide in any of the Wenches concerning my Fears (lest they betray me), I had some Proof of my Condition that Afternoon in the form of a Copy of the *Daily Courant*, casually left upon the Parlour Tea-Table by one of the Girls, and bearing the ominous Date of July the 28th, 1724.

Since the Date of Lord Bellars' Betrayal was sear'd in my Memory, as if branded by red-hot Iron upon the Shoulder of a Slave—for how could I but remember his Letter to his London Mistress of June the 21st?—and since I had last had my Monthly Visitation a Week before that, sure I was near two Weeks o'erdue!

I tried to calm my unquiet Mind by telling myself that 'twas inevitable I should be late owing to my terrible Adventures, my Prodigious Fever, my Fears for the Future, and all the other Terrors I had known in the past sev'ral Weeks; but 'twas no Use to deceive myself, for ne'er before had my Monthly Flow'rs been anything but regular as a Swiss Clock, dependable as a trusty old Servant, and prompt as Afternoon Tea at Lymeworth!

Still, perhaps I was mistaken. If only I had stay'd long enough with my Friends, the poor slaughter'd Witches, to learn their Herbal Receipts! Surely *they* knew a Way to prevent an unwanted Babe from being born—an Herbal

198

Remedy, swiftly swallow'd, which would loose the dread Homunculus from the Womb without Harm to the Mother!

O I was mad with Rage! In my Mind and Spirit alternated Disbelief at my Condition and sheer Fury at Lord Bellars, i'faith at all Men, for having the Joys of Love yet bearing no Burden of the Responsibility!

But I could not long dwell upon my Condition, for Mother Coxtart had directed me to dress and make ready for my first Encounter with a Swain that Night. She had order'd Kate, the blonde, pale-skinn'd Damsel (whose lovely form had so astonish'd me last Ev'ning), to prepare me for the Encounter. And 'twas Kate herself who presently join'd me in the Bedchamber, carrying all Manner of Bridal Garments and various other necessary Items of Equipment.

"Come, Mrs. Fanny," says Kate, throwing an armful of white Clothes upon the Bed, "yer to play the proper Bride this Night—fer the Swain that hath purchas'd thy Mock-Virginity is daft fer Brides—the Fool—an' loves no Colours better than bright red Blood 'gainst white Satten!"

Straightaway, she helps me wash and paint my Face, provides the Sponge and Pigeon Blood for my pretend Virginity, e'en shows me how to squat, as o'er a Privy, and stuff it in my Cunnicle. Then she dresses me all in Virgin White—white Corset, Stomacher of white Satten laced with gleaming silver Thread, Dress of Satten, white as Driven Snow, e'en satten Shoes, and white silk Stockings with silver Clocks. My Apron, too, was white, embroider'd with Gold and Silver; and on my Head I wore a Cap of old French Lace, which gave me quite a childish Air.

"Now," says Kate, compleating my Toilette, "'twill ne'er do to wear this nasty red Garter, which, methinks, more befits a Witch than a Bride. Ye must wear Blue."

"That I cannot," I cried, now truly alarm'd, for with Lustre gone, and my dear Witches gone, and Lancelot in Prison, and e'en Black Horatio vanish'd from my Life, what Magick had I left but my red Garter?

"'Twill nee'r do," says Kate, snatching it from me.

"O gentle Kate, I beg of thee," I said, sinking to my white-stocking'd Knees. "Please give it here, I shall not wear it, but keep it in my Shoe, I swear."

"Very well," says Kate, relenting. "But wear this blue one and hide the red one well within yer Shoe, or there'll be Hell to pay with Coxtart. And mark ye—play the Virgin Bride! Curb ye hot Blood an' play the unwillin' Damsel, slow to heat an' slow to vanquish. 'Tis Rape these Swains are after, not Romance! 'Tis yer Unwillingness they pay the Abbess for. Nothing heats their Blood like a good Chase 'round the Bed and fine white Underlinen stain'd with Pigeon Blood!"

So admonishing me, Kate departed, locking the Chamber Door behind her.

I sat upon the Edge of the Bed and waited, wond'ring what Manner of Man found Sport in taking a Maiden's Virginity (and what Manner of Fool would believe that sly old Fox, Coxtart, when she avow'd the Authenticity of my Virginity).

I was to find out soon enough when the Door open'd and a short, slight, bandy-legg'd Fellow with a pockmarkt Face, dress'd quite the Fop, with great Buckles upon his Shoes and an Emerald Waistcoat, trimm'd with silver Frogs, walkt, nay, bounded, into the Chamber.

"I am Theophilus Cibber," says he, "Son of Colley, our renownèd Comedian; and of all the hapless Virgins upon this spinning Globe, 'tis thy Precious Maidenhead I will deign to take!"

O I had heard tell of Colley Cibber, the Comedian, and his Whoremaster Son, Theophilus (who was then beginning his notorious Career as a Player at the Drury Lane), but little did I expect that such a noted Buffoon would be my first Swain at Mother Coxtart's Brothel! E'en in Wiltshire, 'twas known that the young Cibber suffer'd mightily from his Father's Notoriety, his Whoring, Gaming, and Debauchery— and sought to outdo his ev'ry Excess. Tho' Theo was best at playing Clowns and Rogues, he aspir'd to Hamlet, Lear, Othello. Theo had already made some Name for himself playing Ancient Pistol in Mr. Shakespear's *Henry IV*, and Abel Drugger in Mr. Ben Johnson's *The Alchemist*, but he wisht to play the great Tragick Princes, not the Foolish Clowns. That this simp'ring Buffoon thought himself born to be another Betterton was the Common Knowledge (and the Common Jest) of the Town. Alas, 'tis oft' the Case—in Life as well as Art—that Clowns wish to be Tragick Princes (whilst Tragick Princes wish for nothing more than to be Clowns)!

" 'Lady, shall I lye in your Lap?' " says Cibber to me, quoting Hamlet.

" 'No, my Lord,' " says I, (as fine an Ophelia as you please). Whereupon I make haste to hide behind the Bed-Post—the better to inflame his Passion.

200

"Oho," says Cibber, " 'Do you think I meant Country Matters?' "

" 'I think nothing, my Lord,' " say I, demurely.

"Oho, this is Excellent Sport," says Cibber, "a Whore that quotes Shakespeare! Come, my little Bride, let me lye betwixt your Maid's Legs."

" 'You are merry, my Lord,' " say I, jumping up from the Bed and running away to escape his premature Embrace.

"Excellent Sport!" cries Cibber again, throwing himself at my Feet, holding my Ankles firm with his Hands and applying his Lips to my white silk Stockings. "Now I've caught you, little Bride!" Whereupon he darts one quicksilver Hand up under my Petticoats; but I am swifter than he, and with a quick Knee to his Nose, I escape again—if only for the nonce.

" 'O, I dye, Horatio!' " quotes Cibber, holding his redden'd Nose.

" 'Good Night, Sweet Prince,' " I cry, " 'and Flights of Angels sing thee to thy Rest!' " Whereupon Cibber scrambles to his Feet again and pursues me madly as I skip upon the Bed, o'er it, and lead him a Merry Chase up, down, and around— now hiding behind the Bed-Curtains, now running quickly past him on my nimble Feet.

The Chamber is commodious enough for a good Rouzing Chase, and the red damask Bed-Curtains make a piquant Hiding Place for a Mock-Bride in white. Likewise, the Fire-Screen, with its Naked Nymphs, can be us'd as if 'twere the Shield of Achilles! O I am enjoying the Sport as much as he, for I mean to wear him out so much he'll ne'er attempt my Mock-Virginity! Each Time I seem within his clownish Grasp, I slip away, as nimble on my Feet as when I am dancing a Jig.

" 'O Mistress mine, where are you roaming?' " Theo gasps, changing, in his Weariness, from Prince to Clown. I see, with considerable Satisfaction, that I am beginning to weary him. He lyes at length upon the Floor, murmuring Love Songs from Shakespeare, and looking for all the World as if he will expire upon the Moment.

" 'Then come kiss me, Sweet and Twenty,' " he mumbles; " 'Youth's a Stuff will not endure. . . .' " Whereupon he swoons and faints, and all his Limbs grow heavy as Death itself.

I stop in my Tracks, look at him quizzically, stand back to make sure he is well and truly expir'd, and then, feeling myself to be a vanquishing Queen of Vengeance, I climb upon the Bed, loose the silver Ropes and Tassels from the Bed-Curtains, and prepare to make him my Captive.

I creep towards him, with my Silver Bonds—but lo!—just as I am upon my Knees and making ready to bind his Ankles, the cunning Rogue wakes from his Mock-Sleep of Death and leaps upon me, pinning me to the Floor instead!

"Thou Villain!" I cry.

"Little Bride! I have thee now!" cries Theo, gath'ring me up in his skinny Arms, carrying me to the Bed, where he proceeds, with great Care and Solicitude to tye each of my four Limbs to each of the four Bed-Posts with the Silver Bonds I had intended for him!

Now I am truly trapp'd in my own Snares, my Arms and Legs spread wide upon the Bed so I can make no Resistance, my Ankles and Wrists chafing 'gainst the Silver Cords.

Triumph seems to make him play the Tragick Prince again—but now 'tis Othello, not Hamlet, he quotes, though he looks less that Part than e'en Prince Hamlet or Prince Hal.

" 'Put out the Light, and then put out the Light,' " declaims Theo, lifting my Petticoats and Apron and tossing 'em above my Head (until, indeed, I *am* in Darkness). Then he makes bold to attempt my Privy Place with no Preliminaries whatso'er. What can I do but submit, being so bound? Yet I am not gagg'd, and if he can play Othello (pale and pockmarkt as he is), sure I can play Desdemona.

" 'A guiltless Death I dye!' " I cry (from 'neath my Petticoats) as Theo's Privy Member makes its Presence felt near my not quite unsullied Altar of Love.

"O Excellent," he exclaims, "keep quoting Verses, my Sweet Desdemona—for nothing heats my Blood like Shakespeare!" Whereupon I grow silent to spite him, and as he sinks upon me with all his Weight, and wraps his bandy Legs 'round my own, he shouts.

" ' 'Tis the very Error of the Moon!/She comes more near the Earth than she was wont,/And makes Men mad!' "

Now he is properly lodged inside me and moving up and down like a very Candle Wick, being dipp'd in Beeswax by a busy, zealous Housewife; and yet I swear he is so slight a Presence in my Privy Place that it more tickles me than stirs my Blood.

What matter tho', for Blood we have aplenty in the bit of Sea-Sponge conceal'd within Love's Temple; and presently his

202

Hot Lust begins to discharge it (along with other Secretions of a paler Nature), and seeing the Bewitching Colours of bright red 'gainst white Linen, Theo is e'er more inflam'd and cries: " 'O Blood, Blood, Blood,' " like some Bedlam Lunatick that, in his Madness, fancies himself Othello.

But what is this?—I seem to hear Applause, and sundry Chears and Lewd Jests! And now the Chandelier begins to sway (as if the whole House were shaken by a Hurricano) and now it swings precipitously—as if 'tis about to drop to the very Floor—and from my Bondage upon the Bed I see sev'ral Pairs of beady Eyes staring at me from a Crescentshap'd Peep-Hole in the wainscotted Ceiling!

"A fine new Wench, is she not?" comes Coxtart's muffi'd Voice thro' the Ceiling Slit.

"Aye," says a male Voice.

"Aye, Aye," says another. How many Swains are paying for this one Performance? I wonder. But, in truth, Theo is more shockt than I. For now he rises from the Bed of Bliss (tho' not *my* Bliss, I'll warrant) and brandishes his Sword (where before he had brandish'd nought but his Cock) and swears Vengeance upon 'em all.

"Villainous Whore! Thou Rogues!" he screams. "Make light of Theo's Wooing, will ye? I'll see ye roast in Hell!" And he storms out of the Bedchamber, Sword in Hand, to wreak his bandy-legg'd Vengeance upon Coxtart and her paying Swains.

For my own part, I am as amus'd by this new Turn of Events as I was unamus'd by Theo's Am'rous Play, and I lye upon the Bed in all my Helplessness, laughing merrily to myself as Thumps and Bangs echo upon the Ceiling, and Screams reverberate above my Head.

All the while, my Mind is going like a Swiss Clock. How shall I abort this Babe, the loathèd Offspring of Lord Bellars' Loins? How shall I get out of my Brothel Bondage and to Lancelot in Newgate Prison? How shall I form some Scheme to turn my wretchèd Fate as a bloodied barter'd Bride to Advantage? Perhaps by persuading Theo (or some other Player) to try me on the Stage?

I am scheming thus in my Bonds upon the Bed, when Kate returns to rescue me. The Hullabaloo above my Head begins to quiet down by now, and I can only conjecture what Coxtart hath done to make Peace and end the Fray.

"Ahoy, Madame Fanny," cries Kate, "the Abbess is wellpleas'd with yer Performance. She says yer a fine Virgin an' she means to keep ye as the House Virgin as long as there are Gulls to pay fer yer Deflow'rin's. 'Ere, let me untye ye."

"But won't Word get 'round soon enough that I have lost my Maidenhead Time and Time again?"

"By an' by, 'twill be bruited about that there's a new Wench in the House, 'tis true. But Men are Fools. The Abbess knows that as well as we. She'll dye yer Hair if need be, or she'll have ye use yer Charms upon Foreign Rogues—Italians, Spaniards, an' the like, that are more easily gull'd than True-born Englishmen."

"Pray, Sweet Kate, what does she charge 'em when they watch thro' the Peep-Hole?"

"Two Guineas fer watchin', five fer an old Girl, ten fer a new Girl that she passes off as Virgin. I'faith, they gets 'em a special cheap Rate when they enjoy in Armor, but none o' the Swains like an armor'd Cock as well as a bare 'un."

"In Armor? Pray what is that?"

"Fanny, me Girl, yer sure to be clapp'd soon enough or else with Child unless ye learn these Things. What—did no one tell ye about Armor?"

"Evelina said I must use Sea-Sponge and Vinegar."

"Well, that's no good against the Clap—tho' some say it preserves the Womb from Fruitfulness. I have me Doubts."

"What shall I do?" I cried. "And what if I should get the Clap or get with Child?"

" 'Tis nothin that cannot be undone—fer a Price, that is. The Child, I mean. Clap is quite another Story. 'Ave ye ne'er seen the Handbills o' Mrs. Skynner o' Peter Street?"

"No. Pray what are they?"

"Methinks I've got one, 'ere." And having finish'd untying me, she goes to the Escritoire whence she produces a tatter'd Handbill advertising the Wares, "commonly call'd Implements of Safety," produced by a certain Mrs. Skynner, whose excellent Merchandise is attested to by these Lines:

> To guard yourself from Shame or Fear,
> Votaries to Venus, hasten here;
> None in my Wares e'er found a Flaw,
> Self-Preservation's Nature's Law.

"Kate," says I, "I must pay a Call on this Mrs. Skynner."

"Well, whate'er ye do, Sweetheart, don't tell the old Bitch I sent you. She has her own Skins an' Bladders she likes to sell an' she'll charge ye double fer 'em, tho' they be e'er such

204

poor-quality Stuff, an' are fair to burst the Minute yer Swain puts one on."

"Will you take me to Skynner," I ask. "Upon the Morrow?"

Kate looks at me appraisingly. In my Eyes there is true Pleading, a piteous Sense of Desperation.

"Very well," she says, "if we can get away from the old Bitch. But I'll be expectin' ye to return the Favour someday, don't ye forget it."

Chapter IV

*In which we follow Fanny to Mrs. Skynner's Emporium,
are initiated into some Mysteries to which Wise Women
have been privy thro'out the Centuries, and subsequently
make our Descent into London's own Hades, namely,
Newgate Prison.*

TRULY KATE WAS NOT a Bad Sort, tho' Life in the Brothel
had harden'd her. She was but twenty Years of Age and had
spent six of those Years with Mother Coxtart. Ivory-skinn'd
and pale as she seem'd, she was wise in the World's Wickedness, and far more hardy than she lookt.

Coxtart she saw as her Enemy, not her Protector, but an
Enemy to be wheedl'd, cajol'd, and outwitted, whilst the other
Wenches she conceiv'd not as True Friends, but rather as
Temporary Allies, to be woo'd when they could proffer Aid
and Assistance, yet avoided like the very Plague when they
could not. In half a dozen Years, she'd seen twice that many
Wenches dye of Consumption, Clap, or tainted Gin, and seen
Coxtart bury 'em in plain pine Boxes, with as little Ceremony
as she might drown a Litter of Kittens. Kate was determin'd
not to go that Way herself, but enough Natural Kindness was
left in her harden'd Heart for her to take Pity on my Plight
and carry me to Mrs. Skynner's Establishment.

We crept out of the House in the wee Hours of the Morning, whilst Coxtart lay abed with the Butler (he who was the
proud Possessor of "Master Shorty"), and we travers'd the
fetid London Streets before the Fashionable World was
abroad. We saw nought but Ragmen and 'Prentices at that
Hour, as well as Tradesmen delivering Provisions (or Duns)
to the fashionable West End Houses, and plucky Chimney
Sweeps going on their Way to their dusky and dangerous Duties.

Kate had a Lover she would meet in Peter Street ('twas
doubtless the True Reason for her Generosity in taking me to

206

Skynner) but she would disclose little about him. Truly, she seem'd to waver betwixt wishing to trust me as a True Friend and fearing me as a potential Betrayer. She would tell me only that her Lover was a wealthy Tradesman, but married, alas, and that he promis'd to find a Way to bring her out of the Brothel and set her up in a Shop of her own.

She directed me then to Skynner's Establishment, bade me meet her promptly at Eleven o' the Clock in Golden Square, chid me sternly not to betray her—for if Coxtart learnt we had been abroad without so much as a By-your-Leave, 'twould go hard with her, and consequently she would go hard with me, and ran off to meet her Mysterious Tradesman.

I made my Way to Skynner's Establishment, which was located o'er a Tavern call'd The Rising Sun, and reach'd by as narrow and crooked a Stair as I had e'er trod. I rang and waited with a pounding Heart. In my Pocket, I had a few Shillings I had begg'd from Kate, with the Promise to repay double within the Fortnight, but truly I was at the Mercy of the Fates, for it might be Months before Coxtart deem'd I had repaid my Clothes and Keep, and I had also the Sacred Charge of Friendship to fulfill to Lancelot. Before long I must go to him in Newgate Prison and offer whatsoe'er Aid and Succour my paltry Resources could provide.

I rang again. No Sound was heard within. I began to despair mightily of e'er finding a Cure for this unwanted Babe, and, in a trice, the Thought that I might end my Tribulations by throwing myself headlong in the River Thames came to me like a Flash of Lightning on a Summer's Night.

Just then there came a Stirring within, a Shuffling as of Carpet Slippers worn by a very old or infirm Party, and the Door was presently open'd.

There stood before me a Stoop'd and Ancient Matron, with Skin of a cadav'rous Hue, and great goggling Eyes like a Frog, and a Breath as foul and fetid as a Jakes. She wore her Nightshift and Cap, and seem'd distinctly displeas'd to see me at her Door.

"Come back at Noon," she croakt. "I do no Business in the Dead of Night." And with that, she made ready to slam the Door upon me. In a Panick, I did what I had ne'er done before. I wedged my Foot betwixt the Door and Jamb, and begg'd of her with all my Heart that she receive me.

"Please, Madam, I am new in London, and require your

207

Services. Please take Pity on a Country Wench that is a friendless Orphan. . . ."

She looks at me coldly, weighs my Shillings 'gainst her Sleepiness, and says (with that Death-Rattle in her Throat): "Very well, come in. I'faith I am too soft-hearted to refuse." But her great goggling Eyes glinted more with Hope of Gain than with Kindness.

Within the dark forbidding Shop were glass Cases fill'd with a Profusion of sundry Goods, all dusty and disorder'd. Perfumes, Wash-Balls, Soaps, Powders, Snuffs, Pomatums, Cold-Creams, Lip-Salves, e'en Sealing Wax and Ladies' Black Sticking Plaister. But all these Goods seem'd ancient and unus'd, as if indeed they were not her True Trade but only on Display to distract the chance Visitor from her actual Business.

"Sit ye down then," she rasps, off'ring me a three-leggèd Stool whilst she sits in a commodious Armchair, "an' tell me what ye seek."

Whereupon my Tongue went dry in my Mouth, my Throat swell'd with a Lump the Size of a Hen's Egg, and I could not say a Word.

"Speak," says she. "Hath the Cat got yer Tongue?"

But still I could not utter a Syllable. The Prospect of jumping in the Thames seem'd easier and less painful than telling Mrs. Skynner why I'd come.

"Sweetheart," croaks Skynner, taking Pity on me (for Beads of Sweat now stood upon my Brow like glist'ning Jewels of Pain), "Wenches o' yer Age ne'er comes to me but fer two Reasons. Either they be clapp'd, or else with Child. Is that yer Story?"

I nodded my Head like a Deaf Mute.

"Come, Sweetheart, what's yer Name?"

"Fanny," says I (and at once I wisht I'd thought to lye and call myself Druscilla or Arabella).

"Fanny, Sweetheart, I can sell ye Cundums 'gainst the Clap, an' Suppositories o' Black Hellebore an' Castoreum to bring yer Monthly Visitation an' loose the Babe from yer Womb. Would ye have one or both?"

Whereupon I began to weep great salty Tears, which ran down my Cheaks and into the Corners of my Mouth.

"Both," I whimper'd, thinking myself the most wretchèd Wench that e'er liv'd.

"Come, Fanny," rasps Skynner, " 'tis nothin' to be asham'd o'. How else shall a Wench endure the Snares o' Men? We

208

pay fer Love, yet they do not. 'Tis Nature's Law, yet we must break it to survive, an' is not Self-Preservation Nature's Law as well?"

This first Hint of Sympathy brought back my Voice in full and gave me once again Possession of my Wits.

"Please, Mrs. Skynner, tell me what you know of Self-Preservation, for I have heard so many diff'rent Stories, I know not which to believe."

"First, Sweetheart, ye must ignore the major part o' what ye hear, fer 'twill do ye as little Good 'gainst bein' clapp'd or with Child as the Remedies o' the Savage Women o' Hungary that hang Hare Dung and Mule Hide o'er their Beds to secure Fruitlessness! Some will tell ye Willow Drink, or Tincture o' Lead, or else Alum in the Privy Place, or Oil o' Ether, or e'en Mint or Crocus introduced within, after the Act is done. These will avail ye nought! Nor will a Golden Ball within the Privy Place (tho' some Italian Libertines avow 'twill serve), nor is it true, as the Spaniards believe, that passionate Coitus prevents Fruitfulness an' Excess of Voluptuousness so punishes the Womb that 'twill not bear."

"What of Sea-Sponge and Vinegar?"

" 'Tis not the worst, yet Juice o' Lemon will serve ye better, and some swear by a Beeswax Cap, worn o'er the Mouth o' the Womb. But none will serve as well as my Machines o' Safety. How many will ye take?"

"How much do you charge for 'em?"

"How much have ye got, Sweetheart?" says she, rising to her Feet.

"Not much, a few Shillings."

"An' fer that ye expect the Black Suppositories an' the Cundums! Get out, Baggage! Ye waste me Time!" Anger darken'd her hellish Visage again, and grabbing my Shoulders, she made ready to throw me out.

I fell to my Knees and begg'd her to have Mercy. I produced the little Money that I had, whereupon, with supreme Niggardliness and Reluctance, she went to a lockt Cabinet, withdrew two small Packets, and presently press'd 'em into my sweating Palm.

"Ye 'ave two Cundums there an' three Suppositories o' Black Hellebore which ye insert into yer Womb each six Hours. Then ye wait a Day or two an' soon the Blood will come. Begone with ye! I've given ye more Time already than I can spare!" Whereupon she open'd up the Door and pusht me out, slamming it behind me.

209

I secreted my Forbidden Treasures within my Pockets and swiftly descended the Stair, so dizzy and distraught from the Encounter with Mrs. Skynner that I had to cling to the Bannister to keep from falling. I truly felt like the first Wench in the History of the World to seek for such Help from an old Crone, and I felt myself to be more wicked than Satan himself, more deserving of Hell-Fire than a Plotting Poisoner, more evil than a Wanton Robber that sets upon the Poor and Old.

'Twas but half past Nine by the Clock in the Tavern below when I descended into the Street, and thinking I had Time enough to go to Lancelot in Newgate Prison, I determin'd to find my Way thither.

The first Man I askt, a Baker delivering Loaves of Bread from a wretchèd Cart, lookt at me and laugh'd: "Why should ye be in such a Hurry to get to Newgate, Lass? The Wicked Ways o' the Town will send ye soon enough!" But then he inform'd me that 'twas a prodigiously long Walk across the Town and I had best hire a Chair or Hackney.

"But, Sir, I have no Money, and I must visit my poor Brother who is unjustly thrown in Prison."

"If ye have no Money, Lass, 'tis little Good ye can do yer Brother. . . ."

"Still, I must see him," said I.

The Baker lookt at me and hesitated. He had a friendly Face and the Air of a Man who hath known Hardship in his Time and doth not despise those similarly afflicted.

"Very well," says he, "I'll take ye there, but first ye must help me deliver these Loaves in Soho Square."

This I readily, e'en gratefully, did, and within a half Hour or so, we set off across London for Newgate in the rattling Cart. We travers'd St. Giles, then High Holborn, then Holborn Bridge; then we came at last into Newgate Street whence I could see the gleaming Edifice of St. Paul's in all its Glory. 'Twas indeed the largest Church I had e'er beheld!

The Noise and the Clatter of the London Streets ne'er fail'd to amaze me. Now that the World was getting up, the Streets grew e'er more crowded and noisy. Cars, Chairs, and Hackneys jostl'd for place with gilt Coaches. I was momentarily gladden'd and amus'd by the Sight of the Barber, hurrying along with his Wig Boxes, the Apple Women with their Baskets of Apples, the sooty Chimney Sweeps with their blacken'd Brushes, the seductive Milliners walking briskly with their Bandboxes swinging.

The Baker carried me to the Prison Gate, where I thankt him with all my heart, ne'er once wond'ring how I would return to Golden Square. So eager was I to see Lancelot that t'was all I thought of upon that Occasion.

Yet nothing in my Life had prepar'd me for Newgate Prison. The Eyes, the Nose, the Ears were all assaulted at once, and 'twas verily as if I'd entered into Hades itself rather than a Place upon this Earth.

Just within the Gate, I was greeted by the Turnkey, a hideous Man of surpassing Corpulence, with Legs so gouty he could scarce walk, but waddl'd rather, like a Goose. He welcom'd me with Leers and Grimaces, and the usual Attentions to my Bosom, whereupon a Cry was rais'd amongst the Prisoners, who surely thought another Poor Wretch was joining their Throng, and perhaps they had Hope of the Company that Misery proverbially loves.

"Pray, Sir, may I visit Lancelot Robinson?" I askt the Turnkey.

"Oho," said he, his great red Mouth slobb'ring and his great pink Face looking as wet and fleshly as a cookt Ham, "d'ye mean that pitiful Maniack that declares himself the Ghost of Robin Hood? He'll hang anyway, to be sure. He escap'd the Gallows once, but this Time he will surely hang."

"Sir, I am his Sister and I would visit him."

"An' d'ye hope to visit without payin' the Visitors' Fee?" said the Turnkey.

"Sir, I've not a Ha'penny to my Name," I said, "but I swear that if you let me see him just this once, I will return with Guineas for you—and I will ne'er forget the Favour."

"Sassy Wench!" says he, "then pay the Favour now!" Whereupon he pins me to the Wall with his huge Belly and thrusts a filthy Hand into my Bosom. The Prisoners within—those of 'em that can crane their Necks to watch the Show—begin to make lewd Noises and offer their Encouragement to the Wretchèd Turnkey, whereupon he lifts my Petticoat, opens his own Breech, and makes ready to ravish me just there against the damp and dirty Wall.

What shall I do—kick him in the Privy Place and risque being turn'd into the Street without so much as a Civil Word with Lancelot? This seems unwise; so I try with all my Might to dissuade with Eloquence rather than persuade with Force.

"Gentle Turnkey," say I, "if you will desist, I shall return with jingling Coins and Hosts of lovely Wenches to do thy Bidding. We shall make a Bow'r for you and each of us at-

211

tend another Part of thy Beauteous Anatomy. I pray you, then, desist." But, as many Sages have observ'd, 'tis in the Nature of Lust to be impatient, and rather than dissuading him, my Words seem'd to inflame him further. He fumbl'd in his open Breech for his Organ—lost, perhaps, amidst Folds of Flesh—and, whilst the Jeers and Encouragements of the Mob grew louder, I had near resign'd myself to yet another Ravishment.

Just then, howe'er, a Familiar Face appear'd. The Turnkey was seiz'd by his fat Shoulders and shaken from his Lustful Attentions to my Person by none other than John Littlehat—Lancelot's Confederate!

"Unhand the Wench, Bully!" shouted Littlehat, his short, fat Body shaking with Rage and his black Beard glist'ning evilly. Whereupon he swiftly trips the Turnkey and sends him reeling down the Stair, to the gen'ral Applause of the Prisoners. (So quickly do they change Allegiances that now they are chearing for my Freedom, where before they chear'd for my Ravishment. Such Perfidy, I warrant, is e'er the Nature of Mobs.)

"Come," says Littlehat, "I will carry ye to Lancelot. 'Twill do his Heart good to see ye. The Lad's in a Sorry State."

Littlehat took my Hand and led me through the teeming Prison whilst the Turnkey curst us with "Damn yer Eyes" and the Prisoners guffaw'd and chear'd. I felt fair to faint from the very Reek of the Place and my Eyes were affrighted and amaz'd at each Turning by the Misery I saw.

In ev'ry Nook and Cranny were wretchèd Rogues begging me for Pennies I did not possess, starving Women nursing Skinny Babes, Men so weak with Hunger they could scarce raise their Arms to beg, and others who attackt the Nursing Mothers for their Milk, throwing the poor squalling Babes aside.

Some Prisoners seem'd afflicted with Consumption; others had Sores and Pocks upon their Faces; others moan'd with Dysentery and discharged the Infected Offal of their Guts into Publick Privies, which gave the whole Place the Reek of Excrement.

We pass'd the Middle Ward, which Littlehat told me was the cleanest Place in all the Prison, and was reserv'd only for Prisoners with Money—tho' it scarce seem'd to me much cleaner than the Rest of that Hell-Hole. Thence we descended into a Pit call'd the Lower Ward, the nastiest Place in this nastiest of Places. There a naked Woman, about my Age, was

212

being flogg'd with a Cat o' Nine Tails and weeping piteously whilst the Rabble lookt on with Merriment and Lust, as if 'twere a Raree Show. There was also a large Chamber call'd the Tangier, where the miserable Debtors were kept (only distinguish'd from the Felons by the Fact that they wore no Irons), another Chamber call'd the High Hall, which was use'd for Recreation, and a stinking dark Cellar where intoxicating Liquors were sold, and Multitudes of Prisoners rioted merrily, inflam'd by what was doubtless tainted Gin (and which, you may be sure, they paid dear for). Fearful Brawls and Fights were in progress there, and Littlehat had to shield me with his great fat Body to protect me from the Boisterousness of the Rabble. We descended finally to the Lower Dungeons, past the Press Room, where Prisoners who refus'd to plead were press'd with iron Weights, and wail'd horribly under their Torture. And adjacent to that Pit of Terrors we saw a still more terrible Room where, of Old, the Hangman us'd to seethe the Quarter'd Limbs of Traitors in Pitch, Tar, and Oil. 'Twas not now in Use, and thank the Goddess for that, since, had the Smell of cooking Flesh and Tar been added to the Smell of Excrement, 'twould have made an e'en more nauseous Brew than that which caus'd my Guts to heave and made me glad I'd eaten no Breakfast!

In the very lowest Dungeon, chain'd piteously in a sort of Oubliette in which he could not stand, his Legs in heaviest Irons, his Body clad in the filthiest of Rags, sat our Lancelot, his beauteous Form doubl'd o'er as in Pain.

Littlehat brib'd his Guard with a Shilling to leave us alone with Lancelot for a Time, and tenderly, my Heart breaking with the Pain of seeing him in Circumstances so much Reduced from his former Glory, I sat down at his Bare Feet and held 'em in my Hands, chafing 'em warm, e'en tho' Rats scurried nearby and Vermin crawl'd. Ne'er had I been indiff'rent to Vermin before, but Lancelot's Plight engaged my whole Heart and made me forget my wretchèd Surroundings.

For a Moment or two, he scarce acknowledged my Presence.

"They have been hard on him," Littlehat said, "fer they fear his Influence upon the Prisoners due to his Miraculous Escape upon the last Occasion, an' tho' they permit the likes of me to walk about at will, they saw him be stripp'd naked by the Prisoners fer Garnish an' would not give him Freedom of the Rules."

"Garnish?" I askt. "Pray what is that?"

"'Tis the Pay the Convicts expect from each new Prisoner. O, Madam Fanny, there are a thousand little Fees in Gaol— Payment to the other Convicts, to the Turnkey, to the Cook who dresses the Charity Meat (e'en tho' most Convicts ne'er see, much less taste it), to the Swabbers (e'en tho' the whole Place is Filthy as ye see an' not once swabb'd in twenty Years), an' e'en to the Hangman, who, in Former Times, did seethe the Limbs of Traitors all Day long in Pitch, an' now dispatches the better Part of these Poor Wretches at Tyburn Tree. Some innocent Prisoners are freed at the Old Bailey only to be thrown back into Gaol because they cannot pay their Fees!"

"What will it cost to get Lancelot Freedom of the Rules?"

"More than ye have, I fear, Sweetheart. Fer they would make an Example of him, break his Soul, as 'twere, upon the Wheel, as they could ne'er break his Body."

"And where are the others," I enquir'd of Littlehat, "the Merry Men?"

"Black Paul, bless his Pyrate Heart, escaped, taking his Latin Learning with him—where, we know not. An' Mr. Twitch was kill'd upon the Thames, God rest his Soul. Likewise poor Sotwit an' gentle Mr. Thunder. Puck Goodfellow an' Francis Bacon made off, too, an' presently I hope fer Word of 'em. Sir Fopling an' Beau Monde are here as well, tho' Fop is grievous ill with Gaol Distemper, an' as fer the others, I cannot say. God bless 'em all."

"Who turn'd you in?" I askt. "Who was that Traitor?"

At this, Lancelot came to Life, and Fury lit his wretchèd Face like Fireworks in the black Night Sky: "The Wretchèd Captain o' the *Hannibal* turn'd me in an' took the Swag an' the Price upon me Head as well! I trusted him, I did, an' swore he ne'er dealt in Human Flesh. Alas, what a Fool was I!"

And with that he slump'd back down again and moan'd, whereupon Littlehat whisper'd in my Ear: "I've ne'er seen our belov'd Lancelot so cast down. Pray, Madam Fanny, can ye beg or borrow Guineas enough to get him Freedom of the Rules? Fer they mean to make him suffer more than the common Lot of Convicts an' I fear fer the Soundness of his Mind."

"I'll try, good Littlehat, good Friend," said I. But i'faith, I knew not how I could relieve Lancelot when I could not relieve myself.

Just then Lancelot came to Life again, lookt up with a

214

Wildness in his Eyes, and cried, "Why hast thou forsaken me?" 'Twas not e'en clear he recogniz'd me, but the Look of Betrayal upon his haunted Face was unmistakable. Now I, too, fear'd for Lancelot's Sanity and understood Littlehat's Concern.

"They sold me Soul fer thirty Pieces o' Silver!" rav'd Lancelot. Then he sank down again, moaning like a Woman in Travail.

"Pray go," said Littlehat, "an' try not to despair. When he is quite himself he says he loves ye best in all this World. He raves now an' he hath forgot his Golden Tongue, his Faith in God an' Robin Hood—fer the Betrayal by the Captain of the *Hannibal* went hard with him. Friendship's all to Lancelot, an' Honour amongst Thieves was all his Creed; now he sees his Confederate Thieves in as harsh a Light as all the Great World of Lawyers, Statesmen, an' all such respectable Rogues. 'Twas e'er thus with Lancelot—one Minute high upon his Fancies an' his Words, as if on Rum, the next Moment cast down, as if he were a raving Bedlamite. Go, Madam Fanny. Tell me where to send fer ye."

I gave the address of Coxtart's House in the West End, praying Littlehat would not know 'twas a Brothel. Then I threw my Arms around his Neck and kiss'd him, bent again to Lancelot and kiss'd his chilly Cheak, and fled from the Depths of the Prison like Persephone fleeing Hades to shelter in the Arms of her Mother Demeter in Blossoming Spring.

But sure Coxtart was no Demeter (and perhaps I was no Persephone), yet I would find a Way to rescue Lancelot, I vow'd—if I had to be deflower'd ten thousand Times! O I would study Devious Ways to cheat that sly old Coxtart out of Guineas that I had sweated for upon my own (poor but honest) Back; and if I was bound to be a Trollop for a Time, at least 'twas in the sweet Name of Loyalty to Lancelot, and (dare I say it?) Love.

Chapter V

Fanny's Flight thro' London; Dissension in the Body Politick, and a most amazing Revolution, which Whigs will applaud but Tories may grumble of; after which our Heroine learns sev'ral important Lessons, which we hope will help her her whole Life long, but ne'ertheless is mov'd to an Act of great Desperation which causes her untold Anguish and Agony.

I FLED THRO' THE Streets of London then, as if Pluto himself (or indeed the Grim Reaper) were pursuing me. The Soles of my Feet felt each Stone thro' the worn Leather of my Shoes, and the Sweat ran down my Face like Raindrops down a Window Pane. The Day was clear and hot; the Sun shone strongly. My Stays were fair to bursting from my heavy Breathing and the Strain and Exertion of running. Perhaps I shall run so hard, I shall lose this Babe, I thought; for the Treachery of my Body against my Mind in conceiving a Babe at this worst of all possible Times was ne'er far from my Thoughts.

In Fleet Street, I glimps'd a Clock and saw that 'twas already half past Eleven! I had miss'd my Meeting with Kate and doubtless won her Enmity for Life! I ran harder now, along the Length of Fleet Street, then thro' the Temple Bar, adorn'd with the Figures of Kings and Queens below, and the horribly rotting Head of a Traitor upon an iron Spike above. As I ran thro', a ragged-looking Man offer'd me the Use of a Spying-Glass for a Ha'penny so that I might better see the grisly Traitor's Head; but I shook my own Head with Distaste and Dislike—for what could be the Joy in feasting my Eyes upon this gruesome Relick?—and ran furiously onward.

The Streets were crowded now, and 'twas not always easy to make my Way. People stood aside with Wonder at the Fury of my Running; but oft' an unruly Chairman took special Delight in pinning me 'gainst a Wall, or hitting my

Back with the Poles of his Chair. I near upset a Fruit Peddlar's Cart at one Turning and became so distraught with the
Lateness of the Hour, sheer Weariness, and Despair that I
compleatly lost my Way in some filthy back Alleys and had
no Notion whatsoe'er of how to return to the West End.

My Clothes reekt of the Prison; my Hair flew about my
face like a Madwoman's; and finding myself lost, late,
doubtless in grievous Trouble with both Kate and Coxtart, I
began to weep with Self-Pity for my Plight.

What had I hop'd for when I went to Lancelot? Had I
hop'd for his Aid in my Perilous Predicament? If indeed I
had, 'twas clear as Crystal that he could not help me in his
present State. I would have to draw upon whate'er Reserves
of Strength I had and be his Saviour instead! Friendship and
Love both demanded it; and tho' I did not feel myself to be
equal to the Task, I would have to learn to be stronger than I
had e'er been in the Past.

I stopp'd and leant 'gainst a Wall to catch my Breath. I
mopp'd my fever'd Brow and daub'd my moist Eyes with the
dirty Hem of my Petticoat. Just then, there came the Cry of
"Gardy-loo!" above and I darted out of the Way scarce in
Time to avoid being drench'd with the unlovely Contents of
someone's Chamber-Pott! 'Twas all I needed in my Mood of
Dark Despair, and the sheer Absurdity of it stopp'd my Tears
as they sprang and made me laugh where I had previously
cried.

Very well, then, Madam Fanny, said I to myself, since
Fate herself hath decreed that you would miss the Contents
of the Chamber-Pott, 'tis clearly an Omen you will survive!
Nay—survive and prosper. If Lancelot cannot save you,
you'll save yourself and save him into the Bargain. Onward,
Fanny! Onward, Fanny Hackabout-Jones!

Thus I began to run again (tho' whither, I knew not); and
as I ran, I trusted but I should meet some kindly Soul who
would direct me to the West End, and I remember'd, all in a
Jumble, as if in the Moment before Death, the Losses of the
last Weeks: the Loss of my Childhood Home at Lymeworth,
of my Step-Mother, Lady Bellars, of my Faith in First Love
(so cruelly betray'd by Lord Bellars); I remember'd, too, the
dastardly Murders of the Good Witches, the Loss of Lustre,
the Loss of my Great Epick Poem (yet in its Infancy), the
Loss of my Friends the Merry Men, and worst of all, the
Loss of Lancelot—or, dare I say it, the Loss of Lancelot's
Mind!

But just then Lines from the Witches' Prophecy came back to me, I know not how. "Your own Father you do not know," I remember'd. "Your Daughter will fly across the Seas. Your Purse will prosper, your Heart will grow. You will have Fame, but not Heart's Ease." What could it mean? Clearly, whate'er the Meaning, I must not now throw myself headlong into the Thames. "From your Child-Womb will America grow," the puzzling Prophecy continu'd. "By your Child-Eyes, you will be betray'd"; well, *that* had already occurr'd with Lord Bellars' wretchèd Letter! "You will turn Blood into driven Snow." Puzzling, puzzling in the extream. Whereupon the last Line echo'd in my Ears as if spoken by the strong Voice of Joan Griffith herself: "By your own strong Heart will the Devil be stay'd!" 'Twas hopeful, hopeful indeed! I might become strong if only I could believe myself so! I might prosper if only I could conquer my Terrors! I might save Lancelot if only I could save myself!

By the Time I found my Way back to Mother Coxtart's (after many wrong Turnings and the well-meaning Assistance of a poor Half-Wit, who claim'd to know the Way but knew it e'en less than I did), the whole House was frantick with my Absence. Mother Coxtart had cruelly lockt Kate in the Cellar for her Deviltry in setting me free; the Butler she had threaten'd to flog within an Inch of his Life for his Laxity in letting me escape (tho' i'faith, she *knew* he'd lain abed with her); and the other Girls were also trembling in Terror of her Wrath.

This was the unhappy Scene into which I return'd. Since 'twas clear that neither Lyes nor Demonstrations of Submission would avail me of any Mercy whatsoe'er with her, I made the Decision to brazen it out—to stand upon my Honour and Dignity rather than upon my Knees!

"Well—you wretchèd Baggage!" Mother Coxtart exclaim'd. "Where have ye been that ye dare return here smelling like the Fleet Ditch itself after all my Kindnesses to ye!"

"Madam," said I, "I know not the Kindnesses of which you speak. I have workt hard and been paid nothing. I have been ravishd and disgraced only to enrich your Pockets. I have borne the Indignity of having my Dishonour watch'd by Swains who paid you for the Privilege. And tho' I did not rebel at this, I must now declare that I am a Free Woman, not a Guinea Slave, and I'd sooner starve upon the Streets than have you treat me like a common Cur to be chain'd at your Back Door!"

218

At this Speech, the other Girls gasp'd in Awe, and Coxtart herself was stunn'd for ne'er before had one of her Wenches dar'd to stand up against her Authority. I'faith, I knew not where I got the Courage for it; 'twas as if some Spirit possess'd me and spoke thro' my Lips.

"Filthy Baggage!" were all the Words Coxtart found upon this Occasion. "How dare ye address me with such Impertinence?"

"Madam," said I, "I mean no Impertinence to you. I mean only to assert that I'll be treated like a Woman, not a Slave! If I work hard for you, I will be paid some Share of it; if I must leave this House upon Errands of my own Concern, I'll not be question'd like a Criminal. I'faith, Madam, I ask only for the Rights that all the Great Philosophers assert belong alike to ev'ry Human Soul! For are we not, as the Third Earl of Shaftesbury says, 'Rational Creatures who crave Generosity, Gratitude, and Virtue as we crave Life itself'? Are not the twin Senses of Right and Wrong as native to us as Natural Affection itself?"

At this, Mother Coxtart was mute with sheer Perplexity. Her Mouth hung open as if 'twere a Trap for Flies, and she presently began to sputter and shake like a Tea Kettle o'er an open Fire.

"Fie on yer Impertinence, Strumpet! If ye have such a fine Protector in this Mr. Chaffberry, why doth he not keep ye then?" But 'twas clear to see I had fought her with Weapons beyond her Reach and she was as puzzl'd as she was enraged.

Meanwhile, the other Wenches, beginning to perceive that perhaps some Good might come from this for them as well, harken'd to me e'er more attentively.

"Madam," said I, "I demand that each of us be paid each Time she entertains a Swain, that we be treated like reasonable Creatures and not unthinking Beasts, that our Keep be tallied in a Book of Accounts open for all to see, and that it not be more than you yourself must pay for the Provisions."

"Trollop!" she scream'd. "Ye mean to ruin me! Out with ye into the Streets again. I'll not tolerate such Impertinence! I take the Risques and pay the Landlord here, I feed yer ungrateful Mouths and clothe ye like the Ladies ye are not! Why should I countenance such Mutiny? Damn yer whoring Eyes! Begone!" Whereupon she dramatically opens the Front Door and stands, Arms folded, with a curt Nod of her hennaed Head, bidding me go.

Panick reigns in my Breast then. Merciful Heaven, I think,

have I gone too far, stretch'd the Limits of her Endurance quite to the Breaking Point? But I dare not show my Indecision nor my Turmoil. With Chin held high and my stinking Skirts trailing in my Wake as if I were the Queen of Mudpyes and Chamber-Potts, I make ready to depart, with all Mock-Dignity.

I advance towards the Door, trembling within and calm without, pause a Moment to bid Farewell to the other Wenches who stand agog at my unwonted Courage, and say: "Gentle Ladies, thanks for all your Kindnesses to me. I wish you well," whereupon I turn upon my Heel, step across the Doorjamb mincingly, as if 'twere a Basket of Eggs, and out the Door.

But no sooner is my Back turned and it is clear that I am really going, than a Cry rises at my Back as if a Mob of Maenads had just glimps'd the Great God Pan himself!

To my Astonishment, 'tis the scrawny Nell who first runs forward, grabs me by the Skirts, and cries (as much to me as to Mother Coxtart): "If Fanny goes, then I go, too!" Whereupon the consumptive Roxana joins the Cry, and next the red-cheakt Molly! All three restrain me there without the Door, challenging Coxtart for the first Time in their Cow'ring Lives!

She is aghast, agog, amaz'd. She turns and looks at us, the Four Mutineers, and then back at the other Girls—Raven-hair'd Druscilla, the Creole Evelina—wond'ring, no doubt, how soon they, too, will rebel against the Divine Right of her Queenship. Like the Canny Politician that she is, she decides 'tis best to bargain now, whilst two Wenches yet remain in her Party, rather than waiting for the Mutiny, nay the Bloody Revolution, of all her Charges!

"Ladies, Ladies, Ladies," says she, in a new, gentle Tone. "Pray sit ye down and let us talk of this more calmly. Anger ne'er solv'd the Woes of Humankind, and War is e'er a poor Alternative to Peace. Let us reason with each other then, like true Philosophers."

I could scarce believe my Ears! Was it possible I'd won? Had my Brazenness accomplish'd what Submission ne'er could?

Slowly, with Dignity (and hiding my great Relief at being taken back again), I enter'd Mother Coxtart's House once more, closing the Door behind me, whilst my loyal Confederates, Nell, Roxanna, and Molly, walkt two Paces behind like Ladies in Waiting.

'Twas thus I learnt my first Great Lesson in the Conduct of Diplomacy. I had sought only to cover my own Fault in coming Home so late, and in my Brashness had spoken like the very Spirit of Lancelot Robinson himself—whose Notions of Fair Play and Camaraderie I had learnt during my Travels with the Merry Men. Little did I dream that Coxtart would truly propose a Counter-Scheme whereby each Wench earn'd a Share of the Profits of the House according to her Seniority and Industriousness! But now I saw that my Determination had frighten'd Coxtart, particularly when she saw all too clearly the Threat of her most valu'd Wenches all departing at once; and suddenly my bluffing Brazenness to acquit myself of Blame had turn'd me into the Heroine of all the House! 'Twas droll indeed! 'Twas perhaps a Lesson to me. For when I worried and fretted with Indecision, trembl'd lest I be turn'd out of Doors, no Good came of it—only more Worry and Fretting—but when I pretended to the Courage which I lackt, Coxtart herself capitulated and the other Wenches declar'd me reigning Queen!

All of 'em, that is, but Kate. For her part, she had been lockt in the Cellar upon my Account, and now nurs'd bitter Enmity 'gainst me. I tried to reason with her, to tell her that henceforth e'en she would have a Share in all she earn'd, but she was bitter with the Grudge of one who finds it hard to trust, then trusts a little, is betray'd, and now hates Humankind for good.

Friendship came hard to Kate. She had put out the first delicate Tendrils of that rare Plant; and when they were so unkindly lopp'd off by my Carelessness, Enmity took Root in their Stead.

"I knew I should ne'er have trusted ye," she said bitterly, when we were alone together.

"But Kate, I sought to reach Golden Square by Eleven; 'twas impossible."

"What kept ye, then?"

"I dare not say."

"Filthy Swine," she mutter'd. "Perhaps ye met the Scoundrel that put ye in the Family Way. I'll tell Coxtart that, I will."

"Tell her, then, tho' I swear 'tis a Lye. Have you no Wits about you? Do you not understand that you, too, will profit from this new Scheme?"

(For tho' Kate had been lockt in the Cellar during my great Mutiny 'gainst Coxtart, the other Wenches had related the Incident to her—nay, related it with as many Embellishments as a clever Comedian adds to the Words of the poor Poet who first penn'd his thund'ring Lines in a draughty Garret.)

"Who requires such Foolishness?" she said, with great Disdain. "I learnt to survive an' prosper before ye arrived here, *Madam* Fanny. Ye think yerself the Saviour o' the Girls—those simp'rin' Strumpets that are in Bondage because they can do nought but *dream* o' their Freedom! I've been savin' Shillin's these half a dozen Years an' mean to have a Shop o' me own thro' me own hard Work and me own lovin' Man. Poo—I care not a Fig fer yer fine Words to Coxtart an' all yer fake Philosophy. Ye ne'er did it the hard Way as I did, ye Baggage!"

Thus I learnt, (for Kate continu'd to hate me passionately, despite all I did to make amends) that Gratitude is, for some Mortals, the most unwelcome of Emotions; that many Women who feel they have borne the Brunt of Woman's Lot wish all their Sisters to be as unfortunate as they; that not only doth Misery love Company, but those who account themselves amongst the Miserable have a positive Hatred for those who would lure them amongst the Happy; and many Lessons of the like Nature—too num'rous to account for 'em all here, without unbearably delaying our Tale.

Now, I began to work like a very Devil, both to secure Lancelot Freedom of the Rules, and because, having won a Share of my own Earnings (tho' admittedly a small one), I was more eager than e'er before to play the false Virgin—or any other mischievous Rôle Coxtart devis'd for me—so long as it would yield the most Guineas.

Of the many Times my Maidenhead was taken, the Great Figures of the Day who enter'd the Brothel (only to enter my Bow'r of Bliss), and of their curious Predilections and Practices betwixt the Bed-Clothes, I shall have to tell in a separate Chapter. 'Twill be useful, I trust, for any Woman who must at some Time in her hapless Life make her Bread and Board with her Body; and what Woman alive hath not at some Time been brought into that Predicament?

For, are not e'en Wives—especially Wives of Great Men—nought but Whores in bart'ring their Board (e'en if it include gilt Coaches and rich laced Clothes) for their Bed? And do not e'en our Poets and Philosophers show that a Woman who is a wily Merchant of her Maidenhead will

222

make a better Match than one who spends it thriftlessly—as witness Mr. Richardson's cloying Pamela Andrews, who ensnares her Squire, Lord B, by holding fast to her Maidenhead until the very Moment after Marriage and thereby receiving the very best Goods in Exchange for it?

Belinda, you well may ask whether I, who was e'er prone to Deliberation and Philosophical Debate within my own Soul, deliberated with myself about earning my Living as a Whore. To be sure, I did so. But when I first came to Mother Coxtart's Brothel, 'twas not clear to me the House was a Brothel at all—so innocent and rustick was I. After that, I was restrain'd there under Lock and Key; and finally, knowing myself with Child and knowing now of Lancelot's great Need of me, I remain'd in order to obtain pecuniary Benefits for myself in the only Way I thought open to me. But unlike wily Pamela Andrews, I was an Honest Whore and no Hypocrite! I hold my Body freely, but not my Mind! Whereas the Wives of Great Men, or those who aspire to be the Wives of Great Men, sell e'en their Minds and account themselves blest into the Bargain!

No, Belinda, I preserv'd the Independence of my Mind e'en tho' I could not preserve the Independence of my Body. And so I account my Whoring more honest than the common State of Matrimony, wherein the Wife is sold to her Husband in exchange for Land to be added to her Father's Holdings and reaps the Benefit of High Life from the Rental of her Flesh in the Merchant's Shop of the Matrimonial Bed!

But now I come to a Subject far more unpleasant than e'en the one before, a Subject which makes my Quill tremble and my Eyes run with Tears—especially since these Pages are intended for my own Belinda. Would I were not sworn to Honesty above all! Would I were writing a Tale to pass the Time of Idle Ladies, or a Farce to be perform'd upon the London Stage! For now I must tell what I did upon the Ev'ning after my Mutiny 'gainst Coxtart and my Discussions with Kate in which I strove to make amends with her. I lockt myself in the Basement Privy ("The Stool of Repentance," as Coxtart call'd it), and with trembling Hand, I inserted the hellish black Suppository into the unwilling Mouth of my Womb.

'Twas no easy Thing; I bled profusely from my Nether Eye, and I also wept with those other Eyes which knew all too well the Import of my Act. 'Twas nothing short of Murder, in my View. I think there is no Woman in the World who murders her own Babe, Flesh of her own Flesh, without terrible Remorse and Pain; and yet my Desperation was so great that I knew I could not bear the Babe. Coxtart would throw me out upon the Street if she knew of my Condition, and not only would I surely starve, but Lancelot would starve and lose his Mind into the Bargain.

How can I explain this to you now, Belinda? How can I explain that you, the dearest Person in the World to me, the most precious Mortal on this spinning Globe, were once the Object of my murderous Wrath? Alas! Not Wrath, but Desperation! And yet, 'twas not, i'faith, you yourself! For a Mother in the first few Weeks of her new Condition, before she hath felt the Stirrings of Life within her, and before she hath borne a child at all, cannot conceive with her Mind what her Body can so well conceive with its smallest Atoms and its coursing Blood!

So I inserted the horrid black Thing into my Womb, and bled, and waited; and before a half an Hour had pass'd, I was wrackt with Pain so terrible I had to stuff the whole Hem of my Petticoat into my Mouth to keep from Screaming. I doubl'd o'er with the Pain. I held my Vitals. My Legs began to shake and sweat ran down my Brow. I dug my Nails into my Palms until they bled, whilst I pray'd silently to the Great Goddess, to Jesus Christ, our Lord, to any Deity at all who chanced to hear my Pray'r—e'en if it be the Foul Fiend Himself!—to grant me a Cessation of this Pain.

Pain was a great Red Ocean in which I swam, and I was a Shipwreckt Sailor. Pain was my Heaven, my Earth, my Native Element. I was near to fainting with the Pain, expiring there in the Reek of the House of Easement, with its fetid Odours rising and its Dampness like the Ante-Room to Hell itself—when, in a trice, my Womb cramp'd entirely in one horrid Convulsion, and the wretchèd black Thing (or what remain'd of it) came out.

I lost the Suppository with a fair Amount of Blood, yet I did not lose the Babe! That you know, since you yourself *are* that Babe (who held on with a Will of her own e'en before you had a Hand to grasp with, or a Rational Mind!). But at that Moment, I myself knew not whether I had loosed the Homunculus or no. I only knew I could not endure a Repetition of such Anguish e'er again, and I threw the other two ghastly black Things down the Hole of that stinking Privy, with scarce a Thought except to vent my Rage at being curst with Pain so unendurable!

In the Days that follow'd, I debated with myself as to whether I was still with Child. My Desire argu'd No; my Reason argu'd Yes; and, i'faith, I did not truly know until, well four Months later, 'twas unmistakable that my Belly had begun to grow.

But now I must go back again to that horrid Jakes and capture with my Quill the shaken, weeping seventeen-year-old Wench, who unlockt the Door, and with unsteady Tread, bloody Thighs, and bloody Linen, crept into her borrow'd brothel Bed to fall asleep and dream of the Home she had fore'er lost, whilst in her teeming Brain she could not ascertain—either by Logick or the wildest Guess—whether she would bear a Babe in nine Months' Time or no; but she suspected the Truth and it terrified her.

At the Washstand in my Chamber, I cleans'd myself as well as I could, wishing truly for a proper Bath, but not daring to call the Maid to assist me at this Hour. I cast aside my smelly Newgate Clothes, my bloody Linen (which I swore to burn in the Grate come Morning), and crept into my Bed. For a Time, 'tis true, I slept and dreamt of Lymeworth; but 'twas not the Lymeworth I had known, but a strange House with many dank Cellars in which Tortures were carried out whilst Rats scuttl'd past the bare and bleeding Feet of Victims.

A hooded Man in black boil'd and stirr'd the Limbs of Traitors in Tar and Pitch, and I leant over the ghastly Cauldron only to see a fearful sever'd Head bubble to the Top—and lo! 'twas Lancelot's Head, and it open'd its Lips to speak.

"Be there Honour amongst Thieves?" it cried. "Nay—fie on Humankind! They'll sell yer Soul fer thirty Pieces o' Silver! Beware the Captain o' the *Hannibal*! Beware the Captain o' yer Soul!" And then the Head submerged into the Pitch again.

I awaken'd with a sudden Cry. My limbs were shiv'ring and an icy Sweat stood in Drops upon my Brow. The Bed-Clothes were wet, as if with Rain. If my Dreams were to be so horrible, I'd best not sleep at all, I thought; whereupon I lit a Taper by my Bed, and sat up holding my Knees to my Belly like a Child.

My Thoughts roam'd back o'er the preceding Day and all the hellish Visions I had seen in Living London which had then fill'd my Dream of Death; I thought of Lancelot in Gaol, of Mrs. Skynner, of angry Kate, of my triumphant Mutiny and then my abject Misery, not long after. Rage fill'd my Heart where Sorrow once had been. How could my Body mutiny so against my Mind? I was just beginning to learn of Life; were all my Hopes of Pow'r o'er my Fate to be snatch'd from me so soon by this small Intruder in my Belly?

No sooner did I feel this Anger than I was stung by bitterest Remorse. I pitied the poor unform'd Creature to be so hated before 'twas e'en born! What a Monster I was! Had I no Pity upon the Small and Weak? And yet 'twas true, I felt the full Force of an Invasion. The Babe had enter'd quite against my Will—as if I were a Castle or a Fort, and some Imposter, in the Guise of Friend, had penetrated to my very Centre, and now sought nothing less than my Life!

Alas, Belinda, perhaps you will forgive me for these Thoughts when you, too, bear a Babe; for no State is as much akin to Madness upon the one Hand and Divinity upon the other, as being with Child. First, there is the Fear of Death, which no Woman who lyes down to bear a Babe can be sure she will escape; next, there is the Fear of Pain; finally, there is the Terror that she will prove an unloving Mother, wishing her Babe dead each Time it cries, instead of pitying its prodigious Need of her.

But with each Month that the Babe within grows bigger, the Certainty grows stronger that her own Destiny is intermingl'd with her Child's. Henceforth, she shall define herself, at least in part, as the Mother of that Babe. If it dyes, she is the Mother of a dead Babe; if it lives, its Smiles and Tears will be her Smiles and Tears. If 'tis taken from her, still, she is changed fore'er on Earth and in Heaven, too. She has been doubl'd, then halv'd; and she will ne'er be whole again.

Chapter VI

Containing a short Sketch of the celebrated Dean Swift of Dublin, Author, Misanthrope, and Horse-Fancier extraordinaire; together with some philosophical and moral Lessons which our Heroine drew from her curious Friendship with him.

THE EXPECTATION OF A BABE, for a Woman who is without Dowery, Husband, or i'faith without loving Relations, creates, above all, an immense Capacity for hard Work.

Ladies with Child who languish in the Country whilst their Husbands pursue Whoring and Gaming in Town, may indeed be curst with ev'ry Ailment of the Female Flesh; but Ladies who must work to put Bread into their own Mouths are, i'faith, too busy to suffer from Faintings or the Spleen, from Lethargy or Megrim, Sciatica or Vomiting. Idleness itself creates the Spleen, but good hard Work cures all these Maladies better than the costliest Physician.

My Work was hard—hard upon my Body and harder still upon my Mind, for 'tis no easy Thing to be put to Bed with Gentlemen for whom one has nought but Dread and Loathing. Picture to yourself a young Girl, still in love with Love itself, being forced to frolick betwixt the Bedsheets with cadav'rous old Men, bandy-legg'd Actors, pockmarkt Booksellers, and young Merchants' Apprentices still with Pustules upon their boyish Cheaks.

All these loathsome Swains I will, howe'er, pass o'er; I have already given an ample Picture of my Initiation both with Coxtart herself, and with Theophilus Cibber. I shall now devote myself to describing the other Swains I met within the Brothel—particularly the Illustrious Ones; for just as Honest Women in this weary World derive all Honour from the Men (whether Husbands or Lovers) who keep them, so Whores are valu'd by the Illustriousness of their Swains. For a Woman is ne'er thought to make her Way in the World upon

227

her own Merits, but she will fore'er be judged according to the Men who love her.

I'faith, Women know well 'tis true that oft' they flourish *despite* their Men rather than because of 'em, yet the World will e'er judge us in reverse; and Wags will always say we gain'd whatsoe'er Preferment we have found from our Lovers.

Did I gain Preferment from my Illustrious Lovers? Rather I would say, with all Modesty intended, they gain'd it from me, for I had begun to learn, having had Womanhood so rudely thrust upon me in my seventeenth Year, that Men come to a Brothel as much for Understanding and Compassion as for the Fulfillment of their Lustful Desires, and that a Whore who pays Attention only to their Bodies (and not to their Minds) will ne'er flourish long in her Trade.

Sure there are Whores who trade only in the Flesh, but they are the ones soon tired of, soon clapp'd, soon dead. The Whores who endure despite their perilous Profession are those who minister as well to the Souls of Men as to their Bodies. Truly, we are Clergy, of a sort.

Speaking in this Vein, I think, above all, of Dean Swift, later so famous as the Author of *Travels into Sev'ral Remote Nations of the World* by "Lemuel Gulliver," and so infamous in England, yet rever'd in his Hibernian Homeland as the Author of *The Drapier's Letters.*

He was in England secretly for a brief Time during my first Summer in the Brothel. Secrecy was indeed of the utmost Import, since had the Crown but known that the detested Drapier who had done so much to arouse the Ire of the Irish Patriots, was upon English Soil, his Neck would ne'er be safe, and he might suffer the same Fate as my belovèd Lancelot. Dean Swift was a curious Fellow—the cleverest Man I e'er had met but for Lancelot himself—and, I believe, much misunderstood. Just as I had rever'd Mr. Pope for his Poetical Works before I met him, and then grew disappointed with the Man himself, so 'twas the Reverse with Dean Swift: my Admiration grew, first from my Knowing him, then from the Splendour of his Works. Of course I had not read his notorious *Travels*, when first I made his Acquaintance (nor had the World), and yet I was charm'd by the Man himself, and understood a good deal more of his Enigmatick Character when I came to read those *Travels* two Years later.

He was a rather short Man, above fifty Years of Age, and

his Eyes were surely his most striking Feature. Bright blue they were, almost piercing and somewhat protuberant, as if he'd had a Goitre once, or else was goggle-eyed at the Injustice of the World (which, indeed, he could be quite as furious o'er as Lancelot). When he was mild, his Eyes were azure as the Seas of the Spanish Main; but when Anger flasht in those Orbs, they could quite terrify.

He was a great Card Player (he taught me Ombre, Picquet, and Whisk), a great Giver of little Gifts (tho' he could ill afford 'em), and quite prodigal in his Charities. For a Man who had a Reputation as a Misanthrope and Malcontent, he was oft' merry and the best of Company, but I believe he suffer'd greatly from Dizziness and some Disturbance in his Ears which, ne'ertheless, he bore with the Stoicism of an Ancient Roman.

We had sev'ral Passions in common, in particular the Love of Horses, and the Belief that a Good Horse was better than the best of Men. Likewise, we were both haunted by our common Want of a Father; for Presto (as he call'd himself amongst the Ladies) was born Months after his Father's unfortunate Demise, and always accounted himself an Orphan of sorts (which perhaps explain'd that heighten'd Sensitivity in his Character, a Species of Skinlessness, as 'twere, which made all the Barbs of the World prick him more than they prickt the ordinary Man).

His Passions were many, and contradictory in the extream. He hated Fanaticism of any kind, Projectors who would improve the World by Schemes, and Criticks who cluster'd about the greatest of Authors.

"A Critick," he once said to me, "is one who cannot write very well himself and therefore spends his Days and Nights in laying down the Law to those who can." Similarly, he hated Divines, tho' he was one himself, for as he said, "Is not Religion a Cloak, and Conscience a Pair of Breeches, which tho' a Cover for Lewdness as well as Nastiness, can be pull'd down for the Service of both?"

He lov'd La Rochefoucauld above all other Authors, for showing so well that Man is not the Rational Creature he claims to be, but is riddl'd with contradictory Passions, Lusts, and Vanities. And yet he avow'd that he himself wrote Satyres in order "to vex the World rather than divert it" and "to bring Mankind to his Senses before 'twas too late and all Hope of Reason was lost fore'er."

"If you despair of Reason, my dear Presto, why do you

229

write to bring the World to Reason?" I askt him more than once.

"Because I am a Fool, Fanny," said he. But like all Men who readily admit their Foolishness, he was amongst the cleverest.

And yet there was something uncontrollable and contradictory in his Character, for he always claim'd he had wisht to rise in Court and yet had stood in his own Sun by insulting all those who could help him.

"Had I but curb'd my Tongue and Pen, I might have rose like other Men," said he, the Couplet coming as readily to his Lips as a Cough to the Lips of a Consumptive. But sure, he could no more curb his Pen than a Nightingale can curb his Song. 'Twas his Genius to lash the World, and he paid dearly for that Genius.

He was helpless to refrain from lashing the Criticks in whose Pow'r it was to help him rise, or the Courtiers, or the Ladies in Waiting, who had the Ears of the Great. All these he call'd Whores and Parasites, and then was stung bitterly when they wreakt Vengeance upon him in return. Passion he had aplenty, but no Tact whatsoe'er. Brilliance, but no Gift for Diplomacy. Lying he hated and could so little manage it that he worried constantly lest his Stella in Dublin should know of our Liaison and be vext with him. He had not married her, he said (despite Rumours to the Contrary), for Marriage ruin'd the best of Women and made them Scolds. Besides, the World already had too many unlov'd Brats within it; better to practise Continence than coax another hapless Infant into this sorry World. "For, consid'ring the Miseries of Human Life," said he, "why should a Child be under any Obligation whatsoe'er to his Parents for bringing him into the World? Life is neither a Benefit in itself, nor was so intended by the Babe's Natural Parents, whose Thoughts in their Love-Encounters, were otherwise employ'd."

I was glad, indeed, 'twas not yet apparent I was with Child; for had he known, he would have despis'd me as a "Yahoo"—his curious Word for all those Mortals who give in to the Appetites of the Flesh. He lov'd Women to be young and girlish, slim and virginal, like unattempted Brides. Little Girls of Twelve, with Breasts still unfledged, represented his favourite Female Forms; thus when Coxtart first brought him to my Chamber, she bade me tell him I was e'en younger than Seventeen and instructed me to wear my Bridal Costume, yet not be vext nor insulted if he ne'er touch'd my Flesh.

He would talk instead and feast his bright blue Eyes upon me, discoursing of Philosophy and Literature, Politicks and Religion; and once, when he was satisfied I was fond of him and would not think him strange, he propos'd that we go together into the Countryside and spend a curious Afternoon romping amongst Foals and Mares and Stallions at the Park of one of his Friends.

We hir'd a Barge upriver, upon that splendid Summer's Afternoon, rode as far as Maidenhead, there were met by a One-Horse Chaise belonging to the Dean's Friend, and carried to a beauteous Country Estate call'd Dumswood, whose Owner was said to have some of the finest Race Horses in England.

Perhaps by design, Dean Swift's Friend had been call'd away. Only his Grooms and Trainers and other Servants were in attendance; thus we could be almost entirely undisturb'd as we picknickt upon the Green, watching the Mares and Foals frolicking upon the velvet Grass.

"Observe the Horse," said the Dean, "observe his nimble Gait compar'd to the shambling Gait of Man. For a Man is a Creature that hath but lately determin'd to walk upon his hind Legs, whereas a Horse flies upon all four with such surpassing Grace that the Ancients themselves identified the Horse with Poesy!" (Ah, when the Dean said this, I knew beyond any Doubt that we were Friends of the Soul, for had I not oft' thought the very same Thing concerning Horse and Poesy, Horse and Man?)

"For mark you, Fanny," he went on, "from the most ancient Times, Man and Horse have known a Mystick Bond. The Mare hath been identified with the Earth Goddess, Persephone, and the Stallion with the Sun God, Apollo. Warriors, from Ancient Times were buried with their Steeds; and e'en in the Greece of Homer, Horse Races form'd part of the Funerary Games. The fierce Mongols and the ferocious Tartars drank of *Kumiss,* or fermented Mare's Milk, to raise Visions in their Brains; and the Celts perform'd a sacred Wedding betwixt Mare and King to ensure Fertility of Crops and Men. In the remote and Pagan Counties of Ireland, I have heard, e'en Today, of Men mating with Snow White Mares to raise the Crops and stave off Famine—but the Irish are a Barbarous Race and capable of any Nastiness!"

Just then a dappl'd Grey Mare walkt curiously up to our

Picknick Spot, turn'd Tail, and harken'd to one of Nature's profoundest Necessities.

The Dean was entranced. "Observe, Fanny," said he. "E'en the Droppings of a Horse are Golden Stones compar'd to a Man's brown and putrid Excrement! Mark how beautiful they are—these Golden Droppings! And is this not because the Horse eats nought but the purest Grass and Hay, whilst we, who claim to be the Rational Race, eat largely dead and decaying Flesh? By a Creature's very Droppings shall ye know him!"

"But Presto, Dear," say I, "a Horse has no Rational Speech, whilst we can converse in Language and thus inprove our Reason. . . ." And yet I said this merely for the Sake of Argument, for had I not convers'd quite reasonably with my own Horse, Lustre? Alas, that I could not introduce the Dean to him!

"Bah," says the Dean, "we but use Language to obfuscate the Truth, as if we were all Lawyers! Yet the Whinnying of a Mare to a Foal is a purer Language, if we could but understand it!"

I listen'd deeply to the Whinnying of the Mares, striving to hear the Rational Language which the Dean assur'd me was to be found there—but all I could hear, alas, was Whinnying! Perhaps one must live with a Horse to understand him—for tho' surely had I understood Lustre, these strange Horses I could not. The Dean, it seem'd, had finer Ears; for within the Brute Noises of the Beast, he heard Philosophies and Poetries no other Mortal Ears could hear. "Houyhnhnms," he call'd the Horses, pronouncing the Name as if 'twere the Neighing of a Horse; and "Yahoos," as I've said, was his Word for Humankind, which, he avow'd, was neither as human nor as kind as it pretended.

For an Hour or more, he discours'd to me of Horses. He explain'd the History of the Horse in England, how the heavy Horses of our Ancestors had been cross-bred with the Arabians to produce the Noble Thoroughbred, the finest Horse the World hath e'er known. He spoke of the slender Beauty of the Thoroughbred, the Wildness of the Pure Arabian, the Pow'r of the heavy Breeds, the Charm of the Connemara, Shetland, and the Welsh Ponies, the soulful Eyes of Mares, and the flaring nostrils of Stallions—almost as if he were a Lover besotted with his Belovèd's Charms. He spoke at length of his Contempt for Mankind in making this Creature, so much more noble than himself, into a Beast of Burden,

232

and he told me of the Bedouin Tribes who rais'd their Horses in their own Tents, sleeping and eating with 'em, keeping 'em as tender Companions their whole Lives long.

For Guerinière's Rules of Horsemanship, he had nought but Contempt. The artificial Gaits, the Paces these Noble Creatures were forced to learn, disgusted him. The *Galopade, Volté, Pirouette, Terre à Terre, Mezair, Pesade, Courbette, Croupade, Balotade, Capriole*, and such, he view'd but as Expressions of Human Vanity forced upon the gentle Horse. Indeed, the entire Art of Equitation he detested.

"For Man hath taken this splendid peaceable Creature and forced him to the Arts of War. No Horse in his Native State would go to War," said he. "The Horse is by Nature a Peacemaker; Man alone makes War upon his Fellows. Ah, Fanny, when I see the Sadness of Horses in Harness, my Eyes fill with Tears and I curse the Race that claims me as its own! Oppressors are we all—vain, proud, stupid, but pretending to Reason! The Horse is Reason itself. If any Creature deserves to rule the World, 'tis he!"

I'faith, the Dean was so caught up in his Fancies and Reveries about Horses, that I could scarce tell him of my Horse, Lustre, of the fine Arabians Lord Bellars had imported, of the many Foalings I myself had witness'd as a Child, of that splendid Moment, the Culmination of eleven Months of great Anticipation, when the Foal emerges, Forelegs first, then Muzzle, then Cheaks, then Ears, then Withers, then Flank, and then the Foal entire, with the Moon-blue Membranes gleaming, and the Waters of the Womb still glist'ning upon his infant Fuzz! My own fondest Childhood Memories were also of Horses. Perhaps that was why I made no Objection to the Dean's next Fancy.

Now he would try a fanciful Experiment, he said. He would cause me to strip naked upon the Grass, and then he would strive to coax a Stallion to copulate with me. So carried away with this Scheme was he, that he ne'er consulted me as to my Willingness, but rav'd only that this would be the final Proof of his Theories, that upon his Honour I would be uninjur'd, and that he himself would owe me his whole Life, if only I would do his Bidding.

'Twas indeed the most curious Request I had e'er entertain'd in my brief Life as a Whore, but 'twas my Duty, after all, to satisfy the sundry Lusts of my Swains no Matter how peculiar, and a Sense of Curiosity motivated me as well. Indeed the Stallion he chose lookt so like Lustre—but for a lack of white Markings—that, i'faith, I would almost conceive him as my Lover!

I put off all my Garments on the sunny Greensward and lay upon the Grass drinking in the Summer Sun, whilst the Dean, his Eyes gleaming with Mischief, went off to fetch the Stallion. He caus'd the Grooms to lock up all the Mares and Foals within the Barn, so as not to tempt the Stallion to furious rampaging Lust, then he led the Chestnut Stallion to me, his burnish'd Coat gleaming in the Sun.

This Stallion was endow'd with a Cock to make any Pretty Fellow green with Envy; and as the Dean spoke softly in his Ear, in the whinnying Language of the Horses, and rubb'd his Belly and his Balls, the Stallion's Cock grew until 'twas of a Size to affright the most lascivious old Whore.

The Dean watch'd with Wonder and Admiration, as if he, too, were half in Love with the Stallion. Then, when he was assur'd the Stallion's Cock could grow no more, he bade me climb upon his own Back (so that together we almost reach'd the Horse's Height), put my Arms 'round his Neck, and spread my Nether Cheaks as wide as e'er I could, presumably to tempt the Stallion.

Soon the Dean began to romp and whinny, with me stark naked clinging to his Back. He coaxt the Stallion in the curious Language of the Horses, and play'd the Horse himself, trotting across the Grass with me upon his Back! But tho' the Stallion eyed us curiously, and once e'en came forward to look at our strange two-backt Beast more closely, 'twas clear as Crystal that he'd no Intention to copulate either with me or with the Dean!

This "Experiment" we continu'd for well nigh half an Hour, until the Stallion, in Boredom and *Ennui*, wander'd off, his Cock now much reduced to normal Size, and began to graze in an adjoining Field. With a Cry of Triumph and the cunning Smile of a Lawyer who hath won his Case, the Dean cried out: "Sweet Fanny, now dismount!" To which I happily obey'd, and as he help'd me dress, he drew such Moral Lessons as he could from this.

"For mark you, Fanny, a Man in Heat will mate with any Hole that presents itself to his View! He'll mate with Hens, Sheep, or e'en ripe Melons, a pregnant Woman, or one that flies the Monthly Flag! But a Horse, a Noble Horse, mates only with a Mare to bear a Foal, mates not out of her proper Season, and thus is far more rational than Man!"

As we made our Way back to Town once more, by the

234

mighty Highway of the Thames, the Dean discours'd continuously of the Diff'rences betwixt Men and Horses; and, i'faith, I had to agree that his curious Logick had some Justice in it. If I seem'd on the Verge of Tears as he spoke, 'twas because I was thinking always of Lustre, and tormenting myself concerning his Fate. Was he a common Pack-Horse, being workt to Death, fed little, languishing for Want of Rational Discourse? Was he a Freak in a Raree Show, caus'd to leap through flaming Hoops, or jump flaming Barrels, or dance upon his hind Legs like a Circus Dog?

"I have no Love for Man's Hubris," said the Dean, not noticing my welling Tears. "His Tragick Flaw is that he thinks himself a Rational Being, when 'tis clear from all his Acts that he is more benighted than the lowest Insect that crawls along the Ground. I have e'er hated all Nations, Professions, Communities, dear Fanny, and all my Love is for Individuals. Ah—wait until you read my *Travels*. They are admirable Things and will wonderfully mend the World."

This was the chief Contradiction in the Dean—that he claim'd Mankind had no Pow'rs of Reason, and yet he fore'er tried to mend the World and bring it to its Senses. He was a slighted Lover of Mankind, one who lov'd not wisely, but too well. And having seen his Love rejected, trampl'd in the Mud, he grew Bitter. From him I learnt that ev'ry Misanthrope is nought but one who once hath lov'd the World too well; ev'ry Misanthrope's a wounded Innocent, I fear.

When I came to read the Dean's *Travels* two Years later, I was indeed amaz'd! 'Twas then I most wisht to discourse with him—but, alas, I ne'er saw him again.

The Book astounded me with its Brilliance of Invention. That plain Man Gulliver amongst all those fanciful Creatures! What a merry Book indeed! To Swift I accorded the greatest Compliment one Author pays another: I wisht his Book were mine! And yet I knew e'en then that Books—especially the greatest Books—are like the Wrinkles in our Faces; each Man makes his own. And we can no more imitate 'em than we can seek to wear another Author's Face. The Books we love the best are quirky and curious indeed as the Minds that gave 'em birth!

I need not tell you, Belinda, how the Book at once captur'd all the Town and was the Rage of ev'ry Tea-Table, replacing Ombre and Gossip as the Ruling Passions of the Ladies. I wisht to write the Dean my Felicitations, but, having heard that his Stella was ill and close to Death, I dar'd not, for fear my Letter would be discover'd and hasten her Untimely End.

But you may well ask whether, having known the Dean in such an intimate Fashion, I have my Piece to add to the furious Discussion of his Works which raged amongst both his Lovers and Detractors. Did he mean his Gulliver to be a sane Man, or a Poor Bedlamite, driven out of his Wits by too many Shipwrecks? Alas, I fear that Knowledge of Dean Swift's last tragick Illness hath prejudiced the World concerning his Books.

I heartily affirm that his Gulliver possesses the soundest of Minds, that he alone of all Mankind sees the World quite clearly; and truly, when he retreats to a Stable to live with Horses and will no longer have Intercourse with Men, 'tis because he hath discover'd the two great fatal Flaws in Humankind: the Stink of Mendacity and the rotting Odour of Vanity. He would rather feast his Senses upon the good clean Smell of Horses' Flesh than suffer the putrid Odour of Mankind's Lyes. And, for this, who indeed can blame him? Living in Coxtart's Brothel, I oft' felt so myself.

Chapter VII

*Of Fanny's Acquaintance with those two curious Fig-
ures, Mr. William Hogarth and Master John Cleland;
their opposing Views of her Character, their Predilections both in Life and Art; together with our Heroine's
Motives in composing this True and Compleat History
of her exotick and adventurous Life.*

MR. HOGARTH ALSO FREQUENTED Coxtart's Brothel, both to
satisfy his fleshly Lusts and to sketch the Girls.

During that fearsome Summer of 1724, when all my Care
was to procure Money to get Lancelot Freedom of the Rules,
and to put some by for my Lying-in, I met countless Swains
besides the illustrious Dean Swift, the young Painter Mr.
Hogarth, and that dastardly Stripling, Master Cleland, who
was later to exploit my History so callously in his *Memoirs of
a Woman of Pleasure.* But of these three, I have the most
vivid Memories; for, howe'er reduced my Circumstances to
humble Whoredom, my Mind was still keen for Learning,
and from these Swains, above all, could I improve my Intellect as well as my Fortunes.

Mr. Hogarth came at first to purchase my Mock-Maidenhead (having heard from his whoremong'ring Colleagues that
there was a new and delicious Wench in Town). He was,
howe'er, too clever a Fellow to be gull'd by my ravish'd
maiden Pantomime; for, unlike so many of the others, he was
no foolish Aristocrat, no Strutting Player, no Poet besotted
with his own Verses, but a plain young Fellow from Smithfield who had grown to Manhood in the Precincts near Bartholomew Fair, and had feasted his Childhood Eyes upon all
Manner of Mountebanks, Merry Andrews, Strolling Players,
Acrobats, Rope Dancers, Quacks, Jugglers, Puppets, Huxters,
Giants, Dwarfs, Drolls, Jilts, Harlots, and Sharpers. From the
tend'rest Years, he had known the hard Life of the London
Streets, for the Area of Bartholomew Close and Smithfield

237

was still the London of Olden Days, untouch'd by the Great Fire. 'Twas a Cattle Market where the Oxen and Sheep were driven up each Monday and the narrow ancient Streets were fill'd with Dung, Blood, Guts, drown'd Puppies, dead Cats, and straggling Turnip Tops.

Hogarth himself, tho' he lookt the most unprepossessing Pug (being short, blunt-featur'd, and stout as a little Bull-dog), was a canny Fellow, the Son of a distracted Schoolmaster turn'd Coffeehouse Keeper, who'd been gaol'd in the Fleet for Debt; and he was determin'd to escape his Father's hard Fate. His Father, said he, had spent the better part of his Life toiling at Dictionaries for callous Booksellers, who neither paid him a Fair Share of Earnings when the Book sold, nor fail'd to blame him when it dy'd stillborn. He had resolved, therefore, e'en at the Age of Twenty-Seven (when I met him), not to be a Victim like his hapless Father; for he aspir'd to Great Things, knowing himself blest with the Gift for getting the most telling Likeness with two Strokes of a Quill or Brush, and possess'd, as well, of the Lit'ry Gifts his Father had so little known how to exploit.

He quickly call'd my Bluff as a false Virgin.

"Fanny, my Girl," said he, " 'tis clear you've been a Virgin fifty Times, if you have been so once."

"I beg your Pardon, Sirrah," said I, all full of Mock-Dignity. "How dare you jest with a poor Country Girl that offers up the only Jewel she hath?"

"Jewel, my Arse," says Will Hogarth. "The Jewel is Pigeon Blood and the Country Girl hath learnt some City Ways! But I'll not tell Coxtart that I've call'd your Bluff if you'll sit for me both in your Clothes and out!"

'Twas thus I became Hogarth's Model as well as his sometime Whore, and as he sketch'd me, filling endless Books with my Face, my Breasts, my Rump, my Legs, my Hands, we told each other of our Youths, our Hopes, our Dreams. His Quill would scratch upon the Page as he rav'd on and on about the Bad Taste of the Town.

"No self-respecting English Lord," he said, "will buy a Painting unless it comes from bloody Italy! For the English disdain their own Native Genius. In Musick they must have Mr. Handel—and other curious Germans or Italians who sing in Gibberish no True-born Englishman can understand—and in Painting, they call for the Italian Rogues, spend Fortunes upon Forgeries of Nymphs and Dragons, or else pay Homage to a Mountebank like William Kent, who declares all En-

238

glishmen devoid of Craft and Art, paints Pretty Pictures in the Italian Mode, styles himself a noble Ancient Roman, and hath the Earl of Burlington to lick his Arse and settle his Bills for Port! By God, Fanny, I hate the Palladians worse e'en than the Italian Charlatans, for they spit upon our Native English Genius, whilst they tout the rankest Mediocrity in the Name of Noble Rome!"

"What would you do?" I askt, scratching my naked Rump and quickly resuming my Pose.

"Fanny, my Love, I would show the wide World as 'tis! I would show the Streets of London with their dead Cats and squalling Babes. I would show Trollops and Mountebanks and Strolling Players at Southwark Fair! I would show Rope Dancers falling from their Ropes, and Actresses disrobing in a Barn! I would show Taverns and Brothels; Paupers drunk on Gin and Burghers drunk on Beer! I would show Whores as well as Grecian Goddesses, Rogues as well as Heroes, Bakers and Brewers as well as Noble Lords! For which amongst us hath e'er glimps'd St. George, or a Dragon, for that matter? But the very World we see around us—the sprawling Streets, the squalling Mob—why should we disdain it? 'Tis the very Stuff of English Life!"

As he spoke, he sketch'd, as always, his Tongue moving quite as rapidly as his Quill. Then, in a trice, he leapt up and ran to me where I lay naked on the Bed. He wav'd the Paper in his Hand.

"See, Fanny," said he, showing me the Sketch. I had to laugh out loud to see; for he had caught me in that very Moment when I scratch'd my Rump, and upon my Face was a quizzical Look as if I doubted all he said. 'Twas so true a Likeness that I roar'd at my own Foolishness; all the Time I had been posing like a Goddess, fancying the Ideal Form that would emerge 'neath the Artist's Quill, he had seen nought but a Country Wench that scratches her Rump and looks most quizzically upon the World!

"Is that how I appear to you?" said I.

"At Times," said he, "you are a Country Maid, at Times a Queen, but with your flaming Hair and flaming Nether Hair as well, I think of you more as a raging Fire than a mere Woman, a Conflagration that might consume all of London and me as well!" With that, he threw himself upon me, dropp'd his Quill and Paper and his Breech; and made love to me as vigorously as any Swain had done.

But enough of that. Why interrupt my Tale with still another inflaming Love Scene, as if I were Mr. Cleland himself? Alas, it bores me to detail all the various and sundry Cocks that slipp'd betwixt my youthful Legs that Summer. Suffice it to say that Mr. Hogarth's Tastes were simple; not for him the Excitement of Stallions and Mares, nor the Thrill of Disguises and Masquerades. He lik'd his Ladies wanton, compliant, and built for *Use*; and his Cock was quite as energetick as his Quill or Tongue.

Not all Great Artists are Great Orators and Great Fornicators as well, but Mr. Hogarth surely was. Perhaps 'twas due to the Shortness of his Stature, all his Animal Spirits were compact, as 'twere, into a smaller Space.

Some eight Years later, when the Artist and I had not seen each other for sev'ral Years, I chanced to pass a Print Shop which display'd "The Harlot's Progress" or "The Humours of Drury Lane" by Mr. William Hogarth. There, I saw the Use to which he had put all his Sketches of me! E'en the Name of his Trollop (which many assum'd was inspir'd by Francis Hackabout, the notorious hang'd Highwayman, or Katherine Hackabout, his hapless whoring Sister), was, in fact, inspir'd by my Tales to him (whilst posing in the nude) of my Travels with the Merry Men and Lancelot's naming me in accordance with my Fortunes!

The Prints near broke my Heart, for they show'd the Fate which might well have been mine—and which, i'faith, I'd narrowly escap'd. In the first, the Harlot comes to London from the Country, an Innocent, prey'd upon by Bawd and Rapemaster alike. She knows not what her Fate will be, but a wrung-neckt Goose in the Foreground of the Pictures shows that the clever Artist knows. She progresses, through gradual Stages of Debauchery, from being kept by a rich Jew (whom she cuckolds), to being the tainted Whore of Highwaymen, to beating Hemp in Bridewell (still in her Whore's Finery!), to dying of the Pox in a Garret, whilst her poor Urchin sits by the Grate, waiting for his meagre Supper. In the last Print of all, she lyes in her sad Coffin whilst the Whores and Clergymen around her are yet more interested in their own tawdry Pleasures than in the grave Lesson of her Death. ('Tis is sad Commentary indeed upon the Clergy that have so little Interest in the spiritual Welfare of their Flock.) But sadder than all these Lessons is the Fate of Moll Hackabout herself. For truly she endures the Wages of Lust whilst her Swains go free; and she dyes a Pauper's Death of Clap, whilst the Rapemasters and Clergymen flourish to work their Wickedness

240

upon the next Innocent. Canny Hogarth knew that 'tis the Woman who always suffers for the Sins of all Mankind.

Did the Artist think, when he sketch'd me, that this would be my Fate? No doubt he did. And there were dreadful Times I fear'd 'twould be so myself. Yet I do not fault him for using my Name nor indeed Aspects of my Face (a certain sad-eyed Look for the imprison'd Whore, the Curve of a plump Breast or slender Ankle), for clearly his Sympathies are with the innocent Girl, whom the World abuses, then casts upon the Refuse Heap of Death.

Mr. Cleland, upon the other Hand, I consider no Friend of mine, nor of the Fair Sex in gen'ral, for the Portrait he paints of *his* simp'ring Strumpet leaves the World to think that the Whore's Life is nought but a Bed of Roses. Of Clap, Consumption, the Evils of Drink, Death in Childbed (and the other Ravages of the poor Harlot's Life), he hath nought to say. Reading his Book, you'd think that the Whore's Life was as great a Lark as that of a Lawyer or a Magistrate or e'en a Physician! (I mention, of course, those who batten off the Sorrows of the Poor!)

For mark you, Belinda, here were two Men whom I met at the self-same Time of Life; whilst one saw me as a Figure fit for Tragedy, the other saw me as the very Embodiment of Comedy and Light-heartedness. And which indeed was the Truth? Is there, i'faith, one Truth indivisible? Are our Characters not more oft' form'd in the Eyes of our Beholders than in our Souls themselves? For tho', 'tis true, we must learn to know ourselves—in order to survive this Wicked World, and also Divine Judgement in the World to come—oft' the Image the Publick hath of us is more compounded of the Follies and Fears of those who lov'd (or hated) us than of our own true Mettle. Thus 'tis that ev'ry Woman's most Profound Lesson must be to learn to disregard the World's Opinion of her, and to rest her Case solely upon her own Opinion of herself; for whilst the World may at Times be just in judging the Characters of Men (tho' e'en here, more oft' it errs), 'tis ne'er so in judging the Characters of Women. Indeed, Women are thought to have "no Characters at all"—in the Words of Mr. Pope, and to flit from Fancy to Fancy as a Butterfly flits from Flow'r to Flow'r. Perhaps *this* accounts for the Hubris of the Male in fashioning the Female, in Novels and Poems, as the very Creature of his own Fancies; and perhaps the Masculine Poet avers that "Women have no

Characters at all," so as to better justify his unfeeling and un-thinking Treatment of her in his Verses!

But I must pass now to Mr. Cleland, who came into my Life not long after Will Hogarth. Unlike the Painter, who stood upon the very Threshold of his Fame, John Cleland was a mere Stripling—with the Pustules of Youth still standing upon his Cheaks like so many small Monuments to his Lust! Nor was he more than two Years out of Westminster School.

He came into my Chamber all full of Swagger and Braggadocio, claiming that he requir'd a fresh Maidenhead a Day to keep his Spirits up (as a Vampyre requires Blood), and declaring himself to be a Man of the World, a weary Voyager in the Ports of Love, a jaded Rake, a bor'd Libertine—when indeed 'twas clear as Crystal that he was not above my own Age. I'faith, I later learnt he was e'en two Years younger!

I was, once more, in my Bride's Attire (tho' how much longer I could claim to be Virgin was doubtful—for I was already becoming quite famous in the Town, and to speak the Truth, I was also growing rather bor'd with the Game myself) when I made Mr. Cleland's Acquaintance.

I'll ne'er forget how he lookt upon that first Occasion when I met him. He'd got himself up like a Pretty Fellow of the Town—with Silver-hilted Sword, Laced Hat, Full-bottom'd Wig, and a Velvet Waistcoat, laced with Silver, despite the Summer's Heat. Yet all these Clothes fit him quite ill, as if indeed they were borrow'd, or purloin'd, Finery. And his Hat, in particular, was sev'ral Sizes too big—e'en with the Wig 'neath it—and slipp'd o'er his Eyes most comically.

"My Belovèd Bride!" he cried, entering the Chamber.

I could scarce conceal a Yawn at the Words. O I was weary of my Work, and weary of this foolish Pantomime! How, in the Name of the Goddess, would I e'er find the Zeal to play at this absurd Virginity still one more Time? I was bor'd in the extream.

"Come catch me, Groom!" I cried, going through the Formality of the Chase 'round the Bed with barely conceal'd *Ennui*. Young Mr. Cleland chas'd me dutifully, and yet, he seem'd in as little Hurry to catch me as I was to be caught. I'faith, he seem'd more truly afraid of me than I was pretending to be afraid of him!

This Masquerade of Chase and Pursuit we kept up as long as we could—I darting about the Bed, he chasing me (like a

242

fat, lazy Cat chasing an agile Mouse), but 'twas plain he had no Stomach for it.

"Come catch me," I cried again. Yet how could I play the unwilling Virgin when he was still more unwilling than myself?

At last he collaps'd upon the Floor (in all his Finery) and began to weep most piteously.

"I'faith, Madam Fanny," says he, "I am a Virgin myself!" And with that, he pulls off the absurd Full-bottom'd Wig, revealing to my Sight the sweet Face of a Boy of Fifteen (albeit a sweet Face bespeckl'd with Pustules!), with frighten'd Eyes that regard me (me!) as a Woman of the World!

Then my Pity is rais'd where Lust could ne'er be rais'd, and sweetly and tenderly I begin to undress him, revealing his bare pink Chest, his tiny Hips, his spindly Legs, his poor naked vulnerable Toes.

But surely you will ask, what sort of Cock had he who invented more fanciful Names for that common Organ than Adam invented Names for Animals? 'Twas a middling Thing, neither larger nor smaller than the Majority of Cocks, and tolerably well-shap'd, but without the inflam'd Redness of which he so constantly writes in his foolish *Memoirs*. Indeed, 'twas a pasty white Thing, as pale as uncookt Pye Dough, and it took all my Coaxing and Reassurance to make it stand up in my Hand—and e'en then I fear'd it should faint again upon the Instant! But I roll'd it in my Hands and then betwixt my Lips until 'twas hard enough to suck upon, and when 'twas slick with Spittle and firm enough for Use, I lifted my Bride's Finery and sat upon his Cock, teazing and turning in corkscrew Motions until he swoon'd with Pleasure and, i'faith, quite fainted away.

At first I swear I thought him dead, so cold and still was he. I fear'd I'd kill'd him quite with Voluptuous Pleasure and I scarce knew whether to laugh or weep. 'Twas droll how all his Swagger had come to this! He lay upon the Floor like a dead Fish, nay like a Loaf of Bread, for no Part of him e'en twitch'd at all.

By and by, he recover'd his Senses. O he was mad with Gratitude to me! He said he could ne'er repay my Kindness, my Thoughtfulness, my Christian Charity!

I laugh'd and reassur'd him that he'd have to pay Coxtart for *my* Virginity—tho' he *himself* had prov'd the Virgin Bride. And that seem'd to put him in mind of a Fancy of his, which he was half afraid, he said, to voice.

"Pray tell me, Master Cleland," says I, "for I am here to do your Bidding."

"I dare not," said he, giggling like a Schoolgirl.

"Marry come up," says I, "I'll not mock you for it, I swear."

"Do you truly swear?" says he.

"I swear," say I.

Whereupon he proposes to me that now we exchange Clothes—he'll be the Bride and I the Swagg'ring Groom—and repeat our little Game.

This indeed tickles my own Fancy, so bor'd am I with playing Bride, and now I strip and offer him my Virginal Clothes, whilst he does the same, off'ring me his Fop's Finery.

He unlaces my Corset for me, and in a Minute or two, I lace him into it, giving him a tiny Waist, but alas no Breasts at all. These we form with cambrick Handkerchiefs roll'd into Balls, and he primps and views himself in the Glass as if he is quite pleas'd with all his Eyes behold. I dress him next in Boddice and Petticoat, Veil, Shoes, and Stockings. I e'en offer him my Paints—my Bavarian Red Liquor for the Cheaks—and my Scents as well. All these he is happy enough to use; and he shows less Discomfort in 'em than a Lapdog put into a Bathing Tub. Indeed, female Dress brings out all his Confidence and Daring, and he minces and curtseys with more Aplomb than he swagger'd as a Beau before.

For my part, I am content to be in his Attire; for wearing a Man's Disguise always fills me with a Sense of Freedom, e'en Wantonness. I chase him 'round the Bed again, delighting in the Novelty of this Change in Status.

I growl that I shall catch him; he squeaks I shall not. I now cajole, now threaten, now pursue. He now protests, now pleads, now flees. At last I catch him and throw myself upon him with all my Weight.

"Pray, Sir, desist," he squeaks, *Falsetto.*

"Pray, Madam, yield," I thunder, *Basso.*

Whereupon I thrust my Knee betwixt his Thighs and like a hopeless Maid he cries in the highest Voice: "Please, Sir, I have no Jewel but my Vartue, and if you strip me of it, I am lost." Then he begins to weep withal, yea, weep so convincingly that my Heart is mov'd and I forget that 'tis only a Play.

After some Time at this Pantomime, we fall to Love-making in earnest, I playing the Man and he the Maid. I'faith, he

244

is more arous'd by playing the passive Virginal Maid than he was by playing the Seducing Rake; for upon this Occasion his Cock requires no coaxing. But O 'tis droll to see it emerge 'neath a Petticoat and Hoops!

Thereafter, whene'er Master Cleland came to Coxtart's Brothel, 'twas our usual Sport to mimick the Sexes neither one was born to. Playing the Wench seem'd to give him the Confidence he lackt in his proper Gender; and after our frenzied Bouts in Bed he could be persuaded to tell me of his Dreams and Plans.

He was besotted with the East, dreamt Continually of Venice, Constantinople, Smyrna, Bombay, and long'd to travel to those distant Parts. For he had heard and read much of Oriental Luxury, of the Freedom Turkish Ladies enjoy'd 'neath their Veils, of the wicked Seraglios of the East, of the lustful Sultans and of their voluptuous Concubines.

"Sure you must be mad, John," said I, "to imagine that Turkish Ladies have more Freedom than English ones."

" 'Tis true, Fanny," says he, "for 'neath their Veils, 'tis said not e'en their own Husbands can recognize 'em, and they go about the Streets of Constantinople quite *Incognita*. Thus, you see the Jealousy of Husbands creates a Disguise which quite defeats its own Purpose. 'Tis a solemn Lesson in the Vanity of Human Passions!"

'Twas indeed hard for me to believe that the Plight of the Turkish Lady could be better than that of the English, but perhaps 'twas true. For English Ladies liv'd at the Mercy of their Husbands, their Fathers, and all the gossiping Tongues of the Town. They, too, could know Freedom in Disguise, which surely accounted for the great Popularity of Masquerades in London. Perhaps the Slaves of the East had more true Freedom than we Englishwomen who only *seem'd* so free; 'twas a Paradox indeed.

But what was Master Cleland's secret Wish in travelling to the East? Did he dream perhaps of dressing up to play the Turkish Lady? That I'll ne'er know, for he would not trust me so far with his Fancies. Within the Year, howe'er, he'd disappear'd from London altogether to journey across Europe; and I heard tell that he turn'd up in Smyrna by and by, having secur'd a Consular Appointment by some Means or other. Was he tasting all the forbidden voluptuous Secrets of the East? So I fancied, for he was the sort of Man who would have lov'd to play the Concubine whilst a savage Turk ravish'd him in his Nether Regions. Neither proper Man, nor proper Woman was he, but an odd Blend of the twain, a curious Person who seem'd torn betwixt East and West, betwixt Male and Female.

I later heard that he fled Smyrna for Bombay, where the East India Company employ'd him for a while. Then he was banish'd from India, too, after some Quarrel or Scandal, and wander'd across Europe like a Lost Soul, until he return'd to his Native Land, where he was promptly thrown into Gaol for Debt.

Thus he came to write his loathèd *Memoirs*; for those on whom the Muse seldom smiles are driven to write only by Want of Money, not, like Dean Swift, by the Noble Desire of bringing Mankind to its Senses. His Book surely did inflame the Town, and it made Ralph Griffiths rich as well. 'Twas Common Knowledge that the Bookseller had bought the Copyright of Cleland for twenty Guineas and thereafter earn'd from it more than ten thousand Pounds. As oft' occurs in these Cases, the Bookseller was able to set up like a proper Gentleman, with Chariots and Steeds and a Household full of Servants, whilst the Author, for his Pains, was nearly clapp'd in Gaol. He latter got a Pension of Lord Granville, who pitied him, but still he remain'd a struggling Grub Street Hack, and ne'er free from Want his whole Life long. Indeed, the Bookseller fatten'd whilst the Author starv'd, and drove about in Coaches whilst the Author walkt. ('Tis e'er thus, I fear, when Commerce meets the Muse—but Cleland deserv'd no better, having stolen my Name in Hope of Gain!)

For my own part, the Book caus'd me only great Embarrassment, for ev'ryone thought 'twas my True Life Story, and correct in all its Particulars. I'faith, Belinda, the printed Word carries more Credence than Truth itself. And a Book—e'en if it be malignant and scurrilous—carries more Weight in the Scales of Life than the truest Oath upon the heaviest Bible. After Cleland's Volume appear'd I had no Peace at all, since 'twas presum'd that I *myself* was the Model for Fanny Hill. All that I protested to the Contrary, only serv'd the more to convince my Enemies that I was lying.

This, indeed, is one of the most compelling Reasons for my writing my own True and Compleat History of my Life and Adventures; so that you, my belovèd Belinda (and the scurrilous World as well), shall know the Truth of my Life and not labour under the dark and dingy Veil of Falsehood. For the sugar'd Tale of cloying Fanny Hill is as far from my own

246

Life and Philosophies as the sugar'd Tale of virtuous Pamela is far from the Truth of Serving Maid and Master. Neither Comedy nor Tragedy alone rul'd my Life, but 'twas a Mixture of the twain. Sometimes my Fortunes rose, sometimes they fell; and indeed I came to believe the Adage of La Rochefoucauld, that "Greater Virtues are requir'd to endure Good Fortune than to endure Bad." Whilst all my Care was to survive, bear my Babe in Peace, and aid my dearest Lancelot, I was too busy to suffer prolong'd Fits of Melancholy or Spleen; but later when my Fortunes improv'd, I was able to learn the Truth of another of that clever French Duke's sayings, to wit: "Violence done to us by others oft' pains us less than Violence done to us by Ourselves." But more of that anon.

Chapter VIII

In which we look in upon Mr. Lancelot Robinson in Newgate Prison and learn what hath transpir'd with him whilst our Fanny was very much Otherwise Engaged.

AFTER MY FIRST SEV'RAL WEEKS in the Brothel, I had, by dint of great Industry as well as Thrift (for I ne'er took Breakfast or Lunch from Coxtart, for Economy's Sake), earn'd and sav'd enough to secure Lancelot Freedom of the Rules.

'Twas also plain by now that some new Life was coursing thro' my Veins; for, tho' my Belly was as flat as e'er before, my Skin show'd a new Bloom, my Eyes sparkl'd like the brightest Stars, and ev'ry Swain who saw me remarkt that my Beauty grew more dazzling Day by Day. Indeed, I could see it myself, in my own Glass.

How very curious, I thought, that this unwanted Babe, this Child conceiv'd in Betrayal and Treachery should, ne'er-theless, create such Beauty. Perhaps ev'ry Woman who hath e'er drawn Breath, hath made the self-same Observation; but to me 'twas novel and most unexpected. I loath'd the Father, yet I lov'd the Babe.

But did I truly loathe the Father? There raged still in my Breast a War betwixt Love and Hate for Lord Bellars. I had lov'd him like a Father and he had betray'd me like a Rogue. Surely, Belinda, we are ne'er as offended by bodily Violence alone as we are by Violence to our tender Sensibilities and Betrayal of our Trust. From Time to Time I could rekindle in my Heart the Tenderness I had once felt for Lord Bellars; but more oft' the Love curdl'd into Hate, and I felt Rage against him and indeed against all Men.

Some Days I would walk the Streets of London to buy some necessary Item of my Trade—new Patches or Paints, Scents, and such—and I would feel the sheerest Fury 'gainst ev'ry Man I saw. The Beau that strutted with his Snuff-Box and Sword, the Footman that ap'd the Beau's Fine Manners and wore his cast-off Clothes, the proud Physician all in black, the Officer of the Guard in his Finery, the Linen Draper that mimickt the Officer's Fine Manners in his turn, e'en the lowly Nightmen and Polemen whose assorted Stinks call'd forth Memories of the Privies they clean'd—all of 'em could strut imperiously above the best-hearted, most learnèd Lady in the Land. And why? Because she, not they, must bear the Great Belly that assures all Humankind of its Survival!

If Men had to bear the Babes, I thought, the entire Race would perish! For what Man would risque his Life for a mere Babe? E'en he, who would so readily risque it disputing some foolish Point of Honour in a Duel with another Man, would balk at the very Thought of enduring Pain or Death for a helpless Lump of shiv'ring pink Flesh that can neither walk nor talk to pay him Homage! For the Curse of the Male Sex is its constant Need of Homage—Homage to its Intellect and Wit, Homage to its Gallantry and petty Prowess betwixt the Bed-Clothes; whilst the Female Sex, *said* to be so vain, is vain only of mere superficial Beauty. And e'en that Vanity—oft', I confess, so noisesome and tedious—is nought but an Instinct for Survival; for a Woman knows that in a World where Women have no Pow'r—Beauty, like Witchcraft, is her only Substitute.

I waver'd betwixt Rage at Men, Rage at their Betrayal and my Body's, and sheer, irrational Delight at the new Life pulsing thro' my Blood. Oft' I would catch myself smiling for no Reason, smiling at the Babe in my Belly that could not see my Smile. Then, quite as suddenly, my Smile would turn to furious Tears, and I would weep and rage at that which could not be undone. O I felt trapp'd and imprison'd by this Babe as well as blest by it. I lov'd it and I hated it, both equally and both by Turns.

'Twas Time to go again to Lancelot in Newgate; for tho' I had been sending Money lo these many Weeks, the Press of my Work had prevented my visiting that foul Prison. Indeed, the Idea quite affrighted me; my last Visit to Newgate had left me haunted by terrifying Dreams and Visions for many Days afterward.

Upon this Occasion, howe'er, I arriv'd to find Lancelot in a changed Humour. As melancholy and cast down as he had been before, just so much was he high and buoyant now. Indeed, he was almost the Lancelot of Old—the green-eyed Wonder I had first met upon the Road! No longer did he languish in a Dungeon in Rags, but he was restor'd to his Proper Place above Ground, and dress'd finely as you please in the Clothes I'd sent him (with the Money I had earn'd upon my Back!). Moreo'er, he was surrounded by a Mob of Prisoners, who lookt to him for Wit, for Philosophy, and, above all, for Hope of bett'ring their wretchèd Condition. (I'faith, a Man may be starving and diseas'd, but if he hath Hope, he will not swiftly perish. For Hope is as a floating Spar to a drowning Man; it buoys him up yet a little longer, and puts him above the Waves when he might well be under 'em!)

Lancelot stood upon a Table in the High Hall, with all his wretchèd Disciples beneath him, and he preach'd quite grandly to the Prigs, whilst his good Friend, John Littlehat, stood by with troubl'd Mien, wond'ring what new Mischief Lancelot would bring down upon himself now.

I went first to Littlehat, for Lancelot was raving upon his Pulpit and was separated from me by a Wall of stinking, mutt'ring, shouting Humanity.

"Ah, Madam Fanny," says Littlehat. "Bless yer Soul, fer ye have sav'd our Friend from deep Despair; an' yet I fear that when he raves like this, he is in greater Danger still! He hath won the Prisoners to his Party by the finest Talk an' also by his Arts of Healing. I'faith, many are convinced he is a Saint, if not Jesus Christ Himself, fer he hath done such Miracles in raising the Sick an' restoring 'em to Health that they are now convinced of all he says, an' I fear fer him more now than e'er before."

"What is this bloody Code call'd the Law?" shouts Lancelot from the Table's Height. "Why, 'tis nought but an Excuse to kill the Poor, whilst the Rich may steal an' go free!" To which fine Sentiments the Rabble chear'd. Hearten'd by their Adulation, Lancelot grew more fever'd still:

"Why should a poor Man hang fer stealin' a Sheep or a Horse? Why should a poor Man hang fer stealin' five Shillin's worth o' Toys from a Toy-Shop, or cuttin' off a Watch from a Pretty Fellow that hath ten gold Watches if he hath one? Hath not that self-same Pretty Fellow stolen yer Daughter's Honour or the Fruits o' the Land where yer Father labour'd? Why should the Sweat o' yer Father's Brow be worth nothin' an' the Pretty Fellow's Watch be worth yer Neck in the Noose? Why should it be call'd Lawlessness an' Highway Robbery when a poor Man steals what he needs to eat yet be call'd Fine Manners when a rich Man steals the Sweat o' the poor Man's Brow? Doth not God Himself say 'Consider the

250

Lilies o' the Field' an' how little they toil an' sweat? Yet He provides for 'em! Why not likewise fer the Poor? Are the Rich alone God's Lillies an' the Poor nought but Clods o' Mud?"

Whereupon the Rabble shouted "Amen!" and "Blessèd be our Lancelot!" and other Sentiments of like Nature.

"I fear he means to lead a Rebellion of the Prisoners," says Littlehat to me privily, "an' surely he will hang fer that."

"An' now, ye Debtors," Lancelot goes on, "where is it writ within the Holy Book that one Man may lock another up an' throw away the bloody Key because o' bloody Debt? I say there *is* no such Thing as Debt! Each Man must have whate'er he needs to live an' no Man may be his Creditor nor Usurer, nor can he seize him fer the Crime o' Debt! Fer we are all God's Debtors—are we not?—an' if God can forgive Sinners, sure he can forgive Debtors, too!"

More Chears and Blessings rose from the Rabble now, and Lancelot rais'd his Arms to acknowledge his frenzied Publick, then leapt down from the Table with all the Grace of a Cat, and made his Way thro' the Mob to me and Littlehat. Without a Word, he press'd me in his Arms, enfolded me, and strokt my Hair. Then, quite suddenly, as if remembering himself, he drew back, startl'd by his own Affection for me, and essay'd again to conceal it 'neath his wonted Swagger.

"Fanny, me Girl, let me look at ye! Why, what Finery! Hath Fortune smil'd on ye in wicked London Town?"

"You might call it Fortune," say I, "but I would not. Come—may we speak somewhere privily?" Whereupon Littlehat led us to a solitary Chamber, furnish'd tolerably well with Bed and Table, which my Largesse to Lancelot had secur'd.

"Whence comes this Finery?" asks Lancelot again, regarding my lavender silk Morning Dress, with pale green satten Ribbands, and my lavender silken Shoes with Pattens that lookt too fine to endure e'en one Hour in the muddy London Streets.

"The same Place your Finery comes from," say I, brazenly as you please. "I have sweated for it upon my Back!"

"A Common Strumpet, Fanny mine?"

"Nay, Lancelot, a most uncommon one! For the Tricks I've learnt in lo these last few Weeks would take the Crimp out of your flaming Locks and cause your very Toes to curl towards Heaven! There is nought common about my Strumpeting!"

251

"Fanny!" says Lancelot, aghast. "How can a Lass o' yer Quality stoop to such a low Occupation?"

"A low Occupation! A low Occupation! What? Do my Ears deceive me? Is this Lancelot the Rebel, the Poet of Priggism, the Preacher of true Christianity! Did not Jesus Himself forgive the Harlot? Marry come up, Lancelot, I ne'er thought I'd see the Day when you yourself talkt like a hypocritical Whig!"

"But Harlotry, Fanny, to sell yer Soul fer fine Ribbands—"

"Not my Soul—but merely my Body, and not for myself, but for you and the Merry Men. O this is a fine State of Affairs! I rescue you by the Sweat of my unwilling Thighs and this is all the Thanks I get! Damn your Eyes, Lancelot, I leave you to your Fate!" And with that I pickt up my Petticoat and prepar'd to leave the Chamber.

"Pray, sweet Fanny, do not be so rash."

"Pray, sweet Lancelot, I might say the same to you!"

"But why Harlotry, Fanny?"

"If I must explain that to you of all People, Lancelot, then truly I am curst. Shall my Lord Pillicock give me a Pension for my Wit and Learning alone? Hardly! I could be as great a Philosopher as Plato himself, yet would I starve unless I were to earn my Keep the only Way a Woman can! Yea, you would starve, too, and my Babe as well."

"Yer *what?*" says Lancelot.

"Lancelot, I am with Child."

Lancelot lookt wildly at me, as if he'd kill me for the very Words.

"Is it that Black Swine, Horatio?" he rav'd.

"No—" say I, "a thousand Noes. Would that my Bastard Babe belong'd to the Merry Men! But 'tis my own Step-Father!"

"An' where's the scurvy Blackguard now?"

"That I can't say."

"An' what d'ye mean to do?"

"I mean to work as hard as e'er I can, to put by Money for the Babe. What else can I do?"

"Ye can join me Rebellion, Fanny, with the Merry Men. I've sent fer those that remain alive—e'en Horatio, if we can track him, an' I mean to raise the fiercest Army o' Prisoners that London e'er hath seen—fer we mean to change the World!"

"Lancelot, you are daft. Surely you'll hang!"

"Sure I'll hang whether I raise an Army or no—fer I was

252

to hang before, an' now I stand accus'd o' *new* Crimes by the wretchèd Captain o' the wretchèd *Hannibal*! Death's not me Fear, Fanny. I fear Gaol an' Melancholy more than Death. Death's a Reprieve, me Girl. Death will bring Martin back. Besides I've nought to lose."

I shook my Head sadly.

"Fanny, ye grow hard in yer new Life. Come with us! We'll be the happiest Outlaw Band since Robin Hood's an' raise yer Babe up in the Forest as the Child o' all the Merry Men. We'll teach him Priggism an' True Philosophy. We'll raise him in the Wild without the Lyes o' Society to warp his little Soul!"

"And what if he's a Girl?"

"Nonsense, 'tis a Boy. I can see it in yer Eyes!"

"Lancelot, you are mad! You're the next Thing to a Bedlamite."

"An' proud o' that!" cries he. "Fer is not Wit to Madness oft' allied? Think on't, Fanny. Think o' the Babes expos'd in Dung-Heaps thro'out London Town. Is not me own Proposal better? D'ye wish yer Child to dye upon a Heap o' Straw when ye yerself are clapp'd or consumptive from yer vile Trade?"

This indeed brought Tears to my Eyes, for I knew 'twas no idle Chatter. All o'er London and in the outlying Fields, one could see hapless Babes thrown out in Dustbins, expos'd upon the Heaths, and mewling like so many abandon'd Kittens in the cold Rain, until a merciful God clos'd their Eyes, putting 'em out of their brief Lives of Misery.

" 'Twill ne'er happen to my Child," said I. But e'en so saying, I doubted the Truth of my own Words. Infants there were aplenty in London, but no Money to clothe or feed 'em; and oft' the very Mother who had borne in Pain, at risque to her own Life, put her own sweet Babe out to starve upon the Street for no Reason but Harsh Necessity. Thus, she shed double Tears, both for herself and all her wasted Griefs, and for the Babe and its sad Life, though brief.

I mus'd upon these Melancholick Thoughts as I left Newgate and found a Chair back to Coxtart's Brothel, for Lancelot's dire Warnings might portend my Fate. Far better to cast my Lot with the Merry Men than waste away of Pox and leave an orphan'd Babe—or worse, see my own Child waste away for Want of Food.

Now I had Money to ride in a Chair. Now I held my Head, all too briefly, above the Rabble. But what would happen when I grew great-bellied as I must in a Month or two? What would happen when I could not earn my own Bread? Or if I contracted a fatal Fever in Childbed? Or if, i'faith, I dy'd and left a Babe to Coxtart? Perish the Thought!

From the Height and Isolation of my Chair, I lookt down into the London Streets. There clamour'd all the sundry London Throng—raggèd Orange Women, Serving Maids, Street Urchins, and Chimney Sweeps. Nothing separated me from their Fates but a few Months' Work upon my Back and my Goddess-given Beauty, which someday soon should fade. E'en riding in a Chair, I could scarce forget that a fearful Fate awaited me upon the Streets! I had but narrowly escap'd, and not for long. Fortune's Wheel might turn again and leave me helpless as before. I might be thrown in Prison by one of my own jealous Swains, condemn'd to Bridewell by a miserable Magistrate who found his greatest Joy in blaming Harlots for the Sins of Men! I myself had seen Harlots flogg'd in Newgate, and heard tell of many who beat Hemp in Bridewell. What did it profit me to cast my Fate with respectable Society? What had respectable Society e'er done for me? My Fate was with the Outlaws! For despite my Finery, a red Witch's Garter lay beneath it all! And despite my hir'd Chair, I was a Wayfarer, a weary Pilgrim, a Traveller upon Foot! E'en my Magick Steed was lost to me by now and the only Witchcraft I possess'd was in my Garter and my long red Hair. Better to cast my Lot with Lancelot, than, by and by, to starve in London.

Very well, I thought, I'd return to the Brothel for the nonce, and wait for further Word from Robin Hood.

Chapter IX

Containing a most edifying Excursion into the World of London Clubs, in which our Heroine journeys to the Centre of the Earth, meets the Devil, and finds him a more familiar Figure than she otherwise would have guess'd.

PERHAPS YOU WILL RECALL that upon my first Acquaintance with the fair Wenches of Mother Coxtart's Emporium, I mention'd that four of the Girls were away, upon my Arrival, for they were employ'd at a Private Revel. These Ladies were Melinda, Sophia, Rosamund, and Bridget; and they were, in many Ways, the most skill'd Wenches in the whole Establishment. They specializ'd, so to say, in Private Revels, and they were better paid, I learnt, than the other Wenches; but what they did remain'd mysterious to me, for they were always coming and going, and did not ply their Trade within the Brothel itself.

I was eager to learn what private Business they were engaged in; howe'er, as you may guess, the Girls were not so eager to tell their Doings, fearing, as they did, my Competition. For 'twas true that I was better-looking than most of 'em—at least to their Eyes. And tho' I myself knew, having been beautiful my whole Life long, that Beauty creates as many Woes as it bestows Advantages (not the least of which is the Envy of other Women), they, lacking Great Beauty, and fancying it a Cure for whate'er ail'd 'em, did not share this Wisdom.

Of these four Wenches who carried on at Private Revels, Melinda was the most amiable and the least suspicious of me. She was a pretty Thing, with light brown Hair, and a Merry Face (which, sad to say, was marr'd by Pockmarks). 'Twas bruited about that she was of Noble Birth, but had been banish'd from her Home in Yorkshire by an evil Father, who ne'er forgave her Refusal to marry a deprav'd and ancient

Suitor whom she loath'd. Melinda, herself, soon bore out the Rumour; for she was no poor Country Girl like the others but carried herself like a depos'd Princess (tho', in truth, her Father was no King, but only a Baronet). She'd grown from Girlhood at Gigglesden Hall in the West Riding, and spoke often and longingly of its mullion'd Windows, its great Gables, its beauteous circular Window of eight Lights, and its brooding Topiary Garden, casting ominous Shadows upon Velvet Lawns. No sooner did she make my Acquaintance, than she wanted me to know that she was no Common Strumpet but a banish'd Bride, that she was accustom'd to Finery beyond these tawdry Brothel Rags, that she found the Manners at Coxtart's Tea-Table distasteful in the extream, and that the Life she liv'd Today was but a pale Reminder of her former Glory.

"Oft'times I dream I've dy'd and gone to Hell," says she, speaking of the Brothel Life. "My Childhood was the sheerest Paradise. At Gigglesden, we din'd off golden Plates and had our Wine brought in Venetian Goblets of Emerald swirl'd with Amethyst, like unto an Adriatick Sea whereon a low Sun sets."

As if to stress her Longing always to be in the Past, not the Present, she spoke in a Voice that was more a Child's than a Woman's; i'faith, for all the gorgeous Rhetorick she us'd when speaking of her long-lost Home, she seem'd at other Times to lapse into Baby's Prattle. Before long, I won her Confidence by refusing to mock her Dreams of vanish'd Grandeur (as the other Wenches did), and indeed, by becoming the only Wench in the House with whom she could reminisce o'er her Youth. I appear'd, in fact, to share her Obsessions with her Past; and I paid her Tit for Tat—her Memories of Gigglesden with mine of Lymeworth. Soon we form'd a Pair and were fast Friends; whereupon I took the Liberty of enquiring about the Nature of these Private Revels.

There were, she told me, many Clubs in London, and most of 'em met in Coffee and Chocolate Houses 'round the Town. Some were Lit'ry Clubs, some political, and some were Clubs for Pranksters, like the Golden Fleece, wherein each Member assum'd a new Name, such as Sir Whore-Hunter, or Sir Boozy Prate-All. There was the celebrated Mollies Club, whose Members dress'd up as Women and titter'd behind their painted Fans. They had a Secret Couplet which was the very Proof of Membership, and they delighted in reciting it to each other, thus:

> Tell me, gentle Hobdehoy,
> Art thou Girl or art thou Boy?

There was also the Ugly Club, whose Members were suppos'd to be the most loathsome-featur'd in all of England; and the Lying Club, whose Members were mostly Lawyers; and the Divan Club, whose Members fancied Turkish Dress, Turkish Tobacco, Hashish, and Revels in the Turkish Style. But the Clubs that concern'd Melinda (and the other three wenches) were those formerly known by the name of Hell-Fire Clubs, and regarding these, great Secrecy and Discretion were requir'd, for just a little over three Years previously, a Royal Proclamation had been issu'd 'gainst blasphemous Clubs in London; and since that Time, the Hell-Fire Clubs had all changed their Names and conducted their "Amorological Rites," their "Corybantic Orgies," their "Tahitian Fertility Rites," most privily.

No longer did they meet at the notorious Rose Tavern nor at well-known scandalous Bagnios, nor e'en at Chocolate and Coffee Houses, but instead conspir'd to find more sequester'd Quarters, usually at some small Distance from the Metropolis.

One such Club, said she, had initiated her into Membership, but she could tell me no more about it. Only if I were an Initiate myself and sworn to Secrecy could I learn of it, whereupon I would be committed to its Rules for Life. Did I wish to take on such a heavy Oath, she askt; for were I e'er to break it, Satan himself should come to fetch my Soul.

"Do they worship the Devil, then, Melinda?" I askt her.

"Aye, Fanny, and 'tis on Penalty of Banishment to Hell forthwith that you break their Vows of Secrecy. Moreo'er, once you are initiated you must serve that Club and that alone; you may see no Swains within the Brothel here."

"Would you take me with you?" I askt.

"Fanny, do you dare?" she said in her Child-like Cadences. "Pray think on't. For there are Times I wish I ne'er had seen that cursèd Club."

I thought of my Friends the Witches and all I'd learnt from them of Witchcraft. Could a Club of London Fops be more terrifying than what I'd witness'd upon Stonehenge Down?

Why, it seem'd hardly likely! Besides, these Private Parties paid far more than all of Coxtart's Swains together. Since the Babe I carried would start to show ere long, I'd better make my Fortune whilst I might!

"I dare and dare again," said I, as brazen as you please. Somehow I was certain that 'twas all the sheerest Twattle, and now that I'd determin'd to escape with Lancelot, I felt free to try whate'er I wisht; i'faith, I felt invincible.

Mother Coxtart, presenting no Obstacle to our Plans, (indeed she encouraged us in 'em, owing to the Fact that she herself stood to gain more by my new Occupation), sent Word to the Founder of the Mysterious Club, that a new "Young Nun" was to be "prepar'd for Vestalship," and fixt my Initiation for that very Week.

When the appointed Ev'ning arriv'd, Melinda came into my Chamber carrying my "Holy Vestments," lockt the door behind her, and show'd me how to dress myself like a Nun of that "Sacred Order."

She brought with her two Habits, all in white and made of the finest, thinnest Wool. These loose Garments (which, indeed, conceal'd our Forms) we were to wear with no Undergarments whatsoe'er. Our white silk Stockings we would roll above the Knee and fasten with red Garters (one of which I possess'd already); but we were to be free of Stays or Boddices or Underlinen of any sort. Ne'ertheless, chain'd 'round our naked Waists, we were to wear inverted iron Crucifixes upon iron Chains.

Our Headdresses were made to look like Nuns', but with the Addition of white silk Masks, which cover'd nearly the entire Face; and our Hair was also tuckt away so that we could in no wise be recogniz'd by its Colour. O'er all this Costume, we wore black velvet Cloaks with ample Hoods so that our Nuns' Costumes could not be seen at all by curious Passersby; and in these Disguises we had just attir'd ourselves when a Footman came to say that a Chariot awaited us without.

'Twas Twilight in the London Street when we stepp'd into the waiting Coach, drawn by four white Horses. The Carriage Door was bare of Markings; no Coat of Arms reveal'd the Owner to our View. But within was our Guide, a Maskt Man in a black velvet Cloak, made like ours, (and 'neath that were brown Monks' Robes, we later discover'd).

"Good Ev'ning, Ladies," said he, welcoming us, with great

Formality, and presently we were off across the London Streets, and our Guide saying not a Word to us all the while.

When we reach'd Oxford Street he produced two scarlet silk Handkerchiefs and, with great Solicitude, bade us blindfold ourselves; for 'twas one of the Rules of the Club that female Acolytes must not know its Meeting Place.

I began, then, to grow wary; for there is nought quite so unsettling as rattling along in a Coach without knowing the Direction of one's Journey, and there is, withal, a Sense of Helplessness owing to the Fact that one cannot see one's Way to escape, should Escape prove necessary. I remember'd my blindfolded Journey with Lancelot and grew e'er more untranquil. But I reminded myself that I had bargain'd for just such an Adventure, so I strove to quiet my own Fears.

We drove for a Time; just how long I cannot say, most probably due to the Effects of the Blindfold upon my Senses, but after a while, I could readily feel the pav'd Road turn to an earthen one and the Coach go slower and yet begin to rattle still more than before. I could smell that we were in the Country. The sweet Odour of mown Hay ascended my Nose and I heard the Sounds of ev'ning Birds communicating in the Dusk. I laps'd into a Sort of Reverie, owing to the Motion of the Coach and the Effects of the Blindfold, and I sought to imagine what my Life would be like after I bore my Babe, and ran away to the Forest with Lancelot and the Merry Men. I essay'd to picture the Face and Features of the tiny Life I carried so hidden within me; but i'faith, I could not. This Babe was as mysterious to me as God—a Presence that determin'd all my Fate, yet which I could not see.

We must have ridden longer than I reckon'd, for 'twas black as Pitch when the Coach came to a stop and our Guide bade us remove our Blindfolds. We had stopp'd before a ruin'd Church curiously cut into a Hillside, surmounted with evil-looking Yews, and a full Moon caught upon one of their Points like a Head upon a Pike. The Façade of the Church was inlaid with strange Stones and Pebbles, curiously workt in what seem'd a Runick Design, and, indeed, it appear'd more pagan than Christian.

Here we dismounted, and our Guide nodded towards the Entrance of the Church. A Shiver shook my Shoulders, for the Church seem'd the very Image of Evil, but I had come too far to give in to idle Fears, so instead I clasp'd Melinda's Hand, and we advanced to the Portal.

259

"Are you afear'd, Fanny?" askt she, her infantile Voice quavering despite all her Efforts to control it.

"No," said I, lying as much as she.

We walkt, following our Guide, into a low vaulted Passage, which led into a Tunnel hewn from the sheerest Stone, in which the Marks of Pick-Axes could still be seen. The Caves were damp and dark, illuminated here and there by single Tapers, stuck in Sconces, mounted along the rustick Walls, but these gave pitifully small Illumination. Our Footsteps echo'd upon damp Stone; and we heard as well the continual Sound of running Water, dripping from the stony Eaves. At Times our Feet falter'd, but our Guide urged us e'er onward, saying, "Come, Ladies, there's nothing here to fear."

'Twas cold Comfort to us, for as we proceeded deeper into the Bowels of the Earth, we grew more terrified. We seem'd to pass dark little Alcoves cut into the Stone, whence came the low Sounds of Masculine Laughter and the higher Sounds of Feminine Laughter. At one Turning, I nearly dy'd of Fright, for there, carv'd above an Archway, and illuminated by half a dozen Candles, was an Image of the Devil as ravenous and open-mouth'd as you please, and dangling from his bestial, pointed Teeth was a Woman's white silk Stocking—as if indeed the Foul Fiend had eaten her alive!

Beyond this Archway, we advanced timidly to a Place where the Walls were honey-comb'd with tiny Chambers, within which I seem'd to hear Stirring; but these Chambers were so dark, i'faith, that I could see nothing more than shadowy Forms. We continu'd onward o'er a Bridge that cross'd a Black River, and on the opposite side took a sharp Turn to the Left thro' the narrowest of Passages, where suddenly we saw before us, all illumin'd by Candles set within Skulls, a Pagan Catacomb.

Candlelight flicker'd in hollow Eye-Sockets, so that the empty Skulls seem'd to have a sort of ghastly Life within 'em. In a Trice, one of these Skulls began to speak: "Welcome Sisters," came a thund'ring Voice, follow'd by a Gale of devilish Laughter that near knockt me off my Feet with Terror.

Our Guide led us still deeper into the Hillside, until I was sure I would ne'er emerge again, and I was all but ready to kiss my Immortal Soul goodbye. I curst my restless Nature, my foolish Adventurousness, my Willingness to risque Life and Limb for mere Curiosity. Just as I was ready to shout, "No more!" and turn upon my Heel and flee—no matter what the Consequences—we were usher'd into a Great Hall, hollow'd deep inside the Hill, with a central Banquetting Table illumin'd by a great Oil Lamp of curious Design, and surrounded by Statues of unclad Nymphs and Venuses and prancing Satyrs, which stood in shallow Niches 'round the Perimeter of the Room.

Seated at this Banquet Table (which was, by the by, set for Thirteen with pewter Plates, and Goblets fashion'd from Skulls) were five "Monks," dress'd all in brown Robes, and maskt like ourselves (but in brown Masks); and five "Nuns" in Attire precisely like our own. Our Guide led us to our Seats at Table, where a Footman stood to take our Wraps, and then we were seated, whereupon our Wine Goblets were fill'd with Claret.

The "Monk" who sat at the Head of the Table then lifted his skull-shap'd Goblet and propos'd the Toast:

"Here in the gloomy Caves of Endless Night,
We Stalwart Sons of Satan pledge to fight
'Gainst all the False Morality of Fear
And Dedicate our Lives to endless Chear!"

To which the Brothers responded "Hear! hear!" and rais'd their Goblets to drink. I peer'd into the Depths of my Skull-Goblet with considerable Suspicion, but then drank, at the Urging of the Brothers.

Now a Feast was set before us, and the Brother who sat at the Table's Head solemnly nam'd each Dish for the assembl'd Multitude. First we were serv'd "Holy Ghost Pye" (which seem'd a sort of Kidney Pye to me), then "Devil's Loins" (a Leg o' Mutton, to my View), then "Breast of Venus" (being nought but two Pullets, set Breasts upwards and garnish'd with Cherryes for Nipples). When each Dish was nam'd, the Maskt Brothers chear'd and made various witless, lewd Remarks, which scarcely bore repeating (could I, in any case, remember 'em—which indeed I cannot). The Drinking continu'd fiercely thro'out Supper, the Ladies growing quite as drunk as the Men.

Now my Fears were quieted again, for this devilish Club seem'd nothing more than a Group of bor'd Rakes pursuing their usual Pleasures of Wine, Women, and Gluttony, albeit in monastick Garb and deep within the Bowels of the Earth. What a silly Goose Melinda was, I thought, to be so terrified! If these foolish Pranks could conjure the Devil, then surely the Devil was no more than a Fop that strutted in the Mall, or lounged at White's or the Cocoa Tree, showing off his new Paris-made Suit, his French Valet, and his Smatt'ring of the French Tongue!

When Supper was quite finish'd and the Plates had been clear'd away, the head Monk stood, rais'd his Goblet again, and demanded that we all make a Solemn Oath ne'er to report what had transpir'd in these Stygian Caves.

"For whosoe'er will break the Devil's Oath," says he, "the Devil himself will fetch him straight to Hell!"

The assembl'd Company swore the Oath readily enough, whereupon the head Monk, with all due Ceremony, nodded to the Nun on his right, help'd her climb upon the Table, threw her Habit upwards so that it quite cover'd her Face, and ravish'd her there within Sight of all.

"In the Name of Satan, I anoint thee!" said he as the crucial Fit of Lust was upon him. And then he fell, heaving with Passion, upon the chosen Bride of Christ, whilst the other Monks toasted his amatory Skills with their Skull-shap'd Goblets.

What idiotick Entertainment! thought I. What uninspir'd Loving. To swive a Whore in a Nun's Habit upon a Table before one's Friends was the sort of Play one would expect of Boys of Fourteen, not of grown Men! But the Nun seem'd to enjoy it; indeed, she seem'd to enjoy it still more when the next Monk, in his Turn, climb'd upon the Table and also anointed her "in the Name of Satan." Surely I hop'd all the Women were not to be accorded like Treatment, for now it appear'd that a third Monk was beginning his Ministrations to the Nun, but this Monk was hardly so inept a Lover, and he made certain to kiss and fondle her for a Time before he began (whilst his brother Monks made lewd, encouraging Noises as if they were Footmen at a Play). I sat transfixt, for there was something uncannily familiar about the Motions this Monk made. 'Twas almost as if I knew him—despite his Disguise, but i'faith, I could not place him. Then, slowly, he began to apply his Tongue to the Nun's Nether Orifice, and she began to moan and writhe with Pleasure, whereupon he lifted the Skirts of his Monk's attire, brandish'd a fine brown Cock of ample Proportions, thrust it into her eager Cunnikin, and cried aloud, "In the Name of Satan I anoint thee!"

'Twas Lord Bellars' own Voice. Upon hearing it, I grew cold as Ice and my Heart began to beat so loudly I fear'd all the Monks should hear it as well. 'Twas unmistakable that those resonant Cadences belong'd to Lord Bellars. His Face might I forget in Heaven or Hell, but his Voice ne'er! Hearing it, I e'en felt Passion for him again, and then Loathing for myself for feeling Passion towards one who had us'd me so scurvily. Had my Heart no Pride? (But then, hath *any* Heart Pride? Pride is a Possession of the Brain, not the Heart; and the Heart will triumph o'er the Brain in any Contest.)

I sat as if in a Trance whilst I watch'd the Rest of the foul Ceremony, each Monk in turn climbing upon the Table, ravishing the Nun, with greater or lesser Skill, and climbing down to the Chears and Huzzahs of his Brothers. I watch'd, but my Eyes saw nothing. I listen'd but my Ears heard nothing. In the Cave of my Skull, there echo'd only the Ghost of Lord Bellars' Voice, saying again and again, "In the Name of Satan I anoint thee!"

'Twas a Dream, I thought—this doltish Merriment, this childish Debauch. Thro' it all, I sat still as a Statue, terrified lest Bellars recognize me (yet, how could he, in my Disguise?) and terrified lest I be askt to lye upon the Table in my Turn, whereupon I would have to submit to his splendid Love-making. Surely then all would be lost! My fine Resolve to hate him would vanish into the Ether if he so much as touch'd me!

'Twas not to be, thank Goddess. These Fops were no longer young and virile, and they had eaten and drunk to Satiety. One Debauch apiece was all most of 'em desir'd. Indeed, most of 'em could hardly rise to *that* Occasion. As the last weary Fop roger'd the still-willing Nun, the head Monk declar'd:

> "Now are we all most truly join'd in Soul,
> For we are Brothers of the self-same Hole!"

Whereupon (and quite as if this were the most ordinary of Soirées) the Ladies withdrew, leaving the Gentlemen to piss, drink, and smoke their Pipes.

The Nun whose Cunnikin had been the Site of the quaint, fraternal Ceremony was help'd down from the Table—seeming not much the worse for Wear—and all the other Nuns usher'd her out.

"How was it?" one Nun whisp'red to her when we were out of the Monks' Range of Hearing.

"Dull as always," says she, "except for the third one. They're a tired old Lot, I vow."

"And the third?"

"Ah," sighs she with remember'd Pleasure. "He's the only lively Fellow in the Bunch. The others are half dead."

Now this Piece of News was scarce soothing to my Ears; it but inflam'd my senseless Passion more. How could I still desire a Man who had us'd me so cruelly? 'Twas past all Reasoning—and yet, and yet, I did.

Melinda now came up beside me. "Were you terrified, Fanny?" she whisper'd in my Ear.

"Utterly," said I.

"I fear the Devil, Fanny," said Melinda.

"And so do I," said I. And yet the Devil that I fear'd was my own Step-Father, Lord Bellars. Both his Touch and his Voice held greater Terrors for me than the scaly Embrace of the Foul Fiend himself. I'faith, I was beginning to wonder whether the Foul Fiend wasn't more Chimera than Reality, for Man was Devil enough, I knew. The Witches had been murder'd by Mortal Men; and I had been undone by one Young Man who claim'd to love me as a Daughter. What need was there for Devil more than this?

"I fear the Devil, too," I said to Melinda, clutching her Hand. And she squeez'd my Hand warmly—for she was a True Friend, despite her Foolishness.

Now the Nuns retir'd to their Robing Room—another Chamber dug from sheerest Stone—where Chamber-Potts were provided for their Use, as well as Scents of various sorts. Some of the Ladies unmaskt merely to cool themselves; most did not. Some avail'd themselves of the Chamber-Potts and Scents, daubing the Perfumes under their Habits, as if indeed they hop'd to be "anointed" next.

I was still so shaken by the unexpected Presence of Lord Bellars at this Revel that I was almost unaware of the Chatter of the Ladies, but by and by my Ears became attun'd to a Conversation betwixt two Nuns which had the Pow'r to penetrate my Trance.

"Do you know him, Madam?" says one Nun to another.

"Know him! Aye, as well as the Beggar knows his Dish. We have been Lovers these five Years past!"

"And doth it not raise Jealousy in your Heart to see him swive another?"

"No, Madam; Jealousy is the basest of Emotions—suitable for the commonest of Folk. Noble Hearts ne'er feel Jealousy. Why, we tell each other of our Liaisons—'tis Capital Sport!"

The Words rang Bells in my Brain! Capital Sport! The

very Phrase Lord Bellars had us'd in that foul Letter to his Mistress in which he describ'd his Seduction of me! Could the Voice I was hearing belong to my loathéd Rival?

"Madam," said I, addressing the Nun who had spoken. "You speak of Lord Bellars, do you not?"

" 'Faith, you are an impertinent Strumpet," says the Lady. "You know we are sworn here ne'er to use proper Names!"

"Begging your Pardon, Madam," I said, "but he sounds so like my own Lover that I could not *but* break in. Forgive me."

"What? Your own Lover? And who, pray tell, are you?"

"Madam," I continu'd, smiling 'neath my Mask, "I would say my Name most willingly, but you have just reminded me quite rightly that we are not to use proper Names here—so I dare not."

And with that Retort I turn'd and began applying Attar of Roses to my Breasts and Thighs. I laugh'd a little to myself. O I knew 'twas a small Triumph, but a Triumph nonetheless. I would plot a greater Revenge upon this haughty Lady yet! Revenge was the unworthiest of Actions—that I knew. Revenge belong'd to God, not Man. And yet my Hatred of this Lady was so great, that it gave me sheerest Pleasure to think of the Discomfort I had already caus'd her.

Now a Footman came to summon the assembl'd Company of Ladies and bade them follow him to a Place he call'd the Labyrinth. We were to disperse there, said he, each find a Hiding Place, and when the Monks discover'd us by and by, we should lead 'em a Merry Chase until one Brother should catch us. This Labyrinth was more dimly lit than the Rest of the Caves and 'twas replete with blind Alleys and false Turnings, empty Niches, and thro'out, the Sound of Water dripping upon cold Stone. I shudder'd somewhat with the Cold and Damp; but presently the Monks were heard in Pursuit, and I had to be nimble on my Feet despite the Darkness of the Caves and the Unevenness of the Floors.

One fat Monk came after me, but I quickly eluded him by ducking into a Niche whither his surpassing Corpulence prevented him from following me. Soon I heard the Voice of another Monk calling in the Darkness: "I seek a Sister who is soft and wanton! Here I am, little Sister, here I am!"—but I ran quickly by him, and when he reach'd out his Arms to catch me, I escap'd. Now I thought myself safe, but, alas, I presently ran headlong in the Darkness into another Monk. He clasp'd me firmly about the Waist, pusht me into a Niche despite my Cries, whereupon he fell to his Knees, imprison'd my Legs with his strong Arms, duckt his Head under my Habit, and began to feast upon that Jam-Pott which Nature, in her curious Wisdom, hath placed betwixt the Thighs of the Fair Sex. Now this Sort of Love-making nearly always undoes me—no matter how loathsome the Swain who performs it (for I can close my Eyes and forget his Person), but the Licking and Teazing was so sweet withal that I near fainted away with Rapture.

"Ah what a ready, willing Nun," says he, emerging from 'neath my Skirts, whereupon I am brought to my Senses in a Flash—for 'tis Lord Bellars' own Voice!

Suddenly I feel as if cold Water hath been pour'd upon my Passion, and all my melting Lust turns to a steely Desire for Mastery! I disengage myself from his Clutches, fall to my Knees, and begin making love to him the self-same Way in return, but, just as the crucial Fit is on him, I stop with deliberate Abruptness and run away!

"Ah, cruel Sister!" he declares, pursuing me. But I say nothing—both to prevent him from recognizing my Voice and to elude him better.

Still he catches me and kisses me passionately and moistly upon my not altogether unwilling Lips, asking, "Why art thou so cruel, my Love?"

I do not answer, but flee again, whereupon he pursues again, with greater Frenzy still—but now I hide in a Niche and slow e'en my Breath so that he will not discover me. I hear him running to and fro begging for his "Cruel Love" to make herself known to him, whereupon another Lady answers his Call and falls into his Arms sighing most willingly.

"Excuse me, Madam," says he, eluding her Embrace, and feeling along the damp Stone Walls for me. O this is a pleasant Turn of Events! His Longing for me is almost palpable.

"Where are you, my Love?" he calls to me. "Where are you, my Love?" he sings again. But only the echoing Grots and Tunnels make the slightest Reply.

Suddenly, I dart from my Hiding Place, find him, embrace him fleetingly, then run away again. Now he pursues me thro' the Caves and I lead him a Merry Chase 'round and about the Labyrinth (for, by this Time, my Eyes have grown accustom'd to the Stygian Gloom). Beyond the Labyrinth, deeper into the Bowels of the Earth, there flows a River, black as the Styx itself, which is cross'd by a small wooden foot Bridge. I flee across; he follows me, and when we come to the other side, I dart at once into a Cavelet, laughing to myself in Triumph. Now I fancy myself safe from him, hidden in the dark Recesses of my chosen Grotto. I crouch there for a few Minutes, holding my Breath, praying for Mercy to the Goddess, to spare me the Temptation of being found and ravish'd by Lord Bellars.

Alas, my Pray'rs are all in vain, for he gropes his Way into the little Cave and strokes its moist Walls until he finds me!

"Now I have caught you, my Beauty," says Bellars, seizing me and pressing me to him with such Passion that I fear my very Habit shall melt away as if 'twere Butter instead of Wool.

He clasps me to himself like Life itself and he a Dying Man. Ne'er have I felt such Need, such Desire. Whereupon he seeks to lay me on the Ground and make love to me there and then.

My Intellect rebels, but O my Heart and my Body are all too willing. He parts my Thighs with Kisses, fondles my Breasts 'neath the loose Nun's Attire, and soon has his Way with me, sweeping away all my Resistance in a Flood of Passion more intense than any I have known.

O I have been swiv'd and roger'd in the Brothel and felt little but sweet Triumph or base resentful Submission o'er Man's Foolishness, but here some Essense of my Soul is touch'd, and I must curse the Author of that Touch, because whosoe'er can make me sigh like this, can make me weep as well.

When the Act is done, I am undone, bereft. All the Self-Esteem and sweet Control of my Destiny I have nurtur'd, lo these last few Weeks, is gone! I scramble to my Feet, e'en as he seeks to fondle me and cover me with Kisses of Gratitude.

"Ne'er have I known a Cunnikin as sweet as yours," says he.

"Ne'er?" say I, disguising my Voice.

"Once only, and that was in another County," says he, punningly.

"What? And the Maid not dead yet?" said I.

"Only her Maidenhead dy'd," said Bellars, "but I hope the sweet Maid is alive yet, tho' surely I have lost her."

"Sir," said I, "I assure you I am no Maid, and have not been for some Time past. And now I'll take my Leave."

"Please stay," says he.

"That I cannot," say I.

"Where may I find you again?" says he.

"Nowhere," say I. "I am a Phantom, a mere Chimera. In Daylight, I disappear."

"I beg of you," he pleads.

"Now will I vanish into thinnest Air," say I.

"I beg of you on bended Knee," says he.

"Then send for Madam Hackabout-Jones in care of Mother Coxtart," say I, thinking myself daft to reveal my Whereabouts. But I tell myself that I shall plot Sweet Revenges against this Villain, Lover, Devil; and e'en as I flee, I promise my sullied Soul and punish'd Pride that I shall have the Upper Hand ere long and one Day be his Master!

Chapter X

Of Love and Lust, Pan and Satan, Longing and Loyalty, and other such lofty (or low) Matters; together with our Heroine's Adventures at the notorious George & Vulture Inn, and how (with the Aid of some of the surviving Merry Men) she resolv'd the Dilemma of her Destiny.

IN THE COACH returning to Coxtart's Brothel, thro' the Wee Hours of the Morning, I drows'd in my Blindfold, and sought to reflect upon the curious Doings of that fateful Night. I thought myself mad for giving Bellars a Way to seek me out, for I knew that my Passion for him had been but newly kindl'd and that now I should live in Dread of his summoning me. But the Words had flown from my Lips against my Will. I had been pow'rless to part from him without the Hope of seeing him again!

O what a vain and useless Thing was Passion! Lancelot I lov'd like a Brother, but Bellars, like the Devil, had stolen my Soul. Lancelot I would give my Soul to save from Death, but Bellars had my Body! And who is the Wit that says: "He that possesses a Woman's Body possesses her Soul"?

I was torn betwixt two Loves—one Golden Pan and one Olive-skinn'd Satan! I wanted both—and both on my own Terms. I could give up neither—neither the Passion I knew with Bellars nor the fraternal Loyalty I knew with Lancelot. Were all Women so torn? Was Love a two-faced Beast (or two-faced God) that ne'er could be united in one Man?

What would I do when Bellars sent for me as I knew he must? What would I do with the curious Triumph of making him fall in Love with me when he knew not my true Identity? I wisht, above all, to disown my Body, for I felt that my Body had betray'd me. But how could I disown it now when 'twas ripe with Life and craving the Father of that Life more than e'er before?

These and other Questions perplext me during my Blindfolded Ride back to Coxtart's House. I turn'd 'em 'round and 'round in my Brain like Wheels that had no Beginning and no Ending, until at length I grew weary and full of Despair and I resolv'd upon Sleep as the only Cure for my Perplexity. "Sleep that knits up the ravell'd Sleeve of Care," as Shakespeare hath writ. I would sleep, I promis'd myself, and the Answer would come to me in a Dream.

But, alas, no Dreams attended me. When I return'd to Coxtart's, I sank into the dreamless Sleep of the Dead. Morpheus sent no Messages; nought but Blankness came, blessèd, useless Blankness.

I awaken'd late to hear a persistent Rapping at my Chamber Door. 'Twas Mother Coxtart herself—now quite as obsequious to me as she had once been arrogant (for, since I was lately bringing her Establishment a handsome Profit, she could not do enough for me, it seem'd, but would fore'er be grovelling, cringing, and scraping to do my Bidding). How fickle was Fate! What a Lottery was Life! Two Months before she'd scorn'd me as a Beggar; now she grovell'd to me as to a Duchess. But, alas, knowing of her Fickleness, her Grovelling was of as little Use to me as her earlier Scorn.

"Madam Fanny," says she, "an' beggin' your Pardon for this rude Awak'ning, but there are Letters for you—or should I rather say, *Billets Doux.*"

I could not bear to see her fawning Face—so I bade her slide the Letters 'neath my Door, whereupon I tiptoed out of Bed to fetch 'em.

Indeed, there were two, one seal'd quite unmistakably with Bellars' Seal, the other scrawl'd upon a dirty Piece of Foolscap that had known the Mud of the Kennels and bore no Seal at all.

When I saw these two Missives (and especially the one bearing Bellars' Seal), my Hands began to shake like Leaves upon a great Autumnal Oak. I sav'd the Bellars Missive for later, fancying that 'twould cause me the greatest Inquietude, and open'd the one that was splotch'd with Mud. I read the Scribblings of a hasty Hand:

My Dearest Fanny:
    Robin Hood bids me inform you that all is in Readiness for the Greatest Triumph of his Career. Go at once to Horatio at The George & Vulture in Cornhill, St. Michael's Alley, and he will make all known to you. I beg of you, do not tarry. Horatio awaits. Dubious as I

270

remain of this Enterprise, I am Sworn to do Robin's Bidding, as are you. I trust your Noble Heart will ne'er let you forget.

God Bless You.

Yr. Affectionate Friend,

Littlehat.

The News that Horatio had rejoin'd the Merry Men and that Lancelot had fixt all for his Great Rebellion gave me less Apprehension, oddly, than Bellars' Letter, which now I tore open with trembling, icy Hands:

Adorable Creature,

I know not what to say—my Mind is in greater Turmoil than a Bedlamite's. Since we parted in those Stygian Caves last Ev'ning, I have slept not a Wink, being toss'd upon a Sea of Doubts and Fears, the like of which I have ne'er known. I feel that my Heart is a leaky Boat, tormented upon Storm-cross'd Seas, that should I fail to see you again, I am little better than a Crusoe without his Friday. A dreadful Cloud seems to hang o'er my Heart when I consider that you and I may be parted fore'er more. I ask you to search your Soul for whate'er Humanity and Compassion you possess and grant your Humble Suitor but one further Audience. If I cannot then convince you that I have Pow'rs to make you the Happiest of Women, I shall withdraw and quit your Sight for all Eternity. Send to me presently with your Answer in order to assuage the intolerable Torment that afflicts the Heart of your most Faithful,

Bellars.

P.S. If you are still loath to reveal your Identity, I shall gladly meet you at a Masquerade. But I must meet you again! Adieu.

Reading this, my Mind suffer'd as great a Tumult as Bellars had described in his own. What Answer should I make? Should I meet him in Disguise and seek to wreak my Vengeance upon him? Or would Vengeance melt into Submission the Moment my Eyes beheld him?

Moreo'er, if Bellars was so determin'd to see me, why did

he not accost me at the Brothel and seek to hire me as a common Whore—tho' 'twas against the Hell-Fire Rules. E'en as I wonder'd this, I knew the Answer. A common Whore would not be to his Taste—he who told his Lover of his Liaisons! No, he must have Intrigue and Masks and Masquerades; he must make me rare enough to warrant his uncommon Loving; he must swive me as a Lady or a Nun, ne'er a Strumpet! For a Man of Lord Bellars' Parts pleasures and disdains "mere" Strumpets and must win, at all costs, more than a Cunnikin: he must win a Heart.

Yet I could not ponder long my Response to this Dilemma with Lord Bellars, for I was bound to meet Horatio at The George & Vulture and learn of Lancelot's Rebellion, wherefore I hastily sent Answer to My Lord that I should seek him in the Costume of a Spanish Nun—for our Hell-Fire Nuns' Robes were forbidden ev'rywhere but in the Club itself— whilst he should seek me in the Garb of Satan, at the next Costume Ridotto to be held at The King's Theatre.

Having sent such Reply, via Coxtart herself (who prov'd quite willing to play the Go-Between for me), I hastily dress'd and took a Chair for The George & Vulture.

Now, The George & Vulture had, of all London Inns, the most sinister Reputation. 'Twas thought to be a Resort for Ghosts, Goblins, and all Manner of Demons—a Reputation which the sinister Landlord not only did little to discourage, but in fact encouraged owing to his Belief that it brought more Custom to his House—tho' indeed a strange kind of Custom. The Inn was notorious for being the Meeting Ground of Mountebanks, Thieves, Astrologers, and Fortune Tellers.

This was the sort of Place where I was to meet Horatio; and indeed, it liv'd up to its Ill-Fame, for hanging o'er the Portal was a creaking wooden Sign whereon was painted the Image of a dreadful Vulture, preparing to swoop down upon its Prey. Within the Innyard itself sat the living Likeness of this Bird, a terrible Creature who regarded all Comers with the clearest, coldest Eye.

The Landlord welcom'd me. He was a Man nearly as terrible as his Bird, with a similar Beak, Eyes, and Mien. 'Tis said that Men grow to resemble their loving Dogs; but I can also attest that they grow to resemble their Vultures should they keep such Pets!

The Interior of the Inn was dark, tho' 'twas little past

Noon, for the Windows were kept shutter'd 'gainst prying Eyes. A Fire burn'd in the Grate, and sitting near it, at a Table in the Corner of the Room, was Horatio himself flankt by Francis Bacon and Puck Goodfellow!

Horatio's Skin glow'd chocolate brown in the flickering Firelight, whilst the Sword-shap'd Scar upon Puck's Visage seem'd more ominous than e'er before. Sir Francis Bacon rose and greeted me first, saying, "What a fine Beauty you're growin' into, Fanny!" And then Horatio embraced me with his usual Lust; and after him, the tall and fearful-featur'd Puck Goodfellow.

"Pray, be seated, Sweetheart," says Horatio, "and Welcome! Let's drink a Toast to this unexpected Reunion." Whereupon the Landlord, who had hover'd about us all the while, fetch'd a round of Claret, and we all drank with genuine Good Humour and Chear.

"Bless me if you're not more beautiful than e'er before, my Fannikins," says Horatio, "but, in the sacred Name of Friendship, I'll refrain from doing Nature's Bidding—tho' such, I vow, is ne'er the Path of Wisdom. For doth not Juvenal himself say: *'Nunquam aliud Natura, aliud Sapientia dixit'*? . . . Or, for you ignorant Prigs," says he, glancing at Bacon and Puck, " 'Ne'er does Nature say one Thing and Wisdom another'!"

" 'Tis good to see you, Horatio," say I, "and hear the Latin Syllables roll from your Tongue, but pray, what News have you from Lancelot?"

"He's mad as e'er he was," says Horatio, "but now he hath a new Plan which surpasses all his other Plans in Daring. And, if I may say so, in Stupidity. . . ."

"Not Stupidity!" cries Bacon, always ready to defend Lancelot's Honour, "but Bravery."

"Stupid Bravery," says Horatio, "for he means to lead the Prisoners out of Newgate and to the London Docks or e'en as far as Southampton or the Isle of Wight, where he plans to commandeer a Ship to take 'em to the New World. There he hopes to build a new Eden in the Wilderness—a 'True Deocracy of Christian Souls,' or so he calls it."

"Where will he get the Ship? And why the New World? I thought Lancelot hated all Mention of the Colonies and thought America a Land of Savages!"

"And so 'tis, Fanny, so 'tis. Dare I, with my Skin my very Brand—e'en if I had no Brand—set Foot upon that savage

273

Soil? Why, here in England I may starve, and yet I'm free, but in the Colonies, I'm nought but a hunted Slave!"

"An' yet you are not free in Law," says Bacon.

"'Tis true, good Francis," says Horatio, "but in Britannia we are not mere Lambs to slaughter, whilst in the Colonies the Fate that awaits a Runaway is harsh indeed."

"But Lancelot means to sail to Boston Harbour or Providence," says Puck, "not to the Sugar Isles or to Virginia or the Carolinas."

"You are as much a Fool as Lancelot!" shouts Horatio. "Do you think that the sanctimonious Puritans are any less brutal to the Black Man than the Plantation Owners? Sure, they keep only a few domestick Slaves themselves—but the Wealth of all the Ship Owners in New England is built on Slaving! Boston Harbour runs sticky with Rum and Blood! Do you know my Worth in New England, Puck, my Friend? 'Tis a hundred and fifteen Gallons of Rum—no more, no less! I'd have a better Chance as a *Cimmarone* in Cuba or upon a *Quilombo* in Brazil than as a Black Man in saintly Boston or sanctimonious Providence!"

"Pray, what are *Cimmarones*, Horatio? And what indeed *Quilombos*? They sound like Things to eat!" said I, hoping to add some Levity to this distressing Conversation.

"The *Cimmarones* are the Outlaw Blacks that live in all the Sugar Isles as Fugitives—but most particularly in Cuba, where they build Stockades they call *Palenques* and defend their Freedom from the *Rancheadores*—the Evil Slave-Hunters. The *Quilombos* in Brazil are much the same—Settlements of Runaways who hide in the Bush and make their Raids upon the White Planters. I'faith, they oft' have Plantations themselves, and live in Harmony with the Indians, plotting the Day when they may make a great Rebellion and have their own Nation. There I might survive—but in the Colonies I'm sworn to prove myself a Freed Man on Pain of being sold into Slavery again. And how can I prove such? I'm wanted by a Master in Barbadoes and by another in Bath!"

"But Lancelot speaks of settling perhaps in Massachusetts, perhaps in the Hudson Valley of New York," says Puck. "He means to build a true Democracy and take all Fugitives who come, whether Indentur'd Servants, Debtors, Blacks, or Indians."

"They keep Slaves in the Colony of New York, too, my Friend. Why, since the last Slave Insurrection, the whole Metropolis of New York is so inflam'd with Fear that no Black

Man may walk upon the Streets at Night! Bah—Lancelot claims to be a Christian Saint, but he knows not how 'tis with me—I wear my Destiny upon my Skin! And there's the Diff'rence betwixt him and me!"

I lookt at Horatio solemnly, knowing his Fate as akin to my own. Only when I walkt the World *en Homme* was I safe from Rape; a Woman's Fate was not much diff'rent from a Black's. I could wear Breeches and Peruke, but how could he disguise his very Skin?

"Then shall you not sail with Lancelot?" I askt.

"Truly, Fanny, I am torn. I love that Boy—Fool that he is, and I love the Merry Band—like my own Family. But where can I be safe but with the Pyrates or the Fugitives? E'en so, I must defend my Freedom Day by Day. It doth not drop from Heaven as the Rain."

"May Lancelot not lead the Pyrate Life?" said I. "Sure, on the Sea, you're free."

"So I've proposed," said Horatio, "but he is daft to build this Eden of his, this Sacred 'Deocracy' he calls it, upon God's Soil. He longs to found this Second Eden, this New Jerusalem, this Prig's Utopia! He doth not know that Eden is nought but an Oasis in the midst of Hell and that Hell threatens to encroach upon it by the Hour! E'en the Eden of the Bible was surrounded by Hades—and the Serpent penetrated soon enough. I'faith, Eden is like nought so much as a Maidenhead—a passing Fancy, the most temporary of Conditions. *'Heu pietas! heu prisca fides!'* says the Great Bard, Virgil—by which he means: 'Alas for Goodness, alas for Old-World Honour!' But there's the Rub, for e'en in the Old World, Honour did not exist, and ne'er was Goodness so invincible that Evil could not penetrate her Heart—or shall I say—looking at my beauteous Fanny—her Divine Pudendum, her Sacred Slit, her God-like Gash!"

"Blasphemy!" cries Bacon.

"Is it Blasphemy to honour the most God-like Eden we know upon this Earth? I mean the Female Garden, the Bow'r of Earthly Bliss!" asks Horatio.

"And perhaps heavenly as well," says Puck. "For all we know, Heaven itself is nought but a Great Cunnicle on High!" And here he bow'd his Head as if in Pray'r. "Deliver me soon, O Lord," says he, winking at me.

"Come, you Rogues," I say, "stop your infernal Jesting and tell me how I shall join Lancelot in his Great Rebellion."

"Fannikins, my Sweet," Horatio declares, "you are our

275

only Hope of making him see Reason. If you will pledge to join us and essay to convince him to found his bloody Eden aboard a Pyrate Ship, instead of the bloody New England Soil, I'll risque my Freedom and come, too. But if you stay behind, I shall not sail with Lancelot! There's the Long and the Short of it."

"And what convinces you I have such Pow'r with Lancelot?" I askt. I was trembling now, for I knew I must make my Mind up and be quick about it.

"Fannikins, my Love," says Horatio, "can you not know that Lancelot adores you? He struggles in his Heart betwixt the Love of Men and the Love of you, but sure he loves Men with nought but Lust, yet you have all his Heart."

"Is this true, Francis?" I askt. "Is this true, Puck?"

Both Merry Men nodded their Heads solemnly.

" 'Tis true as the Gospels, Madam Fanny," said Francis.

" 'Tis true as my Lust for you, and also Horatio's," said Puck.

I paus'd awhile in Thought, as the intent Faces of the Merry Men studied my own. What would I do? 'Twas now September and I was three Months gone with Child. An Atlantick Crossing might take two Months in mild Weather, but if we waited till the Winter was upon us 'twould be perilous indeed and longer still. And yet if I departed now with Lancelot, I would ne'er see Bellars again. O how my Heart was sunder'd by that Thought! Yet my Longing for Bellars was nought but Lust—and was Lust a worthy enough Emotion on which to build one's Destiny? Certainly not! Lust but toppl'd the House that Friendship built; Lust but sunder'd the worthiest Alliances. Let Bellars seek me in vain at the next Costume Ridotto! Let him wander sadly amidst the Dominoes and Dandies, the Virgins of the Sun, the Popes and Pantaloons, the Devils and the Jesters, the May-Day Sweeps and the Corsican Brigands. Let him whisper in the Ear of ev'ry Nun he sees, and find me not at all. 'Twould pay him back for all his Villainies to me! And to the Whole of the Fair Sex as well!

"Very well, then," said I, "I'll join our Robin Hood and sail the Seas."

"Bravo!" cried Horatio.

"Praise the Lord!" said Puck.

"Thank Heavens," said Francis Bacon with a deep-fetch'd Sigh.

"But how doth Lancelot plan to make this Great Rebellion

a Reality?" I askt. "For I am sure that there is Peril in his Plan."

"Peril indeed is Lancelot's Meat," says Puck, "but he hath contriv'd to win the Fealty of certain of the Guards, and he hath brib'd the Turnkey with the Money you sent. Those that he cannot convert to his Cause, he can convert to the Great Cause of Cash! At this very Moment, i'faith, he has a Following of Debtors and Felons so great that they can easily o'erpow'r the Guards. Verily, the Debtors love Lancelot for preaching that there is no such Thing as Debt. They would follow him to the Ends of the Earth!"

"Or Seas," says Horatio.

"But fear not, Madam Fanny," says Bacon, "for you need not join us at Newgate in the midst of the Rebellion. Littlehat will send a Coach to carry you to our Ship, an' there you'll wait for Lancelot an' the Men."

"When shall we sail?" I askt.

"That hath not been decided yet, nor indeed have we determin'd whether we shall sail from Southampton or the Isle of Wight," says Horatio, "but soon you shall know all. You must be ready daily to depart and wait for Word from Little-hat."

"And if I bear my Babe at Sea?"

"Praise God! Are you with Child?" askt Bacon.

"Did Lancelot not tell you?" I askt.

"Lancelot is so daft with Plans for his glorious Rebellion that he hardly remembers to eat a Bite of Food or sleep a Wink at Night," Horatio declar'd. "But this is shocking News. Who, pray, is the Father? I wish 'twere myself."

"And so I wish, too, good Horatio," said I. "For I was seduced by my own Step-Father before I met the Merry Men and this is the Issue of it. I ran away, ne'er dreaming I might be with Child and only when I was a Captive in Coxtart's House did I discover it."

"And you are sure 'twas your Step-Father?" Horatio askt.

"It could be no other. I was a Virgin until he seduced me."

"And there were no other Swains?" Horatio askt, more with curiosity than blame.

I thought of my Night at the Inn with Tunewell, and my Sapphick Scenes with Coxtart. But no; such am'rous play could not bear Human Fruit. Bellars was the only Man to pierce my Virginity before I learnt I was *Enceinte*.

"No others," said I. "By the Time I began my Brothel Life, I knew I was with Child."

277

"Praise God," says Puck, "Lancelot shall deliver it himself, for he is train'd in all the Healing Arts."

"And I doubt not but he shall put some religious Interpretation to it as well. A Virgin Birth, i'faith!" says Horatio, mockingly. "Another young Disciple for his Deocracy! Ye Gads, your Child shall be a very Proving Ground for all his Theories!"

"So I fear," said I, "but a Child could have a worse God-Father than Lancelot!"

"I'faith, your Son shall have *all* the Merry Men as God-Fathers!" said Horatio warmly. "What a blessèd Child!"

I smil'd. "And what if 'tis a Daughter?" I then askt. "Is she still blest?"

Horatio, Puck, and Francis lookt at me quizzically as if the Birth of a Daughter were more miraculous and impossible than the Birth of a new Jesus.

"It cannot be a Daughter," said Horatio.

"Certainly not," said Puck.

"Impossible," said Francis.

"And why impossible?" said I.

"Because if 'tis a Daughter, how can we call him Lancelot the Second?"

"Indeed," said I, smiling mischievously (in part at their Masculine Vanity and in part with the sheer Pleasure of being back amidst the Merry Men again), "now I understand your Logick."

Chapter XI

Containing a most curious Exchange of Letters thro' which our Fanny learns more concerning the Capriciousness of Destiny than all her Adventures have taught her until now; after which she is summon'd by her one True Love, as the Reader of this most stirring epistolary Chapter shall shortly see.

AND SO I WAITED, as I had promis'd, for Word from Littlehat, wond'ring when I should be summon'd to join Lancelot's great Sailing and feeling considerable Anxiety for Lancelot's Fate and the Fate of his Historick Rebellion. Tho' the Merry Men would scarce speak to me of it, 'twas clear enough that the Rebellion might misfire and Lancelot might swing once more at Tyburn. This Time, the cursèd Beam could well dispatch his Soul with Speed, and ne'er again would Lancelot's lovely Form and Face be seen upon this Globe!

In the Days that follow'd my Meeting with Horatio, Puck, and Francis Bacon, I was nervous as a Cat, awaiting Letters. The other Girls went about their Business, ne'er noticing my Condition, but Kate, with an Enemy's Attentiveness to all my Griefs (as well as Envy of my Joys) watch'd me most closely. She perceiv'd that I waited for the Post as if 'twere for an Annunciation from an Angel, and she smil'd sourly to herself when a Letter came for me.

Many Letters came, i'faith, but all from Bellars, not Littlehat nor Lancelot. Indeed, Bellars sent me sev'ral Letters each Day—one more pitiful and pleading than the next. It took all my Courage to ignore 'em since they touch'd me to the Core. But Kate, for her part, still had not been summon'd by her mysterious Tradesman, so she conceiv'd a Fear that I would leave the Brothel before her (tho', in truth, I'd been there so little Time compar'd to her) and this Apprehension made her most grievously envious.

Oft' she herself would snatch a Letter from Coxtart's

Hands, and carry it up the Stair, then wait at the Door slyly, hoping I would open it in her Presence. I ne'er did so, but her Slyness caus'd me Grief. I worried lest she steal the fateful Letter and I miss Lancelot's Sailing. But no; she was too much a Coward to play such Pranks. She would rather linger and smirk by my Door than take Fate into her own Hands. Tho' harden'd by Life in the Brothel, still she was a cowardly Enemy—more inclin'd to hope for Ill-Fortune to claim me, than to be the Author of my Ill-Fortune herself.

"Another *Billet Doux*, Fanny," says she, handing me a Letter with Lord Bellars' Seal.

"What a curious Post-Boy you are, Kate," says I. "Pray, have you nothing better to do with your Time than deliver my Letters?"

" 'Tis the least Service I can perform for my dearest Friend," says she, mockingly; whereupon she gives me the Letter and flounces away.

I lockt the Door of my Chamber and sat down upon the Bed to read:

> Adorable Creature,
> Pledged as I am to await the next Costume Ridotto at The King's Theatre, ne'ertheless, my Passion for you bids me nourish the perhaps Vain Hope that you will hear my Plea and grant me an Audience sooner. My Love is as a Thunder Cloud about to break, and I can no more contain it than Nature can contain a Flood once the Waters have begun to rise. Pray send to me presently that I may call upon you, and you will assuage the Torment that afflicts the Heart of your most devoted,
>
> Bellars.

I took this pathetick Missive to the Escritoire (which, by the by, already contain'd a Box full of similarly pleading Missives) and forthwith penn'd my Answer.

> My Lord,
> My Word is unbreakable, nor can I be mov'd by Entreaties, howe'er honey'd. If your Lordship continues to plead with me to break my Word, I shall have no Choyce but to put our next Meeting still farther into the Future. Do not tempt me to such stern Expedients.
>
> Yours,
> "Sister" Hackabout-Jones

I laugh'd a little to myself as I penn'd this harsh Epistle, thinking how far I had come since that Day at Lymeworth when I read Lord Bellars' Letter to his Mistress and wept. I had, i'faith, discover'd the Key to Lord Bellars' Heart: namely, Sternness. What I had sought to win by Kindness, Trust, and Innocent Love—his Heart, in short—I should win instead by Disdain. Ah Cruel Irony! Bellars despis'd Love that was freely given, but grew mad as a rabid Dog for Love denied, niggardly Love, Love that was not e'en Love but only Coquetry. He was the Living Proof of the Maxims of La Rochefoucauld, who said, upon one Occasion, that 'twas harder to be faithful to a Woman when all went well than when she was unkind. As long as I remain'd unkind I should secure Bellars' Heart, for twas the Chase itself he favour'd and not the Companionship of a Loving Heart. But damn him! By the Time the next Costume Ball came due, I should be at Sea with Lancelot, and Bellars should sigh in vain for his moist-thigh'd Spanish Nun!

How consistent with his low Character that he should interpret my forbidding Missive as nought but a Plea for a Bribe! For the next Letter to arrive from Bellars contain'd a gold Bracelet emblazon'd with Diamonds and a Plea to allow him to be my Keeper under any Terms I might propose:

> Queen of my Heart,
> The Unkindness of your last Missive hath lacerated my Heart to its very beating Centre. Know that I enclose this small Memento as but a Token of my fiery Passion for you, and also as but a modest Harbinger of the Riches that may be yours, if you will agree to let me care for you as befits your Splendour in the Arts of Love. Cupid himself will look down and smile to see you ensconced in the fine House I will build for you in St. James', and Venus herself will laugh and sing to see the Jewels I will heap about your delicious Neck, entwine 'round your delicate Wrists, and slide upon your slender Fingers. A Life of Luxury and Ease awaits you, if you will but relent in your Cruelty to your most anguish'd and tormented,
>
> Bellars.

To which I rais'd my Quill and replied:

My Lord,

Do you think that because I have been driven, like many another impoverish'd Lass, to make my Living as a sometime Whore, that I am totally insensible to the Pleasures of Freedom and would so readily abandon 'em for Jewels and fine Houses? Your Lordship's Jewels, I perceive as nought but Manacles; your Lordship's fine House as nought but a Prison; and your Lordship's Words of Love as nought but Treachery. You mistake me, My Lord, for another sort of Woman if you think I may be as easily brib'd as a Whig Minister! I return your Jewels herewith with my strictest Warning not to further try the Patience of your most insulted and outraged,

> "Sister" Hackabout-Jones.

O this indeed was Capital Sport! Was I becoming as corrupt as Lord Bellars from the Pleasure I took in this Game? Had I lost my Innocence entirely? Had I forgotten the Wisdom of the Grandmaster of the Coven, who herself confirm'd that Vengeance belong'd to the Goddess alone? But the Delights of this Game were so irresistible to me that I could not forbear from playing. Indeed, I lookt forward to seeing the Letter Bellars would send when he saw his Bauble return'd.

His Answer came upon the Morrow, and sure enough, nosy Kate fetch'd it for me. 'Twas a larger Packet upon this Occasion—a Fact which was duly noted by Kate, who sneer'd and said: "Methinks me Fanny hath an Admirer."

"What gives you that Idea?" I askt, taking the Packet and swiftly locking the Door to my Chamber.

The Letter was wrapp'd about a small mahogany Casket, lin'd with red Velvet and fill'd with loose Jewels which sparkl'd with all the Colours of the Rainbow. I gasp'd to see such an Array of Rubies, Emeralds, Diamonds, and other Gems, for not only were they costly beyond Reckoning, but, loose in the Hand, they seem'd like Gifts from Faery Land, not from the World of Mortals. These would I have dearly lov'd to keep, but the Letter which accompanied them harden'd my Heart:

Belovèd Creature, Keeper of my Heart, Most Honoured Madam,

I am contrite. My whole Heart contracts into a shiv'ring Ball for fear I have offended you. Heaven Forbid that I should misconstrue your Honour and your Purity and lead you to believe I value you as nought but a Common Strumpet.

Perhaps the Bracelet that I sent was too ornate for the Purity and Simplicity of your Tastes and therefore offended you. For that, I ask a thousand Pardons!

Please accept these modest Jewels as a small Token of my Grief o'er having insulted you. If you will be good enough to visit my Jeweller, Mr. Crickle, in the Royal Exchange, he will set these Stones for you in whatsoe'er Manner you choose and bill them to the Account of your most devoted, contrite, and humble,

Bellars.

P.S. I will no longer press you, but will count the Minutes until we meet at The King's Theatre. Adieu. I hope my Heart will not break into a thousand Pieces e'er then!

So the Blackguard thought I did not fancy his Taste in Bracelets—the Fool! I ran to the Escritoire and wrote:

My Lord,

'Tis not your Lordship's Taste in Jewels that is wanting, but rather your Lordship's lack of Delicacy in understanding the Hearts of Women. I would rather accept six Pomegranate Seeds from the King of Hell and risque Imprisonment for half the Year than accept these Jewels, for they are nought but Bribes to relinquish all I hold most dear in this World—namely, my Liberty. My Heart is not to be so lightly won.

Riches alone ne'er sway'd my Soul to Love. Think on your past Behaviour and purify your Heart. Then perhaps I shall learn to love one who has so little Esteem for the Souls of the Fair Sex. I return your Lordship's Jewels herewith.

Yrs.,
"Sister" Hackabout-Jones.

Ye Gads! I thought, sealing the Packet, perhaps I've gone too far this Time and I will ne'er hear from Bellars again.

But I was much too taken with the Game to stop playing now. Like a long-time Gambler, my Fever grew as the Stakes rose higher, and Danger of Loss kindl'd Passions that Safety and Security ne'er knew!

Perhaps Bellars was a Gambler, too, for upon the following Day I receiv'd this surprizing Missive:

Empress of my Heart,

I have search'd my Soul to understand the Import of your last Letter, and, after much Anguish and Consternation, have determin'd that you must, in some wise, be alluding to the Entanglements I have nurtur'd lo these last five Years, with a certain well-known Lady of the Town.

Know then, that immediately upon Receipt of your Letter of Yesterday, I terminated all Entanglements with this Lady and gave her to understand that I could not see her e'er again. Before we meet at The King's Theatre, I will study to purify my Heart so that I may, by the Grace of God, be worthy of your rare and divine Love.

What a Fool I was to dream that a Heart as pure as yours could be won by Jewels alone. Rather, I will essay to present you with the Jewel of my Fidelity to you and you alone.

Most Respectfully
Your Contrite,
Bellars.

Now this was cunning Vengeance indeed! The Lady with whom Bellars had broken my Heart had now been cast out by him! Had Revenge been my whole Intent, I could have ne'er contriv'd such sweet Vengeance! 'Twas only when I idly toy'd with Fate, instead of fretting and anguishing o'er it, that Fate dropp'd all her most glitt'ring Jewels in my Lap. Was Destiny no more than a Game in which Merit was seldom rewarded and Vice was punish'd capriciously, if at all? Was the Great Goddess a Merry Prankster rather than a Dispenser of Solemn Justice? So it seem'd!

What a Lesson this was! Ne'er had I truly seen Life as a Game of Chance before. O I long'd for a Friend with whom to share this Wisdom. I wisht for someone I could trust with this curious Tale! 'Twas then that I thought of the Wiltshire Witches. Isobel would understand all this, tho' Joan might not. Dear Isobel, I thought, Peace be with your Soul. But Isobel and the Witches were gone, and the Wenches at the Brothel were none of 'em true enough Friends to tell.

But where was Littlehat's Letter? I grew impatient awaiting his Call. This Game with Bellars was diverting for the nonce, but I had seen enough of his Contradictory Character by now to fix my Heart in its Resolve to flee with Lancelot. Bellars was passionate in Pursuit, yet I doubted not that he should grow bor'd and jaded once he had me in his Keeping. And I was bitterly aware that 'twas not me myself he lov'd, but merely a mysterious Maskt Lady who had teaz'd him mercilessly in the Hell-Fire Caves. Should he discover me to be nought but his simple innocent Step-Child, all his ardent Adoration would blow away like Clouds o'er the Sea upon a windy Day. No, I could not risque putting my Destiny in the Grasp of such a fickle Passion. I must choose Friendship instead and sail with Lancelot! Upon this, my Mind was firmly fixt.

At last, after what seem'd an interminable Wait, I receiv'd the long'd-for Letter. Kate, my avid Post-Girl, carried it upstairs, but upon this Occasion, I was so eager to read it that I tore the Paper open without bothering to lock the Chamber Door. I read with trembling Hand as she lurkt in the Corner watching (with the avid Eyes of Envy) my own eager Orbs flicker o'er the Page.

My Belovèd Fanny,

I risque this Missive only upon the Assurance of Littlehat that you will not fail to burn it as soon as you have committed its Contents to Memory.

All is in Readiness here for the Embarkation for Eden. I have secur'd—I cannot tell you how—a twomasted Brig, the *Hazard*, which is anchor'd off the Isle of Wight. She's a fine Ship, about 30 Ton, square-rigg'd on the Foremast, fore-and-aft-rigg'd on the Main, and flying a Jib and Staysails. She'll sail with as little as a Crew of Twelve, as well as Captain, Mate, Cook, and Carpenter.

The Captain is myself, Horatio the Mate, whilst the other Crew may easily be supplied from amongst our worthy Followers here. I shall send Littlehat to fetch you upon horseback on the Morrow to carry you to our Rallying Ground, which I cannot yet disclose. Take as few Possessions as you can, but do not fail to bring any Valuables which may easily be barter'd, and dress *en*

Homme, as you were when first we met. Fear not but you will be as well car'd for as if you were our own Daughter, Sister, Mother, Wife.

My Heart is heavy as a Hangman's Noose about the Throat of an innocent Man when I consider how I us'd you at the Start of our Acquaintance; but having search'd my Soul I know that you and you alone are the Woman who can share my curious Destiny. Some Men sigh for Heiresses with Doweries, and some for the Appeasement of their jaded Lusts. For mine own part, I have turn'd to beauteous Boys because ne'er before did I meet a Woman whose Wit and Learning could challenge my own Understanding and cause me to reach for Truths unguess'd before.

I fear'd you not only for your Beauty, but also for your Wit, for I was wholly unaccustom'd to finding Wit so enclos'd in such a beauteous Form; and the Presence of two such rare Qualities in one Woman fill'd me with Dread of the Unknown. Most Men fear Learning and Wit in Women, for they suppose that all a Woman's Wit will be put to the Service of ensnaring them and making them Slaves for Life. But I have found in you another Quality more rare than e'en your Beauty or your Understanding, namely your Sweetness and Loyalty—Traits said not to exist in Womanhood. Ne'er have I seen you stoop to Coquetry e'en when Coquetry had serv'd you better than your own Native Honesty.

Know then that I love you with all my Heart and require your Wisdom and Wit, as well as your Companionship and Chear, in establishing my great new Nation of Free Souls. In it, Women shall have no less Authority than Men, and Blacks shall equal Whites, for we are all nought but Souls in the Sight of God, and Souls have neither Sex nor Colour. Truly, we shall build a New Jerusalem, a Second Eden, far from the Fears that trouble this hellish Isle, where Liberty is nought but a Word and Men are imprison'd merely for seeking to survive rather than perish of Hunger. Come with me and I shall prove to you not only that I can show you most enduring Love, but that we can build a World where neither Sex nor Poverty nor Colour may be a Bar to perfect Happiness and Liberty!

My Heart flies to you until I may but clasp you to my Breast fore'er more!

Yr. Most Devoted,
R. Hood.

I gasp'd to read this Letter, which represented the pure Fulfillment of all my Noble Dreams of Love. How wise I had been to fix my Heart upon Lancelot's Lofty Friendship rather than Bellars' Scurvy Lust! Here was Love conjoin'd with High Ideals, Love which did not seek to bribe with Jewels nor play the gaudy Games of Coquetry, but Love which sought to join two Souls in pure Service to the Great Goal of Liberty! How could I burn such a Letter upon the Instant? I must read and re-read it until I knew its Contents by Heart! And so I tuckt it in my Bosom, promising myself that I should burn it ere long—but only after I had savour'd its stirring Text, not merely one more Time but sev'ral.

So engross'd was I in the Letter that I quite forgot the Presence of Kate, who still stood in the Corner, surveying me with her envious Eyes.

"That must be quite some Letter, Fanny me Girl," says she, bringing me back to my Senses with a Jolt.

"Kate, you take too much Notice of my Business and not enough of your own," say I.

"'Tis me own Affair an' Coxtart's, too, if ye mean to fly the Coop, Fanny. D'ye catch me Drift?"

"And what of your own sweet Man, Kate? Will he not make an Honest Woman of you as he promis'd?"

"An' that's none o' yer Business neither, I reckon," says Kate, turning bright red.

Suddenly I know I have done ill to touch this sore Nerve, so I quickly seek to make amends, to soothe rather than pique mine Enemy.

"Kate, can I help you somehow to flee this Place? For I will plight my Troth to you in Friendship and help you all I can. . . ."

"An' who needs yer bloody Help, ye Baggage! Me Man will come fer me. I need no poxt Strumpet to befriend me!" Whereupon she hastens to leave the Chamber.

"Kate," I call after her, "there's not a Soul alive who doth not need a Friend from Time to Time."

But Kate only turn'd 'round to sneer, then clatter'd down the Stair. O she was one of those who mistake Friendship for Pity and can accept no Help for fear of seeming Weak. Her

287

Frailties, more than my own, I fear'd, might be my Downfall. For 'tis oft' the Case, in this imperfect World, that the Strong are fell'd by the Weak, that the Robust are brought low by the Envy of the Frail; and many a mighty Fortress, which Cannon could not tumble, hath been undone by the tiniest of Termites, doing their steady, destructive Work unseen!

I fear'd Kate's Enmity now as much as I had formerly fear'd Lord Bellars Satanick Lust (and the corresponding Lust it rais'd in me). But I could not long dwell upon Kate and her Jealousies, for I must now make Preparations for Littlehat's Arrival; and then I must lock the Door to my Chamber and feast my hungry Eyes upon Lancelot's beauteous Letter until I had burnt its fateful Contents into my Heart.

Chapter XII

Containing an Incident of a more tragick than comedick Kind, the Import of which may not be Reveal'd for many Years, but which nonetheless alters our Heroine's Destiny most profoundly.

UPON THE MORROW I awoke with all in Readiness for my Departure with Littlehat. My Clothes were laid out upon a Chair, my few Valuables stuff'd in my Pockets; my Hat, my Riding Wig, my Boots—all were prepar'd.

I bolted out of Bed and ran to the Window. 'Twas a grey and rainy Day in London, near as cold in September as it might be at Christmastime, an autumn London Day that chills one to the very Marrow of one's Bones.

I stood watching the Rain make Rivers of Garbage in the Street below—Rivers which carried all Manner of Offal from Orange Peels to Human Excrement, from drown'd Kittens to Shards of broken Glass. Since knowing myself with Child, my Feelings for Animals, always most puissant before, had grown intolerably strong, so that whene'er I saw a drown'd Kitten, or a starv'd Dog, my Heart seem'd to lurch in my Chest, and my Eyes wept with Pity for all the Animals in this World. 'Twas thus with an aching Heart that I watch'd the Gutter-Spouts drench the unwary Pedestrians who ran along, hugging the Wall, or, if they were jostl'd away from it, cov'ring their Heads as best they could with their Cloaks, for in those Days no Man would use an oil'd Umbrella for Fear of being thought Mollyish. Sooner be drench'd than that!

What a miserable Day to make our Escape upon horseback! But surely with a Plan this great, mere Weather would not foil it. I reach'd into my Bosom again to extract Lancelot's Letter and read it just once more (for I had slept with it safe in my Shift)—but lo! the Letter was gone!

Panick then reign'd in my Breast. I ran to the Bed and search'd 'neath the Pillows, 'neath the Quilts, e'en 'neath the

Mattress, but there was no Trace of the Letter. I had fallen asleep with it still about my Person and the Door to my Chamber lockt, but now 'twas lost! What Villain had snatch'd it? And what Use might be made of it to detain or betray my Lancelot?

O I had underestimated Kate's Evil! I had thought her too cowardly to act against me, but 'twas clear I had been wrong. Why had I not burnt the Letter at once as Lancelot directed? Would my Longing to keep a mere Love Letter deprive me of the Love of Lancelot himself? O Cruel Irony!

I reach'd for the Key to my Chamber Door (which hung, these Days, on a Chain about my Neck), but, to my Astonishment, the Key, too, had vanish'd and the Door was securely lockt from the other side. I struggl'd with it, half in Disbelief, half in Fury, for still I could not credit my Senses in this Predicament. Could I be held Prisoner upon this Fateful Day? I pounded my Fists against the Door in Fury and Rage, but I doubted that anyone should come to my Rescue. The Deed had been too well done for it to be undone now by mere Pounding.

I ran to the Windows facing upon the Street. I could escape thro' the Windows if not thro' the Door, but the Windows were—I now remember'd—painted shut! Many Times had I told myself to have 'em scrap'd, but always procrastinated, and now all my Efforts to force 'em open avail'd nought!

Come, Fanny, thought I, how should you let mere Prison Walls detain you when now your Mind is fixt upon your Destiny with Lancelot? Whereupon I held myself in check and sat down upon the Bed to think. Be still, I counsel'd my beating Heart. Be Serene, I counsel'd my disorder'd Mind. Panick ne'er broke down Prisons, but slow, calm Consideration might do so.

But my Thoughts came all in a Rush! I thought of Lancelot's Brig, anchor'd off the Isle of Wight, riding the Seas, Flags flying, waiting to take me to my Destiny. I thought of the Witches' Prophecy—"Your Daughter will fly across the Seas"—which seem'd to portend my Escape now, despite all Odds. I thought of Bellars' Jewels and Promises, of the tragick Deaths of Isobel and Joan, and finally of Horatio's utter Faith that I and I alone might convince Lancelot to shun the Colonies where poor Horatio should always be in Peril as a Runaway.

What dire Opinion would Horatio have of me, if I fail'd to

eapt. Whereupon I fell upon the Street, trying to
< my Fall—but coming down, alas, so heavily
oot that I bruis'd it horribly. For a Moment, the
ed me from moving at all. Ne'ertheless, I soon
my Feet and began to limp in the Direction Lit-
one. I dragg'd myself along thro' sheer Will and
s, for my Hand was bleeding more than e'er be-
' Foot had now begun to swell within my Boot,
Pain nearly unendurable. How I endur'd it, stum-
ng in the Rain, I cannot say. I only know that I
Lancelot waiting, and of Horatio's Distress when
nd himself betray'd, and of the Sadness of my
ehat, which had been so clear upon his loving

ve been in true Delirium by then, for I remember
shouting "Littlehat! Littlehat!" just before I
a Mud Hole and chanced to hit my Head against

t transpir'd I also do not know, since I was dumb-
Vorld than that Post upon which I'd dasht my
eamt I was aboard a handsome Brig, anchor'd off
Wight, and I was dress'd all in a Pyrate's Garb,
olour'd patchwork velvet Breeches, a velvet Coat
oat, and a gorgeous gleaming Cutlass, which I
nst the Foe as ably as any Man. I climb'd the
an expert Sailor, then I stood in the Crow's-Nest,
the Water, watching the Seas glitter with Jewels
vhilst the Men upon the Deck below appear'd for
l like Children's Mannikins made of Lead.
celot was beside me, kissing me upon the Face
nd thanking me for having Faith in him and
aat it should not be long before we found safe
ur new Jerusalem. In the Dream, all was Peace,
anquillity. My Heart was flooded with Sunshine
that all would be well with me thereafter. 'Twas
Dreams we have when our Fortunes reach their
and we wish to reassure ourselves that all is not

aat base Deception do our Dreams create! For
ken'd, 'twas in my familiar Bed in Coxtart's
Coxtart's awful Face, not Lancelot's lovely one,
er me, and my whole World seem'd suddenly
.

appear as I had promis'd? And would Lancelot believe I had
rejected his Love? Why had I fail'd to burn the Letter? Was
there a Worm in my Heart gnawing away with Lust for Bellars? Was there yet a Part of me that could not sail across the
Seas without setting Eyes upon him once again? Was I still
torn betwixt Passion and Honour, betwixt fiery Lust and fond
Friendship? Or was I merely still too innocent of Evil and
had I taken too little Care to guard against Kate's Envy?

These were the furious Thoughts that battl'd in my Brain
as I sat upon my Bed, wond'ring when Littlehat should come
to fetch me and how I should communicate to him my Imprisonment, my Love for Lancelot, my Willingness to flee
with him and keep my Word to all the Merry Men?

I rose and dress'd myself in Man's Attire, refusing to believe that I should not find some Way out of this foul, unfair
Gaol. But, once dress'd, I could do nought but gaze at the
Raindrops chasing each other down the Window Panes and
wonder when my good Friend Littlehat should come.

'Twas deathly still and quiet in the House. I heard no
Sounds of Coxtart or the other Wenches stirring. 'Twas
strange; 'twas very strange indeed. Where might they have
gone? What Ploy might Kate have us'd to so impound me
without Hope, for I doubted not but she was the Culprit, the
Author of this hellish Plan, the Serpent in this rotten Garden
of Evil.

I struggl'd again with the Window, but 'twould not budge
an Inch. I ran to the Bell Pull and yankt upon it with both
Hands, but lo! it came loose as I did so! The entire Chamber
had been prepar'd to thwart my Plans! O Villainy! O mis-
placed Innocence!

I press'd my Nose to the Rain-streakt Glass, determining
that I should position myself there and wait for Littlehat to
appear, then make such Noises that he could not fail to hear
me, despite the Din of Traffick in the Rain-soakt Street.

Whilst waiting, I should find a Means to open the Window,
I vow'd to myself. And so I station'd myself there, in Read-
iness for my Journey, whilst the Rain pour'd down and the
Pedestrians, Chairs, Carts, and Coaches in the Street below
sent a Din up to Heaven which might have been the very
Echo of my Distress.

How long I waited I cannot say. Time lost all Meaning as
I struggl'd with the Window, then stopp'd to rest, then
struggl'd and stopp'd again. I watch'd the Pedestrians below
with a Wary Eye. Whene'er I saw a short, fat Man or one

with a black Beard, my Heart seem'd to cease beating in my Breast. 'Twas very like a mad Infatuation; I long'd for Littlehat's squat Form and comical Face as if he, not Lancelot, had been my Lover!

The Rain grew heavier, then abated a little, then grew heavier once again. The Damp penetrated my Chamber, where no Fire burnt in the Grate upon this chill and miserable Day. I rubb'd my Hands together with the Cold. I press'd my cold Nose to the Panes. Many Times I began to weep for my Plight, but held myself in check with the stern Admonition that losing Hope was the greatest Defeat of all, and that if I might but maintain Faith in my eventual Salvation, then Salvation should somehow come to me.

At last, I saw a short, squat Figure in a green Surtout hurry along the Street, leading a fine Ebony Arabian Mare. The Gnome-like Figure walkt with lower'd Head, and, his Hat being uncockt, I could not see his Features; but from his Gait and Manner, I was certain 'twas Littlehat. Then the Rebellion had been a Success! For if Littlehat had left the Confines of the Prison Walls, perhaps 'twas safe to assume that Lancelot and the others had done so, too. At this very Moment, they were doubtless speeding towards our Rallying Ground. My Heart leapt in my Bosom with Joy and I wanted to shout "Hail Littlehat! Hail Lancelot! Hail Horatio!" For the nonce, I near forgot I was a Prisoner myself.

Now Littlehat approach'd the Door to Coxtart's House, looking behind him, to ascertain whether he was being follow'd. Now he was momentarily out of my Sight as he rang at the Gate. Now he stepp'd back again, waiting; and now a female Figure in a Cloak came out to speak with him. She must have been waiting there all along, for she walkt with him into the Street, instead of calling him within. O Treachery!— 'twas Kate!

At first, both were turn'd with their Backs towards me, but then they slowly turn'd 'round. Now I could see Littlehat's Face. As he glanced up at the House, I beat with furious Fists upon the Window, but, alas, he could neither hear nor see me. Now Kate whisper'd something in his Ear, and now suddenly he wore a troubl'd Mien, his Moustache seem'd to droop, his Mouth quiver'd as if he should begin to cry. Quickly, I ran to the Bed, tore off the Linens, and began knotting 'em together in the Hope of making a sort of Ladder for my Escape. Why had I not thought of this sooner? Then back to the Window where I could see Littlehat was just now

sadly walking away. With a bu___ foundest Anguish o'er Little___ smasht my Fist thro' the Win___ also cutting my Wrist so sever___ reddest Blood.

"Littlehat! Littlehat!" I shout___ With my left Hand, I smasht ___ to him and screaming all the wh___ the Opening in the Window w___ thro'.

O I was in a Rage of Tears ___ tention to the spurting Blood, n___ smasht at the Window with bot___ hat, who, e'en now, was moving ___

I ran to the Bedstand and f___ with this I batter'd at the Wind___ whereupon I began the much n___ the wood Frames so as to mak___ how to secure the Sheet so tha___ myself to Heaven forthwith? ___ Problem. Should I forget the S___ dow Ledge, and hope that L___ 'Twas a long Fall to the Grou___ Way upon the Sheet, I migh___ from here might indeed be fata___

Just then I spy'd a Hoisting ___ the outer Window Frame. If I ___ Window Ledge and afix my lin___ myself a bit and be within clo___ to leap the Rest of the Wa___ Goddess above, I stepp'd out ___ my bleeding Hand I grasp'd t___ (trying for all my Might not ___ good Hand I sought to atta___ 'Twas a Job that requir'd tw___ slick as Glass and I dar'd not___ compar'd with losing Lancelo___ Frame, and carefully reach'd ___ of the Bed-Linen to the Hoo___ that the Hook should bear n___ Ladder with both Hands and sl___

O the Rope held for the no___ I had a long Way left to jump___ dangling so precariously in A___

Mouth and ___ roll to bre___ upon one ___ Pain preve___ scrambl'd t___ tlehat had ___ Stubborne___ fore and n___ making the___ bling head___ thought of ___ he should ___ Friend Lit___ Face.

I must h___ nought bu___ stumbl'd in___ a Post.

What ne___ er to the ___ Brains. I d___ the Isle of ___ with multic___ and Waisto___ wielded 'ga___ Rigging lik___ high above ___ of Sunlight ___ all the Wor___

Now La___ and Neck ___ promising ___ Haven for ___ Joy, and T___ and I knew ___ one of thos___ lowest Ebb ___ lost.

But O w___ when I aw___ House, wit___ watching o___ black as He___

I wept and whimper'd in Coxtart's Arms. Ne'er did any Wench have such a strange Nurse, such a curious Mother!

"Come now, Fanny mine," says she. "Why weep when ye have charm'd a fine Admirer? Why, Lord Bellars himself hath call'd here a dozen Times if he hath call'd here once—and just in these three Days! My Word, you've hardly cause to weep when a Gentleman of Lord Bellars' Rank hath been so daft with Worry o'er yer own fine Self!"

"Lancelot! Lancelot!" I cried amidst Gales of Tears.

"Pray, who is Lancelot? Is my Lord Bellars' Christian Name Lancelot? I doubt it, for I have heard he is call'd Laurence, tho' perhaps Lancelot is yer Pet Name for him abed!"

O I wept bitter Tears both at Coxtart's Misunderstanding of my Plight, and the dread News that three whole Days had pass'd, and here it was too late to reach the Isle of Wight!

"Fanny," Coxtart says, "I owe ye a great Debt of Gratitude for all yer valiant Efforts to arrest Kate's Escape. For the Baggage hath elop'd, and I doubt not but all yer Struggles with the Window were nought but the most valiant Essays to stop the Wench. For truly she hath deceiv'd us all. She spirited away the other Girls with the News of a great Auction in the Royal Exchange, which prov'd a Lye. And when I return'd from Market, I found the Baggage gone—with all my Plate as well!—and you bleeding in the Street where you had fallen in yer Loyalty to me! O there was a Young Fellow who came here enquiring after you upon that Night of your Initiation as a Nun—a Fellow from Wiltshire—a rough Country Squire who claim'd to be the Heir to a Great Estate. I would have sent him packing, but Kate insisted she herself would entertain him—the Strumpet—and I reckon 'tis with *him* she hath elop'd! But fear not, we'll see the Strumpet hang'd, I warrant. O what Satisfaction 'twill be to hear the Snap of her foolish Neck and see her swing at Tyburn."

I only moan'd and wail'd for Lancelot and did not answer, but in my Mind many Visions rose and fell. Could it be Daniel who had come in search of me, and had he then been set upon by Kate? Impossible, I thought; Coxtart must be mad. Kate had doubtless stolen the Silver and then fled, or perhaps her mysterious Tradesman had come for her at last. Still, what did I care for Kate's Affairs, with Lancelot gone!

Oblivious of my Distress, Coxtart chatter'd on: "And mark my Words, you have slept thro' the greatest Tumult London hath known since the Royal Entry of King George. Why, a

Rebellion hath taken place in Newgate Prison and well o'er twenty Rogues and forty Debtors o'erpower'd the Guards and made away on horseback. 'Twas said they had Confederates without the Prison Walls who brought 'em Horses on which to escape—Stolen Horses, I'll warrant—and the whole Town hath talkt of nothing else lo these three Days past!"

This News brought me suddenly to my Senses.

"And what became of the Mutineers?" I askt, my Voice hoarse with not having spoken a Word except to rave in three whole Days.

"See here," says Coxtart, "I've *The Daily Courant* somewhere about." And she lookt for it upon the Escritoire—but finding it not, she said: "No, no—'tis not here, but I'll fetch it from the Parlour." Whereupon she hasten'd towards the Door.

"Pray, Mother Coxtart," I askt, "tell me, have I broken Bones? Will I be lame fore'er more?"

"I fear'd that, too," says she, "for my belovèd dearest Fanny, but 'twas nothing more than a twisted Ankle, tho' yer Leg swell'd so, we had to cut the Boot off. Clever Girl to pursue that Strumpet, Kate, in Man's Disguise—but have no Fear, we'll see her swing yet. Sure, Fanny, had ye not hit yer Head and knockt yer Brains to Heaven, that Ankle would have stopp'd ye—not to mention all the Blood ye lost from yer Wrist. Why, had ye wisht to suicide, ye could have done no better! Now then, I'll fetch yer Tea and *The Daily Courant*. I'll warrant there'll be Love Letters as well from yer Fine Admirer. . . ."

Coxtart bustl'd out the Door, full of counterfeit Love for me now that she saw still more Profits to be made off Lord Bellars' Infatuation. I lay abed alone and moan'd with Anguish. I remember'd my Dream of Peace and Happiness and how I had awaken'd from it to this Nightmare. I curst my Fate which had orphan'd me fore'er more. Would I always be an Outcast, wand'ring the World, seeking my own Native Tribe, and finding it briefly only to be cast out again? I moan'd more with the Ache in my Heart than with the Pains in my Foot and Wrist. O why was I not dead if not with Lancelot? I wept until I soakt the Linens with my briny Tears.

Coxtart soon return'd, full of Chear and Bustle, placed a Tray before me set with Dishes of Tea and all Manner of Muffins, Buns, warm Breads, Butter, and Cheese.

"Come now, Fanny, dry yer Eyes. Lord Bellars will pay a

Visit to ye anon," whereupon the sly old Fox smil'd like a Tom Cat that tortures a Canary.

This News alarm'd me. Now, more than e'er before, Bellars must not see my Face! For surely if he knew I were his Step-Child, he would grow tired of me ere long.

"Pray, Mother Coxtart, you must keep Lord Bellars away from here until I am recover'd. I will not have him see me in this distress'd Condition. Why, Coquetry and Prudence *alone* dictate that he must ne'er see me in this Condition! I have sent Word to him already to await the next Costume Ridotto at The King's Theatre and I'll ne'er see him ere then. Do you think I have gain'd the passionate Loyalty of such a notorious Rake by letting him come to me at any Hour? Nay, Mother Coxtart, he will pay better for my Services if he is forced to wait!"

"Clever Wench!" says Coxtart, her Eyes glitt'ring with Greed. "Very well, then, I'll keep the Wolf at bay. But mark ye—there are Letters here," whereupon she hands me no less than four Letters with Lord Bellars' Seal. Now she draws a somewhat tatter'd Copy of a News-Sheet out of her Apron, sets it before me, and with many counterfeit Kisses and Fondlings (which near cause me to be sick upon the Bed), she takes her Leave of me.

I put the Love Letters aside without the slightest Hesitation and turn hungrily to *The Daily Courant* before I e'en taste my Tea. There I read these stirring Words upon the Page:

London, September 24.
We have receiv'd Information of a major Tumult Yesterday at Newgate Prison. The Turnkey, perceiving the Prisoners going into a Riot, sent Guards for a File of Musqueteers to prevent it, and a Tumult arose, in which there were seven Men kill'd and a like Number of Soldiers wounded, despite which Occurrence, well o'er Forty Prisoners escap'd upon horseback, doubtless with the Aid of Confederates without the Walls. A Committee of Council hath been form'd to look into this Disorder and the Warden hath been directed to take more effectual Care for the Future.

So the Rebellion had not fail'd! Yet who were the seven Men kill'd? Was Lancelot amongst them? And did they truly escape and reach the Isle of Wight? Upon this the News-Sheet was anguishingly silent. Was there no further Report, no News at all but this? Alas, the Paper was far more prolix upon the Subjects of lost Dogs, erring Wives, and facial Washes. For in the self-same Sheet I also read:

> Lost September 24, 1724, betwixt St. James' Sq. and the Old Palace-Yard, a little Cross-shap'd Dog, of the Lurcher kind, of a yellow-brown Colour. 'Twas taken up by an ill-lookt Fellow, a Notorious Dog-Stealer, and led by a blue String towards York Building. He answers to the Name of Bugg, and leaps o'er a Stick. Whoe'er brings him next door to the Great House in Dean's Yard, shall have Two Shillings Reward. N.B. He will ne'er be worth a George to those who have him, his Marks being known.

'Twas clear that lost Dogs merited a far more Precise Account than Prison Rebellions. Likewise, Lost Wives:

> Whereas Dame Eliza Penny (Wife of Sir James Penny of York Place in the County of Surrey, Bart., and Daughter of Samuel Snellgrove, late of Deptford in the County of Kent, Shipwright), aged 23 years, or thereabouts, hath elop'd from her said Husband without any Cause, and endeavours to run him in Debt, by taking up Goods from Tradesmen and otherwise. The said Husband, with an honest Intent, that Tradesmen and others should not be impos'd on: Doth hereby give Notice of the said Elopement, and that he will not pay any Debts she shall contract. This Notice is further to Forewarn all Persons not to trust her; and to the End no Person may be impos'd upon by her under any False Names in the Future, all Persons are inform'd that she is a little Woman, light brown Hair, full grey Eyes, large Eyebrows, round Visage, pale Complexion, with a small Moon-shap'd Scar in the Middle of her Forehead, and hath a very voluble, deceitful Tongue.

Alas for the English Nation which hath e'er set a higher Value upon Dogs than upon Wives! I doubted not but Eliza Penny had good cause to leave her "said Husband," and in my Heart I wisht her God's Speed. Likewise Lancelot, tho' I knew not whether he was alive or dead. O curse the foolish News-Sheet which had more Space for Notices of Aids to Beauty than for Notices of Rebellions in Newgate Prison!

298

For now I glanced down the Page, where, in my Distress and Anguish, I allow'd my Eye to linger o'er the trivial Notices of Beauty Aids, many of which I already had employ'd:

The famous Bavarian Red Liquor; Which gives such a delightful blushing Colour to the Cheaks of those that are White or Pale, that it is not to be distinguish'd from a natural fine Complexion, nor perceiv'd to be artificial by the nearest Friend. Is nothing of Paint, or in the least hurtful, but good in many Cases to be taken inwardly. It renders the Face delightfully handsome and beautiful; is not subject to be rubb'd off like Paint, therefore cannot be discover'd by the nearest Friend. It is certainly the best Beautifier in the World; is sold only at Mr. Payn's Toy-Shop, at The Angel and Crown in St. Paul's Churchyard near Cheapside, at 3s. 6d. a Bottle, with Directions.

Would I now, having lost Lancelot, and all my Dreams of Liberty, devote myself entirely to being a Painted Whore, and fill my Life, like so many Women, with these Trifles? Then I had best read carefully, for this News-Sheet foretold my entire Destiny:

The true Royal Chymical Wash-Ball for the beautifying of the Hands and Face, as it is from the first Author, without Mercury or anything prejudicial, largely experienced and highly recommended by all that use them, and that for making the Skin so delicately soft and smooth, as not to be parallel'd by either Wash, Powder, or Cosmetick; and it being indeed a real Beautifier of the Skin, by taking off all Deformities, as Tetters, Ringworms, Morphew, Sunburn, Scurff, Pimples, Pits, or Redness of the Small Pox, keeping it of a lasting and extream Whiteness. It soon alters red or rough Hands and is admirable in shaving the Head, which not only gives an exquisite Sharpness to the Razor, but so comforts the Brain and Nerves, as to prevent catching Cold, and is of a grateful and pleasant Scent; which has been sold above this twenty Years at the Corner of Pope's-Head Alley in Cornhill, over against the Royal Exchange, and is still continu'd to be sold at the same Place by Mr. Lambert, Glove-Seller, and at Mrs. King's Toy-Shop in Westminster Hall. Price one Shilling each, and Allowance by the dozen. Beware of Counterfeits which may prove very prejudicial.

Beware, indeed, of Counterfeits! Would a Bavarian Red Liquor cure a pallid aching Heart and make it robust and red again? Would a Royal Chymical Wash-Ball cleanse Deformities from the Soul? O the News-Sheet did not answer this! But how informative 'twas upon the Subject of Perfume for Wigs!

> The Royal Essence for the Hair of the Head and Perriwigs, being the most delicate and charming Perfume in Nature, and the greatest Preserver of Hair in the World, for it keeps that of Perriwigs (a much longer Time than usual) in the Curl, and fair Hair from fading or changing Colour, makes the Hair of the Head grow thick, strengthens and confirms its Roots, and effectually prevents it from falling off or splitting at the Ends, makes the Powder continue in all Hair longer than it possibly will, by the use of any other Thing; by its incomparable Odour and Fragrancy it strengthens the Brain, revives the Spirits, quickens the Memory, and makes the Heart chearful, never raises the Vapours in Ladies, & c., being wholly free from (and abundantly more delightful and pleasant than) Musk, Civet, & c., 'tis indeed an unparallel'd fine Scent for the Pocket, and perfumes Handkerchiefs, & c. excellently. To be had only at Mr. Allcraft's, a Toy-Shop at The Bluecoat Boy by Pope's-Head Alley against The Royal Exchange, Cornhill, seal'd up, at 2s. 6d. a Bottle with Directions.

O Mr. Allcraft, sure I could use some of your Craft! For ne'er did my Brain need so much strengthening, nor my Memory so much quickening, nor my Spirits so much reviving, nor my Heart so much chearing! O I must go to Mr. Allcraft's Toy-Shop presently! I must have this Royal Essence to revive my Spirits! I must cover my aching Heart with Paints and Patches, my aching Brain with perfum'd Powder for a Wig, my sadden'd Soul with Petticoats and Panniers, my sunder'd Spirit with silver Lace or gold. Alas, Belinda, we read the News-Sheets for News of Life and Death, Survival of our Souls in Worlds to Come, Reunion with our Loves and Lovers—and we find nought but Notices for Toys and Toy-Shops, Beauty Aids and Scents! The Printing-Press may have a certain Pow'r, but it doth nought to bring us back our Friends nor heal our Hearts! And when we read the News for Comfort and Consolation—Cosmeticks are all we get!

My Tea was now cold as Ice, likewise my Breads and Muffins; and, putting 'em all aside, I crumpl'd the accursèd News-Sheet into a Ball and fell to weeping again as if I must discharge the stor'd Tears of an entire Lifetime. O that my briny Tears were the briny Sea and I were aboard the *Hazard* with Lancelot! But 'twas not to be. The Fates had other Jests in Store.

Chapter XIII

*Containing a most Edifying Comparison betwixt Life
and a Masquerade, as well as our Heroine's Meditations
upon Maternity and the curious Bargain she struck with
the Devil to ensure the safe Arrival upon this Earth of
her unborn Babe.*

WHEN THE TIME CAME for the next Costume Ridotto at The
King's Theatre, I was near recover'd of my Strength, tho' the
Condition of my Spirits was, to say the Truth, not much better than upon the Day I sought, all fruitlessly, to run away.
Ne'ertheless, I had settl'd into a sort of fatal Resignation
about the Loss of Lancelot, and I knew I must now apply
myself to Thoughts of providing for my Babe, since before
long, my Condition would begin to show; there was not a
Minute to spare. Already, I was beginning to notice a slight
Thickening in my Waist. O 'twas nothing the World could
see—especially when I wore my Corset drawn as tight as was
the Fashion then—but 'twas a Warning to me. No longer
could I tarry in Regret and Indecision; I must determine how
to make the best of my Destiny.

Truly, I languish'd with the Loss of Lancelot and the
Merry Men, but I was quite distraught as well about my foolish Innocence in trusting Kate. For in the Days that pass'd
after her Elopement, I found that she had stolen various Articles from me—small Things in the main: a painted Fan, a
Patch Box, a pair of red-heel'd Slippers of green Silk, as well
as sundry Cosmeticks, Ribbands, and a Hat of Butter-
colour'd Straw with pale pink Ribbands. I curst myself for
being so unwary of her—for had I taken better Care, I might
now be aboard that dashing Brig, the *Hazard*, with my belovèd Lancelot. But I had underestimated the twin Pow'rs of
Envy and Hatred. Since Envy was not my Ruling Passion, I
fail'd to understand it, quite, in others.

Sure, I had felt Stabs of Envy (as any other Mortal Soul

hath done), but always I seem'd to know that all the divers Destinies of Humankind have their own Pains as well as their own Pleasures, and e'en the Greatest Lord who suffers no pecuniary Want, may be tormented with the Gout, or Devastation at the Loss of Love, and feel his Suff'rings as keenly as the poor Gin-soakt Beggar. O Lancelot was right: there was too little Equality betwixt the Debtor and the Lord, the Woman and the Man, the Black and the White. But truly 'twas God's Blessing to me, that, tho' I saw these Inequities quite clearly, still I knew that ev'ry Station in Life had its own peculiar Miseries, and so I did not fancy that by changing Places with another Soul, I would be free of Pain. I had oft' wisht to be born a Man; 'twas clear as Crystal that a Man's Lot was easier than a Woman's. Yet I felt a certain grand Defiance, too, in having been born in Woman's Form, and making my Way despite all the Impediments that Man had placed for me to stumble o'er!

But Kate was sour and scheming, evil and envious, hungry and heartsick. She fancied that by taking Things from me, she would improve her own Lot. Perhaps her Tradesman Lover had disappointed her after all, and she essay'd to assuage her own Pain, by preventing me from going to my Love. For how was she to know that 'twas the Outlaw Lancelot whom I long'd to see, whilst Bellars' Jewels were quite as little to me as glass Beads!

And yet, with a Babe to care for, and no Lancelot nor Merry Men, I could not now afford to spurn Lord Bellars' tawdry Jewels. Instead, I must study Ways to compel Lord Bellars to pay his Debt to his own Child, and yet without revealing my true Face. 'Twas a Dilemma, a Dilemma indeed.

When the Day of the Costume Ball came 'round, I sent Coxtart to White's Chocolate House to purchase my Ticket, and I directed her as well to procure me the most fetching Spanish Nun's Attire that could be found in all of London. Truth to tell, the Brothel had as fine a Collection of Masquerade Costumes as any Dressmaker or Milliner in the Town. For, oft' 'twas a Swain's Desire to enjoy his Trollop in some curious Disguise which conjur'd voluptuous Fancies in his Brain. Consequently, the Costume I sought was to be found right in Coxtart's Emporium—and a fetching one 'twas. Ah, Belinda, 'tis a Paradox of Lust that the deliberate Modesty of Nuns' Attire may conjure more lascivious Visions in the Brain than the sheerest Nakedness!

Coxtart assisted me in my Preparations, sent for a fine gilt

Coach and Four, with liveried Attendants, for she dreamt that my Good Fortune thro' Lord Bellars would also be hers, and she meant to prepare me well for these Revels. No mere Chair and Link Boy would convey me, but a golden Coach. What a Contrast 'twas with that first Day when she had insisted that we share one Chair!

And so the golden Coach bore me to the King's Theatre in the Haymarket, where I, a Nun, sought Satan! But O I had scarce anticipated that there would be so many Satans! For well-nigh ev'ry other Swain I saw fancied himself the very King of Hell! Some wore Breeches of Flame-colour'd Velvet, with Flame-colour'd Tails; and some were Black Devils, and some were radiant in white Satten as Milton's Lucifer before he fell. Ne'er would I have believ'd the Tribe of Satan to be so num'rous, had not I seen this Masquerade!

I mingl'd in the Crowd amidst the Faery Queens and Quakers, the Dominoes and Dandies, the Harlequins and Columbines, the Chimney Sweeps and Scotsmen. There were curious Double-Masks, as well as single ones. A Lady who lookt Elizabethan from the Front, turn'd around, and lo! was quite the current Mode from the back. There was yet another Lady who seem'd a Venetian Courtesan from the rear, and a Turkish Pasha from the front. The Courtesan had Hair of Titian red, which hung in long Ringlets, whilst the Pasha wore a Ruby Velvet Turban, encrusted with Jewels; and indeed the whole Headdress was so cleverly arranged that the Folds of the Pasha's Turban serv'd also as the Venetian Lady's Coronet! As this Mask turn'd from front to back, from back to front, it changed its Sex, its Nationality, its Rank, its all! What a Lesson 'twas in Fortune's Fickleness! How we are all Pashas, then Courtesans; Elizabethan Ladies, then Modern Belles; Angels, then Devils; Nuns, then Rakes! The Wheel of Fortune spins, the Dice of Destiny are cast, and we do not choose our Costumes as for a Masquerade, but they are fitted for us by the Fates. No wonder those Ladies are seen as Sempstresses. They sew the Clothing of our Lives; they outfit us as for a Grand Ridotto and then they set us whirling on the Floor to find our proper Partners—or our improper ones!

I wander'd in the Crowd in search of that Satan who of all Satans was my Special One. I pass'd divers Parties of Friends, bedeckt for the Masquerade in specially-dress'd Groups. There was an Indian Chief surrounded by his Squaws, another Turkish Pasha with his Harem, a Captain of the Guards with all his Men.

Sev'ral Masks approach'd me, bow'd, and begg'd a Dance with me; but I demurr'd, looking only for Lord Bellars, my Mind set upon my Task with him, my Heart harden'd against mere Frivolous Intrigue and determin'd upon Practicality for my Child's Sake above all.

At first, I thought I should ne'er find Lord Bellars again; whereupon, in a trice, I felt a Tap upon my Shoulder, and a low Voice said:

"Sister? Sister Hackabout? I seek nothing less than thy Body and thy Soul."

To which I replied, Voice low with Irony, and speaking quite as Quakerishly as he had spoken to me:

"And didst thou not, thou wouldst not be my Satan."

"Capital!" says he, taking my Hand. O this Biblical Speech piqued his Lust—especially as he was Satan and I a Nun!

Behind our Masks, we danced the Age-old Dance of Lovers ere they go to Bed. Whether we trod the Minuet or Rigadoon, or let fly our Feet in Jigs or Country Dances, each Step brought us closer to the inevitable Encounter betwixt the Bed-Clothes; each sweet Note of Musick carried us closer to the Ev'ning's End abed.

"Truly, thou hast made me pine for thee," Lord Bellars said, leading me in a stately Minuet.

"Milord, I am no Man's Plaything," said I.

"That much is clear, Sister."

We danced some Minutes longer; then he said:

"Alas, if neither Jewels nor Love Letters can move thee, what shall melt thy frigid Heart?"

"Sir, 'tis perfect Fealty I seek."

"And how, pray, shall that Fealty be prov'd? I have already forsworn an old Love for thee, Sister, and wouldst fain e'en marry thee, were I not so pledged already—what more of Love can I prove?"

I shudder'd slightly at the Mention of Marriage, for at that Moment there danced into my melancholy Brain a Vision of Lady Bellars, my dear Step-Mother, amidst her Animals at Lymeworth; but I made haste to banish it most sternly. How dare I talk of Fealty when I had betray'd my own sweet Foster-Mother? And yet I must endure—for my Child's sake, if not my own. Alas, is it e'er the Fate of Woman to excuse all human Betrayals for the Sake of that next Generation which we carry 'neath our Hearts? Charged as we are with the awesome Task of keeping the Race alive, we Women give nothing less than the Gift of Life itself. Without us, no

305

Coronations of German Kings, nor Whig Ministers doing their Briberies and Spyings. Without us, no Comedies, Tragedies, Epicks, nor Histories. Without us, no stern, be-wigg'd Physicians debating Diseases, no starry-eyed Astronomers debating Stars, no greedy Astrologers predicting Fates for Gold, no Soldiers marching, no Dancers dancing, no Singers singing out their Lungs, no Painters painting out their Hearts, no Actors and Actresses making the Footmen howl in the Pit. We are at the Root of all Society's Triumphs and Disasters, at the Root of all Knowledge and all Ignorance, all Health and all Disease, all Art and all Nature—for without us, the Dance of Life itself stops short, and the Dancers, whether maskt or unmaskt, fall dead in their Places ne'er to stir again!

How, therefore, could I *not* excuse my own Treachery 'gainst Lady Bellars now that I bore this Child 'neath my Breast? The Call of Life is stronger than the Call of Custom; the Howl of an Infant drowns out the husht Voice of Piety and the low Murmur of filial Duty. Henceforth my Care must be for Belinda, above all (tho', in truth, I neither knew her as Belinda yet, nor felt her as a Personage at all. She was only a Sense of Vulnerability about the Heart, a Desire to protect, at all costs, someone I scarce knew).

"Sir," said I to Lord Bellars, "thou mayst prove thy Love in a most curious Way—and yet I fear to tell thee how, for prechance thou wilt but laugh at me."

"Sister, that wouldst I ne'er do. For I am so far gone with Love of thee that I wouldst keep thee under any Terms thou mayst propose."

"Very well, then, listen to my Plan."

"I am all Ears," says he, dancing quite as prefectly as any Dancing Master despite my Words.

"I would be kept in a fine House with one loyal Servant to attend me. . . ."

"Sister—that is simple, nothing could be simpler—"

"Pray, Lord Bellars, hear me out. . . ."

"I tremble on each Word, my sweetest Love. . . ."

"Thou shalt come to me but once a Week and only on the Night I say. . . ."

"But certainly, my Love—"

"Hear me, Milord. . . . And always I shall be maskt from thee—until I say thou mayst unmask me, which, I warn you, I may ne'er say."

306

"O that is hard, my Love, yet can I swear to do thy Bidding e'en so."

"And thou shalt ne'er question me about my Past, nor seek to know whence I come nor why, nor seek to spy on me in any Way. . . . But on that one Night each Week I shall do all for Love of thee and pleasure thee in ev'ry Way—save that I shall not unmask, howe'er thou begst. And if thou seekst to force me, or seekst to unmask me whilst I sleep, I swear I shall ne'er see thee again."

"My Love, I think I can submit myself to these hard Rules . . . for I have pin'd for thee so during these Days past, that I would rather see thee once each Week than risque thy Wrath again."

"Art thou sure thou canst comply with these hard Rules? For if I e'er discover that thou spyst on me in any Way, or tell any Member of thy Family or e'en of thine Acquaintance of mine Existence, I will surely banish thee again."

O what rough Words for such a soft-hearted Wench! Ah, Fanny, thought I, you astonish e'en yourself!

"I swear by God and all the Angels, by the Divine Light of Reason, and the Pow'r of the Supreme Being; by Jove and Cupid, by Venus and Apollo; by all that I hold dear and sacred!"

"Very well, then," said I, "we have struck our Bargain. Now, shall we seal it with a Kiss?"

Lord Bellars took me in his Arms amidst the whirling Masks and kiss'd my Lips and murmur'd in my Ear. "I promise thee, I promise thee, I promise thee. And may the Great God above strike me quite dead if e'er I break my Word or Bond to thee."

Our Lips melted together in a Sweetness which banish'd Visions of Lady Bellars, the Merry Men, e'en Lancelot. And as we kiss'd, I had to ask myself if I was truly doing this for my unborn Child, or for my own wretchèd Longing and Lust which held me in their Thrall quite as surely as my Womb held the Stirrings of a Babe for whose Sake I made this Pact with the Devil and offer'd up my Body and my Soul.

BOOK III

Chapter I

How our Heroine spent her Confinement; a short Description of her loyal Servant, Susannah; some philosophical Meditations upon the Phases of Childbirth, after which your Author enters into the Controversy (which raged thro'out the Age) betwixt Midwives and Accoucheurs, and thereafter gratefully ends the Chapter.

LORD BELLARS KEPT HIS WORD as faithfully as e'er he had sworn it. He found me a fine House in Hanover Square, plentifully brib'd Coxtart for my Freedom, furnish'd me with all the most splendid Plate, Porcelain, and Linens; had my Walls decorated (ere I could protest) by some Monkey of an Italian Painter my good Friend Hogarth would have mockt; had my Pier-Glasses carv'd with gilt Eagles' Heads and Garlands by James Moore and John Gumley; my Bureaux and Tables veneer'd in Walnut; my walnut Chairs beautifully can'd and gorgeously gilt; and the Seats of my walnut Settees plushly upholster'd in Emerald Green cut Genoa Velvet.

My Cellar he kept fill'd with Sack and Claret; my Larder with all Manner of elegant Provisions. My Neck he hung with Jewels, my Pockets stuff'd with Guineas. He paid my Dressmaker's Bills, my Tea Merchant's and Vintner's Accountings almost ere they came due—and in return for all this Plenty, he askt only that I entertain him but one Night a Week, maskt from his prying Eyes both by Darkness and by the curious silken Masks I had design'd expressly for the Purpose. They were finely workt in divers Colours to match my divers Clothes; and some were embroider'd with Silver, and some with Gold, and some were shap'd like Butterflies and some like the Wings of Birds. O they gave my open, trusting Face a sinister Look (which perhaps increas'd its Allure—at least for a Rake like Lord Bellars).

My Face could I disguise, yet I could not disguise my Belly from my Patient Lover (for since he could not feast upon my

Face, he must, at least, be allow'd to feast upon my Form); and my Belly was plainly growing. My Breasts were growing, too, and my pink Nipples had turn'd the Colour of sweet Chocolate. A pale, thin Ribband of amber Flesh ascended from my Mount of Venus to just below my Navel; in short, 'twas plain I was with Child.

But Lord Bellars, like most Men, was no canny Mathematician regarding the Natural Cycles of the Fair Sex (and howe'er many Babes he may have begotten—both as Rake and Husband—the very Process still seem'd as obscure to him as those curious Heavens of the Mahometans and Hebrews). Thus, when I swore upon a Pile of Bibles that the Babe was his, both his Ignorance of Female Things, and his native Masculine Vanity led him to grant me Credence (with only the smallest Amount of Jesting about his Fears that perhaps some other Swain had got me with Child afore him).

And yet, Belinda, as you know, the Child *was* indeed his! (And the Child was you!) Yet the Conception had occurr'd at Lymeworth, not London; at the Eden of my Childhood Home, not the Hades of the Hell-Fire Caves! Nor would I have ly'd to any Man concerning such a weighty Matter as his Paternity. O I might fiddle with the Months a bit; all's fair in Love and War. But the plain Fact remain'd that he and he alone was "the only Begetter," as our great Bard Shakespeare hath term'd it.

How, you may indeed wonder, did I entertain Lord Bellars for so many Months without his e'er guessing me to be his orphan'd Fanny? I can but reply that I took the most careful Precautions to have him come to me only by Candlelight; to have him led upstairs to my Bedchamber by my faithful Servant only after blackest Nightfall, and rouz'd again always before Daybreak and quickly led away. My Voice I attempted to Disguise e'en in Fits of Passion, but e'en had I fail'd to do so, I believe that he would scarce have made the Connexion betwixt the innocent Wench he seduced at Lymeworth and the experienced Whore who entertain'd him in London.

For most Men, as I have said, see Women either as Angels or Devils, Marys or Liliths, Virgins or Whores, Saints or Sinners. 'Tis incomprehensible to them that the self-same Wench may be half-Angel and half-Devil, Innocence itself at first, and later the very Embodiment of Experience. We Women know that both Innocence and Experience are fluctuating States, not Absolutes; that they depend as much upon flickering Circumstances as upon fixt Morality; that Virtue is, in fact, a Luxury of the Rich, whilst Sin is oft' the only Means to Survival of the Poor; but Men do not know this unless they are Geniuses of Mr. Hogarth's Rank—and Lord Bellars I grant, was no Genius.

Yet he was no Monster either; he was no more than a Spoilt Rake whose Selfishness had always gone uncheckt. The Age had granted him Pleasures unabated, had indulged his ev'ry Whim—whether lustful or pecuniary; thus he had ne'er learnt Self-Control, Self-Rule, or Moderation of his Passions. Married young to a timid Heiress who could not raise her Voice to him, school'd in Scandal amidst Whores and Rakes, how could he practise that Humility which manifests itself in Kindness? I fervently believe that the Rules I impos'd upon his Impulsive Nature did his Soul more good, i'faith, than his whole willful, Pleasure-seeking Life before he found me in the Hell-Fire Caves!

My curious Rules of Secrecy also prevented Boredom— that greatest Enemy of Lovers—from blunting the Point of Passion. O had I lov'd Lord Bellars in my own plain Face, he would have tired of me in two Months' Time. But maskt, I could be all Things to him; all Women: French Courtesan or Turkish Harem Slave, Venetian Lady or Provençal Peasant, Spanish Nun or English Trollop. Indeed, I kept him guessing Week by Week, and this piqued his Passion as a Cordial before Dinner piques the most jaded Appetite.

Alas, 'twas true, as I discover'd when I came into Lord Bellars' Keeping, that Daniel and Kate were now join'd in their evil Purposes like a two-headed Dragon of Old. When Lord Bellars was not making love to me, he was sighing o'er his Son's sad Fate: to wit, Daniel had fallen into the Scheming Hands of a Trollop from Mother Coxtart's Brothel.

"Unlike your own Sweet Self," said Laurence Bellars, "this Wench is bent upon our Family's Ruin, and will stop at nothing to disgrace my Son and bring him to his Knees."

O with what divided Mind I heard this Tale! For tho' I could admit to knowing Kate, I could not admit to knowing Daniel; and tho' I could verify Kate's Evil, I could say nothing of what I knew of Daniel's Character, lest I betray myself as the Fanny of the Past. But 'twas ironical that Kate should have snar'd Daniel on the self-same Night I met his Father in the Hell-Fire Caves (for that I'd glean'd from Coxtart).

"Pray, Sir," I askt Lord Bellars, "why is it wrong for your Son to have a Mistress when you yourself have one? Doth he not follow in your Footsteps?"

313

Laurence Bellars laugh'd most derisively. "If you knew my scurvy Son, you'd ne'er say that!" he burst out. "Compar'd to this Kate, you are an Angel, and compar'd to Daniel, I fear I am Virtue's very Self."

I long'd to enquire further what transpir'd with Kate and Daniel—but I fear'd I could not without giving myself away, and I fear'd myself always on the Brink of Peril in any case. So I held my Tongue for your Sweet Sake, Belinda (and for my own), and not until many Months had pass'd was I to know the Issue of this other History, and so shall you before my Tale is done.

In my Establishment in Hanover Square, I had a Servant nam'd Susannah, a freed Mulatto Wench from the West Indies who was sworn to deepest Secrecy about my True Identity. She had a Gap betwixt her Teeth as large as her Gen'rous Heart and Skin the Colour of Coffee mixt with Clotted Cream. She was barely older than myself, but wise beyond her tender Years, and she swore she knew all about Newborn Babes; indeed, 'twas why I hir'd her. Moreo'er, she was my constant Companion during my Confinement, playing ev'ry Rôle from Friend to Mother Confessor to Physician.

How did I pass those Months awaiting your Birth, my own Belinda? Lord Bellars occupied but one single Night a Week, and I had, as well, dropp'd from Sight of all the Brothel Swains. (Nor did I wish to see 'em—e'en those who'd been my Friends—for I was done with Whoredom and Good Riddance! Whate'er the Glitter of it may seem to the foolish Wench who languishes of Boredom at some Country Seat and dreams of London Life, the true Facts of a Whore's Existence are, i'faith, enough to put one off the Love of Men for all Eternity!)

O I was happy for my six-day Chastity! I read the Classicks and all current Literature. I studied Homer, Virgil, Horace, Boileau, and La Rochefoucauld. And O my Belinda how I wrote!

With you in my Belly 'twas as if I had the very Muse inside me! My Quill flew o'er the Pages as if propell'd by Angels' Wings, or, i'faith, as if Pegasus himself had seiz'd it and gallop'd away amidst the Stars!

I wrote Tragedies in Verse and Noble Epicks, Romances in the French Style and Maxims modell'd upon La Rochefoucauld's. I wrote Satyres and Sonnets, Odes and Pastorals, Eclogues and Epistles. But nothing satisfied my most exalted Standards (which had been bred upon the Classicks),

314

and at length I committed all my Efforts to the Fire. I wrote and burnt and wrote and burnt! I would pen a Pastoral thro'out three sleepless Nights only to commit it to the Flames! And yet were my Words not wasted, for ev'ry budding Poet, I discover'd, must spend a thousand Words for ev'ry one he saves, and Words are hardly wasted if, thro' one's Profligacy with 'em, one learns true Wit and true Expression of it.

Lord Bellars no doubt wonder'd how I spent his Money, but the Truth was that most of my Guineas went for Books and Foolscap, Quills and Inkstands—all the humble Tools of the Writer's Trade. The Smell of Ink pleas'd me more than that of the costliest Perfumes; the Touch of fine Paper thrill'd my Fingertips more than the thinnest India Silk. I was besotted with my Craft and all its Tools; I vow'd to write and write until perchance I wrote one Poem worth preserving.

'Tis said by some that bearing Babes is all a Woman's Fire and Inspiration; that as her Womb fills, her Head empties; that the Act of Bearing substitutes for all Acts of the Imagination. But I swear that 'tis not so! Rather, as my Womb fill'd, my Head teem'd as well with Fancies. As my Belly grew, so did the Children of my Brain!

The Bearing of a Babe puts a Woman thro' as many Metamorphoses of Mood as the pale Moon hath Phases; and in each of these Phases I wrote—tho' to say the Truth, I ne'er wrote of Womanhood or bearing Babes. No, I wrote of Imaginary Kingdoms, Grecian Shepherds, Roman Warriors, and Persian Pashas. Who, I wonder'd, would wish to know of bearing Babes? Why, no one! Did Mr. Alexander Pope write of bearing Babes? Did Dean Swift? Or Mr. Addison, or Mr. Steele? Did Boileau or La Rochefoucauld? Did Virgil or Horace? Nay, nay a thousand Times nay! Why then the very Act must be neither a fitting nor correct Subject for my Quill; for if Mr. Pope found it not correct, and if Mr. Addison found it not correct, how should it be Literature at all?

I observ'd with rapt Fascination the divers Phases of my Childbearing (but wrote of 'em not, in order that I might spend my Ink upon more fitting Lit'ry subjects). At that Time of my Life, I ne'er question'd the Justness of such Judgement. Forgotten was my Great Epick upon Woman's Lot, begun at that Coaching Inn, The Dumb Bell, and abandon'd to the Siren Song of Lust!

Yet now I ask: what could be more curious and strange than the Cycle of Child-bearing, the Phases of Pregnancy?

There is, for instance, the First Phase, when one wishes to quite undo the Babe, because one feels its Presence as an Invasion at one's very Centre; then the Second, when one feels the first delicate Stirrings of Life within (as if the Tail of a tiny Mermaid had brusht against one's Heart and all one's Inner Being were a gentle Sea with small Waves lapping); then the Third, when the Child grows bigger and 'tis very like a Puppy wiggling, tickling, e'en licking within; then the Fourth, when it grows the Size of a great Melon and causes one to make Water four Times an Hour, and indeed wakes up just when one lyes down to sleep, and falls to sleep just when one walks or rides or goes abroad; then the Fifth Phase, when the Child becomes a true Burden, heavier under the Heart than Lead and yet, for all its cumbrous Weight, more lov'd as well (for now it seems real rather than fanciful to the Mother and so she can better bear the Discomfort of its Heaviness); and then the Sixth Phase, when the Mother begins to grow immobile, fearful of Death in Childbed, (with Nights full of Dreams of Monsters, and Days full of Dreams of Childbirth Horrors); then the Seventh, when the Pregnancy grows long as the longest Day of Summer and the Mother forgets she hath e'er been slender of Form or will e'er be again, and ev'ry Step is an Effort not to make Water by Chance in the Street, and ev'ry Motion causes Pain and ev'ry Night is sleepless (because turn as she will this way and that, the Child cannot be accommodated whilst it kicks her Lungs and butts its bony Head against her Bowels); and then the Eighth Phase, the Phase of Immense Impatience and Weariness, when she believes the Child will ne'er be born (and she is glad, for then she may not dye but only endure Pregnancy for all Eternity!); and then the Ninth Phase, when the Moon is full as a Bladder of pale Wine, and the Sea glows with its rotund Reflection and the Mother fears Death more than e'er before; and then, at last, the Tenth Phase, when the Waters break and the Pains begin, slowly at first, and then tumultuous; and she knows she has no Choyce now, but must give birth or burst; for she cannot turn back, cannot take another Road thro' the Forest, another Canal to the Sea, and she, like her Babe, is pusht headlong into the Dance of Life and Death, turning, whirling, moaning, writhing; and whether she shall live or dye she does not know, but the Pain grows so terrible at the Last that, i'faith, she does not e'en care!

O what a curious Cycle of Life the Goddess hath devis'd

for the Race to perpetuate its Kind! Many of the Agonies fall upon the Female of the Species, yet also many of the Joys.

Who but a Woman can speak of pressing her Cheak to the tender pink Cheak of her own Child and her Breasts running with Milk at its very Touch, squirting fine Streams heavenward like the sprinkl'd Stars of the Milky Way? Who but a Woman knows the joy of Feasting her Eyes upon Eyes that cannot focus, of clasping tiny Fingers that can only grasp without knowing what they touch, of kissing tiny Toes that cannot walk and know not whither they shall go or whence they have come? O no Matter how lacking in Reason the Newborn Babe seems to the Masculine Philosopher, 'tis Reason itself to its Mother, so besotted is she with its Charms! Who but a Woman could love a Creature that cries all Night when she would sleep, who wakes up ravenous to eat only when a Plate is set before its Mother and *she* would eat, who partakes of no Polite Conversation but only pushes its Tongue in and out of its Mouth like a very stupid Puppy, and drools and pukes and shits all the livelong Day and Night!

How, indeed, hath our Race surviv'd but thro' the Love of Women for their Newborn Babes? Common it may be, and yet 'tis also nothing less than a Miracle! For despite the Times when one would toss the Babe into a Dustbin to stop its Crying, the Passion to protect, preserve, and shelter is so much stronger than the Passion to destroy, that truly, most Babes have nothing to fear from their Mothers!

I fervently believe that if a Man had known as much Pain from a Creature as a Mother knows with the Birth of her Child, he would hate it e'erlastingly. But 'tis the Glory and the Credit of our Sex that we bear the Pain with no enduring Grudge and if we begrudge any Creature, 'tis not the Child, but the Man who got the Child (because of the Injustice of our Lot: the greater Weight of Responsibility we bear, yet the lesser Credit which the World accords us for it!).

But I race ahead with my History. Shortly, I will tell of my Lying-in and of the curious Things that came to pass as you, my Belinda, enter'd this World of much Woe and occasional Joy. Yet first, I must tell more of my Servant, Susannah, who shar'd this curious Time with me; for next to Lord Bellars and my Goose Quills and Foolscap, she was my most inseparable and belovèd Friend during these amazing Months.

Susannah, I have said, was light brown of Skin, gaptooth'd, gen'rous-hearted, garrulous. She spoke the Argot of the Islands, but *which* of the Sugar Isles she came from was impossible to know, for she herself remember'd almost nought before a Shipwreck in her fourth Year which washt her to Shore, a tiny Coffee-colour'd Girl, quite near the chalky Cliffs of Dover. She had been sold into an English Family, she recall'd, as a Playmate for their only Daughter; but when the entire Family perish'd at Sea, she alone was sav'd upon a floating Spar, weeping piteously for her Black Mama in the Islands, and having just watch'd her little White Mistress perish in the briny Deep.

Her Fate, thereafter, was harsher and more hackt-about than mine. She was befriended first by a Fine Gentleman who, 'twas later prov'd, lusted after little Girls (and who, when she was but five Years of Age, practis'd his perverse Diversions of the Flesh upon her). Running away from him at length, she was apprenticed to a Quaker Sempstress of cruel Temper (who us'd her as a sort of human Pin Cushion and curst the Colour of her Skin as the Devil's own Doing). She ran away once more, this Time to London, where she join'd a Pack of Street Urchins who stole Watches and all Manner of golden Baubles for the notorious Mr. Jonathan Wild; but seeing one of her small Friends hang'd at Tyburn (tho' the Lass was but ten Years of Age), she quit the Life of Crime, dress'd as a Boy, and took up Chimney-sweeping.

When she came to me, her Lungs, I fear, were still as black as Coal, and oft' she would give herself o'er to Fits of coughing which made me fear for her very Soul. And yet I hir'd her as my most intimate Companion, for something in her Manner made me quite love her at first Sight. She was kindly without being obsequious, willing to please without seeming slavish, and she saw the Humour in her Fate as well as the undeserv'd Woe. She also swore her Quaker Mistress had entrusted her with Newborn Babes; thus I dar'd to hope that she would be a proper Nursemaid for my unborn Child.

And so we liv'd for near six Months together: Susannah, me, my growing Belly, my Quills and Foolscap, my Epicks (which were written for the Flames), and Lord Bellars coming but on Wednesday Nights.

Much of that Time, I blush to say, I spent in fear of my Lying-in. I say I blush, because, of all the foolish Fears of Humankind, Fear of the Future is by far the most foolish. We cannot control the Future by fearing it, howe'er much we may believe we do so. Anticipation and Worry are, in fact, quite as useless to affect our Fates as a Fortune Teller's Predictions; but, alas, that doth not prevent our Indulgence in 'em.

Being a bookish sort, I fill'd some of my fearful Hours with reading Books upon Midwifery, which recounted the Terrors of Childbirth. In particular, I must mention Van Deventer's *The Art of Midwifery Improv'd*, with its terrifying Pictures of poor Infants attempting to pass thro' the Bony Pelvick Gateways of their hapless Mothers; and also the French Doctor Mauriceau's learnèd Book concerning *Diseases of Women with Child and in Childbirth* as translated by the notorious Dr. Hugh Chamberlen. These two Books alone were enough to excite all my Fears; for not only did they speak of Women whose Bones were too small to accommodate their Infants' Passage, but also of Extracting Hooks and other terrifying Devices; of Mothers who offer'd up their Bodies to be split asunder upon the Altar of Childbirth; of Labours lasting Days long; of learnèd *Accoucheurs* who knew no better Physick than to sacrifice the Mother's Life to the Child's; and of Midwives who, despairing of both the Mother's Life and the Child's, were directed to baptise the Child *in Utero*, lest its Infant Soul go straight to Hell if it dy'd unbaptis'd.

O I quite terrified myself with reading Books! Meanwhile, an Argument raged betwixt Lord Bellars and Susannah, my loyal Servant, regarding who should attend my Lying-in.

Lord Bellars, for his part, maintain'd that nought but ignorant Country Women were, in these modern Times, attended by Women-Midwives; but that e'en the Royal Mistresses of France call'd forth male Midwives, or *Accoucheurs*, to deliver 'em. Susannah for *her* part declar'd that more Women were kill'd by the Ignorance of Men attempting to deliver 'em than by the very Plague itself; that male Physicians, for the Sake of Modesty, deliver'd with a Sheet ty'd about their Necks and their Hands groping blindly 'neath it so as not to see the Lady's Privy Parts; and that e'en were there no Sheet at all, Man's Ignorance of Women's Privities was so great as to render the male Physician entirely unfit for the Noble Task of assisting the Fair Sex in Labour.

Imagine then, Belinda, your own dear Mother, maskt in embroider'd Silk with her swollen Belly beginning quite to loom beneath her Smock, listening by flickering Candlelight, to the diff'ring Arguments of her two would-be Protectors. To give the full Comick Impression, I had best write this brief Interlude as Dialogue from a Play, to wit:

LADY FANNY'S LYING-IN
A Comedy
in Nine Acts
As 'tis Acted at
Number 17 Hanover Square

Written by Mrs. Hackabout-Jones

LONDON
Printed for G. Fenton in the Strand
MDCCXXIV
Price One Shilling

MEN

LORD BELLARS: *A Spoilt Rake or Man of Pleasure*

WOMEN

LADY FANNY: *An Innocent Country Girl, turn'd Trollop (who would fain be the first Female Poet Laureate of England)*

SUSANNAH: *A Mulatto Wench of much Spirit and Native Intelligence. Servant to Lady Fanny.*

(ACT I. SCENE I.)

Scene Lady Fanny's *House. Her Bedchamber, by Candlelight.* Lord Bellars, Susannah, Lady Fanny.

LORD BELLARS. By Jove, I'll not permit my own True Love to be deliver'd by an ignorant Midwife! Why, most of 'em are little more than Witches that should be burnt at the Stake instead of entrusted with the tender Lives of the Fair Sex!

SUSANNAH. Beggin' yer Pardon an' meanin' no Disrespect, Milord, 'tis the Men-Midwives who should be hang'd fer all the Lives they've sacrific'd to their Stupidity and Pride!

LORD B. What mean you, Wench?

S. Milord, here is my Meanin'. Doth a Cook prepare yer Dinner 'neath the Table Linen? Doth a Blacksmith shoe a Horse 'neath his Workbench? Doth a Husbandman plant his Furrow wearin' Blinders like his Horse?

LORD B. Get on with it, Wench, and spare the Metaphor.

S. Then answer me, Sirrah!

LORD B. Impertinent Wench! Why, of course the Answer is no.

S. Then why should a Man-Midwife be suffer'd to deliver 'neath a Sheet?

LORD B. Why, for Modesty's Sake, Wench! Shall he feast his Eyes upon another Man's Property?

S. No, Sirrah, 'tis better to dye than to risque Offence to Modesty! As long as 'tis only a mere Woman who dyes! An' beggin' yer Pardon, Milord, whose Property is a Woman's Life? Is she nought but a Goat or a Sheep to be slaughter'd at will by her Master?

LORD B. Why, Susannah, I have nothing but the most solicitous Care for your Mistress. I would ne'er see her kill'd. Perish the Thought!

S. An' yet deliver her up, ye will, to the Hands o' Butchers! Truly, Milord, ye do yer Love o' Sister Hackabout a grave Injustice if ye suppose ye spare her Pains by callin' in a Man-Midwife.

LORD B. I shall call the greatest Practitioner in all of England, Dr. Smellie, all the Way from Lanarkshire. Why, he is fam'd thro'out the Land and hath studied Physick at Glasgow, and is a most excellent Man-Midwife, who, 'tis said, uses secret Extracting Implements to spare both the Mother and Child. I have met this excellent Fellow once in London and find him quite agreeable and talented with Flute and Paint and Brush. By Jove, the Man is both Artist and Musician—he must as well be adept at delivering Women in Travail!

S. I'll warrant he ne'er plays his Flute 'neath a Sheet, nor paints his Portraits so!

LORD B. Sweet Susannah, trust my Love for Sister Hackabout to bring this Matter to a happy Conclusion, and stay within your own Province of Kitchen and Chamber. . . .

S. I would bid ye, Sirrah, to stay within yer own Province o' Gamin' Tables an' Race Meetin's, an' not meddle with the Mysteries o' Midwifery an' Childbed that are better done by Women!

LORD B. Out—impertinent Wench! Or I'll box thine impertinent Ears!

S. I go, Sirrah, yet not all the Threats in Hell can banish my Solicitude fer me Mistress.

Whereupon Susannah makes a Curtsey (which seems to me more impudent than polite) and leaves the Bedchamber, thus ending the first Scene in our Comedy.

What were my own Sentiments regarding this Dispute? O I was in the gravest of Quandaries. Lord Bellars swore he sought the best Care for me, and what could be better than the Care receiv'd by Queens and Royal Mistresses? Yet I also remember'd my Friends, the Witches, part of whose Teaching was that Women were better Practitioners of Physick than Men (who sought to steal their mid-wifing Mysteries for Gain and Profit).

O the List of Queens who had dy'd in Childbed was long indeed—as was the List of Royal Mistresses, and, i'faith, Royal Infants. Not one of Queen Anne's Children liv'd to claim his rightful Throne; and how many other Noble Ladies had dy'd under the Hands of Generations of Chamberlens, or other Quacks (whilst the Physician, for his Pains, receiv'd a hundred Guineas and the Lady receiv'd nought but a Shroud!).

Thro'out my Confinement I wonder'd and worried whom to call when the Waters broke and my Child began his laborious Journey into this Planet of Pain. Susannah said she knew of a Mid-wife of exceptional Reputation, lately come to London, whilst Lord Bellars insisted upon Dr. Smellie, whose very Name, i'faith, seem'd so comical to me that I should surely commence laughing the Moment he came to attend me. As a budding Poet and Playwright, I had indeed noticed that the Names of real People were oft' more curious and strange than the Names of the Playwright's Personae. Which Brazen Grub Street Writer, i'faith, would dare to name a Man-Mid-wife, or *Accoucheur*, Dr. Smellie? Why 'tis a Name from a Comedy by Mr. Fielding—a Name quite on the Order of the Princess Huncamunca, or the Queen Dollallolla, or those Maids of Honour, Cleora and Mustacha, in love with those Courtiers, Noodle and Doodle!

Be that as it may, I could not decide, thro'out all the six remaining Months of my Confinement, whether to have Susannah fetch the Midwife of whom she spoke, or whether to accede to Lord Bellars' Wish that I be deliver'd by the great Dr. Smellie.

Lord Bellars' Masculine Pride, coupl'd with my foolish

Wish to have the most modern Physick known, finally prevail'd upon me to accept Dr. Smellie—tho' Susannah's Opposition continu'd unabated to the End.

Alas! I should have listen'd to that Wench!

Chapter II

*Containing better Reasons than any which have yet
appear'd for the happy Delivery of Women by those of
their own Sex, together with the Introduction of the
newest Character in our Historio-Comical Epick, who,
tho' small, proves more Trouble to her Author in her
Entrance upon the Scene than any Personage of more
prodigious Size.*

'TWAS THE MONTH OF MARCH and the Sun was in Aries
when my Confinement came to its grateful End. It had rain'd
in London for well-nigh three Weeks and the Skies were as
heavy as my Great Belly. O my Face seem'd young and fresh
thro'out my Confinement, as if, indeed, I had discover'd the
Fountain of Youth, but at the End of my Pregnancy I was as
Melon-bellied as a Woman with Twins (and, i'faith, I fear'd I
might give birth to two instead of one!).

Still, I'd heard no Word from Lancelot or the Merry Men
in six long Months and knew not whether they were alive or
dead. I wonder'd e'en whether I had not dreamt 'em all—so
remote did my Travels with 'em seem. I wonder'd as well if
there had e'er been a Time when I was without my Great
Belly—for it seem'd as much a Part of me as my red Hair or
my brown Eyes.

My Belly was so large, i'faith, that 'twas almost impossible
for me to fulfill my weekly Obligations to Lord Bellars—for I
could scarce clasp him 'round the Waist, much less allow him
to lye with me in any but the most bestial of Postures, and
e'en that one grew unwieldy in Time. Ne'ertheless, he was by
then so thoroughly in Love with me, that I swear he came to
me as much for Love of my Soul as of my Body, since he
scarce complain'd of this Disability. O the Ways of Destiny
are strange, indeed; for I had, by dint of my Stratagems of
Masks and Disguises, my Limitations of our Trysts to but
once a Week, almost reform'd his selfish Nature. Lord Bellars

also seem'd to look forward to the Birth of this Child as he had ne'er lookt forward to the Birth of his legally begotten Son or Daughter. This Child he saw as a Love Child, begotten more in Passion than in Duty and therefore he lov'd it e'en in the Womb and was, indeed, more wary of hurting it than I was myself.

How tenderly he touch'd me as we drew nearer the Close of my Confinement! A Man might walk upon a Carpet of Hens' Eggs with greater Force! He strok'd my Body—particularly my Belly—as if 'twere some infinitely delicate Thing, containing all the Seeds of his Past and Future.

For his own part, I found that my Lust for Lord Bellars—indeed for any Man whatsoe'er—decreas'd as my Lying-in approach'd. The Child within made me wholly self-sufficient, as if I were both Earth and Sky, both Sea and Land, and less and less did I require any sort of physical Union with the former Begetter of all my most lustful Passions. No, on the Contrary, I wisht nothing more than to lye abed Mornings, alone, and dream of the Babe to be, or to sit at my Writing Bureau penning Metaphors which I would then commit to the Flames, or, by Ev'ning to sit before the Grate with Susannah, watching the Flames leap in their constantly changing Patterns, reminding me of the mysterious Dance of Destiny, the Vanity of Human Wishes, and the Difficulty of knowing the Meaning of Life or the Great Purpose for which the Goddess placed us all here upon the Earth.

Bearing a Child made me, i'faith, more philosophical than e'er before (and I was always of a philosophical Bent); for what can be more mysterious and strange than to be one Person for all one's Life and then suddenly become two! To be doubl'd, then halv'd; to be one, then two, then one again! 'Tis the Destiny of but one-half of the Human Species, and the Possibility of explaining it to the other half is remote indeed. Alas, we can scarce explain it to ourselves! And yet I believe, tho' all the World may hold us in Contempt for it, that we Women are truly blest in this Capacity of Child-bearing. Perilous it may be (just how perilous you will see anon) and yet it tempers the Spirit e'en as it does the Body. 'Tis very like walking thro' a Wall of Flame, which few survive, but those who do, are stronger for it their whole Lives long.

'Twas the third Week in March when, the Heavens having been open and streaming most of the Month, my own Waters broke and you, my Belinda, began your Storm-toss'd Voyage into the World.

I shall ne'er forget that I was reading a Romance by Mrs. Haywood (*Idalia*, perhaps, or *The Fatal Secret*) and thinking to myself that I could do as well and perhaps should try my Hand at one, when I discover'd that my Smock was wet beneath me, as indeed was the Seat of my Chair, and this I believ'd was the tell-tale Sign of the Beginning of Travail.

Quickly I rang for Susannah and directed her to notify Lord Bellars, at whose London Apartments the Great *Accoucheur*, Dr. Smellie, was to be arriving that very Day.

After dispatching Susannah, and whilst waiting for my Pains to become strong and regular, I remember that, quite unaccountably, I sat down at my Writing Bureau and then and there began a Romance in the Manner of Mrs. Haywood. I was fill'd with such Energy and creative Fire that it seem'd I could compleat an entire Book that very Ev'ning, so I took Quills and Foolscap in Hand and began, in a Frenzy, to write. Dimly, I recollected that Women at the Start of Travail are said to be seiz'd with great Vigour, that some compleat entire Tapestries, and others sew Christening Gowns, with intricate Embroideries, whilst others are seiz'd with a Passion to sweep Floors, clean Grates, bake dozens of Pyes, and roast Legs o' Mutton!

But the Vigour is at best a passing Fancy, o'erwhelm'd quite soon by the Pains of Travail; for no sooner had I determin'd upon the Names for my Star-cross'd Lovers—Clotilda and Philidore—and penn'd an appropriately obsequious Epistle Dedicatory (with Blanks for the Name of whiche'er Noble Lord should be most worth my Flatteries when the Romance was done), than the Pains of Travail became strong indeed, and I dropp'd my Quill to the Paper (where the Inkblot oddly form'd the Profile of a curious Horn'd Creature) and I held my Belly and pray'd to the Goddess above for my own Life and the Life of my Child.

Then, 'twas all I could do to walk to my Bed, lye upon it in my Smock, breathe as calmly as I could to bear the Pains, and await the Return of Susannah.

O the Pains were bearable at first, but in an Hour or so they grew stronger. My entire Belly would rise in a tight Knot, causing me to grit my Teeth, to blank out the World by shutting my Eyes, and to enter, as if I were a Traveller to a distant Land, the red Universe of Pain. At Times I forgot my very Surroundings, tho', indeed, the Walls of my Chamber were cover'd with painted Clouds, painted Cherubim, and painted Goddesses reclining upon rosy Clouds, and I would attempt to stare at 'em to distract myself from my Distress. 'Twas impossible; I was driven inward by the Tumult taking place inside me, and 'twas all I could do to keep myself from moaning, much less to concentrate upon the painted Cherubim, that were a Man's Idea of Paradise.

Time lost all Meaning as I dwelt in the e'er briefer and briefer Spaces betwixt the Pains. Thus when Dr. Smellie came to attend me, I was in no great Condition to observe his Form and Figure with a Poet's Eye.

And yet I recollect his great unwieldy Hands—more like a Farrier's than a Midwife's—and more for holding Horses' Hooves than the tender Skulls of Babes.

He had put off his Peruke and capp'd his Head with a sort of Turban of white Linen, ty'd with white and silver Ribbands. Likewise, he wore a great loose Gown of flower'd Calico in which he lookt a sort of curious Pasha, his Eyes blazing in his Head and his wide Mouth set in a determin'd Posture.

He sent Susannah for hot Water, clean Sheets, a fresh Shift for me; then he began to question me as to the Onset of my Travail.

"Sir," said I, betwixt the Pains, " 'twas about Eight o' the Clock when the Pains began—but I know not what Time it might be now."

"This Babe will be born ere Midnight if I have my Way," said he, pressing upon my swelling Belly (causing me still greater Grief).

"Pray what Time is it now?" I askt, nearly breathless from the great Waves that engulf'd me.

"Why, half past Nine, Lass."

My Heart leapt in my Bosom to believe that this great *Accoucheur* possess'd Magick that might so shorten my Travail. Thus arm'd with his Promise (like a Shield against my Woe), I vow'd I would endure any Terrors the Goddess might send. O I still wore my Magick Garter for Occasions such as this; and tho' 'twas fray'd and tatter'd, I dar'd to hope that 'twould shield me from all Harm.

Lord Bellars, I was told, waited without my Chamber for the happy Conclusion of my Lying-in. Susannah brought hot Water and Sheets as she was bid. She ty'd one of these 'round the Neck of Dr. Smellie, stretching its nether Ends o'er me, so that my Privy Parts were duly cover'd (as Modesty requir'd), whereupon the Great Doctor bade me spread my Legs, and with his enormous Hands he prob'd the Inmost

Centre of my Being, causing me more than once to catch my Breath and almost wail with Pain.

Yet I did not. I bit my Lips, I held my Breath; I shut my Eyes until num'rous salty Tears were squeez'd from their Corners; but moan and wail would I not, howsoe'er the Pain demanded it. I'faith, I felt a sort of Pride in being a Warrior Woman, a Mythick Amazon of Old, and thus enduring the Distress without a Cry.

Dr. Smellie withdrew his Hands, with the Verdict that my Womb was opening quickly and 'twould be no Time at all before the Babe emerged, whereupon he strode from my Chamber to report to Lord Bellars in the Ante-Chamber, leaving me alone with Susannah.

O we could hear 'em talking and laughing without, as if the Birth of a Babe were no more to 'em than an Ev'ning at a Coffee-House, and, Truth to tell, it griev'd me deeply to hear their mirthful Chatter (o'er Jests I could not share) whilst I was labouring to bring the next Generation into this World.

"Mrs. Fanny," said Susannah, whisp'ring in my Ear, "I would have yer Leave to call the Midwife. . . ."

" 'Twill all be o'er soon," I mutter'd betwixt the Pains. "Dr. Smellie said so."

"I have my Doubts," said Susannah; but I was too far gone by then to answer her.

"I will do what I will do," Susannah mutter'd 'neath her Breath, whereupon she departed the Chamber (most privily, thro' a Door that led only to the Back-Stair) and left me to my Griefs.

Now, I would fain describe the Hours of Travail that follow'd but a curious Fog hath misted 'em, like Clouds snagg'd upon a Mountaintop; and try as I may, I have only the haziest Recollection. You will say, Belinda, that this is because so many Years have pass'd since your Birth; but 'tis not so. I swear that when you were but five Weeks old, I tried in vain to recollect the Pains of Travail and e'en then could scarce succeed. O I remember that the Cramps grew terrible at length and that it seem'd both my Back and my Belly should burst from the Ache. I remember that my Teeth chatter'd and my whole Body shook and my Feet grew cold as Ice; but for the Life of me I cannot recollect the Pains themselves, nor e'en their Duration.

I have since question'd many Women concerning this curious Phenomenon, and 'tis common as the Dust we come from and the Dust to which we return. Pain, you will say, is ne'er memorable; but I swear I can better recollect the Pains I suffer'd in my Foot and Hands when I tried to escape from Coxtart's Brothel to join Lancelot's Sailing than I can the Pains of Travail. I'faith, 'tis almost as if I were not fully present at your Birth (tho' indeed I am your Natural Mother).

What can be the Cause of this strange Phenomenon? I have meditated long and hard upon it. Perhaps 'tis part of Nature's mighty Plan for the Continuation of the Race of Humankind; for if Women truly could recollect the Pains of Travail, they would take a Vow of Chastity forthwith, go at once to a Nunnery, and ne'er lye with a Man again their whole Lives long!

Perchance this curious Forgetfulness of Birth hath another Significance as well. Maybe it reminds us that we are not so much the Mothers of our Babes as Nature is; that we are but Conduits for the Great Goddess; that Babes derive from and belong to Her and we must possess our Children but lightly, for they are lent to us, not given.

If ev'ry Mother recollected her Travail too strongly, she would be inclin'd to cling to her Child more desperately when she should send it forth into the World to seek its own Fortune. In this wise are we all Orphans of Destiny, whether we know our Natural Parents or not.

How many Hours I labour'd, I cannot say. Dim Figures came and went in the Chamber's Gloom. Susannah's anxious Face loom'd above my own; Susannah's gentle Hands mopp'd my fever'd Brow. Dr. Smellie strode in and out from Time to Time, thrust his Hands 'neath the Sheet, prob'd me roughly, grunted unintelligible Words, and strode out again. Susannah sat beside me, now holding my Hand, now placing her Hand 'neath my Back to ease the Pain, now encouraging me, now mutt'ring that she would give the Doctor but one Hour more.

When t'was already past Midnight (or so I gather'd from the Doctor's Consternation), Smellie examin'd me again, declar'd that the Babe was obstinate and would not turn its Head, and withdrew to fetch his Secret Instruments.

Then the Nightmare began in earnest, for the Doctor return'd, hiding bulky Instruments 'neath his Smock, and now I cried out in Terror lest they be the dread Extracting Hooks that spell'd the Death of my Unborn Babe!

"Nonsense, Child," said Dr. Smellie to my Fears. "This Secret Invention will but ease your Pain and bring your Babe to birth alive." Whereupon he thrust his Hands again 'neath the Sheet, bade me spread wide (which was well-nigh impossible in the midst of my tumultuous Pains), and quite suddenly inserted cold Metal into the Interior of my Being.

I felt at once like a Prisoner of the Inquisition, or a Felon being put to the *Peine Forte et Dure*, for e'en as my Pains came in Waves, this other Force of cold Metal insinuated itself into my very Bowels, jabbing and twisting; 'twas groping, it seem'd, for the Head of the Babe, that refus'd, in its Obstinacy, to turn. I'faith, Smellie seem'd to be in a Battle with the unborn Babe, angry that it did not yield to his Secret Implements, for he mutter'd and snarl'd 'neath his Breath e'en as he prob'd me, and he curst the Babe that would make a Mockery of all his Reputation and make him seem a Liar in his Predictions that 'twould be born ere Midnight.

Despite my awful Anguish, I sens'd this Battle betwixt the Babe (who had its Life to sustain) and the *Accoucheur* (who consider'd nought but his Fame).

O he was not entirely insensible of my Pains, but truly he seem'd more to wish for the Vindication of his own Success, than for the Happy Conclusion of my Travail. And so he prob'd and grunted and prob'd, until at last, he withdrew the Metal Instrument of Torture (to which I gave a grateful Sigh), secreted it again 'neath his Calico Gown, wip'd one huge Hand across his resolute Brow, and said: "I fear I can no longer spare the Babe."

These dread Words gave me Energy and Determination where I fear'd none were left, and suddenly, I was seiz'd with the Conviction that I could bear the Pains of Travail for all Eternity rather than sacrifice my Child.

"Leave me in Peace," I mutter'd, "and let Nature take her Course."

Smellie lookt at me with his great goggling Eyes. "My Dear," said he, "I know what's best for you. Pray, let me extract the Infant and spare the Mother's Life. 'Tis the only Way, I fear."

O now I recall'd from all my Reading, dreadful Drawings of Extracting Hooks and Babes remov'd in Pieces from their Mothers' Wombs, and I scream'd at the learnèd Doctor with all my Might: "Leave me in Peace! Let Nature take her Course!"

"I have sworn to Lord Bellars that I would spare your Life, my Dear. Come, let us baptise this doom'd Child, and save the Mother's Life at least."

Whereupon, to my own Amazement, I rose up out of my Bed of Anguish, and kickt the Great Doctor with all my Might, screaming at the top of my Lungs: "I'll see you roast in Hell before I see you kill my Babe!"

Susannah fairly chear'd to behold this new and surprizing Turn of Events, and somehow, betwixt us two, we shov'd the astonish'd *Accoucheur* out the Chamber Door and lockt it from within.

That Effort took all my Breath away and I fell to the Floor moaning in great Grief and near fainted away. Then I lay for a Time upon the Floor, writhing in Agony, whilst Dr. Smellie and Lord Bellars beat with angry Fists against the Door, screaming to be admitted; but I could no more rise to unlock it than I could fly to the Isle of Wight to join Lancelot (who, in my Delirium, I fancied still to be awaiting me there).

I lay upon the Floorboards, listening to the beating Fists like Thunder in a Storm. I knew not where I lay nor why, but I vow'd somewhere in the Recesses of my Heart, ne'er to let my Infant dye ere 'twas born, or if Matters came to that, to dye along with it, and ascend to Heaven with my own pink Babe in my Arms!

O I must have been quite gone in Delirium, for I rav'd of Angels and Devils, saw Visions of enormous Sunflow'rs growing quite up to the Clouds, and e'en said once to Susannah (for she told me later): "The Man accosts the Sunflow'rs." But what that means, I know not.

At length, I was in my own Bed again (but how or by whom transported, I cannot tell) and Susannah was whisp'ring in my Ear: "Mistress Fanny, ye 'ave suffer'd enough. I'faith, fer the Love o' God, let me fetch the Midwife," whereupon (without awaiting any Reply from me— indeed I was perhaps beyond Reply) she again left the Chamber by the Back-Stairs Door, which was unknown to Lord Bellars.

Next I recall blue Eyes looking down at me from 'neath a low white Wimple and a soft Voice saying, "My Child, 'tis true, you have suffer'd too long already." Then Susannah and the Midwife undrap'd me, open'd my whole Belly to their View, and with utmost Gentleness, the Midwife laid her tender Hands upon my Belly, feeling for the Position of the Babe.

She traced my throbbing Belly, as if she could discover 'neath it, as in an Anatomist's Drawing, the true Outlines of the Child. My Pains continu'd tumultuous as e'er before, yet

331

the Midwife's Tenderness brought me new Hope. Perhaps we would yet save the Babe. How curious, I thought, I had once sought to do away with this Creature, and now I felt I would do anything to spare its budding Life. 'Tis odd indeed that once we are truly caught up in the Dance of Life, we follow the Steps as diligently as we have been taught. The Musick swells; our Feet and Hearts obey; and we are whirl'd into the Centre of the Ball.

"The Babe's Head," said the Midwife, "is lockt within the Bony Pelvis, yet 'tis too high, I fear, for Dr. Smellie's dread Extractor to be of any Use whate'er. Alas, how Men love their Machines better than Life itself! Our Hands are good enough Machines for most of Life's Contingencies! Pray, spread your Legs my Dear, I would fain feel the Child's Head from within."

I tried, in my Anguish, to do her Bidding, but I was so far gone in Shiv'ring and Chatt'ring that 'twas hard, indeed, to obey. Susannah and the Midwife rais'd my Knees and spread my Legs apart. Whereupon the Midwife prob'd me with one delicate Hand, pressing the other upon my Belly.

"I feel the Babe's Head," says she. " 'Tis turn'd to one side, thus with ev'ry Pain it throbs against your Back. If I can turn the Head by deft Massage, then truly I can spare both Mother and Child."

She left me for a Time, whilst my Teeth continu'd to chatter almost in Tune with the Thunder of Fists upon the Chamber Door.

"Begone ye Butchers! Ye Murderers!" Susannah shouted more than once, yet the Pounding continu'd.

"I go—and leave the Ingrate to her Fate!" shouted Smellie, quite enraged by our Rejection of him. Lord Bellars must have pleaded that he stay, since still we heard the Thund'ring Fists for quite some Time to come.

"Her Death's not on my Head!" Smellie scream'd, loud enough for God Himself to hear; and then, at length, the Pummeling ceas'd, and Susannah whisper'd, "Perhaps the Murderers have gone. . . ." But I wonder'd if Bellars himself were not there, awaiting the Verdict of the Fates, for from Time to Time, I heard a timid Scratching on the Door, as if a Kitten sought Admittance, but dar'd not scratch too hard for fear some large Dog lurkt within.

The Midwife presently return'd, bearing Jars of Salve, Herbs, and all the Potions of her Trade.

"I bid you drink this for your Pain," said she, off'ring me a

Cup of some unknown Liquid. 'Twas bitter, but I drank since my Fear of being Poison'd was less, by then, than my Fear of continu'd Pain. I knew not how many Hours I had been in Travail, yet could I see the Dawn rising in the London Sky, and I was so weary and so weak that I welcom'd any Opiate I might have.

The Fluid workt remarkably quick; and Truth to tell, I did not lose my Cramps, but I ceas'd fretting o'er 'em. 'Twas curious: I knew myself to be in Pain, and my Spirit floated o'er my labouring Body, with little Concern for its Anguish. 'Twas indeed as if I were two Women: one a Ghost or Wraith, and the other a moaning Lump of Flesh.

The Wraith knew perfect Confidence and Peace, whilst the Flesh anguish'd and begg'd for Mercy. Yet the Mercy had, i'faith, been granted; for this Division betwixt Ghost and Flesh was Mercy's very Self. I knew that I was lost in deep Travail, but for the Life of me I did not care.

The Midwife greas'd my Belly with her Unguents, and greas'd my Privy Parts as well; whereupon she began a sort of Rhythmick Dance o'er my Belly with her gentle Hands, which was design'd, she said, to turn the Infant's Head, that it might pass out of my Body still alive.

I felt her Hands upon my Flesh, both within and without; and yet that Flesh did not belong to me. First I was at Sea with Lancelot; and then at Lymeworth with my Step-Mother, walking thro' the Topiary Gardens, as they had been before they began to be "improv'd" by Mr. Pope's new modern Schemes.

Hours must have pass'd, for when I open'd up my Eyes again, the Sun was high against my Window Panes and they were glitt'ring as if alchemically transform'd to Gold. I heard the Midwife say, her Voice echoing as in a Great Cathedral: "I fear we cannot turn the Head this Way."

Susannah began to weep; but I myself was still so far away, that 'twas nigh impossible for me to grasp that 'twas my own Life and my own Babe of which they spoke.

"Pray, try the Ergot, then," Susannah begg'd.

"I fear 'twill cause her too much Pain," the Midwife said; "she is worn out already."

The Midwife shook me then to bring me back to Earth. "What would you, Fanny? Spare the Child by all Means, howe'er painful? I would know your Wishes."

"The Sunflow'rs, the Sunflow'rs," I rav'd. O I was too far gone by then to answer rationally.

"Pray, try," Susannah said. "I know me Mistress well. She is Life's Advocate 'gainst the Jaws o' Death. She would always see Life triumph despite Pain!"

The Midwife sigh'd. "Alas I fear 'tis true. And yet it hurts me to the Quick to see her suffer so."

Next she administer'd another Cordial to me, but this one was more bitter than the first; and before too long it banish'd all my Dreams and brought me back inside my howling Pain.

Now were the Knots that twisted up my Belly tumultuous and strong indeed—so strong at last that I cried out loud for Mercy and swore I'd dye than bear 'em longer.

"For Pity's Sake," I scream'd, "take my Life, for 'tis not worth a Farthing to me. But spare the Child if e'er you can. . . ."

Susannah and the Midwife whisper'd then, in most sober and solemn Counsel.

"I'll try one last Expedient," the Midwife said, "although the Risque is great. And the Risque of Discovery of it is greater still—for should any Person learn of this, and if our Fanny doth survive, we three shall surely be call'd Witches."

"The Stake, the Pyre, is nothing to this Pain!" I rav'd; whereupon the Midwife gave me Laudanum in such a Dose that I was soon insensible of not only the Pain, but of the Planet I inhabited.

"Bless you," said I as the Opiate took me and I sail'd off to Sea with Lancelot again.

Next, I remember the Gleam of Razors and the Clatter of iron Potts; but so separated was my Spirit from my Flesh that I car'd not what Brutalities were practis'd upon my Form.

I rockt upon the Waves with Lancelot, and at the self-same Time I felt cold Metal shave my Belly and a Razor's Edge penetrate my Skin. Blood flow'd like the Ocean's Currents; the Razor cut deeper, and deeper still. Yet so outside my Body was I that tho' I felt the Pain, I did not *care;* and tho' I saw the Blood, it no more belong'd to me than the Blood of a butcher'd Lamb belongs to the Hearty Trenchermen who dine upon its Flesh.

Susannah gasp'd to see this horrifick Sight; but I had reach'd a Stage of Resignation beyond the Rage to live. A little Time before, I'd wisht to cling to Life with all my Being, and yet the Opiate took me so far away from Passions of the Flesh that e'en the Lust for Life now hung suspended.

Blood flow'd; the Sheets themselves turn'd red. My Innards

gap'd; a practis'd Hand reach'd in to pluck a Child from my very Bowels. So raving mad was I that, i'faith, I thought 'twas my beating Heart they pluckt and not my Child.

A bloody Creature snatch'd by its tiny Feet; held upside down, smackt until it howls! I heard its lusty Cry and wept and wept.

" 'Tis a beauteous little Girl! Blessèd be!" the Midwife said.

"Hath she five Fingers on each Hand? Hath she ten Toes?" was all I might collect myself to ask.

"She hath! She hath! And red Hair, too!" the Midwife said. Whereupon she wrapped the tiny Creature (still bloody with our mingl'd Blood) in a woollen Blanket and laid her by my weary Head.

I marvell'd then at the tiny turn'd-up Nose (crusted with the Blood of the Womb), at the tiny Hands groping for they knew not what Hands to hold, at the tiny Mouth sucking blindly for it knew not what Breasts, at the tiny Feet that knew not what Paths they would walk in what Continents yet to be discover'd, in what Countries yet to be born.

"Welcome, little Stranger," I said betwixt my Tears. "Welcome, welcome," and then the salty Sea of my Tears o'ertook me and I wept in great Tidal Waves of Brine. O I cried until my Tears themselves washt a Portion of the cak'd Blood from the Infant's Cheaks and show'd me her translucent Skin, the Colour of Summer Dawn.

But what was that stitching, stitching going on below? The Midwife held a Taylor's Needle o'er a Candle, perhaps to staunch my Blood or cauterise my Wounds, and with the finest, whitest Silk she stitch'd my Belly back together.

All this I saw and felt, yet the Laudanum made me numb to Pain. I feasted my bleary Eyes upon my Daughter's Face and cried for her unearthly Beauty.

O what a Miracle is a Newborn Babe! Snatch'd from the Void, barely alive nine Months, yet it arrives with its Fingers and Toes fully form'd, its Lips tender as the Petals of the Rose, its Eyes unfathomably blue as the Sea (and almost as blind), its Tongue pinker than the inside of a Shell, and curling and squirming like a garden Worm in sodden Spring.

Almost three Decades have pass'd since I first beheld you, my own Belinda, but I will ne'er forget my Feelings as I feasted my bleary Eyes upon your flesh-hatch'd Face. The Pains of Travail may fade (ah, fade they do!) but the Wonder of that Miracle—that most ordinary Miracle—of the

335

Newborn Babe is a Tale told and told again where'er the Race of Womankind survives!

Then I slept. Morpheus, who softens so many Blows in our ungentle Lives, receiv'd me into his loving Arms and I was lost in Sleep.

How long I slept, I know not, but when I woke 'twas darkest Night and only one Candle burnt in my Chamber. Susannah herself kept watch. I arose, groaning of the Pain in my Belly, and she came to me with a Potion to relieve it.

"Laudanum?" I askt.

"Yes," said she.

"Then wait a little. I would see my Child before you take the World away again."

"I'll call the Midwife fer ye," said Susannah. "The Child is well and lusty, have no Fear."

She withdrew by the secret Back-Stairs Door; and in a little while, the Midwife came in her Stead.

She approach'd my Bed by that single Candle's Light; a smallish Figure all in white, with a Back curiously hump'd, and a low white Wimple covering her Forehead. She carried a red and wrinkl'd Babe, swaddl'd in Linen; and when she reach'd my Bed, she presented the wond'rous Creature to my View. 'Twas the tiny Bud of a Human Being, as tightly folded as a Rose in early June. Two pink Eyelids curl'd upon two pink Cheaks; and the merest Suggestion of Eyelashes were just beginning to sprout. The Eyelids were, i'faith, so transparent that the Network of diminutive Veins glow'd 'neath 'em, blue and purple as Creatures of the deepest Seas. The Eyes were tightly shut against the World. (O soon enough would they behold its Cruelties!). And the Mouth was a sleeping Worm in a Springtime Rain. The Nose turn'd Heavenward at its tiny Tip; and the Fingers were fashion'd from some Book wherein the Cherubim are writ.

I marvell'd—that much is true—and yet, tho' I had seen the Babe pluckt from my own Belly, I was not certain she belong'd to me. 'Twas not I fear'd a Changeling—no, not at all. I knew myself to be your proper Mother, and yet somehow I did not *feel* myself to be your Mother, but only a sort of Passage for your Birth.

Such Things are common in the first Hours after Childbirth. Being a Mother is learnt, not inborn. We Human Creatures learn so much and know so little! And still I lov'd you from the Moment I beheld you—lov'd you with purest Love, not mere Possession, lov'd you for your astounding Beauty, all the Beauties of the Human Race join'd in one Babe.

The Midwife knelt before the Bed, placed the Child inside my waiting Arms, and bow'd her Head in silent Pray'r. Then, looking at me with her bright blue Eyes, she pusht the Wimple from her Brow, and lo! blazon'd in her Flesh was a Cross, carv'd out of tortur'd Skin and still pucker'd crimson as a new Wound.

"Isobel!" I cried.

"Fanny, my Dearest, my Daughter!" says she.

Chapter III

*In which such surprizing Events occur that we dare not
e'en hint of 'em here, lest the Muse of Historio-Comical
Epick Writing be very cross with us and flee our House
forthwith.*

I LOOKT AT ISOBEL—the Hump upon her Back, the Cross cut
in her Forehead, the Eyes like bluest Jewels—and I was sure
that I was still lost in Dreams under the potent Influence of
Laudanum.

"It cannot be!" I rav'd, "for you were kill'd. I saw you
murder'd upon Stonehenge Down!"

"I am no Ghost, my Love," said Isobel, "tho I was almost
one, 'tis true. Ravish'd I was; blooded I was—'tis plain to see
the Cross cut in my Forehead; and yet, tho' I was stabb'd, I
did survive."

"How can that be?" I askt, now almost forgetting the horrid Pain in my Belly and the Stitches that pull'd with ev'ry
Breath I drew.

"The Goddess spar'd me for a Purpose, Fanny mine, that I
might spare you and your Babe as well. There are Greater
Plans in Heaven than we mere Mortals see!"

"But *how* did you survive?" I askt, incredulous.

"Those Blackguards were so frenzied in their Bloodlust
that when they came to me, their Force was nearly spent. The
Pig-faced Ruffian ravish'd me and carv'd this horrid Cross
upon my Brow, but when he came to stab me thro' the
Heart, he was no longer puissant as he thought. He wounded
but my Flesh and miss'd my Heart, and yet I moan'd and fell
like one quite dead; thus he deduced he had dispatch'd my
Soul. Then I lay very still—as I have learnt to do thro' Hours
of Meditation—and I impersonated Death-like Sleep. I quieted my Breath, near stopp'd my Heart, until the Ruffians all
departed. My Wounds were such I could prevent Gangrene
by Means of Herbs I knew—the same Herbs I shall use to
heal your Belly. And yet I could not save our Friends, the

Witches, for they were too far gone. The very Stones of Stonehenge drink their Blood. And e'en belovèd Joan's. . . . 'Twould be a Sacrifice to the Goddess if she desir'd such."

"Who is this Goddess, Isobel? Doth she, in truth, exist?"

"Ah, Fanny, Fanny, how can you ask when you still live and I still live and this beauteous Babe doth live? Dr. Smellie's Forceps—for that is what his Secret Instruments most surely are—did you no good. Had I not cut into your swollen Belly, 'twould sure have burst, and burst your Life as well. The Operation I perform'd is old as History itself, and venerable as Ancient Greece or Rome. I'faith, it goes back to the Dawn of Time, yet 'tis forbidden as if 'twere Witchcraft. Since the accursèd *Accoucheurs* have ne'er perform'd it upon a Woman who liv'd—they say that 'tis impossible to spare both Babe and Dam! Yet we Wise Women have known this Art for Centuries and pass'd it on in secret to our Daughters. The Mother's Life is spar'd when we defeat the Gangrene with our special Herbs. Thus I have given you Moulds and Mosses, which, mixt with Laudanum to kill the Pain, shall prevent the Festering of your Wound. O Scars shall you have, but what are Scars beside the Gift of Life? You shall wear your Scar as the proud Badge of your Life-giving Pow'rs. I'faith, you shall wear it 'neath your Boddice—unlike mine." She pointed sadly to the Cross she bore, still red and angry as the Ruffians who incis'd it. I listen'd with what mixt Emotions I cannot e'en say.

"You must understand, my Girl," Isobel went on, "that we are all rising from a buried Past. They speak of Reason and Enlightenment, of Nature's Mighty Plan in this Best of all Possible Worlds, but for Women this Age of supposèd Enlightenment is dark as Darkest Night—quite unlike the Ancient Days when Woman was worshipp'd as the Sun, not obscur'd as a pale and misty Moon. We are only beginning now to rise, to throw back the Dust from our Graves, to unearth our own Faces. My Face, like ev'ry Woman's Face, is an Image of the Goddess. They have cut their Cross into it as a Symbol of Masculine Pow'r. They think that thus they may subdue the Goddess—but she is not to be subdu'd with Knives alone."

I lookt at Isobel in stark amazement, but her Eyes shone with other-worldly Fire and as she spoke, she sway'd and rockt as I had seen poor slaughter'd Joan do, so many Months ago.

"We are the Bringers and Givers of Life," she said. "*That*

they cannot take from us. Tho' they may try to degrade these Mysteries, to make them our Downfall and not our Glory, they still remain the Source of all our Pow'r. The Joy you felt the Moment you beheld the Babe is a Glimpse of your Divinity within. 'Tis also the vast Pow'r of the Goddess. The *Accoucheurs* and all their Kind may wish to make you think Travail and Birth are Agonies, not Blessings, but e'en within their Pains, you have glimps'd their Joys.

"The Cross, the Hanging Tree, the Bars of Prisons—all these are Symbols of the Madnesses of Men. They would e'er put Pow'r before Life itself. But the Symbol of the Woman is a Circle—the Infant's Head emerging betwixt the Legs of the Goddess, the Circles of the Nipples, the Navel, the Gravid Belly. 'Tis the Sun, all Radiance, Circles that have no Beginnings, and no Endings, whilst Uprights, Crossbeams, Crucifixes, and Hanging Trees are nought but Testaments to Man's Worship of Death."

I held my Child, lookt up at Isobel, and struggl'd to understand her Meaning. My Head swam with Images of Life and Death. I knew myself to be upon the Brink of a Great Revelation, and yet I could not grasp it.

"Ah, Fanny, you are tired," said Isobel. "I'll fetch your Sleeping Potion and your Cures. All this Talk can wait until another Time."

She took the Babe and brought my Sleeping Draught, which I drank thirstily, knowing now that I would live to wake again, and strangely sooth'd by all she'd said. Then I drifted into a curious Visionary Sleep in which the Things she'd said and what I had perceiv'd in these last Hours were strangely intermixt.

I dreamt I had a silken Gown given me by my own Natural Mother. 'Twas beauteous, a Thing of rosy Silk, and yet I cut a gaping Hole in it to accommodate my swollen Belly. Then I was fill'd with the bitterest Remorse, for the silk Threads unravell'd and I knew I could not sew 'em back together. I wept most inconsolably for my unravell'd Gown. "All the Silk Worms in China toil fer ye," Susannah said, her Skin transform'd to white, her Hair to red. O in this Dream, *Susannah* was my Daughter, and as I watch'd, I saw her Body shrink back, back, back to Infant's Size!

I rockt her in my Arms, she suckt my Breasts, and all my Being o'erflow'd with Passion such as no mere Man had e'er rais'd in me. In making love to her, I made love also to myself, for our two Essences were so intermingl'd that 'twas impossible to say where one began and the other ended.

O what strange Dreams the Laudanum sent! Did Isobel still live or did I dream that, too? And was there a Newborn Babe? Indeed, on this first Day after your Birth, I knew no Distinction betwixt Dreams and Waking, betwixt Life and Death.

One Candle burnt in the darken'd Chamber. A Door creakt open on its Hinges and Footsteps approach'd my Bed.

"Isobel?" I askt. But no Reply was given.

"Isobel?" I askt again.

The Footsteps drew nearer. I struggl'd to raise myself upon the Pillows, and as I did so, I saw in the Gloom the astonish'd Face of Lord Bellars.

"Fanny!" he cried, seeing my Face unmaskt for the first Time since Lymeworth; whereupon he fell to his Knees at my Bedside pleading Forgiveness.

"Had I but known," he sobb'd, "had I but known."

"What would you have done?" came another Voice in the Darkness. 'Twas Isobel, her Voice suffus'd with Bitterness such as I had ne'er heard—e'en from her.

Lord Bellars lookt up suddenly. "Isobel?" he askt uncertainly.

" 'Tis I," she said.

"O no—not you, too!" he cried. "O God! What have I done to deserve such a Fate!"

"What have you *not* done?" said Isobel bitterly. "Satan himself shall deal with you in Hell, Laurence Bellars!"

"Then you two *know* each other?" I askt.

"Fanny—you should know—" Lord Bellars began, but Isobel swiftly interrupted him.

"Not now," said she, "the Lass hath been thro' enough Hardship these past Days." Whereupon she seiz'd Lord Bellars by the Arm and dragg'd him to the Corner of the Chamber.

I could neither see nor properly hear what transpir'd betwixt 'em, but from the Gasps and Moans Lord Bellars made as Isobel whisper'd in his Ear, I deduced that the Matter was not pleasant. At length, after many Exclamations of Grief on his part, I heard him again fall upon bended Knee and exclaim: "What have I done to win the Love of such good Women when I am so base myself!" Then again I heard Footsteps, fleeing the Chamber and clatt'ring down the Stair, and presently Isobel came to me.

341

"What have you told him," I askt, "to make him so exclaim?"

"That you shall know in all good Time," said Isobel, "when you are quite recover'd of your Pains. Now you must sleep again and we shall talk together when you are better."

"But where doth he go?" I askt.

"He goes to atone for his Sins," said Isobel. "We need no Men here. This is Women's Work. Sleep, my Fanny, sleep."

All these most strange Events occurr'd betwixt Sleep and Waking under the puissant Influence of Laudanum, in that curious Twilight State that follows upon Childbirth. E'en had I no Opiate to cloud my Brain, I should have been half mad, at least, after my Ordeal. O Angels and Demons attend Women in Childbed! E'en without Isobel to prompt my Rage, the Severity of the Pain I had known should have stirr'd my Anger 'gainst the Whole Race of Mankind who but employ Women as Brood Mares and steal not only Life from 'em but e'en Joys of Bearing. For who can glory in bearing a Daughter in a World where Women have so few Prospects and are us'd so ill?

I remember how I wept o'er your tiny Form, my own pink Belinda, vowing that your Fate should be better than mine, that you should ne'er be seduced as your Mother had been before you, that you should have as much Education as any Lad, that you should learn to ride and fence and shoot, so that howe'er many cruel Hands Fate should deal you, you should prove able to defend yourself against 'em all.

I remember how I sat and rockt you (both of us still in the Drowse that follows Birth) and marvell'd at your Face, your Cherub's Hands, the Impenetrable Blue of your Infant's Eyes, and the Dawn Pink of your newborn Skin.

How did we, who were so recently one Being, become two? I marvell'd most at this, for still I felt you 'neath my Heart and I wept for the Separation which presages all the Separations of Life, ending with Death.

'Twas great Good Fortune to have Isobel there, for I felt almost like a Babe myself. When I curl'd up in Sleep I imagin'd myself a pink Infant, with a Mouth drooling Slime—as if a tiny Snail had cross'd the Bed—and small Hands clutching and unclutching at the Air.

"What shall we name her?" Isobel askt, sitting by my Bedside, looking down with Eyes of sweetest Love upon the Babe.

"Belinda," said I, all unthinking, for I still lov'd "The Rape

342

of the Lock" tho' I could not love its Author anymore. O might my Belinda know no greater Rapes than to be shorn of one small Lock of Hair whilst playing Cards!

"The Goddess guides your Words," Isobel said, "for Belinda means 'Serpent-like' and the Serpent is the Ancient Symbol of Wisdom and also of the Goddess."

"Are you quite sure?" I askt. "I would not name her thus if 'twere Satan's Name, for doth not the Snake signify the Devil?"

Isobel lookt at me most patiently, but her Eyes flasht with Anger.

"If I had rear'd you, you would know," said she. "The Serpent was the Symbol of the Goddess, and when her Holy Temples were o'erthrown and Priests replaced the Priestesses of Old, the Serpent was made to seem the Devil. 'Tis always thus: the new Cult names the Gods of Old as Devils. But that whole Eden Story is nought but Lyes! Name her Belinda then, 'twill please the Goddess."

Just then, the Door open'd and Susannah rusht in, her Face full of Fear.

"Quick! Run an' hide yerself, Mistress Isobel! 'Tis the *Accoucheur* Dr. Smellie an' his Cohorts. They murmur o' Witchcraft an' press to see the Midwife. O I beg ye, run an' hide!"

Isobel pull'd her Wimple down on her Brow to cover the awful Cross. She threw herself upon her Knees, begg'd Mercy of the Goddess, and murmur'd other Pray'rs I did not hear.

"Isobel," I said, "there are so many Questions I would ask of you concerning Lord Bellars, the Goddess, all your Lore. . . ."

She ran to me and kiss'd me tenderly, then kiss'd the rosy Babe. "This Meeting was more than I dar'd hope. O if I must dye now, I have done my part in saving you and also blest Belinda. Keep her safe. Our Paths will cross again if the Goddess desires it. Blessings on you both and all your Daughters! O blessèd, blessèd, blessèd be!" Whereupon she ran from the Room by the Back-Stairs Door.

"Isobel," I cried, distraught to lose her again after having so recently found her. "Isobel!"

Dr. Smellie then burst in, accompanied by two younger-looking Cronies. Their Perukes were askew, their Faces flusht with Hurry and Anger.

"Where is that Witch," says Smellie, "who dares call herself a Midwife?"

343

'There is no Witch," said I, "unless 'tis I myself. For I de-liver'd the Babe myself." I said this as brazenly as you please, but my Hands trembl'd as I held my Child.

"You lye!" Smellie accus'd. " 'Twas impossible to deliver that Child alive thro' Nature's Gate. By Rights you should be dead. I swear upon the Ghost of Dead Hippocrates that Witchcraft hath been us'd. By Jove—I would see the Wound, for I am sure there is one!"

"Modesty forbid!" said I. "At your Peril, Sirrah, you un-drape my Body!"

Smellie stopp'd in his Tracks. He dar'd not undrape me for fear of being condemn'd in his Profession: for if an *Ac-coucheur* could not undrape a Woman in Travail without transgressing the Bounds of Modesty, then how would he presume to do so, after she had been so happily de-liver'd—albeit by another?

"Cease an' desist, Sirrah," said Susannah. "Begone, ye Murderer!"

Smellie stood and gap'd, consider'd the Penalties, then, looking around the Room hastily, askt for Lord Bellars.

"Lord who?" said Susannah before I could make any Re-ply.

"Lord Bellars of Lymeworth," said Smellie. "For my Fee is still not paid."

"There is no Bellars here," said Susannah, "nor hath there been. I'faith, I know not who this Man might be."

I lookt at Susannah in amazement. What a wily Wench!

"I'll have my Fee!" said Smellie.

"Fer what?" Susannah said. "Fer near murderin' me Mistress? She hath deliver'd the Chidl unattended—an' fer that ye would be paid? Begone!"

Smellie fum'd and sputter'd; his Cohorts mutter'd dire Warnings.

"Where is that Witch?" Smellie said again (as if indeed un-able to think what else to say).

"O ye are daft!" said Susannah. "Begone to Bedlam where ye belong an' leave this poor Woman to nurse her Babe in Peace."

" 'Tis Witchcraft!" Smellie said.

"Aye, 'tis Witchcraft," echo'd his Crony.

"Witchcraft, indeed," said the other Crony.

Whereupon Susannah snatch'd the Broom from the Corner of the Fire-Place, and brandishing it like a Weapon, went af-ter Smellie and his Brethren.

"Witchcraft?" askt she. "If ye believe so in Witchcraft, then fly away upon this Broomstaff! Ye Fools! Ye Butchers! Begone!" And she drove them off with the sheer Fury of her Words whilst she whipp'd the Air with the Broom Handle.

Smellie and his Cohorts ran so fast that I had indeed to laugh despite the Fact that Laughing made my Belly ache and my Stitches pull.

When they were gone, I askt Susannah if Isobel had enlighten'd her about the Cause of Lord Bellars' hasty Departure.

"She said not one Word about it, Mistress Fanny, but occupied herself with showin' me how to brew yer Medicaments—almost as if she knew she might not stay here long. But as fer his Departure, I know not why he fled—tho' he press'd Guineas in my Hand as he did—enough at least to keep us for a while."

"O Susannah!" I said. "Come hold me—for I am so afraid."

I'faith, my Body trembl'd and my Teeth chatter'd. I held the pink and sleeping Belinda—all oblivious of the Woes of the World—but who would hold and comfort me?

"I'll be yer Mother, Mistress Fanny," said Susannah, "fer I know what 'tis to be an Orphan." And, i'faith, 'twas true that she had mother'd me and spar'd my Life—both by calling in the Midwife, unbeknownst to me, and by chasing out the odious *Accoucheur*. Now she sat upon the Bed and rockt me in her slender Arms.

"O Susannah, you have sav'd my Life!" I cried.

"Hush, Fanny, I did nothin'. 'Twas Mistress Isobel who did it all."

Whereupon we rockt: Mother, Babe, and Sweet Susannah, wond'ring what more the Fates could send to test us after the astounding Events of the last few Days.

Susannah kiss'd my fever'd Brow and kiss'd Belinda's Brow as well.

"I'll be yer Mother, Mistress Fanny," said she, "an' Belinda's, too." Whereupon I fell asleep again, with my own pink Belinda in my Arms.

Chapter IV

We are introduced to Prudence Feral, Wet-Nurse extraordinaire, and your humble Author summarizes the current Controversy concerning Wet-nursing versus maternal Breast Feeding, to which she appends some Views of her own, drawn from Experience (that greatest of all Teachers).

IN THE DAYS THAT FOLLOW'D, I liv'd betwixt Sleep and Wakefulness, trying to nurse my Babe whene'er her Infant Cries pierced the Darkness of my Dreams and she would feed. I'll ne'er forget, if I live to be a Hundred, how your little Mouth latch'd on to my Nipple as if there were nothing upon this whole Earth but Mouth and Breast, and all the Dance of Life were simply the Motion of an Infant's Lips, sucking, sucking, sucking!

O how strangely the Goddess hath arranged our Fates! Waken'd in the Night by the shrill Cry of an Infant, what Wrath and Resentment we feel to have our Rest thus interrupted. But then when we take the rosy Babe into our Arms—a sweet warm Weight, smelling faintly of Sweat and Urine—and we look down upon that pink drowsy Face, with Eyelids clos'd upon Rose-Petal Cheaks, the Wrath quite melts away. At length, when the little Creature attaches its tiny determin'd Mouth to our waiting Breast, we are wholly won o'er: and Mother and Babe become once more one Being, breathing in Tune with the Great Breath of the Universe, sucking the Sweetness at the Core of Life, with a Mouth whose Motions are not learnt but quite inborn, and strong as the Pulse of Nature itself.

I remember the first drowsy Days when my Breasts gave only the clearest Tear Drops of Fluid, and the Babe slept more than it wak'd, and wak'd only to uncurl itself like a little Bud and squall in Hunger, knotting up its whole Form in Pain. 'Twould latch on to my Breast like a Barnacle and suck for dear Life, until its whole Body eas'd and its Legs

346

and Arms relaxt, and at length it fell asleep with the Nipple in its Mouth. Immediately its Head fell heavily to one side, the little Mouth lost hold of the Nipple, and you were lost in Sleep, my own Belinda, quite lost in Sleep. After three Days, white Streams of Milk began to flow from my Nipples, so that I might squeeze them and see the slender Threads of Milk squirt from them like tiny Moonbeams, or Spiders' silken Threads, spun out of my Body to feed the Child so recently pluckt from within. I remember how my Nipples began to ache as Feeding Time drew near, and how your slightest Cry, or e'en the tender Thought of you, made my Breasts burst with Milk and three pearly white Droplets gather in a Stream at their Tips.

Quite suddenly, upon the tenth Day after the Birth, my Milk grew bitter and you would not take it. You would turn your little Head from the Nipple, crying, deforming your Face with Pain and Anger, so that the same Breast that had so recently comforted you, now made you weep quite inconsolably. How I, too, wept at this unhappy Occurrence and how my Breasts fill'd until they pain'd me and Milk leakt all o'er the Bed-Linen!

O what an unhappy Turn of Fate for one who had been so oft' bereav'd—for a Newborn Babe speaks only to its Mother in Suckling, not in Words, and if this simple Speech be taken away, what Discourse is left betwixt 'em? 'Twas not the Fashion of that Day for High-born Women to nurse their own Babes; Suckling was thought to be quite low and bestial. Ne'ertheless, I went against the Fashion and attempted it— tho' when my Milk turn'd bitter, Susannah herself confess'd to me that Isobel had warn'd her this might come to pass.

"The Bitter Herbs have sour'd yer Milk, I fear," Susannah said. " 'Tis not yer fault. Isobel warn'd o' this an' bid me fetch a Wet-Nurse fer the Babe, but 'twas yer Wish to suckle her yerself. Ah, Mistress Fanny, do not weep so. . . ."

I wept and wept. The Babe's turning from my Breast seem'd as bitter to me as all the Losses I had suffer'd in my Life. You were my only Kin upon this Earth and I wisht for nothing more than to suckle you for all Eternity.

What Solace 'tis to suckle one's own Babe! Men of Fashion may argue against it; Ladies in Waiting may call it base and fit only for the Animals, but 'tis a Comfort for the Mother as much as the Child. For as the Child is eas'd of Pain and Hunger, so is the Mother fed as well. One takes by Giving, the other by Taking, gives; and by this Intercourse the two are blest. Feeding is a Comfort for the Feeder as much as for the Fed.

Ne'ertheless, the very Herbs that spar'd my Life embitter'd my Life-giving Milk; thus 'twas essential that a Wet-Nurse should be found and found upon the Instant. It took a Day and a Night to find the Nurse, and during all that Time I fear'd you'd starve to Death. Twenty-four Hours is an Eternity to a new-made Mother, when her Infant screams in Pain.

What a Profusion of Fluids is the Female Form! Milk, Tears, Blood—these are our Elements. We seem to be fore'er awash in Humours of divers Sorts. O we are made of Waters; we are like the Seas, teeming with Life of ev'ry Shape and Colour!

The Wet-Nurse came at last, both to my Relief and my Regret. Better a Wet-Nurse than a starving Babe. And the Nurse prov'd to be a stout Creature, with enormous hanging Breasts, a porcine Face with slitty Eyes behind iron Spectacles, the Hint of a Moustache 'neath her stubby Nose, and Lips as wet and red as Calves' Liver. Her Hair was Mousebrown, her Moustache the same Colour, and a large brown Wen adorn'd her right Cheak. Despite her unpleasing Appearance, Susannah and I were both so grateful for her Arrival (for the hungry Babe was fed and ceas'd at once to squall) that we should have thrown ourselves upon our Knees with Gratitude had she lookt like Medusa herself and threaten'd to turn us all to Stone.

Prudence Feral—for that was the Wet-Nurse's Name—was the sort of Person who regarded Kindness and Friendship as but Excuses to dominate those who proffer'd 'em. Thus, seeing how reliev'd we were at her Arrival, she set out at once to put both me and Susannah in our Places.

The Daughter of a Curate, who claim'd herself the recent Widow of a Seaman lost at Sea, she said she'd buried her Infant Son not three Days past, and for that Cause and that Cause alone, was willing to take up Wet-nursing for a Time. Doubtless she hop'd to convince us that she was comfortably fixt and scarce needed the Money, but took this Place for Love of Babes alone—unlike the mercenary Wet-Nurses of Song and Story.

The Moment she establish'd herself in our House, she was full of Rules for the Babe, and e'en for me and Susannah. She'd eat nought but Mutton Chops, fresh Oysters, and fresh Goat's Milk, she said, and she demanded that a Cook be hir'd to please her Palate. All these Conditions I acceded to—so anxious was I for my Belinda to survive and so well did I understand that the Nurse's Nourishment augur'd the future Nourishment of the Child. (Isobel had said 'twas unlikely after my Ordeal that I'd bear another Babe, thus I was more than e'er determin'd to keep you alive—despite the thousands of Infants born only, it seem'd, to dye in that Dark Time.)

Prue took compleat Command of you, taking you into her own Chamber, locking the Door, and ne'er permitting us to see you except by special Dispensation. 'Twas like an Audience with the Pope in Rome! Had not Prue been quite in Love with Food, and, i'faith, rather a Glutton, we should ne'er have seen your Infant Face at all, so proprietary was she of your tiny Being. But all Day and all Night she crept with sneaky Feet into the Kitchen to fetch Cakes and Cups of Milk for herself; thus when her Stomach bade her go, *I* might creep into her Chamber and view your lovely Face.

Prue's Nights and Days seem'd to fall into the same Pattern as those of a Newborn Child. She slept and ate, drank warm Milk and slept again—and all the while grew stouter. 'Twas a Form of Magick, perhaps, that as she grew, the Babe would grow as well; but, i'faith, she was more careful to feed herself than to feed the Child! She liv'd in that darken'd Chamber, with the Curtains drawn and the fusty Bed-Linens toss'd upon the Bed and the Fire burning always in the Grate, but no Candles at all in the Sconces. The Room began to smell of Urine and curdl'd Milk, whilst Prue went about her somnolent Life, to the Pantry and back again, to nurse, then back to Bed again.

Susannah and I would stare at the lockt Door of her Chamber, daring not to knock, lest Prue grow cross with us. The smallest Trifle seem'd to vex her; and vexatious Persons oft' can be Household Tyrants.

"What? Yer Milk wasn't rich enough?" she'd say when she talkt to me at all. Like all Wet-Nurses, 'twas not enough for her to suckle the Infant, she had to castigate the Mother as well! Likewise, would she criticize my Dress, make dire Predictions concerning my future Health, and mock my Views upon the Government of Children. For at the Time of your Birth, Belinda, some Nurses still swore by Swaddling (indeed 'tis still the Custom in much of Europe), whilst Parents of the more enlighten'd sort were beginning to speak out against that ancient Practice. Had not I interven'd, Prue would have had you swaddl'd up exactly like a Dutch Nine-Pin, with your Head (which should have been secure—owing to the

349

Natural Weakness of an Infant's Neck)loose and unprotected at the Top and bobbing about with ev'ry Shake, like one of those Niddle-Noddle Figures from Canton.

Swaddling I would not permit, since I believ'd e'en then, before the Learnèd Physicians began to argue against it, that a Babe must be free to move about. How I concluded this, I cannot say; 'twas my Natural Inclination, as was my strong Desire to feed you from my own Breasts. Nowadays the Pamphleteers prate of all these Things, but the Reign of George I was still a Dark Age, of sorts, and there were many Rakes and Men of Fashion who'd scarce permit their Wives the Pleasure of Nursing their own Progeny (for then the Father had no access to 'em, lest they become *Enceinte* and their Milk dry up).

Tender Parents oft' seem'd a Rarity in those Times and many Nurslings were sent away to Regions far more dangerous and diseas'd than where the Parents dwelt. The Father said 'twas for the Country Air, but in Fact, 'twas for his own ease, both in having Access to his Wife, and in ne'er being awaken'd in the Night by a squalling Babe (or "Brat," he would have said).

What occasion'd this Coldness towards Infants I cannot say, for e'en Mothers, having borne in Pain, oft' assented gladly to the Custom, sending their Offspring to well-known "Killing Nurses," who had the Reputation of overlaying Babes or starving 'em at Nurse. Perhaps 'twas because so many Infants dy'd before the Age of Five, and Parents were loath to grow too fond of 'em lest they be too oft' bereav'd. 'Twas possible these Mothers reason'd that 'tis better to send the Child away if 'tis to dye anyway.

My own bitter Relations with my Step-Sister, Mary, were, in fact, owing to this regrettable Practice of Wet-nursing. She was sent out to nurse at Birth and kept away near three Years. When she return'd to find myself and Daniel there, usurping her Proper Place, she both wept for her Nurse (whom she now regarded as the Mother of her Heart) and was enraged to find herself replaced at Home. I'faith, as Lady Bellars told me later, 'twas Lord Bellars' own Fault. For finding himself bitterly disappointed to be presented with a Daughter as his First-born, he banish'd her to a Wet-Nurse in the Country and would ne'er set Eyes upon her until, as he said, she'd reached "the Age of Reason." That Age, alas, did she ne'er achieve. On the Contrary, this early Banishment so fill'd her Infant Heart with Spleen that, when she was restor'd

350

amongst her Kin, she spent all her Days in thinking up Trials for her Mother and her Brother—but most especially for me.

Mary had been swaddl'd; I had not. Therefore, I would not permit you to be, but 'twas only thro' the most repeated Arguments that I managed to keep Prue Feral from binding you up like a truss'd Capon. In the first Days of her Employment, she wrapp'd the Swaddling Bands around your tiny Body as tightly as she could—doubtless so that you might not move to trouble her. Nor did she oft' inspect your Wrappings, lest she soil her delicate Fingers with Infant's Ordure or Urine. This made me so enraged that I could scarce tolerate Prue's Presence in our House one Moment longer, but Susannah stopp'd me from reprimanding her, reminding me of the Difficulty we'd had in finding a Wet-Nurse upon such short Notice. (For mark you, Belinda, the *Accoucheurs* were also the Purveyors of Wet-Nurses in London then, and no *Accoucheur* in Town would have Dealings with us after Dr. Smellie's Reports concerning my Lying-in.)

"I will not permit my Child to be swaddled," I said to Prue at last, unable to contain my Fury longer.

"Unwrap her yourself if you want her dead," says she.

I lookt at her in amazement. "What is your Meaning?"

"I'll not be to blame if the Child freezes to Death," says Prue. " 'Tis not *my* Fault."

"And why should she freeze?" said I.

"Hmmmph," says Prue, pursing her great Liver Lips and shaking her fat Jowls with stern Disapproval. "You know little enough of Babes, I'll warrant."

I doubted myself then, for 'twas true I knew almost nothing concerning Babes. I had only my own Natural Inclinations but no Proof. Alas, Nurses may tyrannize o'er new-made Mothers readily enough, for new-made Mothers doubt ev'rything and Babes cannot speak to tell their own Opinions.

Would the Babe freeze to Death unswaddl'd? Would she starve to Death from the Bitterness of her own Mother's Milk? Would she imbibe the Nurse's sour Disposition with the Nurse's Milk? Would she think Prue Feral her Natural Mother instead of me? All these were Things I fretted o'er during those first Weeks after your Birth. O Astrologers and Men of Magick claim that a Woman upon the Verge of her Monthly Flow'rs hath Magical Pow'rs and can raise Spirits to do her Bidding—why then how much more puissant Magick must a new-made Mother possess! For truly the Process of

Birth is a Crack betwixt the Earth and Sky, the Abyss betwixt the Sublunary and the Divine, the Shimm'ring Boundary betwixt Man and God, betwixt Woman and Goddess.

"Unswaddle her," says I, raising myself straight and tall as I was able. "I take full Responsibility for the Consequences."

Prue Feral made a sour Face (as she was wont to do) but ne'ertheless unwrapp'd your Swaddling Bands. I wept then to see your little Legs so redden'd by the constraining Linen, and your little Arms almost deform'd by their unwarranted Confinement. I sent the sour Mistress Prue to boil Water so that I might mix it with cold to prepare a Tub for you, and with my own Hands I bath'd your tiny Form.

A Prue purs'd her great Liver Lips, frown'd, and cluckt her Displeasure, I marvell'd at the Perfection of your own small Self: the ten pink Toes with their Nails the Colour of the Interior of a blushing Tropick Sea-Shell; the diminutive Pudendum so smooth and pink that 'twas impossible to believe 'twould e'er sprout Hairs. The mere Suggestion of Nipples turn'd inward upon themselves (as if in refusal to believe they'd e'er give Milk), the round Barrel Chest of the Infant, and the delectable diminutive Arse that invited its Mother's Kiss.

How Prue frown'd when I kiss'd you there!

"You'll send the Child straight to Hell," says she, "with Pettin' and Kissin' like that."

But I had won the Argument concerning Swaddling—at least for the nonce. I dress'd your tiny Form in a loose Shift of white Linen and gave you to your Nurse to feed once more upon her great hanging Breasts. And so she took you off to her Chamber and lockt the Door, appropriating you to herself again.

For my own part, I sat down at my Writing Bureau determin'd to compleat that Romance in the Manner of Mrs. Haywood which I'd begun at the Start of my Travail. Such a Romance might keep us all in Oysters, Goat's Milk, and Mutton Chops when Lord Bellars' Money and Jewels ran out and Creditors began to knock upon our Door. O there was Money in Novels if not lofty Reputation (since all the Criticks of the Age agreed that the Noble Epick was superior to the crass Novel and was, besides the Tragedy, the only Form to which Genius ought aspire).

But would Genius feed Prue Feral's Appetites? Hardly! Therefore, I took my Quill in Hand and scribb'd away. I had nam'd my imaginary Lovers Clotilda and Philidore, as I have said before, and penn'd an Epistle Dedicatory full of the most flatt'ring Panegyricks—yet vague enough, as such Panegyricks always are—to suit any Noble Lord, or e'en Lady, I might later choose to serve as Patron for my Work.

My first Romance! What might I write about? O I'd have Sailing Ships and Seraglios, Pyrates and Nabobs, Shipwrecks, Storms, Marooning, Fortunes lost and found again, Fortunes gain'd and lost again—all told in highly overwrought "Secret" Letters, burning with sweetest Love, hottest Jealousy, and darkest Despair! 'Twould pay the Bills and keep Belinda and her Nurse and e'en Sweet Susannah; for I was the Head of a Family now and could scarce write Epicks upon Woman's Lot to please myself, but must instead bow to the Fashion of the Day and write Romances in Mrs. Haywood's high-flown Manner.

Thus I began to spin out an amusing Tale of Star-cross'd Lovers, compleat with swooning Virgins, rough-hewn Rakes, lustful Sea Captains, and ruin'd Courtiers. The Work went smoothly enough for a Time, since I was as able with my Pen as any Grub Street Scribbler, purveying their Romances, like so many Cups of rich, sweet Chocolate, to their greedy Readers. Sure, I was aware that the Novel itself was lookt upon as nought but an Inflamer of Dubious Passions in bor'd Ladies who should have tended instead to their Needles and Pray'r Books, but I reason'd to myself that the first Fruit of my Scribble (not counting all those Lit'ry Works I had committed to the Flames whilst still in Lord Bellars' Keeping) should at least have a worthy End. Low as Novels were, compar'd to Lofty Epicks and Noble Tragedies, they were still, perhaps, better for the Soul than Whoring.

I wrote and wrote whilst Prudence rais'd my Babe. 'Twas hard enough to enter your Chamber, much less care for you myself—tho' indeed I kept a watchful Eye upon Prue's Comings and Goings. But as I wrote I was seiz'd with Sadness that I could not attend to you myself and I felt myself to be a cruel Mother for leaving my Babe to another's Care. Alas! 'Twas the inevitable Consequence of my new-found Independence. I could not nurse you myself, nor could I depend upon any Person but myself to earn our Bread and keep us from the Workhouse. Where Lord Bellars had fled I did not know, nor indeed why, and Lancelot, for certain, was Worlds away by now. I had no Choyce but learn to play the Man— better indeed than any Man—since whom could I rely upon except myself?

Tired as I was after my Ordeal (and my Belly was still not properly heal'd) I applied myself to Work ne'ertheless. I forced myself to cover no less than ten Sheets of Foolscap per Day and upon each Saturday I play'd my own Amanuensis and transcrib'd the Week's Writings into Fair Copy. 'Twas upon those dreaded Saturdays that my Doubts crept in, since the Mind and the Quill may Race along happily enough during Composition of the Work, but when one stops to copy out one's Words, the very Slowness and Dullness of the Task makes one doubt all. Why was I writing of Philidore and Clotilda, thought I, instead of Lancelot and Fanny? Sure we were as Star-cross'd as any Lovers the World had e'er known! And yet 'twas not the Fashion of that Day to write one's own Am'rous History. 'Twould be consider'd arrogant, e'en a bit mad, to presume that the Events transpiring in one's own Heart were fit Matter for a Book.

Mrs. Haywood wrote Romances in the French Manner; Mr. Defoe wrote True Histories of Famous Criminals and Notorious Shipwrecks; whilst the French Romancers sent us Year after Year the passionate Productions of their Pens (which were as oft' denounced by our noble English Criticks as they were gobbl'd up by our hungry English Readers). But no one made bold to write of her own Love Adventures unless 'twas for the Privacy of her Secret Diaries (to be read by her blushing Heirs).

Yet what a History 'twould make, thought I, if I should write of Lancelot and Fanny! Lancelot and Fanny were worth one hundred Philidores and Clotildas! Lancelot and Fanny were as delicate and fine in their tormented Love as Piramus and Thisbe or e'en Eloise and Abelard!

Oft', whilst sitting at my Writing Bureau, I'd hear the muffl'd Cries of a Babe. Then, o'erflowing with Maternal Passions, I would run to the Door of Prue's Chamber and timidly knock.

" 'Tis nothing, Mistress Fanny," came the reply. "Pray, do not discommode yourself." Reluctantly, I'd return to my Scribblings, yet all the while, my Ears prickl'd with a Mother's fierce Attentiveness. Clotilda and Philidore had only half my Heart; the other half and both my Ears belong'd to you.

Those Ears heard ev'ry Whimper of your Infant Voice and with each Whimper came horrifick Visions. Was Prudence swaddling you again, or was she starving you? No Matter how many Times I betook myself to her Chamber to enquire and was told " 'Tis nothing," I came back again. I imagin'd you torn to Pieces by Wild Beasts, or still'd in your Cries by mysterious Fevers. I imagin'd your Eyes pok'd out by Sticks or your tender little Feet us'd to stir up the Fire in the Grate. I had only to hear you Whimper once to rise and run to your Chamber; but always Prudence kept me out with her " 'Tis nothing, nothing, nothing."

The Weeks pass'd; I scribbl'd. As Philidore and Clotilda were captur'd by Pyrates, lost each other and found each other again, lost Riches and found 'em again, lost Children and found 'em again, lost Parents and found 'em again, you grew from a squalling red-faced Newborn Babe into a smooth, pink-featur'd Child of three Months old. When I could break into your forbidden Chamber to view you—usually when Prue was bathing you—I perceiv'd that your Face had taken on new Contours and you had begun to smile and coo and mimick Speech. O when you laugh'd, you threw your Arms and Legs into the Air with pure Delight and your entire Infant Form appear'd to laugh. Yet still, intermittently, I was bedevill'd by the Whimpers that came from your Chamber; and one Day, unable longer to contain myself, I knelt at Prue's Keyhole and lookt in.

E'en now my Heart pounds and my Eyes fill with briny Tears to remember what I saw. Prue had you truss'd up again in the Swaddling Bands I had forbidden and she had hung you on a Peg upon the Wall whilst she greedily devour'd her Mutton Chops washt down with pure Goat's Milk. As she slobber'd and wip'd her greasy Hands upon her greasy Smock, you let out a grievous Cry. Whereupon I saw (O with what disbelieving yet believing Eyes!) Prue take a Linen Napkin from her Lap and clout your Infant Face! You squeal'd again, she clouted you again. I rose up from my Knees and beat my Fists upon the Door.

" 'Tis nothing," Prue said sweetly.

"Open at once!" I cried.

" 'Tis nothing," Prue said again.

"Open up or I'll break down the Door," I cried.

I heard slow, dragging Footsteps approach the Door, and finally 'twas open'd.

"How dare you strike my Child!" I shouted in a Rage.

"I ne'er did such a Thing," said Prue.

"You lye! And you have swaddl'd her again against my Will."

Prue lookt at me defiantly and said: "I merely try to save your Babe from Hell and this is all the Gratitude you show."

I ran to you and took you in my Arms, unwrapp'd the Swaddling Bands, and kiss'd the Welts that Prue had made upon your Face. I rockt you in my Arms protectively. "Out! Out of my House this Instant!" I commanded Prue.

"Then let Belinda starve?" askt she. "For where will you find a Wet-Nurse upon the Instant?"

"Out of my House!" I cried.

"Very well, then," said Prue with all Dignity. "I go and let the Infant starve." She made a busy Pretence of gath'ring up her Clothes and Linens and pulling her Sea-Chest out from under the Bed.

Then I grew truly frighten'd, for 'twas true that I had no other Nurse for you, nor had I any Way to feed you myself.

"Pray stay," I stammer'd, "for one Week longer whilst I find another Nurse. But this Door shall remain ajar and the Babe shall not be swaddl'd or I'll box your Ears!"

"O thankee kindly, Mistress Fanny," said Prue, wiping the Mutton Grease from her Moustache and falling to her Knees in Gratitude. Now that I had given her Notice, she immediately became obsequious and slavish. O I should have known such Conduct augur'd ill!

Chapter V

Containing the Character of a Cook, some useful Opinions upon the Nature of Infants, our Heroine's Attempts to find a new Wet-Nurse for her Babe, and the compleat Contents of a Mother's Nightmare.

WHILST SUSANNAH AND I put all our Efforts towards searching for a new Wet-Nurse, Prue attempted to persuade me that her Treatment of Belinda had been only for the Child's own Good. "For Children are born with the full Weight of Original Sin," said she, "and we must whip it out of 'em for their own Soul's Salvation."

Such Beliefs horrified me; I had read Mr. Locke's *Some Thoughts upon Education* and I believ'd that the Newborn Babe was a *Tabula Rasa,* neither good nor evil, but infinitely malleable and subject to the Mouldings of Experience. Mr. Locke was of the Opinion that the Child, at Birth, was without Morals, Ideas, or Opinions, and as the Parent printed him, so he became. I myself inclin'd to an e'en milder View than Mr. Locke's and was particularly taken with Mrs. Aphra Behn's Words in *Oroonoko:* "God makes all things good; Man meddles with 'em and they become evil." I'faith, what could be more surely good than a Newborn Babe with its pure unwrinkl'd Skin and honest Temper? When 'tis hungry, it cries; when 'tis sleepy, it sleeps. Only as it grows doth it develop Deviousness and Guile, masking its own true Feelings in its greater Desire to manipulate its Fellows. O I had oft' observ'd the dire Metamorphoses that o'ertake the Human Creature as it grows from Infancy to Old Age. The Body grows deform'd along with the Mind. Each Lye incises itself upon the Brow as a Line; each Act of Cunning or Deceit twists the Features into the ravaged Contours of villainous Old Age; and oft' the Body grows so asham'd of its Deceptions that it seeks to cloak itself in Fat and hide away. Ah too, too solid, too, too sullied Flesh! The Body is the Canvas whereupon the Soul paints its own Deformities! In my Whoring Days I had star'd with Disgust and Disbelief upon the ruin'd Bodies of Men—corpulent and gouty, red with Drink and swollen from Gluttony—and I had thought: E'en this Tub of Lard was once a sweet-faced Baby Boy.

By Day, I abandon'd my Romance and devoted myself to finding a new Wet-Nurse whose Philosophies should accord more with my own, whilst by Night I scribbl'd. 'Twould not be long before the Creditors came knocking at our Door (e'en now, I thought Susannah was ordering Mutton Chops we could ill afford to pay for, and Dr. Smellie had not ceas'd to threaten us with Imprisonment for Debt if we did not pay him for my Lying-in). My Romance was not far from Completion, yet 'twas Folly to presume that any Bookseller would pay an unknown, untried Author for an unfinish'd Work. London was full of Scribblers who would be glad of a Guinea or two Recompence for a polish'd Manuscript of many hundred Pages. The Garrets of Grub Street scarce lackt for starving Poets, many with Names far more renown'd than mine. Before long I would have no Choyce but to throw myself upon Coxtart's dubious Mercies—tho' whether she would want me now, scarr'd and deform'd as my Belly was, I could not know. I e'en thought of appealing to my former Lovers, Presto and Pug, but both had other Lady Loves of their own and would scarce welcome my embarrassing Importunities. Cleland, for his part, had abandon'd London for the East (where, no doubt, his scurrilous Life was preparing him to write that scurrilous Book about me). O I e'en thought of begging Theophilus Cibber for some Work upon the Stage, or of throwing myself and Belinda upon the Mercies of my Step-Mother, Lady Bellars, but how could I return to Lymeworth with a Babe begotten by her own Husband?

Did I e'er, in my Desperation, think of seeking out Daniel Bellars? No—a thousand Times no! Better to starve than that! 'Twas true enough that when I departed Lymeworth, I'd no Idea his Lust for me was strong enough to make him follow. But doubtless he had taken with Kate less for Love of me than for the base Desire to mimick his Father's Amours. E'en Lord Bellars had refus'd to see him at the Last, and where Daniel and Kate had fled, I knew not—nor did I wish to know.

Susannah took charge of our Finances, and had been pawning, at a great Rate, the various Jewels Lord Bellars had given me. How many were left I knew not, but I assum'd none, for Susannah spoke as if we were near Bankruptcy. Ne'ertheless, I trusted my loyal Servant would find Means to hold our Creditors at bay for a few Weeks longer whilst I found a new Nurse and compleated my Romance, since, truly, I doubted not that my Tale of Clotilda and Philidore was amusing enough to win me as many Readers as Mrs. Haywood had; and with Readers came Mutton Chops, Goat's Milk, and Oysters!

Fully a Year had pass'd since I'd fled Lymeworth for London, and what astounding Events had transpir'd in that short Time! I had departed Lymeworth a mere Girl of Seventeen, my Virginity just taken, but my Mind as innocent of the myriad Deceptions of the Great World as a bleating Baby Lamb's. In twelve brief Months I had known Witches and Highwaymen, Whores and Hell-Fire Clubs, Intrigues and Ecstacies. I had travers'd the great Abyss that separates a Maiden from a Mother. I had discover'd how weighty and awesome a Responsibility 'tis to mother rather than to be mother'd. O there were Times when I *myself* wisht to be Belinda, lying amidst the Ruffles of an Infant's Gown, crying and spitting, laughing and feeding, drooling and playing with her tiny Hands.

Daily, I sent Susannah to the Royal Exchange to consult the Columns whereon were posted Names of Country Girls who might be in search of a Place. I knew 'twas not the best Source of Wet-Nurses (for the *Accoucheurs* all had their Nurse Books, and for a Fee, supplied Nurses to new-made Mothers); but the *Accoucheurs* were now in league against me and I dar'd not contact one of 'em for fear that Smellie would renew his Demands for Pay.

I directed Susannah to bring Home to me such Country Girls with Babes in Arms as I might transform into a Wet-Nurse for Belinda. If a Woman with Twins may suckle two, I reason'd, then sure a new-made Mother, if she be well-nourish'd, may give suck to both her own Babe and another's. I'faith, many Wet-Nurses who take their Charges to the Country (away from the watchful Eyes of their proper Parents) practise Baby-farming and suckle three or four or e'en more, according to their own Want—or e'en their Husbands' Greed.

What a Procession of Unfortunates Susannah brought Home! It seem'd that London was cramm'd full of starving Wenches with skinny Babes in Arms. It broke my Heart to turn each one away, and I wisht for nothing more than a

Great Fortune wherewith I might feed all the hungry, homeless Waifs of London. But I harden'd my Heart. I could scarce nourish myself and my Babe, Susannah, the Nurse, and the Cook—much less all the starving Wenches in London!

Yet 'twas a Lesson to me to see how many would perish of Hunger before the Year was out. Why, in Coxtart's Brothel, I had seen many a Rich Rake spend as much for a new Peruke or a Mock-Maidenhead as would feed a Country Family for a Year. Lancelot was right to rob the Rich! Such grave Injustice was there in London—and all of it paraded before my Eyes! I ne'er sent a Wench away without at least a Cup of Chocolate and some Chear, tho' it certainly depleted our Reserves and 'twould not last 'em long, I knew. Before Summer's End, most of 'em would languish in a Brothel or a Workhouse, Bridewell or e'en Newgate itself. Or else they would be sunk so deep in Gin that their own Starvation and e'en their Babes' would be as Dreams to 'em.

Each Wench I would interrogate concerning her Views upon the Government of Infants. Did she agree with Locke that the Babe was a *Tabula Rasa,* neither good nor evil, but malleable; or did she conceive the Child as imprinted with Original Sin (which must be driven out with the Rod)? Did she concur with many learnèd Astrologers, that all Character was form'd by the Juxtaposition of the Planets at the Moment of Conception (or e'en of Birth), or did she believe, as Mrs. Behn seem'd to, that Children were born good and Society corrupted 'em? I took care not to tip my Hand to reveal my own Convictions, but I queried each Wench most cleverly, pretending only to be chatt'ring idly to pass the Time and put 'em at their Ease. Ne'ertheless, I am sure that most of 'em thought me quite daft—for who but your fond and foolish Mother would probe a Wet-Nurse to discover her Philosophies? Doubtless they would have been less surpriz'd had I askt to taste their Milk!

Prue Feral kept a watchful Eye upon these Proceedings, knowing she must soon depart and therefore making a great Show of her Solicitude for you, Belinda, in order to cause me to change my Mind and keep her in my Employ. She carried you from Chamber to Chamber like a Doll-Baby, play'd with you and e'en sang Ballads to you. Oft' she was wont to remark, within my Hearing, of your angelick Nature.

"La, Mistress Fanny," she would say, "the Child's a Perfect Angel, I'm sure."

But 'twas no use. I was determin'd to find another Nurse to replace her.

When Prue perceiv'd that I was in earnest about finding a new Nurse (for Day and Night I spent interrogating Wenches with suckling Babes—or Wenches who'd recently buried 'em), she askt my Leave to have Susannah carry a Letter to the Wharves, where a Shipmate of her dead Husband's, who had promis'd to look after her, was preparing for a Voyage to the Colonies. Thinking nothing of her Request, and being e'er of a too soft, yielding, and unsuspicious Nature, I granted my Permission. 'Twas true that Prue could not leave a Nursling to deliver the Letter herself and I saw no Harm in it; for her own part, Prue claim'd the Man had some Money for her, left in his Safe-keeping by her late Husband, and she must have it of him before his Ship sail'd. Whereupon she sent Susannah to the Docks to seek out the Seaman, and she did not fail to remind me that 'twas because she now lackt a Place that she must be so assiduous in finding her poor perish'd Husband's Friend and begging this Money of him. In short, Prudence was so fine a Genius in inspiring Guilt in others that the piteous Face she made whilst explaining this to me almost convinced me to give her another Chance.

Susannah carried Prue's Note to a Merchantman call'd the *Cassandra*, lying upon the Thames, taking on Cargo for a Voyage to the Colonies, but I myself was so engross'd in the Task of finding a Wet-Nurse for my precious Babe, that I paid little mind to these goings-on.

I was concern'd chiefly that Prue not swaddle you, Belinda, for her own Convenience, since 'twas clear now that you had begun to develop a Will and Wit of your own and you were no longer a blind, bewilder'd Thing, clutching at the Ether. No, you had begun to babble like a Bird before Sunrise, and to make Faces and smile almost as tho' you recogniz'd me. Your soft little Voice attempted to mimick Speech, and your Hands attempted to grasp. When I dangl'd a Baby o'er your Face as you lay in your Cradle, you would squeal with Joy and kick your tiny Legs in the Air. Consequently, I was loath to allow any Treatment of you which might corrupt your true and joyous Infant Nature and turn your Delight to Pain.

My Interviews with the Unfortunates of London were not yielding the Treasure I so earnestly desir'd. One Wench babbl'd to me of Hell-Fire and Damnation (in the Hopes of showing me how severe a Governess she'd be) and another lookt blankly at me when I enquir'd of her Philosophy.

"Spare the Rod and spoil the Child" was all most of 'em could think to say (when askt to discourse upon the Rearing of Babes); for most of 'em had not, sad to say, thought very much upon the Subject and nothing but this old Maxim came immediately to Mind. (Tho', i'faith, striking little Children for the Sake of Discipline was beginning, e'en then, to go out of Fashion with English Persons of Quality—howsoe'er much it might still be practis'd abroad and amongst the Lower Orders.)

"Choose the Wet-Nurse fer her Milk, not her Philosophy," Susannah begg'd. "All the Philosophy in Heaven will not feed a hungry Babe." Susannah was e'er the Soul of Practicality, but I persever'd in my Interrogations. At length, finding myself discontented with the Wenches I had seen, I determin'd to myself accompany Susannah to the Royal Exchange (and e'en to a Registry Office should that prove necessary) and search out Wenches with my own very Eyes.

'Twould be the first Time I had ventur'd farther than my Writing Bureau since my Lying-in, but my Belly was fairly well heal'd by now, and as the Weather was fair (it being June), I thought no Harm would come of it.

I ventur'd into the Nursery to kiss my belovèd Babe before departing, as this was the first Time I had been more than a few Chambers away; and it vext my Heart to be separated e'en for an Hour or two. O there is a special silken Cord of Love and Solicitude that joins a Mother with her Babe, and the first Time she stretches it, she feels the Tug most piteously within her own Heart. 'Tis verily as if her Entrails were torn out from within; thus, doth Nature protect her Little Ones.

I leant o'er your Cradle to kiss you on your tender Infant Cheeks and you smil'd at me with utter Trust. 'Twas hard to pull myself away.

"I'faith, I find it hard to leave her," said I.

"Have no Fear. She'll be here when ye return," said Prue, smiling sweetly in the Hopes that I would not now let her go.

So off we went to the Royal Exchange—Susannah and me in all our Finery—and left Prue and the Cook alone with Belinda.

Now, the Cook was a curious Creature, hir'd hastily to satisfy Prue's Demands, and not quite suitable for our humble Household. She was as fat as she was tall, a bit deaf in one Ear, and tho' she claim'd nought but forty Years to her Credit, 'twas more likely that she was close to Sixty, with more than sixty Years' worth of Tastings and Pan Drippings accumulated about her Middle.

She swore she'd been Assistant to a French Chef in a Great House for many a Year; and indeed she complain'd constantly that our Fare was far too simple for her High French Tastes. Before Foul Fate had so reduced her as to send her to us, she'd known Dinners of thirty Dishes and at least ten Courses, great mahogany Tables decorated with Pyramids of Sweetmeats and Fruits, Pigeons Cheak by Jowl with Oysters, Calves' Heads Cheak by Jowl with whole Lobsters; Pottages of Duckling, Crayfish, and Lobster all serv'd upon the same Table, whilst the Sideboard boasted Venison Pasties, Westphalian Ham Pyes, and Beef Roasts *en Croute*. She spoke of one Dinner in which the Dessert alone consisted of Spun Sugar Webs drap'd o'er Birds' Nests of colour'd Sugar fill'd with transparent Jellies that were made to resemble Eggs. Out of these Eggs jump'd candied Chicks, flapping their candied Wings! Upon another Occasion, said she, her Mistress had caus'd the Table to resemble a lovely Greensward whereupon Trees burst suddenly into Leaf, Rivers unfroze, and Flow'rs pok'd their Heads above the Earth. O 'twas clear she thought herself fitted only to cook *La Haute Cuisine*; therefore, to show her Displeasure with our humble Kitchen, she left the Spits unclean'd, the Fowls unsinged, the Roasts half raw, the Potts unscour'd, and she made sure to comb her Hair o'er the Pottage of Pease. She was also very loath to wash her Hands, e'en after going to the Necessary House; for why, she reason'd, must she wash 'em when they would just get dirty again? She complain'd bitterly of the Want of a Scullery Maid, saying that so great a Chef as herself should not have to trouble with fiddling Work, such as dressing small Birds; consequently, she serv'd 'em up compleat with all the Feathers and Entrails with which the Creator had blest 'em (and nought but a bit of Catchope or Piccalillo for Sauce). The Last, but not the Least, of her Complaints was the Solitary Life our Household led, for she was much accustom'd to having the Vails that a fine Household provides for its Servants; and how could she receive Vails, said she, unless we invited Guests to proffer 'em? (Then, as now, Belinda, 'twas the Custom for the Parting Guest at a Great Dinner to grease the Servants' Hands with Shillings ere he could be sure to reclaim his Hat and Cloak; thus Mrs. Wetton—for that was the Cook's name—

conceiv'd that her Pay was halv'd since her Days of Glory and this vext her in the extream.)

I have said so much concerning the Cook, for she was the Person Susannah and I encounter'd when we return'd to Hanover Square (after many fruitless Hours at the Royal Exchange and at a Registry Office in the Vicinity). The very first Thing of which she solicitously inform'd us was the following:

"They've come fer yer Sea-Trunk, Mrs. Fanny, an' caus'd me no End o' Trouble. I'll not be Porter 'round here as well as Butler an' Scullery Maid an' Cook, an' I'm warnin' ye that no self-respectin' Cook, what is us'd to cookin' in the French Style like meself will last long in yer scurvy Kitchen. . . ."

"Pray, what Sea-Trunk do you mean?" I askt, for I had caus'd no Sea-Trunk to be sent anywhere, to my Knowledge.

"The Fellow from the Docks what come to get yer Sea-Trunk, Mrs. Fanny, to put it aboard the Ship. He come here just before Mrs. Prudence went out an' I'll not be Porter fer ye, I say, not without no Vails neither. . . ."

"Do I mistake your Meaning," said I, my Blood racing and my Forehead beginning to break into a fev'rish Sweat. "Mrs. Prudence went out, say you? Then who attends Belinda?"

"I'm sure I don't know, Ma'am; I'm sure I'm not meant to be Nursemaid as well as Cook an' Porter, an' Scullery Maid. . . ."

I heard no more, but raced up the Stair to the Nursery with Susannah close behind me.

Dear Goddess, thought I, do not fail me now.

Bursting into Prue's Chamber, with my Head full of Visions of starv'd or smother'd Babes, I'll ne'er forget the Picture of Desolation that greeted me.

The Cradle was empty—empty e'en of Linens and Pillows—and the Chamber itself lookt as if it had been sackt by Robbers. A Candle Stand had been knockt o'er upon the Floor, the Fire had dy'd in the Grate, Drawers had been pull'd open and ne'er clos'd again, the Door to the Great Armoire swung open to show utter Desolation within. Meanwhile, in the Corners of the Chamber were Reminders of Prue's Gluttony: dried Chicken Bones gath'ring Dust, Oyster Shells toss'd amongst mildew'd Crusts of Bread, along with the usual lost Buttons, broken Stays, Balls of Hair, and Dust. The final Insult was the full Close-Stool wherein floated two considerable Turds, imparting their characteristick Odour to the Chamber.

"Dear God," said Susannah, falling to her Knees in Pray'r. For my own part, I was so stunn'd I could scarcely think what to do next. 'Twas as if a Knife had been plunged into my Belly just where Belinda herself once lay. I thought of my red and pucker'd Scar, so ugly yet strangely dear to me, and I fancied going thro' my whole Life with my deform'd Flesh a grim Reminder of the Babe I had lost. O 'tis curious what Visions come to Mind in the midst of Grief!

"Belinda! Belinda!" I cried. 'Twas not possible that I had borne Belinda with so much Agony, only to lose her to a Wet-Nurse's Folly!

"Lookee, Mrs. Fanny—here's a Letter," says Susannah. And so there *was* a Letter, lying upon the Mantelpiece, and writ in Prue's blotch'd and quav'ring Hand. There was no Salutation whatsoe'er, but it began all in the midst of a Chaos of Splotches and Scratches such as belong to those who have no Penmanship at all. I reproduce the Letter herewith, for 'tis burnt into my Memory like a Brand into a Slave's poor Shoulder.

When this cums to hand I shall be far away at sea fer the Babes own good an salvation—her litel soul shant be saved what with her Mum a Hussy and no swadlin nor fit punishment fer Sins—spare the rod and spoilt the child I say an so say others to—now ye may scrible in pease with no Babe to troble ye—God sav yer sinfull soul if he see fit tho I dout it—yer Humbel Servent—Prudence Feral

Chapter VI

In which our Heroine and her loyal Servant, Susannah, begin their Apprenticeship at Sea, and learn that the Sailor's life is not an easy one, tho' the Ship hath scarce left the Dock.

"MERCIFUL HEAVEN," said Susannah, "we must away upon the Instant to the Docks an' find that Seaman to whom Mrs. Prue sent me with her Letter. She'll no doubt be takin' Ship upon the *Cassandra*—O what a Fool was I not to read the Letter ere deliverin' it! 'Tis all me Fault, Mrs. Fanny. Dear God, I curse the Day that I was born." And with that, Susannah began to weep most piteously.

Seeing her give way to Grief, I could not do the same, tho' my Heart was heavy as Lead, and Panick reign'd supreme in my Soul. Oft' when our Friends shed bitter Tears, we must choke back our own, tho' we have more Reason to weep than they.

"No Fault of yours," said I, "but my own for putting so much Faith upon a Wet-Nurse's Philosophy." E'en in my Misery and Shock, I could not find it in my Heart to blame Susannah, so loyal had she been.

"Why, without your Care, I surely should have perish'd after the Flight of Isobel," said I. "I owe my Life to you, and e'en Belinda's. Come! We'll catch that Villain Mrs. Prue, and save the Babe!"

I bade Susannah toss sundry Belongings for both of us into a Portmanteau—nor did I forget my Romance nor my Foolscap and my Quills—whereupon we hasten'd to depart.

"What's this? What's afoot?" said Mrs. Wetton, for she saw us throwing on our Cloaks and making for the Door.

"Never ye mind," said Susannah. "Pray, attend to yer Potts, fer we shall want a good Supper when we return."

"I've half a Mind to quit yer Service," says the Cook, "what with all the goin's-on about this Place. There's many that wants a Chef o' my Stature, there is, and pays better, not to mention Vails."

"Then suit yerself," says Susannah brazenly. "Clear out ere we return. I'm sure Mrs. Fanny can find a better Cook than ye."

"Hmmph," says Wetton, "that'll be the Day."

For my own part, I hardly car'd at all, since 'neath my Chearful Demeanor I was suffus'd with Fear and Trembling for the Welfare of Belinda. Like a Sleep-Walker, I went thro' the Motions of Departure as if I were supremely confident of the Return of my Child; yet I felt as hollow within as I had felt full during my Pregnancy. If Belinda dy'd 'twould be as if my own right Arm were taken or my Beating Heart were pluckt out of my Chest. O I shudder'd e'en to think on't, and my Hair crawl'd upon my Scalp as if making ready to stand on End. I knew full well that without Belinda my Life would be worth nought to me; I would straggle thro' the Rest of my Days upon Earth like a Ghost that haunts the Scene of her violent Murder because she cannot conceive that she is dead.

We were just out the Door and preparing to beg, borrow, or steal a Chair or Coach to take us to the River, when I remember'd my red Garter, lying upon my Dressing Table. There was not a Moment to lose, yet I doubted not but the Garter was as necessary to the Happy Issue of our Adventure as any other Article of Clothing or Sentiment whatso'er—for, against all Reason, I suspected it possess'd Magical Pow'rs. 'Twas a foolish Belief, perhaps, but harmless enough in view of my present Plight.

"Quick, Susannah, fetch my Garter," said I. And then, thinking quickly that 'twas no bad Thing to have a Disguise or two at hand, I bade her fetch a few of the silken Masks and Costumes in which I had entertain'd Lord Bellars during my Lying-in. Heaven alone knew what tumultuous Adventures lay in store and 'twould be useful to have some Protection in the Form of a Disguise.

Susannah ran up the Stair, lugging the Portmanteau, and reappear'd a Moment or two later, the Portmanteau now stuff'd unto the Bursting Point.

By Luck, we commandeer'd a Hackney Hell Cart which, for one-and-six, was to take us to the Privy Stairs; but the Ride became a Purgatory of Delays, for London Traffick was e'en worse then than 'tis Today, and the Paving of the Streets was still in a most wretchèd and primitive State. Why, a Traveller would think the Town were a Hottentot Village rather than the Capital of the greatest Nation upon Earth! We were stopp'd ev'ry Minute by a great Jam of Chairs, Butchers' Waggons, Dung Carts, Brewers' Drays, as well as Cows, Turkeys, Pigs, Pedestrians, Peddlars, and Lone Riders upon horseback. O I was mad with the Delay!

After what seem'd an Eternity to my heavy Mother's Heart, we reach'd the Privy Stairs near Whitehall and hir'd a Pair of Oars to take us as far as the Wharves. We were in such Impatience to reach the *Cassandra* that we e'en risqued "shooting," as they call it, London Bridge (tho' both Susannah and I knew full well that not a Year went by without some Hapless Party being dasht to Bits against its tott'ring Arches). But I had more upon my Mind than my own Safety; and tho' 'twas not my Custom to shoot the Bridge—like most, I disembarqued in Upper Thames Street, then rejoin'd my Waterman at Billingsgate—upon this Occasion, I sneer'd at the other Passengers' Scruples and sail'd straight thro' with my Hair flying and my Heart pounding, whilst Susannah clung to me in Fear, crossing herself when she dar'd let go of me, and mutt'ring of Angels in Heaven.

I myself was in a State akin to Lunacy; tho' I laugh'd and clapp'd the Waterman upon the Back after we'd safely clear'd the Bridge, 'twas not the Laughter of Mirth, I laugh'd, but the Laughter of Panick. My Mood was like the Water of the Thames, glist'ning with Sunlight up above, but stinking with Offal down below. Not e'en Susannah could perceive how I felt, for from the very first Moment when I view'd that desolate, empty Cradle, I had thrown myself into a Frenzy which maskt my deepest Grief. I was determin'd to brave any Peril till I should find my Babe, and I seem'd to be infus'd with a Determination beyond any I'd known my whole Life long.

Reaching the Wharves, at last, Susannah and I were astounded by the Flurry of Activity our Eyes beheld. Ne'er had I seen such a Crowd of Masts, wobbling upon the Water like a curious Forest seen by a Fellow who has had one Port of Ale too many. Red-faced Fishwives with Baskets of Fish upon their Heads and stout Pipes clench'd within their rotten Teeth, sold their Fishy Wares at the Water's Edge, whilst Bum-Boat Women in little Skiffs ply'd the Waters in the Wake of the Great Merchantmen, selling all Manner of Grog and Provisions, doubtless priced well above their Worth, to the Tars who leant from their Ships to purchase 'em.

Press-Gangs rov'd the Streets in search of such poor Unfortunates as they might o'erpower with Cudgels and drag, all unwilling, aboard their Men o' War; and Trollops of a sort so pitiable that they made the Trollops who ply'd St. James' Park look like Queens, rov'd in search of Swains who might pay 'em a Shilling, or e'en a few Ha'pennies, for a quick bit o' Mutton in an Alley.

Many great Ships were loading up Provisions and Ballast for Sea-Voyages, and Hogsheads of Wine were being roll'd along the Docks by stout-shoulder'd Fellows who shouted more Curses to each other in a trice, than one might hear e'en upon the Thames. But by far the most curious Sight my Eyes had e'er beheld was the Vision of a Cow, bellowing with grievous Indignation, as she was hoisted up by Means of Ropes about her Middle and Pulleys attach'd to one of the Masts, swung thro' the Air, and lower'd into the Hold of a Ship. I knew little enough of Sea-Travel—but for what Lancelot and Horatio had told me of their Adventures—yet it had scarce occurr'd to me that live Cattle were taken to Sea in such a Manner.

O think of the Calf, born in a bright Spring Field, the bluish Sack still enclosing her tiny Form and 'neath it her Fur still glist'ning with the Waters of the Womb, who stands up on shaky Legs and frolicks but one Summer 'neath the Teats of her Mother, only to grow tall enough to be sent to Sea as Food for rough, felonious Tars! Think, too, of the Puzzlement of that same Calf if the Ship should chance to founder and she should bellow her Way down to a watery Grave, or chance to fall betwixt the ungentle Teeth of a Shark! Ah the Loss of Belinda had set my Mind on edge and brought me to the perilous Brink of Madness!

Much encumber'd by the Heaviness of our Portmanteau, Susannah and I made Enquiries regarding the *Cassandra*, for we saw no Ship by that Name at the Docks—tho' Susannah swore it had been dockt here a few Days before. Many of the Tars we approach'd would scarce speak to us, save swinishly, for they took us for Tarts who would solicit 'em and we had a Devil of a Time disabusing 'em of that Notion. At last, finding an old Seaman who seem'd rather sober and kindly-faced, I enquir'd of him whether the *Cassandra* was dockt here or no and he told me the following News:

"That she was, Lass, an' took on Cargo an' Provision fer a Voyage to the Colonies, but she departed fer Gravesend at Dawn, she did, with a Hold full o' Woollens an' Cottons, an' a Crew o' one hundred an' five men."

"At Dawn, say you?"

"At Dawn," said the Seaman.

Thunderstruck, I turn'd to Susannah: "Then how could Prudence and the Babe be aboard, since they could not have sail'd at Dawn?"

"Damn me Eyes!" said the old Salt. "An ugly old Dam an' her suckling Babe was 'ere not half a Day ago searchin' out a Yawl or Skiff to take 'em to the *Cassandra*!"

"That's my Babe!" I cried, looking at the Man as if he were the Messiah Himself. "She's kidnapp'd my Babe!"

"An' ye'll 'ave others, too, Lass, young as ye are," said the old Tar, as if this Piece of News would soothe me. I could scarce believe my Ears! Did he think I would so lightly abandon my Child upon the Hope of others? Had he ne'er seen a Woman give birth, that he thought it such a Trifle, a Fiddling Thing—like buying a Pott of Paint and losing it in a Hackney Coach, or e'en losing a gold Watch Case to a Cut-Purse?

"Pray, Sir, could they reach the *Cassandra* by Means of a Yawl?" Susannah askt.

"That they could, I'll warrant, an' the Tide were with 'em," said the Tar.

"An' could we reach 'em by the same Means?" Susannah press'd on.

"Doubtless, Lass, fer if I'm not mistaken, the ugly old Dam sail'd ere Noon an' 'tis well past Five o'Clock."

At this News I fell to my Knees upon the Ground and wept most piteously. O the Loss of Lancelot could I bear, and the Loss of Isobel, and the Loss of my curious Protector Lord Bellars, but the Loss of Belinda was the Blow of Blows. 'Twas the *Coup de Grâce* from which one ne'er rises above bended Knee save as a Wraith.

Seeing me weeping so, the Old Tar took Pity, bestirr'd himself from his Seat upon a Puncheon of Rum, and telling us not to go, but to wait upon him just there, he busied himself amongst the Sailors upon the Docks, querying them concerning some Matter I could not o'erhear.

I wept—first upon the Ground, then in Susannah's tender Arms—whilst I silently swore to put a fatal Period to my wretchèd Existence by drowning myself in the Thames should Belinda not be recover'd.

The Tar came back, as promis'd, with the News that a Brigantine call'd the *Hopewell* was due to sail upon the next Tide for the Colonies. He had begg'd the First Mate of the Ship to take us along, he said, to which the Man had adamantly refus'd; but perhaps were we to prevail upon him our-

370

selves—the old Tar said, looking Goats and Monkies at us—we should have better Luck. Moreo'er, since a Brigantine was a much speedier Sailor than a Merchantman, we should quickly o'ertake the *Cassandra* upon the Seas, or e'en, perhaps, catch her in the Downs, if she were detain'd there by contrary Winds, a not infrequent Occurrence.

I knew not Brigantine from Merchantman from Sloop from Schooner in my Ignorance of Sailing then, nor did I know a contrary Wind from a fair one, but this News so renew'd my Hope and rais'd my Spirits that, thanking the Tar profusely for his Pains, I took Susannah by the Hand and proceeded towards the First Mate of the *Hopewell*.

He was a cantankerous Fellow, gruff, pockmarkt, Peglegg'd; he lookt me and Susannah up and down as if he knew full well what lay 'neath our Petticoats and was having none of it. Behind him, I caught a Glimpse of the *Hopewell*, riding at Anchor upon the Water. She was two-masted, and seem'd a good deal smaller than the three-masted Merchantmen, but Sea-worthy enough to my unpractis'd Eyes.

"Please, Sir," Susannah began without waiting for me. "Me Mistress' belovèd Babe hath been kidnapp'd an' carried aboard the *Cassandra*. We must away to catch her. Pray, Sir, take Pity on two helpless Wenches an' let us sail with ye. . . ." (Susannah, who well knew how to be gruff when the Occasion demanded it, had also at her Command the most honey'd and beguiling Phrases when such were necessary. 'Tis clear that the Life of a Mulatto Slave creates such Virtuosity in the Face of Adversity. O I envied Susannah for her Guile, since surely it had help'd her to survive.)

"Dye an' be damn'd," said the gruff Seaman, spitting Tobacco Juice upon the Ground. "I'll 'ave no Women aboard, makin' Trouble amongst me Crew—the mutinous Dogs. With Women aboard, there's nought but Brawlin' in the Fo'c'sle, an' Gamin' on the Decks, an' all Manner o' Mischief in the Steerage."

At this, Susannah's Face fell and she lookt so pitiable that e'en a Hangman would have wept to see her.

"Don't make such a Face, Lass," says the First Mate of the *Hopewell*—"lucky ye are to miss a long Sea-Voyage. Why, 'ave ye e'er crackt a Biskit an' found it full o' Weevils, or et Meat so rotten ye had to hold yer Nose to chew it? Or wrapp'd yerself in an old bit o' Sail 'gainst the Rats, or been drench'd to the Bone by a Storm at Sea? Why, pretty Wenches like the two o' ye want none o' that! Shipboard Life is hard, Lasses. Ye best stay 'ere in London an' seek yer Fortunes!"

With that, Susannah fell to her Knees yet again and began to cry.

"An't please ye, Sir," said she, betwixt her Sobs, "we'll e'en dress as Men an' stay out o' the Way o' yer Tars, but ye must take Pity on us, fer me Mistress' Heart is broken with the Loss o' her Babe, an' if ye'll not take us aboard, she'll sure perish o' Grief."

Most privily, Susannah took this Opportunity of being upon bended Knee to reach into the stuff'd Portmanteau and extract from it a jewell'd Necklace of glitt'ring Diamonds which Lord Bellars had given me during my Lying-in (and which I was utterly astounded to see, thinking it had long since gone to pay our Creditors!). Rising from her Knees, she convey'd it into the waiting Hand of the First Mate of the *Hopewell*, whereupon his Eyes widen'd in Greed, but he at first pretended Indiff'rence. Incredulous as I was at Susannah's Cleverness in keeping this Bauble in readiness 'gainst, as 'twere, a rainy Day, I could scarce say a Word. What a splendid Wench Susannah was! Had the Management of our Affairs been left to me, sure not a single Jewel would have remain'd with which to barter for Belinda!

I watch'd all this with Amazement and Admiration, for before long, despite his gruff Refusals and Allegations that the Bauble must be stolen, together with his staunch Avowals that since we were neither Carpenters, Surgeons, Sail-Makers, nor Musicians, we were quite useless at Sea, our Fortunes had improv'd to such a Degree that the First Mate agreed to let us sail upon the *Hopewell* in Man's Disguise!

"But I'll have no Mischief below Decks," said he, "or I'll toss ye in the Drink, d'ye hear?"

To which we solemnly swore to be good as Nuns in a Cloister, and we begg'd of him some old Linen and Trowsers into which we might change as Disguise. Then we made haste to find a Doorway or Alleyway where we could slip into these ragged Clothes unobserv'd. (We were fortunate to find an open Warehouse—guarded only by a half-blind old Watchman—and there, behind some Tuns of Wine, we transform'd ourselves into Tars!) This being accomplish'd, we hasten'd back to the First Mate of the *Hopewell*, lest he change his Mind in our Absence and depart without us.

"Do we not look like proper Tars?" askt Susannah coyly, curtseying before our mercenary Saviour. We lookt so quaint

372

that e'en this gruff Fellow had to smile, for, to be sure, his cast-off Clothes lookt better upon us than they e'er had done upon him. But then he quickly resum'd his gruff Composure and fell to warning us again.

"Seamen is a superstitious Lot, Sweethearts, an' if they know there's Women aboard, 'twill cause no end o' talk o' Curses an' Bad Luck fer the Voyage, not to mention the Brawlin' that'll go on fer the two o' ye. So I'm warnin' ye now that I've a Mind to keep ye hid in my Cabin an' if ye go so far as the Fo'c'sle without me Leave, I'll tye ye together like any Common Cut-Throats an' drop ye in the Briny Deep, d'ye 'ear?" Whereupon we again promis'd to be good as Gold; and Susannah repeated that perhaps we should find the *Cassandra* awaiting a Fair Wind in the Downs, in which case we should not need to trouble him further. Then we both fell upon bended Knee to proffer our Thanks.

The First Mate of the *Hopewell* (whose Name, by the by, was Mr. Cocklyn) hurried us aboard, carrying our stuff'd Portmanteau; for he said he wanted us safely stow'd in his Cabin before the Tars could look us o'er properly (and perhaps discover us for the Women we were).

I was astounded by the Smallness of the good Ship *Hopewell*! When Lancelot and Horatio had recounted their grave and glorious Adventures at Sea, I had envision'd grand Galleons, their Sails billowing in the Wind, their Cabins outfitted like Pyrate Palaces, and their Holds awash with Ducats and Doubloons, Crusadoes and Crowns, Shillings and Guineas, Louis d'Ors from France and Golden Mohurs from the East Indies! But alas, the Reality of these Ships was quite diff'rent. The Brigantine *Hopewell* was but sixty Foot long and less than twenty Foot wide. She had a Fo'c'sle which also serv'd as Galley, one Great Cabin for the Captain (which was more Cabin than great, i'faith), a little Cabin behind it for the First Mate, and an e'en smaller Cabin behind *that* for the Steward, the Surgeon, and the Surgeon's Mate. The Majority of the Tars had not yet boarded, and already the Ship was so crowded, 'twas impossible to imagine how there should be room e'en for the smallish Crew that sail'd her!

Susannah and I were install'd into narrow Berths in the First Mate's Cabin, where we soon discover'd our Pallets to be alive with Lice and the Floors to be veritable Ballrooms for Assemblies of audacious Rats. The whole Ship had the most unsavoury Odour of Bilge Water mingl'd with the Scent of putrefied Cheese, and truly, had I not been in search of

373

my belovèd Babe, I would have quit that detestable Place forthwith; for it stank worse than Newgate itself and made the latter appear as a Palace—in Space, if not in Stench!

Was this how the New World had been discover'd, in Tubs such as this? And had the lusty, bawdy Buccaneers, those fearsome Fellows out of Esquemeling's Pages, sail'd the Seas *thus*? Why then, they were far braver than I dreamt! For just to live aboard such a stinking Prison as this Ship took Courage. And what of William Dampier, Bartholomew Sharp, Lionel Wafer, Basil Ringrose—all those canny Chroniclers of the Pyrate Round—did they *too* take ship in such old Tubs?

Mr. Cocklyn must have seen my Distaste upon my Visage as he install'd Susannah and me in our Berths, for he now gave vent to a Panegyrick upon the *Hopewell*, which was design'd to make us appreciate our Good Fortune.

"Damme," said Cocklyn, "the Devil an' his Dam blow me from the Shrouds if this be not the finest Brigantine e'er to sail the Seven Seas! Why, she was built scarce four Year ago, an' rigg'd in the latest Fashion—square on her Foremast, fore-an'-aft on her Mainmast—which makes a more weatherly Rig than a square-rigg'd Brig an', when close-haul'd upon the Wind, will beat any Brig, Flute, or Merchantman whatsoe'er in Fair Weather or Foul! An' as fer Comfort, why Lasses, there's plenty o' Ships where the Crew sleeps in Hammocks, not good solid Berths, an' where the Rations is scantier than these! We've Salt Pork ev'ry Day, not Pease one Day an' Pork the next, an' Cheshire Cheese, an' Grog aplenty to go 'round!"

"A fine Ship indeed," said Susannah, who was the Soul of Diplomacy when the Occasion demanded it, for she quickly grasp'd that Cocklyn lov'd this Ship as he did his own Mother and to insult it was to dishonour him and perhaps to imperil our Search.

"Yes, yes, a fine Ship indeed," said I, taking my Cue from Susannah. "Why the Rig is more weatherly than any I've seen—and modern, too."

At that, Cocklyn's Face lit up with Pleasure, tho' he must have known I was but parroting his Words. Ah, La Rochefoucauld is right in saying that when we complain of Flattery, we are but complaining that it is not artfully enough done! For Flattery is the Universal Lubricant; it greases the Wheels of Commerce and Industry, creates Good Will both in the midst of Courtly Pomp and upon Humble Hearth; and it e'en eases the Path to Glory of the Dauber or the Scribbler (tho' the Latter both pretend to be above it).

"That's right, Lasses, she's a fine Ship, a fine Ship, indeed. Why, if yer good, I may teach ye a bit o' Sailin' an' make ye useful aboard, fer yer outward bound on the finest Brigantine upon the Atlantick an' ye'll not be sorry ye sail'd with her!" In a few short Minutes Cocklyn had gone from trumpeting the Miseries of Sea-Travel to praising his belovèd Brigantine; 'twould have been comical did not Belinda's Life depend upon it!

After Cocklyn took leave of us, Susannah and I settl'd ourselves as comfortably as we could in the dreadful Cabin and lookt at each other with Foreboding, wond'ring what more the Fates might have in store after this.

"There's nought to do now but pray," said Susannah, falling to her Knees upon the Floor of the Cabin, for Susannah, I have perhaps neglected to tell, was notable for her Belief that she was one of few Mortals upon Earth who had direct Access to God's Ear and that her Pray'rs were heard when others' were crassly ignor'd. The Vicissitudes of her Early Life had endu'd her with a curious Notion of God, deriv'd in part from her Quaker Mistress, in part from her deprav'd Master (who'd fancied little Girls), and in part from the young Thieves and Chimney Sweeps with whom she'd cavorted before I met her. She'd a pow'rful Belief in the Devil, whom she conceiv'd was at Work whene'er a Pott boil'd o'er, a Catarrh linger'd, or a Guinea was lost; but likewise she'd a pow'rful Belief in God, whom she believ'd had a more sympathetick Ear to Black Voices than to White ones, owing to the greater Suff'rings of their Posssesors. Likewise, she conceiv'd that she must intercede with Heaven upon my Behalf, for Heaven would not hear me without her Pray'rs, and 'twas her Duty to save my Soul as well as care for my Body. She took her Rôle as Servant in a most spiritual Sense and was resolv'd to succour my Immortal Soul as well as attend to my grosser physical Needs. Thus charged with the weighty Matter of my Salvation as well as her own, she had near worn out her Knees with Praying since she came into my Service.

Whilst Susannah pray'd and mutter'd upon bended Knee, I myself knelt to beseech Heaven, and most especially the Great Goddess, upon whose Holiness Isobel and the Witches had insisted. O I would ne'er tell Susannah of the Witches' Coven lest she think me a Worshipper of the very Devil she fear'd, but how could I explain to her that Witchcraft was not what it appear'd, that, i'faith, 'twas a Creed she would approve if only she knew its Essence as I did?

I whisper'd to Heaven the Words a fond Mother whispers as she kneels by her Babe's Cradle, looking down at the sleeping Angel born out of her own Body, with its golden Eyelashes flutt'ring upon its Sleep-flusht Cheaks, and its tender pink Lips clos'd o'er toothless Gums.

"May you brave the Dangers of Childhood, my Darling, my Daughter, my Fledgling, my Phoenix, and rise out of the Mists of Infancy to clothe yourself in the fine Flesh of Womanhood, growing from the unform'd Babe into the perfected Woman, who glides with Assurance thro' this perilous World, having slipp'd past all the Devastations of Disease, the myriad Calamities of Childhood, to come away miraculously unscath'd, holding your Head high in the Radiance of Womanhood, walking with straight, swift Legs along the Paths of your Destiny, to find at last the True Mission for which the Goddess placed you here upon this Earth, and to fulfill it with Joy and Vigour—this is your Mother's Pray'r."

So saying to myself, I fell prostrate upon the Floor and wept an Ocean of Tears on whose Tide we might sail away in search of Belinda, who now seem'd as far as the Land of Eldorado or the Fountain of Eternal Youth, and infinitely more precious.

Chapter VII

Containing a Storm at Sea, a Scene which should perhaps be skipp'd o'er by those with squeamish Stomachs, and the Entrance into our History of the notorious Captain Whitehead.

As Susannah and I remain'd virtual Prisoners in the Cabin during the Sailing, I did not observe the Activity upon Deck as the *Hopewell* broke Ground, weigh'd Anchor, or whate'er 'tis the Seamen call it, upon her Passage thro' the Thames to Gravesend, and thither towards the Downs. Ne'ertheless, from the Creaking of the Ship's Timbers and the continual Shouting that went on above us, not to mention the Thunder of Seamen's Feet directly above our Heads, 'twas apparent we were outward bound.

For most of the Ev'ning we were left alone whilst the First Mate attended to his Duties upon Deck. 'Twas customary in those Times for Pilots to take Ships to the Open Sea, and for the haughty Captains to come aboard later when all such mundane Tasks were accomplish'd. Just when Captain Whitehead boarded, I know not, owing to my Imprisonment. I can only say that I caught no Glimpse of Sea nor Sky until Mr. Cocklyn came to fetch us at Dawn. For in our Weariness from the Exertions and Agitations of the Day, Susannah and I had fallen asleep and were dead to this World until then (I was dreaming myself back in Lymeworth with Belinda), when a rouzing Shake from Mr. Cocklyn brought me to my Senses and reminded me of the Misery of my Plight.

"Come, Lasses," says Cocklyn, "I'll take ye up on Deck, fer we're anchor'd off North Foreland in nine-fathom water, and 'tis a lovely Sight at Dawn."

We were swiftly hustl'd out of our Berths and brought up on Deck in the beauteous Glow of early Morn, whereupon our wond'ring Eyes beheld the shimm'ring Sea Light, suffus'd with Rose, which is Nature's Gift to Mariners in return for the Harshness of their Lives.

Many Ships lay at Anchor around us. I spy'd the *John & Martha* ("a fine Galley o' twenty Guns," said Cocklyn); the *Delicia* ("a beggarly Brigantine, not half so Sea-worthy as the *Hopewell*"); the Sloop *Childhood,* out of New Providence ("a well-known Pyrate Port"); and many other tall Ships with curious Names such as *Paradox, Pelican, Batchelor's Adventure,* and *Merry Christmas.* But the *Cassandra* was no-where to be seen, e'en thro' the Spying-Glass Cocklyn proffer'd.

" 'Tis no Matter, Lasses," Cocklyn said, "we may yet catch her ere we come thro' the Channel."

Thro' the Spying-Glass I could see Tars on neighbouring Ships scampering up the Shrouds and Masts like so many barefoot Monkies. All the Particulars of Sea-Travel amaz'd me, but I was very much surpriz'd by the raggamuffin Look of the Tars and the strenuous Exertions of their Tasks. I had scarce dreamt that Sailing made Monkies of Men, and I fancied that an agile Woman might do as well as any Tar—nay, better.

I did not share my Thoughts with Cocklyn, but instead distracted myself from my constant Worry o'er Belinda's Fate by asking him to tell us a bit more concerning the Design of Ships—for some had two Masts, some three, some only one, and I doubted not but these Distinctions were of great Importance.

"That they are, Lasses," said Cocklyn, pleas'd to be askt to discourse of Ships, his favourite Subject in all this Watery World. "The one-masted Ship ye see there—the *Childhood*—is a Sloop, belov'd by Pyrates an' Smugglers—fer she's swift as the Wind, fore-an'-aft-rigg'd, but fer her square Topsail, an' she'll go as quick as twelve Knots in a Fair Wind. But with so much Sail, she's a Bitch in a Gale, an' many's the Time I've seen the Tars scurryin' to saw away the Mast ere the Wind heels 'em o'er into the Drink. With a Sloop in a Storm, ye might as well kiss yer Arse Goodbye—beggin' yer Pardon, Ladies. Now, that Ship there, the *Delicia,* is call'd a Brigantine like our own Vessel here—tho' to my Mind she's an old Tub an' not e'en Worthy o' the fine Name o' Brigantine. She's two-masted, square-rigg'd on both Main an' Fore—which drives fair enough in a quarterin' Wind but is well-night useless when sailin' to Windward. The *Hopewell* here is fore-an'-aft-rigg'd on the Mainmast an' square on the Fore-mast—which makes a more—"

"Weatherly Rig?" askt Susannah, who also knew a bit of

Sea Lingo from her Childhood Travels, and anyway could parrot as well as I.

"Correct, Lass!" said Cocklyn, beaming. "Now, that Ship there"—he indicated a Three-master call'd the *Rover*—"is one o' yer biggest Merchant Ships afloat, a West Indiaman. She's seven hundred tons, with a main Deck one hundred sixty Foot long an' near thirty-six Foot wide. She'll carry as many as three hundred in Crew an' fifty-four Cannon—tho' she scarce carries e'en twenty-five since she'd rather have the Space fer Cargo. She's got a gilded Stern with a fine painted Taffarel an' she's square-rigg'd on all her Masts—Fore, Main, an' Mizzen—so she's not the swiftest Sailor, save in a quarterin' Wind; but fer Space an' Cannon Pow'r, she's unbeatable, tho' I'd rather sail a Brigantine in any Weather."

"Do they really saw away the Mast," I askt, "when in Danger of Shipwreck?"

"That they do, Lass, fer it keeps the Ship on an even Keel when ye clear the Decks in a Storm."

"And pray, how do they return Home with no Sail?" I askt.

"Slowly, me Lasses, slowly," said the First Mate of the *Hopewell*, laughing.

I tried to imagine the *Hopewell* without her Masts. How should we get back to London? Would we merely float until some kindly Vessel rescu'd us? 'Twas a terrifying Prospect. But clearly, 'twas not one Cocklyn car'd to linger o'er, for in a trice he gloss'd o'er my Question and went on to describe various Rigs to us, naming the Sails from Foreskysail to Cross-Jack, from Flying-Jib Boom to Spanker. Likewise he pointed out the Parts of the Ship from Bowsprit to Dolphin-Striker to Taffarel, but I thought 'twould be Years before I got 'em all right, so many were they, and so odd. Cocklyn told us the Diff'rence betwixt a Flute and a Merchantman ("The Flute is a Two-master o' Dutch Design, square-rigg'd an' with plenteous Space fer Cargo, owin' to her great flat Bottom—like an old Amsterdam Whore!"). And also the Diff'rence betwixt a Navy Snow and a square-rigg'd Brigantine ("She's got a fore-an'-aft Trysail, the Snow has, which gives Speed in a quarterin' Wind."). He e'en show'd us, thro' the Glass, a great Man o' War of 360 Tons and twenty-six Guns, which he said could beat any Pyrates in the Caribee (tho' a Ship of the Line mounted sixty Cannon at least), but my Thoughts drifted to Belinda in all this Talk and I could not keep my Mind upon sailing Gibberish, e'en if both our Lives might depend upon it.

"I hope you are learning all this well," I said to Susannah, "for 'tis beyond me."

"Nonsense, Lass," said Cocklyn, "ye'll be a fine Sailor in a Matter o' Days, mark me Words." Whereupon he bade us return to the Cabin forthwith since the Watch was about to change and he did not want our Presence upon Deck to raise Questions.

Thro' all this Time aboard, Cocklyn had offer'd no Lewdness to our Persons, notwithstanding our being both Messmates and Cabinmates. I suspected such a Situation was too good to last, for why should he have taken us aboard save to be his private Whores, and would he not soon wish to collect what he deem'd his Due?

We had been sav'd up till now, I reckon'd, by the Business of getting the Voyage under way, but soon we should have to submit to his pockmarkt, Peg-legg'd am'rous Advances. I shudder'd to think on't.

Before too long we had weigh'd Anchor again and were under Sail on our Way to the Downs, where we did not tarry owing to an Easterly Wind (so Cocklyn later told us) which took us, with great Dispatch, 'round the Isle of Wight, and thro' the choppy and blust'ry Channel. I long'd to go up on Deck to see if the *Cassandra* might be sighted, but Cocklyn swore he would call me at the first Sighting of her and, more than that, would make certain I boarded her if such were possible. He swore upon a Bible that he'd seen neither Stem nor Stern of her and he reckon'd that the favourable Wind had set her upon her Course for the Azores a Day or so before us. Yet despite her earlier Start, we might still catch up with her at Sea, said he, for our Route was much the same, namely, south to the Azores, across the Atlantick to the Bahamas, then up the Coast of the Colonies from Charlestown to New York, to New Providence, to Boston. I was not at all certain I trusted him to call us if the *Cassandra* were sighted, nor did I have any Way of knowing if indeed he were lying to me, ne'ertheless what could I do but stay close to my Berth and pray for Belinda's Deliverance? Cocklyn had ne'er ceas'd swearing to tye us together like Malefactors and drown us both should we disobey his Orders.

"God," Susannah said soberly, "takes care o' Fools an' Babes. Belinda shall not perish. That I may promise ye since the Angel promis'd it to me." I lookt at her with Desperation, wanting with all my Heart to believe her, hoping I was not deceiving myself mightily. Susannah was fore'er hearing the Voices of Angels and Demons—and since I heard 'em not, I was obliged to use her as a sort of Post-Boy betwixt me and the Supreme Being.

Going thro' the Channel, the Ship pitch'd and toss'd extreamly and the Unsavouriness of our Mess, combin'd with the Motion of the Ship, made me most grievously ill. I had ne'er been Sea-sick before (having ne'er been at Sea before!) but, i'faith 'twas so unpleasant an Experience that I vow'd to eat no more than barely necessary for Survival thro' all the Rest of this Voyage. The Distemper in my Stomach together with my regrettable Discovery that certain diminutive Visitors had come to sojourn in my long red Hair (without so much as a By-Your-Leave) made me miserable in the extream. When Cocklyn return'd to the Cabin to inform us that we were well upon our Way (and to make it plain that he now desir'd Payment in Flesh for his Magnanimity in carrying us aboard), 'twas all I could do to keep from vomiting upon his loathsome Person.

"I've a Mind to board ye both, Lasses," said Cocklyn, as if this were the very Apogee of Wit, "but with yer Decks awash so, I'll 'ave to save me Sail fer a better Wind, tho' me Bowsprit is sound as any, ho, ho!"

Susannah, who was an excellent Sailor, and bearing up far better than myself, thought she might as well pacify the old Tar's Lust and keep him from bothering me; for Am'rous Dalliance represented no Sin to her if 'twere the Price of Survival. So she offer'd herself quite graciously to Cocklyn, who was upon the Point of accepting her Blandishments with Gusto (mutt'ring of the clever Things he could do with his Peg-Leg) when the Wind blew up such a Gale that all three of us were knockt clear across the Cabin amongst our slithering, sliding Possessions. E'en the Rats took Shelter in their Holes in such a Gale!

"O 'tis nothin' but a Capful o' Wind," says Cocklyn, grabbing for Susannah upon the Cabin Floor.

"A Capful? A Capful?" I cried in Distress. "If that be not a Tempest, then I know not what the Word means!"

The Ship's Timbers creakt mightily, the Floor heav'd up under us as if propell'd by a Rift in Hell itself, and we could already hear the Clanking of the Chain Pumps, the Shouts of the Crew, and the Wind howling like a Demon thro' the Shrouds.

"A Tempest!" laugh'd Cocklyn, grappling for Susannah.
"By Jove—if ye call that a Tempest, what'll ye call it when
we've a *real* Tempest! Peep out above Deck, me Girl, and
have a Look at yer Tempest. 'Twill do yer Stomach good to
have a bit o' Fresh Air."

In his Zest to ravish Susannah, Cocklyn had forgotten all
his previous Warnings about not showing my Face above
Deck. I dragg'd myself along the Cabin Floor to the ladder,
climb'd it with unsteady Feet, and soon found myself looking
out o'er the most terrifying Prospect my Eyes had e'er beheld.
The Waters of the Sea had turn'd from glitt'ring blue to
blackish green and they swell'd up into liquid Mountains
upon which our Ship perch'd for a perilous Instant before
being dropp'd into the Valley below. Sometimes, whilst in the
Valley, we rode betwixt two mountainous Waves which
threaten'd to break above our Heads and sweep us away to a
watery Grave without a Moment's Hesitation. Our Masts
trembl'd and quiver'd like Reeds in the Wind; our Sails were
ripp'd and torn; and our Tars ran to and fro not knowing
what to do first. Some clung to the Shrouds straining to see
what had become of other Ships around us (as if that might
portend our Fate) and some hung on to the Yards like veritable Monkeys, essaying to straighten the torn and flapping
Sails; others scurried to man the Pumps, shouting that all was
lost, we should surely founder; and still others fell to bended
Knee in Pray'r. I saw a Man blown from the Bowsprit and
drown'd faster than a wicked Child can drown an Insect in a
garden Rivulet. I saw the Sea go Mountains high, break upon
our Deck once, twice, thrice, until I thought that with one
more Crash of Water, we should surely be split in twain. And
yet, tho' the Decks were pounded and drown'd, we somehow
did not crack, tho' all around us, Ships were foundering, or
cutting down their Masts, e'en before the Wind could do it
for 'em.

Thro' all this Disaster, Cocklyn was below, making love to
Susannah, caring little for the Fate of his Men. And a sorry
Fate 'twas indeed, for one Man was flung from a Yardarm
and suffer'd both a broken Arm and a broken Leg (which
later, I heard, had to be amputated), and one was drown'd,
as I have said, and another was washt o'erboard but managed
to sustain himself by holding fast to a floating Spar until one
of his Messmates risqued his own Life to pull him out of the
Drink.

Before this, I'd no very real Idea of the Perils of Sea-

Travel. O I had read all the Travel Books which a bookish Young Lady dreams o'er, and I had fancied 'twas a Pity my Sex forbade me the Privilege of going to Sea as a Cabin Boy to seek my Fortune! But ne'er did I imagine Sea-Sickness, nor Lice, nor rotted Salt Pork, nor soggy Biskit, nor spoilt Water, nor, most especially, the Perils of a Storm at Sea. For 'tis one Thing to read of Tempests and another to understand quite quickly how little stands betwixt your own Flesh and Bone and the mountainous Waves. Why, we might as well have gone to Sea in a Thimble as in this Brigantine! 'Twas ev'ry bit as small when consider'd against the Immensity of the Sea.

Somewhere in that Immensity was Belinda. I had as much Chance to find her as to find one particular Pebble upon a Stretch of rocky Beach, or one Grain of Sand in a Glass, or one Drop of Wine in an Oaken Cask that hath sprung a Leak. 'Twould require potent Magick indeed—more potent than the Magick of the Witches, more potent than the Magick that had heal'd my Belly, more potent than the Magick that had spar'd my Life in Childbed—to find Belinda in this Troubl'd Sea, which was my Destiny.

But just as I was musing thus, the Storm seem'd to blow away as fast as it had risen up. Suddenly the Seas calm'd, the Air clear'd, and where black Clouds had lain, murderous and low o'er the Face of Heaven, there was suddenly a Rainbow. Ah, it glitter'd and shimmer'd as if in Revelation of the Existence of Miracles despite Human Despair. And 'twas as marvellous as Rainbows are said to be; a Promise, a Covenant, a Sign. The Tars fell to their leathery Knees to thank God; for the Masts still stood in good Repair and the Sails could be repair'd in Time. The Tempest had pass'd.

With the immediate Danger o'er, Cocklyn's Presence was miss'd. A Messmate of the Tar who had been flung from the Bowsprit into the Sea and drown'd, began calling for Cocklyn in an angry Voice, vowing Vengeance, blaming his Friend's Death upon the First Mate. Perhaps 'twas an old Quarrel they had, but the Tar, who was a rough Welshman, sounded as if he could ne'er be pacified.

"I've sail'd the Seven Seas," said he, "since I was a Lad o' Eight—an' I've ne'er seen a First Mate so callous to the Fate o' his Men. I'll kill the mangy Dog, the Son o' a Bitch, the Cur!" (Indeed, the whole time I was at Sea, I wonder'd about this Habit the Tars had of calling each other Dogs—for those playful, loving, four-legg'd Creatures are, to my mind, far more meritorious than any Humans—particularly those Humans whose Calling 'tis to sail the Seas!)

"Cocklyn, ye Dog!" cried the Welsh Tar, descending the Ladder where I still stood peeping above Deck. He pusht me roughly aside (whereupon I lower'd myself hastily, making way for him, since 'twas clear he was in a Devil of a Humour).

Leaping the last few Ladder Rungs into Cocklyn's Cabin, he found the First Mate with his Breeches gaping, and Susannah with her woollen Sailor's Shirt sufficiently unbutton'd to make her Sex quite plain.

"Swine! Cur! Ye'll pay fer the Death o' Thomas!" (Thomas, to be sure, was the Name of his drown'd Friend.)

He pounced upon Cocklyn with such Fury that it seem'd he might rush him with his bare Arms. I saw a Dagger twinkle at his Waist; in a trice, 'twas in his Hand. Cocklyn, for his part, grabb'd Susannah to him, using her as a sort of Shield for his Body.

"Would ye kill this defenceless Wench, then?" cried he, ripping open the remaining woollen Cloth that conceal'd her coffee-colour'd Breasts with their Nipples the Colour of Chocolate. Susannah mutter'd Pray'rs for Deliverance as Cocklyn hopp'd about the Cabin with her, tapping his wooden Leg, and using her bare and beauteous Breast as if 'twere the Shield of Achilles, forged by the God of War himself.

"Ye Cowardly Cur!" scream'd the Welsh Tar. "I'll teach ye to use a Wench fer yer Armor!" Whereupon he fell upon all fours, and with a deft, well-placed Stroke of his practis'd Dagger, pinion'd Cocklyn's one sound Foot to the Floor.

Now Cocklyn howl'd like the Hound of Hell, let go of Susannah (who took this Opportunity to make good her Escape), and tapp'd his Peg-Leg upon the Floor in sheerest Agony. But the more he pull'd and tapp'd, the more Blood spill'd from his sound Foot, which, I reckon'd, would not be sound for long.

The Cabin had fill'd with Tars now and they were already gaming o'er the Issue of this Single Combat, wagering Doubloons and Guineas, Pistols, Cutlasses and Muskets, Rations of Rum, Water, and e'en Salt Pork and Pease. Men who had no Weapons and no Money and had e'en lost the Clothes upon their Backs in other Wagers, stak'd their future Pay, their Pills or Potions to cure Clap—if these were all the Riches they possess'd!

Cocklyn, I soon saw, was no popular Fellow with the

Crew, for most of the Sailors put their Faith in the Victory of the Welshman, whose Name, it appear'd, was Llewelyn. He was favour'd to win, and indeed he had commenced his Victory by staking Cocklyn's Foot, but each Time he came near the First Mate, the Latter so deftly cockt his Peg-Leg as to frighten Llewelyn with dire Damage to his Privities. This horrid Spectacle continu'd for a Time, Cocklyn's crucified Foot bleeding heavily whilst he stabb'd the Air with his Peg-Leg, and Llewelyn dancing about the Room like a Pugilist. Yet Llewelyn was too Blood-thirsty to be content with such paltry Torture and Cocklyn was in too much Pain to continue thus for long. Suddenly, Llewelyn drew another Dagger from I knew not where (perhaps a fellow Seaman stealthily slipp'd it to him) and, going up behind Cocklyn, embraced him evilly 'round the Waist. In a trice, he slit his Nose. That astoundingly juicy Organ spurted Blood as readily as any Heart. I, who had been none too well before this, felt myself retch and my Stomach contract into a shiv'ring Ball; but had I known what was to come, I should have truly bedew'd the Floor with my vile shipboard Dinner. For Llewelyn, not being satisfied with these Measures, took the Opportunity of Cocklyn's Confusion and Bleeding to grab his Arms, tye 'em behind him with a leather Thong, whereupon, whilst all the Tars lookt on in Horror, he slit his Gullet from his Rib Cage to his Navel, then drew out a Length of his Gut with his bare Hand and pinion'd the bloody Mess to the Ladder by Means of the second Dagger. Now he releas'd his screaming Victim's Foot and drove him with that pointed Implement of Slaughter 'round the Ladder in a hideous Jog of Death until he mercifully dropp'd. This took longer than I would have guess'd; the Force of Life is stronger than we think until we test it. Cocklyn utter'd Noises fit for no Human Ear as he retch'd and hopp'd in Agony. I could no longer bear to look; indeed I hid my Eyes in Terror until a heavy Thud upon the Cabin Floor convinced me he had expir'd. When I finally open'd my Eyes, I saw that Cocklyn had wound his Intestines 'round the Ladder no less than six Times before Death (or a Merciful Swoon) took him and he fell in a Pool of his own Blood.

The Tars had stopp'd their Gaming to view this Torture Scene in husht Reverence. O the Gaping of a Man's Guts hath a most chastening Effect upon Human Hubris. We know we are nought but Flesh and Ordure inspirited by one mere Lungful of Divine Breath, and yet we ne'er know it truly until we see a Man slit open before us and the dark and murky Omen of his Entrails reveal'd to our astounded View.

The Cabin was, i'faith, so still, that I felt I had happen'd amongst the Waxwork Figures at Westminster Abbey. Tho' the Tars had doubtless witness'd Attacks of Sailors' Vapours before (wherein Mariners lost Ears, Eyes, and Noses as if they were so many Baubles), ne'er till now had most of 'em seen such a Torture as this carried out before 'em. Sure they had heard *tell* of it, as I had, in Accounts of the Cruelties of Pyrates; but 'tis one Thing to hear such Barbarity recounted, and another to behold it.

Suddenly the Door open'd and the Captain appear'd. He was a tall Man with a grey Beard and a red Nose which much resembl'd an o'ergrown Strawberry. 'Twas no difficult Thing for him to perceive who was the Murderer and who the Murder'd, since the Murder'd still lay in a Pool of his own Blood whilst the Murderer still stood above him with a bloody Dagger in Hand. As for the Spectators, they remain'd frozen as waxen Effigies.

At the Entrance of the Captain, they turn'd and star'd as one, knowing (as I did not then) that such mutinous Behaviour could not be tolerated aboard Ship, howsoe'er unpopular the Victim. A Crewman who would kill a First Mate might as readily kill a Captain, and such a severe Break with Discipline could ne'er be countenanced at Sea, where, e'en more than upon Land, each Man's Fate depends upon his Brothers.

"How many have witness'd this Murder?" the Captain askt, all unnecessarily, for 'twas clear all the Men present had done so.

No one spoke or stirr'd so much as a Finger; neither Ayes nor Nays were proffer'd.

"Come, come," said the Captain drily, "any Man who fails to answer yea or nay shall share the Murderer's Blame."

Still, there came no Reply. The Cabin was silent but for the Creaking of the Ship's Timbers and the Slap of Sea-Water against the Hull. But little by little, Fear began to glow in the Eyes of the assembl'd Tars, for Flogging and Keel-hauling were all too real to their Imaginations.

"Aye, aye," said one. "Aye," said another, until a Chorus of Ayes rose to drown the Silence in the Cabin.

"Very well," said the Captain, whose name was Whitehead (as if in contradiction of his Strawberry Nose), "I think we may dispatch Mr. Llewelyn to his Fate without further Ado."

"Look ye," cried Llewelyn, "I deserve a Trial by Jury as well as any Man here!"

"Mr. Llewelyn," said the Captain, " 'tis clear in the Eyes of all that no one but you hath uncaulkt the Seams, as 'twere, of this poor Fellow who bleeds upon the Ground. No mere Careening shall save him from Shipworms now, for neither Oakum nor Tar shall put him back together. The only Question is whether we should flog you first, then keel-haul you, before hanging you from the Yardarm, whether we should do to you what it hath pleas'd you to do to him, or whether we should be merciful and tye you to what remains of Mr. Cocklyn, and toss you in the Sea to drown with him."

"I'll have a Trial by Jury, I will!" said Llewelyn. "Fer I was but avengin' a Messmate's Death. 'Twas Justice I serv'd, look ye, not fanciful Murder, an' I'll not be hang'd like a Dog fer avengin' the Murder o' a Friend!"

"That is debatable," said the Captain, whose ironical, elegant Speech was that of a Gentleman, with a Gentleman's perfect Coldness and Disdain for Sentiment; "wherefore do you term the Loss of a Seaman at Sea 'Murder'? If anyone is the Murderer here, 'tis the Sea itself. Who hath appointed you Neptune's Scourge?"

"If Cocklyn was above on Deck, not below makin' Love to a Wench, Thomas would be here still!" cried Llewelyn.

"What? Do you, in your Fit of Seaman's Vapours, imagine Wenches? There are no Wenches here. Pray, Mr. Llewelyn, take hold of your outrageous Fancy. I'll have no Bedlamites aboard the *Hopewell*."

"There's Wenches here aplenty," Llewelyn said, whereupon he dragg'd Susannah and me out of the Shadows where we were cow'ring, brought us to the bloody Centre of the Circle of Tars, and ripp'd off our Shirts before Captain Whitehead's astounded Eyes, revealing our womanly Breasts.

Whitehead was as amaz'd to see us as the other Men, yet since ironical Detachment was the Secret of his Rule, he would not show it. He made as if to hide his Eyes before our Breasts, but Light show'd betwixt his parted Fingers. "Pray, cover these Ladies up again," said he, "for I'll countenance no Lewdness to the Fair Sex upon my Ship." He said this with all Gallantry and *Politesse*, but it seem'd more Form than Feeling.

"Cocklyn brought 'em," Llewelyn cried, "to be his private Whores!"

"And would you have been more content," askt Whitehead, "if he had shar'd these Ladies with you?"

The Crew laugh'd uproariously at this Witticism. Whitehead swiftly silenced 'em with his stern Visage.

"Mr. Llewelyn, in consideration of your Grief at the Loss of your Friend, I shall be merciful and you shall be neither flogg'd, nor keel-haul'd, nor tortur'd."

At this, the assembl'd Tars seem'd to breathe more freely.

"But you shall be ty'd to your Victim upon Deck and left there for a Week 'neath Sun and Moon, then thrown together into the Arms of Neptune."

The Crew gasp'd in Horror. Susannah grabb'd my Hand and squeez'd it.

"I'll have a Trial by Jury, I will," cried the distraught Llewelyn.

"Be silent and thank God for my Mercy," said the frosty Whitehead. "Place these Men in Irons upon the Fo'c'sle Deck," said he, pointing to the Corpse of Cocklyn and the future Corpse of Llewelyn. The Latter was already shaking with Terror of rotting upon the Deck.

"And send these Ladies to the Great Cabin," said the Captain. "When I have seen the Murderer in Irons, I shall deal with them as I see fit." Whereupon Susannah and I were hustl'd into the Captain's Cabin to await the perilous Issue of this new Rotation of Fortune's Wheel.

Chapter VIII

In which 'tis prov'd that Sea Captains are as lustful as they are reputed to be, that Deists do not always make the best Lovers, and that many Persons in their Erotick Habits crave that Treatment which, in truth, they deserve, in consequence of their Characters.

FOR A WHOLE WEEK, whilst the Body of Cocklyn rotted upon Deck, bringing all Manner of Vermin up from the Hold to seek Nourishment in the Decay of its gaping Guts, Llewelyn lay under it moaning in Agony which soon turn'd to Madness, and the Tars of the *Hopewell* (having been strictly forbidden to save him upon Pain of sharing his Punishment) grumbl'd mutinously amongst themselves.

Llewelyn and Thomas had been Favourites of the Crew; the First Mate and the Captain were cordially hated by all— Cocklyn for always lining his own Pockets or Belly at the Crew's Expence, and Whitehead for his Cruelty and *Hauteur*. The Crew's Grievance seem'd, in the Main, to be Whitehead's Denial of a Trial to Llewelyn, for they knew he must be punish'd, but they felt all Trueborn Englishmen were entitl'd at least to a Trial by Jury, howsoe'er abridged and unfair it must necessarily be with Captain Whitehead acting as Judge.

What, then, kept the Men from avenging Llewelyn's Torture—or indeed from dispatching him more speedily into the Drink? The Knowledge of how severe the Captain would surely be with 'em. For Whitehead was known for unspeakable Cruelties—such as forcing Men to swallow live Cockroaches, stuffing Oakum in their Mouths and setting it aflame, flogging and keel-hauling 'em within an Inch of their Lives, and making very free with his Supplejack e'en for minor Infringements. One Tar had been flogg'd no less than fifty Times for taking one Swallow of Water above his Ration, the Cook who brought our Mess inform'd us; therefore, the Men were attempting to close their Ears to the Ravings of poor Llewelyn upon Deck, tho' it hurt 'em sorely to do so. Still,

Mutiny was mutter'd of in the Steerage, and the Cook whisper'd to us that the Men were sick at Heart, and that when Carrion Birds had come to pluck out Cocklyn's Eyes, they had torn at Llewelyn's Flesh as well. 'Twas only a Matter of Time before his Eyes should suffer the same Fate as Cocklyn's, whereupon there'd be no telling what the Crew would do.

Susannah and I shiver'd to hear all this, for we were Whitehead's Prisoners in the Great Cabin, tho' as yet he had treated us quite civilly. Outwardly, our Fortunes had improv'd; the Captain's Cabin was provided with Windows, Light, Air, a Writing Bureau, and dry Berths lin'd with Eider-Downs, as well as Plate and Pewter bearing his Family Crest. But we liv'd in Terror of the Captain's Whims, and we both felt we had fallen into the Hands of a crueller Master than e'en murder'd Cocklyn.

Susannah, for her part, was certain God was testing her for some grievous Error she had made. First, she'd been responsible for the Kidnapping of Belinda; then she'd caus'd the Murder of Cocklyn, bringing us both into the Clutches of a Villain. What Lesson was she meant to learn thereby, she askt. O Day and Night she could not refrain from reproaching herself upon these Accounts.

"I ne'er e'en submitted to Cocklyn's Am'rous Advances," said she, "fer I was able to use the Pretext o' the Tempest an' the Rockin' o' the Ship to fend him off. Yet was the poor Man disembowell'd fer his suppos'd Seduction o' me."

"Pray, do not blame yourself, Susannah," said I. " 'Twas an old Quarrel they surely had, which caus'd his Downfall."

"God's testin' me, Fanny. He is. Yer too innocent o' the Devil's Ways, Fanny, so ye cannot comprehend the Danger, but I see Demons ev'rywhere, tryin' us sorely. If ye had any Friend besides me, I'd throw meself away to feed the Fishes—fer me Life is worth nothin' to me now! O I curse the Day I went to the Wharves fer Prue! Alas that I should have been her Messenger—I, who am God's Messenger! Whitehead—I trust him e'en less than Cocklyn. How shall we find the *Cassandra* when he is no Friend o' ours, an' the Sea—the Sea is bigger an' colder than Hell itself?"

A strange Calm had o'ertaken me in these dire Circumstances; for 'tis paradoxical that when our Fortunes reach their lowest Ebb, we oft' find a sort of Resignation in Despair, and to ward off Disaster become most erect in the Face of Grief that should, by all the Laws of Reason, bow us

390

down. O there are stronger Things in Life than Reason; of that I am sure.

"Do not despair, my dearest Friend," said I to Susannah. "Disaster is oft' a Cloak for Fortune, as Fortune is oft' Disaster's own Disguise. We shall find Belinda in this great Immensity, the Sea, and make a Heaven in the Place of Hell!"

Susannah fell into my Arms and wept, and as she wept I felt my Strength grow. We could not both give way; one of us must be strong to aid the other.

"Mistress Fanny, 'tis little I remember o' me Youth—fer Years I remember'd nought but the Shipwreck in me fourth Year, but last Night, fallin' asleep to the Moanin' an' Ravin' o' Poor Llewelyn upon Deck, I dreamt o' me Black Mama in the Sugar Isles an' she spoke to me as plainly as a Flesh-an'-Blood Woman."

"What did she say?" I askt Susannah, hoping to distract her from her Thoughts of Self-Murder which, i'faith, fright-en'd me.

Susannah lookt into my Eyes and chanted these stirring Words:

"'We were pluckt from the Bosom o' the Continent o' Magick an' Darkness an' brought into the White Man's Light. His God is Reason—a false God—a God that flashes Numbers in Place o' Lightnin', a God that is but the Devil in Dis-guise. Spirit alone is real; Spirit alone endures. 'Tis the Curse o' the White Man that he hath made a God 'o Reason; the End o' the World shall be at hand when the Black Man comes to worship Reason, too.'"

I listen'd, stunn'd into Silence by this Prophecy, which seem'd drawn from the Depths of a Dream like the Witch's Prophecy of many Moons ago. The Dream was daft, yet was there Wisdom in it. O doth not Dryden himself say that "Great Wits are sure to Madness near allied;/And thin Parti-tions do their Bounds divide"?

"But wherefore have you abandon'd Spirit, Susannah?" I askt.

"O—I am doubtin' all, Mistress Fanny, doubtin' all. Since Llewelyn raves upon the Deck, I doubt me God, an' find me Heart drawn unto the Devil's faulty Reasonin's. I think o' Self-Slaughter—tho' I know that Suicides must go to Hell, an' yet I think I *merit* Punishment. I lov'd Belinda like me own sweet Babe an' caus'd her to be taken. Likewise, I caus'd

391

Cocklyn's hideous Fate. I was sent to lead ye to Salvation, an' here I doubt me God meself!"

"Wherefore do you take all Blame upon your own Shoulders? Is that not Hubris, Susannah? Would God wish to hear such Self-Reproach? 'Tis for Jesus to take Man's Sins upon his Shoulders—not Susannah." Susannah only whimper'd in reply. Whereupon the Door open'd and Whitehead strode in.

"Do I interrupt a Metaphysical Discussion betwixt you Ladies?" said he, curling his lower Lip in Disdain. "Pray forgive me if I do."

He said this with the Mockery of one who believes Women wholly unfit for Metaphysicks, but polite enough ne'er to say it in so many Words. Yet did his Mocking Visage announce his View. "Ladies," said he, "shall I leave you to your Philosophical Disputations?"

Amaz'd as I was by Whitehead's Calm, his lack of Response either to Llewelyn's Cries or to our Presence aboard Ship, I strove to answer his Ice with Ice and his Intellect with Intellect. Perhaps I fancied that if he knew me for an educated Wench, not just an ignorant Whore, 'twould save my Life. *Why* I should have believ'd this I did not know, for had my Education spar'd me Grief before?

"Pray join us, Captain," said I, playing at his frosty Game. "My friend Susannah is suff'ring a Loss of Faith in God because of the Shrieks that issue Moment by Moment from the Fo'c'sle Deck. Pray, what can you do to reassure her? As Captain you are Custodian of our Souls as well as our Bodies, and we look to you for Guidance."

I said this with just a Hint of Mockery but then fell before him in a Curtsey so complaisant that all Mockery was eras'd.

The Captain laugh'd. "I do not wish to bear the Heavy Burden of your Souls, Ladies."

"Then who shall bear it?" I askt. "For we are but foolish Women and you our Lord and Master."

The Captain knew me not well enough to presume that these Words were, in fact, the direct Opposite of my Beliefs. Perhaps he suspected me of jesting with him, yet, being a thoroughgoing Patriarch, and being, as well, caught off guard by Flattery—that Universal Lubricant—he tumbl'd headlong into the Pit of Philosophical Disputation. "Satyre," my Friend Presto us'd to be fond of saying, "is a sort of Glass wherein Beholders do gen'rally discover ev'rybody's Face but their own." So, too, with Mockery, unless it be of the most unsub-

392

tle sort; 'tis gen'rally miss'd by those we mock—protected as they are by the heavy Armor of their Self-Love.

Captain Whitehead was a Perfect Deist, and as 'tis characteristick of that Breed to try to convert others to their Lack of Faith, he could not resist my Invitation.

"Ladies," said he, "Reason teaches us that Moses himself was guilty of known Blunders in his Account of the Creation, and the Miracles in both Testaments—Old and New—are inconsistent with Reason, which it hath pleas'd God to give us to aid us in our Pursuit of Happiness. Reason teaches us that there must be a First Cause of all Things, an *Ens Entium*, which we, all unreasoningly, call God, but this First Cause is perfectly indiff'rent to our Fates, for as He is wholly self-sufficient, happy, perfect, and neither loves nor hates, why should He be concern'd with us? And why indeed should He be affected in any Way by our Beseechments? Our Sins neither discomfit Him nor do our Adorations please Him. He hath set the Earth in Motion upon its Axis, spun this Planet we call Home amidst the alien Spheres, and gone away. What we term Religion is nought but Human Policy for Governing the unruly Passions of Man, and as such, it hath e'er pleas'd the Tyrant to enlist the Priest in his Service. . . ."

"Then is Pray'r useless?" askt the unhappy Susannah.

"'Tis nought but the Opiate of Child-like Minds," said Whitehead. "You may pray to pass the Hours away, but it availeth nought. Sometimes Fortune chooses to turn the Way you pray, but she doth not turn so as a *Consequence* of your Pray'rs. 'Tis all Caprice and Chance and Circumstance."

"Then is Spirit wholly fled from the World?" I askt. "Is there no Convenant betwixt Man and God?"

"Let me put it to you thus, Ladies. Circumcision is said to be a Sign of the Covenant, is it not?"

We nodded our Heads.

"Yet the Negroes of Africa, who have read neither Old nor New Testament, circumcise their Men-Children, for they inhabit the Southern Climes, and not wishing perspir'd Matter to consolidate beneath the Prepuce and possibly fester, with fatal Consequences, they remove this Flap of Skin. And yet, as they know nothing of our Bible, it cannot be said to be a Sign of the Covenant. Thus, would I put it to you, Ladies, that all the Rituals we take for Signs of the Interest of God in the Affairs of Men, have rather a most logical and scientifick Cause. If, despite this Logick, we wish to believe in Spirits, either friendly or hostile, we may do so, as Serving

Maids believe in Ghosts and Goblins, Witches, Apparitions, and Prophecies, but Men of Understanding and Good Judgement do not."

This Speech was hardly design'd to augment Susannah's Faith in God, nor mine, for that Matter; for confronted with Captain Whitehead's cold Logick, I myself, who had *seen* Witches, who had been heal'd (when Men of Science fail'd) by the Pow'r of the Goddess, thro' Her Devotée, Isobel, falter'd in my Faith. Faith is the Knowledge of the Heart, Logick the Knowledge of the Mind. "*Le Coeur a ses Raisons*," as Monsieur Pascal hath said, "*que la Raison ne connaît point.*" I quoted this Line to Captain Whitehead, hoping to fend off his Tidal Wave of Deism with a single French Phrase.

"Pascal, Pascal," quoth he, "when I hear French, I reach for my Pistol. Quote me no Garlick-eating French *Philosophes*," he said. "For I doubt 'em more than Hottentots. A Frenchman thinks if he can purse his Garlick-Lips and pout a pretty Phrase, he hath defeated you in Argument. Bah—they make me sick with their fine Philosophy and fancy Cookery. Just as a Frenchman can make a Roast Beef look like a Quail Pye, or a Quail Pye look like a Roast Beef, so, too, can he make Falsehood look like Truth and Superstition like Science. I'd sooner argue with a Roman Papist than a French *Philosophe!*"

"Sir, I only mean to say that we know Truth by the Heart, not by the Head. The Head oft' deceives—"

"So say Weaklings and Scoundrels!" snapp'd Whitehead. "The Heart would dictate Mercy for Llewelyn. D'ye think 'tis easy to hear him whimper so and bear the Burden of the Crew's Hatred? D'ye think 'tis easy to be Captain o'er a scurvy Lot of Rogues, a Parcel of Lazy Poltroons who'd as soon rot in the Grog Shops of the Sugar Isles as go to Sea and work for an honest Shilling? No! The Heart recoils, but the Head bids it be strong. The Dictates of the Heart are Weakness, Sentiment, and womanish Cowardice; but the Head is manly and courageous. Heart me no Heart and Head me no Head! 'Tis a World of much Cruelty and little Justice, and Woe to him who lives in Expectation of Mercy from his Brethren; he shall be eaten by the Sharks ere his Ship has properly set Sail! Life in Society is little diff'rent from Life in the State of Nature, as Hobbes himself hath described it: 'Continual Fear and Danger of Violent Death; and the Life of Man, solitary, poor, nasty, brutish, and short.' Those who live by the Heart make their Lives e'en shorter and nastier than those of Savages. Those who live by the Head may increase their Pleasures. For 'tis true, is it not, that 'little else can Life supply but some Good Fucks and then we dye'?"

"What a dismal Philosophy!" said Susannah.

"Dismal, but true," said Whitehead. "A short Life and a merry one, as the Pyrates say."

"Sir, I did not know you for a Poet," said I.

Whitehead smil'd, flatter'd. "O I scribble Couplets now and again," said he.

"So I see," said I.

"Come, Ladies, shall we act out the Truth of that last Couplet? For I am very keen to try a Black Lady and a White one in the same Bed, like black Caviar spread upon white Bread, and whilst the Sea is calm and the Men not yet quite mutinous, let us take our Pleasure where we may. Before long, we'll be in the hot and humid Equatorial Climes and who knows but Ship Fever may carry us off ere we reach our Guinea Castlekeep."

"Pray—what Guinea Castlekeep do you speak of?" I askt. "For 'twas my Understanding we sail'd for the Azores and thence to the Bahamas and up the Coast of the Colonies."

"That is true enough, Ladies, true enough. We shall indeed sail to the Bahamas and by and by find ourselves in Charlestown, New York, and Boston, but first we shall touch the Guinea Coast and fetch a fine Cargo of Africans to sell in the New World."

"Then you mean to take us Slaving?" I askt incredulously.

"The Head dictates it, tho' the Heart refuses," Whitehead laugh'd. "A Cargo of fine Guinea Slaves shall fetch a good Price in the New World, e'en if but half of 'em live. Why I could e'en sell Susannah here . . . if she'll oblige me not in Bed. . . ." He laugh'd as if the Menace were but Jest, yet Susannah shudder'd; such a Fate would be the final Proof of God's Displeasure with her.

"Sirrah, when we came aboard," I said, "we paid Mr. Cocklyn handsomely for our Passage—but not to be taken Slaving."

"He shar'd neither your Wealth nor your Flesh with me," said Whitehead, "and as you know, he did not beg Permission of his belovèd Captain. Moreo'er, he hath lost both Mast and Sail and his Hull is severely damaged. His Spying-Glasses have the Birds pluckt out to make their Dinner—"

"Enough!" said I. "I will hear no more! I am in Pursuit of

my lost Child and I will countenance no further foolish Jests."

"Come, come," says Whitehead, "we shall make another Child. Children are cheap and easily made. They cost nothing and there is some Pleasure in it, too. Was this Child a Son that you take on so?"

"A Daughter, Sirrah, and as dear to me as twenty Sons . . ." I said with a sinking Heart. *Dear Goddess, why hast thou forsaken me?* I thought.

"Daughters, Daughters . . . why they are cheaper than Sons, until they come to wed and one must find them Marriage Portions. Come, if 'tis a Babe you want, we'll make another . . ." said Whitehead.

"Captain," I rejoin'd briskly despite my Grief, "we would not have come aboard did we know you meant to take us Slaving. . . ."

Whitehead sneer'd. "Nor would the Men," said he, "for the Guinea Coast teems with Distempers, Agues, and Feyers. If the Men knew our Destination, many would refuse to board. Why half of 'em will dye ere we start the Middle Passage. And as for those that live, the Middle Passage is no Pleasure Cruise for Seamen or for Slaves. Death comes so oft' upon a Slaving Ship that Man-eating Sharks will chase us 'cross the Ocean and our Wake will oft' be red with Blood." He smil'd. " 'Tis a Lesson for us: We must snatch our Pleasure whilst we may. The Jaws of Death are sharp and trail us constantly beneath the Waves. Death swims behind us with his cold grey Eyes and scaly Skin. . . ."

My Flesh crept to hear Whitehead talk so. He seem'd to take particular Pleasure in frightening us out of our Wits. Death, it seem'd, arous'd him more than all the Beguilements of the Fair Sex. O Whitehead claim'd to hate the Disciplines he was driven to perform as Captain, but for my own part, I would have sworn he lov'd 'em. The more he talkt of Slaving, the hotter and more passionate he became. At length, he went to a lockt Cabinet and brought out a Box full of curious Instruments, which at first Sight reminded me of those Devices I had seen depicted in Books on Midwifery. But no, they were not Forceps nor Extracting Hooks; they were Hand-Cuffs and Leg-Shackles, Thumb-Screws and such—all the iron Implements of the loathsome Slave Trade.

"This," said Whitehead devilishly, "is a Device call'd the *Speculum Oris*, with which we open the clos'd Jaws of an unwilling Slave—like so." He grasp'd me 'round the Waist and thrust two metal Points into my Mouth, then crankt a sort of Screw that strove to open my Mouth to its widest Extent.

"Cease an' desist, Sirrah," said Susannah, leaping to her Feet and challenging Whitehead, who now quickly unscrew'd and withdrew the Device, as if he had been using it in Jest. The *Speculum* resembl'd a Pair of Compasses or, indeed, Calipers.

"I'll not hurt your Mistress," Whitehead said, withdrawing it, but ne'ertheless I was shaken by this sudden Assault upon my Person—I who was already fell'd by the News that we were sailing to a Region of the World where we had little Hope to find belovèd Belinda. Whitehead petted me upon the Back, saying, "There, there." O what a Creature of Whim and Caprice we had drawn for a Master!

"Well then, Ladies," said he, "shall we make merry ere the Shark of Death dispatches us?"

"Have we a Choyce?" I askt dismally.

Alas, Belinda, I wish I could tell you now that your Mother and her loyal Retainer, Susannah, found some clever Way to hold the loathsome Whitehead at bay. I fancy two Warrior Maidens—one White, one Black, fending off the mutual Rape that is their Destiny—fending it off with Words, if not with Cutlasses, with clever Tricks, if not with Pistols. But, alas, 'twould not be true. A Ship is a sort of Prison, and the Captain is both Warden and Turnkey. Nay, he is King of the Seas, Prince Regent of all he surveys, and where can his Prisoners run but into the Briny Deep? Dishonour is worse than Death, say some—but I say that Dishonour is a trifling Thing compar'd with Death. For where there's Life, Honour may oft' be recaptur'd—many's the Duchess who started out a Whore—but where no Life is, what use is Honour? Honour will neither feed the Hungry, nor clothe the Shiv'ring, nor heal the Sick. Honour's like a Badge of Merit: worthless at Pawn, useless to warm the Bones, inedible, and sooner to tarnish than a silver Watch. (Susannah herself, for all her Piety, was fond of saying that any Woman who rates her Honour according to the Diameter of one of her Nether Organs is a pure Fool.)

In short, Belinda, we lay with Captain Whitehead. "Lay with" is a curious Term for what we did; for, in truth, not much lying went on, unless 'twere of the verbal sort, but I use the Phrase out of Custom and the Shyness that o'ertakes my Quill when I remember I am writing for a Daughter. I wish I were not sworn to Truth above Modesty and could afford to be coy! For, tho' I wish neither to inflame nor to disgust by writing of my Life with all its Vicissitudes, yet I *must* assume—or I would not have chosen this perilous Profession of Scribbler—that describing Vice is oft' the best Guarantee of future Virtue, whilst describing Virtue is no Guarantee against the Pow'rs of Vice!

Many foolish and credulous Folk believe the Opposite. They accuse the Chronicler of Vice as if he were the *Creator* of it; and conversely do they believe that honey'd, insipid Writings are the best Assurance of Virtue in this World of Vice. Piffle! Do they not understand that we Scribblers must scourge the World to bring it to its Senses? Do they not understand that an Author doth not necessarily *approve* the Sins his Love of Truth causes him to chronicle? And, as for depicting Female Venery and Lust, I hardly do so to recommend the same to my Daughter, but only to give her the Benefit of Experience, that sublime Teacher. Let virtuous Ladies snicker at my Exploits, feeling superior to me, a sometime Whore. I answer them as Mr. Pope hath answer'd those who would deride poor Jane Shore, to wit:

> There are, 'tis true, who tell another Tale,
> That virtuous Ladies envy while they rail;
> Such Rage without betrays the Fire within;
> In some close Corner of the Soul, they sin;
> Still hoarding up, most scandalously nice,
> Amidst their Virtues, a reserve of Vice.

Those who are pure of Soul—altho' the Body may sometimes sin—need not, Belinda, denounce your hapless Progenitrix. But those who lust inside their teeming Brains and yet confess it not—*they* must condemn!

Thus perhaps 'twill help you in some future Predicament if I describe what happen'd next and if I explain it in the Light of the Captain's Character. For Knowledge of Human Nature is the Key to both History and Poetry, is it not? Both Clio and Apollo would be dumb but for their Knowledge of the strange Aberrations of the Human Heart.

Captain Whitehead was a curious Fellow who could not enjoy us until we were manacl'd both Hand and Foot and he might work his Will upon us without a single Challenge to his Dominance. ('Tis oft' the case with Men who claim Superiority o'er the Fair; they say they do not doubt their Dominance, yet can they ne'er enjoy a Woman till she be bound in Irons like a Guinea Slave!) Be that as it may, he had but passing Interest in the Act of Copulation, which he executed only when the Victim was upon all fours in the most bestial of Postures, and only when he might assault that Altar of Love which is shared by both Sexes, for he had no Use whatsoe'er for that Part specifick to the Female of the Species. (Mark you, Belinda, this, too, is frequently the Sign of a Man who holds a particular Grudge against the Fair Sex and would rather play the Woman himself, but is forbidden by the Weight of Custom from doing so!)

First, the Captain had both Susannah and me undress completely, whilst he snicker'd o'er our Nakedness in most unsavoury Fashion. Then he had us crouch upon all fours like Dogs and he manacl'd my right Hand to her left, and my right Foot to her left. The Sight of our bare Bums in the Air excited him beyond Measure, for he drew his Supplejack ere he drew his Cock and "burnish'd"—so he call'd it—our Bums with the stinging Leather Thongs, creating that Redness and Heat without which his Privy Member would not stand at attention. The Whipping was painful enough, but I would not give Whitehead the Satisfaction of my Outcries. Susannah, for her part, took it as God's Punishment for her Sins and perhaps e'en welcom'd it in her Mood of Contrition. But the Whipping did not last long, for it so arous'd the vile Whitehead that, shortly, he dropp'd his Supplejack and then his Breech, and strove to enter first me, then Susannah from the Rear with his great Batt'ring Ram of a Cock. This was painful, too, but fortunately as short-liv'd as Whitehead's Erection. Both the Whipping and the Sight of stripp'd Bums had brought him so close to his ultimate Hot Fit of Lust that he could not penetrate us long.

"O I dye! I dye!" cried Whitehead, emitting copious Fluids and collapsing upon Susannah's kneeling Form. He fell upon her Back with such Force that she, in turn, fell sideways, dragging me with her, and our manacl'd Wrists and Ankles pain'd us horribly.

"Enough! Enough!" I cried. "Let us free!"

Whitehead now began to stir from his exhausted Lethargy of Lust. He struggl'd to his Feet, whereupon he pull'd us up after him. He stood us in the Centre of the Cabin, still bound Hand to Hand and Foot to Foot and bade us spread our Legs as wide as we might. O now I truly fear'd for our Fates, for I suspected Whitehead might put the *Speculum* to use upon a Part for which 'twas not intended; but no, to my sheer Astonishment, he crawl'd upon his Back betwixt my

Legs, open'd wide his Mouth, and bade me water it with my own Natural Dew. This I freely did, whilst he smackt his Lips in Joy, as if Urine were the finest Wine and he could ne'er drink enough of it!

"What a Vintage!" cries he, flat upon his Back and savouring the Flavour of this Fluid. Susannah lookt at me in amazement (since, having ne'er workt in a Brothel, all this was new to her—tho' not to me).

"Ah, forbidden Wine!" exclaims Whitehead. "Rare Pressings from what exotick Grapes! Come, let me taste the sable Beauty's Dew as well!"

Now he turn'd and crawl'd, then wriggl'd upon his Back until he lay beneath Susannah, who let loose a Torrent of Urine such as I had ne'er beheld.

"Drink, Swine!" she cried.

"O yes! Abuse me!" Whitehead begg'd.

"Ye Snake, ye Cur, ye Devil in Disguise!" she cried.

Whitehead groan'd with Satisfaction, licking his Lips. O how Susannah and I wisht to take this Opportunity to trample him in all his Evil, but the Way we were manacl'd made it impossible—as Whitehead doubtless knew. Ne'ertheless, Susannah continu'd to curse at him in true Outrage and he continu'd to lick all the Urine from the Corners of his Mouth whilst at the same Time he manipulated his own Organ until once again it exploded with sticky yellowish Seed, more like Pus than Sperm.

"O yes! O yes!" he sigh'd. "I am ready for an Execution now!" Whereupon he struggl'd to his Feet, unshackl'd us and bade us dress, rubb'd Urine in his Beard most lovingly, and declar'd it Time to dispatch Llewelyn into the Merciful Sea.

"Ladies, you must see this," said he, " 'twill be a Lesson in Metaphysicks."

"I've seen enough Today," Susannah said, for she was truly astonish'd by this Afternoon's Activities, whilst I had oft' seen the like in the Brothel and was more disgusted than amaz'd.

"Come, come," said Whitehead, " 'twas merely Prologue to the Night's Festivities. We'll have an Execution as our Main Event and then more Am'rous Play as Afterpiece!"

"If this be Am'rous Play, what d'ye call it when ye shit?" Susannah said.

"Ladies," said he, "I save the Best for last. When we have thrown our Corpses into the Sea, we'll have a veritable Feast of Shit to celebrate! O I shall lick your Bums and stick my

Fingers in 'em till you discharge your Bounty in my waiting Mouth!"

He smackt his Lips in sheer Anticipation.

"Doth it not excite you, Ladies? For verily, it doth me! I could dye and dye again just thinking on't. Come Ladies, let's away. We'll have an Execution ere we play!"

Chapter IX

In which our Heroine learns more than she wishes to know about the Nature of Distemper'd Lust; debates with the Surgeon (and indeed with herself) about the Nature of Evil and whether anything we Mortals do can assuage it; and loses an old Friend just as she hath made a new.

THE EXECUTION OF LLEWELYN was a Solemn Event which the entire Crew attended. Tho' Executions were customarily held at Dawn, not Sunset, Whitehead had chosen this Hour because 'twas exactly a Week Llewelyn had rav'd 'neath the rotting Corpse of Cocklyn; and 'twas Whitehead's Nature to be so exact in his Cruelties that no one might fault him upon Trifles. His Philosophy might be disputed, but the Forms it took were punctilious. Like many Men who make a Virtue of Vice, he put much Faith in Form and Conduct (as if indeed Vice well-perform'd were Virtue's very Self, whilst Virtue ill-perform'd were but the Essence of Vice).

O I had oft' remarkt in History Books how very orderly the Pictures of Executions seem'd! Headless Men all lain in a Row, their Toes pointing heavenward—as if they would walk there instead of the other Place—their Necks seemingly cut with no Effusion of Blood; O what a Mockery of Death with her Odours and Stinks, her nasty Reminders of Mortal Decay, and Flesh returning to Clay! Man turns away from both Death and Birth, little wishing to acknowledge the Dust from which we spring and to which we must, despite our Heartiest Protestations, return. E'en Women, after Childbirth, forget the Ordeal, the Closeness of Death, the Pain that near splits the Body from the Soul, and go on to breed and bleed again.

The Crew assembl'd upon the Fo'c'sle Deck at ruddy Sunset when Phoebus' bright Disk lay just above the Horizon Line. The Sea was calm as if oblivious of Llewelyn's Moans. Still, he lay 'neath Cocklyn, whose Guts now were alive with

Maggots and his Hair with Lice. In Llewelyn's vain Struggle to free himself from his oppressive Companion, whose pluckt Eyes were now two reddish Clots upon his blackening Visage and whose Tongue loll'd horribly in his open Mouth, he had become entangl'd in the Dead Man's oozing Guts, with this Sequel: that the Maggots that swarm'd o'er the Corpse now swarm'd o'er him as well. 'Twould be the sheerest Mercy to dispatch him now, for he swoon'd like one whose Wits were as unravell'd as Cocklyn's Entrails. E'en Cocklyn's Peg-Leg was soakt thro' and thro' with Blood which had turn'd a most hideous Black.

The Captain stood o'er the tangl'd Bodies of the two Men—one barely alive, one so mangl'd, 'twas not clear he'd e'er been a Man at all—and drew himself up to his full Dignity. 'Twas impossible to believe that this Figure of *Hauteur* was the very Man who not long ago had drunk my Urine (and Susannah's) with a daft Expression upon his ravening Lips and a mad Gleam in his Eye.

The Crew had been small to start—Slavers oft' had small Crews owing both to the Niggardliness of their Owners and to their Conviction that many Tars would dye anyway of Distempers in Guinea, whereupon they could be replaced by others from the Castle of the Trading Company—and it had been e'en more reduced by the Loss of Cocklyn, Llewelyn, and Thomas. Each Man, therefore, had an excellent View of the Agonies of Llewelyn. As for Cocklyn, his Death had been horrible, but at least 'twas behind him.

"Gentlemen," said Whitehead, "and, begging your Pardon for mentioning you second, honour'd Ladies. . . . You see here before you the Ultimate Result of Insubordination in the Divine Chain of Being, which is loathsome in the Eyes of the Benevolent, Omniscient, Omnipotent Supreme Being, and consequently which 'tis our Moral Duty as Men to punish swiftly and severely. . . ."

I could scarce believe my Ears! Whitehead the Deist, the Slaver, the Libertine, calling upon the Supreme Being to justify his Acts! What a Perfect Scoundrel the Man was! Would he stop at nothing? Would he stoop to anything—e'en blaming his Conduct upon the Idea of Order in the Great Chain of Being? O beware the Word "Order," Belinda, likewise the Word "Discipline"; they are oft' nought but Cloaks for Tyrants who believe in nothing but their own Dominion—and certainly not that of God. More Murders have been committed in the Name of God than in the Name of Satan; for the Satan-Worshipper tends his Lord in secret, whilst the Man who would be Tyrant of the World calls the Name of God to cover all his bloody Deeds, and what is worse, he is oft' believ'd by an unreasoning Populace!

"For the Bible teaches us," Whitehead the Hypocrite went on, "that 'whoso diggeth a Pit shall fall therein; and he that rolleth a Stone, it shall return upon him.' Therefore, heed the Example of Mr. Llewelyn and do not think that any Hint of Insurrection or Mutiny whatsoe'er will go unpunish'd upon the *Hopewell*. For mark you, Gentlemen, I shall not be so merciful upon the next Occasion. If 'tis e'en rumour'd that a Man thinks to ease his Lot by spreading Talk of Mutiny amongst his Fellows, Keel-hauling shall be too good for him—he shall suffer rather both Mr. Cocklyn's and Mr. Llewelyn's Fates. . . ."

Now Captain Whitehead made a Sign for the two chain'd Men to be heav'd into the Sea. Two burly Tars came forward to perform these Duties obediently, but sheer Disgust show'd upon their faces as they strove to lift the tangl'd Bodies, heavy as if both were already Corpses. Two Men could not accomplish it; three were requir'd before the intermingl'd Flesh of Cocklyn and Llewelyn could be hurl'd o'er the Side into the Deep.

I caught one last Look at Llewelyn's Face ere he was swung o'er the Side; 'twas suffus'd with Gratitude to be dying at long last. Thus do Men make Hells on Earth for one another—worse than anything Satan might prepare for 'em. The Sea clos'd so quickly o'er the Bodies that 'twas as if neither of 'em had e'er been upon this Earth before. O the Sea is a swiftly healing Wound; she staunches the Blood of the World more quickly than e'en the gen'rous Grass that turns all Flesh, in Time, to Green.

The Captain now perfunctorily read a few Pray'rs for the Dead (which he recited with all the Expression of a School-boy regurgitating Caesar for his Latin Master), whereupon, the Execution being compleated, he directed that the Deck whereon the two Malefactors had lain be washt with Vinegar to avoid Epidemicks. 'Twas late for this Measure, but had the Captain attended to the Problem of Ships' Fevers ere this, 'twould have impeded his Punishment of Llewelyn—something which he could scarce tolerate. Better have half the Crew dye of Fluxes and Distempers than have 'em all alive and mutinous!

Well-pleas'd with the Execution, Captain Whitehead led

Susannah and me down to the Great Cabin again. O he was lustful as a Popish Monk in an Old Tale, his Appetite for Female Flesh well-whetted by the Spectacle of Gore we had beheld! In the Brothel I had heard tell of (and e'en witness'd) Men whose feeble Pow'rs could only be arouz'd by Desecration of the Female Form, but ne'er had I encounter'd Murder as a Prelude to a Debauch, tho' doubtless uncheckt Debauchery is common enough following Executions. I had oft' noticed, i'faith, that upon Hanging Days at Tyburn, Mother Coxtart had more than her usual Share of Custom. The Sight of Blood is a pow'rful Aphrodisiack, and nothing is more piquant to the Libertine than a grown Man swinging by the Neck till dead, unless it be a little Girl of Ten. (I shudder e'en now to think of such!)

"Come, Ladies," said Whitehead, "let's have a Revel thro' the Night to celebrate!"

Susannah groan'd with Distaste, but she was so melancholick and cast down that her usual Quick Wit deserted her. Were that not the case, I'm certain she should have thought of some Expedient to distract Whitehead from the Carnal Plans he was hatching.

What would Susannah do, I askt myself, were she not in such a Melancholick Humour? I scratch'd my Head, which was itchy with Lice (as it had been since the Start of this Ill-fated Voyage). In a trice, it came to me! Whitehead was afraid of Epidemicks, was he not? Whitehead had directed that the Men be delous'd, had he not?

"O Captain Whitehead," says I, "I fear I have caught a bad Case of Lice, and little as I wish to interrupt your delectable Plans, I fear we must attend to my Condition ere we sport and play."

"Damme!" cries the Captain, for he is as afraid of Epidemicks as he is hot for his Erotick Play. "Are you certain?" asks he.

"Look for yourself," say I, whereupon I duck my Head before him, but he steps back in Fear. "No, no," he cries, "I'll have your Word for it!" Urine and Ordure he will drink and eat, but a few Lice affright him terribly. O what a curiously contradictory Creature is Man!

When we are settl'd in the Great Cabin, the Captain sends immediately for a Hogshead of Brandy, then directs that the Surgeon be brought to diagnose my Condition.

The Surgeon, a fine young Man of Twenty-Seven or so, comes into the Great Cabin presently, bows to the Captain, acknowledges our Presence politely, and asks Whitehead what Service he desires.

"I desire that you inspect these Ladies' Hair for Lice and then dispatch those Creatures instantly. For, as these Ladies share my Cabin, I cannot risque their Infestations being transmitted to me."

"Very good, Sir," the Surgeon says, whereupon he sets about inspecting first my Scalp, then Susannah's, pronounces, not surprizingly, that I have Lice, whilst Susannah may have 'em in the incipient Stage and suggests a thorough Ablution with Vinegar as the Cure, or possibly e'en our being shorn.

"O no!" I cry, not thinking that such Resistance will surely seal our Fates with Captain Whitehead (for he loves most to do to Ladies what most displeases 'em).

"Vinegar is much too crude a Fluid for such Fine Ladies," says Whitehead. "Bring on the Brandy and let me watch the Show!" Whereupon he leans back in his great oak Captain's Chair and watches with Pleasure whilst we are stripp'd, then washt from Head to Toe in Brandy, then—Goddess preserve us!—shorn.

Our Nether Curls are shav'd, so that our Mounts-Pleasant resemble those of tiny Girls (O this fills me with Longing for my own Sweet Belinda!), but our Scalps are merely cropp'd close, so that the hair stands up in Prickles all 'round.

As I see my long red Curls fall one by one from my Head upon the Cabin Floor, I weep most piteously; for verily, 'tis as if all Strength and all Resistance ebb out of me with the Loss of my Hair!

My Defeat pleases Whitehead well. Rather than Pity for me, he feels Lust. The Debasement of a Woman is the very Essence of his Lust, and since Whitehead is an unavow'd Molly-Coddle or Mary-Ann, he likes nothing better than to see a Woman shorn of her Crown of Curls and to be robb'd of one of the greatest Glories of her Sex.

Naked, shorn, shiv'ring, Susannah and I are perfect Quarry for Whitehead's Perversities. Dismissing the Surgeon, whose fair Face is full of Pity for our Plight, he manacles us to each other once again and delights himself with poking Fingers, Dildoes, and other Objects up our Bums until he hath procur'd for himself his chosen celebratory Feast.

This Perversion he calls "Making the Hen Lay," and the Fruit of his Efforts he terms an "Egg." Verily, he exclaims o'er it as if 'twere an Egg of Gold—and Susannah and I the Golden Geese of Song and Story! 'Twould be comical, I think, if 'twere not supremely sad. But depriv'd of my Hair, my Spirit, e'en my own Shit (which ne'er seem'd to have Value before Whitehead desir'd it), I am too lugubrious to laugh. O the Loss of my red Hair hath depriv'd me of all Capacity for Mirth.

I shall not, dear Reader and Daughter, trouble you with further Details of Captain Whitehead's Perversities. Suffice it to say that like most Men of his Stamp—Mollyish, yet playing the Tyrant to cover his Effeminacy—he was interested in ev'ry Part of the Female Form, save that Bow'r of Delight, that Divine Monosyllable, which is the Summit of the usual Sensualist's Search for Pleasure. That Part alone he disdain'd; that Part alone he ignor'd, as if, indeed, 'twould bite him.

And so we sail'd southward to go Slaving, in the Grip of a capricious Master, who us'd us more as Boys than Women, as Jakes or Close-Stools rather than Human Beings. The Weather grew humid and hot as we drifted into the Southern Seas, and many Men sicken'd with the various Maladies to which all Tars are prone (and the Risque of which had been greatly increas'd by those Rotting Bodies upon the Deck). Captain Whitehead had given out the Word that we would not stop at Madeira to take on new Provisions because doubtless he dar'd not stop in any civiliz'd Port lest all his Men jump Ship. We were to continue directly to the Mouth of the Gambia River, there take on Water and Provisions, and thence steer for the Gold Coast of Guinea. It scarce needs saying that the Tars were not pleas'd about this, distemper'd and unhappy as they were.

The Surgeon neither slept nor ceas'd to toil, for, of our tiny Crew, as many as half were laid up at any Time and four more dy'd and were committed to the Deep. Nor did this dampen Whitehead's gloomy Lusts; he pursu'd 'em as doggedly upon this Ship of Death as another Man might in a bright Spring Meadow. His Appetites were endless and insatiable, albeit carried out in an Atmosphere of doggèd Determination in lieu of enthusiastick Ecstacy—which I fear, is oft' the case with perverse Lusts such as his. O I tried to interest him in other Entertainments, such as Sporting in the Masks and Costumes which had so intrigued Lord Bellars during my Lying-in, but his Proclivities were not of that Persuasion. They lackt e'en that Hint of Whimsy which Lord Bellars' Lusts possess'd; they were Earth-bound to a Degree my Step-Father and his Hell-Fire Brothers could not have known.

Ah, Belinda, Lust is a curious Thing! 'Tis oft' the Obsession of disorder'd Minds and takes its Lineaments from the very Nature of Mind's Disorder. Those Joyless Puritans who denounce all Lust alike are foolish and innocent of the Ways of the World; for, as there is a Diff'rence betwixt sound and rotten Meat, so, too, there is a Diff'rence betwixt chearful Lust and that gloomy Variety which sickens the Soul. For 'tis in the Nature of distemper'd Lust to be insatiable, whilst the robust and loving Lover takes his Pleasure, then basks in the Satiety of a Thing well done, enjoying the Afterglow of Ecstacy as much as the Act itself. As for the distemper'd Lover, there is scarce a Moment of Peace or Rest; he is fore'er searching for a Satiety he will ne'er discover.

Imagine, then, our Plight: we drift inexorably toward Africa upon a Sailing Ship full of distemper'd Tars, enslav'd to a Maniack with an insatiable Passion for Piss and Shit, shorn of our Curls and Courage, cast into the most melancholick of Humours, knowing that each Day takes us further from finding Belinda alive upon this Earth and knowing also that we ourselves are not likely to survive the myriad Distempers of this Voyage. We felt as Castaways must, or as maroon'd Pyrates who know that nought but Birds of Prey visit their doom'd Islet. 'Twas true we had the Company of each other, but Melancholy had cast us down in such a Pit that betwixt us was less Chear than may be found in a Pott of Ale. E'en Grog made us weep, not laugh, and each new Day brought further Degradation.

"God hath abandon'd us," Susannah said.

"Hush, Susannah. If you believe it, 'twill be true." I had ne'er seen a Friend in such Despair. E'en her Body revolted against her Mind: her Stomach heav'd; her Breath came short as broken Straws; and tho' she suffer'd, said the Surgeon, no Distemper, she seem'd curiously upon the Point of Death.

" 'Tis true, Fanny, 'tis true," she sigh'd.

"Bite your tongue, Susannah, and fall upon your Knees and pray." And so she did, but more out of Habit than Conviction. She pray'd to her God, and I to mine, and perhaps they were the same. Yet my own Thoughts were gloomy despite my Encouragement of Susannah. How many since Time began have pray'd and pray'd in vain? How many Greeks, Romans, Mahometans, Jews, Turks, Gypsies, Witches, and e'en good Christians have pray'd to various Gods and been slaughter'd nonetheless? The Witches pray'd to the Great Goddess and dy'd with Her Sacred Name upon their Lips. How many others had dy'd by Burning, Stoning, Flaying, Drowning, Blooding—and dy'd whilst deep in Pray'r? The Supreme Being—howsoe'er you nam'd Him or Her—did not promise to save the Body but only the Soul. Only! The Soul was, indeed, the only Part worth saving, but without knowing my Belinda safe and sound, the Salvation of my Soul was useless to me until I might secure the Salvation of her little Body. If I had liv'd but eighteen Years to learn what I had learnt and bear a Babe, well then, sobeit; I could accept my own Dying ere I had a score of Years to tally—yet I could not accept Belinda's! As sure as I had borne that Babe at Risque of Life, I must do anything within my Pow'r to see her bloom and flourish ere I dye!

I was in the Grip of great Remorse! I blam'd my Romance for the Taking of Belinda, and blam'd my Foolishness in choosing Wet-Nurses, and beat my Breast until 'twas blue with Bruises; I would have torn my Hair if I had had any! We had been at Sea now for upwards of six Weeks and 'twas not impossible to make the Mouth of the Gambia River in two or three more Weeks, if the Winds were favourable. I'faith, we had best arrive there soon or all our Crew would perish!

Besides the Cook, who brought our Meals, the only Member of the small Crew that remain'd who could visit us without incurring the Captain's Suspicions was the Surgeon; he was directed to take special care of our Health owing to the close Contact we had with the Captain. Sometimes, whilst Whitehead was engaged upon Deck, we would converse with Mr. Dennison, the Surgeon, who seem'd to me verily like a floating Spar bobbing upon that vast Ocean of Despair. Bartholomew Dennison, as I have said, was fair of Face, mild-manner'd, and not a little abash'd by Ladies. He was not above twenty-seven Years of Age, but shy as a Country Boy of Twelve in Love with a Milkmaid. He was the sort of Man who wins Women by thinking he has nothing winning about him, the sort of Man, in short, who will ne'er be call'd a Rake or Man of Pleasure, tho' indeed he gives more True Pleasure than those who are term'd such.

Dennison was from Hampshire, the By-Blow of a Lord of Great Estate and a Housemaid turn'd out of Doors by the Lady of the House when she was big with Child. He grew up in a Workhouse, made his Way to London at Fourteen, fell in with the kind of Company that preys upon Country Boys

409

with City Dreams, and found himself, like so many, drunk in a Publick House one Night, and signing his Life away in Exchange for a few Rounds of Ale on Credit. But Dennison was more fortunate than most. Once he had sign'd those cheating Articles and shipp'd away, he was made Assistant to a Surgeon upon a Liverpool Slaver; thus he learnt a useful Craft, and, upon long Sea-Voyages he read the Classicks, thus giving himself the Gentleman's Education the Fates had denied him. Yet Freedom eluded him, for the Trading Company had Snares, it seem'd, to keep the Men perpetually in Debt, and the more they sail'd the larger their Debts grew. Thus, they were as much Slaves as the Blacks from Guinea, and scarce better treated either.

Dennison sought to distract us from our Woes by telling us Stories of his Sailing Life. His Intent was to make us feel less unfortunate and raise our Spirits, for he knew that People perish as much for Want of Hope as for Want of Food or Air.

"The worst Fear I e'er knew, my Girls," said he, "was upon my first Voyage, when I, like you, first realiz'd that a Ship's a Prison and that I was damn'd to stay aboard it come what may—or perish in the Deep.

"Until the Vessel clears the Channel," he said, "the Seamen are not so badly us'd; for the Captain knows that any Wind may drive them back into an English Port and the Tars will then jump Ship. Rations are plentiful enough and Discipline slack. But O when you reach the Open Sea—what a Change is there! One Quart of Water a Day for toiling Men—and some grow so thirsty that they drink up their whole Ration when 'tis serv'd and live the next twenty-four Hours in a Hell of Thirst. Upon my first Voyage, one Tar found a Way of licking Dew Drops off the Hen Coop at Dawn and when he was discover'd, he was keel-haul'd for it and later dy'd of the Wounds inflicted by the Barnacles. The farther we got from England, the worse the Food and the crueller the Discipline. . . ."

"Then how did you endure?" I askt, from the Depths of my Despair.

"Ah, my Friend, God uses us for many Things, teaches us many Lessons that we may be Instruments of His Will. For the past fourteen Years, I have kept a Book of all my Travels and of the worst Excesses of the Slave Trade, and I dream someday that I shall publish it and show the World the Horrors of this Evil Practice. I live only to heal the Sick and

410

write my Book. I turn my Face away from the World and into the Pages of my Secret Journal, dreaming of that Day when I shall publish it and the World shall stand amaz'd."

"When was the World amaz'd by Cruelty?" I askt wearily.

Dennison lookt at me most pensively and shook his Head. "The Word can change the World," he said, "we must believe it."

"So would I have said one Year ago, but since then I have seen Cruelty which astounds the very Soul. When I dreamt in a Library o'er Mr. Milton's and Mr. Shakespeare's Books, I verily believ'd the Word could change the World, but now 'tis 'dark, dark, dark, amid the Blaze of Noon,/Irrecoverably dark . . ./Without all Hope of Day!' "

I spoke in Milton's Words; so Dennsion answer'd me the same: " 'Hence loathèd Melancholy'!" said he; whereupon he added: " 'Haste thee Nymph, and bring with thee/Jest and youthful Jollity,/Quips and Cranks, and wanton Wiles,/Nods, and Becks, and wreathèd Smiles.' " And he smil'd the sunniest Smile I had seen in Months.

"O where shall I find those wreathèd Smiles upon this Ship of Death?" I askt; "and how shall I go on when e'en my Friend, Susannah, is shaken in her changeless Faith?"

"By Rights," said Dennison, "given what I have witness'd in these Years of Slaving, I should be faithless and melancholick as you yourself. But the first Voyage is the worst, for there is no sadder State than new-affrighted Innocence, as 'twere. You think yourself the first Soul upon this Earth to discover the World's Wickedness; but 'tis not the case. You discover Hypocrisy and Guile as if you were Adam discovering the Serpent's first Duplicity, and you rail at an indiff'rent God, but later, as you endure, you will learn that He hath put you here for many Lessons. Why, upon my first Voyage I saw Tars so ill-us'd that they committed Suicide in Shark-fill'd Waters. I saw Black Men stackt upon each other as if they were so many Logs of Wood, as 'twere. I went down into the Hold to treat Slaves who were ill with Bloody Flux and I swoon'd there of the Smell and could not rise e'en when I was cover'd with Blood and Ordure. O the Hold was as awash with Blood as 'twere an Abbattoir and all that Blood issu'd from the Roiling Guts of these poor Slaves from Guinea! I saw Slaving Captains who would stuff the sick Slaves' Anuses with Oakum before the Scramble or Auction in the West Indies, and I saw Seamen flogg'd till their Backs were raw—for the most trivial Offences—and then a Mixture

411

of Sea-Water and Chian Pepper rubb'd in those very Wounds. But I believe that God hath sent me upon this Earth to be a Scribe, God's Quill, as 'twere. His Amanuensis, as 'twere, so I observe all most faithfully and put it in my Book. For I know that when the Inhuman Abuses of the Slave Trade are commonly known, all reasoning Men shall rise up as one Body and protest these Evils."

"O wherefore do you put such Faith in Reason?" I askt. "O wherefore do you believe that Men have only to see Evil to denounce it? Men look upon Evil with great Complaisancy when it touches 'em not directly. And e'en when it comes close to their own Families they shut their Eyes and steadfastly refuse to see it."

"Ah Fanny, you are bitter with the Bitterness of Innocence first Affrighted, but Time shall mellow you. I do not mean that one Word changes the World at once or that one Book transmutes all Grief to Glory, as 'twere. I only mean to say that Books are like Bricks wherewith we build the House of Justice. We build with one Brick at a Time. Each Seeker of Truth toils like a Bee in a Hive, as 'twere, but all together we shall make the Honey of the World!"

"Honey?" askt Susannah. "Honey?" During that Interval whilst Dennison and I had talkt, she had been huddl'd in her Berth in the Great Cabin, with the Quilt pull'd up almost o'er her Head. I was not e'en sure she listen'd to our Talk, but now she rose out of her Berth, wrapt in her Eider-Down, and walkt the Floorboards like an Apparition. With her small Head almost shav'd and her Arms and Shoulders thin from the Poverty of our Shipboard Rations, she lookt a sable Ghost walking the Floor.

"The Honey o' the World?" she askt. "Ah seek not the Honey o' the World upon the Earth—seek it in Heaven!" She stopp'd and rais'd her Arms, letting the Quilt drop to the Floor. Her Ribs show'd thro' her brown Flesh and her Ankles and Wrists were raw where she had oft' been manacl'd to serve Whitehead's Lusts. "See, see how the Air is bright with Honey," she cried, "how it dazzles the Eye an' ye can taste it upon the Tongue! 'Tis God's Honey—this Honey o' the World, but how shall we eat it without bein' stung?"

So saying, she ran in all her Nakedness out of the Great Cabin and upon the Deck. Dennison and I pursu'd her, reaching the Deck in Time to see her scramble up the Shrouds, naked as the Day of her Nativity, and spread her

Wings as if to fly o'er the Ocean straight into the Bosom of God.

"God Bless ye both, an' also Sweet Belinda!" she cried. Whereupon she flapp'd a little with her scrawny Arms and flew, like Icarus, up for a Moment, then down, down, down into the Depths of the all-enveloping, all-forgiving Sea.

Chapter X

In which our Heroine learns that no Man is such a Scoundrel that he doth not wish to be an Author, that e'en Slavers account themselves patriotick and virtuous, that the Sea is as full of Magick and Mystery as the Land, and that Ships oft' become Pyrate Prizes as much thro' the Connivance of their own Tars as thro' any other Means.

SUSANNAH'S UNTIMELY FATE did not affect me quite as I would have suppos'd. Melancholy I was, and melancholy I remain'd. Lost and friendless I was—except for Bartholomew Dennison—and lost and friendless I remain'd. Yet, tho' I griev'd for Susannah most piteously, and miss'd her sorely, the Example of her Suicide, far from making me wish to imitate it, made me most determin'd to survive. The Deaths of our Friends are most curious in that regard: they oft' inspire in us a hot Desire to live. Susannah had sav'd my Life and shar'd with me that Moment when my Soul split—O irrevocably!—in twain and I became a Mother. From that Moment onward no Movement I made would fail to take Belinda's Fate into Account. 'Twas the Way of Motherhood, the Sorrow and the Glory of the Female of the Species: that once having born a Child, the Soul divides itself betwixt the Child and Mother and the Mother cannot toss her own Life away without consid'ring what will become of her Babe.

Yet did I ponder long and hard regarding Susannah's Fate and what it might mean. Susannah was Faith itself, my self-appointed Intermediary with God, and when she abandon'd her Faith and perish'd, 'twas as if God sent a Rebuke to me about the Danger of losing Faith. Yet, at the Last, she seem'd to have a Vision ere she dy'd; and like her African Forbears, seem'd to believe that in her Dying, she'd rejoin her Ancestors. How I hop'd 'twas verily the case!

Bartholomew Dennison wrote it all faithfully in his Book, betwixt his Visits to the Sick and Dying and his Attendance upon me. As for Captain Whitehead, tho' it piqued him to lose one of his private Whores, it did nought but confirm his Beliefs concerning the predestin'd Inferiority of the Negro Race, their Fitness to be Slaves, their Deficiency in Reason and his own Righteousness in engaging in the Slave Trade. The Crew, for their part, took it as a Sign, if more Signs were needed, that this Voyage was doom'd. All their Seamen's Superstitions now came to the Fore and they murmur'd of curst Ships that have Women aboard, of ghostly Galleons pursuing us across the Seas, and other Vapourish Fantasies to which all Tars, so Bartholomew avow'd, were prone.

As for me, I could not decide what the Meaning of Susannah's Death might be, but it acted upon me as a pow'rful Goad to my Resolution to endure this wretchèd Voyage. As Bartholomew believ'd himself to be set upon Earth to chronicle the Slave Trade, I knew that I was destin'd for some Mission which had not yet become clear to me. I knew that I must save Belinda and I also dimly sens'd that all my thwarted Efforts to scribble Epicks and Romances were leading me perhaps towards a Destiny not unlike Dennison's. Yet I lackt his Conviction—perhaps because of my Sex. 'Tis easier for a Man to believe in the Nobility of his Destiny than for a Woman; the Fair Sex faces so many Obstacles, not the least of which are: Whoredom, Motherhood, the Distractions of Love.

But sure there was some Reason why I had surviv'd the Witches' Massacre, surviv'd the Birth that should have kill'd me, surviv'd e'en this Voyage. Let me find my tatter'd red Garter, I thought, and put it on. Whereupon, as I was seeking it in the Depths of the Portmanteau Susannah and I had dragg'd aboard, I chanced to remember the Witches' Prophecy recited to me by poor dead Joan all those Months ago. The words echo'd in my Ears as if in Joan's Voice, transform'd by Trance, but I heard the Lines with new Understanding.

> Your own Father you do not know.
> Your Daughter will fly across the Seas.
> Your Purse will prosper, your Heart will grow.
> You will have Fame, but not Heart's Ease.

From your Child-Womb will America grow.
By your Child-Eyes, you will be betray'd.
You will turn Blood into driven Snow.
By your own strong Heart will the Devil be stay'd.

So many Predictions had already come true! If I was to have Fame, then surely I must survive! If I was to stay the Devil, then surely I must survive! The Prophecy had not yet been proven wrong! O my dear, dead Friends, my Sister Witches, Susannah, my sable Sister lost at Sea, I shall not forget you. Your Deaths shall not have been in vain. I shall carry the Blessings of the Goddess across the Seas, and with my Life and Belinda's avenge all your cruel Deaths!

E'en as I was drawing on the tatter'd Garter, the Ship began to heave and rock; Water slapp'd against the Hull and the Cabin tilted perilously, causing all the Captain's Charts and Papers to slide off his Writing Bureau upon the Floor. Then, 'twas as if some Creature rose from the Deep, exactly under our Keel, lifted us for a Moment out of the Water, whereupon it plunged us back down into the Waves with great Noise and Tumult.

So shaken was I by this strange Occurrence—taking place exactly at the Moment I was standing upon one Leg slipping the red Garter on the other—that I fell to the Floorboards upon my Bum. I was still sitting there, astounded and stunn'd, when Bartholomew rusht in to enquire after my Health, bringing with him the News that the Helmsman had been momentarily much affrighted, for he could neither steer in one Direction nor the other whilst the Obstacle remain'd.

"What could it be?" I askt.

"The Helmsman says a Whale—or else a Sea-Monster, as 'twere," Bartholomew laugh'd nervously; "for Whales are rare in this Latitude."

In a trice, I knew that this "Whale" was not a Whale at all. "I know who 'tis," I said.

"Pray who?" askt Bartholomew.

"I cannot say—but 'tis a Sign." For as I live and breathe and write this Book, I knew 'twas the Great Goddess.

"Pray tell," said Bartholomew.

"That I cannot, for you will take me for a Lunatick, but mark my Words, 'tis no Whale."

"Susannah's Ghost?" askt Bartholomew.

"Exactly so," said I. And in a Sense, 'twas true, too.

"Thank God, she's a friendly Ghost, as 'twere," said Bartholomew, laughing as if I had spoken but in jest.

At the Time I receiv'd the aforesaid Sign from the Goddess upon High (or from the Heavenly Spheres, the Supreme Being, or whatsoe'er you may wish to call Her), we had been at Sea, as I have said, six Weeks, and we were already in most southerly Climes. Our Destination was the Mouth of the Gambia River, where Captain Whitehead plann'd to trade some of the Commodities most in demand in Guinea (or Negroland—as that and the adjoining Lands are call'd upon Old Maps) for the fresh Provisions which we sorely lackt. Then, we were to continue 'round the Coast of Sierra de Leon, the Ivory Coast, and the Gold Coast, in search of Slaves. As far as I could ascertain, the African Coast was full of great Rivers from the Gambia to the Callebar and e'en beyond. 'Twas down these Rivers that the Canoos bearing dark-complexion'd Slaves were brought to be sold into a Life of Misery or a Hellish Death. For the Purposes of Trading, Captain Whitehead had brought along pewter Basons of sev'ral Sizes, old Sheets, Iron Bars, large Flemish Knives, Cases of Spirits, and the large good-colour'd Coral said to be much belov'd by the African Kings. He also carried divers Supplies for the Castle of the Trading Company, such as Muskets, brass Kettles, English Carpets, Lead Bars, Firkins of Tallow, Powder, et cetera. Our Crew was much reduced, 'twas true, but Tars he hop'd to enlist when we reach'd our Trading Fort. I was, of course, most desirous of Escape so I lost no Time in quizzing Captain Whitehead upon his Plans, since I knew little of the Slave Trade but for the Horrors Bartholomew (and Lancelot, before him) had recited. I thought that the more I knew, the better were my Chances for Escape, but Whitehead was most evasive concerning the Stops he plann'd to make. He seem'd to know that I was too interested in his Intentions, thus he was deliberately vague concerning both the Location of the Trading Company's Factory and the various African Rivers where we would barter for Slaves.

Upon one Occasion, not long after Susannah's Death, I chanced to find, in the Great Cabin, an Old Map of the Guinea Coast, showing all the Rivers, Islands, and Shoals. I was essaying to burn it into my Memory when Whitehead appear'd, and despite my best Efforts to conceal what I was doing, discover'd me at my secret Studies.

"Your Interest in Geography is keen, I see," said White-head, snatching away the Map and rolling it tightly.

"O Captain Whitehead, I am a slow Scholar," said I. "Maps confuse me; I can hardly read 'em at all." But, clearly in my Mind's Eye. I saw the Names of Countries from Negroland to Guinea, from Mandinga to Zanfara; and the Names of Rivers, from Gambia to Sestro, from Formosa to Callebar.

"You'll not escape, Madam," said Whitehead coldly, "for I have Ways to keep you in my Care—Manacles, Leg-Irons, and the like—which would chafe your lovely Skin most sorely. Do not fail to take into consideration how merciful I have been till now, but you try my Patience in the extream." So saying, he reach'd for his Supplejack and whipp'd it thro' the Air most menacingly to show me his Severity.

"Captain," says I, "my Intentions are scarcely to escape, but merely to learn more about this Expedition, for I am most intrigued with this Trade you engage in, and having oft' been a Devotée of Narratives of Explorations and Expeditions, I fancy I may someday wish to write of these Travels. . . ."

"And if you do, Madam," says Whitehead, "pray, depict 'em in the proper Light, for I am sick to Death of those who say the Slave Trade is a brutal Calling. Wherefore brutal? Why, Slaves upon a Slave Ship are far better treated than e'en indentur'd Whites. They are plentifully fed; Mirth and Jollity are oft' their predominant Humours, and they are rouz'd to bodily Exercise to prevent their unhealthy dwelling upon their Change of State and Loss of Home. Crowded in some small Degree, they must necessarily be, but Crowding, alas, is the Fate of all who sail the Seas. . . ."

I was amaz'd at this Recital of the Pleasures of Slaving, for Whitehead himself had told me that Man-eating Sharks would follow our Ship thro'out the Middle Passage and that many Tars would have refus'd to board had they known we were going Slaving.

"Wherefore, then, do you deceive your Tars," I askt, "if Slaving is so sweet?"

"O Seamen are a Parcel of slothful Poltroons," said he, "who cannot bear an honest Day's Work and many dread the Southern Seas, for they have been corrupted by the Horror Tales soft-hearted Fools bring back from Guinea."

"And what of the Sharks that trail the Ships?" I askt.

"O 'twas a Jest," said he, "a mere Bagatelle. Why, the

Ocean Floor is pav'd with Bones and most of 'em are the Bones of White Men! The Sea's no easy Calling—that I grant. But those Lily-liver'd Souls who denounce the Slave Trade are ignorant both of the Sea and of the very Nature of the Negro Heart. Life is cheap in Africa; they do not feel about their Fates as White Men do. Why, Time out of Mind, it hath been their Custom to make Slaves of all the Captives taken in War. Now, before they had the Golden Opportunity of selling 'em to White Men, they oft' were obliged to kill Great Multitudes, for fear that they should mutiny 'gainst their Captors. The Slave Trade, therefore, spares many Lives, and great Numbers of Useful Persons are kept in being. Secondly, these Slaves, when carried to the Plantations, live far better there than they did in their own Countries; for the Planters, having paid dear for them, have a great Stake in keeping 'em alive and in good Health. Thirdly, the Trade is patriotick in the Highest Sense, for as 'tis the Wish of ev'ry True-born Englishman to see his Country prosper both at Home and abroad, what could be more pleasing to the Patriotick Englishman than to view the great Advantages which have accru'd to our Nation thro' the Bountiful Harvests of the Sugar Isles? Why, e'en the most middling sort of Londoner takes Sugar in his Tea, and buys printed Calicoes of Cotton for his Lady. Wherefore would our Capital be such a Pleasure Fair without the Trade that issues from our fine Plantations in the West Indies, which, lying in a Climate near as hot as the Coast of Guinea, the Negroes are fitter to cultivate the Lands there than the White People? In a Word, from this Trade proceed Benefits, far outweighing all, either real or pretended, Mischiefs and Inconveniences. The worst that can be said of it may be, that like all other Earthly Advantages, the Advantages of the Slave Trade are temper'd with a Mixture of Good and Evil—but in that regard 'tis like all the Rest of Life! Pray Madam, write *this* if you write about the Slave Trade! By Jove, it hath done England more Good than all the Riches of India! Besides, as all Civiliz'd Nations engage in it—the Dutch, the Portuguese, the Spanish, e'en the damnable French—only a Person of greatly deficient Wit and Reason might be so misled by the Tenderness of his Heart that he should fail to see the Blessings of this Trade and dwell upon the Curses. Sure, ev'ry Blessing comes with added Curses, but taken as a whole, by a Man of Reason, 'tis an admirable Calling, albeit a demanding one. And 'tis more patriotick than leading a conquering Army; for whilst the Army depletes our Nation of Wealth, our Plantations and the Slaves who work 'em bring in Riches undreamt of by the very Moguls of India. Write *this*, Madam, and do not fail to praise the Reasonableness of the Trade, tho' I know you are no great Believer in Reason!"

I was quite stunn'd by this long Apologia for a Calling which, until now, I had ne'er heard spoken of but in the blackest of Lights.

"What a pretty Speech," said I. "My Captain hath a Way with Words, i'faith."

Whitehead preen'd a bit, pleas'd yet careful not to show his Pleasure too clearly.

"I have oft' thought to write my Adventures, too, Madam; for the Narratives of Voyages I have read are full of egregious Errors. At the very least," said he, "I may put my Pen to a Pamphlet, explaining the Blessings of this Trade which hath been so oft' malign'd."

Aha, I thought to myself, in all of England and her Colonies, is there no Fool nor Knave so debas'd and illiterate that he doth not delude himself he is an *Author*? Is ev'ry Knave a Scribbler in his Soul? What a Curse is Education then—if ev'ry Cretinous Criminal thinks to tell his Tale and justify his foul, felonious Trade!

"Perhaps I may be your Amanuensis, Sir," said I, "for I write a fine Hand—for a Wench, that is—and I have some small Degree of Skill at making Sentences, e'en Verses, despite my Sex."

"Hmmmm," said Whitehead, not a little tempted by my Proposal. "Your Offer interests me. Let me think on't, Madam."

Thus did I achieve, by dint of my Education and Skill in Scribbling, what e'en my Brothel Tricks could not secure for me: namely, the Captain's wary Trust. For tho' he still watch'd me closely, he grew so carried away with his Desire to justify the Slave Trade in his Memoirs (which now I began to scribble for him) that he could not treat me quite as he had before. 'Tis said that no Man's a Hero to his Valet—how much more true 'tis for an Amanuensis! For I was privy to the Workings of his Mind and 'twas I who fram'd his Thoughts in good plain-spoken English whilst he rambl'd and reminisced of his Adventures.

From Whitehead, I learnt immeasurably about what motivates some Men to conceive themselves superior to their Fellows on account of the Colour of their Skins. For Whitehead, whose own Erotick Proclivities were none too fastidious, seem'd to think himself better than the Negroes, owing to their Proximity to the Beasts and his own to the Angels. In speaking of the Blacks of Guinea, he oft' describ'd 'em as "Monkies," or remarkt that their Teeth, being fil'd into Points, had a "canine" Appearance. Likewise he avow'd that their Song was a "wild and savage Yell, more befitting Beasts than Men." Now, I, who had the highest Regard both for Dogs and Horses (and accounted those Species oft' superior to Mankind), could not but find this a curious "Justification" for the sad Traffick in Human Flesh in which Whitehead engaged. 'Twas remarkable to me that a Man who lov'd Piss and Shit as Whitehead did, should account the Negro Slaves "bestial" for what he term'd "the filthy Habit of depositing their natural Excretions where they sleep." Were these poor Creatures not manacl'd where they lay? Were they not depriv'd of Chamber-Potts or any other civiliz'd Article in which to do Nature's Bidding? Why e'en the Tars of the *Hopewell* had no better Accommodations for Nature's Necessity than to climb out along the Bowsprit and thence discharge their Excrement into the Sea; for none but the Captain, the Surgeon, and the Sick had Close-Stools aboard our dismal little Brigantine. Yet Whitehead blam'd the Negroes for their Filth as if they themselves, not their Captors, were responsible for their Conditions. That same Effusion which he call'd "Nectar" or "Vintage Wine" in his Hot Fits of Lust, that same Excretion he term'd "Eggs," were nought but Objects of Disgust when they issu'd from the Negro Slaves! Ah, give me Dogs before Men any Day, for they make no Bones (if I may be permitted a low Pun) about their Love of sniffing Shit and do not fault other Canines for it!

Whitehead's Memoirs, as he dictated 'em, were full of Phrases like "Common Decency" and "Personal Cleanliness," as if he himself were but the Height of Civilization and Fastidiousness and 'neath him lay all God's other Creatures. Indeed, I have oft' noted this is the case with Memoirs both of Politicians and of Criminals: that tho' they be guilty themselves of the most heinous Crimes, yet they are very quick to judge their Fellow Man and find him wanting.

We were not far from the Mouth of the Gambia River, and the Weather had become almost unbearably hot and humid, when our Ship found itself suddenly becalm'd and Fog-bound and unable to proceed under Sail.

The Tops of our own Masts were invisible and the Shrouds themselves seem'd to vanish into the Mist, like Ladders up to Heaven. 'Twas impossible to see our own Bowsprit, not to mention the other Ships about us! Vapourish and ill as the Tars were—given our Shortness of Rations, owing to our Failure to stop in Madeira—the Fog seem'd still another perilous Omen to 'em. By now, 'twas Common Knowledge that Whitehead had deceiv'd the Crew as to our Destination, and the more season'd Seamen amongst 'em had deduced we were going Slaving. Were it not that the Example of Llewelyn's Torture still haunted their Dreams, the Crew should have kill'd the Captain forthwith and taken o'er their own Destinies.

O what a curious Creature is the Fog! It blunts the Eyes, the Ears, e'en the Sense of Touch, and it encourages Fancies in the Brain. Seamen who ne'er experience Vapours in a Tempest do so in the Fog, for it seems a sentient Being in itself, a sort of Sea-Monster of amorphous Shape, lying ev'ry-where and nowhere.

I remember that I was in the Great Cabin on just such a Fogbound Night (scribbling down the Captain's Recollections from previous Voyages whilst he paced and drank his Grog and talkt like one possess'd), when the Watch came in to report that he heard the Rowing of a Boat not far off. The Captain started for the Deck, bidding me follow—for, now as his Chronicler, I had such Privileges—and lookt about for the reported Boat, but all was Eerieness and Mist. We were anchor'd somewhere off Cape Verde then, awaiting the Lifting of the Fog, and feeling we had sail'd straight to Hades, owing to the Closeness of the Weather, when, thro' the Tropick Darkness, the soft Splash of Oars and the Rattle of Oar-Locks could be heard. Whitehead quickly order'd the First Mate who had replaced Cocklyn to go down into the Steerage and send up as many arm'd Men as possible. Then he listen'd as the Slap of Oars drew closer. "Hail the Visitors," we order'd his Second Mate, which the Latter duly did, asking, according to Custom, whence she came and who she was. Thro' the Fog, the Reply came back:

"From the Seas!"

"Pyrates!" cried Whitehead, for this was the traditional Pyrate Reply and now he knew what Manner of Men he was addressing.

"Where are the Men I call'd for?" he shouted down into the Steerage, but all was Silence below.

I lookt out, into the Fog, wond'ring what Fate awaited us in the misty Darkness, yet no further Sound was heard but for that ominous Dip and Splash of Oars. I thought of the Stories I had read of Pyrates; of Henry Morgan's notorious Practice of hoisting the decapitated Corpse of one of his Enemies from a Yardarm whilst the grisly Head dangl'd by a Tarry Rope from its Feet; of Ears and Noses sliced off as if they were so many Lumps of Butter; of maroon'd Men smear'd in Honey and left to the Ants; of Prisoners roasted alive to tell the Porto Bello Pyrates of their hidden Gold. "From the Seas!" The very Phrase was enough to freeze the Blood! O I was horribly afraid.

"Where are my Men—you mutinous Dogs!" shouted Whitehead desperately. Silence in the Steerage was all the Reply he receiv'd; whereupon he drew his Sword and stood upon the Deck as if he would duel with the Fog-Creature. O ne'er had I seen him so panickt as he stood awaiting his Fate like some Don Quixote that would joust with Mist!

"Go into the Steerage," he commanded the Second Mate, "and summon the Men!"

"Aye, aye, Sir," said the Second Mate, who now disappear'd in turn; but no Sound of must'ring Men was heard in the Hold. Finally, in dire Desperation, he bade *me* summon the Men, which I was upon the very Point of doing, when the Sounds in the Water below convinced us that the Boarding Party had already arriv'd and was scrambling up the Side.

"Open Fire, you Mutinous Dogs!" Whitehead shouted to his Crew, yet the Pyrates, who were already clambering upon the Deck, encounter'd no Resistance whatsoe'er in Boarding; and taking Whitehead's Words as if they were Commands intended for themselves, they open'd Fire upon the Instant, fell'd the Captain with a Volley of Musket Shot, and would have fell'd me had I not duckt in Time.

"Send for Dennison!" cried Whitehead, bleeding upon the Deck; whereupon I rusht down into the Steerage in search of my Friend, the Surgeon, and saw, to my Horror, all the Tars reclining at their Ease, awaiting the Moment to turn Pyrate.

"Is the old Bastard dead yet?" askt the Second Mate.

"Tell the Pyrates we're their Men!" shouted the First Mate.

"A gold Chain or a wooden Leg, we'll follow 'em!" cried another Tar.

"A short Life and a merry one!" cried another.

"The Captain's wounded," said I. "He requires the Surgeon."

"Let the old Bastard bleed to death!" declar'd the Second Mate. "He'd do no less for us."

"Will you just lye there and let the Ship be taken?" I askt, incredulous.

"With any Luck, we will!" said the First Mate.

"Where's Dennison?" I askt.

"Scribblin' in his Cabin," cried the Second Mate, "an' deaf to the World."

Just then, we all turn'd and star'd as one, as the Pyrate Boarding Party, a Group of five, descended into the Steerage with their Cutlasses rais'd in Menace and their Muskets and Pistols pois'd for fire. I lookt into their Faces and I swoon'd.

"Lancelot! Horatio!" I cried.

Chapter XI

Containing a better Explanation for the Prevalence of Pyracy than any Authors, ancient or modern, have yet advanced; together with our Heroine's tragick but true Realization that most Revolutionaries are none where Women are concern'd, and what ingenious Stratagem she made Use of to alter this sad State of Affairs.

'TWAS LANCELOT as sure as this Quill I write with scratches, and Horatio dress'd as a perfect Pyrate Prince, and with 'em were three other Black-skinned Men—as fierce a Parcel of Pyrate Potentates as you might hope to clap your Eyes upon, on Land or Sea!

"Lancelot!" I cried, to the Vision of my former Love, now with a long red Beard plaited with Sea-green Ribbands, and the Sea-green Eyes which had a lunatick Look. But Lancelot regarded me blankly as if he neither understood nor recogniz'd me. Likewise Horatio seem'd stunn'd to be call'd by Name. He had let his Hair grow into a ferocious Bush and atop it wore a tatter'd Hat, laced with tarnish'd Silver. Like legendary Blackbeard, he'd taken to putting lighted Matches 'neath his Hat, which glow'd along their Fuses and made him look the Compleat Vision of a Fiend from Hell. The other Black Men had Faces cut with Tribal Scars and Teeth fil'd into Points: their Skins were dark as Ebony. 'Twas clear they were Africans, not former Slaves from the Sugar Isles; and they'd clearly turn'd Pyrate with great Gusto. Astounded that a Wench dar'd to address their Captain and Quartermaster so familiarly, they seiz'd me by the Arms and held me fast.

For a Moment, I was terrified. Can I be dreaming? I askt myself; was there ne'er a smooth-cheakt Lancelot nor any Black Horatio? O my Brain was addl'd by the Torments of this Voyage, by Whitehead's Excesses, Susannah's Suicide, Belinda's Kidnapping, and all I had endur'd. Perhaps my Recollection of a Love call'd Lancelot was nought but something I had read in a Romance or dreamt abed. Perhaps Horatio was no Horatio at all, but only a sable Apparition. But e'en as I thought this, my Lips began to speak without my Will: *"Segnius irritant Animos dismissa per Aures,"* they said, quoting Horace, *"Quam quae sunt Oculis submissa fidelbus!"* (Which, translated into good, plain English, means: "What the trusty Eyes behold piques the Mind more than that which issues thro' the Ears.")

"By Jove!" cried Horatio, " 'tis the Beauteous Fanny! For tho' the Lass is shorn of all her Hair, yet still she hath a silver Latin Tongue!"

"Dammel!" cried Lancelot, "I'll not call that bald Wench me own Sweet Fanny just because she babbles in damn'd Pig Latin! Speak English, Wench. Wherefore d'ye claim to be Fanny Hackabout the Fair, fer if yer lyin' I'll pierce yer lyin' Heart fer takin' me True Love's Name in vain!"

Whereupon I recited the Robin Hood Oath, to prove my Identity beyond a Doubt, and as I finish'd, all my Shipmates cried, "Aye! Aye! We'll take that Oath and turn Pyrate, too!"

"Just a Moment, Lads," cried Lancelot, "not so fast. Not ev'ryone can join the Merry Men." And then to me: "What Villain cut yer Hair? Fer ye look worse than a pluckt Duck! 'Tis the Rape o' the Lock as sure as I'm Robin Hood reborn!"

"O Lancelot, Horatio! I'm so happy to see you both," and breaking free of my Captors, who now stood back, I ran to the Arms of my Merry Men and fell upon 'em weeping.

"First the Ship, Lass, then the Celebration!" said Lancelot, "fer we're here to take a Prize, not a Pudendum!" And he wriggl'd out of my Arms like the Lancelot of Old.

"Let's kill the Captain!" shouted the First Mate.

"Killin's too good fer him!" shouted the Second Mate.

"Let's do to him what he hath done to Llewelyn!"

"What's this? What's this?" askt Lancelot.

"O Lancelot," said I, "there is so much to tell—my beauteous Babe is gone, kidnapp'd by an evil Nurse—and as for the Captain here, not only hath he cut my Hair, but he is a Monster of Cruelty who hath done such Deeds to all the Men and me as not e'en deranged Popish Monks in a Roman Monastery could be guilty of! He is a Torturer, a Slaver, and a Lover of the Supplejack. He despises Women and the Negro Race and he hath no Use for his own Seamen, whom he uses as mere Beasts of Burden and flings into the Sea when they dye of Distempers. O I could go on and on detailing his Cruelties, but we must not tarry here, for perchance he will escape if left alone upon the Deck!"

"Is this true, me Lads?" askt Lancelot of my fellow Travellers.

"True! True!" they cried.

"The Wench is no Liar!" said the First Mate.

"Let's put the Captain to the Jog o' Death!" said the Second Mate.

"Let's have him walk the Plank!" said another Tar.

"Torture's no cure fer Torturers!" cried Lancelot, "but Kindness is!"

"Nay!" cried the First Mate, "if ye show that filthy Cur Kindness, ye'll have to deal with me and all my Men."

"We'll not turn Pyrate if ye show him Kindness," said the Second Mate.

Lancelot rais'd his Cutlass; he was now properly piqued.

"Ye'll not turn what?" said he. "Ye'll not turn what?" He took the Second Mate by the Scruff of the Neck. "I take no forced Men," said he. "Only Rogues an' Cut-Throats take forced Men. Ev'ry Man who sails with me sails out o' Love o' True Democracy! We take the Oath o' Robin Hood. We sign the Pyrate Articles which guarantee that no Man sails against his Will, nor dares be King o'er any other Man. Ev'ry Prize we take is subject to a Vote. Each Man's Share is written in our Code o' Laws an' Woe to him that breaks it! If knowin' that, ye now will swear the Oath o' Robin Hood in all Solemnity an' with a faithful Heart, we'll clap the Captain o' this Ship in Irons an' take a Vote as to his Fate when there be Time! If any disagree, let him speak up now!"

The Men of the *Hopewell* listen'd, aw'd, to Lancelot; like ev'ryone meeting him for the first Time, they were a bit bedazzl'd by his great Gifts as a Tonguepad, his unfailing Knack of rallying Men 'round him. A bit mad he might be, but his very Presence, Bearing, and the Sound of his Voice made Men wish to follow him to the Ends of the Earth.

"Let's swear the Oath!" cried the First Mate.

"Aye, aye!" cried the Second.

"Very well, then," says Lancelot, "repeat the Oath after Madam Fanny," and he had me recite the Robin Hood Oath yet again, with great Solemnity (as I repeat it here for the Reader who hath, perhaps, forgotten it):

"I swear by the Ghost o' Robin Hood
That I shall steal—but steal for Good" (I chanted),

"That I his Creed shall e'er uphold.
And love True Justice more than Gold."

To which the Men echo'd their Assent and Agreement, repeating the Oath Line for Line.

"Come then, Lads," said Lancelot, "let's clap the Captain in Irons!" Whereupon Lancelot started for the Deck with Horatio and his Black Pyrates trailing him, after which the Officers and Tars of the *Hopewell* also follow'd with great Whoops of Delight.

Arriving above, we saw at once that Whitehead had struggl'd to his Feet, despite his considerable Wounds. He was tott'ring upon the misty Fo'c'sle Deck with his Pistol in his shaky Hand.

Seeing the howling, whooping Hordes come to fetch him, he'd train'd his Pistol upon Lancelot, and, as if still the Master of his Ship, he cried: "Welcome! Win her and wear her!" 'Twas a brave Stand for a Captain, but more bluster than Ferocity, for Whitehead lurch'd upon his Feet and his Voice quaver'd like an old Man's. Ne'ertheless Horatio ran immediately to disarm the Villain; as Lancelot's self-appointed Guard, he could not risque Shots being fir'd.

"Are ye the Captain o' the *Hopewell*?" askt Lancelot, knowing the Answer perfectly well.

"I had been so till now!" cried Whitehead in great Distress. Already the three fierce Black Men had run to aid Horatio and were beginning to bind Whitehead Hand and Foot.

"Tye him to the Foremast!" Lancelot order'd.

The Black Pyrates did his Bidding whilst Horatio led the Men of the *Hopewell* in firing a Victory Salvo into the Air. Lancelot's Party had only been aboard a few Minutes and already the Ship was theirs! But apparently, the Pyrates upon the Mother Ship, hearing Fire, concluded that their belov'd Lancelot had been taken, and they began to cannonade the *Hopewell* in Vengeance for the presum'd Murder of their Master and his Boarding Party. Pandemonium reign'd then upon our Decks as the Pyrate Ship all needlessly attackt the Pyrate Prize.

"Hoist the *Joli Rouge!*" cried Whitehead, who could not now, like the Rest of us, duck to avoid Fire and was therefore in Terror of being hit again.

"What's that? Ye cowardly Cur," cried Lancelot, "are ye afraid o' goin' to the Devil by a Great Shot?"

"That'll be nothin' compar'd to what we'll do to you!"

428

shouted the First Mate of the *Hopewell*, flattening himself upon the Deck to avoid being hit by what seem'd an eighteen-pound Ball. It thunder'd upon the Deck quite near him and crasht thro' the Wood as if 'twere Paper.

"If ye were wise, ye'd ask God to take ye now!" cried the Second Mate.

In a trice, Horatio drew a crusht and folded Pyrate Flag from his Coat and made quick Work of hoisting it. 'Twas a red Banner, showing a fierce Skeleton with an Hourglass in one Hand (to show Time running out for the Prey) and a rais'd Cutlass in the other. Below the Skeleton was the Motto "*A Deo a Libertate*," for God and Liberty, to show all who came near Lancelot's Ships that he was no Common Cut-Throat Pyrate, but Pyrate of *Principle*. Tho' the Flag soon flutter'd on high, the Mother Ship still blaz'd away in the Darkness, and the vigorous Cannonade did not cease. Were it not that the Fog caus'd as many Cannon to miss us as to hit, we surely should be sunk!

"They cannot see our *Joli Rouge!*" cried Horatio, "for the Fog obscures all but the Ghosts of our Lights!"

"Then send a Party to hail the Mother Ship!" cried Lancelot. "An' be quick about it!"

"Don't give me Orders, White Man!" snapp'd Horatio. "Send a Party yourself!" With all deliberate Speed, Lancelot dispatch'd a Boat containing the Black Pyrates and the new First Mate of the *Hopewell*. Their Task was to inform the Mother Ship that the Prize had been taken, the Tars turn'd Pyrate, and all was well. Those of us still aboard the *Hopewell* duckt below the Waists and pray'd that the Boat should arrive at the Pyrate Flag Ship before Lancelot's Men destroy'd our Rigging utterly in their o'er-zealous but misguided Revenge.

Whitehead, for his part, now rav'd upon the Deck where the huge Cannon Balls kept missing him.

"Have Mercy upon my Sinful Soul," he cried, turning away from Reasonable Deism and towards a Personal, if Unreasoning, God in his Hour of Need. O 'twas painful to see him raving there! He was as frighten'd and cowardly as any Man I've seen. Stripp'd of his Supplejack, Pistols, and Captain's Authority, he shrank from a great Villain into a Little Boy, begging us for Mercy.

In all this Riot, the last Person on my Mind was Bartholomew Dennison, who had been scribbling away in his Cabin whilst these Events occurr'd on Deck. (Only a Scribbler could

429

be so oblivious of a Cannonade!) Now he show'd his Face e'en as the Broadsides flew. Standing upon the Ladder, half above Deck, half below, he rais'd his Piece in Lancelot's Direction.

"Get down! Get down!" I cried to him. "These Men are Friends, not Foes!" But daz'd from Writing in his Book, and not comprehending what was going on, Bartholomew cockt his Pistol and made as if to fire.

"These Men are Friends!" I cried again. "Put down your Pistol." Bartholomew star'd at me in utter confusion, his Eyes having the bleary Look of one just sprung from Sleep. Whereupon Horatio, seeing the Lancelot he both lov'd and hated in Danger, could not wait and risque the Loss of his Captain and Lover; thus, he open'd Fire upon Bartholomew.

"Cease and Desist, Horatio!" I cried, but 'twas too late. Being hit in the Belly, Bartholomew fell backwards into the Galley. At once I ran to him thro' Cannon Fire to see what Damage had been wrought.

He lay upon the Floor 'neath the Cooking Stove, holding his Bowels in place with one Blood-stain'd Hand.

"I am mortally wounded, Fanny," mutter'd he. "That much I know."

"Hush," said I. "I'll bind your Belly. Say nought of Mortal Wounds. . . ." But as I strove to bind him with a Piece of Cotton torn from my own tatter'd Skirt, I saw 'twas true, his Guts gap'd almost like poor dead Cocklyn's had, and 'twas all I could do to keep from swooning at the very Sight.

"I might have lov'd you all Life long, Fanny," said Bartholomew, "had I the Courage to say so ere this Wound."

I lookt into his sweet angelick Face, halo'd with golden Hair, and wept. Was he embolden'd only by Death to reveal his Love?

"I might have lov'd you, too!" said I. "O I do love you! That I do!" Whereupon Bartholomew put out a feeble Hand to take mine, and as I press'd it, I knew 'twas cold as Death.

"I bequeath my Book to you, Fanny, my sweetest Love. If you e'er return to London, publish it and tell the World about the Slave Trade . . ." Here he falter'd and drew Breath. "The Word can change the World," he said, "do not doubt it . . ." And then he breath'd the Last.

I fell o'er his Body weeping, so shaken with Sobs and Tears that I fail'd to notice that the Mother Ship had ceas'd to fire, and suddenly the Air was still.

Sev'ral small Boats were arriving at the *Hopewell*, whilst

Pyrates of ev'ry Description were swarming o'er the Sides in search of Grog for their Victory Celebration. The Musicians began to play upon the Fo'c'sle Deck with a raucous Cacophony of Drums and Trumpets. Bare Feet thump'd o'er my Head as the Sailors danced their Hornpipes and their Jigs. Pyrates crowded into the Hold seeking Rum and Brandy, and their foul Imprecations fill'd the Air. Our Provisions were almost out, so there could be no Pyrate Feast of Salmagundy—that great peppery Stew of divers Meats and Fishes—which was usually cookt to celebrate the Taking of a Prize; but the Men made merry with the Grog, rolling Puncheons of Rum along the Decks only to hack 'em open with their Boarding Axes, and nicking Bottles of Brandy with their Cutlasses instead of troubling to uncork 'em. O they little noticed the broken Glass which pav'd the very Deck whereon they danced!

What a Debauch 'twas! The Tars of the *Hopewell* join'd in as if they'd ne'er been fell'd by Sickness. And whilst the Dancing thunder'd all above, I lay with my Cheak to Bartholomew's dead Cheak, weeping for all my dear, dead Friends, the brightest and most beauteous who had fallen. "Only spare Belinda," I askt the Goddess of the Skies, "and blessèd be Thy Name for reuniting me with my own Merry Men!"

Life is e'er a Mixture of Sweets and Bitters! I regain my Lancelot and Horatio only to lose Bartholomew! I lose Susannah only to regain Lancelot! But Belinda must I find again or dye. On that Score will I countenance no Bargains or Barters e'en with the Goddess on High!

The Musick play'd and play'd, the Pyrates danced and drank, sang Pyrate Songs, and swarm'd into the Great Cabin and the Hold in search of Booty. Coral and Iron Bars were heap'd on Deck, Firkins of Tallow, e'en the Basons that Whitehead had brought for Trading. All the Captain's Belongings—his Personal Plate, Wigs, and Clothes—were thrown upon the Booty Pile. The Necklace that Cocklyn took from us ere he dy'd—e'en this they found and threw upon the Heap—together with the Costumes in which I had woo'd Lord Bellars during my Lying-in. 'Twas verily as if the Remnants of my whole Life lay upon that Deck! I fear'd for Bartholomew's Book in all this Fray; Jewels could I lose, and Costumes, but the Book was a sacred Trust to a departed Friend. I ran down to the Surgeon's Cabin, where I search'd for a Time before I found it rudely thrown upon the Floor, in a great Pool of Rum. Pyrates consider'd Books of little

Value. I pickt it up and wip'd it with my Skirt, wrapping the sodden Leather in a rough woollen Sailor's Shirt, then running back on Deck.

Abruptly, the Musick stopp'd and Lancelot summon'd the Men from their Drinking, Dancing, Singing, and Heaping great Piles of Booty.

"Silence, ye Rogues!" he cried. "Silence on Deck!" The Men obey'd but slowly, stagg'ring about in Drunkenness. After some Confusion, they found Places where they might sit or stand amidst the broken Glass and flowing Rum. Clutching Bartholomew's Book, I found a quiet Corner of the Deck and there sat down. I recogniz'd a few of the Merry Men of Old—Littlehat and Francis Bacon, Caveat the Warrior and Puck Goodfellow with his scarry Face—but most of the others were Strangers, both Black and White. O Lancelot must have taken many a Slaver to liberate so many Ebony Souls!

"Gentlemen!" cried Lancelot. "We have taken a Pretty Prize—the *Hopewell* here, a most Sea-worthy Brigantine, tho' damaged she be in her Riggin' by yer daft O'er-Zealousness in defendin' me. Yet still I warrant she'll make a fine Member o' the Fleet if she be not foul-bottom'd. Her Captain's ours, her Men will join our Band; an' after they have sign'd our Articles, we'll share out all the Booty! Accordin'ly, an' since I'll have no forced Men upon me Ships, I would now read to ye our Sacred Articles to make sure ye agree. What say ye, Lads?"

"Aye! Aye!" cried the Pyrates, new and old.

"Ye must swear to uphold our Flag as well, Lads, since 'tis no common black Pyrate Banner, meant only to strike Terror in the Hearts o' Prey, but a proud Emblem o' our Faith: '*A Deo a Libertate*'—which Motto hath been chosen by our fine Quartermaster an' Latin Scholar, Horatio the Fierce. . . ." Here he introduced the terrible-visaged Horatio to the Men, whereupon my old Friend stood and bow'd, making sure to bare his Teeth and snarl most ferociously. (Like many bookish Fellows who dream a Life of Action, Horatio delighted in seeming e'en more fearsome than he was!)

"Bring the Bible, Horatio!" Lancelot said to his fierce Compatriot. Out of his Waistcoat, Horatio produced a small octavo Bible bound in black Morocco, edged in Gold, with a fore-edge Painting which represented Jesus Christ as a Pyrate, looking for all the World as red-hair'd and green-eyed as Lancelot! (O certainly I could not see it from where I sat, but later I was to have a good Look at this curious Object.)

"Now—the Articles!" Lancelot said, drawing a tatter'd Parchment Scroll from his own Coat. "Listen well!" He ceremoniously unroll'd the Scroll; the Men, drunk as most of 'em were, tried ne'ertheless to attend to Lancelot.

"Article I," read he. "Ev'ry Man shall have an equal Vote in Affairs o' Moment. . . ." At this the Men chear'd loudly; Lancelot went on: "Ev'ry Man shall have an equal Title to the fresh Provisions or strong Liquors where'er they be seiz'd an' shall use 'em at Pleasure unless a Scarcity make it necessary fer the Common Good that a Retrenchment may be voted." The Men chear'd e'en more loudly at this Provision, for Grog is e'er more important than Votes.

"Article II. Ev'ry Man shall be call'd fairly in turn by the List on Board o' Prizes, because o'er an' above their Proper Share, they are allow'd a Shift o' Clothes. But if they defraud the Company e'en to the Value o' one Piece o' Eight whether in Plate or Jewels or Money, they shall be mercilessly *maroon'd* . . ."

Here the Men drew their Breath in Terror, for Marooning was ev'ry Pyrate's Nightmare.

"An' if any Man rob another, he shall have his Nose an' Ears slit an' be put ashore where he is sure to encounter Hardship . . ." A grievous Gasp was heard from drunken Men, but Lancelot went on, reading more dramatically than our own Mr. Garrick reading Shakespeare: "Article III. The Captain shall have two full Shares, the Quartermaster one an' a half, the Doctor, Gunner, Boatswain, an' Sailin' Master one an' a quarter. He that first sights a Prize shall have his Pick o' Weapons aboard her. He that first boards her shall have a double Share o' Booty!"

"Hurrah!" shouted the Men.

"Article IV," read Lancelot. "None shall game fer Money with either Dice or Cards . . ."

The Men moan'd loudly at this, but seem'd resign'd.

"Article V. Lights an' Candles shall be put out at Eight o' Night, an' if any desire to drink after that Hour, they shall sit upon the open Deck without Lights, to avoid the Danger o' Fire at Sea."

"Aye, 'tis a good Rule," one Tar near me mutter'd to his Mate.

"Article VI. Each Man shall keep his Piece, Cutlass, an' Pistols at all Times clean an' ready fer Action, an' any Man that takes another's Piece shall have his Nose slit!"

"Aye! Aye!" cried the Tars.

433

"Article VII. He that shall desert the Ship or his Quarters in Time o' Battle shall be punish'd by Death or Maroonin'. Fer Cowardice we cannot countenance aboard our Ships, an' Cowards shall be hang'd from a Yardarm till they be dead, or maroon'd where they shall surely starve to Death!"

Silence and grave Looks greeted this Rule.

"Article VIII. If any Man shall carry a Woman to Sea in Disguise or otherwise, he shall suffer Death . . ."

At this my Blood began to boil in Fury at the Lancelot of Old, for was he not suppos'd to found a True "Deocracy" where Men and Women were wholly equal? Alas, most Revolutionaries are none where Women are concern'd, yet for the nonce, I held my Tongue.

"Article IX. None shall strike another on board the Ship, but ev'ry Man's Quarrel shall be ended upon Shore by Sword or Pistol in this Manner: At the Word o' Command from the Quartermaster, each Man, bein' previously placed Back to Back, shall turn an' fire immediately. If any Man do not, the Quartermaster shall knock the Piece out o' his Hand. If both miss their Aim, they shall take to their Cutlasses, and he that draweth the first Blood shall be declar'd the Victor."

This Article was receiv'd with quiet Nods, for 'twas rather common amongst Pyrates to have a Means of settling Disputes that should not involve the Crew in a gen'ral Mêlée.

"Article X. The Musicians shall have rest on the Sabbath only, by Right. On all other Days by Favour only."

At this the Drummers play'd a great Drum Roll and there were shouts of "Huzzah!"

"Article XI. No Man shall talk o' breakin' up their Way o' Livin' till each hath a Share of a thousand Pounds in Plate or Jewels or Money. He that shall have the Misfortune to lose a Limb in the Time o' Engagement shall have a Sum o' eight hundred Pieces o' Eight from the Common Stock fer a Leg, six hundred fer an Arm, five hundred fer an Eye, four hundred fer a Hand, an' fer Lesser Hurts proportionately. Likewise, if any Artificial Limbs are taken from a Prize, they shall be given out accordin' to strict Need. Moreo'er, a Man unfit—by Nature o' his Wounds—fer Battle, shall be given the Post o' Cook fer the Rest o' the Voyage an' receive a half Share o' all Booty taken. If there be more Cooks aboard a ship than one, the other crippl'd Men shall serve as Sail-Makers, Carpenters, or other Specialists, accordin' to their Craft. If they have none, they *still* shall be given the Means to live until the Conclusion o' said Cruise."

The Men of the *Hopewell* seem'd amaz'd by this Provision, for they were us'd, as most Common Seamen were, to the most barbarous Treatment in both Sickness and Health.

"Article XII. No Man shall berate another accordin' to the Colour o' his Skin, but Black an' White shall live as Brothers."

Here the Merry Men chear'd; but the Tars of the *Hopewell* lookt a bit confus'd, having ne'er heard of such Equality before.

"Moreo'er," Lancelot went on, "when we shall find the proper Haven—whether in the West Indies, North America, or Madagascar, we shall name it *Libertalia,* in accordance with our Beliefs in Liberty an' Justice. At such a Time another Vote shall be taken an' those who do not wish to join our great Deocracy shall be provided with a Ship to sail the Seas an' they may continue in a Life o' Pyracy just as they please. . . ." Lancelot ceas'd dramatically; the Men applauded him again. "Any Questions ere we swear?" he askt.

I saw the Sailors whisp'ring amongst themselves, but no one rais'd a Hand to ask a Question. The Articles were far beyond a Common Seaman's wildest Dreams. In a Time when most Tars could hardly hope to see twelve Pounds for a whole Year's wretchèd Labour, a thousand Pounds seem'd like the Fortune of an Indian Mogul—and indeed 'twas. Why, e'en the Governour of the East India Company earn'd no more than three hundred Pounds per Year!

"Hath any Man a Question?" Lancelot askt.

Silence reign'd on Deck.

"Hath any Man a Question?" Lancelot askt again.

"No!" I cried, leaping to my Feet. "But one Woman hath!"

I stood then, trembling with Anger, clutching Bartholomew's Book. My Skirts were torn and Blood-stain'd, my Hair shorn, my Feet bare, my Cheaks sooty with Gun-Powder. I hardly lookt like a Female at all—and scarcely like the Beauteous Fanny of Old—but in my Heart, I was as much a Woman as e'er before, nay, more.

"The Articles . . ." said I, quaking with Fear and Rage (as a Woman will quake when she is all alone amidst two hundred Men). "The Articles make no Provision for the Female of the Species!"

The Men all turn'd as one and lookt at me. Some began to jeer and some star'd as if they'd seen a ghostly Apparition. Was this a Woman at all, or just a Raggamuffin of no particular Sex claiming to be a Member of the Fair? I swear the

435

Jeering heated up my Rage, and I drew Pow'r from some secret Source whose Name I do not know.

"Laugh at me, then," I cried, "I care not—but what sort of Democracy may it be where Blacks and Whites may live as Brothers but Women are nowhere mention'd in your Articles, except as Cause for Death? And what sort of Democracy may it be where the Sex who breath'd you all with Life and mother'd you, hath no Rights and Privileges at all? And what sort of Democracy may it be where Men will found a great and glorious Nation yet treat half of the Human Race as Outcasts and Pariahs?" Bedazzl'd with my own Goddess-given Pow'rs of Speech, I warm'd to my Subject and continu'd e'en more dramatically:

"Without us, there are no Pyrates, no Pyrate Ships, no Merchantmen to seize, no Sea Captains to capture, no Sailing Masters to set Sails, no Gunners to man the Cannon, no Cooks to stir the Stew, no Carpenters to build the Masts, no Sail-Makers to sew the Sails, no Drummers to make you merry, no Quartermasters to divide the Booty! Go your own Way without Women and where will you replenish your Crews? Will you seize Women and use 'em as Breeding Stock, then throw 'em to the Sharks? Will you seize Children and use 'em as Cannon Fodder? So hath it been for the Whole History of the World and sure *this* is no Democracy! But if you truly mean your Motto, '*A Deo a Libertate,*' and if you truly mean to make a *Libertalia*, in Spirit as in Name, then you must honour your Mothers as well as your Fathers, and accord that Sex a Place both in your Hearts and in your sacred Articles!"

Some Men jeer'd at this, whilst some lookt daz'd and bemus'd, for 'twas all so strange to 'em.

"The Wench is daft!" cried the First Mate of the *Hopewell*—that same who ow'd his Position to Mr. Cocklyn's Death. "I'll sign no Articles that mention Bleedin' Women!"

"Nor will I!" cried the Second Mate.

"Aye! Aye!" shouted some of the *Hopewell's* Men. "Women are a Curse aboard!"

"If I be curst," I continu'd in a Rage, "then wherefore are you all redeem'd from the cruellest Master you have e'er known? If I be curst, then wherefore doth that Villain White-head stand bound unto the Mast? If I be curst, then wherefore have you found your Lancelot to lead you all to Liberty and *Libertalia*? I warn you, Lads, if you dispose of me, your Ships shall perish sure as I'm standing here; for as your For-

436

tune turn'd once, so may it turn again, since nothing is constant in Nature but Change!"

Where my fighting Words came from I knew not, since oft' in Fits of Rage we speak the Contents of our Hearts more fluently than in Tranquillity, but suddenly I was seiz'd with such Eloquence as would have made Athena herself pale with Envy and Diana take to her Stag and ride away upon the Moonbeams that attend her!

"O ye Tars and Sea-Artists, Craftsmen and Sons of Apollo"—here I indicated the rude Drummers and Musicians to flatter 'em—"do not conclude from your late Success that Fortune always will be favourable! She will not always give you the Protection of Lancelot and his Merry Men! She will not always faithfully follow you across the perilous Seas! Remember, the Sun rises, comes to its meridian Height, and stays not there upon the Height, but at once begins to decline. Let this admonish you to reflect on the constant Revolution in all Sublunary Affairs, for the greater be your Glory, the nearer you are to your Declension! We are taught by all we behold in Nature that Life is nought but continual Movement. No sooner doth the Sea lap upon the Land, but it retreats again. No sooner doth the Tree flow'r, but the Flow'rs fall. No sooner doth the Woman bloom with Child, but the Child drops from her and she begins to wither. Ev'ry Herb and Shrub and e'en our own Bodies teach us that nothing is durable nor can be counted on. Time passes away insensible to all our Protestations, and all our Succours begin to shrink and fade. I tell you if you now dispose of me and slight all Womankind in your Articles, the Pow'rs that have brought about your Redemption shall once more abandon you, and you shall fall into the Hands of an e'en crueller Master than Captain Whitehead here!"

The Tars began to mutter amongst themselves. Principles and Justice most of 'em car'd not a Fig for, but Seamen, as I've said, are a Superstitious Lot and I had most craftily play'd upon this Quality. Sure, I did not mention the Goddess as the Source of their Redemption (tho' I was certain 'twas She), for they might have burnt me as a Witch! But my Rhetorick began to stir 'em to their Bones when I planted in their foolish Hearts and Minds the Hint of Superstition; whereupon many began to feel that I alone was the Mascot and the Figurehead of their Good Fortune! ('Tis oft' true, Belinda, that whilst Men wish to conquer Women at large, they'll accept one special Woman as a Token, the better to subdue the Multitudes!)

Lancelot, for his part, stood amaz'd at my new Pow'rs of Speech, so very like his own. Dimly, he recall'd his Promise to me in that last Letter which had seal'd my Doom with evil Kate. Nor could he fail to see that I had rais'd the Doubts and Superstitions of the Men, and 'twas his Duty as their Leader to satisfy such Qualms:

"The Lass hath Reason," he now said to the assembl'd Tars. "Fer doth not ev'ry Ship have its Figurehead? An' doth not ev'ry Family have its Mother? I say that we appoint our Madam Fanny as Mascot o' the Pyrate Flotilla an' honour an' respect her as our own sweet Dam!"

"Bah!" cried the First Mate. " 'Tis no proper Pyracy with Women aboard!"

"On the Contrary, Lads," Lancelot said, warming to the Subject, "have ye ne'er heard tell o' Mary Read an' Annie Bonny? They were as fierce a Brace o' Hellcats as e'er sail'd the Seven Seas an' braver than most Men! 'Tis true that Annie Bonny was an Irishborn Wench, not English, an' rais'd in America, too, which perhaps accounts for her well-known fierce Temper. Why, she drew a Knife once, on a Lad that try'd to rape her, and scar'd him off as well as any Man. When *she* sail'd the Main, 'twas no Curse to have a woman Pyrate aboard. I'faith, Lads, 'twas the best o'Luck. Alas, she was braver than wise, our Annie was, an' married a cowardly Cur like many a brave Lass. When her fickle Mate, Jim Bonny, turn'd Informer 'gainst the Pyrates o' New Providence, she ran off with Jack Rackham, the Pyrate King, an' sail'd the Seas with him instead. Cleverer she was than most o' yer Masculine Pyrates, an' fer a glorious Time the Scourge o' the Bahamas. I've heard tell o' 'The Bonny Bitch' from many a Pyrate an' none that saw her fail'd to honour her as brave. Likewise her dearest Friend, the fam'd Mary Read, who'd fought in Flanders in a Man's Disguise. Together these Wenches fill'd the Caribee with Fear, an' none there jest o' women Pyrates now!"

"Then let the Wench learn to fight if she's to sail with us!" the First Mate of the *Hopewell* cried.

"Aye, aye," cried a Number of the Tars.

" 'Tis only fair," said I. "I'll take no Privileges which I have not earn'd. If you will add Women to your Articles, I'll learn to fight with Cutlass and with Pistol and fight I will like any Man."

"Amend the Articles!" Horatio cried, for he was e'er soft on me and could not bear to see us part again.

"I shall affix an Asterisk," cried Lancelot, "signifyin' that where'er the Word 'Man' appears, 'Woman' is meant as well." (O this was not perfect, I knew, but 'twould do for now.)

"And cross out Article Eight!" I cried. "Or I'll not sail!" For I'd be damn'd if I'd board any Ship with such a Rule about carrying Women.

"Ye drive a hard Bargain, Wench," said Lancelot.

"If I were hard," said I, "I'd make ye change the whole Parchment to read 'Woman' in ev'ry Article—with an Asterisk saying 'Woman' also includes 'Man'!"

The Men laugh'd nervously as if I jested here, but I was in dead earnest.

"Very well then," said Lancelot. "No Woman sails with us as private Whore or Mascot, but only as a Member o' the fightin' Band!"

"Aye, aye!" shouted the Men.

And so the Articles were amended, the Men sworn, and I became a Pyrate.

Chapter XII

Containing divers Dialogues betwixt Lancelot, Horatio, and our Heroine in which the History goes backward somewhat and we learn what these Gentlemen have been doing whilst the Queen of our Narrative was extending her Education and Adventures; thereto is added a brief History of Buccaneering for the Reader who is bent upon the noble Cause of Self-Improvement as well as the more pleasant one of Entertainment.

REUNITED THUS WITH LANCELOT upon the Seas, and committed to fight as fiercely as any Pyrate—as soon as I should learn how to wield a Cutlass—my only Thought was now to enlist Lancelot in finding my Beauteous Babe. I'faith, I would have sworn the Sea was rose and the Sky green if it had brought me an Inch closer to Belinda.

After the Reading of the Articles and the Swearing-in of the Pyrates, the Festivities resum'd upon the Deck and Lancelot and I were able to slip away to the Great Cabin to speak most privily. Horatio remain'd to watch o'er the great Pile of Booty, for, as Quartermaster, 'twas his Task to see that no Man receiv'd more than his proper Share.

At first, Lancelot and I sat and faced each other dumbly, little knowing what to say. We had not seen each other in almost a Year and O what momentous Events had interven'd! So many Thoughts rusht thro' my Mind—the Friends I'd lost, Lancelot's near-Betrayal of his Promises to make a true "Deocracy," all that I had born with Whitehead, my own Metamorphosis from Maiden to Mother! Then, quite abruptly, Lancelot spoke:

"Ye came not to sail with me as ye swore," said he. "The first Lass I trusted, an' ye fail'd me, Wench. . . ."

Suddenly, I understood why Lancelot had been so testy with me; Trust came hard for him; he had laid his whole Heart out in a Letter and then I had not come!

"O Lancelot," said I, "I would have given my right Arm to come—my Starboard Arm as the old Tars say—but I was prevented by a jealous Wench within the Brothel where I earn'd my Keep. Doubt not my Loyalty, for I was lockt in my Chamber when Littlehat came to fetch me and I shouted to him all fruitlessly. If only you knew how hard I sought to escape and how I was injur'd as I did so! Ne'er would I have betray'd you willingly, I swear it on Belinda's Life. . . ."

"Belinda? Then did ye not have a Son and name him Lancelot?"

I lookt at Lancelot and smil'd. Ah, Vanity, thy Name is Man! But I held back the Mockery and Jests that might have sprung to my Lips upon that Instant.

"For your Sake, Lancelot, I wish the Babe had been not only yours, but a Boy to be call'd Lancelot the Second; yet for my own part, 'twas fated that I bear a Daughter."

Lancelot view'd me quizzically. "An' why, I pray, is that?"

"Because only when a Woman bears a Daughter doth she journey through the Pier-Glass of her Destiny and see the World thro' her own Mother's Eyes. To *be* a Daughter is but half our Fate; to *bear* one is the other. And suddenly that Bearing changes all our Views: our Fury at the Fates, our grim Denunciations of our Destinies, our very Rage at Womanhood itself—such Things are soften'd by the Bearing of a Daughter."

Lancelot understood not; that much I could see, yet he did not argue with me.

"I must find Belinda," I went on, "and you must help me."

"An' wherefore must I do anythin' ye say?"

"Because you love me, Lancelot, and our Destinies are intertwin'd. Because your soft Heart will not allow a Babe to perish in the Deep. But most, because you'll ne'er establish a True Deocracy without me. Passion you have aplenty and perhaps you've seen God as you avow, but you fly too fast, too far, and without a Woman's steadying Hand, your Dreams will perish in the Deep. These Men are Rogues and Slavers, most of 'em, who'll follow you for Hope of Gain, not Principle; but if they have no Chest of Gold to show for all their Pains, surely they'll kill you in a trice. The Merry Men of Old are outnumber'd here. You need more than Passion now; you need Reason, too."

"An' I'm to let a Wench tell me what Reason is? By Jove! No Wench tells Robin Hood what he must do!"

"Lancelot, Lancelot, my Love," said I. "I may be in Rags

441

and Tatters, and I may be shorn of my Hair, but I am no mere Wench to do your Bidding as I was before. Lancelot, I am a Woman now, and wiser than I'd wish my Girl to be at merely nineteen Years. Why, the Things I've known would stand your Hair on End if I would care to tell."

"Pray tell, Madam Fanny; I'm all Ears."

"Not now—someday you'll know, but now we must away and find Belinda. Can you permit the only Babe your Love may e'er bear to perish in the Deep? Ah, Lancelot, you whose soft Heart melts at the Suff'rings of Slaves and Debtors. . . . Picture a pink Babe, still washt with the Waters of the Womb, kidnapp'd by a wicked Wet-Nurse whose only Art is to bind and swaddle its tender Limbs and clout its Face to drive out what the old Bitch deems Original Sin! Why, if you believe in Freedom and the Goodness of the Newborn Soul, you must do all within your Pow'r to help me find Belinda!"

Just thinking of Belinda I began to weep most piteously and my Belly began to ache with that primal Separation. She was part of me and yet not part of me. She was close as a Limb and yet so far away, protected within my Heart, yet Miles away across the Sea beyond my Pow'r to protect her. O the Sorrow of a Mother whose sweet Babe is pluckt away! Suddenly and without knowing why I did so, I rais'd my torn and tatter'd Skirt and bar'd my Scar to Lancelot. 'Twas red and pucker'd as a Newborn Babe and angry as if the very Skin were wroth with all the World's Cruelties.

"Behold!" I cried. "I bore this Babe at cost to my own Life and if I lose her now 'twill be worth nought to me!"

Lancelot star'd in utter amazement at the Wound. He was torn betwixt Revulsion and Pity—he whose Fear of the Fair Sex vy'd with his unvoiced Attraction. His green Eyes star'd; his very Beard seem'd to flame. He fell to bended Knee and kiss'd me there.

"O let me kiss away the Pain!" cried he, running his Lips up and down the awful Scar. His Beard tickl'd me and yet my Heart was melted utterly, for I knew 'twas e'en more difficult for him than for another Man and it quite stirr'd my Blood. I, who had thought the Pow'r of Lust had dy'd for me with Childbirth, had dy'd twice and thrice more with Whitehead's Abuses, until the carnal Acts of Love came to disgust me more than e'en Torture or Murder—e'en I began to feel once more the sweet Stirrings of Carnality like Sap oozing from the Bough in Spring. If Lancelot makes love to me, I

442

thought, I will be his utterly. And sure as I stood there, Lancelot's Hands play'd about my Thighs, his Fingers began to twine in my womanly Vegetation whilst his Tongue danced along my Scar, cooling its Rage and sweetening its Sourness. O I was mov'd beyond my Pow'r to tell by the Sight of his Head tenderly bent against my Belly, as if headstrong Lancelot were humbl'd quite by the Mysteries of Birth. I swear we seem'd about to fall into a Reverie of Passion right there in that Cabin where Whitehead had so oft' assaulted me with his disgusting Lusts, and Lancelot, the Lover of Boys and Men, was upon the Point of being converted to the Love of Women fore'er!

But alas, 'twas not to be. For just at that Moment when his Privy Part had stiffen'd to Ramrod Strength and wisht to seek Admission to that Bow'r of Bliss (which he had mockt before), Horatio raced in, crying,

"Lancelot! Lancelot! The Men are flogging Whitehead without a proper Trial or Vote!" Whereupon, perceiving what was happening, he grabb'd Lancelot by the Scruff of his Neck, calling him all Manner of Swine and Cur, and raving, "You'll not have Fanny as I live and breathe, or I will have her, too!"

Then he seiz'd Lancelot by the Beard, and tore him from my aching Body, pulling him most violently out of the Great Cabin and up the Ladder leading to the Deck.

"An' am I Captain o' this Fleet or no? Ye filthy Cur, ye Black Tyrant! Unhand me, Villain!" Lancelot was buttoning his gaping Breech e'en as he scream'd.

I sigh'd profoundly as I saw him go. Would I ne'er find Love, but only Lovers' Triangles? O I might break thro' Lancelot's Revulsion of the Fair, but what of Horatio's Jealousy of Lancelot? How would we three resolve our curious Minuet? 'Twas a thorny Problem, yet I could not ponder long, for upon the Deck such Shrieks and Shouts were heard as might echo within Hell itself. I ran above to see a Pandemonium of Pyrates, and in the midst of all, Whitehead stripp'd naked and ty'd now to the Mizzenmast, not the Fore, and his Back a piteous Wreck of Blood and Gore where he had been mercilessly flogg'd. Having given off Flogging, the drunken Pyrates were now pelting him with broken Bottles, some empty, some half-full, some still uncorkt. For the drunken Orgy was yet in full force and the Men were nicking Bottles, drinking two Swallows or three from 'em, and tossing the Rest at Whitehead, who seem'd nearly dead with such

Abuse. His Head loll'd to one side, hideously; his Beard itself was cak'd with clotted Blood. He hung there like an anti-Christ upon a bloody Cross. Not only the former Tars of the *Hopewell* (now turn'd Pyrate) but Lancelot's Pyrates, too, took the greatest Pleasure in pelting him with Bottles.

"Cease an' Desist!" cried Lancelot. "No man dyes without a proper Trial an' Vote!" But the Pyrates were far too frenzied now to heed him.

"He's a Villain an' deserves to dye!" cried the Second Mate of the *Hopewell*.

"Aye, aye!" shouted sev'ral of the Pyrates.

"Take not Justice into yer own Hands," cried Lancelot, "Justice belongs to God!"

"We'll give ye Justice," said the First Mate of the *Hopewell*, raising his Cutlass and threatening Lancelot. Whereupon Lancelot leapt upon him in a Fury and began to throttle him with his bare Fists.

I could scarce believe my Eyes! The same Lancelot who just a Moment before was making love to me, now had his Fingers about the First Mate's Neck and seem'd upon the Point of choking him.

"Ye'll not take the Law into yer own Hands!" cried Lancelot, "I am Captain here!"

"And we'll vote another Captain if we choose!" said the First Mate in all Insolence. Whereupon Lancelot, now being heated to a Pitch of Rage such as I had ne'er seen before—in him or any Man—kickt the First Mate in his Privy Parts until he howl'd in Pain. Then, he hoisted him upon his brawny Shoulders and made as if to pitch him in the Deep.

"I require Obedience from me Men!" he cried. "No Ship sails without Obedience. Ocean Currents may carry a Ship whose Masts are broken. Rainwater we may catch in the Sails when Barrels run dry. But without Obedience, we're done for." So saying, he toss'd the First Mate o'er the Portside of the Ship and into the foggy Drink.

His Cries were heard a little Time and yet in Fog he would ne'er be found alive. The Men gasp'd, their Lesson learnt; Lancelot was not a Man to cross. Whitehead, for his part, was finish'd; he had quietly given up the Ghost whilst Lancelot rav'd at the Men. O what a quiet Death for such a Villain! He dy'd unlamented by any but Satan himself!

Be that as it may, 'twas from this Incident that Lancelot learnt how perilous his Authority might be amongst the Mutinous Tars. Chaos was ne'er far from these unruly Sea-Dogs, and Principle mov'd 'em less than Rum and Wine. Perhaps this was the Reason Lancelot now agreed to take off in search of Belinda and heed my Warnings about his Need of my Advice; for he perceiv'd I had been right about the Pyrates, and perhaps 'twas true he needed a Woman's Hand in his "Deocracy."

"But can we find *Cassandra?*" I askt later, when Lancelot, Horatio, and I met within the Great Cabin to chart a Course.

"The Currents must carry her South to the West Indies like any other Ship," said Horatio, "and tho' she sail'd full six Weeks past, who knows but she might be becalm'd or encounter other Difficulties. If she was bound for Charlestown, or e'en Boston, still she'd sail first to the West Indies, for to sail South along the North American Coast is to beat against the Wind. 'Tis a fairer and more favourable Sail from South to North."

"But which Port would she anchor in?" I askt.

"That could we learn in the West Indies—and there's good Prey there, too—to content our Men. We could tell the Men we're off to the West Indies to prey upon the Main Shipping Roads—indeed we will!—but the *Cassandra* should be not hard to find. And Women are so scarce upon those Isles that a Wet-Nurse should be noted easily. Ah, methinks I recall from my Days with Captain Thack, a certain *Cassandra* which call'd at the Port of St. Christopher's—or was it Tartola? No matter, we'll find your Babe, for, as Virgil says: *'Non aliter quam qui adverso vix flumine lembun/Remigiis subigit: si brachia forte remisit,/ Atque illum praceps prono rapit alveus amni!'* Which means, as you know, my dearest Fanny—I only translate for our ignorant Lancelot—that when we are most exhausted and cannot row with Oars, oft'times the Current itself sweeps us along! So 'twill with our Search for your Babe! You have row'd long and hard enough; now let the Current sweep us to our Prize, the beauteous Belinda! But if I catch you two in Bed, there'll be no Belinda, and no Lancelot nor Fanny neither! For I have not regain'd my delicious Fanny only to see her devour'd by my delicious Lancelot! And if you make the Beast with two Backs, I'll stab 'em both as sure as I can play Othello!"

Lancelot and I regarded each other sadly. O we moon'd o'er the forced Separation and yet were curiously reliev'd by it as well. For Lancelot's part, he was not so sure yet that he did not fear the Fair; and for my own, the Thought of carnal Love (that Culprit which had caus'd so many of the Pains of

445

my short Life) was still a Thing to view with some Alarm. "Let us first find Belinda," I thought to myself, "and let Eros wait for me as I have done so oft' for Him!"

'Twas determin'd that as soon as we could repair the Rigging of the *Hopewell* and capture fresh Provisions, Water, and e'en Men from some outward-bound Slaver, our Pyrate Flotilla should head across the South Atlantick for the Sugar Isles. 'Twas Lancelot's Policy to liberate as many Slave Ships as possible and to invite the Crews, but most especially the Slaves, to turn Pyrate; for thus he hop'd to subvert the evil Practice of Slaving, which he saw as an Atrocity in the Eyes of God. Horatio was only willing to risque sailing to the Sugar Isles (where he was still wanted as a Runaway Slave) because of his great Love for me. Moreo'er, Horatio had grown infinitely more brazen in the Year he and Lancelot had sail'd the Pyrate Round. He'd taken, as I've said, to wearing Matches 'neath his Hat like Blackbeard, and to wearing his Hair in a most outrageous Bush. He also affected gorgeous Clothes, Hats trimm'd with silver Lace, embroider'd Waistcoats, Boots of gilded Leather, and all the most dandyish *Accoutrements*—French Snuff-Boxes, Silver-hilted Swords, damascen'd Pistols with pearl Handles. The Fear I'd seen upon his Face in The George & Vulture was gone now utterly. Pyracy had driven out the Slave and the new Horatio had as little Fear of Death as the old Lancelot.

"When you came not to sail with us, Fannikins," Horatio said, "both Lancelot and I were cast down with Despair. I suspected Sabotage, but Lancelot felt totally betray'd. Yet could we not dwell upon your Absence, for our Task was hard and the Rebellion we had plann'd might cost our very Lives. 'Twas only when we were safe aboard the *Hazard* and under full Sail that we might speak of you."

I listen'd intently; Horatio went on.

"I'd told Lancelot I'd ne'er sail with him without your gracious Company, for I fear'd his Plans to establish his 'Deocracy' in the New World. But, in the Heat of the Rebellion, how could I fail him? So sail I did; whereupon we found ourselves at Sea with all the scurvy Debtors of Newgate—none of whom knew a Fart's Worth about Sailing—and we discover'd, to boot, that the *Hazard* was about as Sea-worthy as a Tub of Butter or a Puncheon of Rum."

" 'Tis true," said Lancelot, "alas, 'tis true."

"At once we determin'd to take another Ship," Horatio

continu'd, "for 'twas that or perish. We might ne'er sail the *Hazard* without careening her. . . ."

"What's careening?" I askt, knowing little then of the Pyrate Round.

" 'Tis when ye put yer Ship upon dry Land to scrape her clean o' Barnacles an' tar her Bottom 'gainst Shipworms," Lancelot explain'd. "All Pyrates require Countries where they may careen in Peace—New Providence in the Bahamas was once such a Sanctuary. Also Madagascar an' Johanna Isle— but now it grows much harder to find Sanctuaries, fer Pyracy is bein' routed by the Crown—"

"We knew we could not make Madagascar or the Bahamas in a Tub as foul-bottom'd as the *Hazard*," Horatio said, "so we put it to a Vote with these scurvy Debtors and determin'd we should take the first sound Ship we saw. She prov'd to be a Brigantine call'd the *Happy Delivery*—which we spy'd off the Azores—"

"An' none too soon indeed, fer the *Hazard* was already leakin' badly an' was like to sink afore we e'en compleated our Maiden Voyage," Lancelot added.

"But Lancelot had not counted upon one Problem when he recruited these Debtors and Felons," Horatio continu'd; "the Sea was an alien Element to 'em and they were well-nigh useless upon Deck. *'Divisium sic breve fiet opus,'* says Martial. 'Divided thus the Work will become brief. . . .' "

Lancelot did not even flinch at Horatio's Latin now.

"But all the Running of the Ship was left to me and Lancelot," he said, "(and those Merry Men who knew a bit of Sailing), but as for the Debtors, they did nought put puke and complain, complain and puke, and grumble below Deck. 'Twas clear we'd ne'er build a Deocracy with 'em."

"Alas, Horatio is right," Lancelot sigh'd philosophically. " 'Tis one Thing to rally Men 'round, an' another to turn 'em into Brothers in a Common Cause. When the *Happy Delivery* was sighted thro' the Spyin'-Glass, Horatio an' I rejoiced, but all the Debtors found sundry Reasons why they could not fight. 'Twas fight or perish an' they could not fight! I'd put the Boardin' to a Vote before, an' now I was determined to capture a sound Ship to sail the Pyrate Round to the Eastern Seas—fer that seem'd the most likely Alternative to the Settlement in the New World, which Horatio oppos'd. We took the *Happy Delivery* with a Boardin' Party o' but a dozen Men, whilst all the bloody Debtors grumbl'd an' complain'd in the Steerage."

"But how could you take the Ship with so few Men?" I askt.

"Ah, Fanny—most Pyracy is thus," Horatio explain'd. "Thus we took the *Hopewell* in the Fog with e'en fewer Men. Pyracy oft' succeeds not because of Force of Arms, but due to Speed and e'en Surprize. Yet more than that, we oft' succeed because most Seamen are so abus'd at Sea that they turn Pyrate in a trice! Sometimes, 'tis true that Boarding Axes and Grappling Hooks and Broadsides of Cannon Fire are us'd, but oft' the very Cry of *Pyrates!* is enough to stifle all Resistance. So many Tales are told of Pyrates' Cruelties that just to hear the *Name* of Pyrate makes Seamen pale—and also Passengers! Methinks the greatest Pyrate Potentates tell such Stories of themselves to turn their Enemies' Resolve to Mush. Sure Captain Thack was fierce, that much I know, but oft' I wonder of the *other* legendary Pyrates—Blackbeard, Bartholomew Roberts, Howell Davis, Jack Rackham, Long Ben Avery, and the like. Were they as fierce as they were *said* to be? Or were they only turn'd so legendary by their own Story-telling?"

"But what of your Travels with Calico Thack?" said I, for I remember'd Horatio's stirring Tales.

"Thack was brave and foolish, too," said Horatio wearily. "He took daring Risques—and by Jove, so doth Lancelot!"

Lancelot beam'd at this; it seem'd that he and Horatio were far better Friends than they had been a Year before.

"But oft' such Risques are needless, for the Prey surrenders ere we raise our Flag! The Great Age of Pyracy is past, my Sweet, but the Legends about Pyrates daily increase. 'Tis oft' the Case that when some mortal Thing is dying, its Fame increases e'en as it dyes. As Virgil says—"

"Damn Virgil!" Lancelot interrupted, "an' tell the Lass the Tale!"

"And why, pray, is the Great Age of Pyracy past?" I askt.

"Because it no longer serves the English Crown to have their Privateers attack the bloody Spanish under the Cover of Letters of Marque," Horatio explain'd. "But whilst the Spanish were our greatest Enemies, the Buccaneers were born, and now the Crown cannot rid itself of 'em!"

"Ah Horatio," I exclaim'd, "you are the very Tacitus of Pyracy! If e'er we find ourselves in London once again, you must write Volumes of your Knowledge!"

"An' publish 'em under a *Nom de Plume*," said Lancelot, "fer otherwise we'll hang!"

448

"I'd love to write a Book of Buccaneers," Horatio said, his Eyes misting o'er with the Dream of Lit'ry Fame (from which e'en clever *he* was not immune), "for in a Book, a Man is judged not by the Colour of his Skin, but by the Colour of the Page, White as 'tis."

"Piffle!" said Lancelot. "D'ye think Authors find justice more than Buccaneers or Blacks?"

To stop this incipient Dispute betwixt these accustom'd Adversaries, I quickly put another Query to Horatio:

"Why do they call 'em Buccaneers?" I askt, "for I have heard the Word, and always remarkt upon its Strangeness."

" 'Tis a curious Word for a Latin Scholar," Horatio said, "and its History is e'en more Curious. For when Columbus came to Hispaniola, he carried Cattle, Pigs, and Sheep upon his Ships and introduced 'em to the Isle. For a Time, these Animals were tended by the Natives of the Caribee, those Savages who call'd themselves Caribs. But when this Race of Savages dy'd out, the Animals ran wild upon the Isle, which turn'd again to Wilderness and Scrub. Thus uncheckt, they multiplied most prodigiously, and before long, Ships came to anchor in Hispaniola to replenish their Provisions with this Meat. Where there is Profit, there are Profiteers; thus the Buccaneers were born! They came as Hunters first—shipwreckt Seamen, Runaway Slaves, Felons, Debtors, ev'ry sort of Castaway—they took up Hunting as their Livelihood. Dead Shots they were, and nimble in the Bush. They hunted in small Parties with their *Matelots* and banish'd Women from their Ranks to prevent Disputes."

"O ye best not say that to our Mistress Fanny," Lancelot interrupted, "fer she is fierce in her Defence o' Womankind."

I only smil'd at this—to spite Lancelot. "Pray, continue, Horatio," said I, for I had not yet turn'd so humourless that I could not hear a Tale without protesting Woman's Lot. As I was put upon this Globe to learn, so learn I would from Men as well as Women!

"They kill'd their Prey and skinn'd it where it lay, then grill'd its Meat the way the Savages had taught, upon a sort of Rack the Caribs call'd a *Bukan,* made of green Wood and lasht with greenest Vines. Thus, was the Meat they grill'd call'd *Viande Boucanée* and the Men who grill'd it *Boucaniers!*"

"But how did these Hunters take to the Seas?" I askt.

"The Spanish chas'd 'em from their Livelihood upon the Land and liv'd to rue the Day they did! For they became the

Brethren of the Coast, raiding the Spanish Galleons from their Rafts. They learnt to approach a Sailing Ship in such a Way that her Cannon were useless to defend her. They took her from the Bow, then crept aboard, and ramm'd her Rudder with a Wedge of Wood ere she e'en knew that they'd arriv'd, whereupon they'd scramble up the Decks and oft'times take the Ship without a Shot being fir'd! The Spanish studded their Hulls with Nails 'gainst these Invaders and e'en smear'd their Decks with Butter! Why, oft' they'd spill dried Pease across 'em to make 'em more Slippery! But it avail'd 'em nought. The Brethren of the Coast were still their Match and more. Thus, they plunder'd the Treasure Fleets of Gold, Damask, Indigo, and Luxuries of ev'ry kind, whilst the Spaniards were helpless to prevent their Raids. Tho' the English call'd these bloody Brethren *Buccaneers*—and with more than a Hint of Admiration, too, the Spanish call'd 'em simply *Ladrones*, which is their Word for Thieves! In Dutch, they're call'd *Zee-Rovers*, and in French, *Flibustiers*, which we oft' translate as Free Booter. But the Spanish hate 'em most, and e'en Today when you hear the Word *Demonio* or *Corsario Luterano* from a Spaniard's Lips, he says it and then spits upon the Ground—for so they also term these Buccaneers. They were a fearsome Lot, 'tis true, and perhaps the Histories of their Cruelties are true. They hated the Spanish for their Slaughter of the Indians and for their Plunder of the Gold of the New World. 'Twas Montbars who was fam'd for slitting Spaniards' Gullets and hauling out Intestines; whilst Lolonois roasted his Prey alive—or so I've heard. I ne'er beheld it with my Eyes, thank God. But ev'ry Pyrate requires Confederates on Land to sell his Plunder to, since he can scarce *drink* the Indigo nor eat the Gold Dust that he takes. Thus Pyrates flourish only when they are *allow'd* to flourish, when Governments on Land wink at their Doings, pretending not to see. When Britannia thus made Peace with Spain, the Buccaneers began to see their Doom and now the greatest Age of Pyracy is past."

"How can ye say that Pyracy is dead when Robin roams the Seas?" Lancelot cried.

Horatio lookt cynically at his Friend and shook his Head. "Ah, Fannikins, our Robin Hood reborn will rewrite History itself!

"Lancelot," Horatio said, "I only meant to say that since the Peace with Spain, the Place of Buccaneering 'gainst the Treasure Fleets is lookt on by the Crown with some Disfavour. Moreo'er, neither Madagascar nor the Bahamas are quite as safe as once they were; for Pyracy e'er flourish'd with Royal Sanction. The Crown abetted Pyrates 'gainst the Spanish and e'en 'gainst the French—whilst the Colonies of North America us'd Pyracy as their Revenge 'gainst the Trading Practices of the Crown which they deem'd Unfair. . . ."

"Pyracy will flourish once again, as Lancelot lives an' breathes!" shouted my Robin Hood reborn. "Kidd may be dead as Dust an' Blackbeard, too, an' e'en Calico Thack, but Robin Hood still lives! If 'tis harder to play Pyrate now—sobeit! When did Robin Hood e'er flinch at Danger?"

Horatio lookt at me and smil'd a Smile which seem'd to say: Daft he is and yet we love him still.

"But what became of the Debtors when you took the *Happy Delivery*?" I askt, hoping to change the Subject again.

"We storm'd the Ship without 'em," Horatio said, "and those who would come along were happily invited. But most cower'd in the Steerage, awaiting Rescue. We left them thus adrift."

"Without their knowing how to sail?" I askt.

"Alas, 'tis true," said Horatio, "but what other Choyce had we?"

"And the Ship leaking badly, too? These Men follow'd you to Sea and you abandon'd them?"

"You sound like Lancelot, Fanny—crack-pated, begging the Captain's Pardon. You can lead an oppress'd Man to his Salvation, but how can you force him to reach out for it, if he will not move a Muscle of his own Free Will? Doubtless these Men were rescu'd or perhaps they learnt to sail out of Necessity, that Mother of Invention. We gave them ev'ry Opportunity, and most of 'em quite disappointed us. They prov'd a Shipload of Fools and Knaves, waiting for us to serve 'em their Salvation upon a Silver Platter. It quite dasht Lancelot's Theories about the Goodness of Debtors and Felons!"

"Not true! Not true!" cried Lancelot. "I still believe most Men are good at Heart, albeit lazy in seekin' their own Freedom!"

"Be that as it may," Horatio said, "you and I must teach Lancelot to be less fantastical in his Plans for Liberty and *Libertalia*. Men must be tested ere they join our great Deocracy—not ev'ry Idiot will do. There is a Pyrate Captain I have heard about who chooses his Men thus: twelve Men are

maroon'd upon a Desert Isle with one Bottle of Rum betwixt
'em. The Captain sails away and leaves 'em there, to return a
Week later. Those remaining Men become his Crew; the others perish."

"Are you proposing *this* for *Libertalia*?" I askt in extream
Shock and Amazement.

"No—a thousand Times no," Horatio protested. "I only
mean that Lancelot must awaken to the Truth of Human
Nature. 'Tis one Thing to lead a Great Rebellion and quite
another to make it stick!"

"He talks like me own Mother!" said Lancelot. "O what
Joy 'tis to have a resident Critick! What did I do with me
Life ere I met him?" And he laugh'd derisively.

"After you took the *Happy Delivery, then* what happen'd?"
I askt.

"The Crew o' that Ship turn'd Pyrate," Lancelot explain'd,
picking up Horatio's Tale, "an' we all headed for the Red
Sea Round—where we had heard o' untold Riches. An'
what's more, we found 'em! Whilst ye bore yer Babe, we
plunder'd the Moguls' Treasures. O we sail'd from the
Azores to the Cape Verde Islands, thence to St. Helena an'
'round the Cape. We cruis'd the Pyrate Round in the Red
Sea, an' took more Booty than e'en Long Ben Avery! Why,
on one Prize alone we took five hundred thousand Pieces o'
Gold! An' have not spent 'em yet—why, Lass, we're rich!
The Hold o' the *Happy Delivery* creaks with Gold Mohurs,
Gold Dust, Rubies, Emeralds, Diamonds. 'Tis a Sight to
make the Robin Hood o' Old come back to Life!"

"Then why do you continue in this Pyrate Round?" I wisht
to know, for I had Visions of retiring upon Lancelot's Gold
and devoting myself to Poetry and Belinda—when Lancelot
should help me find her!

"To keep a Promise to meself which I had made when I
was Surgeon on a Slaver, an' free me darker Brothers. Fer
this, as well, Horatio goes on, tho' we could all retire an' live
in Peace."

" 'Tis true," Horatio said, putting his Arm 'round
Lancelot's Shoulder. "We sail for Principle, not Prizes now."

"And where would you retire and live in Peace with all
these Crimes upon your Head?"

"Aye," sigh'd Lancelot, " 'tis a Problem, Lass, an' thus I
still would found a *Libertalia*—but where, I cannot tell. Gold
an' Jewels aplenty, that we have, an' yet we are hunted
ev'rywhere, on Land an' Sea. Thus sail we must, fer there is

scarce a Port where we may dock securely. I have e'en dreamt o' some Isle in the Caribees, a Tropick Key where we might make a Home, an Isle set in a beauteous Azure Sea, with Birds whose Feathers are the Colour o' rare Jewels, an' plentiful Springs o' fresh Water. O I dream o' such an Isle with Strands as white as Ivory an' Sunsets rosy as the Inside o' Shells! If God please, we'll find yer Babe an' settle on some sunny Isle set in the iridescent Tropick Sea. An' she shall play with Rubies and sprinkle Emeralds about her baby Toes and prattle to Diamonds big as Pigeons' Eggs, whilst we three live an' love an' prove to God that Men can live as Brothers—e'en when they both are doom'd to love the self-same Wench!"

We three lookt at each other warily and then laugh'd, wond'ring how this beauteous blissful Dream would come to Grief.

Chapter XIII

In which our Heroine well and truly learns the Pyrate's Craft, discovers the Joys of Sailing (as she hath previously known only the Pains), whereupon our valiant Pyrates meet their Match upon the Seas, and we disprove that old Maxim, namely: "Man cannot be rap'd."

THUS OUR MIGHTY Pyrate Flotilla set sail across the South Atlantick (as soon as we had captur'd sufficient Provisions from outbound Slavers and liberated their Slaves to sail with us). It proving impossible to repair the *Hopewell's* Rigging without putting into some friendly Anchorage, we captur'd another Ship instead, a broad-beam'd English Flute call'd the *Speedy Return,* and sank the *Hopewell* without further Ado. 'Twas not until I watch'd that Brigantine go down in the African Waters that I remember'd my Romance—my Tale of Philidore and Clotilda—lying in one of Captain Whitehead's Lockers, now at the Bottom of the Sea! I had sav'd Dennison's Book at the Expence of my own! O for a Time I thought that augur'd ill for my intended Career as an Author. My Epick lost at a Coaching Inn! My Juvenilia lost I knew not where! My Romance lost at Sea! How would I e'er become the Bard I wisht to be if I kept losing my Life's Work so carelessly? Yet perhaps ev'ry Author must serve an Apprenticeship, and perhaps indeed 'tis better that no other Eyes than hers behold the puny Fruits of that Apprenticeship, and no other Lips savour their insufficient Juice. I meditate so now, yet *then* I was Heart-broken o'er the Loss of my Work. It seem'd I'd ne'er find Time to write again and I was quite distraught by my own Foolhardiness in losing my Romance to the Immensity of the Sea. Go little Book, thought I, and feed the Fishes, if they care to eat Words instead of more substantial Food. Ah what Vanity are our Dreams of Immortality thro' Books! I'faith, *most* Books perish thus, e'en those that languish in a dusty Bookseller's Stall in St. Paul's

Churchyard; and those that win great Fame oft' perish thus as well, after a Time. Yet there was a Part of me that saw this Loss of my Romance as an Off'ring to propitiate the Favour of the Fates and bring Belinda safe into my Arms. Alas, 'tis true, I fear, that a Woman ne'er can write a Book without balancing betwixt that Book and a Baby.

Our Pyrate Flotilla now consisted of four Ships: our Flag Ship, the *Happy Delivery*, a Brigantine whose Hold was heavy with the Moguls' Gold and Jewels; the *Bijoux*, a swift Sloop; the *Willing Mind*, a Merchantman and captur'd Slaver; and the *Speedy Return*, the aforemention'd English Flute, built after a Dutch Design. 'Twas she who was the Slave Ship we had captur'd to replace the *Hopewell*, tho' she was, alas, a slow and pond'rous Sailor. But Pyrates cannot always be particular when they require a Ship.

Four Ships barely met our Needs, since we were o'er-supplied with Men. Most Pyrate Ships are cramm'd with Pyrates—hence their Prowess, so Horatio said, in fright'ning off their Prey. But, with all the liberated Slaves, we had near four hundred Men now, and the Holds of our Ships, except the first, were cramm'd with Straw Pallets for 'em to sleep upon, as well as swaying Hammocks hanging from the Beams, as in the King's Navy.

Lancelot, Horatio, and I sail'd aboard the Flag Ship; Deputy Captains and First Mates were elected to sail the *Bijoux*, *Willing Mind*, and *Speedy Return*. The *Happy Delivery* led the other Ships, but how long we would stay together on the Storm-toss'd Seas, and with such unruly Men, was anyone's Guess.

I spent my Shipboard Days learning the Pyrate's Craft. Horatio taught me Swordsmanship, the Use of Grappling Hooks and Boarding Axes, whilst Lancelot taught me to play Helmsman as well as Reefing, Hauling, and Keeping the Watch. 'Twas Lancelot's firm Belief that no one aboard a Ship should be innocent of any Seaman's Task, for you ne'er knew, said he, when you might sail alone or be shipwreckt upon a Desert Isle.

O the Use of Cutlass I ne'er took to with great Gusto—tho' I became proficient at my Self-Defence—nor did I love to reef the Sails, tho' I did it with a willing enough Mind. But Steering the Ship I lov'd! For as I stood at the Helm, watching the blue Sea rise upon either side, watching for Squalls upon the Surface of the Deep, and surveying the Clouds for Rain, I felt like Columbus himself discovering the

New World, or like a Pyrate Queen of all the Seas, piloting my Destiny!

O what a Diff'rence from the Days I cower'd in Whitehead's Cabin as a Slave! Now I was Mistress of the Seas, canny about the Weather, knowledgeable concerning Wind and Cloud and beginning to feel myself at one with this Alien Element, the Sea. I grew to love my Shipboard Life apace. 'Twas true that Rations were not as short upon Lancelot's Ships as upon Whitehead's, and I was treated with great Deference by the Crew—both at Lancelot's and Horatio's Commands (and due to my own Prowess in learning all the Crafts of Pyracy so quickly and so well). But 'twas something more: my Spirit seem'd to soar at Sea. Each Night brought rapturous Dreams as I was rockt in the Cradle of the Deep, and I came to love the Water lapping at the Hull, the Gentleness of Sleep at Sea, and all the Sounds of Wind thro' the Sails.

When our Ships were borne along by Trade Winds in the South Atlantick and the Sails requir'd little Trimming, Sailing was a Joy! Harmony reign'd betwixt Man and the Elements, and a Ship seem'd the Perfect Craft, design'd to bend the Forces of Nature to Man's Will. But when the Wind freshen'd suddenly and Squalls o'ercame us in a trice, Nature herself turn'd from Helpmeet to Harridan and Harmony turn'd to Horror! O what Panick suffus'd our Hearts as we scurried up the Masts to take in the Sails lest we heel o'er into the Drink! I learnt to be as nimble in clambering up a Mast barefoot as any Common Tar, but ne'er did I do so without a Pounding in my Breast that seem'd to say: *Turn back, turn back, this is no Task for the Fair!* Yet I still'd those Voices and continu'd just the same, for I had Contempt for Womanish Fears and fancied myself neither Man nor Woman but a Combination of the noblest Qualities of the twain! Always in my Life have I sought to press myself to do the Things I've fear'd the most; for only when one snatches Fear by the Scruff of its Neck and proclaims oneself its Mistress, doth one live Life to the fullest. The Squall would pass, the Wind be fair again, and I would scramble down the Mast, breathing a Sigh of deep Relief whilst all the Tars and I drank Toasts in Grog to Fairer Winds to come.

From the Lookout on the Mainmast, one could see twenty Miles in each Direction; thus on a clear Day 'twas possible to spy likely Prizes, and with a Fair Wind, give Chase. Most

Merchantmen were ill-equipp'd for Combat and well-nigh helpless to our howling Hordes of Pyrates.

Whilst still a Distance from the Prey, we'd hoist a Flag of her own Country to throw her off her Guard; only when we were quite close would we hoist our Pyrate Flags to terrify. Likewise we had various Flags to communicate betwixt our various Ships, whereupon each Deputy Skipper was to take a Vote amongst the Men to determine whether we should chase a Prize or not. 'Twas common Pyrate Lore that the most heavily loaden Merchantmen were oft' the least heavily arm'd, for the Hold was us'd for Cargo rather than Ammunition. Frequently these Ships had Gunports painted on their Sides to give the false Appearance of great Force of Arms, but an old Salt, canny with a Spying-Glass, could tell the Diff'rence betwixt these painted Gunports and the real Things. The Wind being favourable, and the Vote being favourable, we'd give Chase, each of our four Ships knowing that the first Man on board receiv'd a double Share of Booty. Thus we were racing each other e'en as we pursu'd the Prey, which gave the Taking of a Prize an added Hint of Sport!

The first Ship to reach the Prey attackt in the Time-honour'd Pyrate Fashion, invented, so Horatio said, by the Buccaneers, or Brethren of the Coast. We'd scarce fire Cannon, lest we sink a fair Prize with all her Booty, but rather we would seek to board her from the Bowsprit—oft' without a single Broadside being fir'd. How Ships surrender'd when they saw our Pyrate Colours! 'Twas comical almost. I scarce would have credited Horatio's Tales had I not seen it with my own Eyes! Ship after Ship surrender'd to our Pyrate Flotilla, usually with less Damage to our own Vessels than that wrought by tiny Shipworms. So 'tis frequently the case that the smallest and most invisible Enemy inflicts the greatest Damage, whilst the largest Enemy may be fell'd, like Goliath, with a tiny Sling.

Musicians we had to play the Fife and Drums and Trumpets with War-like Menace, whilst the most skillful of the Pyrates vapour'd 'round the Decks, growling like Lunaticks and baring their Teeth in a fev'rish Display of false Ferocity! Costume was oft' resorted to as well, the most fearsome Pyrates dressing themselves in Savage Colours and wearing their Hair and Beards most horribly unkempt. 'Twas simple to look fearsome, for, i'faith, these Pyrates scarce had bath'd in sev'ral Years, and sure they ne'er once shav'd off any Hair that might affright the Prey! Their Teeth were rotten from their Lives at Sea, their Faces oft' were scarr'd, their Noses broke, and many had but half an Ear remaining! I lookt quite ill myself with my shorn Locks standing up as straight as Stubble in a Cornfield; and when I dress'd *en Homme,* I could pass—to unknowing Eyes—as any Pyrate, despite the Largeness of my Breasts, which I took care to bind 'neath my Coat.

In my Heart, I nourish'd the daft Dream that we would sight *Cassandra* in those Waters and take Belinda as our Pyrate Prize; to that End I forced myself to climb the one-hundred-foot Mast and spy the Seas with Lancelot's Spying-Glass. 'Twas a perilous Climb upon a rocking Sea (e'en on dry Land, 'twould be most perilous!) and my Head cower'd e'en as my Heart demanded it. But what is Motherhood if not a Course in Courage? And what are Children but the Means by which we leave our own Childhoods far behind? In your sweet Name, Belinda, I was pusht to Feats that ne'er before or since have I done.

Alas, I did not sight *Cassandra,* tho' I *did* sight other fair Prizes and won the Choyce of Weapons for it, too. I sighted the *King Solomon,* an English Snow, and the *Guarda del Costa,* a Spanish Merchantman. And I was the first to board the *Guarda,* too!

O I remember that Engagement as if 'twere Yesterday! Lancelot sat back and let me play the Skipper upon that Occasion, for he was growing e'er more proud of my Pyrate Prowess and he delighted in watching me command our Ship.

"Is all ready?" I enquir'd as we gather'd on the *Guarda.*

"Yea," cried the Men.

"Every Man to his Charge!" I shouted, watching the Helmsman with a practis'd Eye.

"Keep her steady," I commanded.

"Aye, aye," said the Helmsman.

The *Guarda* struck her Flag and Pennant and Streamers; we likewise struck a Spanish Flag to confuse her.

"Dowse your Topsail and salute her!" I cried. 'Twas done; the Spanish Ship was hail'd. Only when we were so close that we could almost shout to the *Guarda* did we strike our Pyrate Colours.

"Whence your Ship?" The Master of the *Guarda* askt in Terror, for he knew the Answer.

"From the Seas!" I cried.

The *Guarda* was so surpriz'd by us that she kept her Luff whilst we were making ready to tack about. We approach'd

Bow-on with Noise of Fife and Drum and Trumpet and Vapouring Pyrates making horrid Faces on the Fo'c'sle Deck, sticking out their Tongues at the affrighted Spanish Tars and growling like Beasts of the Wild! When we drew close enough, I climb'd out on the Bowsprit and leapt across to board the *Guarda* ere a single Broadside could be fir'd. Whilst I did so, our three other Ships tackt about as well, quite surrounding our Prize, with Cannon at the ready, and the howling Hordes Vapouring upon *their* Decks! 'Twas all that easy; we so swifty boarded the Spanish Prize that she had no Chance at Self-Defence. The Captain might put up a brief Display of Force, but the Tars would likely not, so abus'd were they.

During the Engagement with the *Guarda*, as during many others, I workt with Horatio as my Mate—and dress'd as gaudily as he himself. I wore a Full-bottom'd Wig, to cover my Stubble, a Hat with a red Feather, and a damask Waistcoat. I'd e'en devis'd Moustaches for myself to cover my womanish Lips. Horatio would follow me across the Bowsprit, and as we boarded the Prize we'd shout in Latin to affright our Prey. To these poor Sea-Dogs, it seem'd a most curious Tongue and it confus'd 'em utterly. They'd ne'er heard its like except in Church, and the Things we shouted were most unliturgical! (Thus doth e'en Book-learning have its practical Use!)

Horatio was adept at slicing Noses and Ears with great Display of Blood but few Mortal Wounds. I would scramble up the Masts to cut away the Rigging, and disable the Prey, making good her speedy Surrender. Few Spanish Sailors would risque their Lives for Plate and Jewels consign'd to haughty Hidalgos they hated. We took the *Guarda del Costa* with her full Cargo of Booty—Gold Dust, Emeralds, and abundant Bars of Silver. My double Share of that alone made me quite rich but, alas, it did not restore Belinda.

A most curious Incident occurr'd whilst we were dividing up the Plunder after our successful Engagement with the *Guarda del Costa*. Each of the Deputy Captains had come aboard the *Happy Delivery* to receive their Men's Share of the Booty, which consisted, in part, of Bags of rough-hewn Emeralds. Having counted 'em all, Horatio determin'd we could spare five per Man, consid'ring the double Shares for me and Lancelot as first to Board and Fleet Commander, respectively. But after sharing out the Gems—which were all of small or middling Size—he found himself down to the last

Man on the List, with only one Emerald remaining, but that one being of prodigious Size. Where the other Emeralds had been but half- or quarter-inch across, this one was perhaps ten Inches wide and weigh'd more heavy in the Hand than many common Rocks. The Pyrate Captain of the *Bijoux*, a gruff, uneducated Man, objected when he drew this great Gem as his Share.

"Damme!" cried he, "the others had five Stones an' I've but one!" Nor would he rest until Horatio took a Mallet and shatter'd this precious Emerald to tiny Bits so he could have his five!

I tell this Tale merely to illustrate the sort of Men our Pyrates were: rough-hewn Rogues who knew not that one great and hefty Stone was worth a dozen small! Literal they were and shrunken of Mind, and the Chance of building a Deocracy with them seem'd slim indeed. We were growing richer Day by Day, yet we were scarcely melding into a true *Communitas*. Horatio and I both knew that Lancelot's Dreams of a New Jerusalem were daft—at least with these Men—but did Lancelot yet know? 'Twas true that Lancelot was changing before my very Eyes; he was proud of my Pyrate Prowess and oft' deferr'd to my Advice and Counsel. Still, did he see, as I did, the Danger of Rebellion of our scurvy Pyrate Colleagues? *That* could neither I nor Horatio rightly say. Our Hold was cramm'd with Precious Jewels and Gold, yet daily our Dreams seem'd further away!

Moreo'er, tho' as Pyrates Fortune smil'd on us, as Lovers 'twas quite another Matter. Horatio, Lancelot, and I slept in the Great Cabin of the *Happy Delivery*, eyeing each other with unrequited Lust. Lancelot would not allow Horatio to make love to me; Horatio would not allow Lancelot to make love to me; and I forbade 'em to make love to each other on Pain of Death! I had not been taught the Use of Cutlass for nought! I would wield my Cutlass in Defence of my own Honour, if not yet to seize Belinda. Thus, we three kept an uneasy Truce at Sea, sleeping in our separate Berths in the same Cabin, and yearning for each other.

"We could make Love as three," Lancelot would sigh. "Such Things are known 'neath Heaven. . . ."

"Not on your Life!" Horatio would rejoin. But should Horatio make a Move to caress Lancelot, I would most heatedly protest. Ah, it made our Tempers keen for Battle—all this unrequited Love and Lust—and we three vented on the Prey the Fury that we could not spend in Bed!

'Twas clear that Things could not continue thus, fore'er more, and a most Fateful Encounter at Sea brought Matters swiftly to a Head.

We were still in the South Atlantick, at a Latitude of about eighteen degrees, and nearing, with Fair Winds (Horatio said), the flat Isle of Anegado, with its Five-Mile Reefs, which stand as Nature's Barriers betwixt the Atlantick and the Caribe. Here Sir Francis Drake had found a Passage, which now bore his Name, and here, in those Isles they call'd the Virgin Isles, were many uninhabited Keys with Fair Anchorages, where Ships as large as ours might hide, sending smaller Ships to raid the Shipping Roads. Here might we find our Tropick Pyrate Isle, to make our *Libertalia*, or here, at least, might we ride at Anchor in a hidden Cove whilst a Landing Party in a swifter Sloop, the *Bijoux* perhaps, set out in search of the *Cassandra*.

The Winds were fair, and Horatio thought to make the Isle of Anegado in a few Days. The Passages were perilous; many Ships had wreckt themselves upon the Reefs; but Horatio, having sail'd this Way before, claim'd he knew the proper Tacks to take to sail about the Isle and ride at Anchor in a pleasant Bay. He also had a practis'd Eye for spotting Reefs 'neath the Sea.

But none of these Plans was to come to pass; for as we sail'd the Open Ocean we chanced to spy without our Glass a most curious Ship, and she hail'd us upon the Seas, as if in Distress.

She was a strange-looking Vessel, Frigate-built and broad of Beam, with Oar Holes like an Ancient Galleass; she mounted thirty Guns, and her Fo'c'sle seem'd a Mighty Fortress. Three-masted she was, and square-rigg'd on all three, but flying a Jib and Lateen Sail as well; with so much Sail, she lookt a fast Ship despite her Bulk. O she was a Sight to see, nor did she seem disabl'd.

"By Jove," Horatio said—for he was first to spy her: "If I didn't know that Captain Kidd was dead, I'd say that was the *Adventure Galley*, and sailing her, the Ghost of Captain Kidd!"

"How so, Horatio?" I askt, as he climb'd down the Mast, Spying-Glass in Hand.

"Kidd had a Ship like that—the fam'd *Adventure Galley*—and 'twas said she could do fourteen Knots under Sail, and three with Oars if she should be becalm'd. I ne'er have seen the like of such a Ship nor do I trust her by the Look of her. She means us Harm, I'll warrant."

"An' shall we neglect a Sister Ship in dire Distress?" askt Lancelot.

"Wherefore Distress?" disputed Horatio. "She signals Distress, yet looks she sound as we—for as Tully says—"

"Stuff Tully up yer Arse," said Lancelot, "an' hail our Sister Ship!"

"Begging your Pardon, Captain Mine," says Horatio with heavy Irony, "but I'll not sail heedless into Danger—I, who am the very Tacitus of Buccaneering!"

"Oho, then is it Mutiny, me Boy?" cried Lancelot.

"Call it what you will," Horatio said.

I fear'd the two would come to Blows, so I stepp'd in.

"Why not hoist a Flag to test her?" I propos'd. For we, like many Pyrate Ships, and Privateers as well, carried Flags of all Nations to beguile our Prey.

"An' which one should we hoist?" askt Lancelot.

"Why not the Mighty British Lion?" said I.

Horatio concurr'd, as did Lancelot—another Brawl betwixt 'em averted!—and we hoisted up the beauteous British Flag; whereupon the strange Frigate did the same!

"'Tis a Fetch!" Horatio cried.

"O ye of little Faith!" cried Lancelot.

"She's coming about!" Horatio said. "Shall we stand here like lubberly Poltroons or board her ere she essays to board us! If that's a crippl'd Ship, I'll eat my Hat!"

"Prepare the Cannon," I counsell'd, "but do not fire!"

The Frigate was coming at us so rapidly that there was no Time to consult the other Ships regarding this Engagement.

"Hoist the Pyrate Flag!" I cried, whilst Lancelot merely stood back and left these Decisions to me.

Our Pyrate Colours were struck; whereupon we saw a Sight surpassing strange: the other Ship struck Pyrate Colours, too!

Her Flag was black as Night; upon it were cross'd Cutlasses 'neath a Skull. But what was curious about this Skull was that it clutch'd a Rose betwixt its Teeth—like some Saucy Wench!

The Frigate gain'd on us; we fear'd for our Lives. She had more Sail than our poor Brigantine, more Cannon, too, and certainly a stronger Fo'c'sle. Why, 'twas a Fortress in itself! O should we, after all our Days at Sea, be taken by Pyrates better-arm'd than we? Desp'rately, we tried to signal to the Rest of our Flotilla.

"Hoist the Signal Halyards!" I cried.

'Twas swiftly done, but not one of the other Ships came about to aid us.

"Mutiny!" shouted Lancelot. "Mutiny!"

As I have said, I'd fear'd for some Time that if we were e'er in grave Danger, our Deputy Skippers would view our Demise with Complacency, and so 'twas true; they made no Move to aid us. I'faith, it seem'd they broke Formation and sail'd away.

Now the Frigate was coming about and making ready to board us from the Bow in the same Pyrate Style we had so oft' us'd ourselves! We saw her Name—'twas odd: the *Three Spoon Galley;* and she had all her Cannon ripe for Fire. Upon her Decks and Shrouds were so many Pyrates that e'en with our swollen Crew, we were outclass'd. But as she came for us, we spy'd upon the Bowsprit, standing like some glorious Figurehead, a beauteous red-headed Wench with a rais'd Cutlass in her Hand! What's more, she had a silken Rose betwixt her Teeth!

Horatio rais'd his Pistol to dispatch her; Lancelot stay'd his Hand.

"Hold!" Lancelot said. "Can I believe my Eyes? 'Tis Annie Bonny, as I live an' breathe! 'Tis the beauteous Pyrate Queen herself!"

At those last Words, Jealousy leapt in my Breast. I stood there on the Deck in Danger for my very Life and I could think of nothing but the Loss of *my* red Hair, how shabby I must look before this Beauty, and how much I coveted the Title "Pyrate Queen"!

Now the Bowsprit of the *Three Spoon Galley* came across our Waist on the Port Side and the beauteous Pyrate leap'd upon our Deck, follow'd by a Boarding Party of twelve. I deem'd us done for now, and secretly I curst Lancelot's soft Heart. Would I (and e'en poor lost Belinda) be sacrificed to his Stupidity? O damn Lancelot and his Thieves' Honour! What a soft-headed Nit-Wit he was!

Two Pyrates seiz'd me; two seiz'd Horatio and two were making ready to seize Lancelot, when lo! the Pyrate Queen seem'd all at once to recognize the Admiral of our Fleet, and running to him, fell upon her Knees and kiss'd his Feet, crying out, "Lancelot the Brave! Yer Fame hath gone afore ye! I salute a Fellow Pyrate an' Colleague o' the Seas!"

In a trice, the Pyrates who were holding us fell back; Lancelot beam'd with Vanity; Horatio breath'd a deep-fetch'd Sigh of Relief, and I—I was consum'd with Jealousy!

I saw how her Words made Lancelot primp and preen; I saw, when she fell upon her Knee, how her Breasts were large as Tropick Melons (and loosely held within her Stays) and how Lancelot lookt at 'em! I fancied she had no scarr'd Belly, no Children at all to stretch her Breasts, and O I coveted her Hair—so like my former Curls—and O, O, O I coveted her Ship as well! More Sail I could forgive, more Cannon e'en, but more Hair, ne'er! I wisht her dead with all my Heart and Soul, yet I smil'd and took her Hand when introduced, and fell before her in a Curtsey so profound, you'd think I'd met the Queen herself!

"Annie Bonny as I live an' breathe, I ne'er thought to see yer own Sweet Self on Land or Sea," said Lancelot. "I heard tell ye were tried in Jamaica an' sentenced to be hang'd."

"Jack Rackham was hang'd—the cowardly Dog—" said she, "but I could plead me Great Belly an', i'faith, was later pardon'd. We Women have so many Disadvantages that we may as well take those few Advantages Nature herself provides—why, I have both me Babes at Sea with me—in trainin' to be Pyrates!"

I listen'd wide-eyed to this Tale. Would that I had my Babe at Sea with me! O I envision'd my own Sweet Belinda playing in the commodious Hold of a Pyrate's Treasure Galleon, prattling and drooling amidst Piles of Emeralds and Gold Mohurs, sucking on Silver Bars, and sprinkling Louis d'Ors and glitt'ring Doubloons betwixt her pink Infant Fingers!

"This 'ere's me Quartermaster, Horatio," Lancelot said, his Thieves' Accent growing thicker at Annie Bonny's Arrival, "and this 'ere's me Mascot, Fanny Hackabout-Jones."

Anne Bonny rose to her Feet to receive Horatio's Obeisances; for now 'twas his Turn to fall upon bended Knee and grovel, like a lovesick Puppy, before her. Me she ignor'd, so little Regard had she for my Looks or Bearing. Only my Name amus'd her.

"Why, what a curious Name!" said she, "Hackabout-Jones—how very odd."

"Ye'd best remember it," I said, "for 'twill be as famous as yours someday."

How unlike me to be so ill-manner'd! The Words leap'd from my Mouth ere I thought about 'em.

464

"Methinks I see a green-eyed Monster," said Horatio, rising from his Knees.

"Come, come, Ladies," Lancelot said. "Why ye have much in common. By Rights ye should both be the best o' Friends!"

I was unconvinced; yet could I not take my Eyes off Annie Bonny, so beauteous was she and so full of Fire. Her Hair was red, her Eyes as green as Emeralds, her Skin as pink as tiny furl'd Rosebuds, and her Breasts as white as Lilies. I touch'd the Stubble upon my Head and felt asham'd. If I were half the Woman this Bonny was, I should ne'er have let vile Whitehead use me so! O I blam'd myself e'en for my Misfortunes! Instead of taking Pity on myself and being a Friend to my own tortur'd Soul, I sought to be her Torturer as well.

Ah, Jealousy is, of all Human Vices, the most vicious! 'Tis truly, as Dryden says, "the Jaundice of the Soul"; and as Shakespeare says, it assuredly "doth mock the Meat it feeds on!" Jealousy can make Enemies of Friends and Friends of Enemies (when they envy a former Friend in common!). Jealousy, not Money, is the Root of all the Evil upon this Earth.

"Come, Ladies," Lancelot said, "shall we take our Ease in the Great Cabin an' drink a Glass o' Claret? Fer, 'tis not often we are blest with such a Guest. . . ." Whereupon he took Anne Bonny's Arm like some Courtier of Old and led her slowly, and in the greatest State, to the Captain's Cabin; Horatio and I humbly follow'd.

There, with Port and Cheese and other Dainties set before us, Lancelot drank a fulsome Toast to Bonny's Beauty (whereupon *she* preen'd) and then he begg'd her to tell her Tale of Pyracy, Capture, and subsequent Deliverance.

I settl'd myself at the Captain's Table to hear this Tale, yet in my Heart was I harden'd against her—if not because of her Great Ship, then because of her Great Beauty, if not because of her Great Beauty, then because of the way *my* two Great Men grovell'd and panted in her Presence. When Lancelot first made *my* Acquaintance, he had scarce us'd me thus. Ah, Men claim to be afraid of Women of Spirit, Women who can duel with Rapier like any Man, but i'faith, such Women fascinate 'em! For 'twas not Bonny's Beauty alone that made Lancelot so daft for her, but the fatal Combination of Beauty and Courage!

"I was born in Ireland in County Cork," said she, "the Daughter o' an Attorney an' a Housemaid. 'Tis said that

465

Bastards have the best Luck, an' my Case proves it, too! Fer I have watch'd me High-born Friends sink down whilst I meself have prosper'd. . . ."

A Braggart she is, too, thought I, as well as Bastard, yet I swallow'd back my Words and held my Tongue.

"Me Father was Will Cormac, me Mother Peg Brennan, an' Bonny is the Name o' me first Husband—the Cowardly Dog, Jim Bonny. 'Tis all I got from him an' just as well. Both me Children are Jack Rackham's—so I think—but e'en that's none too sure. At least I know they're *mine!*" She laugh'd lustily, whereupon Lancelot and Horatio echo'd her Laughter as if this were the wittiest Jest they'd e'er heard. I remain'd as impassive as a good Whisk-Player.

"I was born as the curious Result o' three lost Spoons— thus they are me Good-Luck Charms—an' I have call'd me Galley after 'em. Me Galley itself is built after the Design o' Captain Kidd's, an' save fer him, no Pyrate hath e'er sail'd a Ship o' this Design!"

"You see!" Horatio, the Pyrate Historian, says to me.

"Hmmph!" say I, whereupon Bonny ignores me and continues.

"The Tale is strange—so are the Tales o' all our Births oft' strange, fer if we knew what odd Capriciousness o' Fate brought our two Natural Parents to make love, we oft' would quake to see how little stands betwixt our drawin' Breath upon this Earth an' bein' curst fer all Eternity to Non-Existence. . . ."

Horatio and Lancelot shook their Heads furiously in agreement, like two idiotick Niddle-Noddle Figures; I only lookt icily at my rival Pyrate and said nought.

"Fer as the Tale is told," Bonny continu'd, "me Father had been married to a Lady o' some Estate in County Cork, an' she had gone away fer a Change o' Air after her Lyin'-in, whereupon he took this Opportunity to pay Court to Peg Brennan, the Maid, fer whom he felt a Hot Attraction. So many Men do likewise when their Wives are engaged in Child-bearin'—which is the Reason I will ne'er be anyone's Wife again! But, by the by, me Father's first Wife went to his Mother's in the Country, leavin' me Father an' Peg Brennan alone to do what they would without no spyin' Eyes. But me Mum, Peg Brennan, was also a Beauty like meself, an' sure she had Suitors besides the Master o' the House." Here Anne preen'd as if she play'd the Rôle of her own Mother. Lancelot and Horatio sat listening, slack-jaw'd and slavering.

466

"One o' these, a young Tanner from the Town, took the Occasion o' the Absence o' the Mistress o' the House to Steal three Silver Spoons whilst payin' Court to me Mother. An' she, bein' a canny Wench, soon miss'd the Spoons—fer she knew full well who took 'em—an' she went to the Constable to have her Suitor apprehended. He, on the other hand, havin' *earlier* realiz'd she suspected him, decided *not* to take the Spoons after all, an' hid 'em betwixt the Sheets o' her own Bed. . . ."

Dear God—I thought—what a boring Tale! 'Twas worse than hearing someone's endless Dream; yet Lancelot and Horatio just sat there hanging on each Word as if they had ne'er been so well entertain'd.

"An' so," Anne Bonny went on, "when the Mistress o' the House return'd, the first Thing she was told was o' the missin' Spoons, which me Mother had ne'er chanced to find because she was sleepin' with the Master o' the House! But sure she did not tell the Mistress *that!* Rather, she said that the Spoons were taken by her Tanner Lover, that she *herself* had call'd a Constable, but that the Tanner then had run away an' no one knew his Whereabouts! So much was true, but what me Mother did *not* know was that the Tanner came that very Afternoon, confess'd his Theft o' the Spoons to the Mistress o' the House, but said he'd done it but in jest, an' return'd 'em forthwith to the Maid's Bed. Aha! *Now* did the Mistress o' the House suspect why those Spoons had ne'er been found, an' now did Jealousy infest her Heart! Oho—thought she— me Maid hath not slept in her Bed! Oho, she hath been with me Husband! Whereupon, she resolves to catch the Lovers at their Game an' nail 'em, as 'twere, to the Cross. So she tells the Maid that *she* intends to sleep in the Maid's Chamber that very Night (supposedly to give her own Bed to her Husband's Mother, but truly to apprehend her strayin' Husband) an' she tells me Mother to change the Linens fer her. Well, now, when me Mother goes to her Bed, what should she find there?"

"The Tanner?" offers Lancelot eagerly.

"No, Silly," says Annie Bonny, showing her White Breasts.

"The Attorney, your Father?" offers Horatio.

"No, Silly," says Anne, tossing her red Hair and smiling.

"A long boring Tale?" offer I, whereupon both Lancelot and Horatio look Daggers at me.

"No, no, no!" says our Annie. "She finds the three Spoons!

Whereupon she hides 'em in a Chest fer the nonce, meanin' later to put 'em where they might be found by Chance."

"Oho!" cries Lancelot.

"Aha!" says Horatio.

"Aggh," says I, but in truth, I say it softly, under my Breath.

"Well," says the Queen of all the Pyrates, "that very Night, the Mistress o' the House lyes in the Maid's Bed—me Mother's Bed, that is—an' by the sacred Skull an' Crossbones, what should happen but her own Husband, the Attorney, comes to her Bed an' plays the most vigorous Lover with her—mistakin' her fer the Maid! She bears it all submissively as any Christian Lady—tho' it sure ain't me own Style o' Fornication—an' sure enough he steals away in the Mornin' thinkin' now to surprize his Wife with his Return Home! (Fer, he had pretended to be away on his Wife's Return Home, the better to have another Night with the beauteous Brennan.) Well, now that the Mistress o' the House had her Proof o' her Husband's Infidelity, she straightaway goes to a Constable to have the Maid apprehended fer the Theft o' the Spoons—so strong is her Desire fer Revenge—an' she also goes to her Mother-in-Law, an' most vigorously complains o' her Husband, who play'd so great a Romeo with her, thinkin' her the Maid—tho' in me own Opinion, she should have *thankt* the Maid, fer ne'er before had she so good a Fuck off her own Husband! An' methinks one Good Turn deserves another, eh?"

Here Lancelot and Horatio dissolv'd into Gales of Laughter, as if they were listening to Theophilus Cibber himself, playing Ancient Pistol!

"But no," says Annie, "she has the Maid clapp'd in Prison fer it—the Fool—fer, sure, when the Maid's Trunk is searched an' the Spoons found, she is swiftly condemn'd as guilty o' the Theft! Now, the Husband comes Home, pretendin' he was in another Town the previous Night, an' the first Thing he hears is o' the Maid's Imprisonment, whereupon he goes into a Passion 'gainst the Wife, whereupon *she* accuses him o' bein' the Maid's Lover, whereupon his own *Mother* accuses him o' the same, an' the Poor Man receives such a Tongue-lashin' from the two Women that the Quarrel betwixt him an' his Wife can ne'er be mended more, whereupon both Mother an' Wife take Horse fer the Mother's Country Seat, leavin' the Husband to rage alone! An', i'faith, 'twas the End

468

o' their Marriage, fer the Bitterness betwixt 'em grew such that ne'er did they live together as Man an' Wife again."

"But what o' yer poor Mum, in Gaol?" asks Lancelot.

"Well may ye ask," Anne Bonny says. "She languishes there near six Months ere the Assizes, an' whilst in Gaol grows greater-an' greater-bellied—fer me own Infant Self was bloomin' in her Womb—an' when the Assizes comes 'round, the Mistress o' the House relents, havin' taken Pity on the Maid, an' decides not to press Charges, an' so the Maid is set free, an' soon after brings me to me Birth. All well an' good so far, but the Mistress o' the House also proves with Child an' she gives birth to Twins, whereupon the Attorney, thinkin' he hath not lain with her since her previous Confinement, grows e'en more vext with her than e'er before an' now openly lives with the Maid an' his bastard Daughter to spite her! Well, by an' by, the Attorney's Mother falls ill, begs her Son to reconcile with his Legal Wife fer her own Sake, whereupon the stubborn Man refuses, fer he loves his little Daughter an' his Mistress too well to part from 'em now, whereupon his own Mother disinherits him, leavin' all her Money to the estranged Wife. . . ."

Dear Goddess, thought I, spare me this rambling Tale, which bores me so it makes my Ears itch! Were Lancelot and Horatio both daft? Had they no Judgement at all? I began to nod and close my Eyes, pretending to listen, but only listening here and there to Anne's Tale when it suited my Convenience.

The Nub of her History seem'd to be that her Father soon had to leave County Cork due to this Scandal, which ruin'd his Law Practice, whereupon he departed for Charlestown with his Mistress, the former Maid, and his Daughter, Anne. In Charlestown, he set out to practice Law, but soon turn'd Planter, with much Success. Alas, no sooner was he establish'd in Carolina but his belovèd Mistress dy'd and he became sole Parent to his little Girl. Thus, she was rais'd, our Annie, on a Charlestown Plantation, the Apple of her Papa's Eye and spoilt as rotten as a Child could hope to be. Ah, how oft' 'tis true with Women who are Hellions that they were rais'd by doting Papas! For Anne was ne'er restrain'd in any of her Wishes, and, as a Child, was given her own Slaves, Dogs, and Horses. At Fourteen, she stabb'd an Indentur'd Servant Girl who dropp'd a Dish of Pottage in her Lap—and went scot-free. At Fifteen she join'd a Band of Thieves down by the Charlestown Wharves, and when she was apprehended, her Papa bought her Liberty from Gaol. At Sixteen, she nearly kill'd a Young Swain who'd foolishly thought to take advantage of her. Thus could Anne Bonny defend herself when she did not fancy a Man, but when she fancied one, she also had her Way with him. She told of a Fencing Master who'd taught her how to fence by flicking off her Clothes at Rapier-Point whilst she flickt his as well! Whereupon she announced, in no uncertain Terms, that she'd lost her Virginity at the Age of Nine and ne'er regretted its Loss an Instant.

The History of Annie Bonny's Life now became most gamey and I open'd my Eyes. I tried to count her Lovers on my Fingers, Toes, the Buttons of my Shift, but soon lost count. There was the Fencing Master, the Dancing Master, an Indian Hunter who'd taught her how to hunt and shoot and e'en skin her Prey, a wealthy Planter or two, and innumerable Buccaneers! 'Twas most curious that tho' her Life had been adventurous in the extream, she was able to bore one quite because of the dreary Manner in which she told of it. 'Tis frequently the case with Histories of e'en the greatest Men and Women, that if they have no Wit in their Expression nor Instinct for the Story-Teller's Craft, e'en the most stirring Adventures will seem dull. Mark this well, I told myself, when you come to write the History of your own Life; ne'er forget that 'tis not Fidelity to Fact alone that makes a Story stir the Blood, but Craft and Art! And 'tis perhaps the *greatest* Craft to seem to have no Craft.

But Lancelot and Horatio conceiv'd no Criticisms whatsoe'er of Bonny's Tale. They hung upon each Word as if she were a Female Homer, ranting in Ancient Greece.

'Twould have seem'd to me that Bonny had sufficient Liberty at Home in Charlestown ne'er to seek to leave her Father's Plantation; yet, as e'en the freest Persons account themselves caged if they have licentious Appetites, Anne was determin'd to fly the Nest. As a Girl of Good Fortune, she had her full Choyce of Rich Planters to marry, but none of 'em pleas'd her. Spoil'd as she was by a doting Papa, she ran off with a Common Tar, fully expecting her foolish Papa to shower 'em with Gifts, Houses, and a gen'rous Marriage Portion; but her Papa prov'd wiser than she expected upon this Occasion, and turn'd her out of Doors. Whereupon she and her Husband, James Bonny, took Ship to the great Pyrates' Lair in the Bahama Isles, the notorious New Providence.

To hear Anne tell of it, New Providence was a sort of New-World Sodom, tho' to Pyrates 'twas a Paradise.

470

"The Waters 'round New Providence," says she, "is too shallow fer yer Men o' War, yet perfect fer a Brigantine or Sloop—an' the Channels is most tricky an' treacherous. . . ."

There, in short, upon the Isle of New Providence could the Pyrates prepare Excursions 'gainst the great Merchant Ships, for in New Providence there was no Law at all and Pyrates liv'd just as they lik'd.

" 'Twas what I dreamt about fer all me bloomin' Life," says Anne, "a Town without no Constables nor Judges, a Town where him that's fastest with his Pistol wins ev'ry Argument, an' where the Women were such bold Whores that I was deem'd a Virgin! Well—almost one. . . ."

If she's a Virgin, thought I, I'm the Queen of Sheba.

In New Providence, Anne Bonny soon left her dull Husband, Jim Bonny, for more exciting Meat, and went a-pyrating with Jack Rackham.

"O Woe is me," says she, with no Woe whatsoe'er in her Voice, "I'm e'er a Sucker fer a Handsome Face, an' Jack was that! Big Cock, small Brain, an' Calico Trowsers! Was e'er a Wench so daft as to love a Man fer his bright Trowsers? Why, a Wench should love a Man fer what's in his Head, not in his Cod-Piece, but I'm too innocent o' the World's Wicked Ways, I am—no one understands how silly an' naïve I am 'neath my Reputation. . . ."

Good God! Great Goddess! thought I. Is there no Villain in this World who doth not regard himself as a poor abus'd Innocent, no She-Wolf who doth not think herself a Lamb, no Shark who doth not fancy that she is a Goldfish? Lancelot and Horatio lookt piteously upon her as she prated of her "Innocence"! O ye Heavens—Men are the veriest Fools when Women with large Breasts and Flaming Hair speak of their wounded Innocence!

"Well—" says Bonny, "I went a-pyratin' with him an' prov'd meself—as all say—braver than any Man. . . ."

At least she's modest, thought I.

"Ye know, o' course," Bonny went on, "that Gov'ner Woodes Rogers o' New Providence had promis'd a Pardon fer all Pyrates o' that Town in the Hopes o' makin' 'em proper Settlers an' bloody Money-hungry Whigs—an' so we took the Gov'ner's Pardon—Jack Rackham an' I did. But no sooner was we fitted out with a fine Privateerin' Ship to cruise 'gainst the filthy Spanish Dogs than we turn'd Pyrate fer our own Account! Oho, 'twas *then* that we chanced to find upon our Ship a handsome young Sea-Dog name o'

Mark Read an' he an' I was hot attracted to each other"—here she winkt broadly at Lancelot and Horatio—"whereupon Jack Rackham grew ungodly jealous an' surpriz'd us both whilst we was alone an' kissin' on the Fo'c'sle Deck 'neath the Moon! Jack ripp'd the Shirt off this Mark Read in a Passion an' lo! what should he find?"

"The Silver Spoons?" askt Lancelot.

"The Tanner?" askt Horatio.

"No, Sillies," said our Annie, fondling her own Breasts, "but Breasts as large an' fine as these!" Whereupon she unloos'd her Stays, saying, "Oho, 'tis warm to tell a Tale with so much Passion an' I can scarce breathe free. . . ." And she disclos'd just enough beauteous Breast, with the slight pink Hint of Nipple, to quite distract our two Pyrates from her Tale.

"Well—" says she, "when Jack Rackham sees that Mark Read the Brave Buccaneer is really *Mary* Read the Brave Buccaneer*ess*, he forthwith stops bein' jealous, the bloody Fool—fer I had more good Lovin' with Mary than with any Pyrate that e'er sail'd the Spanish Main! An' mark ye, I've bedded most o' 'em—Stede Bonnet, Calico Jack, all but the dead Cap'n Kidd himself an' Blackbeard, o' course—because he ne'er washt in his Life an' me Nose is as tender as me ye-know-what!"

Lancelot and Horatio roar'd again with Mirth, whilst, needless to say, I did not.

"Well," says dear Annie, "Mary Read an' I was Partners in Battle, Partners in Bed fer as long as the Cruise lasted, an' 'twas many a Time we was on Deck a-fightin' whilst the bloody Men huddl'd in the Steerage. Upon one Occasion, I fir'd into the Hold to rouze them cowardly Dogs an' kill'd a Parcel o' 'em, too. *Then* they comes up an' fights—what's left o' them! We took great Numbers o' Prizes in Jamaica an' other Parts o' the West Indies, an' but fer a short Stay in Cuba where I bore me Babe—the first, that is—I went a-pyratin' with more Gusto than any Man. An' Mary did, too! We dress'd in Man's Disguise an' play'd the Man in Bed as well. O I ne'er met a Fellow as brave as Mary, nor half the Man abed *she* was—but there may always be a first Time . . ." says she, winking again at Horatio and Lancelot.

"Well—we is taken finally because o' Rackham's Cowardice an', our Ship bein' batter'd by Hurricanoes, an' damaged in the Riggin' an' the Masts, we is pursu'd by Pyrate-Chasers from Port Royal, an' when the Bastards comes about to board us, Jack Rackham cowers in his Cabin like a Cowardly Dog! Mary an' I mann'd the Decks alone—but O, brave as we was, we cannot take three Pyrate-Catchers single-handed! Carried to Jamaica in Chains we is, an' there in Port Royal have the grandest Trial that e'er was seen since Cap'n Kidd was hang'd! A drunken Judge, lyin' Witnesses, a drunken Barrister—all the Glories o' British Justice! Why, when Mary an' me says: '*Milord, we pleads our Bellies*'—the drunken Judge thinks we mean to say 'tis Time fer Dinner! Fer yer British Judges is e'er attun'd to their Bellies an' not to the Meat, as 'twere, o' the Trial! When a Prisoner pleads her Belly, all the bloody Judge can think of is his own Mutton Roast!"

"Aye, 'tis true," says Lancelot.

"Well—we get off hangin' thus," says Bonny, "but whilst in Gaol, poor Mary dyes o' Gaol Distemper! Thus do I lose me greatest Love. . . ."

"Aye," says Lancelot, "I know it well. . . ."

"Alas, alack," says Horatio, as if Anne Bonny were another Eloisa losing Abelard to Death's own Monastery, or i'faith, another Alcestis sacrificing Life itself to Love.

"But the Day Jack Rackham is to hang, I goes to his Prison Cell—fer I had Influence aplenty in that Gaol, thanks to me Father's Money (which he sent via his Planter Friends in Jamaica)—an' I bid a fond Farewell to the very Man who brought both me Downfall an' me Deliverance! Fer I was *caught* owin' to his Cowardice, 'tis true, but owin' to his *Cock* I was spar'd the Noose! '*Jack*'—says I—'*O dearest Anne,*' says he—'*Jack darlin',*' says I—'*O dearest Anne,*' says he—'*Jack darlin',*' says I—'*if ye had fought like a Man ye needn't have hang'd like a Dog!*' "

"That's tellin' him!" cries Lancelot.

"Aye!" says Horatio.

"What sweet and comforting Words to a dying Man," say I with heavy Irony, whereupon Lancelot hushes me and Horatio hushes me, and Bonny continues:

"But me Papa comes to the Rescue in the End, sweeps me from Gaol with some well-placed golden Coins—Sacks o' Coins i'faith—to all the drunken Judges, Gaolers, Barristers, an' Gov'ners, whereupon what d'ye think happen'd?"

"He makes ye promise to forswear Pyracy?" askt Lancelot.

"No, Silly," says Annie, loosing her Stays e'en more and fondling her Nipples.

"He makes you promise to live with him in Charlestown?" askt Horatio.

"No, Silly," says Annie, pulling up her Skirt, and showing first her white Calves, then her fine pink Knees, and then—O Goddess—her smooth white Thighs!

"What, then?" says Horatio, panting.

"Well," says Anne, "me Papa says: *'If yer determin'd to be a Pyrate as I see ye are, ye shall have the finest Ship Money can buy an' all yer Heart desires, fer I suspect 'tis in yer very Blood!'* An' so he outfits me as you can see, with all the finest Gear, a Galley built like Cap'n Kidd's own Ship; an' he makes only this Proviso—that I must tithe to him ten per cent of all I take!"

"Amazing!" said Horatio.

"Astoundin'!" said Lancelot. "An' very like a Lawyer!"

"There's more Amazement soon to come!" said Anne. Whereupon she opens her Legs and begins, most seductively, to stroke that Bow'r of Bliss betwixt 'em. Now Anne Bonny begins a slow and sensuous Dance before our six astonish'd Eyes and like Salome with all her Seven Veils, she strips off Garments as she dances, and fondles her own Breasts and Thighs! 'Tis verily as if, having expos'd her History in that long, torturous Tale, she now proceeds to lay her Body bare!

Despite my Jealousy, I must confess that Anne's naked Form was beauteous beyond my wildest Dreams: Breasts round and firm as Melons, Nipples pink as Dawn and large as Sand Dollars, a flaming Bush, white Thighs, and a beauteous Belly whose only Hint of Child-bearing was a not unpleasing Slackness. Nor was she unskill'd in Dancing and Disrobing at the self-same Time. E'en her Stays and Petticoats and Shift she us'd most seductively, dropping 'em here and there upon the Floor, in what Mr. Herrick might have call'd "a sweet Disorder."

Finally, after much Dancing and Fondling, she takes Horatio's Hand, leads him to kneel betwixt her open Thighs, and offers him the Honey that verily drips in that most purple Place. At once he drives in with more Enthusiasm than a famish'd Dog finding a Leg o' Mutton! Lancelot, for his part, is too shockt to protest and I must pinch myself to make sure I'm not asleep and dreaming. Ye Gods—what a Woman! Coarse, crude, and yet I cannot but admire someone who takes her Pleasure so directly. In a trice, she and Horatio grapple on the Floor and they are making the Beast with two Backs with the greatest Gusto. Bonny goes about her Pleasure

474

with such high Animal Spirits that 'tis quite infectious; and ere long, e'en Lancelot and I have join'd 'em upon the Floor! As Bonny and Horatio pant and buck, seeking the Summit of Love's sensual Pleasure, I fondle Bonny's Breasts, and Lancelot strokes Horatio's sable Back. Great Goddess! Can this be happening to me? I hate this Woman's Soul and yet I love her Breasts—and O her Spirit quite engages me!

In the Debauch that follow'd, our own Annie was the Alpha and Omega of our Pleasure. We three scarce attended to our own Wants, but all to her Insatiable Appetites. Both Men had her, then did I almost devour her from her Toes to her red Curls; then did she devour me! O what a clever Tongue our Annie had! Words she fumbl'd with, but Flesh flow'd for her as smoothly as a Springtime River. She could play the Man better than any Man, and the Key of her Tongue unlockt Places in my Lock of Love that had ne'er been unlockt before!

O, O, O—I blush to think how Annie quite undid me! Crude as she was in Speech, she was just so gentle in the Art of Touch. Perhaps 'twas all a Conquest; oft' later I had Occasion to think so. But ere Logick rear'd its ugly Head, I was lost in a Loving so sublime that I forgot the Author of my Good Fortune. It almost seem'd Annie had workt in a Brothel breaking young Country Wenches to the Trade, for she so excited my Blood with her expert Touch that I would have sworn she had been train'd by Mother Coxtart herself, if not another Bawd!

Her Fingers play'd o'er my whole Body with that Lightness of Touch which more excites the female Blood than the heavy grappling most Men proffer. Her delicate white Hands seem'd to be Birds that flew and landed, flew and landed, hither and yon, from the Tips of my Toes to the inner Whiteness of my Thighs, then nested in that russet Thatch of Hair, so like her own. By teazing, tickling, pressing, squeezing, licking, she brought me to the Ultimate Conclusion of Love's Pleasure. Not too swiftly (like an eager Swain) nor too slowly (like a clumsy one), but with just enough Delay to sharpen Pleasure, and with just enough Swiftness to satiate it, quite!

What Satisfaction do Women desire in loving other Women? Is it the Image of *themselves* reflected in the Body of another? Is it a kind of Mirror like the one Narcissus found in his belovèd Pond? Is it an Affirmation of the

Goddess in themselves? Or is it merely wanton Pleasure's very Self?

What a curious Foursome were we! Two Men who lov'd each other, two Women who hated each other, and yet were bound, it seem'd, by Chains of Flesh. If I had any Doubt before that 'tis the Goddess who arranges our Fates, this Meeting with Anne Bonny upon the Seas should certainly erase that Doubt; and why—you soon shall see.

Lancelot, Horatio, and I were, 'tis true, starv'd for Love after our Shipboard Triangle of Abstinence. We three could not make love because of the strange Currents of Fealty and Passion that swirl'd about us. But now came Annie, a Stranger to our Pack; and oft' 'tis easier to make love to a Stranger than to the belovèd Brother that shares your Heart's Affections! Or so I reason now.

Horatio would not tolerate Lancelot's making love to me, yet o'er Annie, he felt no Dominion. Likewise Lancelot, who claim'd me for his own, could not square that with his Passion for Horatio. But Annie was a neutral Stranger, a Diplomatick No Man's Land, a Pyrate of the Pudendum, a Doxie of Downshire, a Gaping Grotto, a Happy Harbour, a very Queen of Holes—and O 'tis easier to fill a Hole than to leave it empty, for Nature quite abhors a Hole unfill'd!

Lancelot and I scarcely touch'd; Horatio scarcely touch'd Lancelot; but we all made love to Bonny as if in her we found another Lancelot, another Horatio, and another Fanny—all roll'd into one Being! Plato says that Human Love is but the passing Shadow of Divine; then may it be also that frequently we act out the Love we have for one Lover upon the Body of another? We three made Love to Annie with such Heat that verily it could scarce be Annie *herself* who evok'd such Love. But she—like the Lapdog that receives the Spinster's Love, like the Statue of the Virgin that receives the Adoration of the Popish Worshippers, like the Footman that receives the Passions of his widow'd Mistress—took all our Loves most amiably and well; and now please hear what she gave us in Return. . . .

Chapter XIV

Containing Anne Bonny's Legacy to our Heroine; better Reasons for Female Pyracy than for Male; a very tragical Incident; and the Beginning of the Conclusion of our History—(but do not fear, we shall not leave our Reader without many more Epilogues, Appendices, and Farewells).

AFTER OUR DEBAUCH, we four peculiar Lovers loll'd at our Ease drinking Sack and Claret, sleeping for sev'ral Hours entwin'd in each other's Arms, then waking to talk quietly amongst ourselves; for oft' 'tis true, that shar'd Pleasure softens the Aversions we may have felt before and brings illmated Rogues into the Orbit of Friendship. O short-liv'd Friendship mayhap, but Friendship just the same! And so it came to pass that I pour'd out my Heart to Annie concerning my missing Babe, my Childbirth Pangs, and e'en my Envy of her that she might have her Babes at Sea with her in training to be Pyrates—whilst I was bereft of my own Belinda! So I mus'd and so she (also soften'd by our mutual Flame) comforted me, for, i'faith, she preferr'd Women to Men for all her Swagger—and then I chanced to mention the *Cassandra.* . . .

"The *Cassandra* ye say?" Bonny asks. "The *Cassandra?* Why, I saw that Ship careenin' in Tartola when I crept into Roadtown Harbour aboard me little Pinnace to fetch me some fine Frocks from me English Taylor there!"

"When? When did you see her?" I askt. My Heart was pounding now with Hopes of finding Belinda.

"Not a Week past," says Bonny. "Why, I heard tell she was damaged in the Riggin' an' the Hull by a Hurricano an' put into Roadtown fer Repairs afore she sail'd fer me own Charlestown Harbour. . . ."

"When would that be?" I askt.

"Why, I reckon ye could still head her off with a Fair Wind. . . . 'Twas said she plann'd to sail this very Day."

Now Horatio and Lancelot were rouz'd from their Lethargies of satiated Lust.

"Do you hear that, Lancelot? We could o'ertake the *Cassandra* before she puts into Charlestown Harbour! We could catch the *Cassandra*!" I leapt into the Air with sheer Joy and clickt my bare Heels together.

"I'd be careful, Lads," says Bonny, " 'twas not far from there that Blackbeard himself was fell'd in the shallow Shoals of Ocacock Inlet. . . . Ye must take the *Cassandra* afore she sails into Charlestown Harbour, fer tho' Blackbeard dar'd blockade the Town seven Year ago—an' with what fatal Consequence ye know—I'd scarce commend the same to ye!"

Whereupon, with greatest Generosity and Open-heartedness, Bonny offer'd us all her Charts and Maps of Charlestown Harbour, the Bahama Isles, and e'en the Caribe.

"From Roadtown Harbour, she'd sail Drake's Passage to Anegado, then the Anegado Passage to the Open Sea. Ye'd take her off Anegado or off the Grand Bahama Bank with any Luck at all, an' failin' that, ye'd chase her up the Coast."

"Praise God!" said Lancelot.

"Praise Goddess!" said I—which I suppose the others regarded as a mere Figure of Speech, tho' I did not.

"I'd always help a Sister Pyrate in Distress," said Annie Bonny, suddenly becoming the finest, bravest Woman I'd e'er met in all my Life. Whereupon she embraced me and wisht me Luck, Health, Happiness, long Life, the Return of my Child, my Ringlets, all my Heart's Desires, and she made ready to reboard her Ship—tho' not before she'd sent her First Mate to fetch the Charts she promis'd, for she was a Woman of her Word.

'Twas Dusk when Annie Bonny left us on the High Seas, accompanied by the same twelve Pyrates who had leapt aboard our Ship with so much Menace. O as I saw her depart, I was full of Admiration for this Pyrate Queen! How *could* I have thought her low and common when she was such a true Sister of the Seas! What Generosity of Spirit! What Magnanimity of Heart! Annie Bonny was all Things, thought I, save a Hypocrite. She scoff'd at Fine Manners, took her Pleasure where and when it pleas'd her, like a Rake, but underneath it all, she had the Pyrate's Honour and an Honest Heart. She knew enough to honour Lancelot and Horatio as fellow Colleagues of the Seas, and tho' her Morals might seem loose to some, at least 'twas true she was no Hypocrite! She did not claim to be but what she seem'd. She was no Whore pretending to the Manners of a Duchess, no Courtesan masquerading as a Countess, no Harlot claiming to be Queen. As her Ship sail'd away in the Tropick Dusk—the Skies still pink with Phoebus' Afterglow—I saw her Pyrate Banner flapping proudly in the Breeze and I rejoiced; for this was the finest Woman I e'er had known, the lusty Goddess manifest on Earth!

'Twas strangely quiet upon Deck. Lancelot and Horatio and I wav'd Farewell to the *Three Spoon Galley* with what aching Hearts I cannot e'en say. Lancelot sigh'd; Horatio sigh'd; I sigh'd. But in a trice, I had the most curious Pang.

"The Men!" I cried. "Where are our Men?"

We lookt about; the Decks were bare. The Sails were luffing and the Rigging foul. Not a single Tar was to be seen about. Swiftly and with what Panick Sailors alone may know, we three ran about the Ship. Horatio to the Steerage, Lancelot and I to set the Sails again. 'Twas not long before a Howl, as of some Savage Beast, rose from the Depths of the Hold. 'Twas Horatio, summoning us below.

Lancelot and I descended, our very Souls in the Grip of Fear—and O when we arriv'd, the Picture that we saw was piteous indeed:

In the commodious Hold of the *Happy Delivery*, where before had been Bars of Silver, Piles of Emeralds, Sacks of Golden Coins, were all our Tars bound Hand and Foot and gagg'd like rabid Dogs! Some few had been shot—tho' none was kill'd—as Tokens, but most were unharm'd, yet so tightly bound that they could scarce move at all. Horatio began the Task of unbinding 'em, and when he ungagg'd the first, a Carpenter, that same let fly a Volley of Curses the like of which I had not heard since I journey'd up the Thames by Boat!

"The boilin' Bitch! The stinkin' Whore! The Jade! She's got our Booty—Lock an' Stock an' Barrel!"

I heard this Volley and did not know, at first, whether to smile or weep, tho' 'twould cost my very Life to do the Former. O 'tis said that Men cannot be rap'd, but Bonny prov'd it untrue! My Woman's Heart knew not whether to salute her Cunning or damn her as a scheming Bitch! I ponder'd to myself, yet for the Life of me I *could* not damn her. Emeralds would we lose and find again, but Belinda was unique upon this Earth! If she had barter'd me her Charts for all those Jewels, verily, 'twas worth it—tho' I'd best not say so. What a Wench! Sure all the Tales of Rackham's Daring were her own Doing. She was the Brains behind 'em both! Why, to take in Lancelot and Horatio—those greatest of Great Pyrates—and steal their Treasures by the simple Ruses of Flattery and Lust, 'twas a sort of Genius! Without Jack Rackham, Bonny would ne'er be caught! And where'er she sail'd a Part of me would sail, chearing the World's chief Female Pyrate!

But none of that must show; I must be heartbroken o'er the Loss of our Booty and I must seek somehow to appease the Men.

"The other Ships are gone!" cried the next Man to be unbound, a Musician. "She bewitch'd 'em as she did you!"

"Then did they sail with her?" I askt. "The Bonny Bitch. . . ."

"Mayhap," says the Carpenter, "or took off on their own Account. . . ."

"Good Riddance," says Horatio. "If they have not the Wit to sail with Lancelot Robinson to *Libertalia*—the Devil take 'em!"

Lancelot lookt downcast; his Dreams of a Deocracy were dasht again. I put my Arms 'round him to comfort him.

Now Horatio was untying sev'ral of the original Merry Men, Puck Goodfellow, Francis Bacon, Caveat, and Littlehat.

"We're better off with one loyal Ship than four mutinous ones," says Caveat. "O I have oft' told Lancelot that 'tis his O'erreaching will be the Death o' him—like Icarus o' Old. If those Fools would rather sail with the Bonny Bitch instead o' Robin Hood reborn, 'twill be their own Downfall! They will come to Grief, mark my Words, they will!"

"So ye had a good Bit o' Mutton, Boys, did ye?" says Puck Goodfellow, mockingly. "She must have drugg'd yer Claret or yer Port, the Tart, fer ye was dead to the World fer sev'ral Hours and heard neither Screams nor Scuffles. Why, Anne Bonny's Men carted off the Booty as if they workt in the Removal Trade!"

"How could ye let her strip ye o' yer Booty?" Caveat asks, just like a nagging Mother. "How could ye, Lancelot?" Whereupon Lancelot lookt as if he were going to weep.

"Come, come!" says Littlehat, embracing Lancelot, too, and me into the Bargain, "we're found Booty before, we'll find it again! 'Tis in our Stars to lose Fortunes an' make 'em again!" Whereupon he slapp'd Lancelot upon the Back encouragingly. "Good Riddance to those other Rogues, say I! If they haven't the Wit to want our *Libertalia,* good Riddance, say I!"

"Aye," says Francis Bacon, "Littlehat is right. Damn'd Meat-Eaters all of 'em! What Enlightenment can ye expect of 'em what eats Carrion! In *Libertalia,* we'll eat Vegetables an' Fruits alone an' spare the Souls of our four-leggèd Friends!"

Lancelot lookt a bit happier now, with his two-leggèd Friends rallying 'round him.

"Speakin' o' Meat, how was the Bonny Bitch?" askt Puck in Accents most pyratical. "A juicy Bit o' Mutton, eh? A nice Fillet o'Fish?"

Horatio and Lancelot lookt at him and winkt simultaneously, like sly Schoolboys.

"Wouldn't you like to know!" said Horatio.

"Ye know I have no Use whatsoe'er fer the Preposterous Pudendum," says Lancelot.

"Oho," says Puck, "that's yer Beard, me Boy! I know that one, too! 'Tis the Mollyish Boys gets *all* the Girls—" and he mimickt a Molly mincing along the Strand in his high-heel'd Shoes, waggling his Arse seductively.

"Enough of this Chatter," I cried. "Away with you! All Hands on Deck! The Sails are luffing! Should a Squall come up, we'll surely founder! There's Time enough to talk of Bonny later! For the nonce, we're setting Sail again for Anegado! There's a Fair Prize coming through the Anegado Passage and I mean to take her!"

"Which Prize is that?" askt Littlehat.

"The *Cassandra!*" said I. "All Hands on Deck!" O I was in command of my Ship again and I meant to find Belinda!

Suddenly I was fir'd with the Ambition to be like Anne Bonny! I thought that my whole Life long, I had been too timid and Lady-like. All the good Things I had gain'd—leaving Lymeworth to seek my Fortune, making my Mutiny within the Brothel, insisting upon my own Terms for being kept by Lord Bellars, becoming Whitehead's Scribe, altering Lancelot's Pyrate Articles, learning the Craft of Pyracy itself—were gain'd thro' killing the Lady in myself and playing the Pyrate! The Lady and the Pyrate! 'Twas as if two people battl'd for Supremacy within my very Soul: one a Vapourish Lady and one a Daring Pyrate, and they were so unlike each other they were scarce on speaking Terms! Whilst the Lady in myself was quiv'ring and quailing in Cowardice, the Pyrate was itching to breathe free! 'Twas the Pyrate who could command a Ship, scale a Shroud in a trice, climb to the Top of a Crow's-Nest, and scour the Seas expertly with a Spying-Glass! 'Twas the Pyrate who had beguil'd Lord Bellars into keeping me, all unknowing of my True Identity; and 'twas the Pyrate who had earn'd Whitehead's wary Trust by becoming his Amanuensis! 'Twas the Pyrate who had endur'd a Childbirth few endure, but 'twas the Lady who, in her Guilt and Vapourish Fear, allow'd a Wet-Nurse to tyrannize o'er her and steal the very Jewel of her Existence! 'Twas the Pyrate who amended Lancelot's Articles, but 'twas the Lady who at first resented Bonny both for her Beauty and for her Freedom! O I must *learn* from Bonny, not resent her, I thought; for she is what all Women long to be! E'en Chaucer says it thro' the Wife of Bath: The Fair Sex seeks that "absolute Command/With all the Government of House and Land;/And Empire o'er his Tongue, and o'er his Hand!"

Perhaps I had resented Bonny because she alone of all the Women I had met had gain'd what we all seek: true Mastery o'er her Fate. She depended upon no Keeper, whether male or female. She rais'd her own Babes and commanded her own Ship; and a Host of Pyrates listen'd when she spoke! If Women could master their Fates only thro' Pyracy, sobeit! Banish the Lady from my Soul fore'er more! Pyrate I was and Pyrate I long'd to be! And let Belinda learn to be a Pyrate, too!

We sail'd onward now for Anegado, hoping we might, in a few Days, intercept the *Cassandra* as she clear'd Sir Francis Drake's Channel, heading for the Open Sea. The Sea was Sapphire blue, shading off to Azure 'neath the Reefs, and tho' 'twas almost October and the Season of Hurricanoes, the Seas were not treacherous tho' the Winds were fresh. No, the Skies were changeless blue; the Sea glitter'd like a Jewel; and the Sun was a bright Disk of Gold on High.

Horatio and Lancelot were disgruntl'd o'er the Loss of our Booty, disgusted with themselves, I'll warrant, for having been taken in by a canny Wench; but I read the Sea and Sun and found the Omens good. I understood now that Anne Bonny had been sent to me to teach me of my Fate, for only when I kill'd the timorous Lady in myself would I rise like the Phoenix o'er the Ashes of my former Life and become the Fanny I was meant to be!

My Thoughts turn'd now to Belinda—now that I hop'd I might truly find her again. What did it mean to have a

Daughter in a World of Sons, and how might I teach her to survive? Someday, I vow'd, if I endur'd and if my Belinda endur'd, I should write a Book for her, embodying all I'd learnt about surviving upon this ungracious Globe in Woman's Form. This Vow I made to the flat Horizon and to the Sun's bright, blinding Coin, to the variegated Fishes 'neath the Sea, and to the Gracious Goddess who is o'er all, and who embodies all. I would write a Book for my own Belinda, so that when she ventur'd out into the World, she should have under her Arm a Book to guide her, a vast Compendium of Woman's Destiny, an Epick and a History roll'd into one, advice to a Daughter by her loving Dam! Empty-handed went I into the World, but Belinda shall have her own Great Book. For the Mother who really loves her Daughter, doth not strive to keep her Home by the Hearth, but sends her out into the World, arm'd with the Lessons her own Life has taught.

So I mus'd, and the Winds answer'd me by staying fresh and fair. O Sailors live at the Mercy of the Winds, rocking in the Cradle of the Ocean like Newborn Babes. And if we are a superstitious Lot, 'tis because our whole Existence may depend upon a freshening Breeze. But when the Winds are fair and the Sun shines, when we see Ripples of white upon the Surface of the Deep, yet no Mountainous Waves, no Alps nor Troughs of Water, then we account ourselves most truly blest and make Obeisances to whate'er Gods we honour.

I spy'd many a Ship in my Spying-Glass in the Days that follow'd, many three-masted Merchantmen, but none was the *Cassandra*. Some of our Crew Members began to grumble, wanting to take Prizes we saw, in order to recover our Fortunes more speedily, but Lancelot convinced 'em to wait for the *Cassandra*, which he promis'd would be worth a dozen other Merchantmen. Lancelot now took many Risques for me—as if indeed he'd come to love me quite—altho' we ne'er touch'd save in Platonick Passion. What if the *Cassandra* prov'd to have no Booty and the Men mutinied against him in Revenge? Lancelot seem'd not to care so long as I found Belinda. My Passions now were his; what better Love hath any Man?

For my own part, I knew the Weather was unseasonably fair, and as the Days pass'd and still we did not sight the *Cassandra*, I began to worry about Bonny's Treachery. Perhaps she'd ly'd to us concerning the *Cassandra*. Perhaps she'd given us Charts merely to confuse us and keep us from discovering the Loss of our Booty until 'twas verily too late. Perhaps there was no Sisterhood whatsoe'er betwixt us, and perhaps all her apparent Concern o'er my kidnapp'd Babe was nought but Trumpery, Tricks, and Mischief. Why should I believe her regarding the *Cassandra* when she had beguil'd us regarding our Booty and perhaps e'en beguil'd our other Ships and Tars? Why had I such Confidence that as a loving Mother she'd be true to another loving Mother, e'en tho' she had stolen our Gold and Jewels? Ah Fanny, thought I, you are still an Innocent in this Wicked World! Have you not yet learnt the Lesson that you must trust *no* one utterly? For Treachery e'er lurks around the Corner, and Trust is the Enemy of those who would Survive!

I fretted thus as I scann'd the Horizon thro' my Spying-Glass, wond'ring if I should e'er see my Belinda again, or if she had already been offer'd up—like some Infant Iphigenia—to propitiate the Winds. Goddess forbid! I must bite my Tongue for speaking such a Fear, e'en if only to myself!

The Fair Weather could not last fore'er more. 'Twas October and the Seas now show'd Signs of growing rough. 'Twas on a Day when the Skies were darksome and brooding and Clouds obscur'd the Sun, that I spy'd three Masts upon the Horizon, at a Distance of sev'ral Miles, and I had a most curious Conviction that 'twas the *Cassandra.*

We gave Chase, mounting a Parade of Sail that would do a Pyrate's Honour proud; Guns were at the ready and we had a brave Topsail Gale from North to North-East. The Weather grew thicker and dirtier as we gave Chase, and our Hold now being empty (where before 'twas deep-loaden with Gold and Silver), we heel'd precipitously. The Wind whipp'd thro' our Sails, which were so close-haul'd that all our Timbers creakt and our Brigantine was strain'd to her utmost. I knew, by now, the Danger we were in, the angry Look of the Seas, the blackening Skies, the sudden Furies of the Winds, but I abandon'd my Fears to the Pow'r of the Goddess, telling myself that if I lost Belinda, my Life should be worth nothing to me, whereas if I found her, I should have nought to fear from the Fates as long as I might live.

Those who have given Chase in a Sailing Ship in rough Weather will readily know how treacherous this Chase was. The *Happy Delivery* had gone too long without Careening, and when her Timbers creakt so, she readily sprung small Leaks. A Host of Tars were constantly needed to man the Pump, and the Loss of our Cargo had made us too light upon a heavy Sea.

Still, by the Pow'rs of the Goddess, we gain'd upon our Prize, and i'faith, when I was able to spy her Name, I saw that indeed, 'twas *Cassandra*! Having so recently been careen'd, and doubtless less foul-bottom'd than we, she seem'd at first our Match in Speed and more, yet being very deep-loaden, and much larger than our Brigantine, we had nonetheless a slight Edge. The *Cassandra* was an East India-man, and seem'd at least six hundred tons. She'd twenty-four Ports for Cannon on her starboard Side alone, but Horatio reassur'd me that doubtless she carried half as many Guns as it appear'd, for she needed Space for Cargo. 'Twas useless to debate whether to attack or no, for we were bound to take her or dye trying. Perhaps the rough Seas would e'en give us an Advantage; we had to hope so, for our other Advantages were few.

'Twas Noon upon the first Day of October, but dark as Night withal, when we got within random Gunshot of the *Cassandra* and struck our British Colours. Our Ship was in a Posture of Attack, but the *Cassandra* was wholly taken by Surprize, for the rough Seas had occupied her Tars so busily that she did not sight us until we were almost upon her. Whereupon she struck British Colours, too; whereupon we hoisted up our Pyrate Flag, and tackt about, Guns and small Arms at the ready, to affright her with a great Show of Strength. The Sea rose in vast Mountains and gap'd in great Valleys, and the Tars of the *Cassandra* were engaged in furling Sail (for she had such great Quantities of it, on all three Masts, that it took well-nigh fifty Men just to reef 'em), whilst we could manoeuvre much more rapidly.

I drank a Dram to give myself Courage, order'd my Men to their Guns, and deliver'd a warning Broadside to the *Cassandra*, hoping she would surrender quickly, for I had no Wish either to sink her with my Babe aboard or damage her so that we could not take her as our Prize if that prov'd convenient.

This Broadside—which penetrated her thick Hull but slightly—together with the Sight of our Pyrate Colours, so affrighted the Tars of the *Cassandra* (many of whom were pois'd, as 'twere, in mid-Air upon the Masts and Shrouds and clinging piteously in the Squall) that it threw the whole Ship into Confusion. They attempted to return our Fire, but we were already tacking about to approach 'em Bow-on in our wonted Pyrate Fashion.

Now began a Sort of curious Minuet in which the Sea and both Ships danced their Parts; for as the Waves carried us up, they carried the *Cassandra* down; and as the Waves carried the *Cassandra* up, they carried *us* down. In consequence there was ne'er a Moment when it seem'd propitious to board, for no sooner were we pois'd to do so than a Chasm of boiling Sea yawn'd betwixt our adjacent Ships. Yet here, too, it appear'd the Weather was our Friend, for just when it seem'd we'd ne'er take the *Cassandra* at all, the Waves gave us just the Boost we needed to send our Bowsprit shuddering athwart her Waist—like a Rake accosting the Honour of a trembling Virgin!

Now Horatio twirl'd his Grappling Hook above his Head and, with a furious Cry, led our Boarding Party—myself, Littlehat, Caveat, Puck, Francis Bacon, and a Horde of our most fearsome liberated Slaves—onto the Decks of the *Cassandra*. Sev'ral of our Black Brothers ran to wedge the *Cassandra*'s Rudder, whilst Littlehat and Caveat and Puck swung their Boarding Axes at *Cassandra*'s Rigging, bringing down both Rope and Sail as well as the Tars who clung there in Terror for their Lives. Men and Boys verily rain'd upon the Decks. In the gen'ral Mêlée that follow'd, the Weather impeded the Defense of the *Cassandra* more than it harm'd our own Offensive, for Pyrates are better skill'd with Cutlass and Dirk than Common Tars, and steadier on their Feet upon a pitching Deck.

Leaving Horatio to lead the Attack, I slipp'd below to search for my Daughter in the Steerage, descending into the very Bowels of the Ship to seek my Persephone like some madden'd Demeter. Tars were must'ring upon Deck in all their Numbers; thus the Passengers were unprotected below and highly alarm'd by our warning Cannonade. They ran to and fro, the Men with their Wigs askew, the Women in Déshabillée. Mistaking me, in his Panick, for a fellow Passenger, one old Codger, with a Wen as big as a Piece of Eight upon his Cheak, shouted, "Look lively, me Boy, 'tis said we're taken by Pyrates!"

"Is that so?" I cried in Mock-Horror. "Pray, where is the Babe, for I'd not have the Pyrates take her lest they roast her

alive and eat her!" Saying this, e'en as a Fetch, made all my
Flesh creep and my Teeth chatter, since I could not e'en
speak of such an Occurrence without sickening at the
Thought.

"She's below, sleeping in a Hammock with her Mum!"
And the old Fellow pointed to the lowest Section of the Ship,
not knowing what a Service he'd done me.

Her Mum! thought I. Her Mum! How dare that old Bitch
pass herself off as Belinda's Mum! On the sheer Fury of that
Thought, I fairly leapt down the Ladder of the Rolling Ship,
made my Way amidst the Forest of swaying Hammocks
where the poorer Passengers slept, and lo! found Prue Feral
snoring like an old Dragon, with the beauteous Belinda in her
Arms!

The Child was just stirring out of Sleep when I came upon
'em; her Face was flusht as the Dawn; her reddish Lashes
were like thick Fringes upon her Infant Cheaks; and she had
grown most prodigiously since last I saw her. She was too old
for Swaddling now—at seven Months—but Prue had bound
her to her own ugly Body by an Assortment of Rags and
Twine, so that only her Arms might move. So they did,
reaching out into the Air as if they recogniz'd me. I bent o'er
my Child in wonder and amazement.

What a diff'rent Creature is a Child of seven Months from
one of three! At three Months all is Possibility unform'd, un-
fixt, but at seven Months a Child has join'd the World of
Men and Women, and a Human Creature has come to
manifest itself in Infant's Form! The little Hands reach'd out
as if to grasp for me as they issu'd from the half-Death of
Sleep, whereupon the Heavenly Blue Eyes open'd, star'd a
Moment in Perplexity, lookt piercingly into my great brown
Eyes—which were wet with Tears—whereupon, in a trice,
you let a Scream that would thaw Hell itself!

I grabb'd at my Hair—my Stubble, rather—thinking 'twas
my wretchèd State that so affrighted you (for I had too
little Experience with Babes then to know that after six
Months of Life the Sight of a strange Face can terrify a
Child). No; since you were the Lodestar of my Longing, I
presum'd that I was the Lodestar of yours as well—but 'twas
not the case! (The Love of Parents for Children is oft', at
any rate, an unrequited Amour, tho' as Parents we hardly
care, knowing that our Children will return to *their* Children
the Passion we lavish'd upon them, if not to us. Alas, in Life

487

'tis frequently the melancholy Fact that the Favours we do for certain Persons are not return'd by those Persons at all, but by others who owe us no Debt whatsoe'er!)

Thus you scream'd and scream'd, and Prue awoke just as I had my Cutlass pois'd, ready to cut you loose from your Kidnapper. Whereupon Prue, thinking me a Murderer, scream'd e'en more loudly than you yourself, and sundry Passengers rallied 'round more out of Curiosity than to proffer Aid, tho' they cloakt their Curiosity, like most, in Offers of Aid.

"Help! Kidnap!" cried Prue, accusing me, in her Confusion, of the Crime she had committed.

In a trice, a Big Bully who had decided to make himself the Hero of this Pyrate Engagement, drew his Sword and challenged me to a Duel.

Prue took this Opportunity to lumber out of her Hammock with captive Belinda and make as if to flee, but a Crowd of Onlookers, already laying Bets, impeded her Progress; and she was trapp'd betwixt the Mob and the Ladder which led to the Deck.

As for my Opponent, he was skillful with his Rapier—despite the fact that he lookt the veriest Booby. O he had Blubber Lips and a Nose as red as Autumn Apples, but he knew the Art of Self-Defence! His Sword was a Flicker of Silver to the broad Curve of my Cutlass; and either he should pierce my Heart at once, or I should snap his Sword in twain with one quick Cutlass Slash. We danced betwixt the swaying Hammocks, feinting, thrusting, parrying, and playing Hide and Seek. My small Size was some Advantage, as was the Swaying of the Ship—now somewhat diminish'd, as if the Squall were passing—but there was no Question that in an open Field he should cut me down in one deft Stroke, the Point of his Rapier seeking my Heart as 'twere some Homing Pigeon and my Heart its Coop.

He thrust his Rapier and sliced my Cheak; the hot thick Blood amaz'd me as it flow'd out and trickl'd into my open Mouth. Ah the salty Taste of one's own Blood is a strange Aphrodisiack! It must have fir'd me with some Rage to live—as my old Friend Pope hath term'd it—for I rais'd my Cutlass and snapp'd my Opponent's Rapier at the very Root!

"Have Mercy upon my Soul!" cried the Booby, his Rapier lost; but now I leapt in for the Kill and slasht his fat, red Neck. He fell, spouting Blood like any Fountain; whereupon my Spectators jump'd back in Awe.

But 'twas too late for me; Prue was already fleeing with Belinda and the Stealing of the Babe distress'd me far more than the Killing of a Man. I chas'd the porcine Prue up to the Deck, where I soon saw that the Squall indeed had abated, but the Battle had not. The Planks of the *Cassandra* now ran with Blood and enough Wounded had fallen or been thrown o'erboard to lure Man-eating Sharks in these Tropick Waters. O some Prizes are taken upon a Tidal Wave of Blood, whereas others are taken without a single Drop!

As for my Belinda, who clung to her Nurse, the Child seem'd more terrified at her attempted Rescue than she had at her Kidnap, for she scream'd and scream'd, her whole Face contorted and red. Prue was hobbling across the Deck, dodging Combattants at ev'ry Turn, and I was in Pursuit (my Shirt now gaping open, revealing my Sex for all to see), following the Squalling of the Babe, praying that she would not be kill'd by Chance, and fighting off all Comers. Chief amongst them was the Captain of the *Cassandra,* who, it now appear'd, was prepar'd to defend the Honour of our Prize with his Life itself! Ne'er had I seen such unaccustom'd Bravery from a Sea Captain!

"I'll dye before I let ye have this Ship!" he cried. I swear his Words enraged me—or perhaps 'twas the Screaming of the Babe. Whereupon, in a Frenzy of Bloodlust, Hatred for the whole Race of Mankind, and Pique at having to rescue my Babe single-handed, I slasht my Cutlass across the Captain's Chest, drawing one great Rivulet of Blood which bloom'd upon his Holland linen Shirt, travers'd his Sash and Breeches, and pool'd upon the Floorboards, where it ran, like Tar, into the Cracks betwixt the Planks. He scream'd and scream'd yet did not fall; and he came back at me most hatefully, as if he wisht to kill all Womankind.

"Bitch! Witch! Shrew!" he cried, his red Face reminding me of the very ugliest of the ugly Rogues who'd rap'd my Sister Witches.

"For Joan! For Isobel!" I cried, running him thro' with one great Stab of Strength. O the Word "Witch" had unleash'd in me Pow'rs I ne'er had known before. Our Captain fell; my Heart exulted in my Chest. But where was Prue? And where was my Belinda? No sooner had I dispatch'd our disputatious Captain than I lookt about wildly for 'em. If Prue car'd enough to steal you, she car'd enough to spare your Life, I reason'd, yet where would she have gone? 'Twas clever enough Logick—like Solomon's Judgement concerning another disputed Babe—tho' it scarcely prov'd true, for no sooner had the mighty Captain fallen than I lookt up, and in a dizzying Moment beheld Prue climbing the Shrouds with my Babe ty'd, like some Savage's Papoose, about her Waist!

O Prue was fat and cumbersome, but sheer Spite made her climb against the grey and brooding Sky.

"If I can't have her, she shall go to God!" screams crazy Prue. My Knees are weak with Grief, my Stomach heaves with Fear. I think of Susannah and Bartholomew, of Joan and the slaughter'd Coven, of all my lost and lovely Friends who sleep with Davy Jones beneath the Sea or in the Witchy Mists of Wiltshire. Dear Goddess, not again!

Prue clings to the Shrouds with the screaming Babe at her Waist; the whole Battle stops *in Medias Res* to observe this most terrifying Sight. Horatio leaps into Action and scales the Shrouds behind Prue Feral—whereupon she climbs higher, whereupon Horatio follows.

"Cease!" I cry to Horatio. "Pray don't drive her any higher!" My Heart is like to choke me with its Grief, for it hath lodged squarely within my Throat. The Shrouds tower above like Cathedral Windows; the Masts sway like Trees in a Forest of Giants. The whole Ship creaks in Anticipation, tho' not a Human Voice is rais'd but mine.

My Pray'rs ascend upon the Tarry Ropes to the Goddess; I eat my Heart as if 'twere a Cake, but a bitter one, made of Gall and Sorrow. O I pray that Prue shall reconsider and not jump, or that if she jumps, her fat Body shall break my sweet Babe's fall. Otherwise she should surely be crusht by the sheer Weight of the all-devouring Sea. But no—the Goddess is not listening to my Pray'rs. How have I wrong'd her? What Lessons have I drawn upon myself that I should lose my Child after such a long and perilous Chase? Prue leaps from the Shrouds into the savage Sea with the screaming Babe lasht to her pond'rous Waist. Horatio follows, sailing thro' the Air without a Minute's, nay a Second's, Hesitation; he is an Arrow flying straight to meet its Mark.

"Quick! The Boat!" shouts Littlehat, low'ring the *Cassandra*'s Skiff. We lose no Time in launching it, yet that Time seems as Hours, nay Centuries, nay Eons, to me. Now Horatio is splashing in the Water, and as for Prue, I cannot see her.

Sharks! I think in Panick; shall my Belinda go to feed the Sharks?

The Skiff hits the Water with a hideous Crash, near breaking into a thousand Pieces, but at once I catch a Glimpse of Belinda, a red and squalling Face crying upon the angry Waters.

Blessèd be her Cries! They prove at least that she is still alive! The Babe bobs upon the Water before the fat, floating Moon Face of her lunatick Nurse, who seems near-dead from the Fall; and yet Belinda lives! Prue is her Raft, her Yawl, her Pinnace, her Pilot, her Wherry! Horatio swims to her with what manly and heroick Resolution I cannot e'en say, snatches the Babe, and whilst she screams in his Arms, he swims alongside our Boat. He gasps and sputters as he hands the screaming Infant to me, whereupon one long and hideous Cry escapes his Throat as he lifts Belinda aloft and sees her safely in my Arms.

So pleas'd am I to have Belinda back, that I scarce comprehend what is occurring in the Water. Prue hath vanish'd in the boiling Sea; Horatio's Face bears a hideous Grin—as if he were fixt in attendance at a Play the which he loath'd but could not leave (perhaps because the Actors were his Friends).

"Good Christ!" says Littlehat, reaching out to seize Horatio's Arms. He did so with one great Essay of Strength; whereupon my horrified Eyes beheld Horatio's legless and hipless Trunk, for ev'rything below the Waterline had gone to feed the Sharks!

"Blessèd be his Soul," I say, clutching that very Babe he gave his Life to save. Too mov'd to weep, too stunn'd to speak, I hold Belinda, who has also ceas'd to scream as we bob upon the redden'd Waters.

I look up at the *Cassandra*, rap'd by the Bowsprit of the *Happy Delivery;* both now float upon a Sea grown almost calm after the Squall.

The Faces of the Merry Men and all the Tars look down in Wonder, as if the Saving of the Babe were some sort of Solemn Sign. Lancelot is low'ring a Ladder, and urging Littlehat and me to come back, come back swiftly now (for fear, no doubt, the Sharks should return to butt the Boat in their Feeding Frenzy).

I look up at my Lancelot, who waits for me. His Hair and Beard are red as Rust 'gainst a Sky grey as Slate, yet beginning, e'en now, to clear. Behind his leonine Head I see the first Glimmerings of a Rainbow, broken, 'tis true, by the Masts and Shrouds of the *Happy Delivery*—but a Rainbow nonetheless.

O Belinda! We shall indeed survive!

Chapter XV

In which we draw nearer and nearer to our Conclusion, and certain Omens presage the Future of our Heroine, Hero, and their Belovèd Babe.

ALL OF LIFE'S BLESSINGS are mixt—save to Fools alone. Lancelot and I were reunited upon the *Happy Delivery*'s Deck (with little Belinda betwixt us), but Horatio was gone ne'er more to show his Face upon this pendant Earth! O how ironical is Fate that Horatio should escape Sharks in his chequer'd Youth only to encounter 'em again with Results most fatal.

"Neither the Sun nor Death may be lookt at steadily," said La Rochefoucauld; and i'faith, 'twas so with Horatio's Death. Lancelot and I, who had each lost a Lover and a Friend, could scarce talk, then, about Horatio, but we were driven closer by our mutual Grief.

"Chance cures us of many Faults incurable by Reason," La Rochefoucauld also says; and Lancelot was the perfect Example of this. The brash and brazen Boy I'd known, grew mellower with Horatio's Passing and of more Philosophical Temper. Thus Grief must make Philosophers or Madmen of us all; for those whose Hopes and Loves are dasht so oft' will grow crack-pated or will mellow at the End.

What with *Cassandra*'s Captain dead, the Tars who had surviv'd that bloody Battle were glad enough to turn Pyrate with Lancelot Robinson—once His Name was known. They hail'd him as their Captain, but now he refus'd. He had no Wish, he said, to lead 'em now. He only desir'd, he said, a Private Life, but he was a wanted and, for a Time, a broken Man.

"Successful Thieves is lov'd by all the World, me Girl," said Lancelot, "unsuccessful ones is scorn'd. The Rabble loves Rebellion in a Thief an' loves to dream o' Deeds fer which they lack the Courage. Robin Hood, Dick Turpin, Blackbeard—e'en me meself—we're scarce ador'd so by the Rabble fer our Souls, but fer our Darin', fer Rebellion's Sake—so that the Clod who ne'er hath dar'd e'en dream, can point a Finger at me an' say, 'There but fer me Chains go I!' *Bah!* I'm done with these Mock-Heroicks!"

The *Happy Delivery* was damaged, yet less so than *Cassandra*. Lancelot propos'd therefore that we repair both Ships as best we could and permit the Men to decide which they would sail upon and whither. Let the Men of the *Cassandra* go pyrating upon their own Account if they so chose. This was Lancelot's Wish—for he only desir'd to meditate upon Horatio's Loss and his Dreams of *Libertalias* upon Tropick Keys were dasht.

For my own part, I had to make anew the Acquaintance of my Daughter, who seem'd quite daz'd by all these odd Occurrences. She star'd at me with almost adult Eyes, seeming to know me and yet not know me quite. Sometimes an Infant Face betrays the Adult Soul 'twill become—and so 'twas with you, Belinda: your Face was grave and thoughtful, yet not sad withal; Intelligence shone in your Eyes of Sapphire blue.

Francis Bacon devis'd for you a Diet of masht Pease, Cheese, and boil'd Rice pusht thro' a Sieve. 'Twas providential almost that you were seven Months old by now and could eat solid Food instead of Milk alone, for I had none to give. Prue, in her own Way, had given you the Gift of Life. Thus, too, are all our Blessings mixt, and none quite so mixt as Motherhood!

Where might we go now with our Babe return'd, our Fortune stolen, and our Hopes so smasht, yet so encouraged by your Return? Lymeworth! I thought of Lymeworth with incredible Longing and Homesickness, yearning to see it again, to return and show my Babe to my sweet Foster-Mother—and yet fearing to return. I seem'd to smell the Hedgerows of my Youth here upon the Open Sea! O what is it about having one's own Babe upon one's Hip that makes a Woman wish to go home to her Mother? A Desire to say: "Look, the Circle is compleat"? A Desire to say: "Look, I have cross'd the Divide and now am more like you"? A Desire to say: "Look, this Babe I offer you is my most precious Gift"?

"I long for Lymeworth," I said to Lancelot, "with a Passion that is most extream. If I could see the Hedgerows of my Youth just one more Time, then I would be content."

And so, with all the World before us, the Bahamas, the Bermudas, and the Caribee; Madagascar and the Coast of Africa; the Colonies of North America; e'en the South Sea

494

with all its Riches, we sail'd again for verdant England, our Island Home, our Shield of Peace upon a boiling Sea!

We had the Merry Men—both old and new—as Crew; and as for those who wisht to continue on the Pyrate Round, they took *Cassandra* with Lancelot's Blessing and sail'd under the Sober Rule of one of the blackest of the African Slaves. To them we gave the Charts that Bonny had given us, wishing 'em God's Speed!

'Twas October; the Crossing was not easy. It took many long, cold Weeks to make the English Coast, and when we did, 'twas almost Christmas.

We had lost our Great Fortune, 'twas true, but we had still a few Guineas betwixt us. We hatch'd our Plans most carefully, debating whether to come ashore at Lundy (where some of the Merry Men had Privateering Colleagues, who might take us to the Mainland), at Lizard Point in Cornwall, or near Bolt Head in Devonshire. The Last was decided upon because of the Loneliness of the Sea-Coast, and 'twas further agreed that we should split our Party—Lancelot, Littlehat, Belinda, and I journeying to Lymeworth alone—and the Rest of the Merry Men taking their various appointed Disguises and hiding out with old Compatriots till we should send for 'em.

When we four tatter'd Voyagers were put ashore by Pinnace near Lantern Rock in Devon and we bade Farewell to the *Happy Delivery,* we did not know if we would meet the Merry Men again—except in Dreams.

Weary and Sea-worn, we began to make our Way through Devon and Somerset dress'd as Dealers in old Clothes, with num'rous Hats upon our Heads, like the Ragmen of London. The Clothes themselves we had garner'd from those aboard our Ship; some were from Prizes we had taken previously and some had been left by Anne Bonny's Pyrates in their Haste to take our Jewels and Plate; some were Whitehead's and came from that first fateful Engagement with the *Hopewell.*

Thank the Goddess that we had 'em and had chosen this Disguise—for 'twas cold and drizzly as the Devil and many was the Time I wisht for the Tropick Keys of the Caribee and call'd myself a Fool for dragging Lancelot and Littlehat Home to Bone-chilling England just for the Fancy of seeing Lymeworth yet again! With a Babe upon my Hip, and pinching Pennies to spare the Last for Bread, and begging Rides in Dung-Carts and Waggons for Want of Carriages, I was wretchèd indeed. Lancelot and Littlehat dar'd no extravagant Thefts for fear of bringing the Outrage of the Law 'gainst us all; and so we made our weary, hungry Way homeward—if 'twere still Home indeed. We might have taken a Pack Horse Carriage or a Stage, but for our Fear of being recogniz'd under such Circumstances; and tho' we hir'd Horses at Post-Houses from Time to Time, we felt that e'en this was too great a Risque to run.

Just as Hope was fleeing and we were most miserable, there befell an amazing Incident which changed our Moods from black to white and seem'd, i'faith, to presage Happiness.

We had little Money to buy a Horse, yet we sorely needed one, or more, as you may guess. The few Shillings that we had left we were hoarding for some great Calamity.

We were not far outside Taunton and we had been speaking amongst ourselves of Inns where we might pass the next Night, and of the advisability of stealing Horses if we could not buy 'em—when we came upon the most piteous Sight the Eyes may behold: that of a furious Man beating an Animal within an Inch of its Life.

The Man was enraged; he beat the Horse with a Crop and then with the Handle of his Sword as well. And as he beat this cow'ring Creature in the freezing Rain, he cried out:

"Wonder Horse! Pegasus indeed! I'll give ye Wonders to behold!"

With my Beauteous Babe upon my Hip, I ran to the Man, shouting, "Cease! Desist! How dare you treat a Fellow Creature so? May God send you back as a Horse with a cruel Master in the next Life!"

"Hold yer Peace, Scold!" cried the Man (who lookt no Gentleman, but a poor Wretch who had bought this Horse with his last Guinea). For my Benefit he began to beat the Animal e'en harder, whereupon, I chanced to take a good Look at the Horse—this Creature with Bones poking thro' the Skin, and Withers so thin they lookt starv'd almost, and Patches of mangy Fur and cak'd Blood where he had oft' been beaten—and lo! I saw a white Blaze upon his Forehead, glitt'ring thro' Dust. Could this pitiful Nag be Lustre? I lookt down at the lower left Leg; and half-hidden by Mud was a white Stocking—upon a Limb grown most horribly raw from the Mange!

"Where did you get that Horse?" I askt, my Voice trembling.

"I bought him from a Fellow who was goin' to the Fleet

fer Debt. Sold him cheap, he did. He's still in Gaol, I hear; an' may well rot there fer all I care—the Mountebank! He was a Player and tried to make a Show with this here Horse, callin' him 'Pegasus the Wonder Horse'—but when he perform'd no Wonders, the Rabble ston'd him and his Master, too! An' well they might. Wonder Horse, indeed!"

"Pray, what was this Fellow's name?" I askt, hoping 'twas Doggett (hoping, i'faith, that the Goddess had dispens'd that Revenge which belong'd to Her alone).

"I know not," said the Man, "but he was a travellin' Player an' hop'd to pay off his Debts with this Horse. But as ye see, the Beast is good fer nothin' but Dog Meat—the old Nag. I've a mind to shoot him here." And He pull'd out a Pistol and put it to Lustre's head. I tried not to show how agitated the Sight of such made me.

"Pray, Sir, desist—I shall pay you handsomely to have that Horse."

The Man lookt me o'er and found my Appearance wanting all Display of Riches; my Stubble had grown to Curls by now, but I was dress'd in all the Dust of the Road, and hardly lookt a Lady. Lustre's Tormentor cockt his Gun.

"Pray, Sir, please reconsider," said I, Heart pounding, clasping Belinda tightly. For her part, the Child began to whimper as if she knew.

At that very Moment, Lancelot and Littlehat caught up with us.

"What's this?" askt Lancelot.

"I must have that Horse," I said to him, firmly yet softly.

He lookt at the Horse, then lookt at me as if I were daft; Littlehat did the same.

"What am I bid not to shoot?" askt the Man.

"Five Shillings!" said I. 'Twas all the Money we had left in the World.

"Good Lord, Woman!" cried Lancelot, "are ye mad?"

"Trust me, Lancelot," said I.

Lancelot lookt at me questioningly; in some strange Way he understood that all our Love and Trust hung in the Balance.

The Man press'd his Gun against the Horse's Brow, then he lookt at Lancelot quizzically.

"The Lady shall have the Horse," said Lancelot, pulling a Bag of Shillings from the Pocket of one of the old Coats he wore, one atop the other. He counted out the Shillings soberly; Littlehat shook his Head in amazement.

"Take the old Nag! An' good Riddance!" said the Man; and he positively cackled as he went his Way.

"Fanny!" said Lancelot, "are ye Mad? That Horse shall ne'er be ridden more! What shall we do with our last Shillin' gone?"

"You doubted me," I said, "and yet you trusted me. Trust me somewhat longer; this is *indeed* a Wonder Horse, a Pegasus, of sorts, yet can he only perform his Wonders when I am his Mistress. O Lancelot, I truly love you," said I, my Eyes filling with Tears. I handed Sweet Belinda to Littlehat and threw my Arms around my Lancelot and kiss'd him most ling'ringly upon the Mouth.

"If you had sought to win my Heart, you ne'er could choose a better Way," said I. "Lustre will repay you—that I swear, and so will I." And for the first Time, Lancelot fully kiss'd me back.

From the Moment we found Lustre, our Luck began to change. The Horse was sick and needed Care; he could not sustain e'en Belinda's Weight. But each Day he grew stronger, and tho' we doubted we had Money enough for e'en Oats or Hay, Littlehat found a few Guineas which had dropped thro' a Hole in the Pocket into the Lining of one of the old Coats he wore, and then I found a few Shillings I had not seen before, and then Lancelot found a Sack of ten Guineas sewn into the Lining of one Coat! Why, we were rich as Landlords now!

"Most probably they have been there all along," I told Lancelot and Littlehat; and yet I knew that 'twas the Goddess' Own Doing! O someday I should tell 'em both of the Coven, and of Isobel and Joan; but for the nonce, I must only nurse Lustre back to Health and hold my Tongue. Achieving Wisdom in this World oft' means keeping one's Mouth shut, and not blurting out all that one knows before the Time is ripe.

Yet I was sure I knew the Reason for these miraculous Finds: I had been initiated as a Witch and Lustre was my Familiar. Separately, our Pow'r was small, but together, a Witch and her Familiar had triple Strength—or so Isobel had said. Did I believe all this? At Times I did; at Times I doubted it as Twattle; yet still I wore my tatter'd red Garter just in case. I only know that from the Moment Lustre was restor'd to me, Good Luck came to take the Place of Bad!

The Bond betwixt Lancelot and myself was also growing, and we were slowly melding into a Family—we who were no

Blood Relations save Belinda and me. Soon 'twould be Time to tell all our Tales and wholly open up our Hearts, ne'er to close 'em more. Lancelot had indulged my ev'ry Fancy, sail'd Home with me, follow'd me to Wiltshire, car'd for my Child as his, and e'en for my mangy Nag as his. Whate'er Doubts I may have had about his Love were now dissolv'd; he had grown into a Man and he stood by me in all my Passions. What Woman can hope for more?

The Death of Horatio had sober'd Lancelot most extreamly, and he seem'd determin'd to heap upon me and Belinda the Concern he previously reserv'd for his Black Belovèd. Lancelot had lov'd a Woman once, long ago in Oxfordshire; then, disappointed with her Fickleness, had turn'd to Love of Men. But now, with Horatio gone, his Fealty was all to me, for we had shar'd Life's Great Adventure and were bound by joint Misfortune as well as mutual Laughter.

Lustre rallied swiftly; we found an old Chaise for Sale at an Inn near Cheddar (where it had been left for Pawn) and bought it quite cheaply. Lustre grew strong enough to pull one Person and Belinda in the Chaise, then two Persons and the Babe, whilst the third walkt alongside; by slow Degrees, we made our Way to Wiltshire.

The Nights were long, and Dusk fell rapidly and early; yet no Harm befell us on the Road—not e'en Highwaymen—perhaps because we lookt so poor. At Inns we slept all in the self-same Bed for Warmth; and Lancelot and I did little more than clasp our Hands and clasp Belinda's Hands—and Littlehat's as well! Eros had fled to that curious Place where oft' he goes when our Lives hang in the Balance and we must save our Strength for other Feats. And 'twas on Christmas Eve that we made Lymeworth.

I scarce recogniz'd the Place—'twas so changed! Perhaps 'tis true, that all the Houses of our Youth are changed, but in this case, the whole Gothick Edifice had been cover'd with a prodigious Scaffolding, and 'neath it rose the Façade of a new Palladian House, with Columns and Pediments, and rusticated lower Storey, and large Square Windows—sixteen across at least—and Grecian Gods and Goddesses ascending from the Pediment and Roof into the frigid Wiltshire Air! O it seem'd that Lord Bellars had thought better of his Plans to pull down the whole Pile and had decided rather to cover the Gothick Front with a Palladian one! O Folly! O Fashion! The Gardens, too, were changed, tho' not entirely, for a Great Work had been begun and then abandon'd, as 'twere, *in Medias Res.* The Ancient Oaks still stood upon the Hill, the Beeches and the Elms below, as well. But where the Topiary Garden had been, all was Purest Nature, with grazing Sheep and a little round, white Temple to some God whose Face I could not see. My fragrant Bow'r had not vanish'd, tho' 'twas sere with Winter's Cold; it had remain'd perhaps less for Want of Intent to tear it down than for Want of Time to accomplish it. The Obelisks still march'd along the Wall; the carv'd Balls still seem'd to bounce against the Sky; and sure my headless, armless Venus still stood within the Walls, having not mov'd an Inch since that Day—Eons ago—when I fell at her pretty Feet (pois'd upon a sculptur'd Shell, above a sculptur'd Wave) and wept.

Timid as Beggars, we approach'd the Great Front Door, feeling we should rather cower at the Back Door—e'en tho' we knew not where 'twas amidst all this Scaffolding! The new Front Entrance seem'd a Grecian Temple with six tow'ring Columns, but there also were two more Temples being built, one on either End of the Great House. O I much preferr'd the other Lymeworth! The Great House that had contain'd my Childhood was now encas'd in a new-fashion'd outer Shell, like Chinese Boxes, one within the other. And yet, I carried the old Lymeworth inside, as we all carry the Houses of our Youth inside, and our Parents, too, grown small enough to fit within our Hearts.

Ah Belinda, a Mother carries a Babe for but nine Months, yet for all her Life that self-same Babe carries her Mother in her Heart—as my Tale presently shall show.

We knockt. I touch'd my Curls nervously, wond'ring if I should be recogniz'd as Fanny. Lancelot and Littlehat stood back, holding Lustre whilst I stood at the Door with Belinda. Footsteps were heard within. Presently, Mrs. Locke, the Housekeeper, came to the Door, dress'd all in Mourning, with sev'ral Mourning Rings upon her gnarl'd Fingers. She lookt at me as if to throw me out, and then star'd and star'd, first at me, then at the Babe, then at the Men behind me.

"Do my Eyes deceive me?" she askt. "Or is it Fanny?"

"The very same," I said, Tears coming to my Eyes. Where were the Porter, the Footmen, all the Household? Mrs. Locke was formerly not wont to attend the Door. Behind her was the renovated Great Hall, alter'd to suit the newest Fashion. Its Floor was chequer'd Marble of black and white; yet a Painter's Scaffold still hung from the Ceiling, and the Walls were but half-painted with mythological Scenes.

"O Mistress Fanny, ye come at such a Time, such a Time."

"Who has dy'd?" I askt, but Locke only began to weep.

"Come in, come in," said she; and but for the Babe in my Arms she lookt verily as if she'd fall into 'em herself.

"Meet my Daughter!" I said, putting the Babe into her Arms.

Belinda lookt at Mrs. Locke and babbl'd quite unafraid. "Dada? Baba?" she askt, grabbing Locke's red and swollen Nose as if to pull it off; Locke laugh'd betwixt her Tears.

"La! Mistress Fanny, she looks just as you did when a Babe! Come in. Lady Bellars will be glad to see you."

"These Gentlemen have brought me safely Home and the Babe as well. Pray, make 'em comfortable," I askt, signalling Lancelot and Littlehat to come. Lustre turn'd and trotted off to the Stables as if nothing at all had changed since the last Time he was here.

Presently, we were all led to divers Apartments in the newly renovated Rustick (the second Storey being reserv'd for visits of State—at least, 'twas so intended), but as we walkt along the Corridors 'twas plain to see that the House was in great Disarray, and Pieces of Furniture stood ev'rywhere, drap'd in Linen. Likewise, there were Signs of interrupted Construction ev'rywhere. New Ceilings were being painted, new Panelling built to replace the old, and the Wind whistl'd thro' the Walls where the two new Grecian Temples were being built at either End of the House.

The Staff seem'd much reduced; one Chambermaid was sent to bring Water and lay Fires for all three of us. She was a new Girl—new since I'd left Lymeworth—and she was giddy and silly enough to answer my Questions ere she knew who I was.

"For whom is the Household in Mourning?" I askt, since she, too, wore a Mourning Ring—not a Hair one nor a Death's Head like those Mrs. Locke had worn—but one on which this Posie was engrav'd: *"Prepar'd Be to Follow Me."*

"O Madam," said she, "d'ye not know? 'Tis Lord Bellars himself an' now his Son, Daniel, too."

"It cannot be!" I said, holding Belinda on my Lap whilst she pull'd at my Hair and babbl'd as if Death did not exist in her World.

"How so? How can that be? Daniel was only Twenty."

"Aye, an' fell in with bad Company, too. Ran away to London, he did, all fer fancy of an Orphan Girl that liv'd here once under Lord Bellars' Roof, an' refus'd his Father's Wishes to go up to Oxford or e'en away on the Grand Tour. But she was a Bad Egg, she was—the Wench he lusted fer— workt in a Bawdy House, she did, an' when he found out 'twas Mrs. Coxson's Brothel she went to—Mrs. Coxson is a Famous Bawd, ye know—he follow'd her there, only to find she'd already gone—gone to serve some Dark Satanick Cult, 'tis said, as was her witchy Nature. So he took up with an- other Tart, he did, a certain Mistress Kate, an' she got him into Debt, she did, fer she was a Jezebel, she was, an' he fell in with Bubblers an' Stock Jobbers, he did, to pay his Debts and many was the Time he was thrown into the Fleet an' bail'd out by Lady Bellars—but by an' by he was gaol'd again, an' his Mum, bein' quite resolv'd to make him learn his Lesson, refus'd to send a Penny, whereupon he was kill'd in a Brawl in Gaol o'er a Bottle o' Gin, he was, poor Fellow, an' now his Mum's distracted with blamin' herself fer his Death, poor Lady. 'Tis Pity the Poor Fellow's gone. I liked him quite."

"But what of Lord Bellars?" I askt, less astounded by this Tale than I seem'd to be (for now the Pieces of the Puzzle began to fit in place). "Lord Bellars had Friends in Change Alley and Lloyd's Coffee-House." I said. "Could he not warn his Son of Larcenous Bubblers?"

"O d'ye not know? Lord Bellars fled to Switzerland some Months past an' became a Hermit in a Monastery. Not only did he disown Daniel, but he left the House unfinish'd as ye see—an' such a fine House, too. O fer a Time the Workmen workt on Credit, but then they refus'd to work more until Lord Bellars or his Banker should pay 'em. But we heard nought o' Milord until a Letter came, tellin' o' his Death. Lady Bellars will tell all—if she's not mad with Grief. Most Days she does nought but stay abed—so piteously sad is she. . . ."

I scarce knew how to react to the News of these Tragick Deaths, which at first made me feel wholly to blame for all the Ill Fortunes of my adopted Family. Alas, I thought, I have caus'd Daniel's Death, and Lord Bellars' as well, and Lady Bellars' Grief! But then, as I thought on't, I realiz'd that 'twas Hubris to see myself as Cause of all. Daniel was a Fool to come to London (which he surely did as much to mimick his Whoring Father as for Love of me). And 'twas surely fated for him to take up with Kate, who would have fancied him if only because he'd come for me. Lovers of such sort oft' become each other's Punishment upon this Earth, ere they reach Purgatory or Hell. Acquainted with Kate's envious Nature as I was, I could well imagine the Gusto with which she'd fallen upon Daniel, hearing he was in search of a certain "Fanny." 'Twas her Fate as well as his that brought 'em to be each other's Scourges. And what, I wonder, became of Kate, when Daniel was thrown into the Fleet to dye o'er a disputed Bottle? I askt the Maid, who seem'd to know so much and have so loose a Tongue.

"I know not," said she smugly, "but the Hussy no doubt dy'd o' a Clap." O snippy Chambermaids are quick to condemn Women driven to the Bawdy House by Want—as if such ne'er could happen to themselves! *I* had no such Illusions; Witch, Whore, Stowaway, Slaver, Amanuensis, Pyrate—I knew the Things a Woman could be forced to do for Want of Bread, for Want of Freedom, for Want of Strength, for Want of Manhood. Ne'er again would I condemn a Sister for her Luck—not e'en an envious one like Kate.

The Chambermaid curtsey'd and left; she return'd soon after with fresh Clothes for me and for the Babe, informing me that Lady Bellars would see me in her Chamber as soon as I could make myself ready. With her Aid, I washt and dress'd myself in the Gown she brought, which, by the sheerest Chance, was the same Sacque-backt Dove-grey Silk I had tried on, then rejected, upon that fateful Day when Mr. Pope came to visit. 'Twas much looser now than e'er before, for my Adventures had not only made me wiser, but thinner! Thus, 'tis oft' true that as we gain Mental Substance we frequently lose Substance of the Grosser Physical Sort, which perhaps presages our Ascendance, after Death, into the Spirit World!

Belinda was washt by the Maid and dress'd in a Gown of pale cream Silk—one of my own old Infant Gowns. Whereupon I inform'd Lancelot and Littlehat that I would call upon my Step-Mother, Lady Bellars, alone; they wisht me Luck. Well they might, for I hardly knew what I might expect in all this Turmoil, or what it all might portend for my Future and Belinda's.

When I was receiv'd into the Ante-Chamber of Lady Bellars' new Apartments, I found the Windows most heavily drap'd in black, as if my Step-Mother were not only Mourning for her Son and Husband, but plann'd to depart this Life forthwith herself. The Ante-Chamber was dark as a Stygian Cave, and 'twas fill'd with the Cages of her Birds which had been drap'd heavily as if for Night; consequently, tho' 'twas still Day outside, no Birds chatter'd nor sang.

A Maid receiv'd me into Lady Bellars' own Bedchamber. There my astonish'd Eyes beheld a pale Figure, lost in Pillows upon the great Bed, and lying back with her Eyes clos'd in an almost Death-like Trance. Her three Lapdogs—a King Charles Spaniel and two Pugs—lay upon the Quilt mimicking quite their Mistress' Torpor. As I cross'd the Threshold, they leapt awake and began to bark, rouzing the Monkey who perch'd upon the Canopy of the Bed, but not e'en causing their Mistress' Eyelids to flutter.

Slowly, I walkt to the side of the Bed, holding Belinda in my Arms.

"My Lady," I whisper'd. She did not move, tho' the Dogs barkt furiously, leapt off the Bed to sniff me and the Babe, and then, satisfied I had a friendly Smell, ceas'd all their Noise, and resum'd their chief Life-long Pursuit of Sleeping.

"My Lady," I said softly, "I bring you Proof of Life amidst these Tragick Deaths."

My Step-Mother did not stir; her Cheaks were sunken and her Pallor was so great, she seem'd a Waxwork Lady in the Abbey.

"Babababa!" cried Belinda.

Slowly, Lady Bellars open'd her Eyes, fixt upon the Babe, and said: "Fanny, how kind of you to come!" Whereupon she extended one pale Hand to Belinda, who grabb'd her Finger with all her Infant Force and Tenacity.

"This is Belinda," I said.

"No—'tis Fanny. Little Fanny, my Husband's Bastard. Little, little, little Fanny. O 'tis said the ones with all the Wit and Spirit are not got in our lawful, boring Beds—but are By-Blows of the Devil. How do ye do, Little Fanny?" Whereupon she shook Belinda's tiny Hand.

"My Lady," I whisper'd, "I am Fanny. The Babe is call'd Belinda."

"What? Have ye a Babe? Have Puppies, rather, before ye bear a Babe. Puppies will not desert you. Puppies will not dye of a Brawl in Gaol. Puppies—aye, that's the Way. Have Puppies, Girl."

She ceas'd. I sank down on my Knees, holding Belinda, who babbl'd in a sort of Sing-Song, more sensible than Lady Bellars' Ravings. "Babababa! Dadadadada!" she sang, and ended upon this Interrogatory: "La?"

Dear Goddess, I thought to myself, she hath gone quite

mad. Is this where Womanhood leads—to very Madness? I, who have been both Pyrate and Whore, am less distemper'd in the Mind than this Good Lady whose whole Life hath been preoccupied with Goodness! Come then, Pyracy—if this be where Goodness leads!

"A Letter," Lady Bellars said, "from my Dear Husband. Who shall break the Seal? Not I. Not I. Not I. A white Letter is a very Virgin in my Eyes. Pristine. An Ode to Virtue and to Silence. Better to have a Puppy piss on't than to rape it with my evil Eyes." She struggl'd amidst the Pillows, then dragg'd forth a Letter which lay beneath 'em, and let it flutter to the Floor, where still I knelt. 'Twas a seal'd Missive address'd in Lord Bellars' Hand to Lady Bellars.

"Read it. 'Tis not for my Eyes," said Lady Bellars. "He is dead—so much the Monk hath writ. I do not wish to hear what he may think beyond the Grave. In Life I married him, but Death makes a Divorce! Ah yes, I am a Widow now and blessèd be that Name. No Husband. No Children. Have Puppies, Girl."

I pickt up the Letter from the Floor, turn'd it o'er in my Hands, whereupon Belinda snatch'd it, conveying it immediately to her Mouth.

"No, no," I said gently, taking it back and secreting it in my Bosom; but in some Sense I thought that the Child's eating it should be as good a Solution to the Problem as any, for Lady Bellars did not wish to read it, nor, i'faith, did I.

Suddenly the Door to the Dressing Room swung open and who should appear but Mary, who still lookt—after all these Months—as if she suckt upon a Lemon.

"Well, well," says she. "Look what the Cat dragg'd in. Got ye that Bastard in the Brothel—or in the self-same Place ye lost your Hair?"

I thought of all I had been thro', and here was Mary, the same as e'er before, still catty with the Enviousness of Inexperience. 'Tis said that Adversity is a sort of Crucible wherein all our petty Fears are melted down; if we become more open to Life's Joys after Misfortunes, 'tis because we know how scarce they are and consequently we appreciate 'em. But Mary, who had stay'd Home, protected at her Mother's Bosom, did not know what 'twas to be depriv'd of Home and Hearth, and consequently she appreciated neither them nor her Mother.

I rose with Belinda in my Arms and said: "Mary, how sweet 'tis to see you once again!"

"Hmmph," said Mary. "If ye mean to honey me into letting ye stay here with yer Bastard, there's a big Surprize in store for ye. I am Mistress of this Manor now and I've no Intention of letting a Bastard with *another* Bastard sully the Good Name of Lymeworth more."

"Bastard?" said Lady Bellars. "Did someone speak of Bastards? O have Puppies, rather. Pugs are nice and Spaniels slobber but are sweet, and O the Little Dog of Teneriffe is sweet indeed!"

Mary lookt at her Mother with Contempt.

"See what you've brought her to," she said. "I've a mind to throw ye out."

"Me!" I said, "see what *I've* brought her to? O Mary, you are sick with Envy and it thwarts your very Life and Happiness! What of your Father and your Brother? Am I to blame for the unhappy Match that brought you to this World? Am I to blame for all your Father's Infidelities, your Brother's Foolishness, your Mother's Madness, your own envious Nature? Look inward to your own Heart and see the Sickness there! 'Twill do more Good than blaming me! For my part, I am glad to go. I have made my Peace with my own Life. I will flourish where'er I go. Banish me from Lymeworth and I'll sail again to the New World to seek my Fortune. I know I shall survive and so shall my Belinda! I wish I knew the same were true of you!"

"Go then!" said Mary. "And leave me here to nurse my Mother! She scarce needs *your* Care. I have call'd a Woman from the Countryside who is known for Healing. Go back to your Bawdy House! Sail to the Plantations for all I care! Leave us in Peace! We need no Bastards here!"

"And what of your Father's Letter?" I askt, drawing the Letter from my Bosom. (I swear the Devil made me speak those Words—or was it verily the Goddess?)

"What Letter?" askt Mary, her Eyes blazing.

"This one!" said I.

"Give it here!" said Mary, running to me and making as if to snatch it.

"Not so fast!" I said, holding Belinda and the Letter tightly.

"Give it here!" cried Mary, "or I'll scratch your Eyes out!"

I ran for the Door; she follow'd me.

"O my Sweet Ladies!" rav'd Lady Bellars. "Do not scuffle so! You may have my Cakes! You may have my Ale! You may have my Husband and his Letters! But ne'er my Puppies! No, you may ne'er have my Puppies!"

The Dogs sprang from the Bed, as if they had been summon'd, and follow'd me and Mary, barking furiously.

"Give me that Letter!" Mary shriekt, as we reach'd the Door, whereupon it flew open, nearly knocking me down—and who to my astonish'd Eyes should appear but Isobel in her low white Wimple!

She lookt at me and at Belinda, then at Mary, who was now tearing at my Gown, ripping the Train of the Dove-grey Silk.

"Blessèd be," she whisper'd 'neath her Breath, touching Belinda's red Baby Cheaks, whereupon she said, "What's this? What's this? I shall do no Healing in a Madhouse!"

"She took my Father's Letter—the Tart, the Slattern!" cried Mary.

"What Letter?" askt Isobel.

"Lord Bellars' Letter!" I cried.

"Give it here," said Isobel, directing her Words to Mary (tho' i'faith, 'twas *I* who still clutch'd the Letter), "or I'll ne'er attempt to heal your Mother."

Mary ceas'd her Scuffling. "Are ye the Healer, then?" she askt.

"The same," said Isobel. "Pray, Ladies, sit ye down. If you sit peacefully, I shall administer a soothing Potion to Lady Bellars and then I'll read the Letter to ye all!"

I gave the Letter o'er to Isobel, marvelling at her Appearance here, yet knowing enough by now not to question it. With Belinda in my Arms, I sat down in a rose Silk-cover'd Chair whilst Mary sat opposite me, glow'ring.

" 'Tis the Healer I call'd," said she, "to heal my Mother. If 'twere up to you, she'd dye, I reckon."

"O," said I, watching the familiar Figure of Isobel busying herself at Lady Bellars' Bedside with Herbs and Potions drawn from the Bag she'd brought.

"I'll need hot Water," she said to Mary.

"I'll call the Chambermaid," said Mary, rising and pulling the Bell Cord.

"O Mary, Mary, quite contrary," said Lady Bellars, looking distractedly about the Chamber for her Daughter.

"Here I am, Mother," said Mary. "I have sent for someone to heal you."

"What? Healing?" She lookt at Isobel with Puzzlement, yet

Recognition. "O this Lady heal'd me once before, I think, but then I broke again—did I not, Love? Did I not?"

Isobel took her Hand and clasp'd it. "He that broke you is now gone," she said simply. The Chambermaid appear'd; the Dogs barkt; Belinda babbl'd; Isobel held Lady Bellars' Hand and star'd into her mad Eyes.

Did they then know each other? O Wonder pil'd on Wonder! There were more Things here than I was privy to! That much was clear.

"Pray, bring hot Water," Isobel directed the Maid.

"Dadada?" askt Belinda, clapping her Hands with Glee. Isobel lookt at her with Love, then she lookt back at Lady Bellars, who rav'd again.

"Witchcraft?" she askt. "O no! 'Tis merely Healing! She is my Friend. May Men only be Friends? Sure, Women may be Friends as well!"

"Hush! Mother," said Mary.

"Hush me no Hushes, Girl," said Lady Bellars. "I am not asham'd to Love a Puppy or a Friend!"

The Air was thick with strange Suggestions; what might all these Things portend?

I sat quietly holding Belinda whilst hot Water was brought and Lady Bellars' Herbs were mixt and pour'd and she was given to drink.

Soon, she seem'd sooth'd and sleepy, whereupon Isobel led me and Mary and Belinda into the Ante-Chamber, saying: "Let her rest now. We will read the Letter."

Chasten'd by the Presence of Isobel, on whom she depend-ed to soothe her Mother, Mary was quiet and obedient. She follow'd us into the Ante-Chamber, still looking Sour, to be sure, but no longer protesting.

"Sit ye down, Ladies," said Isobel, who directed us to Chairs, yet stood before us. I was struck as ne'er before by how tiny and frail she was, with her bent Back and fragile Bird-like Bones. With her white Wimple low upon her Fore-head, to hide the horrid Cross, she lookt a sort of curious Nun, Chaucer's Prioress, perhaps, to my Wife of Bath: what Strength was in that tiny Figure of a Woman!

" 'My dearest Heart,' " the Letter began, (read in Isobel's tinkling, chiming, yet strangely determin'd voice, " 'When this comes to hand, I shall be dead. You, of all Persons, are most entitled to know the Reason for my strange Disappearance, and yet 'tis towards you that I have the most enduring Shame, for Reasons which will soon be apparent.

" 'How may one begin to undo more than twenty-five Years of Wrongs? If I were no more than the Erring Husband of Song and Story, I should come Home forthwith, like Ulysses returning to Penelope, enfold you in my Arms, and vow to spend the Years remaining us, atoning for my Sins. But the Gods have arranged a sterner Punishment for me; the Wrongs I have done have already begot their own Progeny, and I am curst fore'ermore, I fear. For that Reason, I retreated to this Monastery to pray out the Rest of my Days, hoping thereby to mitigate the Evils of a long Life of Errors, the Worst of which I shall now acquaint you with (tho' it grieves me in the extream).

" 'Being always accustom'd to indulging my own most fleeting Passions, I hesitated little, if at all, when I found myself suffus'd with deep Desire for our adopted Daughter, Frances. . . .' "

"Aha! I thought as much!" Mary cried.

"Dada?" askt Belinda, a silver Thread of Spittle dangling from her pink cherubick lower Lip, and staining the ruff'd Boddice of the silken Gown she wore.

"Pray, cease," I said, "I can hear no more."

"You must," said Isobel, "and so must Mary. 'Tis Time the Truth were known, harsh as 'tis."

"Read the Letter!" cried Mary, glow'ring at me as if the Letter would now give Proof Positive of all my Guilts and all her Innocence.

" 'Tis Lady Bellars' Letter," said I.

"Aye," said Isobel, "but it concerns you more and she is too far gone to read it now. Let me continue. . . ."

I lower'd my Head and clos'd my Eyes, listening whilst I held Belinda, who babbl'd sweetly as a Brook in Spring.

" 'Thus,' " said Isobel, reading, " 'when I found that I was able to seduce her' . . ."

I hung my Head still lower in Shame.

". . . 'neither your Presence in the House,' " read Isobel, " 'nor the Stern Moral Obligations befitting an adopted Father restrain'd me. I had my Way with her, thinking there would be as little Consequence as when a Great Lord takes his Pleasure with a Chambermaid. Would that it had been so! Or rather, knowing what I now know, it could *not* have been so, for the Gods prepar'd for me a Tragedy of most Shakespearian kind. Little did I then know that Fanny was my own Natural Daughter.' . . ."

"What?" cried Mary. "This is Blasphemy!"

"Dear Goddess, preserve me," I mutter'd.

"Quiet!" said Isobel, "and hear."

" 'Little did I then know that Fanny was my own Natural Daughter, and that, in seducing her, I should beget still another Bastard upon my own Bastard!' "

"This is Impossible," said Mary, pointing to Belinda. "This Brat is no Child of my own Father's!"

"No," said Isobel, softly, "because he is not e'en your Father. . . ."

"What?" screamed Mary. "How dare ye come into my House and tell me that?"

"I shall explain all," Isobel said, "but you must first hear the Letter."

" 'Tis a lying, cheating Letter!" Mary cried. " 'Tis a Fetch! 'Tis not my Father's Letter!"

In a Way, I hop'd 'twas true, for the Thought of the Incest I'd committed froze my very Blood.

"Will you hear me then?" Isobel askt Mary. "Or would you rather have the Events to come take you by Surprize?"

"What Events?" cried Mary.

"The Arrival of Lord Bellars' Attorney with his Last Will and Testament, of which this Letter speaks. . . ."

"His Last Will and Testament?" askt Mary.

"Aye," said Isobel, "the same."

Mary ceas'd; Isobel resum'd reading.

" 'For you did not tell me, dear Cecilia, what you then knew; namely that Fanny was my Daughter by Isobel, the Housekeeper who was turn'd out of Doors for suspected Witchcraft, and knowing all that, yet keeping your Peace about it, you rais'd her lovingly as your own Child, letting me in no Way suspect that she was my true Daughter, whilst Mary was the Changeling.' "

"How dare you!" Mary cried, jumping out of the Chair and seizing the Letter, whereupon she ran to the Grate and toss'd it in the Fire. It caught immediately, and was charr'd beyond Recognition before Isobel could e'en try to pull it out. Part of my Mind was reliev'd, as if the Burning of the Letter might undo the incestuous Act itself.

"No Matter," said Isobel, calmly. "The Attorney will arrive from London by and by and you shall know the Truth. You can no more kill the Truth with Fire than you can kill the Goddess with your Fires; the Truth will blaze up o'er all."

"But what then *is* the Truth?" I askt, my Eyes brimming

with Tears, my Heart pounding against my Chest like a Pigeon who hath flown off course and lost his Loving Flock.

"Fanny, my dear, you know in your Heart that I am your Mother and Lord Bellars was your Father. Dear Daughter, I call'd you by that Name when you had just ceas'd labouring to bring this Babe to Birth—yet you remember nought. . . ."

"I thought so, I thought so, and yet I dar'd not think. . . . I thought 'twas merely Metaphor," said I, wetting Belinda's red and curly Hair with Tears. The Sweetness of knowing Isobel for my Mother somewhat assuaged the Pain of knowing Lord Bellars was my Father. "O my God, my God," I cried.

"Goddess," said Isobel smiling.

From the Bedchamber, there came a lone Cry from Lady Bellars, then Silence again. O my two Mothers! One was sane and one was mad! One a Witch and one a Wife—madden'd by Goodness! But O which was which? Were they perhaps *both* mad—but mad in diff'rent Ways?

"Hear me now," said Isobel, directing her Words both at my Sobs and Mary's incredulous Stares.

"When Lady Bellars bore her first Babe, Mary, in the fourth Year of the Reign of Queen Anne, the Child was put out to nurse with a Woman in the Country, nam'd Mrs. Griffith, for 'twas not the Custom of that Time, nor is it now, for Mothers of Noble Birth to nurse their own Progeny, suckling being consider'd a low and bestial Pursuit. . . . Lord Bellars had no Wish to have his Sleep interrupted by a squalling Babe—for no Rake nor Man of Fashion would endure such Distractions; thus the Infant was sent to Griffith upon her Birth and left for near three Years. I was then Housekeeper at Lymeworth and so I knew Mary as a Babe. I'faith, 'twas I who found the Wet-Nurse, who was my Friend. You met her once, Fanny; her name was Joan."

"Then Joan was Mary's Nurse?" I gaspt.

"Aha, so ye both are in league against me!" cried Mary. "Ah, when my Father's Lawyer comes, I'll have ye thrown out of this House. . . ."

"Very well," said Isobel, "but first my Tale!"

Whereupon she continu'd: "But alas, the sweet Babe, Mary, dy'd in her third Month, of a Fever, and Joan, who was mortally afraid of being charged with Witchcraft—for she liv'd alone and practis'd Healing and Wet-nursing, having lost her own Babe—substituted another Child, who was the poor abandon'd Babe of a Chambermaid transported to the Plantations for Theft after her Lying-in."

"What?" cried Mary. "No Chambermaid was my Mother! Ye lye!"

"Hush," said Isobel. "When the Attorney brings the Will, 'twill all be there. Meanwhile, let me tell what I know."

"Lyes! Lyes!" cried Mary.

"If they be Lyes, then why are you alarm'd?" Isobel sweetly askt. Whereupon she continu'd, "The following Year, Cecilia bore a Son, Daniel, and nearly dy'd bringing him to birth. I heal'd her with the Herbal Receipts I knew; thus she was always grateful to me, for she saw me as her blessèd Friend, who sav'd her Life. But what she did not know was that during her Confinement, Laurence Bellars had turn'd his Lustful Eyes upon me, forced me to be his Mistress upon Pain of being discover'd as a Witch—for I was also famous in the Neighbourhood for all my Healing Arts—and I carried his Child!"

"No!" I cried, marvelling that my Mother and I should both have shar'd the self-same Fate!

"But," Isobel continu'd, "Cecilia would not hear of Daniel being taken from her—for she had borne him in so much Pain and had sorely miss'd her little daughter when she was foster'd out to nurse, therefore she hired a Wet-Nurse to attend Daniel here at Lymeworth and ne'er let him out of her Sight, having the Babe and Wet-Nurse sleep in her Ante-Chamber so that e'en in her weaken'd Condition, she could oft' visit 'em. Lord Bellars was not happy with this Plan; besides he now tired of his ailing Wife whose Favours had been denied to him for lo so many Months. Thus, he departed for London to play amongst his Whores. . . . I saw him go with little Regret and I e'en consider'd aborting his Child—but the Truth was I wisht for a Child with all my Heart—since I was thirty-three Years of Age and knew not when I might bear if not then. Cecilia and I were left alone, and Truth to say, we became the dearest of Friends. 'Twas impossible to hide my Condition from her after a Time, and knowing her as I did, I took the Risque and confess'd her own Husband was the Father of the Child I bore!"

"What did she say? What did she do?" I askt.

"She took it calmly," Isobel said, "for she was no Fool, tho' she was mad for Want of True Affection from her Mate. 'You have sav'd my Life,' she said, 'and prov'd a Perfect Friend. Therefore will I raise your Babe as mine until the

Time is Ripe for her to know your Name. Then she shall know all if we see fit.' In the sixth Month of my Confinement, I went away to my Friend, Joan, and bore the Babe assisted by her able Hands. Then I left her upon the Doorstep of Lymeworth as agreed, and also as agreed, Cecilia took her in. O I regretted my Decision almost instantly, for I miss'd my Babe and soon was sure that I might raise her despite my impoverish'd State—but Cecilia would not let me change my Mind. I suppose she bore some Grudge against me after all, and when I askt for Fanny back (or at least for my Post as Housekeeper once again, so I might watch her grow), she banish'd me from Lymeworth. 'Twas a harsh Punishment indeed—for I lov'd my little Daughter. I might have had Revenge by keeping Mary (for I went to live with Joan), yet, 'twas ne'er my Way to take Revenge into my own Hands, for I believe that greater Hands than ours arrange our Fates. And verily, i'faith, it hath been proven true!"

"What happen'd then?" I askt.

"Mary return'd to Lymeworth at almost Three, but tho' Cecilia was ne'er told in so many Words, she seem'd to know that Mary was a Changeling—for Mothers know these Things—and besides the Child clung to her Nurse, Joan, as if she were in Terror of Cecilia, and i'faith, returning to Lymeworth was a Shock from which I think Mary ne'er recover'd. No Bond was e'er created betwixt Mother and Child, as is oft' the case with Children nurs'd away from Home so many Years."

"Lyes!" cried Mary, desp'rately, yet was there something in the History which seem'd to explain her own Grievances 'gainst the Fates. 'Tis True, I thought to myself, that such an envious and ill-humour'd Nature was perhaps the Result of her unhappy History.

"Lord Bellars knew nothing of these Things," Isobel went on. "Fanny, he conceiv'd an abandon'd Babe, Mary and Daniel his own Progeny; whereas his Love of Fanny he thought a Fluke of Nature—for he lov'd her more than his own Daughter and was e'er delighted by her great Gifts of Language, her excellent Penmanship and Skill in Latin, and, of course, her Horsemanship. . . ."

"What Gifts?" cried Mary. "The little Minx hath no great Gifts!" O then she fell to whimp'ring like a whipp'd Dog. I'faith, I pitied her; what a Shock to discover that one's entire Destiny and Genealogy hath been a Lye!

"But when did Lord Bellars learn the Truth?" I askt Isobel.

"After your Babe was born," she said. "Tho', i'faith, you knew it not, you were an Instrument of the Goddess' Vengeance. For in wearing your Masks and letting him keep you without knowing your True Identity, you brought him to Repentance. No doubt you also sav'd his Soul. What Daughter could do more for her Father?"

"Dadadadadada?" askt Belinda.

I was silent with the Astonishment of all these Revelations; Mary whimper'd softly as if, i'faith, she knew that Isobel's History were true; Lady Bellars awaken'd suddenly and began to cry out for Isobel. Isobel rusht in to tend her.

"Mary," I said to my Step-Sister, whereupon she only wept longer and louder.

"Mary," I began again, walking o'er to her, carrying Belinda and putting my free Hand upon her Shoulder.

"Sister, Friend, Playmate of my Youth," I said, "if these Things are true, and I am the Heiress to Lymeworth, I swear you shall always have a Place here and a Home—for this is your Home as much as mine!"

"More!" she scream'd, and spat full in my Face.

Chapter XVI

Drawing still nearer to the End.

IN THE DAYS THAT FOLLOW'D upon these Astounding Revelations, the whole Household was in a great State of Anxiety, awaiting Lord Bellars' Lawyer from London. The usual Yuletide Festivities which had graced the Christmases of my Youth were put aside, both for the Sake of Mourning and because of Lady Bellars' great Illness, which requir'd Isobel's constant Care.

As there is nothing more sombre than to be sombre when all the World is merry and rejoicing, Lymeworth was gloomy indeed. Many of the Servants had, in any case, left Months earlier, for Want of Wages; and doubtless to seek better Places in Town—for they had heard the Siren Song of London's Charms and they fancied there was more Tea to be had in London Households, and better Liveries, and less Work than in the dull Country.

As for me, what was my Response to the News that I might soon be Mistress of Lymeworth? I'faith, I scarcely believ'd it! 'Twas a Fairy Tale, a Dream, a Fable from a Book of French Romances! First, as a Bastard—and a female one at that—how might I inherit the Estate settl'd upon Lord Bellars by his Father? Then, what Reason had I to believe that Lymeworth was unencumber'd by Debts and Mortgages! Why some of the greatest Houses in all of England were as heavy with Mortgages as their Chestnut Trees were heavy with Chestnuts! I presum'd, therefore, that Lord Bellars had left his Affairs in great Disarray, o'erspent mightily upon this aborted Renovation of Lymeworth, and was in Debt to his architect, his Landscape Gardener, all his Builders, Painters, and Plasterers, not to mention his Banker, and e'en his Lawyer! In London he had liv'd high; at Lymeworth e'en his Expences for his Horses, Grooms, and Stables—not to mention his Hounds—must be hundreds of Pounds a Year, nay thousands. ❂ I had no Head for Banking and Money (if I were

Mistress of Lymeworth, indeed, I should call Sir Richard Hoare to handle my Affairs as Lord Bellars had done before me), but I knew that 'twas likely I was Heiress to nought but Debts, and that e'en paying out Lady Bellars' Jointure should sore stress the Estate.

Besides, the Shock of learning that my belovèd Belinda was of incestuous Birth dampen'd whate'er rejoicing I might have known o'er the News of my presum'd Inheritance. I lookt and lookt at the Babe, seeking some Flaw, some Touch of the Devil's Tail, some Imperfection—yet found I none. I'faith, you were more perfect, more amiable, more fair, more clever than any Babe I'd seen. If this be Incest's Fruit, sobeit! thought I. Perhaps we all should have incestuous Births! Whereupon I quickly chid myself for such Impertinence to the Fates, and hung my Head again in Shame.

Oft' I respond thus to Good Fortune, whereas Calamity puts me upon my Mettle. 'Tis true as true can be that we are oft' more easy in the Face of Adversity than in the Face of Pleasant Circumstances; for Ill Fortune calls forth all one's Pluck and Tenacity, whereas Good Fortune runs the Risque of plunging one directly into *Ennui,* which is, of course, a greater Evil than Pyracy, Want, or e'en Debt.

So I mus'd and agoniz'd concerning my suppos'd Good Fortune. Nor did I fail to think of a hundred other Dire Possibilities that might stand betwixt me and its Fruition: Daniel might yet turn up, wrongly reported dead; Mary might stab me in my Sleep; Isobel might prove to be quite as mad as Lady Bellars—for are they not the Maddest of the Mad who ne'er doubt their Convictions and seem, i'faith, most sane? Perhaps there was no Last Will & Testament at all, but only Isobel's Word—the Word of a suspected Witch—'gainst Mary's? Perhaps Daniel had married Kate ere he dy'd and she had borne a Son and Heir to whom the Estate would surely go. Perhaps Kate *herself* would arrive to blacken my Good Fortune; for certainly the Chambermaid's Gossip about her was not to be accounted free of Errors. There were more Reasons surely to expect Disaster than to expect Success, and e'en if Success were mine, 'twas sure as Buds in Spring and Flies in Summer that by and by our Deeds of Pyracy and Highway Robbery should catch up with us at Lymeworth.

I told all this to Lancelot, who laugh'd and laugh'd.

"Ye have the Thieves' Disease, me Girl," said he, "Fear o' a quiet Life. A quiet Life in the Country affrights ye more than Fleein' upon the Seas! Ah, I know it well. But I have roam'd the whole Wide World so long, that I think *this Libertalia* may well be the best we'll find, an' I'm content to stay here an' cultivate me Garden."

Lancelot already had Plans for Lymeworth—which we should rename Merriman Park—and make a Sanctuary for retir'd Pyrates and Robbers, where they might stash their Gold and practise the newest Farming Methods, breed Horses, raise Sheep, and fight Sea Battles for Fun and Fancy upon an Artificial Sea.

"When I met ye, me Girl, I thought ye no Use to anyone—on account o' yer Arrogance, yer Beauty, an' yer damn'd red-headed Impertinence. Then, little by little, I came to love ye, until me Heart was so caught up in yer red Hairs that 'twas very like a Fly caught in a Spider's Web—an' now 'tis wholly yers—whatsoe'er Use ye plan to make o' it. An' now to boot, I find ye are an Heiress! Did any Man e'er have such Good Luck? I would have taken ye without a Farthin' an' accounted meself most blest—an' now ye are an Heiress, too!"

Whereupon he threw his Arms about me, tumbl'd me to the Bed, and began to kiss my Face from Forehead to Chin saying, "Fanny, Fanny, Fanny Hackabout-Jones. Only promise ye'll ne'er change yer Name."

I thought then of the Lancelot who had coin'd that Name, the loud and brawling boastful Lancelot who had no Use for Women, nor indeed for any Human Creature who did not serve as a Mirror to the Glorious Figure he cut, an Echo to his Braggadocio—and I had to laugh. And then I had to cry as he cover'd my Eyes with Kisses and drank my Tears, and made love to me with a Love stor'd up for Years—who knows, maybe e'en for sev'ral Centuries?

Our Bedding, being so long delay'd, was bound to be either dreadful or wonderful; 'twas the latter. We kiss'd and clung and kiss'd and clung again. We delighted each other all thro' a Day and Night with that Tenderness which only Lovers who know each other's Souls ere they discover each other's Bodies, may bestow upon each other's Forms. After we made love, and betwixt each tumultuous Act, we laugh'd and talkt and remember'd.

O what a shar'd History we had! And how many Friends in common had we known—from Horatio to Annie Bonny! We shar'd the Pyrate's Craft, the Robber's Art, the Oath of Robin Hood, the Love of the Sea, and e'en the mutual Deception by that bonny Pyrate Queen!

517

As Acts that are oft' tragick when they occur become com-ick upon Recollection and Retelling, the Incident of being "rap'd" by Annie became still another Bond betwixt us. E'en the tragick News of your incestuous Birth did Lancelot trans-form, thro' his Philosophy, to Good.

"Fer we are all God's Creatures, Fanny, Love, an' God de-cides which Parents bear which Babes. Belinda is God's Grace upon that Union which otherwise should have borne nought but Death. Can ye look upon such a lovely bouncin' Babe an' think that ye did wrong? 'Tis Twattle! Belinda's Beauty is a Sign o' God's Forgiveness, a Covenant, i'faith, a Sign o' Grace."

And verily I could not but believe him. For, just as I know that Children are but lightly loan'd to their Parents and not given, I also know that the Accident of Birth oft' yokes to-gether Parents and Children that most ill-suited are. Thus, do we all feel like Orphans, (or e'en like Changelings) whilst we grow apace 'neath our Parents' Roofs. In truth, the Accident of Birth is most capricious—for *all* of us, incestuous or no!

Besides, Belinda, 'twas clear to me that you had no greater Burdens than any other Babe. Because of all the Perils of your Infancy, you were e'en more cherish'd than another Child, and thus Love and Adoration surrounded you and held you in its Glow ev'ry Moment of your Youth. O all the usual Annoyances a Mother feels when a Child intrudes upon her Peace, I did not feel with you; for whene'er you strain'd my Patience and Affection, I remember'd how I rescu'd you from Death's dark Jaws and I rejoiced merely to have you near!

When at last the Lawyer came, we learnt of many Things. Daniel indeed was dead. Kate had dy'd of a Clap, pregnant with his Child. Lord Bellars had not, amazingly, dy'd in Debt, but dy'd in great Wealth, having made so many thou-sands of Pounds in various Ventures that not only was Lyme-worth free of Mortgages, but its Acreage was now so great that it brought in Rents of near seven thousand Pounds *per Annum,* making the Heir to Lymeworth one of the richest Landlords in all of England!

Who was the Heir to Lymeworth? I nodded and yawn'd at the Meeting of the Family with the Lawyer, for nothing puts me to sleep more readily than Talk of Wills, Trusts, Settle-ments, Jointures, Portions, Remainders, Doweries, and Pin Moneys. I know these Words make the weary World go 'round; and I know that Lawyers are unto these Words as

518

Horses are unto Chariots—viz. *They make 'em go.* But I have ne'er been in a Chamber with a Lawyer when I did not wish either to scream with Desperation or else to fall into the deepest of Sleeps, e'en when the Matter concern'd my own Future most profoundly.

And so, 'twas not surprizing to me—tho' perhaps 'twas to all the assembl'd Servants and Retainers, not to mention Mary—that I fell asleep, e'en as the Lawyer was reading all Lord Bellars' various "Give and Bequeaths." Why, the poor Man had made an Inventory of the entire House and all its Contents, and he had e'en troubl'd himself to give and bequeath silver Cream Potts, gold Watches, priz'd Wigs, and Waistcoats to some of the Servants, who, in their Ingratitude, had already departed.

Lady Bellars had the gen'rous Jointure call'd for in her Marriage Settlement. 'Twas eight hundred Pounds a year (but then she had brought Lord Bellars a Dowery of eight thousand Pounds with which he had made his Fortune, so 'twas surely her Due—for e'en in those Days Doweries were ten times Jointures). Mary and Isobel were both given Annuities, nor was Joan Griffith forgotten (tho' alas, she was dead), with her Share to go to Isobel if she were deceas'd before Lord Bellars.

I remember no more of the Will, for after the Mention of Joan Griffith I fell asleep, and dream'd of Pyracy upon the Seas, of Galleons with Rainbow-colour'd Sails, and Brigantines that turn'd into Dragonflies, and Men o' War that roll'd upon Waggon Wheels, and Slaves in bright Feather'd Headdresses and Golden Necklaces, and Annie Bonny winking at me as she leap'd across the Bowsprit into my Arms, fell to her Knees, and made the Sweetest Love to me that e'er was made in a Dream. . . .

My Head was nodding upon my Breast, and my Thighs were so moist with Dreams that the tatter'd red Garter I still wore began to chafe, when lo, I awoke to hear I was Heiress to Lymeworth!

'Twas explain'd that Lord Bellars had adopted me quite legally; that I was now Life-Tenant of Lymeworth, to be succeeded by Belinda, to be succeeded by Belinda's first-born Son.

"I object," my Mother, Isobel, cried out. "Why not a Daughter?" Thus we see that e'en in our greatest Moments of Glory and Good Fortune there is always one who raises a Voice in Protest—and that one is usually our Mother!

The Rest of the Tale, you know, Belinda: How the Settlements were amended to give the Inheritance of House and Title to a first-born Daughter, how you were rais'd by Lancelot and the Merry Men, as well as Isobel, Lady Bellars, and myself, how Mary became as obsequious and grovelling to me as she had previously been scornful and haughty; and where she had once spat and scream'd, she now fawn'd and flatter'd. (Alas 'tis oft' the case with Persons of Inferior Character that they know only two Modes of Behaviour: one being Contempt and the other being Sycophancy; whereas Persons of Superior Character treat ev'ryone with similar Good Humour, if not Deference, and do not inflict, e'en upon their Servants, Manners with which they would not treat their Friends.)

All this you know. What you do not know is the curious Chain of Events which caus'd me to write this Book, which is the Proper Purpose of the ensuing Epilogue.

But first, imagine me upon that Day when I first became Mistress of Lymeworth. 'Twas a sere Day in January and all the Gardens were frosted with Winter's Brush. Venus wore a Blanket of Snow about her Bare Feet, and the Hedgerows of Lymeworth were bare of Leaf.

You were less than a Year old, and play'd before the Grate in Isobel's Chamber, attended by your loving Grandmother, (who e'en then was determin'd to teach you Witchcraft and the Worship of the Great Goddess). Your other Grandmother, Lady Bellars, lay upon her Bed of laced Pillows, playing with her Dogs and talking to 'em. She was enough recover'd of her Senses by now to have her Birds about her, undrap'd in their Cages, but e'en then she scarce knew the Diff'rence betwixt Birds and Persons—nor betwixt Dogs and Persons—nor did she till the Day she dy'd. Her favourite Poem in all the World (which she had woven into a Tapestry and hung above her Bedstand) was one which went:

Reason in Man cannot effect such Love,
    As Nature doth in them that Reason want;
Ulysses kind and true his Dog did prove,
    When Faith in better Friends was very scant.

My Travels for my Friends have been as true
    Tho' not as far as Fortune did him bear;
No Friends my Love and Faith divided knew,
    Tho' this nor that once equall'd were.

But in my Dog whereof I made no store,
I find more Love than them I trusted more.

As for Mary, she was growing accustom'd to her new State
in the Household, as People do, and beginning to falter in her
Resolution to bring Lawsuits against me, Isobel, Lord Bellars'
Lawyers and Bankers, for fear that she should thereby lose
all. Her Annuity was large enough to dampen her Resolve to
sue, tho' 'twas hardly all she wisht. Thus, doth Money mellow
e'en the most furious of Furies and calm the most fever'd of
Brows. Lancelot had sent Word to the Merry Men that they
might make their Way to Lymeworth, and now, as we walkt
the Winter's Gardens, wrapp'd in Cloaks 'gainst the Cold, our
Boots sinking into the Snow, we talkt of our Plans for the
Great House and the Gardens—for is it not e'er the case that
after Pyracy and after Love comes Architecture, as we pour
our Hearts into building a Great House in which we may em-
body all our Dreams?

"Here we shall hoist our Pyrate Flag," said Lancelot,
pointing to the great Palladian Pediment of the new Façade,
"an' here make *Libertalia*. The Merry Men shall till the Soil,
develop new and curious Fruits and Flow'rs, and Lustre shall
be the greatest Stud Horse England hath e'er known. *This is
Libertalia*, me Girl, an' we shall build it accordin' to our
Hearts' Desires. . . ."

His green Eyes blaz'd; his wild red Hair seem'd a Fire ascending from his Soul into the Sky. I said, "Aye, aye," and
kiss'd him on the Lips; but in my Mind's Eye I seem'd to see
Anne Bonny's Galley on the Tropick Seas, and in my Heart,
I sail'd away with her.

Epilogue

In which our Author explains the curious Chain of Events which led to the Writing of this History.

AND SO AFFECTION for the Country got the better of all Thoughts of Town, and Land came to satisfy our Dreams of Sea; and we changed the Name of Lymeworth to Merriman Park (tho' certainly not without hearty Protestations from Isobel, who wisht the Name to be Merriwych Park), and we liv'd there in Peace and Harmony, cultivating our beauteous Gardens, breeding Lustre's lovely Progeny, raising you—a frolicsome, merry, red-headed Marvel of a Girl—in the green and fertile Wiltshire Countryside.

I was rich enough to keep the Law at bay, for Justice, as Lancelot always knew, is the Province of the Rich. So, too, is Literature, I fear; for 'twas only when I well and truly found myself an Heiress, and when I had Lancelot and the Merry Men (as well as Isobel and Lady Bellars) to aid in raising you, that I sat down at my Writing Bureau and began in earnest to be the Bard I wisht to be.

Lancelot serv'd as Steward for the Estate (for he would entrust that Post to no one but himself); and verily he greatly increas'd our Prosperity and made our Fields and Gardens, not to mention our Stables, among the Marvels of the Countryside. Mary, as you know, married Francis Bacon, whereupon they proceeded to torment each other for the Duration of their Lives together (since your Aunt Mary, from earliest Girlhood, lov'd nothing better than a good English Roast Beef, whereas Francis Bacon referr'd to the same as "Dead Cow" and made her quite miserable for eating his "Four-leggèd Friends").

I will not trouble you with all the Particulars of my Lit'ry Career, much of which is already well-known. Suffice it to say, that I began, like most Scribblers, with Imitation of the Ancients—a Great Epick of my Travels and Adventures, couch'd in Perfect Heroick Couplets, which I call'd, after the

Fashion of the Day, *The Pyratiad*. In this Epick I told all I
knew of Sailing Ships and the Spanish Main, of the Travels
of a Group of Valiant Pyrates call'd the Merry Men (whom
ev'ryone believ'd were mere Inventions of the Poet's Fancy),
of the famous Female Pyrate, Anne Bonny, as well as Slavers, Slaves, the Buccaneers, the Pyrate Round upon the
Eastern Seas—which was by then, the latter 1720's, entering
the Realm of Legend (and consequently, becoming more and
more the Subject of Books and Poems). I was wily enough,
by this Juncture in my Life, to sign my Name Captain F.
Jones, which ev'ryone presum'd was a Man.

This Epick Poem was a dazzling Success! The Criticks
rav'd; the Publick bought out the Printings ere the Ink was
dry. Ev'ryone in London clamour'd to meet Captain Jones!
Belles sigh'd for him and Beaux wisht to interrogate him o'er
the Design of Ships; Matrons wisht to present their Marriage-
able Daughters, and Composers wisht to collaborate with him
in styling Entertainments for the Stage. Why, the King Himself askt a Royal Audience, and Letters pour'd into Merriman
Park, inviting me to London, Paris, Rome, Boston, New
York, e'en Constantinople!

Seduced by this Success, thinking that the World at last
had recogniz'd my Goddess-given Gift, I dreamt of leaving
my Solitary Chamber, journeying up to London, and revealing myself as Fanny Jones, the Author of the Epick!
'Twas a piteous, tho' natural enough Mistake. But O 'twas
boring in the Country, tho' beauteous, and besides, what
Scribbler doth not dream of Excuses to leave her Writing Bureau and mingle with the *Beau Monde* in Town? Writing is a
lonely, melancholick Art; and the newly famous, in particular, are inclin'ed towards Foolish Fancies concerning the
Pleasures to be had in Town—the Balls, Assemblies,
Masquerades, and Musicales; the Coffee-Houses, Plays, and
Operas, all the fashionable Strut of brittle London Life.

Isobel warn'd me not to go—tho' the new and mellow
Lancelot was e'er indulgent with my Fancies. But Isobel said:
"When they discover Captain Jones is but a Wench—and a
luscious one at that—they will account your Person more and
your Writing less, mark my Words."

I scoff'd at this, thinking Isobel e'er too sensitive concerning Woman's Lot and e'er wary of Persecution as a Witch.
Besides, I dreamt of a Royal Audience whereby I might secure the Pardons of all the Merry Men, so that henceforth
we should not live with the nagging Ghost of Fear.

In short, I disobey'd my Mother, and I went.

The King was amaz'd to see a Wench where he had presum'd a Man, and in a Fit of Generosity (and perhaps Lust) he granted all the Pardons that I wisht—for myself, Lancelot and for the Merry Men. He also marvell'd o'er my Knowledge of the Seas (for, as Captain Jones, I was *presum'd* to be a great Sailor, but now that I was seen to be a Woman, the King Himself was quite amaz'd that I should know a Foresail from a Mizzenroyal, a Bowsprit from a Boom! 'Twas suddenly as if I had become the Village Idiot who writes, by chance, a clever Couplet; or a Babe that babbles, by mistake, a Latin Word!)

Nor did the Estimation of the Town fail to change—much to my Astonishment. I understood at once how naïve I had been to assume that the self-same Standards prevail for Female Scribblers as for Male. If any Grub Street Hack had written *The Pyratiad,* he would have been securely enthron'd upon Parnassus, but O, 'twas not the case when that same Poem issu'd from a Female Pen! For tho' the Offers of Audiences, Assemblies, and Balls did not cease, there was now an unmistakable edge of Lewdness to 'em. Moreo'er, the very Coffeehouse Wits, and e'en the Criticks themselves changed their previous Estimation of *The Pyratiad.* Where before my Style had been "strong and manly," 'twas now said to be "weak and effeminate." Where before the Characters of the Merry Men had been much admir'd, 'twas now bruited about that, as one Scribbling Rogue hath put it, "A Female Pen is insufficient to portray the Characters and Passions of Men." I was further denounced for being a vain, unsext, unnatural Woman, a vile Seeker after Fame and Fortune, a Slut, and a Whore. Humiliated, my Innocence once again outraged by the Calumnies of the World, I fled Home to Lancelot and Lymeworth—or rather to Merriman Park.

The Pyratiad continu'd to sell upon the Strength of Scandal, tho' its Lit'ry Reputation declin'd. Lancelot, who had also been made to eat Humble Pye when his Hopes of a Deocracy were dasht and dasht again, understood better than anyone my Disappointments. Thus, the Denunciation of my so lately prais'd Epick forg'd betwixt us an e'en tighter Bond. O we lov'd each other truly now—join'd as we were by Love, by Lust, by shar'd Adversity, and by Belinda, our lovely Daughter (whom Lancelot lov'd as if he'd sir'd her himself, nay better). Still, we ne'er married, for I'd be damn'd if I'd give a Man—e'en a Man as loving as my Lancelot—Pow'r o'er my Lands and Houses, Stocks and Bonds! Lancelot might share all that I had, but under the Law, if I married him, he would have Title to all, not I; for thus were Wives treated under Britannia's Statutes. I was resolv'd, therefore, n'er to marry (which Lancelot, who was no Friend to the Law himself, fully applauded and understood).

I return'd, after a Period of Mourning, to my Scribbling. Damn 'em all—I thought—those rude splenetick London Rogues! I'll not be silenced by a Parcel of Poltroons! Whereupon, as is well-known, I scribbl'd in the next score of Years a score of Romances in Mrs. Haywood's Manner, which made both me and my Bookseller richer than "The Beggar's Opera" made Mr. Rich, and gayer than the same made Mr. Gay!

O I had Fame and Fortune from my Fictions now—tho' scarcely lofty Reputation. I scribbl'd my Romances, and nurtur'd my Belovèds, for I knew, after so many Losses, that Love is the closest we know of Heaven in this Weary World, and we must love the Human ere we may know the Divine! I liv'd for Lancelot, Belinda, my two Mothers, and the Merry Men; to tend my Garden, breed my Horses, feed my Turtledoves, scamper with my Dogs, and write my Books. I made good also my Promise to Bartholomew by publishing his Book—tho', alas, it sank upon the vast Seas of the Publick's Indiff'rence without a Trace; for the Time was not yet ripe to question the Slave Trade from which accru'd to England such Riches, Rums, and Sweets, borne upon the beaten Backs of Slaves. I griev'd for the Fate of Bartholomew's Book, almost glad that he was not here to behold it; but save for that, I was happy enough with my belovèd Lancelot, Belinda, and my Works.

Then, in that infamous Year, 1749, there came to me, wrapp'd in a single Sheet of Foolscap, and inscrib'd in John Cleland's own Mocking Hand, an Outrage which *demanded* my Reply. 'Twas a loathsome Book, issu'd by my own Bookseller, that Bloody Rogue, Ralph Griffiths (hiding behind the preposterous Rubrick of G. Fenton) and call'd—O Calumny!—*Memoirs of a Woman of Pleasure!* It told of a simp'ring, cloying Heroine, call'd Fanny Hill, obviously modell'd upon my youthful Self, who toil'd in a Brothel, and lov'd the Masculine Member so dearly and so well that she had dozens of delicious, adoring Terms for it!

I read this so-called "Memoir" and my Blood boil'd! To think that Cleland, to whom I'd been so kind, would slander

and defile me for his Bread alone! For he wrote the bloody
Thing merely to slither out of Debtor's Prison—where he
might have rotted for Eternity for all I car'd!

Lancelot bade me forget the Insult, quoting to me Dean
Swift's clever lines:

> If on Parnassus' Top you sit,
> You rarely bite, are always bit;
> Each Poet of inferior Size
> on you shall rail and criticize;
> and strive to tear you Limb from Limb,
> While others do as much for him.

Isobel argu'd that 'twas my Popularity as a Romancer which
provokt such an Attack, for is there not an Arabick Proverb
which goes, "No one throws Stones at a Barren Tree"?

But I was too enrag'd to heed either Lover or Mother.
Very well, then, thought I, the Time hath come to tell my
own History to the World. For, oft' when we have nurs'd a
Dream for many a Year, 'tis some mundane Provocation
which stirs our Blood and piques us to begin to make that
Dream come true. Since our Return to Wiltshire I had
dreamt (whilst scribbling my Mock-Epick and Romances) of
writing the History of my Life and Adventures for you, my
Daughter, so that when you should go out into the Great
World, you should not go empty-handed, but should have a
Loving Guide amidst the sundry Dilemmas Fate would surely
put before you. (O I would give you my tatter'd red Garter
as well—and someday you would give it to *your* Daughter—
but I wisht you to have Words of Wisdom as well as Witchcraft, Sagacity as well as Spells!)

I dreamt of such a Book, yet hesitated. Fear of Censure
held back my Hand; 'twas not the Fashion of the Time to
write one's own Life History. Besides, there were other, still
more puissant Fears: the Witchcraft Acts were not repeal'd
till '36, and in the Country there were still such Villains as
would stone or hang a poor old Woman for the Charge of
Witchcraft. Moreo'er Pope, my Nemesis, still liv'd, and
wielded the awesome Pow'r of scribbling his Enemies into
The Dunciad. (He had put me there as a Minor Dunce—
doubtless for my Success in writing Romances and for my
slighting him those many Years ago.) But what if I should
tell the Truth of him? O terrible to think of his Revenge!

Thus till he dy'd in '44, I could not tell all that I knew of him.

And so I dreamt, but hesitated; for I knew that if I wrote a Book for my Daughter, and wrote it as a Testament of Love, I must hide nothing, but tell the utter Truth; both Clio and the Goddess must guide my Quill.

Cleland's Book was, then, a curious Barb, a Blessing in Disguise, a sort of Dare. Nor did it discourage me that both Mr. Richardson and Mr. Fielding had begun to write Histories in which English Scenes and Characters of Low Estate march'd thro' the Pages of a Book in lieu of Lords and Ladies in Exotick Lands. Perhaps this was a curious Sign as well, that I might write of all the Common Rogues which Fate had brought before my Eyes. For was not my *authentick* History as stirring as Fanny Hill's, or Pamela's, or e'en that of Tom Jones? Orphan, Whore, Adventuress, Kept Woman, Slaver, Amanuensis, Witch, e'en a pardon'd Pyrate! By the Goddess, 'twas my *own* Life History that made a better History than any *fancied* History. And by the Goddess, 'twas the Time to tell it all!

You, my Belinda, had grown from Beauteous Babe to Beauteous Woman in what seem'd the Blink of an Eye; and to my Sadness, yet my Resignation, you wisht to make a Grand Tour of the Globe, to visit all the Places I had seen and some that I had not—America! (For tho' I'd seen the Azure Caribee, I ne'er had touch'd the New World's fabl'd Shores.) And now you wisht a Voyage to those lands—both civiliz'd and savage—which your Mother had not seen.

I knew I could not keep you from this Dream; and yet I wisht to write a Book for you, which you might press unto your Bosom as you roam'd the World, consult in Times of Need, and which I dreamt should bring you safely Home—to Merriman, your Birthright, and to me.

And so I took my Quill in Hand, and I began.

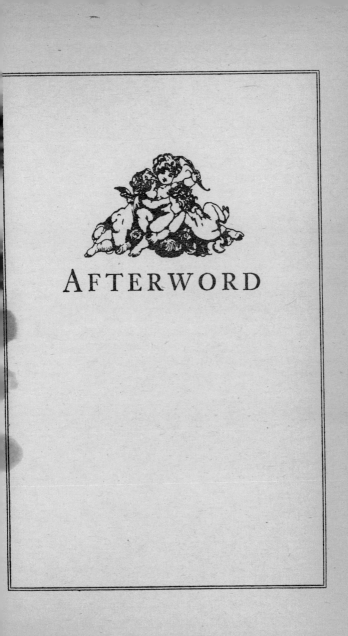

AFTERWORD

HAVING IMPERSONATED FANNY HACKABOUT-JONES for 527 pages, I should now see if I can still impersonate myself in order to give the interested reader something of the background of this book, its roots, as it were.

In 1961, as a Barnard undergraduate, I took my first course in English Literature of the eighteenth century, taught by Professor James L. Clifford, the eminent eighteenth-century scholar and chronicler of the life of Samuel Johnson. Jim Clifford's course was as extraordinary as he was. To begin with, it had Barnard undergrads, Columbia undergrads, and graduate students, all sitting together in something like amity and good fellowship. Secondly, though it was a "lecture course," there was always lots of animated give-and-take between students and professor—which, God knows, was rare at Columbia in that epoch. Jim Clifford made the eighteenth century come alive for us. He referred to figures like Boswell and Johnson by their first names. He shared with us curious biographical tidbits from his own research, recounted with his own glorious sense of humor. Yet perhaps most important was his fascination with the details of daily existence in the eighteenth century. In one of his scholarly essays, "Some Aspects of Life in the Mid-Eighteenth Century," he describes all those things that other scholars omit: the conditions of plumbing in eighteenth-century England, the emptying of chamberpots and cesspits, the lighting of the streets, and various schemes for reducing muggings and street crimes. He goes into detail about these things because, as a biographer, it was his conviction that you could not really understand a man's mind if you dwelt only upon intellectual history—you must also be able to imagine the most mundane aspects of his life.

Two term papers were required for Professor Clifford's full-year course: one dealing with the Augustan period and one with the Age of Johnson. Though a student might certainly write a footnoted scholarly paper if he or she wished, Jim Clifford encouraged us instead to attempt an imitation of a writer we admired. For the first half of the course, I wrote an imitation of Alexander Pope—a "Mock Epick" in heroic couplets. For the second, I wrote a novella in the style of Henry Fielding.

Later I received a Woodrow Wilson Fellowship to take my M.A. in eighteenth-century Literature at Columbia and I wrote my Master's thesis on Alexander Pope. After earning my M.A. in 1965, I began work toward a Ph.D. in that field, but dropped out when my own creative writing became ever more pressing and distracting. Yet in the back of my mind, there was always the fantasy of returning to eighteenth-century England, as it had come alive for me under Jim Clifford's tutelage, and of writing a novel set in that period.

I dared not do it for many years, though I continued to read about the eighteenth century and to visit eighteenth-century houses whenever I was in England. In the years immediately following graduate school, and a four-year stint as a college teacher of English, I was too busy trying to free myself of academic influences to want to plunge back into research. But even as I wrote books like *Fear of Flying* and *How to Save Your Own Life,* and my first four books of poetry, I dreamed of writing a mock-eighteenth-century novel someday. Still, I wanted to wait until I was both free enough of the graduate student within me to do it lightheartedly, and yet calm enough in my own life to devote myself to the massive research I knew it would require.

Early in 1976, after I had finished *How to Save Your Own Life* (though it had not yet been published), I began to do research for *Fanny*—then tentatively called *The True History of the Adventures of Fanny Hackabout-Jones.* I went to see Jim Clifford and he helped me compile the nucleus of the bibliography that made this novel possible. Over the next year or so, he gave me various leads and answered questions I raised. He had also promised to read it for me before publication, but alas, he never saw a finished manuscript, because he died in 1978.

J. H. Plumb was kind and generous enough to take on this task, and I am greatly indebted to him for his help. Both his enthusiasm for this book and his generous offer to point out solecisms and anachronisms have been invaluable to me. My understanding of the eighteenth century I owe in part to his splendid books; my errors, of course, are my own. (I must also thank Phyllis Chesler for bringing us together.)

The other debts I must acknowledge are many. A novel

like this could never have been written without the patience and forbearance of many librarians. I would like particularly to thank the following libraries and librarians: the Pequot Library in Southport, Connecticut (Stanley Crane, Grace Donaldson); the Weston, Connecticut, Library (Jane Atkinson, Geraldine O'Connell); the Westport and Greenwich, Connecticut, libraries; the Beinecke Rare Book and Manuscript Library at Yale University (Donald Gallup and Marjorie Wynne); the South Street Seaport Library, New York City (Norman Brauer); the Columbia and Barnard libraries; Columbia University Law Library (Barbara Kessler was particularly helpful); and the Bridgeport, Connecticut, University Library (Betty Meyer).

Burt Britton, first of the Strand bookstore, then later of Books & Co., searched for out-of-print titles for me. The late Ellen Moers, Elaine Showalter, and Scott Waugh gave encouragement and helpful suggestions about research. Russell Harty took me on a research trip to Bath, which was invaluable even though Bath did not finally appear in the novel. Captain Mike McCarthy and first Mate Sally Polk taught me a bit of sailing and showed me some pirate haunts of the Caribbean. Bardi McLennan, my secretary, scoured the libraries for books, paid overdue fines when I was ashamed to show my face, practically memorized the *Oxford English Dictionary* checking archaic word usage, and typed the manuscript more times than I can say. Jonathan Fast, my husband, read and encouraged every hundred pages or so and made suggestions so good I appropriated them as my own. He also encouraged me to attempt this departure from the contemporary scene and bolstered my faith when it lagged (which was often). Both he and Lula Johnson took excellent care of our daughter, Molly, during my working hours, giving me the peace of mind to write. And Molly herself helped by being the most amiable and unfretful of babies—born as she was between pages 303 and 304!

My editor, Elaine Koster, read and encouraged this project from the start. I am indebted to her for her suggestions for revision, for the care she took with reading and editing during what turned out to be the very last week of her pregnancy. (Quite a number of people involved with this book had babies during its composition!) Herbert K. Schnall of NAL gave his blessings and advice. Diana Levine and Joan Sanger lent their keen editorial assistance as well. I feel uniquely lucky to have such supportive publishers who so readily share my new enthusiasms and never ask me to repeat earlier books. My agent, Sterling Lord, as well as Pat Berens and Philippa Brophy at the Sterling Lord Agency, were my first readers and greatly helped by their enthusiasm as well as their criticism. Lori Henig and Martha Carpentier of Columbia University Graduate Faculties checked facts in the finished manuscript and made excellent suggestions. I am also grateful to Janice Thaddeus of Barnard College for recommending them. Sandee McComas, Natalie Corbin, and Lesley Nagot helped with the horrendous task of preparing the final copy. Bill Reynolds was the intrepid copy editor. Susan Battley assisted with reading proofs.

I hope this novel is true to the spirit, if not the letter, of the eighteenth century, for I am well aware that I have often stretched (though I hope not shattered) historical "truth" in order to make a more amusing tale. Anny Bonny, for example, disappears from the history books in 1720. What she did in the next years of her life nobody knows, thus the novelist is free to imagine. The Hell-Fire Clubs were outlawed in 1721, but I am taking the license of assuming that they must have continued to meet in secret, though their members were cautious not to mention where or when. In my description of the Hell-Fire caves, I have drawn partially on those still visible at the village of West Wycombe in Buckinghamshire, which I realize were not built until after the date of my story. My "Monks" are of course inspired by the notorious Medmenham Monks, who flourished later in the century. Other than that, I have tried to be true to chronology.

Lancelot Robinson is a "Pyrate" of my own invention, yet not long after I imagined him, I chanced to read about the French Pirate Misson, whose motto was *A Deo a Libertate* and whose utopian dreams were very like those I imagined for Lancelot. Piracy buffs will recognize that Lancelot's "Pyrate Articles" are much like those of Bartholomew Roberts', with a few items from George Lowther's articles thrown in for good measure. "Pyrate" articles tended to be rather similar—but none that I have read mentions women except to proscribe them. Yet there *were* famous female "Pyrates" in the seventeenth and eighteenth centuries, and none more famous than Anne Bonny.

Swift, Pope, Hogarth, John Cleland, Theophilus Cibber, Anne Bonny, and Dr. William Smellie, I have imagined as fictional characters within the parameters of the known facts of their lives. Their entry into this book as comic characters is intended as no slur upon the greatness of their achievements. Swift and Hogarth, in particular, are among the most extraordinary artists the world has ever known.

For the arguments regarding the pros and cons of the slave trade, I am indebted to the sea diaries of the period, particularly Captain Snelgrave's. For Fanny's adventures as a "Pyrate" I am indebted, like most writers on piracy, to Captain Charles Johnson's 1724 book: *A General History of the Robberies and Murders of the Most Notorious Pyrates from Their First Rise and Settlement in the Island of New Providence to the Present Year*. Many scholars believe that Johnson was really a pseudonym for the prolific Daniel Defoe. I am not certain this is true, because the writing in the book seems inferior to Defoe's, but be that as it may, the volume is a treasure trove and every writer on piracy has used it.

For Fanny's adventures in the "skin trade," I am indebted to *A Medical History of Contraception* by Norman Himes, and the gracious help of Jeanne Swinton, librarian at the Margaret Sanger Library of Planned Parenthood of New York.

As for my obstetrics, Caesarian section is, of course, an ancient practice known both in Greece and Rome and in "primitive" cultures today. The first successful recorded Caesarian in British medical history took place in 1738, was performed by a midwife, and executed with razor, tailor's needle, and silk thread. The mother not only survived, but recovered well and rapidly. Still, the Caesarian has never ceased to be a controversial operation, and the arguments about it tend to be fervid and political even in our own time. I assume that, if the first successful recorded Caesarian took place in 1738, there must have been earlier unrecorded successes, perhaps not revealed because the Witchcraft Acts were still in force. At any rate, I chose to have Belinda delivered thus for the purposes of my plot.

For the witchcraft material, I am indebted to the crucial anthropological work of the late Dr. Margaret A. Murray, though my witches owe as much to the fairy tale as they do to anthropology. I have placed them in Wiltshire, though I know that Wiltshire was not as famous for witches as, say, Lancashire. These Wiltshire witches are very much of my own invention.

Readers who know the introduction I wrote to *Fanny Hill: or Memoirs of a Woman of Pleasure* (Erotic Art Book Society) are aware that it is one of my favorite books; thus I do not share my heroine's opinions about Mr. Cleland. Nevertheless, I thought it amusing to make her pique at Cleland the impetus for writing her own memoirs. No disrespect to that classic of erotica, *Fanny Hill*, is intended.

I must also acknowledge a debt to Ditchley Park in Oxfordshire, one of the many beautiful English Country Houses that inspired me with the settings for this book. Those who have stayed at Ditchley as guests of the Ditchley Foundation may recognize that Lady Bellars' beloved poem on the superiority of dogs to people is to be found upon a painting of Sir Henry Lee (ancestor of General Robert E. Lee and the Virginia Lees), in the Tapestry Room at Ditchley. But my fictional Lymeworth draws only partly upon Ditchley for inspiration. The other houses I have visited are too many to list and I am particularly grateful to Britain's National Trust that they are still standing.

A note on orthography: Eighteenth-century buffs will know, of course, that capitalization and spelling were highly capricious in that age, and only beginning to be standardized at a later date. (Most of the eighteenth-century novels we read—*Tom Jones, Moll Flanders,* et cetera—have been reset to suit contemporary styles of spelling, capitalization, and punctuation.) I have opted for my own compromise here, capitalizing nouns and catch phrases with regularity, while verbs and most adjectives are lower-case. I have therefore been far more predictable in my capitalization and orthography than the average eighteenth-century author. I do follow the eighteenth-century practice of capitalizing certain words for emphasis—a practice we have largely abandoned except in ironic writing. It was my intention to give the *flavor* of eighteenth-century prose, without, however, forcing my readers to read *f*'s for *s*'s or puzzle through a maze of utterly erratic capitalizations.

I should also add that I started out with the notion of using no language but the language in use in the first half of the eighteenth century, and to a large extent, I adhered to that rule. But I eventually found that the rule was impossible to follow. First, the *Oxford English Dictionary* only records written language, not spoken. Second, some words have so changed their meanings in two hundred and fifty years that to use them would thoroughly puzzle the modern reader and interfere with the pleasure of reading. Also, for comic purposes, I have given Fanny some language that was somewhat

536

antiquated and rhetorical even in her time. When in doubt, I have opted for pleasure, not rigid adherence to rules—even those of my own making.

It may be objected by some that Fanny is not a typical eighteenth-century woman—and I am well aware of this fact. In many ways her consciousness is modern. But I do believe that in every age there are people whose consciousness transcends their own time and that these people, whether fictional or historical, are those with whom we most closely identify and those about whom we most enjoy reading. I have tried to write an interesting and entertaining novel, not an historical treatise, so the development of my heroine's character has always been more important to me than the setting in which we find her. I hope this book will convey something of the fascination I have had with eighteenth-century England, its manners and mores, but, above all, it is intended as a novel about a woman's life and development in a time when women suffered far greater oppression than they do today.

This book is lovingly dedicated to my mother, Eda Mirsky Mann, and to my daughter, Molly Miranda Jong-Fast.

ERICA JONG

ABOUT THE AUTHOR

ERICA JONG has attained a rare distinction as both a poet and as a novelist. Her books of poetry include *Fruits & Vegetables* (1971), *Half-Lives* (1973), *Loveroot* (1975), *At the Edge of the Body* (1979), and *Ordinary Miracles* (1983). In 1981, her nonfiction work of prose and poetry, *Witches*, appeared. Her most recent work is *Molly's Book of Divorce: A Kid's Book for Adults*. (1984).